TWO MINUTES

First Published in 2025 by Echo Books

Echo Books is an imprint of Superscript Publishing Pty Ltd
ABN 76 644 812 395

Registered Office: PO Box 669, Woodend, Victoria, 3442

www.echobooks.com.au

Copyright © Jon Michael Springer

National Library of Australia Cataloguing-in-Publication entry.

Creator: Michael Spring-Springer, author.

Title: Two Minutes

ISBN: 978-1-923441-25-5 (paperback)
ISBN: 978-1-923441-26-2 (ePub)

A catalogue record for this
book is available from the
National Library of Australia

Book and cover design by Andrew Davies.
Cover image: Shutterstock

MICHAEL SPRING-SPRINGER

Two Minutes

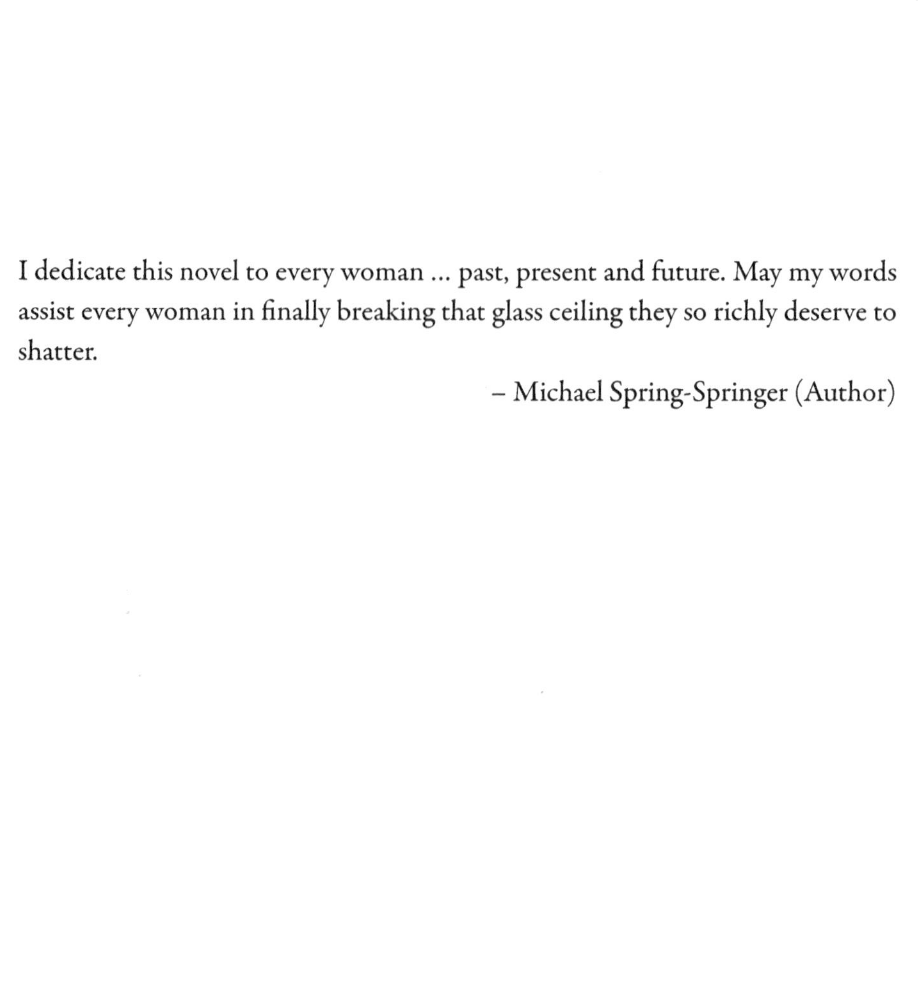

I dedicate this novel to every woman ... past, present and future. May my words assist every woman in finally breaking that glass ceiling they so richly deserve to shatter.

– Michael Spring-Springer (Author)

PART 1

"The Light"

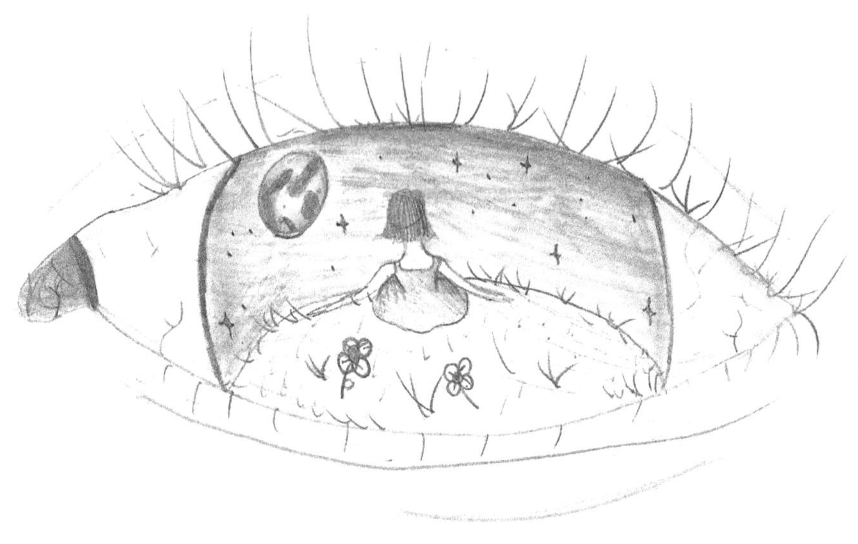

'A Gaze Into The Future'
by Emilie Springer

CHAPTER 1

The lights had been dimmed to complete darkness within the auditorium, making it so dark, cold, and quiet that one might have thought oneself trapped in a lifeless and endless void of intergalactic space. Indeed, it was so dark that one could not see one's hands in front of them. It might have been the nether regions of space, save for a terrestrial circumstance that does not occur naturally within the cosmic void: the sounds of breathing. Oxygen was being consumed, and the sound it generated revealed the surroundings were on terra firma. Then the screen lit up with the first celestial image of the cosmos, almost as though an omnipotent and ubiquitous presence decided that there should be light, and with those images came the primeval sounds of gasping, as the mere mortals present saw on the screen what existed outside in the space beyond their atmospheric bubble.

And then there came the sound, as the starstruck audience was brought back down to terra firma again, because the nasal tones of the announcer shattered the peaceful and quiet universe of the auditorium. "Welcome to history being made by the marvels of science. The light beams of the dawn of creation continue to radiate throughout the heavens in an eternal journey that knows no conclusion in the vast universe, ladies and gentlemen. When the artificial light of our world is absent, the heavens are revealed without any optical interference, as ancient lights can be seen in all of their infinite glory through our spacecraft's lens. Yet, because those photons travel at the speed of light, time is removed as a consideration for them. It is when we transmit images from the cosmic darkness that these spectacles of our universe, these wonders of physics, become crisper, more defined and indomitable as they perpetually embark on their endless journey from their origins."

The images on the screen panned as the lens, one hundred and forty million miles away, scanned the cosmos. The gasping of wonderment was again interrupted by the nasal tones of the announcer. "Folks, in the surrounding darkness of that endless stage of the cosmos, Andromeda features in the background of the screen as its magical display of light is accentuated by its bright core. Still, it is its vast spiralling arms that engage our eyes in a performance that eventually upstages the brightest stars of its core. At this time in the universe, Andromeda's solar brilliance could not be replicated in the Neoplatonic masterpiece of creation, as its huge clouds of gas only further illuminate its beauty. There is a tranquillity to be absorbed by the heart and mind as one gazes upon Andromeda's ethereal existence, and it is that tranquil quality of the appearance of this magnificent galaxy that can otherwise overwhelm any terrifying contemplation of the machinations of this chaotic combustion of science."

Then, the audience broke out into cheers of delight as the lens panned around again, this time revealing the main attraction. "Quiet, please, ladies and gentlemen, quiet." And like serfs, the audience obeyed the nasal-toned announcer's command, as he continued delivering his monologue commentary, while the images alone more authentically described the scene. "Not to be overshadowed in this heavenly dance is Mars. The god of war will not submit to being a supporting player in the dark and frozen abyss. Its rambunctiousness is displayed in its angry, red soil, a uniform feature of its surface, which it presents to whoever may be bold enough to invade its territory. Whether it once nursed life in its antiquity is irrelevant to the respect one must pay to the station it carries within its inner sanctum of celestial friends, performing the same perpetual rotary dance around the central solar furnace that sheds its light into the cosmos and beyond. Mars the powerful, Mars the bold and Mars the warrior; so close you are and yet so inhospitable you can be. What lies beyond you in the heavens is what you portray in your fiery-red surface, the inhospitable, eternal expanse of that stage called space."

Space; the word does no justice to the alien environment it describes. However, the audience's slight murmurs were interrupted again by the announcer's auditory offensive tone. "There are no barriers in that space, nor are there any restrictions. Objects appear to move at equilibrium in that cosmos; they do not seem to fall and do not need wings to fly. Newton's apple would not fall on his head in space, and whilst his laws of physics are fulfilled in the cosmos, no paradox attaches to the universe's perpetual motion. Gravity is the song being played on that unique pianola of space. Still, its rhythm is like no other form of music, and celestial bodies perform neutron dance steps to a multitude of heavenly drums to which each movement may differ from its molecular neighbours."

Finally, the announcer explained to everyone why there were only images on the illuminated screen. "And yet, despite all of these vastly different optical delights that are on show for the audience of this auditorium, there is one sensory element missing from this performance: sound. The absence of sound is a compelling element of terror that one is confronted by in that vast cosmos." On cue, yet also unexpected, a sound contradicted the announcer's previous statement. "However, is that sound occurring now? A beeping sound is squealing out and around this abyss; how could this be?" The beeping was now an overwhelming noise that kept repeating. "What is that beeping noise?" The audience looked at each other as the deafening sound grew louder, causing their eardrums to ache. They were confused by the noise. One member of the audience began to make his way towards a side door of the auditorium, and he exited the room as the beeping noise continued.

PART 2

"End of Innocence"

CHAPTER 2

Within the Earth's atmosphere, objects do not act in equilibrium, and the Earth's gravity draws objects towards its surface. During the day, the atmosphere on Earth impedes the naked eye's view of the celestial objects in the heavens, depriving all life that exists on the molten rock from experiencing the complete performance of light that otherwise exists in that endless cosmos. The people on Earth believe their aeroplanes separate them from all other creatures. However, people are no different from the flying insects they detest; every creature is a captive within the air that gives them life, and the gravity pulling them down.

Felicity Bennet sat keenly by her father's side in his two-seater Cessna 195 aeroplane as he waited for the tower radio to confirm he could take off at Earls Colne Airfield. It had been a cold April morning at Colchester, as it had been at Samuel Bennet's Essex farm the previous night, when he eventually acquiesced to his daughter's importunate requests over dinner for her father to teach her more about how to fly an aeroplane as her birthday present. The aeroplane's aluminium exterior finish shone brightly as the morning sun began parting the cold grey clouds that had delivered the icy cold winds the night before.

Felicity was born in London at Queen Charlotte's and Chelsea Hospital on April 12, 1941. Her 35-year-old father, Samuel, was serving as a Pilot Officer in the Royal Air Force during World War II, flying Hurricane fighters, which were the frontline of aerial defence against the German Luftwaffe. Her mother, Bridget, was born in Dublin in 1916 to an unmarried mother in whom the trauma of childbirth took her life, thereby leaving the infant to be raised as an orphan in an Irish convent. She met Samuel in the early autumn of 1936 when he was visiting Dublin, and although there was a decade in age that separated them, they fell in love immediately. Bridget had died only four days after Felicity's birth when a German bomber regrettably dropped a bomb on the hospital ward where her bed was located, and it was fortuitous for the newborn Felicity that the hospital nursery narrowly avoided the damage.

Samuel was devastated by the loss of his wife, and he was honourably discharged from the Royal Air Force to raise his daughter on his beef and grain farm in Essex, where he continued to do so on this cold Saturday morning, April 12, 1958. Samuel was the tenth generation of Bennet grain farmers, and the *1947 Agriculture Act* assisted him in expanding the family's holdings of land so that grazing beef became part of their commercial enterprise. He had purchased the aeroplane to re-engage with his love of flight, a love which he had lost for many years as another victim of a horrific war.

The Bennet family were also devout Catholics, so the schedule for the following morning would be dedicated to the Sunday mass at the Catholic Church of Saint James the Less and Saint Helen in Colchester. The family were recusant, and their ancestral land holdings suffered because they remained devout Catholics after the English Reformation. Felicity was boarding at Woldingham Convent School in Surrey and would return to boarding school in two days. Therefore, she was desperate for her father to start teaching her more about how to fly a plane on her birthday, so that she could share her excitement with her fellow school colleagues.

The genesis of Felicity's desire to learn how to fly was because of the Soviet Union launching Sputnik 1 into space the previous October, an event marking the commencement of the space race. Felicity had been dreaming of space ever since that moment. The American president's attempt to downplay the significance of Sputnik 1 as a 'useless hunk of iron' was quickly dismissed by the Soviets' launch of Sputnik 2 the following month, so that by the end of November 1957, the world then braced itself for the era of the space race. Samuel had thought his daughter would only have an ephemeral fascination with space since Sputnik 1 beeped its way around the planet. Still, after the successful launch of Sputnik 2, she remained steadfastly committed to the idea of space as her future career path. The United States' launch of Explorer I in January 1958 heralded that country's entry into the race for space, and it further entrenched Felicity's desire to become involved in space flight as her chosen career.

Then, the tower radio message crackled within the cockpit of Samuel's Cessna. "All right, Charlie 2 5 Echo Bravo 3, your path is clear for take-off, over." Samuel raised his microphone to his mouth. "Roger tower, over and out." Felicity's excitement began to bubble inside her as Samuel lined up the Cessna on the runway for take-off. The lesson began.

They flew around East Anglia for two hours that morning as Felicity looked out upon the delightful landscape below this enchanting area of England. She loved the sensation of flying, and she gazed up into the sky, wondering what it was like to be able to escape Earth's atmosphere into the unknown depths of space. Felicity had been allowed to fly the aeroplane for about five minutes before Samuel took back over the controls. About half an hour after she experienced her momentary joy, Samuel instructed her on the necessary steps to land eventually. He took Felicity through the process of calculating the distance to the airport using the flight map, and Samuel informed Felicity throughout the flight to be aware of the distance travelled since departing the airport, the direction of flight vis-à-vis the intended destination, and, most importantly, how far away the aeroplane was from that destination.

And then it came time to land the Cessna. Felicity's adrenaline increased in excitement as the aeroplane slowly descended. Like the seasoned master of flying, Samuel safely landed the Cessna and then parked it in his designated hangar at Earls Colne Airfield. As they disembarked from the plane and walked towards the car park, Felicity was a bundle of excitement and happiness about the flight, but Samuel had one more surprise in store for her that morning. "How did you like that?" Felicity grabbed his left arm and pulled it up and down in glee. "Oh, Dad, that was great. Thank you so much. Can we fly again after church tomorrow, please?" Samuel smiled at his daughter, slightly shaking his head to let her down gently. "Oh, come on, I have already given up time away from my work today; I'm running a farm, not an amusement park. In any event, I have one more surprise for you?"

Felicity's eyes lit up like the headlights on a car. She tugged even harder on her father's left arm. "What is it, Dad? Are we going out for dinner?" Samuel scoffed through his laugh as he pulled his arm away. "God help me; give me my arm back before you dislocate it. No, your grandmother is preparing your birthday feast back at home as we speak. I was going to give you a few quid as a birthday present, but then, whilst we were flying, I thought the money should be spent on something you like." He paused in his speech for a moment as they approached the passenger door of his Rover 105, and as they reached the passenger door of his car, he grabbed her shoulders and spun Felicity around to face him. "I'm going to pay for you to have five flying lessons when you finish secondary school this coming July. And, if you matriculate to attend Oxford University, I will increase those lessons until you are granted a licence to fly. How do you like that?" Felicity was delighted as she could skite at school about her learning to fly. "Oh, Dad, thank you so much. Will you buy me an aeroplane if I am made dux of the school?" Samuel turned away, laughing out loud as he spoke. "Give me strength. Come on, let's get home before your grandfather drinks all my whiskey."

CHAPTER 3

With 'heaven' above and 'hell' below,
A young woman's life, and nowhere to go.

Catherine and Albert Bennet had handed the reins of the farm to their son, Samuel, not long after the war had finished. Their daughter Anne married an Australian pilot who was redeployed to England during the war. Hugh Fraser's father was Scottish, but he emigrated to the Adelaide Hills at the start of the century to purchase land for a vineyard that, by the outbreak of World War II, had grown in size and was producing crisp white wine; however, when Hugh volunteered for the Royal Australian Air Force in 1941, he had to serve with the Royal Air Force as he was only a first generation settlor. Still, Hugh and Anne emigrated to Australia immediately after the war in Europe concluded, choosing to live in the Adelaide Hills. Despite having two sons, they did not return to England.

Catherine and Albert had lost their other sons during World War II; Neil was killed in action as an inexperienced lieutenant at Dunkirk, and their other son, Peter, died on the beaches of France on D-Day. As their eldest son and by their adherence to the ancient right of primogeniture, Samuel was always going to receive the prime one hundred acres of farming land, which he had now expanded to two hundred acres. Still, the deaths of their other two sons had spared them as parents from any protestations their now-deceased sons may have made about Samuel's right. Like so many different English parents, they grieved the loss of their children; however, the bombing of the hospital that took Bridget away from their eldest son could not be forgotten or forgiven.

Any mention of the war would spark flames within Albert's seventy-five-year-old veins, which could only be extinguished by dousing his kidneys with ample doses of whiskey. When he was younger, Albert had been a gifted athlete. He was a champion four-hundred-yard runner at Oxford University, where he had commenced studying Rural Economy, until a right knee injury in his twenties robbed him of an opportunity to compete at the highest level of competition as a member of Great Britain's 1912 team, for the Stockholm Olympic Games.

His knee injury would also fortuitously excuse him from military service during World War I, a war that claimed the lives of his older and younger brothers. Instead, Albert returned to the family farming tradition, working for his father until the Spanish flu claimed his father's life in 1918. He met Catherine at the Colchester Church when they were teenagers, and they married in 1904, before Albert injured his knee, and before the outbreak of World War I. His knee injury left him with a slight limp in his right leg; however, Albert never mentally recovered from his lost opportunity as an athlete, and he would live vicariously through his sons to no avail and otherwise soothe his soul by consuming scotch each day after 5:00 p.m. He now forced his athletic dreams on Felicity, encouraging her from an early age to run each day, hoping she might one day run for her country. Still, he was oblivious to any physical consequences that may arise for his granddaughter by making her run each day from an early age.

Catherine came from a rigorous Catholic family who lived in Colchester. From an early age, her mother instilled in Catherine's mind that she had two pathways available in her life. She either matured into a young woman for whom nature would attract the opposite sex for her to marry, or if nature were not so kind, then she would have to serve the Catholic Church by joining a convent to be ordained as a nun eventually. Nature favoured Catherine with looks, making her a prize for the eligible Albert to take her hand in marriage by the time she was nineteen. She attributed the loss of two of her sons during World War II to being 'God's will'; such was her devotion to her faith. Since the birth of Felicity and, in particular, the conclusion of World War II, Catherine had progressively put on weight because she was constantly preparing meals in the kitchen, including from the day Felicity first began eating solid foods as a toddler. Along with baking biscuits or cakes, Catherine continually grazed in the kitchen. Whilst she might not have been morbidly obese, the once slender young woman had been replaced by an older, rotund version whose food consumption was unwittingly becoming a health hazard. Still, her size made her an imposing presence in Felicity's formative years.

Catherine's family were not heavy drinkers; she tolerated Albert's drinking habits as a dutiful wife. In keeping with their Catholic faith, Catherine would only consume a mere little glass of sherry on special occasions, a treat she looked forward to that evening to celebrate Felicity's birthday. Both grandparents assisted Samuel in raising Felicity, but Catherine had the final say regarding Felicity's morality and spirituality. Before a mouthful of dinner could be consumed, she required Felicity to say grace, and her views about a woman's place in society were too conservative, even for the 1950s. It did not matter how many urgent farming duties had to be undertaken, because attending the Catholic Church in Colchester for Sunday morning religious services took precedence over the work to be done on the farm. Catherine's stoic Catholicism even extended to explaining the late onset of Felicity's development to her. In contrast, other girls of Felicity's age were menstruating and developing breasts; Felicity seemed to be cocooned in a child's body. Catherine had told her it was God's will, and one day, the Lord Almighty might permit her to develop into womanhood, which was another reason why she must remain vigilant in her faith.

Catherine had commenced her work in the kitchen at midday to prepare Felicity's birthday dinner. The first cooking task was to make a chocolate cake for Felicity, and she had just made a tray of ham sandwiches for Samuel and Felicity's lunch before she had started mixing the cake recipe, so she was already slightly flustered in the kitchen. Felicity ran into the kitchen after she and her father had returned from Earls Colne Airfield. Her excitement was palpable after her morning flight, and then Samuel informed her about her birthday present. "Grandma! Grandma! You will never believe what Dad has given me for my birthday!" She startled her grandmother, causing her to drop the two eggs she was about to crack open for the cake recipe onto the floor. "Felicity!" Catherine's angry tone of voice could have stopped a Panzer tank, but it certainly caused Felicity to stop dead in her tracks. "Look at what you made me do!" Felicity's disposition of excitement had now become one of regret. "I'm sorry, Grandma." Notwithstanding her granddaughter's apology, Catherine continued to chastise her about her behaviour. "How many times have I told you not to run through the house? Now I will have extra work to do, cleaning up this mess."

Felicity may have just turned seventeen that day, but now she was being treated like a six-year-old child. "I'm sorry, but I just wanted to tell you about the surprise birthday present Dad just told me about." A surprise birthday present was also a surprise for Catherine. "Surprise birthday present? What is it?" By now, Catherine had scooped up the broken eggs from the floor with an old tea towel, and she was rinsing that cloth out in the kitchen sink as she awaited Felicity's response to her question. "Dad has given me flying lessons." Flying lessons did not align with what Catherine believed a young woman's life should be. "Flying lessons? What on earth for?" Before Felicity could reply, her grandmother interrupted her as she entered the pantry to select two more eggs.

"Sounds like a silly thing to me, Felicity. We will discuss it at dinner tonight. A tray of sandwiches is in the fridge for you and your father. Please take them into the breakfast room and tell your father his lunch is ready." Felicity rolled her eyes as she obeyed her grandmother's command, reflecting her current attitude towards her. "Silly thing! She'd better not tell me again tonight to be a nun!"

Catherine worked very hard in the kitchen that afternoon because she cooked Felicity's favourite dinner: pot roast beef and roasted vegetables, followed by a chocolate sponge cake for her birthday dessert. They had all bathed and dressed for dinner, and Felicity had to wear her 'old woman's' dress that her grandmother had sewn for her birthday. Samuel said grace before they ate their dinner, and then only he and his father spoke as they ate. After dinner, Catherine brought out Felicity's birthday chocolate cake, and Albert sang Happy Birthday. However, he was pretty off-key, as he had already consumed four glasses of whiskey. After Catherine had served a piece of sumptuous chocolate cake, which was accompanied by a freshly made dollop of whipped cream, Samuel then poured his mother a glass of sherry, signalling to Felicity that she could finally speak. "So, Grandma, may I now please talk about the birthday present Dad gave me?"

Catherine carefully placed her sherry glass on the white linen tablecloth, but her attention was directed to Samuel rather than her granddaughter. "Yes, Samuel, what is this nonsense about you paying for Felicity to learn how to fly?" Samuel had hoped it would be a pleasant evening, but now his mother was gearing up to give Felicity the speech: Be a good Catholic girl. "She likes flying, mother, so it seemed a practical gift." Catherine's dismay was evident as her eyebrows rose to their fullest extent. "Practical? It would be more practical if you paid for her to go to deportment school to win a man's hand. Goodness, she does not have her aunt's good looks to catch a man's eye easily."

Felicity was offended; she may have been a plain girl, but she was not ugly. "Grandma!" Before she could say another word, Samuel intervened. "Mother! Do not be rude, for goodness' sake; she is sitting right here!" Samuel's outstretched hand, pointing towards his daughter, did not prevent his mother's disapproving face from focusing on him. "Samuel, if she cannot win a nice man's heart with proper deportment, then her only other choice is to become a nun."

Felicity's ironic tone of voice conveyed her frustration. "Oh, really, not the nun speech again!" Samuel glared at Felicity to display his disapproval of her behaviour. Now, Felicity had also garnered her grandmother's disapproval and attention. "Yes. Really! What possible use can you be as a wife if you do not know how to act like one?" Felicity crossed her arms as an act of defiance towards her grandmother. Still, before she could speak, Albert decided he should intervene in the discussion to change the subject matter of their discussions, whilst simultaneously pouring his fifth liberal dose of whiskey for the night. "So Felicity, have you decided what you wish to study at university?" Felicity's jaw dropped as she turned to face her grandfather, having told him numerous times which tertiary courses she wished to study upon matriculating into university. "Science and maths, Grandpa. It was science and maths when I came home from school on holidays, and it will be science and maths when I return to school tomorrow." Felicity had now drawn her grandmother's disapproving ire. "Science? Maths? How may you do God's work as a young Catholic woman if you are studying those subjects?"

Felicity's eyes opened wide in an incredulous response to her grandmother's rhetorical question, but her father felt compelled to intervene before she could speak. "Oh, cripes! Mother! She wishes to study those subjects because she is interested in the new frontier of space travel, and learning to fly may also assist her." Felicity self-righteously nodded, approving her father's comment, but Catherine's piety could not be subdued. "Space? What a ridiculous notion. The only thing in space is heaven, the Lord our Father, and his son Jesus Christ. Space! I have never heard such a silly idea in my life!"

Catherine had completed her derisive statement whilst she contemporaneously started to clear the dessert plates from the dining table. Not a further word was spoken until she had left the dining room, and then Albert decided he would try to restore some cheer to the occasion. "So, have you been training for the four-hundred-yard sprint?" Felicity was still stewing over the browbeating she had received from her grandmother, so her disenchanted response did not reflect her desire to win that athletics race. "Yes, Grandpa, I jog each morning at 5:00, just like today." Albert persisted with the topic, even though it was apparent Felicity was not in the mood to be cheerful. "Are you going to win the inter-house competition?"

Felicity had endured enough indulgence for the evening, so she stood up to leave the table and muttered her response as she left the room. "Yes, Grandpa, I will do my very British best to beat the Jerries like we did." The mention of the Jerries stirred Albert. "What did she say about Jerries?" he asked his son incredulously. Samuel shook his head to dismiss his father's inquiry; it was meant to be a nice birthday dinner for his daughter, but his mother's conservative Catholic ideals had spoiled the evening.

Felicity stormed through the dining room, saying on top note, 'my very British best' before she eventually entered her bedroom and slammed the door behind her. She was disappointed with her grandmother's submissive Catholic ways that night. She changed her clothing to go to bed and looked at herself in the wardrobe mirror. "I'm not ugly, and I'm not going to be a nun, Grandma." Her disappointment with her grandmother's pious beliefs was one thing, but the old woman's derogatory comment was another. Whilst she may not have been a Rita Hayworth in the looks department, Felicity had an athletic body that compensated for her plain face. The whole notion of being a nun offended her independent feminist beliefs; however, she displayed her ongoing faith in her God by saying her prayers before going to sleep that night.

The following morning, Felicity awoke at dawn and went for her daily jog of about three miles. After her run, as she returned to the house, Felicity came across her father, who was working on the chicken coop. Samuel briefly talked to Felicity about her behaviour that she displayed the previous evening towards her grandpa. She accepted that she must display more respect towards her grandparents, and Samuel assured her that if either of his parents treated her poorly, he would intervene on her behalf. If only he knew what his daughter had to endure from her grandmother's derisiveness when he was not present. Later that morning at church, the tension between Felicity and Catherine could have been cut with a knife. Father O'Leary's Sunday homily did not ease the stress because he warned his parishioners about the evil that loomed in society if the female parishioners read any feminist literature written by Alva Myrdal or Viola Klein. Father O'Leary's fist thumped the pulpit as he spoke about the virtues of a woman's role: being one of service to the church or servitude as a wife.

During the priest's misogynistic homily, Catherine would look out of the corner of her eye at Felicity and self-righteously grunt whenever the priest mentioned the words service or servitude regarding a woman's role in society. Felicity's thoughts expressed her inner frustration. "They will be sorry if God turns out to be a woman!" However, Felicity maintained her composure regarding the priest's chauvinism and otherwise dutifully participated in the religious ceremony following her faith.

After lunch that Sunday, Albert drove Felicity back to the boarders' dormitories at Woldingham School because Samuel had urgent work to complete on the farm after sacrificing his Saturday morning to take Felicity flying. During their two-hour drive to the school, Albert discussed with Felicity many mundane matters, such as the importance of her continuing to train each morning in preparation for the inter-house athletics carnival; however, it was apparent to Felicity that her grandfather had another, more important topic on his mind, which he wished to discuss with her.

When they arrived at Woldingham School, Albert helped his granddaughter lift her luggage out of the boot of his Riley. Before she said goodbye to him to walk towards the dormitories, the old man finally spoke about the issue that had been on his mind. "Do not be too upset with your grandmother, Felicity, as she has your best interests at heart." Her grandfather patronisingly patted her on the shoulder as he said these words, resulting in an incendiary effect on Felicity's already thin nerves. "Well, see, Grandpa, that is the problem, right? It's always her opinion as to what is in my best interests. Why doesn't she treat me with a modicum of respect?"

The slight hostility in her tone conveyed to Albert that he should not discuss his wife's attitude about Felicity's best interests any further, and he held up his hands in a conciliatory display of his not wishing to enter into an argument with his granddaughter. "Very well then, I will not discuss the issue any further with you. In any event, you keep up your daily training regime so that you may be victorious in that four-hundred-yard race." That damn race! She did not want to upset her grandfather, but the four-hundred-yard race had been a burden during her secondary schooling, and Felicity found the training regime very tiring. Albert kissed Felicity on the cheek, then drove off, leaving her staring at him quizzically. "Why do my best interests have to be determined by somebody else?" Her disheartened voice was generated by her mental exhaustion from enduring 17 years of her overbearing grandmother's best intentions for her.

She slowly turned around, picked up her two luggage items, and walked towards the senior girls' dormitories to prepare for her final term of secondary schooling. Felicity would not have to endure her grandmother constantly chastising her about being a good Catholic woman. However, her life at school for the impending new term would challenge her morality while simultaneously opening a new door to her future.

CHAPTER 4

Like the other senior boarders at Woldingham, Felicity was afforded the luxury of having a room to herself, but it came at the price of carrying her luggage up four flights of stairs. She was relieved to finally reach her room after a long, exhausting journey with her two heavy bags. The senior boarders' rooms were adjacent to one another on either side of the long hallway on the fourth floor of the dormitory building. There were forty rooms on that floor of the boarding house, and midway down the hallway, there were bathroom facilities on either side for the young women to use. Felicity's room was the last one down the hallway on the right-hand side. Like the adjacent room on the left, it had the additional luxury of an extra window, allowing her to enjoy a view from her study desk. As she reached the end of the hallway, she saw that the door of the room opposite the hallway was closed, indicating to Felicity that she had returned to face her foe.

A girls' boarding school is always a melting pot of the hormonal emotions of young women whose lives are judged by their appearance rather than their brains. Woldingham was no different from any other girls' boarding school, except that for Felicity, there was one other girl in her senior year in whom mutual feelings of rivalry and angst were held. Amelia Speranza. When they first met, they were friends, but later became rivals, beginning on the day of the inter-house athletics carnival when Felicity won the Third Form four-hundred-yard race. Felicity had tried her hardest to be Amelia's friend since then, as she genuinely liked her; however, Amelia's competitive spirit, pride, and vanity were obstacles that seemed to militate against maintaining a friendship. Over the years, there had been glimpses of sunlight returning to their initial relationship, only to be thwarted by Amelia's entourage of fawners, in whom vanity eclipsed substance.

Each subsequent inter-house athletics carnival from Lower Fourth Form to Lower Sixth Form had been won by Amelia, and she took great delight each year in boasting about her success. Amelia belonged to the successful Stuart House, which would win most inter-house sports carnivals. Felicity belonged to the unfashionable runner-up Duchesne House.

Their rivalry had also transformed into a popularity contest amongst their teenage peers, where Amelia emerged as the most triumphant. Her parents were immensely wealthy because her grandfather, an Italian merchant, had wisely emigrated from Italy when Mussolini was on the verge of taking power in 1922. Amelia's grandfather had shrewdly maintained his market connections in Europe and the East. After the war, her father seized on the opportunities available to import products to help rebuild English society. Amelia's parents were well-known faces within the stratum of London's post-war 'high society', and it was because of their busy social lives that she boarded at Woldingham. Her parents' social page fame and wealth had now propelled Amelia to the helm of the school's student body, making her the Head Girl. Felicity had missed out on being selected for a prefecture.

There were also physical differences that intensified their rivalry. Whereas Felicity had small breasts, Amelia had developed adult breasts. Felicity's hair was straight and fawn-coloured, whereas Amelia had a beautiful head of wavy black hair like a Hollywood goddess. Amelia was the prettiest girl in the school, whereas Felicity was plain-looking as her face was still maturing. Amelia's presence on the school grounds was perpetually surrounded by an entourage of other pretty girls wishing to be just like her, and it was rumoured amongst the other girls that she was now dating the school captain of Worth School in Sussex, being the very eligible Antony Browne of the Montague line of noble Catholic families.

It was only in academia that Felicity excelled over Amelia, but even that success had been turned against her by her rival taunting her. After Sputnik 1 had soared around the heavens, Felicity had confided in her fellow science class students that she aspired to fly in space. The word then quickly spread around the school, and the teasing began. Amelia, from thereon, referred to Felicity as the 'Space Freak', and the unfortunate nomenclature had stuck. Even Felicity's close Sixth Form friends Natasha Grace and Heather Riddell would occasionally call her Space Freak to her face, but at least they did not use that name with malicious intent.

Amelia heard the sound of Felicity dropping her luggage on her boarding room floor, and she quickly opened the door to her room to taunt her inferior rival. "Space Freak! Welcome back. Did you meet any Cosmonauts during the break?" Amelia's condescending tone of voice echoed down the hallway, and a smirk accompanied it on her face. After enduring the belittling of her grandmother's conservative Catholic opinion, Felicity was now in no mood to be teased; however, she restrained her emotions to give back to Amelia. "You look like you put on a bit of weight during the break. When is the baby due?"

Felicity's retort only motivated Amelia to taunt her further, and some of the other senior boarders who had already returned to the dormitory that afternoon were now peering out of the doorway. Amelia's mocking laugh foreshadowed her next derogatory taunt, which was on its way. "Well, well? Isn't that the kettle calling the teapot black? Your boobies look like they have shrunk during the break, Space Freak. If they become any smaller, you might be able to join the RAF!" The sound of some other girls giggling behind their doors only intensified Felicity's shame about her physical development, and the initial restraint of her emotions was now gone. "Well, at least my father is teaching me how to fly! The only flying you will do is as a stewardess!" The other girl sensed her opponent's vulnerability and delivered the final humiliating taunt, her mocking laughter in unison. "Teaching you how to fly? Will he also introduce you to your prom partner, Space Freak, the man on the moon?"

The sound of the other girls giggling became a little louder, and Felicity's humiliation was now complete. She slammed the door to her room shut and kicked one of her bags in anger, causing it to fall on its side. She would not give Amelia the satisfaction of hearing her breaking into tears, but that is precisely what she felt like doing now. She calmed herself down, and after a few short moments, she opened her bag, which she had previously kicked over, and retrieved her copy of the latest publication of the *New Worlds* science magazine. She sat down at her desk and then turned to the magazine page that reported the news about Wernher von Braun's Redstone rocket successfully launching into space the American satellite 'Explorer 1', an event that heralded that the United States had now joined the space race. As she read the article, Felicity would occasionally glance out the window towards the sky, thinking about her impending flying lessons and dreaming about space.

Later that evening, Felicity sat down in the dormitory dining hall to eat dinner. She was joined at the table by Natasha and Heather, as well as some of the younger girls who were boarding on the lower floors. The three of them talked about what they had done during their respective breaks. Heather's family had travelled up to Scotland to see some of their relatives, and she regaled her two friends about how she had also seen Loch Ness. Natasha told her friends that she had been caught by her mother one afternoon snogging the boy next door, a story which caused some mirth amongst the three of them. Felicity was intrigued by Natasha's tale of French kissing a boy, as she had never done so. Indeed, she had never even kissed a boy. Felicity spat out her mouthful of dinner when Natasha described how the young man's tongue almost went down her throat as he slobbered on her face.

During dinner, Felicity would occasionally catch a glimpse of Amelia sitting at another table in the dining hall, holding court with her fawning followers as she discussed her adventurous life during school breaks, experiencing her parents' social life, and, of course, meeting up with Antony Browne. Towards the end of dinner, Felicity caught another glimpse of Amelia again, but on this occasion, she was not regaling her group of boarding house followers. On this occasion, Felicity saw Amelia staring at her, and once Amelia saw her, she caught her rival's attention. She smiled at her. It was not a mocking or condescending smile; instead, it was a friendly and inviting smile on her face. Felicity felt an unusual flutter in her heart, and she quickly looked away.

Later that night, Felicity was lying on her bed after she had said her bedtime prayers. Amelia's teasing taunts had initially been gnawing away at her mind. She was determined more so than ever before to humiliate her by winning the four-hundred-yard race, and she set her alarm clock to wake her up at 5:00 a.m. the next day so that she could train before breakfast. However, just before she fell asleep, her mind turned to the momentary incident towards the end of dinner when she saw Amelia smiling at her, and she couldn't understand her reaction to Amelia's smile. She could not understand why she had felt that flutter in her heart, but she remained resolute in her mind as she drifted off to sleep that she had to win that race.

Her last term of secondary school lay in front of her that next dawn, but after the weekend she had just experienced, she needed her sleep.

CHAPTER 5

A woman dressed in a uniform should not be scorned,
As, after all, they've had to fight from when they were born.

The first few weeks of Felicity's final term at Woldingham passed her by with its consistent routine. Each morning before class, the school assembly would be held by Mother Superior Sister Shawnessy, during which the girls would sing hymns, say their prayers, and then be lectured by her homilies about the evils of the flesh and the importance of maintaining their holy virginity. To watch the Mother Superior on one occasion would be enough to scare a child into submission; to experience her sanctimonious piety each morning was oppressive, and the older girls all longed for their graduation day when they did not have to hear the old nun's voice again.

Each Sunday morning at Mass, the school priest, Father Roper, would require the boarders to participate in the ritual of Holy Communion. Each evening during confession, he would hear at least one of the girls wail away that they had impure thoughts, and he would then tell them to ask for God's forgiveness while they prayed. If you had paid the man a dollar for each occasion he heard such a confession since joining the cloth, he would have been a millionaire by now, but on he would go each night, sitting in the confessional box, listening to privileged Catholic school girls pour out their hearts.

Felicity would be awake by 5:00 a.m. each day to commence her athletics training, and each afternoon and night, she busily studied away at her desk in her room. Each day, Felicity would be stirred by Amelia, whether it was just a glare, a giggle or the gibe of the unwelcome words of 'Space Freak'. She had not smiled at her again since the end of dinner a few weeks beforehand, so that event had drifted to the background of Felicity's mind.

You could almost set your watch to the drudgery of daily life at Woldingham, but then at the school assembly on the Monday of the third week of that term, an unexpected event occurred. Felicity had been intending to submit her application to study science and mathematics at Oxford University, an institution that she believed would offer the best tertiary science courses in

England. However, this particular Monday morning, a young woman dressed in a Women's Royal Air Force uniform was introduced by the Mother Superior to the assembly of students. "Good morning, girls. You are probably all wondering who the young woman in uniform is sitting behind me. Her name is Pilot Officer Joan Wilberforce, and she is studying medicine at Cambridge University and is also a reserve officer of the WRAF."

For most of the girls in the assembly, the idea of serving in any British armed service was not a career path they were interested in, but Felicity was. "Pilot Officer Wilberforce can complete her studies and serve as a reserve officer in the WRAF because she is a member of the University Air Squadron, or, as they refer to it on campus, the UAS. Listen carefully to her girls; after she has spoken, she is willing to answer any questions you may have about studying at Cambridge University, the UAS or the WRAF. Now, please welcome the Pilot Officer to the lectern as usual."

The clapping of the assembled girls was dispirited and lacking enthusiasm, but that reception did not daunt Pilot Officer Wilberforce. "Good morning, girls, and may I thank your Mother Superior and Woldingham School for allowing me to speak to all of you girls this morning. What I am about to discuss with you, young women, is mainly relevant to the upper sixth students, but it will also be relevant for you, younger girls, in the years to come. Now, first of all, have any of you heard about National Service?"

Including Felicity, there were perhaps a dozen students who nodded. The young woman on stage was undeterred by the lack of audience interest. "National Service is your way of helping Britain, girls. Our armed services need smart young people like yourselves, and British women played a crucial role in helping us win the war. Mother Superior mentioned the UAS, and yes, at Cambridge, you can serve your country by joining that reserve corps of the WRAF while also completing your degrees. It's a wonderful way to help our nation, and if you are accepted into the UAS as a cadet officer, you do not incur university tuition fees. Who likes that idea?"

Save for Felicity's nodding head, the speaker otherwise saw a sea of disinterested faces staring back at her. It was now time to try to inspire at least one of the girls. "I have been able to learn additional skills as a member of the UAS girls; one of those skills is that I have learnt how to fly, and I have been awarded a Preliminary Flying Badge. In combination with my future medical degree, I hope to one day be able to fly to remote areas of the world to provide urgent medical relief to disadvantaged people."

Felicity was impressed with the speaker's philanthropic ideals, but the rest of the girls were uninspired. She realised it was time to conclude her speech. "The opportunities now open to women at home and abroad are plentiful if you perform National Service with the UAS. Being a reserve officer in the WRAF even provides an opportunity to serve with the United States Air Force as part of the United Kingdom's defence collaboration with the United States. Thank you for listening to me this morning. If you wish to learn more about Cambridge University, the WRF and the UAS, I shall return to speak to girls personally after this assembly concludes."

The young woman then left the lectern, accompanied by the sound of the assembly's facile applause. Felicity was the only student who enthusiastically displayed her gratitude to her. For the next twenty minutes, Mother Superior bombarded the young girls' psyches with her scornful taunts about the evils of their flesh, their need to seek God's forgiveness each day and to be careful of teenage boys because their sole intentions at that age of their lives were to steal a girl's virginity before God had sanctified such a union in marriage.

The conclusion of the assembly could not come quickly enough for all the students, but for Felicity, it was because she wished to speak to Pilot Officer Wilberforce. She waited for the rest of the students to leave the hall before approaching the now-lonely figure of the guest speaker, who sat behind a desk set up for her by the school next to the stage. Felicity became slightly timid as she approached her, but the Pilot Officer's warm smile reflected her genuine intention to answer any student's questions about the subject matter of her speech. "Don't be afraid to speak to me; come sit down."

Felicity examined every inch of the woman's uniform, and she was impressed by it. She sat down in front of her, and a shy grin overcame her face. "No need to be shy now; we're all mature women here. What is your name, my dear?" The woman's tone was respectful, and that encouraged Felicity to speak openly with her. "It's Felicity, miss, Felicity Bennet." The Pilot Officer dismissed any need for formalities on this occasion. "We are not on parade here, Felicity; please call me Joan. What questions would you like to discuss with me, or do you wish to take one of these UAS brochures I brought with me today?" She patted a pile of about thirty brochures, each displaying the respective seals of the university and the WRAF on their cover.

Felicity decided to ask the most pressing question on her young mind. "Thank you, Joan. During your speech, you mentioned that being a reserve member of the WRAF provided an opportunity to serve with the United States Air Force. How can I do that?"

Joan was pleasantly surprised by the girl's question, which she felt may have emanated from a misunderstanding of her final statement to the assembly. "Whoa, Felicity, I did not mean to mislead you. You have to matriculate into the university curriculum at Cambridge before the UAS will consider your application. Do you wish to study at a university after secondary school?"

The young girl genuinely nodded to affirm her intention, but she did not elaborate beyond that. "What do you wish to study? Have you thought about a university you would like to attend?" Her response displayed a deeper intuitiveness regarding her future study and career path. "I wanted to study science, mainly physics and mathematics, at Oxford and become involved in the American space programme. I know this will sound silly, Joan, but I want to be the first woman to fly into space."

The young girl's desire to fly into space did not seem silly to the older woman, as even she secretly desired to be the first WRAF pilot to fly the rapidly developing technology of Royal Air Force jet fighters. Her reassuring smile conveyed to the schoolgirl her acceptance of the emerging space industry as a possible career path. "It's not silly at all, Felicity. Cambridge offers a master's degree in astrophysics and mathematics. WRAF officers can serve with the United States Air Force as part of our joint efforts in an officer exchange initiative to fight in the Cold War. I gather there would eventually be an opportunity to join the Americans' rocket programme. My fiancé and I want to serve with the Royal Flying Doctors in Australia when I graduate from medical school next year." She had revealed a portion of her personal life, a revelation the young girl could not resist. "You're engaged?" Joan quickly nodded as she spoke, unequivocally indicating that she did not wish to discuss her personal life too much. "Yes, I am. Still, let me get back to the genesis of my attendance here today. Are you interested in planes?"

The young girl's eyes displayed her enthusiasm for the topic. "Yes! My dad was a World War II fighter pilot, and he flew the Hurricane in combat missions during the Battle of Britain. He now owns a Cessna and started teaching me how to fly during the last school break. He has even paid for me to learn how to fly privately when I finish the school year!"

Joan nodded her head in approval of Felicity's imminent plans to learn how to fly before applying to the UAS to be an officer cadet. "Goodness me. That is impressive. I can tell you now, Felicity, if you have learnt to fly before applying to the UAS, your prospects of acceptance into it will be excellent. So do you want to give old Oxford the cold shoulder to come and study at Cambridge and maybe be accepted into the UAS?" The young girl's adamant response left no doubts. "Absolutely. I will tell my dad tonight. He will agree, but maybe my grandmother won't be happy about it."

The young woman was intrigued by the girl's failure to refer to her mother's response to her joining the UAS and the WRAF. "What about your mother? Does she get to have a say in your life?" Felicity's face quickly transformed from one of delight to another, now revealing a touch of sorrow in her heart. "My mum died during the war, Joan. A German bomb hit the hospital she was in, only days after I was born." Joan was mortified by her intrusion into the young girl's personal life, and she brought her right hand up to her mouth in a sign of her contrition. "Oh, I am so sorry for intruding, Felicity. I should not have asked that question."

Felicity's left hand touched the older woman's left hand to reassure her that she was not offended. "That is fine, Joan; I am not upset with you. I came to terms with this fact of life long ago." The young girl's soft and gentle touch was reassuring, and Joan felt like an older sister who had to protect her. She took the young girl's hand in her left hand to thank her for being so gracious and to encourage her to persist with her life aspirations. Felicity felt at ease with the soft touch of the older woman's hand; she, too, felt like the older woman was her older sister.

There was a moment afterwards of the mutual exchange of sisterly emotion, but Joan then resumed completing her task for that day. She then broke her left hand free of Felicity's hand and proceeded to hand her a brochure. "Alright then, how about you take one of these brochures for you to read about the opportunities available to you at Cambridge? Inside the brochure are the application forms to apply to study at Cambridge, as well as to join the UAS." Joan then stood up to bring their discussion to an end. "There we go, cadet. I look forward to seeing you on campus." Felicity eagerly took hold of the brochure, and she got up out of her chair to leave the hall. "I look forward to being a member of the UAS." She saluted the Pilot Officer as she hurriedly walked out of the hall.

It was an unbelievable dream come true for Felicity. She could study for her science and maths degrees at Cambridge while also gaining the additional skill of being a WRAF officer, which may lead to a career in the American space industry.

Her mind was occupied for the rest of that day by the thoughts of her joining the UAS at Cambridge and becoming a WRAF officer, and when the school bell rang at 3:00 p.m., she raced to the boarding house to telephone her father. She was so excited to speak to her father that it took her two attempts to insert the 4d coin into the slot of the public telephone. When she had finished dialling the number, her heart raced as she waited for her father to answer the phone.

His telephone had rung for the seventh occasion when Samuel answered it. He had not even taken off the gloves he was wearing while cleaning out the chicken coop at the back of the house. His dirty boot marks had left a long trail behind him on the finely polished hallways that eventually led to the drawing room. He was slightly out of breath from racing through the house to answer the telephone, having done so because his mother and father were staying in their separate accommodation that afternoon due to the cold and wet weather that had blown in earlier. "Hello, Samuel speaking." He had barely finished his last word when he then heard the excited voice of his daughter talking over the top of him on the other end of the line. "Daddy, guess what, guess what? I have wonderful news." Her loud and excitable tone of voice slightly took him by surprise. He wondered why his daughter's voice seemed so excited on a Monday afternoon, but he had to settle her down first. "Just settle down, please, sweetie, because my ear is still ringing. Is there a problem at school?"

On the other end of the telephone line, Felicity shook her head because she had good news, not bad. "No, Dad, there isn't a problem, but I have wonderful news." She was still overwhelmed by excitement, so her father continued to try to calm her down. "Just slow down there, please, sweetie, because I can hardly understand your words. Now, what is this news?" She held her breath briefly to settle her nerves before speaking. "I'm going to become a WRAF officer, which will eventually give me the chance to go into space." This was surprising news for Samuel. He was aware of the existence of the WRAF and the UAS, but he never anticipated that his daughter would join the Royal Air Force's reserve corps. "You are going to do what?" His disbelief and confusion made her realise her story needed to be adequately explained. "Okay, okay then. I will start at the beginning. This morning at assembly, a WRAF officer spoke to us about joining the UAS at Cambridge University, and I am going to do it, Dad. I am going to apply to study at the University of Cambridge and join the UAS. You won't even have to pay for my university tuition."

Even after hearing his daughter's explanation, Samuel remained surprised and uncertain about the news. "I still don't understand what you are saying, Felicity. How does the WRAF lead to space? And what about Oxford University? I thought you wanted to study science and maths there?" She now tried even harder to calm her excitable nerves so that she could adequately explain herself. "All right. I shall do my best to explain it. Pilot Officer Joan Wilberforce spoke to us this morning about the opportunities available to women students who study at Cambridge and do National Service at the same time by joining the University Air Squadron. You have heard of the UAS, haven't you, Dad?" Well, of course, he had heard of it because he was a former Royal Air Force officer. "Of course, I have heard of the UAS Felicity, but please, go on. How does this lead to space? And what about Oxford? I wanted you to follow in my footsteps."

Felicity could hear the slight disappointment in her father's voice, so she did her best to indulge him while she also tried to explain the link between the WRAF and space. "I know, Dad, I, too, did want to follow in your footsteps at Oxford, but my future lies ahead of me at Cambridge. In any event, if I join the UAS and become a WRAF officer, I will eventually be able to serve with the US Air Force through a joint officer exchange programme. Cambridge is offering a master's degree in Astrophysics, Dad, so it makes sense for me to go there rather than Oxford. The flying lessons you will pay for me to complete during the summer break almost certainly mean that I will be accepted into the UAS. This is not some silly little dream for me, Dad. This is my future career. You do understand, don't you, Dad?"

Samuel now understood what Felicity wanted to do by studying at Cambridge and joining the UAS and the WRAF. As much as he was slightly disappointed she would not be studying at Oxford, he loved his daughter too much to allow his will to overbear her life choices. "I guess I understand, sweetie. And yes, I do understand you have your heart set on flying in space. So, if studying at Cambridge and joining the UAS is what you really want to do in life, then I support you, sweetheart, but I don't know how I am going to explain these developments to your grandmother." Her father's dry wit caused her to laugh as she tried to speak. "Oh, spare me, Dad! I am glad I will not be present for that discussion. Just tell the old grumpy soul I am doing my National Service because she won't be able to argue with that." He now chuckled, but he begged to differ with her. "Oh, my little girl, you don't know your grandmother. She could argue with a brick wall. Anyway, I am glad you called me first before applying to Cambridge. You have my blessing, sweetie. I love you." It did not matter how old she was now; hearing her father's affectionate words brought a warm glow to her heart. "I love you too, Dad."

She was about to hang up the telephone when she heard her father's voice quickly interrupt her. "Oh, Felicity, I do have some news for you from your grandmother. She has spoken to Timothy MacDougall's mum and they have arranged for him to be your partner for the Woldingham Promenade." Felicity was now surprised; she did not have a boy in mind to take to the prom, but now her meddling grandmother had even taken that opportunity of choice away from her. She had known Timothy since she was a little girl, as his family also attended the same church, but she did not really care for him. "Oh, poop, Dad. Not him! He picks his nose and eats it. Do I have to go with him?" He smiled, but he knew the answer would have to be yes to make his mother happy. "He was a young child when he did that, and yes, you have to take him to the prom. It will make your grandmother happy, and goodness knows I will need something to make her happy after I tell her your news. Now, go and do your homework," She reluctantly agreed. "Okay, Dad, if it makes her happy, I will take Timothy, the snot eater, to my prom. Bye, Dad." She hung up the telephone and shook her head. Timothy MacDougall!

Later that evening, Samuel told Catherine about Felicity's news concerning her intention to study at Cambridge University and to become a WRAF officer. Catherine was not amused! "Why on Earth are you indulging her in this fantasy, Samuel? She is not like your sister, whose beauty enticed the hand of wealth; Felicity needs to be directed to the Sisterhood rather than space!" Samuel had heard enough of his mother's constant disparagement of his daughter's dreams. "For goodness' sake! Mother!! Let my daughter live her life the way SHE chooses!" Samuel's harsh tone towards his mother brought an uncomfortable silence to the dinner table, and the daggers continued to be stared between them long after the words had drifted off into the night. Samuel was no longer hungry, and he angrily pushed his plate away from the dinner table while simultaneously sending his dining chair crashing backwards to the floor as he left. Catherine swung her head defiantly away in the opposite direction to Samuel's route of departure from the room as Albert quietly emptied his whiskey tumbler in the direction of his liver.

Samuel stormed outside into the backyard, disregarding the crisp night's air. He kicked the ground in anger, which sent a lump of turf flying through the air to land smack-bang on top of the chicken coop, causing the hens no end of alarm to be unexpectedly awoken like this. Samuel looked up at the clear night sky, and as he searched the stars with his eyes, he sought clarity of thought: "Bridget, my darling love of my life. Please tell me I am right to let our little girl choose her destiny. How I wish you were here." There was only silence, but Samuel remained undeterred in his unconditional love and support for Felicity. As for his mother? "She can go to bloody purgatory for all I care! It's Felicity's life, not her's!"

CHAPTER 6

Run faster than before and win that prize,
Still, will the victory be thy only surprise?

Junior Sister Patricia O'Toole was the nun in charge of Duchesne House. However, among the girls of Duchesne House, she was happy to be referred to as Sister Pat. She was a member of Great Britain's 1952 Olympic team. She had qualified for the final of the 200 metres at the Helsinki Games; however, she injured her calf early in the race and finished in a disappointing last place. Sister Pat's calf did not heal enough to participate in competitive athletics again. By late October 1953, at 23, she had decided to follow the path her parents had initially envisaged for her to join the cloth. Sister Pat saw the potential athlete within Felicity. She had encouraged her over the years to keep trying, hoping she might eventually beat Amelia again, as Felicity had done in her first school year. Sister Pat was also the assistant coach to Sister Clare, who was the school's athletic coach for its interschool athletics carnival. This event was held one week after the inter-house championship, and only one girl from each form would be chosen to represent Woldingham, making the winner of an inter-house event the school's representative. The inter-school carnival was held the week before the school prom, so a specific prestige factor was attached to being known as a senior form representing Woldingham. Amelia was perceived as the 'favourite' to be selected to represent Woldingham for the final form, but she had not trained as much as Felicity had.

The four-hundred-yard trial was the precursor to the inter-house final. The trial was an opportunity for Felicity to display her improvement in the race she had lost in previous years, and it was also an opportunity to get inside Amelia's head. Sister Pat oversaw the girls' limbering up before the time trial to ensure they did not injure themselves during the trial run. She noticed that Felicity seemed to be far more flexible than Amelia, and the former had a steely determination in her eyes, as opposed to the latter's girl's blasé approach to warming up. Eventually, Sister Clare blew her whistle to signify that the time trials were beginning for each form. Still, Felicity stayed with Sister Pat for a few moments as the other girls, including Amelia, began to wander over to the start line, and Sister Pat's words were prescient. "Felicity, it is now or never to take the steps needed to win this race. Amelia has become complacent; she has not trained nearly enough, and I don't mean to be harsh, but she is carrying a bit of extra weight. Run this time trial like the actual race; every opponent, yes, even Amelia, will be unnerved by your speed."

Felicity continued stretching as Sister Clare blew her whistle for the second time, signifying that the time trials would begin in one minute. Sister Pat looked at Felicity, and in her eyes, she saw the focus and discipline that many months of rigorous training and complete faith in her ability had produced. "Do you have any questions?" Felicity shook her head to dismiss the enquiry. "Great! Well, you give it your all, and don't be afraid to chase the fastest time because only six of you can compete for the inter-house crown." Sister Pat gave Felicity a pat on the back, then nudged her shoulder to head over to the trackside enclosure where the other girls were also waiting.

Ten upper sixth-form girls lined up at the staggered starting line. Felicity had Amelia to her immediate left side, which meant she would not know until the last one hundred yards whether she would finish ahead of Amelia. The other upper sixth-form girls were not a concern for either Amelia or Felicity. "On your marks!" Sister Clare's calls were obeyed as each girl took their mark. "Get set!" Felicity's mind focused on the finishing line while she waited for Sister Clare's whistle. Then the whistle blew, and like a greyhound out of its box, Felicity sprang immediately into top gear, and she ran as though it was the inter-house race, driving her legs with all their might. At the one-hundred-yard mark, she could hear some of the student spectators beginning to call out her name, but she did not reduce her pace. By the two-hundred-yard mark, she could feel her lungs starting to strain, but her legs did not slow. As she passed the three-hundred-yard mark, the screaming excitement of the student spectators she could hear suggested to Felicity that she was well out in front of Amelia. Time seemed to slow down over those one hundred yards, and even though her leg muscles ached, Felicity kept pushing her body further and further out in front. She galloped across the line at least twenty yards ahead of Amelia, whose shocked face matched her falling over the line in a worn-out second place. She had never been beaten by such a distance in this race at the previous inter-school carnivals, let alone demoralised like this in the time trial for the inter-house carnival. The paltry Duchesne House girls watching from the sidelines raced over to congratulate the heroine of the moment, and even Sister Pat could not contain her excitement as she, too, raced over to congratulate Felicity. Amelia was still lying on the ground in her exhausted state, as the gravity of her comprehensive loss in the time trial began to sink in, because she knew from the start of the race that she was behind Felicity, and even running at her top speed, she could not catch her.

Eventually, Felicity went to the public telephone to call her father. The excitement of her father and grandfather about her time trial result was palpable, but as usual, her grandmother would not congratulate her; not even a 'Well done!' could be heard. Her father told her both he and her grandfather would come to school to watch the inter-house meet, and the pride in Samuel's voice over the telephone warmed Felicity's heart. That night in the boarders' dining room, the excitement about Felicity's time trial run had not abated among the other girls. While the Stuart House girls glared over at Felicity's table with disapproval, Amelia did not display any hostility towards Felicity. Indeed, Amelia's eyes met Felicity's from across the expanse of the dining room, and there was a hint of approval in Amelia's eyes that fluttered Felicity's heart rather than firing the furnace of her ego.

The following day, Sister Clare declared to the assembly that the four-hundred-yard race was now an event well worth watching and that Felicity would start in the favourite's lane, which was lane one. Amelia had hardly blinked an eyelid when this announcement was made; instead, she had turned her head to look down the row towards Felicity, and the slight grin on her face seemed inconsistent with any signs of concern.

CHAPTER 7

She lives rent-free in the attic of thy mind,
And no escape hatch can thee find.

After the fanfare of the time trial and Sister Clare's bold announcement at the assembly the next day, Felicity did not stop her morning training routine of getting up at 5:00 to train. During her first morning run, after the assembly, she tried not to think about the inter-house carnival. Instead, Felicity thought about the flying lessons she would take when her life in secondary school finished in about four weeks; she thought about studying at Cambridge, and, of course, she thought about one day being the first woman to travel into space. Her ultimate career goal could not be overwhelmed by any thoughts she had about winning the inter-house upper-sixth form four-hundred-yard race; indeed, if it had not been for Amelia previously taunting her, she probably would not be running right now. Amelia! She could not get thoughts of her out of her head, and Felicity had been wondering, ever since Sister Clare's announcement at the assembly, why Amelia had been occasionally smiling at her since then. The final moment was when, as she was about to walk into her dormitory room the previous night, she caught a glimpse of Amelia smiling at her through the half-open door. Felicity was about to speak to her, but Amelia then slowly closed her door to the room, almost in an enticing manner. This behaviour dumbfounded Felicity. The truth was, the more Felicity saw a semblance of warmth on Amelia's face over the past twenty-four hours, the giddier she felt. It was a strange feeling, and she was now struggling to keep Amelia out of her head.

The same behaviour occurred later that day, after school had finished. This time, it happened on the track and field oval as the girls practised for the inter-house carnival. Felicity was about to practise her starting steps for the four-hundred-yard race, the most critical moment of the race when explosive energy was required, when she caught a glimpse of Amelia standing by the side of the track, about 20 yards away, smiling at her. Enough was enough; Felicity withdrew from her starting stance, and she walked towards Amelia, not knowing what to expect but seeking an explanation. "All right. What is it, Amelia? Why are you smiling at me like that?" As she finished her sentence, Felicity stopped in her tracks about five yards away from Amelia. However, Amelia did not respond to the question; instead, she continued to smile with that most enticing smile, and Felicity took the bait. "Please! Amelia! What is going on?" There was no response, and Amelia then walked over to the starting line for the designated second-place runner. As she turned around to assume her starting position, Amelia displayed an enticing little smile towards Felicity before focusing on her own running technique. "Fine, don't talk to me!" Felicity then stormed over to her running lane to resume practising her starting technique. Still, she could not get Amelia out of her head – so much for Sister Pat's theory of athletic psychology.

During the next ten days, Amelia's behaviour did not stop; she continued her wicked little game of grins, and Felicity became progressively more confused by them. Felicity did not allow Amelia's behaviour to interrupt her schoolwork. Still, most of the upper sixth form examinations had already been completed, save for a few physics and biology practical demonstrations, an exercise that posed no problems for such a bright young woman as Felicity. She would not be the dux of the school, as that honour was awarded to Susan le Spring. Still, Felicity was placed second overall with her marks, which meant she was certain of matriculating into a prestigious tertiary institution, such as Cambridge University. Amelia's strange behaviour towards Felicity continued everywhere around the school. Even Sister Pat noticed something unusual was happening during one afternoon of Duchesne House training, when she was assisting Felicity with stretching. "What is wrong with Amelia, Felicity? Why is she grinning at you like that?" Felicity shook her head from side to side because of the strain of stretching her legs under the pressure of Sister Pat's full strength, pressing them down. "You don't know? All right then, I shall find out for you." Sister Pat hopped up from her crouched position next to Felicity, and she took on an out-of-character stentorian school teacher demeanour as she walked over towards Amelia. "Amelia, why on Earth are you grinning like that towards Felicity? Are you trying to wear her down psychologically? You're not being a good sport if you are."

When Sister Pat finished her sentence, she would have only been a yard away from Amelia, but like a cool cat, Amelia did not flinch, and she instead grinned at Sister Pat and then walked over to the track lane, still smiling at Sister Pat. Amelia then got down to her starting position, and just before she took off for her run around the track, she once again shot a similar little smile over Felicity's way. Sister Pat walked back over towards Felicity, and she was shaking her head in disapproval. "If that girl's parents did not donate so much money to this school, I would demand Sister Clare boot her off the athletics team. Half smart and too much damn money behind her!" Two strong words coming out of Sister Pat's mouth in one afternoon were unusual. Still, Felicity could not now be distracted from wondering what on God's Earth Amelia was trying to do to her, and she just stared at her running around the track as the clueless gallery of Stuart House girls at the training session that afternoon screamed out in support of Amelia.

Subsequently, the girls were brow-beaten by Father Roper three mornings before the inter-house meet. The priest set out in the pulpit above, summoning the fear of God to scare the girls about misbehaving with boys at the school prom. It was when Father Roper said the boys might touch the girls in funny places, but the girls were forbidden to respond, that Felicity almost screamed out in rage. She was just about to call out in anger about the priest's sexist observations when Natasha spoke loud enough for everyone else to hear. "So, what does that mean? They could try to touch my boobies, but I have to stand still like a light pole?" The murmur of girls giggling beneath their hands could be heard, but Father Roper was not deterred. "Yes, don't respond to them or lead them on." Natasha was not deterred, and Father Roper's sexist comments just egged her on. "So, according to your views, I cannot touch the boy, but he touches me like a doll? Is that right, Father Roper?" It was sexist; however, Father Roper did not like being chastised by a school student. "A good, Christian girl would not put herself in that position, and I don't like the tone of your voice, so go to Mother Superior now." Natasha lifted her eyebrows as she glanced at Felicity, and for her part, Felicity was stewing in her mind about the priest's sexist comments. "This is a damn man's world." Felicity watched Natasha leave the school chapel. Father Roper's actions in sending Natasha to see the Mother Superior gnawed away at her, whilst the priest pontificated away about the devil within them. She would not speak these words, but they remained on her mind as Father Roper continued his brow-beating and pious ways: "I bet he has given in to his urges, the hypocrite". When it came time to pray, Felicity bowed her head respectfully and asked her God a simple question. "Please, God, get me out of this school. Get me out of this man's world."

During the lunch hour, Felicity and Heather could not wait to interrogate Natasha about what punishment Sister Shawnessy had imposed on her for speaking to Father Roper in such a defiant manner. "It's unbelievable. I have to say the Rosary ten times a day for the next three days, and I have to clean the chapel every evening until we finally get to escape from this hellhole." Hellhole! Felicity and Heather looked at each other and then giggled as soon as they heard Natasha describe Woldingham in this manner. "Well, it is a hellhole. You agree, don't you, Felicity?" Felicity could not lie to her friends. "As much as I love my God and Jesus our saviour, yes Natasha, I agree. This place is regressive because, after all, it produced my grandmother." Even though they had not met Catherine, both Natasha and Heather giggled as Felicity had described her grandmother in unflattering terms on numerous occasions to the girls. Eventually, the topic of the inter-house carnival was bound to be discussed, as the athletics meet was now only days away. Heather was the unfortunate individual who raised the topic on this occasion. "So, are you excited, Felicity? About the race, that is, are you excited or nervous?" Felicity's crisp response revealed her frustration with Amelia. "No! I wish I had not won that damn time trial." Heather retracted from her line of inquiry, but Natasha immediately detected the underlying tension running through her friend's veins. "What is up, Felicity? Is Sister Pat pushing you too hard?" Felicity shook off the question, but then, after a few moments, she revealed what was on her mind. "No, it's not Sister Pat, and I'm sorry I bit like that, Heather." Heather nodded her head and smiled, revealing she held no grudge. "It's Amelia; she is getting in my head after winning the time trial meant I should have been in hers. Anyway, can we discuss something else? What are your plans for the summer? What are you both going to do once we escape this 'hellhole'?" An embarrassed smile came over Heather's face, as she would not be attending a university. "My parents will probably ship me off to a deportment school to learn how to be a good wife." Natasha lifted her eyebrows in disgust. "Pee-ewe. What bloody century do your parents live in? The 15th century?" Felicity nodded her head in agreement. "Yes, Heather. I agree with Natasha. It is your life, so you should have a say in how you will live it. My grandmother wants me to become a nun, but that will not happen! What about you, Natasha?" The enquiry revealed Natasha's depressing roadmap, which was drawn for her by her parents. "Secretarial college. 'Daddy' is going to find me a job with one of his friends in Whitehall, which is fine, I suppose, except I hope I don't end up working in the Ministry for Education because, knowing my luck, I would have to put up with Woldingham again." All three girls giggled and then fell silent. Felicity did not want to say it to her friends, but she was glad she would not be herded off to a predetermined future, as had been the case for her two friends.

CHAPTER 8

When Cupid's arrow finds the bullseye of thy heart,
Be careful! Sometimes, it's trouble from the start.

It was the day before the inter-house athletics carnival, and notwithstanding the excitement in the air, Felicity's mind was occupied with her final secondary subject assessment. It was an oral presentation for her physics class, and even though Felicity knew her subject matter might attract the muttered comment of 'Space Freak' being directed her way, she decided to present her dissertation on U.S. Air Force Captain Charles E. "Chuck" Yeager's feat of flying at Mach 1 in 1947. The only Stuart House student in the class was Cecilia Campbell, or 'CC' as the other students called her. Still, she would not let an opportunity go by, and belittling Felicity was a character trait imbued into CC's nature just as much as any Stuart House girl.

Sister O'Hare, the ever-dutiful sixth-form physics teacher, called out Felicity's name, and as she rose from her chair, Felicity heard CC's sotto voce remark: "Space Freak's turn." Some other students giggled, but Sister O'Hare would not tolerate such immaturity. "Who said that?" Nobody would snitch, not even Felicity. "Be quiet; stop giggling and let your pupil present her assignment without interruptions!" Sister O'Hare may have been diminutive in her physical stature, but her tongue could cut through steel when stirred. All of the girls sat there silently, and when Felicity reached the front of the class, she took a moment to glare at CC before her speech. Then, she was ready to speak. "On 14 October 1947, at 42,000 feet, near Rogers Dry Lake in the southern California desert, U.S. Air Force Captain Chuck Yeager became the first person to fly quicker than the speed of sound."

Felicity paused for a moment to look around the class, and she noticed CC had a faint hint of a smirk, which only inspired Felicity to deliver a breathtaking speech. "Sure, we have learnt about that fact, but you do not know how he managed to do it only two years after World War II, do you?" Her rhetorical question hung in the air, and then she smiled. "It was one of the great moments of courage in the meeting of physics and engineering. The courage, well, that is not physics; that is just the love of flying. However, the engineering of the Bell X-1, the *Glamorous Glennis*, well, that was physics at its finest. The starting point was the aerodynamics of the Bell X-1 because its fuselage was shaped like a bullet." Felicity then turned around and walked over to the chalkboard, surprising even Sister O'Hare with the direction she was taking her oral presentation in. She picked up the chalk and quickly sketched a bullet. "So, bullets were breaking the speed of sound before 1947, but their design had not really been incorporated into the design of aircraft. A bullet is fired from the muzzle at a velocity of two thousand seven hundred feet per second or, to give some idea of speed, about one thousand eight hundred and sixty miles per hour. It is Newton's second law, as the time rate of change of the bullet's momentum is equal in magnitude and direction to the force imposed upon it." Felicity then drew some lines above and below the bullet, and when she turned around, she could see that her classmates, even CC, were captivated. "When a bullet is fired upwards, it will take approximately 30 seconds to reach two miles high, but its velocity is now zero because of air resistance and gravity. Newton's third law of motion – the air applies forces to the bullet that are equal in magnitude and opposite in direction, and so with gravity, the bullet's velocity is reduced to zero, and it falls back to earth at a much slower speed. However, the Bell X-1 cannot be fired from a muzzle, and that is where rocket engineering technology is brought into the physics of this remarkable feat of human technology."

Felicity paused; she waited to see if the words 'Space Freak' were muttered, but all she saw were the faces of an engaged audience. "Alright, then. So, the X-1's fuselage is shaped like a bullet, and its wings are thin but strong to overcome dangerous aerodynamic forces. This is where the rocket technology plays its part, as the X-1 had a four-chambered rocket engine that provided 26,500 newtons of static thrust when fired. The average thrust exerted on a point twenty-two calibre bullet is 900 newtons, so on this occasion, the X-1 wins." The girls laughed, not mockingly; it was genuine appreciation. Felicity regaled them for another 10 minutes with her presentation about Chuck Yeager, the breaking of the sound barrier, and rocket technology. When she concluded her presentation, the class broke out into rapturous applause in unison, and Sister O'Hare nodded her head in approval as Felicity sat down at her desk. "You see, girls, there is nothing freakish about space. Well done, Felicity, that is a ten out of ten." Felicity nodded ever so slightly back at Sister O'Hare, and then she turned to face CC, who was sitting behind her; the smirk now belonged to Felicity.

With her physics presentation out of the way, Felicity's mind returned to its focus on that damn race the next day, but before she could become too focused, she had to call her father to tell him the news about her physics presentation and, of course, to see if he and Grandpa were still coming to watch the race the next day. The telephone seemed to ring forever before Samuel answered it at the other end. "Hello, Samuel speaking." Felicity detected an ever so slight impatience in her father's tone. "Hi, Dad. It's me. Are you okay?" There was a slight pause, but then Samuel's spirits seemed to spark up. "Hi, Felicity. Yes, I am fine; I just have to fix the chicken coop, and that is always a delightful job when it is damp. Anyway, how are you? I am so excited about tomorrow, and so is Grandpa!" That was the first question out of the way. "So am I, Dad, so am I." She was lying. That damn race had been getting to her mind ever since the time trial. "I got ten out of ten for my physics presentation about the X-1 today." His daughter's love of flight and, in particular, jets, brought a smile to an old fighter pilot's face. "Well done, sweetie! You mesmerised them with your Chuck Yaeger speech." Even Felicity felt proud. "Yes, Dad. No more 'Space Freak' nicknames for me. I'm so happy you and Grandpa are still coming tomorrow because, gee, I could do with your support." Samuel detected the faint hint of perhaps uncertainty in his daughter's voice. "Is everything okay with you, Felicity?" She didn't wish to reveal the psychological warfare she had been enduring with Amelia since the time trial. She took a moment to think. "Yes, Dad. I am fine. It's just the pressure that has been building up since I won the time trial, so I want to get this race out of the way." She did not sound fine, but Samuel would not intrude too much into his daughter's psyche. "All you have to do, sweetie, is give it your best. I will be proud of you no matter what happens." If simple words could ever heal a troubled mind, they did on this occasion. "Thanks, Dad. I love you." Her father reciprocated the warmth of her tone. "I love you too, sweetie. Now, go and get an early night's sleep. Bye." The telephone call ended, but Felicity wished her father could be with her tonight to help calm her nerves.

Felicity did not see Amelia in the dining hall that evening, which was a relief from putting up with her persistent grin. Whereas Heather and Natasha wanted to keep on talking after dinner, Felicity decided to follow her father's sagacious advice and go to bed early for the evening. As she walked down the hallway towards her room, she noticed Amelia's doorway appeared to be open. When she reached her door, Felicity turned to peer into Amelia's room, but she was not within it. "Goodness knows where she could be", Felicity thought to herself as she entered her room. Felicity flicked the switch for the light in her room to come on, and she was immediately startled, as standing there before her was Amelia.

"Oh, cripes, Amelia! You scared the living daylights out of me! What are you doing in my room?" Amelia did not speak. Instead, she walked over to the door and closed it. With her right hand still holding the doorknob, she turned around and leaned back into the door. Felicity, after her initial shock, was now puzzled as Amelia dipped her chin and then looked up at her, almost as though she was trying to entice her. It was working on Felicity as her heart began to flutter. "What is going on? Amelia, what are you doing in my room?" Amelia could detect Felicity's submissiveness in the tone of her voice, and now she was ready to speak her mind, which she did as she slowly walked over towards her. "I know you like me, Felicity. I could tell from the first day we met here at school that you wanted to be my friend. I have caught you staring at me from time to time over all these years." Amelia was now only a foot away from Felicity, and Felicity was overwhelmed with the contemporaneous feelings of nervousness and, somewhat strangely, giddiness. "I don't know what you are talking about..." She did not get to finish her sentence because Amelia placed her elegant and slender index finger over her lips. Shen leaned in towards Felicity so that the tips of their noses were touching. "Shoosh, my sweet little admirer. Your secret is safe with me."

Felicity felt like a rabbit caught in the headlights of an oncoming car, and she realised her pulse was pumping feverishly away. Amelia broke away from her, and she began to circle slowly around her like a shark. "It is fine. I like you too, and I want to be friends." She stopped behind Felicity, and Amelia reached out with her left hand to gently stroke her hair, causing Felicity to quickly turn her head to display her curious, apprehensive expression. "I want to be friends with you as well, Felicity, but I need you to do something for me?" Felicity was like putty in Amelia's hands. Seldom had they been civil, and the mere mention of the word 'friends' made Felicity's heart skip a beat. "What do I have to do?"

Amelia's hand stopped stroking Felicity's hair, and the room became quiet. After a pregnant pause of ten seconds, Felicity could not bear the tension anymore, and she turned around to ascertain what was going on behind her. Amelia was now leaning up against Felicity's chest of drawers; her pose was like a gangster's moll from a 1930s movie. "I want you to lose that race for me tomorrow." Now Felicity was genuinely shocked. "You want me to what? Are you insane?" Felicity's demeanour had changed from that of being the obsequious prey to now being truly mystified. Amelia now leapt at the opportunity, and she walked over to Felicity and kissed her on the lips. Mystery now became terror for Felicity because she had never been kissed on the lips like this by anyone, but another girl kissing her lips was the work of Satan's Lilith. Her heart told her it felt nice, but her head told her it was wrong. Felicity pulled her head back, and she froze in the spot where she stood. Amelia smiled. "Lose for me, Felicity. Let me win tomorrow, and I will make it up to you on the night of our prom." Felicity's mind was twirling with thoughts of utter sin; she had trained for this race, but being close to Amelia was so alluring. "How will you make it up? Will you invite me to your pre-prom party?"

Amelia could see innocence being swallowed by impetuous, unnatural feelings in their environment. However, she was not going to break the mystery now, and she once again encircled her prey before devouring it. "You will see. Lose that race tomorrow, for me. You will not regret it." She then fleetingly glanced at Felicity's eyes and saw a mirror in the helpless soul. Poor Felicity was still frozen in the same spot where she stood. Amelia leaned in again and gently, but also, lasciviously, kissed Felicity's lips. The unknown fire of desire ran through Felicity's veins. Amelia pulled her lips away from Felicity's, but she gently rubbed the tip of her nose against Felicity's nose tip. "I promise you, it will be worth your while." Then Amelia smiled before turning away to walk out the door as though her work had been done.

Felicity stood still for another half minute, then took a deep breath and sat on her bed. She initially felt this impulsive longing for Amelia's gentle touch again, but the oppression of 1950s country conservatism and devout Catholicism took over her mind. It was almost like two voices began shouting in her mind. Her grandmother's stentorian and disparaging voice scolded her for being wicked. Simultaneously, Amelia was taunting her but then seducing her. The piousness of good versus the raunchiness of being evil. Then, she felt guilty about disappointing the hopeful group of Duchesne girls. Even deeper feelings of guilt set in her mind as she thought about her father and grandfather driving all that way, only to be disappointed if she didn't win. "Oh, but being close to Amelia and that kiss! Why did I feel that way about that kiss and, indeed, feel that way about Amelia? There is nothing wrong with me, is there?"

Felicity could not fall asleep that night. She was confused about the amorous feelings she held for Amelia, which then conflicted with her stoic Catholic beliefs. She felt guilty about deliberately losing that race, but if she had won, she wouldn't have discovered what Amelia had planned for her on the night of the prom. Her fear was struck by the rage of Grandma's tone of voice, scolding her and belittling her, telling Felicity she was evil, dirty and a bad Catholic. Felicity then felt angry with herself, and despite her efforts to stay focused on running that race, she just wished it would never occur. Her mind asked a central question: 'What about all of the training? Am I just going to throw that away?' Then, the condescending tone of her grandmother embraced her mind: 'You are such a plain girl. Why would you do anything other than commit yourself to a life with God our Father?' Her grandmother's disparaging voice was amplified in her mind, fuelling her anger. Then, Father Roper's condemning tone seemed to drown out other voices as he piously ridiculed her for her sins. Egotistical desires for success replaced scorn as Felicity had trained every day, and surely that mattered most. However, no matter the depths of fear, anger, apprehension, pride or moral reckoning, Felicity kept on returning to her desire to appease Amelia, to be close to her, and by 3:00 a.m. the following day, she fell asleep with one thought in her mind: "I will follow my heart."

Meanwhile, across the hallway, Amelia had no difficulties sleeping that night. However, she, too, had felt a bond of electricity exchange between her lips and Felicity's, a sensation she had not experienced with her boyfriend.

CHAPTER 9

Felicity's alarm rang two hours after she had eventually fallen asleep. She was exhausted, and all she wanted to do was go back to sleep. Felicity's final thought before she fell asleep was that she would follow her heart. Notwithstanding the pangs of guilt that ran through her mind that morning about her deliberate loss of the impending four-hundred-yard race, her heart swooned for Amelia, and about half an hour later, her alarm clock interrupted her troubled sleep to awaken her for the day. Felicity decided to follow her heart. She had always wanted to be close to Amelia, even though that girl could be a bitch at times, but now she felt differently. Now, all Felicity wanted before the school year ended was to feel Amelia's soft lips kiss hers again. She then considered how she could lose the race without making it obvious to her father, her grandfather, Sister Pat, the spectators and the other teachers.

Amelia awoke at 6:30 a.m. without a care in the world. She was sure that Felicity would let her win, and although she wanted to fulfil her promise and satisfy her pride, she did not know how that would occur. She had had amorous feelings for Felicity for several years, but the genesis of those feelings was attached to events in London when she was fourteen. Amelia had not told a soul what had happened, and she had managed to bury her feelings about that because it was the cold world in which she had been raised in her parents' house of hedonism. However, that kiss the night before was on her mind.

Eventually, at 7:30 a.m., Felicity figured out how she could lose the race without making it evident to the spectators, especially Sister Pat, her father, and grandfather. At the start of the race, it was better to make mistakes when her nervous energy could be blamed; curious minds are lost in the pounding hearts of anxiety. Felicity, dressed in her immaculately clean sports outfit, had her hair pulled back into a tight bun, revealing her full features as she stared at herself in the mirror. Her breasts had not developed any further during that school term, and her lack of cleavage accentuated the lines of Felicity's face.

"I look like a boy, and now I yearn for another girl's heart, just like a boy." The genesis of her despondent tone of voice was not for her looks; no, the genesis of Felicity's despondent tone of voice emanated from the prison sentence of her gender. Felicity took one more look at herself in the mirror and sighed through her words. "Oh, who gives a damn, as it is just a silly race."

Felicity opened the door of her dormitory room to go downstairs for breakfast, and, at that moment, Amelia's dormitory room door also swung open, almost as though destiny was meeting at its uncertain crossroads. Both girls stopped in their tracks, the unexpected rendezvous bringing with it the tension of the moment. Not a word was spoken as Felicity and Amelia stared into each other's eyes before Felicity eventually yielded to her heart. Any element of doubt in Felicity's mind was dispelled by the sight of Amelia, whose similar style of sportswear and hairdo just seemed to make her look ever so more attractive. Felicity ever so gently, with a slight nod, affirmed her willingness to let Amelia win the race. With the surreptitious signal between them now exchanged, Amelia lifted her chin and confidently strutted down the hallway, leaving poor Felicity in a visible state of submission.

During breakfast, the entire dining room buzzed with the voices of excited girls eager to display their athletic prowess and their tribal sense of attachment to their sporting houses. Warcry chants would break out at the tables, only to be quelled by the stentorian tones of the supervising nuns, who were trying to ensure the rivalry did not convert into animosity. Natasha's and Heather's voices were just background noise as Felicity's mind ticked over her decision to lose the race deliberately. Young Margaret Healy, an aspiring third-form Duchesne athlete, came over to speak excitedly to Felicity about Margaret's impending 110-yard race, and the younger girl's enthusiasm began sowing some seeds of doubt in Felicity's mind. However, just when perhaps emotion would overcome reason, Felicity would catch a glance of Amelia, who was seated two tables away, and the meeting of their eyes would capture Felicity's heart and focus her mind on letting Amelia win that race.

After breakfast, when the student body made their way down towards the athletic oval, Felicity's guilty emotions would be challenged twice. The first occasion was immediately after she left the dormitory. Felicity stumbled upon Sister Pat, who was heading to the dormitory building to check on all the girls who had to leave for the oval. Sister Pat's warm and proud smile sent remorse down Felicity's spine, and she had not even lost the race yet to feel this way!

Felicity politely nodded and kept walking, knowing Sister Pat would see through the deception.

After she walked past Sister Pat, Felicity continued her mental wrestle to put her guilt back into the crypt she had locked in, continually telling herself: 'It is worth it; this is right, and in any event, it is only a stupid race'. However, her path towards the oval led Felicity straight to the pathway of her father and Grandpa. She had momentarily forgotten about them after breakfast, and now, as she was completing this mental tug-of-war, Felicity's mental anguish would be exposed by her surprise in encountering the two family members whom she did not wish to disappoint. "Felicity! Our little Olympic champion in the making!" Grandpa's booming and proud voice seemed to startle her further, and Samuel immediately detected by the look in his daughter's eyes that something was going on in her mind. Felicity's guilt began to overwhelm her mind, and she threw herself into her father's arms to try to hide her inner turmoil. "Dad! I am so glad you're here." Albert's egotistical nature prevailed over any modicum of intuition he had for teenage angst. "What about me? I have come all this way as well." Felicity quickly released herself from her father's embrace, but her appreciation of Grandpa's presence was not displayed in the same manner of relief as she had shown towards her father. "And, of course, you too, Grandpa. Thank you for coming all this way." Albert nodded, like a grateful child being given the same attention. Still, Samuel knew his daughter, and he knew from his daughter's embrace that something was up. He turned and looked at his father. "Dad, how about you make your way down to the grandstand? I need to have a word with Felicity, alone." Albert's eyes flicked their attention between his son and granddaughter; he was not sure why he could not stay, but there was a hint of importunity in Samuel's tone of voice that suggested this was a father-and-daughter moment. "Very well then, I shall see you down at the grandstand. Run like the wind, Felicity, and go, Duchesne!" Albert tipped the peak of his hat, turned on his heels and threw back his shoulders to march down in his bombastic English countryside gentry manner, which even caused Samuel to roll his eyes before his focus returned to his daughter.

Samuel slightly bent down in front of Felicity so that he could stare into her eyes. "What is wrong, Felicity?" His inquisitive tone was matched by his unwavering gaze into her eyes. Felicity had to think fast; otherwise, the truth might surreptitiously pass through her lips. "I am just nervous, Dad. That is all; I do not want to disappoint you." Her guilt was rising fast to the focal point of her mind, but she hoped her explanation would satisfy her father. Samuel's gaze into his daughter's eyes seemed to be endless in its duration, but then he placed his hands on Felicity's shoulders to emphasise his following words. "Don't worry about disappointing me, Felicity. I will be proud of you, no matter what happens. You don't have to win to receive my love because it is unconditional. So, just do your best. That is all I have ever expected from you." Felicity remained motionless for a moment as her moral turpitude continued to weigh heavily upon her. Then Felicity threw herself back into her father's arms again, and although she simultaneously became teary, it was almost as though her father's words had set her mind free. "It is so, so good to see you, Daddy. I just want this all to finish and to be flying again." Samuel held his daughter tight to his chest, and his soothing voice brought greater clarity to Felicity's mind. "Hey, don't be upset. Come on, go get this over and done with, and then, in no time, you will be up in the sky, flying around again." Felicity withdrew from her father's embrace, and as she wiped the tears from his eyes, her feelings became resolute in her mind: "Damn this stupid race!" Felicity then walked with her father down the pathway toward the oval, and they discussed flying and, of course, the infinite universe of space.

The other athletic events seemed to flash by that day like high-speed locomotives, and whilst there was a tinge of guilt in her heart, Felicity's decision was now cast in stone. She would lose a race to win Amelia's heart. She had hardly even noticed Mother Superior's announcement of the four-hundred-yard race when the cheering went a notch in its fever as the Duchesne students called out Felicity's name. Like a lightbulb suddenly being turned on, Felicity's mind came to the importance of the moment, and she took a deep breath as she took off her tracksuit and sandshoes so that she could now put on her running spikes, which would be the first part of her deception to appear to lose a race she was favoured to win legitimately. Felicity only tied a very flimsy single knot on her right running spikes, and she knew full well the laces would come apart the moment she applied the force of her foot to the sole of the shoe. Everybody's eyes were focused on the participants' faces, and not even Sister Pat noticed the loose flopping of the laces on Felicity's right shoe. Mother Superior's voice boomed down the microphone, urging the groups of excited girls to quiet down as Sister Pat blew the whistle, signalling the girls to line up in their lanes. One more fleeting glance over her shoulder from Amelia dispelled any nerves in Felicity's body. Then Sister Pat commenced the starting call from the inside of the track. "On your marks!" Each girl took her mark, and as Felicity did so, she could feel her right shoe loosen as the lace's flimsy knot gave way. "Get set!" Felicity lifted her buttocks and placed even greater weight on her right foot, which then caused the knot of the lace on her shoe to loosen further. Then the moment of truth. The starter's pistol went off, and every girl simultaneously pushed off to run. Still, as Felicity did so, the pre-planned disaster went better than anticipated when her right foot broke free from the loose tongue of her running shoe, causing her to stumble as it came off. The gasp of disappointment from the Duchesne girls seemed to be louder than the cheering of the Stuart House students, and then Felicity panicked as she tried to convincingly put on her shoe in a feigned, vain attempt to continue with the race. By the time she put that shoe on, Amelia had already passed the one-hundred-yard marker, and Felicity knew there would be no chance of her even catching up with the other competitors, let alone beating Amelia. She ran her heart out, but she would be in last place. As Felicity ran down the last straight, she caught a glimpse of Grandpa standing up in the stadium, and his hands on his face poignantly revealed his despair.

Amelia crossed the finishing line first, much to the delight of the Stuart House girls, who celebrated by disobeying Mother Superior's commands down the loudspeaker as they ran out onto the track to surround their champion. Meanwhile, Felicity crossed the finishing line ten yards behind the second-last runner, and barely a word of support was spoken by any Duchesne student, except for little Margaret, in whom goodwill prevailed over disappointment. She walked over to Felicity, still trying to catch her breath after the race. Margaret stood before Felicity, and the tears in her eyes were evident, but her innocent, pure heart was compelling. "Do not worry, Felicity. You are still the champion, as far as I am concerned." More tears welled up in Margaret's eyes, and now Felicity became overwhelmed with emotion as her guilty conscience consumed her. "My shoe slipped, Margaret. It was not my fault." Felicity, too, now had tears welling up in her eyes, which she valiantly tried to contain.

Then, the dam walls burst as Sister Pat commenced her noticeably disappointed walk towards Felicity from the grandstand, and tears began to trickle down Felicity's cheeks. In mere seconds, she stood before Felicity, and Sister Pat was still reeling from what she had witnessed only moments before. "Margaret, please leave Felicity alone." The young student quickly withdrew from their presence, leaving Felicity heartbroken and guilt-ridden to be momentarily answerable to Sister Pat. Sister Pat placed her left hand on Felicity's shoulder to console her; however, Felicity bowed her head in shame. "What happened, Felicity?" Felicity began to shake with despair, and her eyes were squinted to hold back her tears. "My shoe came off as I pushed forward at the start, Sister Pat." The young nun was sympathetic with her reassuring touch to Felicity's shoulder, but also blunt in her reply. "Well, I know that, but why didn't you fix your shoe before you took your mark?" Sister Pat should have been a barrister because her question cut through to the very issue Felicity had not thought through properly, and her momentary silence almost gave away her deception. Still, she was brilliant, and Felicity's consternation rose through her grief. "Because I was nervous with the pressure, Sister Pat and the last rational thought going through my mind at the moment was: 'Ooh, is that my shoe?' You try having the hopes of your housemates riding on your shoulders! You try to manage the hopes of your family, especially an arrogant and unforgiving grandfather, peering down on you from the grandstand. My mind was cluttered with anxiety." Sister Pat checked her temperament before responding. "I have been to that place, Felicity. I did not mean to be critical." Sister Pat gave Felicity a consoling hug with her left arm before patting her head to cheer her up. "Well, look at it this way: At least you did not falter at the Olympics!" Her warm smile displayed no malice. "Go on, then. Cheer up, and go and console your grandfather before he has a meltdown." She wiped her eyes and nose with her hand, giving Sister Pat a glimpse of a smile. She then turned around to walk towards the grandstand, where her father waited at the bottom of the stairs while her inconsolable grandfather still rubbed his forehead in disappointment.

When she arrived where Samuel was standing, she was relieved by his immediate sympathy. "Bad luck, my little darling. Do not be upset with yourself; these things sometimes happen in life." Her father's unwavering support caused a new wave of guilt and despair to consume Felicity, and she threw herself into Samuel's body as she started crying. "I am sorry, Dad, for disappointing you and Grandpa. It was my shoe; it accidentally slipped off." The tragedy of losing his wife had made Samuel a vessel of devotion to his daughter, and Samuel did not need to be convinced by his daughter. However, he was still worried that another underlying problem was eating away at her mind. He hugged her tightly. "Heh, come on; do not despair. I will always be proud of you, whether you win or lose. You're going to study at Cambridge, and eventually, you will be the first woman in space. Who cares about a four-hundred-yard dash? Not me. So, come on, my little astronaut, cheer up."

Samuel held Felicity in his arms for a few more moments before she broke away to look earnestly into his eyes. "What about Grandpa? Should I go up and speak to him?" Samuel turned and looked at his father, who was still selfishly consumed with his own egotistical emotions. Then Samuel turned back towards Felicity whilst rolling his eyes. "Do not worry about the silly old blighter. I will deal with him. You go back to the dormitory and have a long, hot shower. That will fix your disappointment." Felicity stared into her father's eyes with innocent love for him; however, that blissful father-daughter moment was broken by the sight of Amelia triumphantly marching by, and she was closely followed by the fawning entourage of Stuart House girls soaking up her glory, which, as always, included CC. Felicity closed her eyes momentarily for fear of displaying her infatuation for Amelia before her father. Then Felicity opened her eyes, giving Samuel a glimpse of a thankful smile. She hugged her father and left him to deal with Grandpa's selfish behaviour. That night in the dining hall, Felicity, Natasha and Elisabeth sat quietly at their table as they endured the unnecessary ongoing celebrations of the Stuart House girls. Natasha's derisive comments made it bearable for all three of them: "Don't listen to them, girls. They will be barefoot and preggers by the middle of next year."

Felicity's guilt that evening consumed her mind. She felt guilty about deliberately losing the race, and she could not get out of her mind the sight of silly old Grandpa looking so distressed in the grandstand. When Felicity reconciled her guilt with the pragmatism of Amelia's promised 'surprise', her guilt would then refocus on her desire to feel the kiss of Amelia's lips again. By midnight, her mind asked: "Is something wrong with me that makes me want to kiss Amelia again? Am I evil for feeling this way and deliberately losing the race?" Her submission to the oppression of conservative Catholicism overwhelmed her, and she got out of her bed, prayed for half an hour, and even said the Rosary at least ten times as a way of purging her soul. However, God did not intervene, and when she went to bed, she still longed to kiss Amelia again. By 1:00 a.m., she was exhausted and drifted off to sleep. When she awoke at 7:00 a.m., Felicity no longer felt guilty about losing the race, but she continued to question herself about her undeniable feelings for Amelia.

The following weekend, Amelia ran a disappointing fourth place in the inter-school athletics carnival. Felicity watched Amelia's uncompetitive form with a hint of ironic disdain in her mind. "I would have won that race." She probably would have, too, but Felicity had already made her bed on that chapter of her life. Still, the school prom week was approaching, and Felicity longed to find out what Amelia's surprise would be. The battle between her heart and mind had not subsided. Her heart told her she needed to feel Amelia's lips on hers again, while her mind insisted those feelings were abnormal. Her grandmother's condescending piety was never far from her mind, reminding her that she was betraying Christ.

CHAPTER 10

There were 24 hours to go until the school prom, yet there was not even a hint of Amelia revealing the 'surprise' to Felicity. They had crossed each other's paths several times over the past five days. Still, as always, it was in the context of Amelia being followed by her fawning entourage. When it seemed they might be alone anywhere on the Woldingham grounds, Natasha and Heather would appear to disrupt the opportunity for intimacy. Felicity's heart still fluttered every time she saw Amelia, and occasionally, it would reciprocate back from the eyes of her idol; however, it was a fleeting moment, and Amelia otherwise maintained her air of the 'Ice Queen' towards the other girls, including Felicity. There had been a rumour sweeping around the school that Amelia was hosting a private party before the prom; however, Felicity had not been informed by Amelia this was her surprise, and it seemed from the whispers of the rumour mill the guest list for Amelia's 'pre-prom' party was her closest group of fawners, which included the mean CC, their prom partners and, of course, Amelia's trophy partner, the very eligible Antony Browne, so Felicity wondered whether this was the surprise – to be a guest at the 'Speranza Spare-No-Expense' private party. The battle between her heart and mind had not been subdued, but as her impending surprise crept closer, Felicity's heart prevailed for her feelings for Amelia.

Felicity had received a letter from Timothy MacDougall at the start of that week, in which he unreservedly expressed his excitement about being her partner for the school prom. He also informed her that he would be wearing the same dinner suit his father had worn to his school promenade many decades earlier. Felicity's thoughts revealed her disposition towards Timothy: "Great, as long as it isn't covered in boogers." There would be no pre-prom arrangements for them to meet up with one another; Catherine's arrangements were for Timothy to meet up with Felicity outside of the Woldingham Golf Clubhouse, from where he would escort her into the Woldingham Suite, and it would be where they parted ways for the evening after the school prom concluded. It would be three hours of frustrating boredom as far as Felicity was concerned, and with a day to go until 'Prom Night', her mind was fixated on Amelia's promise of surprise, so she had not really paid much thought to the event itself. Catherine had even sewn the gown for Felicity to wear and had it delivered to the school, a testament to the control she exerted over this aspect of Felicity's life.

Eventually, on the morning of the day of the school prom, Felicity was finally able to speak to Amelia when nobody else was around. All the other girls on the floor of their dormitory had gone to the dining hall for breakfast except for Amelia, who had deliberately left her dormitory room door open. At the same time, she vainly held her evening gown up against her chest, staring at herself in the mirror. She was unaware of Felicity's room door opening. If she had been aware, it would not have disturbed Amelia as she proudly swivelled her hips in the mirror, mimicking how she planned to enter the Woldingham Suite later that evening after the pre-prom party. Even just holding the gown up to herself made Amelia look beautiful. Felicity watched her quietly from across the hallway momentarily before she embarked upon her earnest quest to break the suspense about the 'surprise'. Felicity gently rapped her knuckles on the doorframe of Amelia's room, a sound that slightly startled Amelia in her narcissistic state. "Oh, blimey! Felicity, you scared me." Amelia could sense an air of disappointment surrounding her unexpected visitor. "What is up, Felicity? Why are you looking so maudlin?" Felicity slowly entered the room, but her eyes did not break away from their fixation on Amelia's eyes. "Why haven't you told me my 'surprise', Amelia? I threw away a race for you, yet it seems your end of the bargain or, more precisely, your 'promise', is not going to be lived up to. So what is my surprise?"

Amelia could see there was the hint of a tear in Felicity's eyes, and she smiled in a friendly manner, the first such hint of emotion since Felicity deliberately lost the four-hundred-yard race. She walked over towards Felicity like a cat, knowing full well that this girl was like putty in her hands. "Oh, don't be upset. It would not be much of a surprise if I gave it away to you now, would it?" Felicity mulled over this response, then reluctantly nodded; however, she still wanted answers. "Well, what about your private little Pre-Prom party everyone is whispering about? I thought you might have invited me to that party by now." Amelia found Felicity's innocent disappointment to be so adorable, and she could not help reacting to it by reaching out to Felicity with her slender right hand and taking her gently by the left forearm. Her touch sent waves of electric delight through Felicity's veins. "Oh, Felicity, you do not know how cute you are when you act like this. But my Pre-Prom is not the surprise, and it would not be the appropriate place for it." Felicity was just about to ask her where the appropriate place would be when both girls heard the raucous laugh and the voice of CC coming down the hallway. "Amelia! Are you already getting ready for Antony Browne?" CC's voice brought about an immediate change in Amelia's demeanour, and she quickly retracted her hand before that girl could see her tenderly touching Felicity. CC arrived at Amelia's doorway, and she came to an immediate halt in her stride because Felicity was in that room. It was evident from CC's face that she was surprised and bewildered to see Amelia's supposed nemesis in the room. Amelia briefly looked at CC and then covered any signs of being caught out by quickly turning back towards Felicity, who was surprised to see Amelia's eyes transform from tenderness only moments ago to now displaying her disdain. "So, let me tell you again, Space Freak, for the final time: I won that race fair and square. Now get out of my room and go back to Mars or wherever you are from!" Felicity was mortified to be spoken to in this manner, but she could not move, let alone speak. Amelia's eyes then displayed rage. "Can't you hear? Get out of my room!" Amelia's extended arm and finger were like a road map of despair in Felicity's heart, and she bowed her head as she walked out of Amelia's room. CC shot the final arrow into Felicity's heart. "And stay out!" CC slammed the door shut behind Felicity, who now proceeded to undertake a walk of shame down the hallway of her dormitory floor, and before she reached the stairs, her tears were already running down her cheeks.

The bus to take the boarding seniors to their school prom was already waiting at the main entrance of the school at 6:00 p.m. as the girls began to get ready for their special night. Felicity had recovered that morning after being so mortally wounded by Amelia's cruelty, but she was still quite sombre. She opened the box, which contained the gown her grandmother had sewn for her and had sent without even tying a bow around it. The dress was made of quality white satin fabric; however, in unfurling it for the first time, Felicity saw that it revealed the design of Catherine's stoic Catholicism. It was a long gown that came down to the ankles, with sleeves that reached the elbows. The top had an inbuilt brassiere for a B-Cup young woman, a design feature that briefly intrigued Felicity until she looked back in the box. Underneath the long satin gloves, there was a large envelope that appeared to contain an item. Felicity took the envelope out of the box, and when she shook it open, to her surprise, a packet of handkerchiefs and a note fell out of it. The note was written in Catherine's hand, and it was dripping with her mocking nature. Its words were blunt and straightforward. "Put three handkerchiefs in each cup; that way, you will look womanly for once in your life." Felicity shook her head in frustration and initially resisted the idea of creating a fake bust for herself. Still, when she put the gown on, she realised very quickly she had no choice: she would look ridiculous in a busty gown without any bust. The ignominy she felt as she put those hankies in both cups of her gown. She sighed as she spoke: "Oh well, they may come in handy for Timmy."

Felicity had finished getting ready for the prom and looked at herself in the mirror, stuffed brassiere and all. She had pulled her hair up into a tight bun on her head and, as Mother Superior permitted, applied minimal makeup, including a very soft plum-coloured lipstick. Felicity looked at herself in the mirror for a while because she had never dressed up like this before, and her thoughts travelled back in time to the night of her last birthday. "I am not ugly, Grandma." She was right; she wasn't ugly, but she did not have her aunt's beauty, and, of course, she did not possess Amelia's glamorous looks. For once in her young life, Felicity felt pleasant about her looks. She gathered up the bottom of her evening gown to walk out of her room. As Felicity opened the door, she saw Amelia's empty room across the hallway and immediately felt betrayed.

On the boarders' bus trip to the prom, the high-pitched noise of excited school girls' chatter and laughter was at a fever pitch. Natasha kept the girls in fits of laughter as she paraded up and down the aisle of the bus, pushing her bust outwards in a slightly risqué gown that revealed the hint of cleavage as she did so. "Look at me, girls. I am about to go on a wild date with Father Roper!" As she over-emphasised the name of 'Roper', Natasha also heaved her breasts towards the ceiling of the bus, and the old male bus driver almost ran off the road because his leering eyes were fixated on the rearview mirror rather than the road ahead. Heather reached out from her seat to pull Natasha back to her seat. "Sit down, you fool. You're going to cause an accident." Natasha quickly retorted to her friend, but her volume was not restrained. "I think our old boy driving down the front just had an accident in his seat." The laughter erupted on the bus, and even Felicity, still feeling a bit glum, broke down into fits of laughter.

Eventually, the bus turned into the driveway of Woldingham Golf Club and slowly meandered down towards the clubhouse. As the bus came to the front of the clubhouse, Felicity could see Timothy MacDougall standing outside, waiting by himself. Nearby, a larger group of eager young men were waiting for their prom dates to arrive. Timothy was dressed in a dinner suit, but the poor lad was awkward because of his thick black spectacles and oiled-back hair. His face lit up when he saw Felicity's face in the window of the bus, but his appearance did not enthuse her. Natasha immediately spotted Timothy, and she was blunt with her opinion. "Cripes, Felicity. Is that 'Booger-Boy? He looks like he fell into an oil well. What on Earth is going on with those glasses as well? Is he trying to spot Pluto in the sky?" Felicity gave her friend a look of slight contempt. "Do you have to make this harder than it should be?" Natasha shrugged, flashed a big grin, and grabbed Felicity's left arm. "Come on, let's go have a bit of fun, boogers and all." Natasha's jovial spirit brought a bit of joy to Felicity's broken heart. When they alighted from the bus, Timothy walked towards Felicity, and he shot out his hand in glee to shake her gloved hand. Natasha and Heather had already raced over to the large group of boys where their respective prom dates were waiting. "Hello, Felicity. I am so excited to see you." Felicity was initially reluctant to extend her hand, not because she disliked Timothy, but because she did not trust where his fingers had been in relation to his nose over the last 15 minutes. Eventually, after a short delay, Felicity acquiesced and held out the tips of her gloved right hand. "Okay, Timothy. Shall we get this night over and done with?" Timothy required no further invitation, and he clasped Felicity's fingers with his left hand, which felt slimy even through her gloves. He proudly marched her towards the clubhouse entrance, just as the other children had started to do.

When they entered the Woldingham Suite, it was clear that the £4 her father paid for the tickets was worth every penny. The tables had been stylishly presented, covered in white linen tablecloths and serviettes, with sterling silver cutlery and beautiful floral arrangements at the centre of each table, surrounded by candelabras. Each place setting had a cut crystal glass for the girls and their dates; however, they were only allowed to drink soft drinks from the glasses, as alcohol was strictly forbidden. Mother Superior greeted each girl and their date as they walked into the Woldingham Suite, and when Natasha entered with her risqué gown, she immediately drew the ire of the old, conservative nun. Natasha brushed it off in her typical carefree state. Still, her prom date, Richard Wallace, did display a slightly ashen face after being caught in the crossfire of Mother Superior's disapproving tongue.

Sister Pat was the 'official' photographer, and each girl had to have their photograph taken with their prom date before taking a seat at their designated table. Felicity cringed when it came to her turn to have her photograph taken as a permanent memento of Timothy MacDougall's oil-slick appearance. It was not something she wished to acquire, but she felt at least somewhat comfortable with herself when Sister Pat genuinely told her that she looked very lovely. After getting their photograph taken, Felicity found their table, which fortunately included Natasha and Heather. Richard Wallace had recovered from Mother Superior's ire. He sat immediately in the boy-girl-boy-girl seating arrangements to Felicity's left side. In contrast, Heather's date, William Newton, sat to the left of Natasha but close enough to Richard to start picking on Timothy. Richard was first off the mark to launch a stinging barb, and looking at Timothy's name card first, he commenced his attack. "So, Timothy, or is it Timmy?" Timothy recoiled his shoulders and shot his chin up, making his oiled hair look even more ridiculous. "It's Timothy, not Timmy." Felicity gritted her teeth because even she found Timothy's over-emphasised response painful. Now, William launched the next attack. "Don't sit close to that candle, Tim-o-thy; otherwise, we will have to call the fire brigade to put your hair out." Timothy began to open his mouth to respond, but Heather quickly intervened to tone down the rhetoric. "That is enough, both of you. This is meant to be a nice night." Felicity turned her head away because she wished the whole evening would be over as soon as possible; indeed, she wanted the school year to end so she could start her flying lessons and put the past eight weeks behind her.

As the last girl and her date had their photograph taken, there was one noticeably empty table; Amelia, CC and the rest of the fawning inner circle of Amelia's were nowhere to be seen. Then, with a great fluster, Amelia entered the Woldingham Suite in tow with Antony Browne, followed by CC and her prom date, followed by the rest of the obsequious girls and their dates, and Amelia led the way over to the empty table without stopping by Sister Pat for a photograph. All of them had been drinking alcohol, the effects of which were manifested in the nonchalant manner in which they all marched into the function room. At the long staff convent table, Mother Superior did not look amused at all. Still, she dared not chastise Amelia because her parents were very generous donors to the school fund, which meant Amelia benefited from differential treatment compared to the other girls.

When Amelia, CC and the others sat down, Mother Superior stood up and walked over to the lectern to deliver her welcoming speech. The special occasion did not subdue her domineering mannerisms, and she cast her steely eyes around the room before speaking into the microphone at the lectern. "Good evening, girls, and your dates. Welcome to this momentous occasion that heralds the end of your secondary schooling and the future lives you will venture into as you embark upon a new chapter. A few rules for the night: there will be no drinking and no smoking." She glanced over to Felicity's table, where Natasha was noticeably becoming a bit too comfortable with Richard as she cuddled into his arm, which was placed around her shoulder. "There will also be no inappropriate touching, including during the waltz after your main course." Her eyes remained fixed on Natasha, and Richard quickly took his hand away as Natasha reluctantly returned to sitting in a prim and proper pose. Mother Superior nodded her chin ever so slightly to convey her satisfaction, and then she resumed her speech. "Father Roper will now lead us in prayer as is custom on these occasions." Felicity rolled her eyes, knowing the priest would use his prayer to lecture the girls who didn't return on the boarders' bus about the evil temptations of the flesh. Sure enough, Father Roper, mid-prayer, began pontificating away about the evil that Satan could lure all of them in with if they gave into their urges. Felicity looked over towards Amelia's table, and when she looked back, Amelia was there, with that same sly grin she had seen before. Felicity's heart fluttered, but her mind remained disappointed.

The evening could not go quickly enough for Felicity, and she was relieved when Mother Superior announced after half an hour of tedious waltz music that the evening's events were over. The boarders' bus would be leaving in fifteen minutes. Thank goodness Timothy's fingers had stayed away from his nostrils within the suite. Still, Richard had returned to the table during dessert in fits of laughter to say that he had caught him 'up to his elbows' in the bathroom mining away for nuggets. This report caused immense embarrassment for Felicity, making her wish the evening would end sooner. Watching Amelia dance around the floor with Antony Browne also made her feel strangely jealous, but she quickly dismissed those feelings, disappointing herself at being let down by her. After politely saying goodbye to Timothy, Felicity was the first boarder to enter the bus. When she returned to the dormitory, she quickly changed into her pyjamas and went to bed. She was disappointed and felt foolish because it seemed Amelia had tricked her.

Felicity was sound asleep; her sorrow about the prom and Amelia not 'making it up to her' with the promised surprise had diminished as she dreamt in bed. It was approximately 12:30 a.m. when Felicity was awakened from her sleep. Notwithstanding that she was in a deep sleep, Felicity had been awoken by what she believed to be something or someone sitting down on the end of her bed. Her room was pitch-black, and she was still half-asleep. She reached out into the darkness and whispered in a trembling voice, "Is somebody there?" Then her fingertips were met in the darkness by the soft touch of another young woman's hand. "Don't panic, Felicity, it's me." Amelia's voice was soft and warm, and before she could respond to her, Felicity felt Amelia move closer to her on the bed while she held her fingertips. "I promised I would make it up to you tonight; however, I had to wait when nobody else was around." With those soft, whispered words being spoken, Amelia's full lips found Felicity's lips; the darkness of the room could not hinder them from finding each other. Felicity's initial surprise about Amelia being in her room and now softly kissing her lips subsided as her lips accepted Amelia's kiss.

They softly, indeed, tenderly kissed each other's lips for thirty seconds. Still, Felicity felt conscience about what she was doing, and she slowly withdrew her lips as her eyes saw the outline of Amelia's face. "What are we doing, Amelia? Isn't this wrong in the eyes of God?" She then felt Amelia's hand gently pull her body closer to her again, and her nose tip touched Amelia's. "Don't be afraid, Felicity. God, Mother Superior and Father Roper can all go to hell. I know you like me; I have noticed you staring at me since the night I kissed you. I like you also, and I will make you feel good tonight." Amelia's lips met Felicity's again, and without any resistance, Felicity gave in to her passion and started kissing Amelia. Then Felicity felt the surprising but also stimulating feeling of Amelia's tongue gently parting its way through her lips, and the tip of her tongue now gently stroked Felicity's tongue. Whilst it was unusual for Felicity, she also found the touch of her tongue on Amelia's to be stimulating. Within a few moments, Felicity opened her mouth to Amelia's to fully allow their tongues to explore each other's mouths. They kissed each other for at least an hour, occasionally stopping to giggle but without a word being spoken. Eventually, about two hours after they had locked their lips together, they both fell asleep in each other's arms.

Felicity's alarm clock fortuitously chimed at 5:00 a.m., just as the sun began to rise and before any other boarders were awake. Both girls awoke at the same time, and Amelia smiled at Felicity. She then kissed her deeply again for about a minute before quickly removing herself from the bed to put on her slippers. Felicity's eyes displayed her inner rapture for Amelia, which then caused Amelia to speak her honest thoughts. "I do like you, Felicity, a lot, but we cannot be girlfriend and girlfriend." Felicity's heart sank as she thought they could remain this way towards each other. She sat upright in her bed, and dismay was written all over her innocent face. "What do you mean? Are you saying this is it? Are you saying we can't spend the night like this again?" Amelia nodded to confirm their passion had been for one night only. Felicity's emotions overcame her, and her eyes filled with tears. "Why can't we do this again? I thought you said you liked me; I like you a lot." Her disappointment rang out loud through her whispered words, and she would only be exposed to further disappointment. Amelia shook her head, almost as though Felicity was crazy. "We are at school, Felicity. I have a boyfriend. I can't drop him for another girl. Imagine what people would say. Imagine what Mother Superior would say. I told you the truth last night; I really like you, Felicity; I can't be in a relationship with you."

Amelia had finished speaking; however, no words came from Felicity's mouth in response. Instead, she sat there in her bed, and her tears then started to roll down her cheeks. Amelia looked at Felicity, and she felt her tears beginning to well up in her. She leaned over the bed, kissed Felicity's lips, and sealed the other girl's broken heart. "Maybe in the future, when we're older and away from this life. I cannot do it now." With those final words being spoken, Amelia left Felicity's room, and the tears continued rolling down her cheeks as she wept.

Amelia entered her room and quickly closed the door, feeling tears welling up in her eyes. She took several deep breaths and managed to hold her tears at bay. She liked Felicity more than she was willing to let on, and a personal history from her time in London played on her mind and challenged her. However, she had an image to uphold, but deep down, she still harboured strong feelings for the heartbroken young woman across the hall.

As she lay on her bed sobbing, Felicity's guilt began to take over her, breaking her heart, and she now felt shamed in the eyes of God because she had been unholy with Amelia. It took Felicity a long while to get out of bed that Saturday morning, and she even missed breakfast. By the middle of the afternoon, Felicity's feelings of guilt, shame and confusion were evident to Natasha and Heather, and they pressed her for an answer as to why she seemed to be so self-consumed. Still, Felicity dared not reveal to them the reason why she was so obviously disturbed. That night at the boarders' mass, she feverishly prayed away. Her mixed emotions of guilt and a broken heart followed her back to her dormitory room that night.

She prayed for forgiveness each day of those two miserable last weeks of secondary school, but every time she saw Amelia, Felicity could not help it; her heart would beat vehemently as she longed for the other girl's desire. Not even the thoughts of her impending flying lessons could cheer her up. She did not know what adult love was, but her heart was tremendous for Amelia, and her guilty and shameful thoughts accompanied that love. Her thoughts were prescient on the final school day: "What is wrong with being in love with another girl?" She would not reveal this thought to her friends, nor had she told them what she and Amelia had done with each other the night before. Whereas all the other girls whooped for joy when the final bell rang that Friday to herald their secondary school lives were over, Felicity remained silent and even glum. The final image of her secondary school life was watching Amelia leave the school. Amelia had walked out to the pick-up zone, her eyes embracing Felicity's eyes, like two lovers dancing a tango. Samuel would be arriving there in the next two minutes, and Felicity's heart met Amelia's in their shared gaze of amour. Felicity felt the desire to throw caution to the wind and, to hell with reputation, she would kiss those beautiful lips of Amelia's once again. Two minutes in which to take a chance in life, and prove their love was pure. However, in those two minutes, Felicity hesitated. Then the sound of the horn tooting on Amelia's father's Jaguar broke their gaze, and Amelia picked up her port, but not before she gave Felicity one last longing look, and then she turned away, entered her father's Jaguar, and the car drove away. Two indecisive minutes in which two hearts could have been one. Still, that look would linger long after the window of opportunity had closed.

When Samuel arrived at Woldingham ten minutes after Amelia left, he could see that something was up with his daughter before he even alighted from his car. When he exited the vehicle, he immediately approached her, showing great concern. "Hey, you. What is wrong? I thought you would have cartwheeled down the driveway in joy at leaving this place." Felicity remained silent briefly; then, she shook her head. "It's fine, Dad; I mean, I am fine. Let's just get out of here." Samuel was unconvinced, so he leaned forward and took his daughter by the shoulders to interrogate her. "No, you're not fine. Did something happen at school today?" Felicity shook her head in anger. "No, Dad! It's fine. Just leave me alone. It is all a bit surreal, that is all." Samuel lifted his hands in the air to acknowledge that he would not invade his daughter's privacy anymore. On the drive home, they talked about the farm, about her flying lessons and Cambridge. They even discussed the latest news about the Americans and Russians racing for space, but as a father, Samuel knew something was not right with his daughter. Still, he respected her privacy too much to interrogate her about what was on her mind.

PART 3

"A Woman Emerges"

CHAPTER 11

During thy life, there are few opportunities granted to open thy heart,
So, once thee proceed down a wrong path, thy can't return to the start.

For the first week of her life after Woldingham, Felicity remained isolated in her despair, confusion and guilt, from Catherine's chastising comments that first night back home about Felicity's so-called foolhardy pipe dream of flying into space to Father O'Leary's piety about the evil that lurked in Catholic society because of Lord Wolfenden's report, Felicity's mind was under siege that perhaps there was something wrong with her for holding the feelings she held for Amelia and that she was evil for spending hours kissing her like she had after the prom. After Father O'Leary's mental blitzkrieg, Felicity would spend most of her time watching Samuel work away with the cattle, which were almost fattened enough to be sold. Watching her father work temporarily distracted her mind from her thoughts about Amelia. Still, as soon as Catherine commenced her brow-beating lectures over dinner, Felicity could feel the war between her heart and mind escalating as her grandmother's endless chastisement continued.

She maintained her regime of early morning jogging. While jogging, she could think about her feelings for Amelia, and she would dismiss the idea of lesbianism because she did not feel that way about any other girl. However, those feelings for Amelia confused her, and her heart was broken because of her rejection. Felicity was also shamed because of her entrenched Catholicism. However, at night, she would dream of Amelia's lips touching hers again, and Felicity's heart would race in her sleep as she dreamt of their sweet and gentle embrace. Then Amelia would be taken away from her in those dreams, calling out to Felicity as she disappeared from her subconscious view, assuring her that one day she would return. Then, the following morning, when Felicity awoke, she would feel depressed. Yet, also guilty, and once again, she would embark on her jogging expedition around the farm to try to dispel from her mind her thoughts and feelings.

By that first Thursday night, when Catherine seemed to be reaching a crescendo of moral lecturing, Felicity finally had enough. It started when her grandmother served steak and kidney pie to each person at the dinner table. Catherine was serving a slice of the pie onto Felicity's plate. "I hope you have been thinking long and hard, young lady, about your commitment to God and his son, Jesus, since you have returned home." Felicity was in no mood for Catherine's pious lecturing. "I pray every night, Grandma! What more should I do?" Felicity's tone was not stern, but it also tapered off with derisive sarcasm, which should have forewarned the old woman that her granddaughter was in no mood for opinions or invasion into her life. "Don't you speak to me in that tone of voice, young lady! You have no right to speak to me in that manner." Felicity's frustration boiled over into anger, and she stood up to confront her grandmother. "Speak to you in what way? Like the silly old subservient pain in the neck that you are!?! What gives you the right to lecture me about my life!?! What gives you the right to determine my future or to question my faith? You should concentrate on the log in your eye before trying to pick a speck out of mine!" Samuel tried to de-escalate his daughter's disrespectful tone. "Felicity, don't speak to your grandmother like that." It was too late.

Catherine's face displayed the indignation of scripture being used to strike her down. Her anger became visible as the old woman's cheeks turned bright red, and then she unleashed her tempest as her free right hand reached out and slapped Felicity's right cheek. "You disgraceful little brat of a child; your mother would be ashamed of you right now!" Felicity felt a mixture of humiliation, sorrow, and extreme anger, and tears began to well up in her eyes. Samuel leapt from his seat, but he was too far away from Felicity and his mother to intervene in time. "You horrible old hag! Why don't you sod off, for good!" Albert began to rise from his seat; however, before he could rise from his whiskey-infused stupor, Felicity left the room. Samuel directed his anger at Catherine, rather than his daughter. "What is wrong with you, mother?! How dare you hit her face like that!" Before Catherine could mutter a word in response, Samuel had already embarked on the journey of trying to get his daughter to settle down and also to scold her for her behaviour. "Felicity, come back here, please." His words had echoed from the stairwell back down the hallway to the dining room, where Albert had finally managed to stand up, and Catherine stood in the same spot as resolute as ever in her convictions. She glared at Albert, in whom alcohol had impaired his tongue as much as it had impaired his legs. "Not a word from you. Where were you when I needed your support?" Albert went slightly ashen in the face, as he was always submissive when Catherine was consumed with anger. "I, I, I…" Catherine cut him off mid-speech before he could cross over the pronoun stage of the English language. "I, I, nothing. Just sit down, Albert, and eat your pie." She then stormed off from the dining room in the direction of the kitchen, mumbling words to Christ as she walked.

Felicity had already made it to her bedroom and locked the door before Samuel could speak to her. She felt so humiliated and angry to be slapped across her face by her grandmother. Still, it was her tears of sorrow that overwhelmed her emotions. Samuel arrived at Felicity's bedroom door, and when he turned the handle, he immediately knew she had locked herself in there. He was highly concerned about Felicity, not only because Catherine had treated her in such an ignominious manner and due to her own disrespectful behaviour, but also because she had not been her usual self since he had collected her from school. "Felicity. Open the door, please." There was no response. However, Samuel was undeterred by the barrier of her locked door. "Felicity, I know you can hear me. Please, sweetheart, understand me because I am on your side. However, you cannot speak to your grandmother in that manner. Still, she had no right to slap your face." Samuel could hear Felicity crying in her room, a sound which alarmed him, given her demeanour for the past six days. "Felicity. Please, I am begging you, my little darling. Please open this door." Felicity did not wish to face anyone at this moment. Her mind was a toxic stream of shame, sorrow and guilt. Instead, she buried her face in her pillow, which muffled the noise. "Just leave me alone, please, Dad. I just want to be alone."

Samuel acquiesced to his daughter's wishes and bowed his head in frustration before walking back down the hallway, down the stairwell, and out the front door. Indeed, Samuel continued walking down the driveway from outside the house, which led to the main driveway that separated the two paddocks where he was currently keeping the yearlings and weaners. The cattle watched on, intrigued, as Samuel stormed down the main driveway, muttering words to the air and kicking the ground. The main drive was almost two miles long, so there was no imminent destination he was heading toward. Then, Samuel stopped abruptly midstride, and he looked up to the heavens and bellowed from deep within his soul. "Bridget! For the love of God, please help me!" Of course, there was no response from the heavens, nor did Samuel expect one, but a startled weaner mooed not long after Samuel's words had disappeared into the abyss of the moonlit sky. He turned and looked at the young animal, almost like a displeased employer would look at an incompetent employee. "Oh, shut up, you, you, big piece of sirloin steak!" It was the thundering voice rather than the words themselves, but the young beast briskly walked away from the fence line to join a mob of weaners fifty yards away. Samuel turned his head back towards the night sky, staring into space as he looked for an answer. "Please, Bridget. Help me understand what is happening in our daughter's life." Once again, the words of wisdom did not filter down from the heavens above, but Samuel knew there was more going on in Felicity's mind than just the usual sparring between her and his mother. Meanwhile, Felicity had stopped crying as she now contemplated what had been a very confusing six weeks of her life. She still held feelings for Amelia; however, the piety of conservative Catholicism told her those feelings were wrong and that she must try to put Amelia out of her mind.

The following morning, Felicity did not leave her room for breakfast. Samuel had a curt discussion with Catherine, telling her, "Do not ever, ever, lay your hands on my daughter's face like that again." Catherine remained resolute in her usual self-righteous manner. Still, she did not respond to her son. Instead, she turned away to clean up the breakfast table where Felicity's plate of toast and eggs had gone cold. In the meantime, Samuel went to his office and called Charles Robotham, the flying instructor.

Eventually, Felicity emerged from her bedroom at 9:30 a.m., but she did not venture near the kitchen or laundry, where her grandmother might be. After having a bath and brushing her teeth, which she had missed the night before, Felicity left the house and wandered out into the paddocks to search for her father. She walked over the hill of the house paddock. Past the old willow tree where her dilapidated childhood swing was still held on the branches by mere threads of the once invulnerable twine, and on the other side of the hill, she could see her father in the distance, with her grandfather, working on the plough that was connected to the tractor in the middle of the large grain field. It was about a six-hundred-yard walk away, and Felicity dawdled over towards the two men, not knowing how either one of them would react. When she was about fifty yards away, Samuel looked up from the plough he had been furiously working away on with a spanner, and he instinctively turned towards his father to dismiss him from being present. "Dad, can you return to the shed and retrieve that new hake for me, please? This one is broken." Samuel's eyes essentially waved old Albert on, who, for a moment, thought he should be part of the impending discussion. The hake was needed, so Albert shrugged his shoulders, sighed, and walked away without speaking to Felicity.

Samuel stood up from where he was working on the chisel plough, and he placed one foot on the frame as Felicity slowly walked towards him. She looked at Grandpa, who had turned his back and walked away without even saying good morning to her. "What is wrong with him?" Samuel turned his head to briefly look at his father walking away before returning to face Felicity with a hint of a smile. "Don't worry about him. My father has always been a vessel for my mother's scorn, but I am on your side, even if you did curse at her, which, I beg you, don't do that again. Now, come here and let me hug that baby who keeps growing up too quickly for me." Felicity almost triple-jumped into her father's arms. When they embraced, she became upset again, and tears welled up in her eyes. "I'm sorry for acting the way I have been, Dad. You see, oh, how do I say this? I had a crush on a..." Felicity momentarily paused because she almost said the word girl. "On a boy, but was it not reciprocated?" Felicity looked up into her father's eyes and could tell he was puzzled. Momentary silence, then Samuel's eyes opened wide, and a quizzical expression took over his face. "What are you saying to me? Timothy does not like you?" Felicity's tears were immediately interrupted by mirth, and perish the thought that it could be Timothy who was the source of her despondency. "Booger boy! Oh, goodness me, Dad! Perish the thought." That peculiar position had been answered. Still, Samuel remained intrigued. "So, who is the boy? Did he touch you?" Felicity shook off her father and lied, fearing the truth would upset him. "No, Dad. I was not touched and won't be in the future because..." Felicity hesitated as the wrong pronoun almost crossed the boundary line of her lips, where the truth would remain at bay. It was a crossroads of her life, revealing that she was in love with a girl and perhaps losing her father's unconditional love. Her mind won out over her heart. Sometimes the mind's reasoning leads a person down the wrong pathway. "No, Dad, it's because he was in another relationship when I thought I was the one he liked the night of the prom." The truth and lie clung to one another in a yin and yang relationship of convenience. Samuel briefly considered his daughter's response, but his curiosity remained unsatisfied. "Well, I would be surprised if Timothy did not hold a bushel out for you, and I am also relieved his snotty paws did not touch you. But who is it?" Felicity had to think quickly, and the convenient answer was close to Amelia. "Antony Browne, Dad. However, he likes Amelia Speranza, and I was silly enough to believe at the prom he might be interested in me."

Samuel's furrowed brow revealed his displeasure. "Antony Browne? Do you mean the Antony Browne, son of Herbert Browne?" Felicity nodded to keep the deception shrouded with the cloak of honesty. "Well, I'm glad he isn't interested in you because I am about to take his father to court if he does not repay me." Now it was Felicity's turn to be surprised. "Taking him to court? What do you mean, Dad?" Samuel's brow remained furrowed as he opened his hands to reveal the news. "Bloody Herbert Browne, pardon my French, has not paid me for the large quantities of grain I supplied to him last summer, so he goes to court or, as the offer of settlement currently stands, he either pays my outstanding account and interest, or hands over Parklands Farm at Chelmsford to me. And Felicity, I think it will be the latter rather than the former." Whatever thoughts Felicity had in her head about her feelings for Amelia were now usurped by this most surprising news. "Are you pulling my leg, Dad?" Samuel shook his head, adamantly displaying commercial rambunctiousness Felicity had not witnessed before. "No, I am not pulling your leg. It seems old Herbert decided to invest a fair amount of money in the Speranza importation business, and without being too unkind, that business was travelling as well as poor old Botswana. So, the Speranza investment was a ruse, and old Herbert owes me a significant amount of money. I think there will be fewer Speranzas attending the Ascot Races in the years to come. However, in the meantime, either Herbert Browne coughs up the quid, which he doesn't have, or hands over to me the deed to Parklands Farm, or I will seek a petition against him in the court." Felicity was stunned to hear this news because it was only a few weeks ago that Antony and Amelia swanned their way into prom like the future Catholic monarchy of East Anglia and London. Samuel then decided to change the topic because thinking about the outstanding account angered him. "Anyway, don't worry about boys liking you or not, Felicity, because when you have graduated from Cambridge, you will be taking your pick in life."

For a moment, Felicity felt sorry for Amelia because her glamorous life in London's party scene would crumble down sooner rather than later. Samuel had more news to deliver. "Now. More important matters, my little future astronaut. I called Charles Robotham this morning, and he can commence those flying lessons at Earls Colne Airfield tomorrow morning. So how about that? You will be earning your wings sooner than you thought!" The excitement in Samuel's voice immersed itself vicariously in Felicity's mind, and at least for now, she was not consumed by her mixed emotions. She was uninhibited in displaying her gratitude as she threw her arms around Samuel's waist. "Oh, thank you, Dad.

That makes me feel so much better." Samuel pulled his daughter back from his waist and earnestly looked at her. "Alright, now, it will take Grandpa half the damn day to retrieve that hake, so let's go and speak to Grandma. I know she is wrong, but until the university year commences, you have to eat at the same dinner table." Felicity was initially reluctant to speak to her grandmother; however, for her father's sake, she agreed, and they walked off, arm in arm, to head back to the house and face the pious one.

Back at the house, the air was strained as Felicity apologised to her grandmother for calling her a hag and telling her to sod off. After some gentle persuasion from Samuel, Catherine apologised to her granddaughter for slapping her face, but she could not restrain herself from her piety. Samuel raised his eyebrows behind his mother's back, which almost caused Felicity to break out into laughter. At least they could all sit down to dinner together that night. However, deep inside her heart and mind, Felicity still felt confused about her feelings for Amelia.

CHAPTER 12

Charles Robotham was almost like a wax caricature of a World War I flying ace for whom Madame Tussauds had permitted him to be displayed at Earls Colne Airfield. Not only did he wear the garb of a World War I flying ace, but he also had a moustache curled upwards at either end. When Samuel's car pulled up close to the Robotham Flying School hangar, Charles was already standing in front of a Hawker Hart tandem trainer biplane outside the hangar. Felicity began to giggle, and she pointed towards Charles. "Oh, cripes, Dad. Is this person the flying instructor?" Samuel was concerned that Felicity's open mirth might offend Charles. "Shoosh, and don't point. Charles is an excellent flight instructor, even if he does look like an anachronism of World War I." Felicity then began to fix her eyes on the Hart aeroplane, and she realised that maybe this was the aircraft she would be learning in. "Sure, Dad. I will be respectful of this old geezer, but please, tell me, that is not the plane I am meant to be learning to fly in, is it?" Samuel turned towards his daughter, and he raised his eyebrows at her as though she were a silly little child. "What do you think I learned to fly in? A rocket? Of course, that is the aeroplane you are going to start learning how to fly in. Once Charles is satisfied with your ability to fly a Hart, then he will train you in a Cessna. However, you have to learn how to crawl before you can walk, Felicity."

Felicity looked into her father's eyes, and when she realised he was serious about her having to fly the dinosaur of an aeroplane, she nodded. "All right, then, if that is the starting point, then so be it." She then shrugged her shoulders and sighed. "Let's go and meet old Biggles." Now, it was Samuel's turn to chuckle like a child because it was an apt description. They both exited the car and walked towards Charles, whose subsequent actions entrenched the stereotype. "Samuel, old boy. So good to see you again. And this must be Miss Felicity, is that right?" Felicity clenched her teeth, and her thoughts were clear: "Miss? I am not a child!" Samuel swiftly turned towards his daughter because he knew Charles' innocent condescension would not have impressed his daughter. "Felicity, this is Mr Robotham. Please say hello to him." If old Charles thought a curtsy might have been included in the salutation, he was sorely wrong, as Felicity extended her right hand to greet him. "Good morning, Mr Robotham. Nice to meet you." Initially, Charles was surprised that a young female would extend her hand to greet him like a man, but then he came to his senses and accepted her handshake. "Nice to meet you as well, Felicity, but please call me Charles because we are going to spend a lot of time together in the air, so we had better get to know each other by first name. Are you fine with that, Miss Felicity?" There it was again; Charles' treatment of her as a child, in his ignorant nineteenth-century mannerism, could not be ignored by Felicity, and she spoke before Samuel could intervene. "Thank you, Charles, and of course, but please, there is no need for the 'Miss' title as I am starting university at the end of this summer holiday, so if it is not too much of an imposition for you, please call me Felicity."

Charles was slightly startled because there was a hint of force behind Felicity's words that suggested she was displeased with the sexist title of 'Miss'. However, she was his student for the next eight weeks, and he considered building a rapport with a trainee pilot to be the most crucial element of the master-student relationship. "Very well, then, Felicity, it is." He then turned towards Samuel to ensure Felicity was safe in his charge. "Well, old boy, I shan't need you to sit in the cockpit for the next four hours, so off you go, and I promise Felicity will be safe with me." Samuel glanced at his daughter to ensure she was comfortable with Charles, which, upon his visual inspection, appeared to be the case. Then, he returned his eyes' attention to Charles. "All right, Charles. As I explained during our telephone discussion, Felicity has been instructed by me on many occasions about the aeronautical factors to be mindful of, so apart from the machinations of this plane's instruments and controls, she otherwise has a head start on other students." Samuel then turned towards Felicity, and he took her into his arms to hug her, which slightly surprised her. "Take care, my darling, and please, listen to Charles." Samuel realised his daughter was now venturing into the early stages of her dreams and, sadly for him, the first stages of her progression into womanhood. Felicity nodded her head, and then Samuel let go of her. He smiled, nodded reassuringly, and turned to walk away. Felicity then turned around to look at Charles, hoping his tutelage would not be as condescending as his manner.

They both began to walk over towards the Hart, and before Charles could say a word, Felicity parted ways from him and made her way straight to the Hart's fuselage. She inspected the Hart's fuselage, and then Felicity turned towards Charles and smiled as she had already located on the top of the fuselage what she was looking for, just behind the engine cowling. Charles was intrigued by Felicity's impulsive actions. "What are you doing, Felicity?" The expression on Felicity's face was slightly derisive of the instructor. "My dad taught me that the first golden rule of flying is always to check the petrol tank to ensure you know how much fuel is in the tank and, of course, fill it up before you fly." Charles nodded his head in appreciation of her existing knowledge. "Very good. Well, I see your father has instilled some good basic training skills in you already, and by all means, use that measuring stick near the right wheel to measure the tank." Felicity duly complied with Charles' instructions, and then, after she had satisfied herself that the tank was full, Charles spent the next forty-five minutes carefully explaining to her the various components of the Hart and its operation. Felicity listened attentively to Charles but was impatient because she wanted to fly.

Then came the moment Felicity had been waiting for: takeoff and flight. Still, Charles was a pedantic trainer, and he initially performed the first takeoff manoeuvre to teach Felicity the basics of the operation. After the takeoff, he performed a short circle before guiding Felicity through the landing process. Then, it was Felicity's turn to perform the same flight procedures of taking off and landing the Hart, which she did with minimal intervention from Charles.

When Felicity landed the Hart, Charles directed her to take the aeroplane back to the take-off position. He would now control the flight again to teach her a vital emergency procedure. He did not reveal what that emergency was before take-off. After takeoff, they flew to a cruising level of ten thousand feet, which they flew at for about thirty minutes before Charles performed the safety manoeuvre without any prior warning to Felicity.

Those thirty minutes had been moments of gradual and careful instruction provided by the instructor as he let Felicity fly the Hart from her controls in the front cockpit. Still, Charles suddenly retook control of the aeroplane from the rear cockpit. He promptly lowered the speed of the Hart to below forty-five miles per hour, and much to her dismay and terror, the aeroplane's engine stalled before Felicity could utter a single word. Then Charles yelled the instructions as he restarted the aeroplane, which had already begun diving. "Now, do not panic, as any aeroplane can stall, so this is how you restart this one if it stalls on you in the future. First, we lower the Nose. Felicity, the first step is to push the control stick forward to lower the nose of the aircraft, as this will help to regain airspeed, which is crucial for recovery." Felicity instinctively complied with Charles' direction, but she was terrified. Then came the following order from the instructor. "Now, throttle up; gradually increase the throttle to provide more power to the engine, but be careful not to overdo it, as sudden power changes can cause further instability." The terrified young student followed her order, and she throttled up as instructed, but the aeroplane felt like it was about to go into a spin. Charles shouted the following urgent command. "Rudder control, Felicity; use the rudder to keep the aircraft straight and prevent it from spinning." Felicity controlled the rudder, and any tendency she had felt beforehand for the aeroplane to potentially enter a spin was alleviated. However, the booming sound of Charles' instructions continued from behind her. "Level the wings, Felicity; use the ailerons to level the wings." Once again, Felicity instinctively followed her instructor's command and used the ailerons to level the wings. Then, the following booming command consumed her ears. "Felicity, now do a gradual pull-up as you have sufficient airspeed; gently pull back on the control stick to level the aircraft and resume normal flight." Felicity gently pulled back on the control stick, and the Hart resumed its routine flight just like it had moments before Charles tested her skills. Still, there was one more instruction he had for her. "Well done, Felicity, you have just saved yourself from crashing an aeroplane when it unexpectedly stalls, but do not forget to monitor the engine performance; keep your eyes on the engine instruments, and this is to ensure that the engine is running smoothly and not overheating." She kept her eyes on the gauges as instructed, and there were no signs of the engine overheating.

They flew around for another 20 minutes before Charles instructed Felicity to return to Earls Colne Airfield. She did so and even landed the aeroplane without Charles's instruction. Samuel waited by the hangar as Charles taxied the Hart towards it. Felicity took off her flying headwear and immediately looked at her father, her face displaying a mixture of joy and astonishment. She immediately alighted from her cockpit and ran over to her father, hugging him immediately when she came to him. "Dad, oh, Dad! What a first lesson. I even restarted the plane after it stalled in mid-air." A look of alarm immediately came over Samuel's face, and after the initial alarm, his intuition came to the fore, and he turned to stare at Charles, displaying his displeasure. Charles could tell Samuel was unhappy, but he was a self-righteous old aviator who stood by his instincts. "Why are you looking at me like that, old boy? She was ready for it."

Samuel raised his eyebrows in surprise. "Ready for a stall that may not have restarted? Are you trying to pull the blanket over my eyes, Charles? That stunt endangered my daughter's life!" Samuel's tone of voice did not deter the old aviator. "Just settle, please, Samuel, and listen to me. Normally, I would only teach this skill after the fifth lesson, but your daughter is blessed with flying skills beyond those of other students who have completed five lessons. So, she was ready, and I would not have put her through the procedure if I did not think she could handle it, which she did." Samuel stared at Charles for a good while before Felicity broke the tension. "Dad, I am fine. Charles is an excellent teacher, and, in any event, I now know how to save myself behind the controls of a stalled aeroplane. Isn't that why you brought me to Charles?" Felicity was right; Samuel brought her to Charles for flying lessons, but he wasn't expecting such advanced training techniques in her first lesson. Samuel conceded to his daughter's wisdom and raised his hands to admit defeat. "Sorry, Charles. I should not have flared up at you like that. Still, next time, forewarn me before you decide to teach my young daughter any other death-defying tricks." Charles chuckled as he tweaked his moustache. "Of course, old boy, and I am sorry to say this, but she is a better pilot than you."

For the rest of that summer break, Felicity participated in her flying lessons as though her life depended on it. She found that the flying lessons had taken her mind off her mixed feelings for Amelia, and she also desperately wanted her flying licence before she commenced her university studies at Cambridge. With each new lesson, Charles would challenge Felicity's flying skills, and without fail, she would prove her exemplary abilities. Indeed, Charles expedited her training in the operation of a Cessna; such was Felicity's skill in flying the Hawker. Before the end of the summer break, she had earned her wings by flying 40 hours. Not surprisingly, Charles wrote a glowing letter of recommendation about Felicity's flying skills, addressed to Pilot Officer Joan Wilberforce.

When Joan received Charles' letter, she smiled, and it warmed her heart to know that Felicity should now be readily accepted into the UAS and WRAF. After that, she fought tooth and nail to ensure Felicity secured a spot in the UAS and the WRAF. From their brief meeting several months ago, Joan had felt a sisterly bond with Felicity, and she had not forgotten about her when Charles' letter arrived. However, Cambridge and the UAS were still a man's world, and there was another young man to whom the RAF had provided their masculine rubber stamp of approval for acceptance into the limited UAS positions, so Joan had to pull her familial strings to seek the indulgence of securing one more UAS cadetship at Cambridge.

Felicity continued attending church services on Saturdays or Sundays with her family. Notwithstanding her delight in successfully obtaining her pilot licence and her enthusiasm for her impending commencement of tertiary study at Cambridge, there was one thought which still niggled her mind: 'I love Amelia, but does that make me dirty or evil?' The frequency of her dreams of the sweet embrace with Amelia diminished as the break continued, but a string still attached her heart to Amelia's.

On the last Saturday evening before her university life was set to commence, Felicity could not endure the mixed feelings and thoughts in her mind anymore. Samuel had arranged for a family dinner at the Old Siege House Bar and Brasserie restaurant in Colchester, for which it was a dual celebration of Felicity receiving her pilot licence and, of course, the impending commencement of her tertiary education at Cambridge University. However, before dinner, Felicity told her father and grandparents that she wanted some time alone at the Catholic Church. She would be at Cambridge the following Saturday, so she wanted some time alone now to light a candle and thank God for her good fortune. Catherine was delighted to hear her granddaughter express her desire to contemplate her faith, as this would not make her indisposed to Felicity's request. Catherine still did not approve of Felicity's decision to study at the University of Cambridge rather than train to be a nun. Still, it was agreed between her and Samuel that she would not express these thoughts tonight. Albert saw the opportunity to scoff some pre-dinner whiskey in the lounge bar, a proposition that sat comfortably with him. However, Samuel was surprised that Felicity wanted to go to the church now, on what was meant to be a celebration for her. Felicity satisfied his concerns by deferring to her need to thank God for her good fortune first before dinner.

When she arrived at the Catholic Church, Felicity took a deep breath to find the courage to do more than contemplate her faith; she wanted to confess her thoughts and feelings about Amelia. She had chosen now to make her confession because Father O'Leary had taken a month's sabbatical in Rome, and in his place, a young Vatican priest, Father Rossi, was Colchester's temporary priest, so Felicity believed it was unlikely her family would ever hear about her confession. The Saturday afternoon service had concluded, and there were only fifteen minutes of confession time left to go when Felicity walked into the confessional box shortly before 7:00 p.m. She dragged back the tiny curtain that revealed the grille, where Father Rossi sat patiently waiting for another member of the flock to display their contrition for their sins. Felicity sat there motionless and still, and her fear of seeking the sacrament of reconciliation on this occasion had overcome her so much that she could not speak. After about half a minute, Father Rossi broke the silence. His thick Italian accent only embedded Felicity's fear. "What is it? Why do you come to confess to me tonight?" Felicity gulped some air, and her quivering voice revealed her internal turmoil. "Forgive me, Father, for I have sinned." Then there was silence. Father Rossi was tired and impatient, so he was not willing to let what he thought would be a trivial confession take too long. "Well, what is it? What do you wish to confess?"

Father Rossi's query was underscored by his impatience, for which poor Felicity felt even graver trepidation about confessing her thoughts and feelings. Still, she had to receive penance, or at least that was what she thought she should receive. Elements of sorrow now accompanied her quivering voice. "Forgive me, Father, because I have feelings for someone I should not, and I am afraid God will be unkind to my feelings this way." Felicity was again overwhelmed by her fear, and the silence in the confessional box was interrupted by Father Rossi's gruff response. "You cannot seek penance unless you fully confess your sin. Who is the person?" His commanding voice compelled an immediate reaction from Felicity. "She was one of my boarding school friends, Father. And I love her." This was a most surprising confession for young Father Rossi, as he had never experienced such a confession as Felicity's. "Her? What do you mean by her? What have you done?" Father Rossi's final question was delivered in a harsh tone of aloof disapproval. "We kissed each other, and I thought she would love me forever, but she doesn't, or can't, and now I feel like I have offended Jesus our saviour and the Holy Father." Girls kissing girls! Father Rossi had never been confronted by such behaviour before, and he considered it the act of the devil, whose presence he felt was in the confessional box next to him. His anger overwhelmed him. "You filthy, dirty little lesbian slut of Satan. Who are you? Reveal yourself?" Felicity had envisaged her penance would be strict; however, Father Rossi's reaction was full of bile. Instinctively, Felicity fled from the confessional box, promptly doing so before Father Rossi could confront her and see her face. As Felicity ran out of the church, she heard some muffled yelling in Italian, which drove her legs to flee faster around the corner and out of sight on East Hill.

She was very upset about what had just occurred during her confessional, and Felicity needed to stop crying before she entered the Old Siege. She sat down on a seat on the Riverside Walk and stared at the sparkling water of the River Colne, which had been illuminated by the full moon that evening. The sparkling water allowed Felicity to look up at the night sky, and the full moon filled her heart with comfort, as she believed she would someday fly in space. She settled her emotions by telling Jesus and God she apologised for her thoughts and impure actions. Still, she did not like Father Rossi's words and was not inclined to allow her contrition to subdue her disgust for him. Felicity became angry and stood bolt upright with purpose as she walked and talked. Indeed, she spoke as if she had never spoken before. "To hell with him, my Holy Father. You can tell him from me, he can go sod off. And I am not a lesbian."

On the remaining short walk to the Old Siege, Felicity, for the time being, came to terms with her thoughts and feelings about Amelia, and she felt she had now moved on. She kept on repeating to herself under her breath: "I am not a lesbian." When she entered the restaurant at the Old Siege, Felicity immediately caught her father's eye, who, intuitively, as only a parent can, detected that whatever clouds had been hanging over his daughter's mind had seemingly cleared. When Felicity sat at the table, Catherine could not help but try to interrogate her granddaughter's reflection on her faith. "So, how was your time at church, Felicity?" Felicity turned to the left to look into Catherine's eyes to see her reckoning. "It was empowering, Grandma." She smiled at Catherine, but Felicity's smile carried with it the thought that she had shared her thoughts with a despicable man of the cloth, albeit from some distance away.

The following day, Felicity informed her father that she would not be going to church because she felt sick, likely due to the food she had eaten at the Old Siege. In truth, Felicity did not wish to be anywhere near Father Rossi again because she felt so angered by being called a slut that she thought she would be unable to contain her tongue around him. Felicity even put her fingers down her throat in the toilet to vomit, a sound that convinced Catherine her granddaughter was indeed too sick to go to church. After her father and grandparents left the house to attend church that Sunday morning, Felicity looked at herself in the mirror, and her words revealed her resolute determination. "No man will ever treat me that way again." She had some brief thoughts about Amelia, but she buried those feelings because her mind was fixated on the university, the UAS, the WRAF, and being the first woman to go into space, where she could tell the people like Father Rossi of this world 'to sod off', or words to that effect.

Later that Sunday afternoon, while doing some bookkeeping work on the old mahogany desk in his office, Samuel was disturbed by the jackhammering ringtone of the rotary telephone, which sat hidden among the piles of paperwork he had let build up on his desk. Samuel was rushing to get his books up to date for his accountant, so he was slightly perturbed when taking the call. "Yes. Sorry, I meant to say hello. Samuel speaking." There was a pause on the other end of the line, as Samuel's tone had initially surprised the caller, so he queried the silence. "Hello, is anyone there?" Very quickly, the nervous sound of a female emerged. "Oh, my apologies, Mr Bennet. My name is Joan Wilberforce. How are you today?" The woman's name did not resonate in Samuel's mind as someone he was acquainted with. "I am well, Ms Wilberforce, but you must forgive me, as I do not believe we have met before. So, how may I help you, and how are you today?" No, Joan realised she had rudely expected the man to recognise who she was immediately. "Oh, my apologies. How rude of me. I am a pilot officer from the University of Cambridge. Your daughter met me at her school many weeks ago." Now, Samuel recalled that Felicity had mentioned she had previously met Joan. "Of course, Pilot Officer Wilberforce. How may I help you this afternoon?" Joan's voice was overflowing with glee. "I was calling to let you know Felicity's application to join the UAS and WRAF at Cambridge has been accepted. Congratulations." Samuel was puzzled as to why he was being congratulated when the words should have been extended to Felicity. "Thanks, but why am I being congratulated? Shouldn't you be conveying these words to Felicity?" Joan quickly replied. "Oh, I shall be when she arrives on campus, but I wanted to let you know in person today, unless you are coming to Cambridge on Felicity's first day?" Samuel was quite matter-of-fact in his response. "Yes, well, I intended to accompany her on her first day of university." Then he had an idea. "I just thought of a plan, so to speak. Why don't I keep this news a secret, and then I could meet with you that day when you can tell Felicity in person? I believe she would enjoy that, and I want to discuss some issues about my daughter with you." Joan was amenable to Samuel's idea and meeting him. "What a splendid idea. Let me check my diary." There was a short delay, during which time Samuel could hear the turning of the pages. "How about midday? Is that convenient for you?" Indeed, it was. "Yes, that works well, as it will give me enough time to drive home. I shall see you then. Have a pleasant evening." Before Joan could reply, Samuel had already ended the call. Joan was intrigued as to why Samuel wished to meet with her directly, but after a few moments, she gave the meeting no further thought that day.

CHAPTER 13

Cambridge, where the mind and heart, contemporaneously, soar with delight,
Blissfully travelling within an infinite universe of intellectual might.

The times were changing in post-World War II England, but some things remained the same due to their antiquity. The grounds of Cambridge University were a testament to its 749-year history, being not only one of the oldest universities in the world but also one of the most beautiful, with its architecture and magnificent lawns. From scholars congregating there in 1209 onwards, the university had a rich history in academia, including the construction of buildings by potentates such as Henry VI. Notably, it was also the home of Frank Whittle's revolutionary jet engine, which was transforming aviation around the world. It was not hard for Felicity to become enchanted with Cambridge, as its beautiful, manicured lawns and the architecturally pleasing construction of New Court of Corpus Christi College painted a picture that none of the masters of the Renaissance could ever do justice to on canvas. New Court's stunning carved sandstone walls, arched windows and wood-lined walls resembled medieval England, a country as patriarchal as it was mighty.

As a first-year undergraduate who was female, Catholic, and studying for a double degree in science and mathematics, she was alone in a predominantly male institution. However, this was the first day Felicity followed her dreams and the first day she ventured into the world of womanhood. Samuel accompanied his daughter on her first day to ensure her room was suitable and that the facilities met his standards for her accommodation. Finally, sentimentally, it was acknowledging that the little girl he raised after the terrible event of her mother dying during the Blitz was now embarking on adulthood.

Felicity had a lot of thoughts on her mind during the drive, including a fleeting moment of wondering what Amelia might be doing at that very moment. However, she archived that thought because there was a question about her father she had occasionally contemplated. Still, she never dared to ask him until this life-changing moment. The question could not be contained from passing her lips anymore. "Dad, I have a question I have wanted to ask you for many years. However, I have been too afraid to ask it." Samuel's attention was momentarily taken away from the road ahead of him as he quickly glanced towards Felicity. "Felicity, you should never be afraid to ask me questions. You are the centre of my world, my purpose in life, and I would never become hostile towards you for asking a question. So, fire away."

Felicity took a deep breath because it was an intrusion into her father's life, but she had to ask. "Why didn't you ever remarry after all these years?" Samuel was not expecting a question of this personal nature, but he contemplated it because it was reasonable. Felicity momentarily thought she might have offended her father because he remained silent; however, he, too, took a deep breath and tried to answer it as honestly as he could. "When I met your mother, it was love at first sight. Your mother had many obstacles in her early life, but those obstacles made her virtuous, kind, and most importantly, patient. Your grandmother had previously made me meet young women she considered to be appropriate Catholic women for me, but they were just mere incarnations of her piety. Understand me, your mother was a very devout Catholic woman, but she had a kind and compassionate heart. Once you meet someone like that in life, it isn't easy to meet a person of comparable qualities. Moreover, I vowed on the day of our marriage that I would love and obey her until the day I died. Then, I had you, as a child, in whom I see so much of your mother's kindness in your eyes, and I did not want to; let me see, what is the best way I can explain it? I did not want to disrupt your life by bringing somebody else into it who may not be able to cherish you like your mother would have done." Now Felicity was the one to be surprised because she never realised how much her father had given up in his life to make her life functional in the circumstances of tragedy. Her emotions began to overwhelm her, and they manifested themselves in her voice as she tried to hold back her tears. "You did not have to sacrifice your happiness for me, Dad. I would have accepted you remarrying to be happy." While keeping his eyes on the road, Samuel reached out with his left arm to cuddle his daughter. "You do not need to feel upset or guilty, my little sweetheart. It was my undertaking to your mother, as I watched her coffin being lowered into the grave that terrible day, that I would always love and protect you, and as I said, nobody else could ever come close to your mother's beautiful heart. Besides, I may not screech it out on top note like your grandmother, but I believe in God, and on the eve of my wedding, I swore to Him that I would always love and cherish your mother. Now, cheer up because today is an important day. Still, I am glad you got that question off your chest." One thought did enter Felicity's curious mind, but after her father's heartfelt candour, she decided it was best to ask the question in her mind: "Why does he think God is a 'him'?"

They discussed other topics for the remainder of the trip, including Samuel telling Felicity he wanted to meet Pilot Officer Joan Wilberforce. Felicity had expressed so much admiration for her during her telephone discussion with Samuel that day when she met her at Woldingham. Samuel had told Felicity not too long before they arrived at Cambridge that he had already spoken to Pilot Officer Wilberforce, and she had put aside her time to meet with Samuel and Felicity at midday after Felicity had settled into her room. Despite Felicity's importunate request in the car to explain why her father had spoken to Joan and, more importantly, arranged a meeting, Samuel remained tight-lipped about the reason for their meeting. He wouldn't even tell her when he spoke with Joan.

The splendour of the architecture at Cambridge University took Felicity's breath away. The pictures she had seen of the buildings could not capture the three-dimensional ambience. The moment was perhaps more compelling because Samuel pulled up the car in front of Corpus Christi on Trumpington Street. Although the sky was overcast with reasonably dark clouds, the majestic architecture of that building created its radiance, which Mother Nature could never overshadow. At Felicity's request, Samuel had arranged for her to be allocated a room with an ensuite, a rare indulgence for a first-year undergraduate. Still, it also came at a price, which was in addition to her UAS exemption. When they opened the door to Felicity's allocated room, the curtains were drawn on the windows, which revealed a view of the stable yard and out to Old Court. Felicity's room was spacious and adequately furnished with a bed, a wardrobe, a chest of drawers, and a study desk and chair, all made of cedar. The walls were painted a clinical white, which perhaps needed a fresh coat to cover the years of marks since the last one was applied. However, the colour of the walls made the room feel far more expansive. The bedding linen was folded up on the bed. Once again, the sheets were a clinical white cotton weave, while the blankets and the bedspread featured various masculine colours: blues, grey, and khaki. However, Felicity had never been partial to pastel colours, and in any event, the colours suited her commitment to the UAS on campus. Once they had finished unpacking Felicity's belongings, Samuel and Felicity left for their scheduled meeting with Pilot Officer Wilberforce.

It was a three-minute drive from Corpus Christi College to the UAS

Headquarters at 2 Chaucer Road, Cambridge. Felicity was slightly nervous on the short drive, mainly because she wanted to make a good impression on Joan Wilberforce, particularly, as far as she was aware, her application to join the UAS was still pending. She did not know why Samuel wished to meet with her. She did not realise until that day that Joan had spoken to Samuel and arranged for him to meet with her on Felicity's first day at university. They pulled up outside the two-story stone cottage, which was UAS Headquarters. Felicity's curiosity had not been satisfied by Samuel's earlier answers. "So, why do you want to meet with Pilot Officer Wilberforce, Dad? I have not even been accepted into the UAS." Samuel only partially turned his head towards Felicity, but a faint smile flickered. "I did not want to meet with her, Felicity, initially. The pilot officer contacted me about three days ago. During our conversation, it dawned upon me that she might like to hear a former RAF officer's opinion regarding whether you are suited to join the UAS, so I requested that I meet with both of you today. So, I will do my best." Felicity was now intrigued, and a puzzling question consumed her thoughts. "Why would my Dad influence Joan?" She didn't realise her father held a secret close to his chest.

The windows of the old stone cottage shone with the rare rays of sunshine that had broken through the cloudy sky at midday. Their appearance at that moment brought a sense of joy to the world as Felicity and Samuel walked towards them. Four concrete stairs led up to a small, covered landing, and the old wooden door, painted a warm woodland green, had a sign that said: "Open. Please enter." They entered the cottage, and sitting behind the desk in the vestibule was a young male, about 21, with fair hair and wearing a pair of thick, black Bakelite reading glasses. Samuel looked at the young man's insignia on his coat and immediately detected his rank. "Good afternoon, Warrant Officer. Would you please inform Pilot Officer Wilberforce that Samuel and Felicity Bennet are here to see her?" Samuel's words carried a tone of authority, a clip that surprised Felicity. The young male was quite a nervous fellow, and he clumsily stood up, tripping over his chair as he responded in his distinct Scottish accent. "Yes, sir. I shall inform her straight away." The Warrant Officer walked down the polished wood-lined hallway and knocked on the last door to his left. The muffled sound projected through the old, polished oak door: "Come in." The nervous Warrant Officer opened the door, entered the room and then closed the door again.

About half a minute later, the door to the room opened, and Joan Wilberforce emerged from it, also to be closely followed by the Warrant Officer. As Joan walked down the hallway, she saw Felicity, and mutual smiles appeared on their faces. Joan entered the vestibule, followed by the Warrant Officer, and her warm welcome comforted Felicity. "Well, this is a pleasure. How nice to see you again, Felicity." Felicity was unusually nervous, and she timidly nodded without saying a word. Joan then turned towards Samuel, and she extended her hand to shake his, a gesture Samuel was not expecting. "And you must be Mr Bennet?" Samuel accepted Joan's handshake, as unnatural as it felt for him. "I am. Thank you for seeing us today, Pilot Officer." So far, neither of them had revealed their ruse to surprise Felicity. "It's my pleasure. Please, follow me down to my office." As Joan turned to walk back down the hallway, she half-turned her head towards the Warrant Officer, who was standing behind his desk. "Warrant Officer Jones, please do not put any telephone calls through to me, nor do I wish to be disturbed while I am meeting with Mr Bennet and Felicity." The young man's subservience was palpable as he saluted. "Yes, ma'am." The three of them then walked down the hallway, and when they reached the door from which Joan had previously emerged, she ushered them in. "Please enter and take a seat."

Joan's office had been the old dining room of the cottage, and, unlike the hallway, it was only lined with polished oak a third of the way up the wall, with the remaining areas of the wall lined in aged, floral and striped wallpaper for which age had been unkind. Nevertheless, two windows let in sufficient natural light so that the old glass chandelier did not need to be turned on. Joan closed the door to her office, then walked over to the mahogany desk, where Samuel and Felicity sat in two old Victorian-era dining chairs. In contrast, Joan's office chair was a more modern wooden swivel chair, likely made just before World War II. She took a seat and initially directed her attention towards Felicity. "So, how are you, Felicity?" Felicity was still slightly nervous. "I am well, thank you, Joan." Samuel was surprised by his daughter's lack of military etiquette. "Felicity, show some respect. Acknowledge the Pilot Officer Wilberforce's rank by calling her ma'am."

Felicity was about to protest her father's chipping of her, but Joan held her hand up to display her comfort. "It is fine, Mr Bennet; when we met at Woldingham, I told Felicity in moments such as these, she could refer to me as Joan, and please, the same circumstances of informality are extended to you." Samuel looked towards his daughter, dipping his eyes to apologise before responding to Joan. "Thank you, Joan. And please, call me Samuel. When you call me Mr Bennet, I feel inclined to look over my shoulder to see whether my whiskey-swilling father is standing there." Joan brought her hand up to her mouth to smother her giggle, and then, after removing her hand, they all sat momentarily in silence before Joan broke the silence. "Well, Felicity, I have some good news for you and some bad news. The good news is that your application to join the UAS has been accepted. Congratulations!" For the first time in quite a while, Felicity had some excellent news, and she somewhat uncharacteristically leapt out of her chair in joy. "That is fantastic news." Her exhilarated and loud voice breached the silence of Joan's closed wooden door, causing Warrant Officer Jones to stop typing the letter on the Remington Rand typewriter. Back in Joan's office, Felicity's delight could not be contained, and she instinctively turned towards her father, believing he would be just as exhilarated as she was. However, Samuel just sat in his chair, grinning at his daughter like a cat who had swallowed a mouse. "Aren't you excited for me, Dad?" Joan, once again, spoke before Samuel could respond to his daughter. "Well, Felicity, that is the bad news. Your father already knew before today, but he wanted me to tell you and, of course, be present." Felicity looked at Joan with an expression she could not hide, prompting Samuel to congratulate his daughter as he rose to his feet to hug her and speak simultaneously. "Well done, Felicity. I am so proud of you, and yes, before you say it, I am sorry for keeping it a secret, but I did want to be present when you received this news."

Felicity felt tears of delight welling in her eyes, and the bad memories of Woldingham, Amelia and Catherine's indifference towards her seemed to be shelved in a vault of her mind. Her dreams seemed to be coming true, and her joy was now expressed in tears, which ran down her rosy cheeks. Samuel released his grip on his daughter and turned Felicity towards Joan. "Don't you have something to say to Joan now, Felicity?" Felicity still could not contain her joy, and she quickly made her way around to Joan's side of the desk to hug her whilst she was still seated, an action which surprised Joan. "Thank you, Joan. Thank you. I am going to be the best pilot in the UAS." Joan briefly accepted Felicity's hug in the same sisterly manner she displayed towards her when they first met at Woldingham. "You're welcome, Felicity." She patted her on the back to signal the end of their contact, and as Felicity let go of her, Joan's right arm rose, and her slender hand pointed towards the door, a gesture to display her authority. "Alright now, Cadet Bennet. You are dismissed; please go and keep Warrant Officer Jones company for a while, as I believe your father wishes to speak with me alone. Isn't that right, Samuel?" Felicity turned towards her father, who had now seated himself, and he nodded. "That is right, Joan. Go on, Felicity, as the pilot officer said, you're dismissed, but on this occasion, show some respect because you are now officially one foot in the door of the WRAF." Initially, Felicity was perplexed by the notion of her being dismissed and the meaning of Samuel's direction to display some respect. Still, it dawned upon her that she had to address an officer who had temporarily dismissed her from her presence. Felicity turned back towards Joan, and in the manner her father had taught her since she was a little girl, she raised her right hand in a circular motion, then brought it back with an open palm facing outwards, one inch behind her eyes. "Yes. Ma'am." She turned to walk towards the door; however, there was one more matter Joan wished to discuss with her. "Oh, Cadet Bennet. One more issue. Please provide your uniform size to Warrant Officer Jones, as he will need to use the measuring tape on you. So, do not be afraid, as it is part of his job. Now you're dismissed." Felicity saluted again. "Yes, ma'am." Felicity then turned around and left the room, closing the door behind her. She wondered what secret her father wished to discuss with Joan alone.

Samuel turned back around in his chair after the door had closed, and the earnest look on his face contrasted with the delight he had displayed only moments before. He briefly contemplated his words as he fixed his gaze on Joan, then commenced to speak carefully. "So, do you think my daughter is cut out for the UAS and the WRAF?" Joan sat forward in her chair, resting her elbows on her desk as she brought her hands together in a combined fist of solidarity. She then nodded, ensuring her eyes did not depart from Samuel's eyes. "I do, and I will tell you how much I do. I had to fight tooth and nail to get her application accepted. Indeed, I had to beg for an extra place to be created for her because an Air Marshal's son had taken the last position. Fortunately, my father is an Air Chief Marshal, so I could pull some strings, so to speak, to have her accepted; otherwise, the world of boys supporting boys would prevail, Samuel. We may be almost at the end of the 1950s, but the bloody sexism is still alive and well in the upper ranks of the RAF, just like when you served."

It was Samuel's turn for a surprise because he had not previously told Joan about his RAF service. "I never told you I flew for the RAF. How did you find that out?" Joan's slight smirk revealed her condescension. "Come on, Samuel. The RAF does their homework. Your full name was on Felicity's application form, so it did not take too long for headquarters to ascertain that you are the same former Pilot Officer Samuel Bennet, honourably discharged from service after the death of your wife. In any event, Felicity mentioned that you flew during the war when we first met, so it didn't take much digging to locate your service file. May I say, before I forget to, how sorry I am about you losing your wife during the Blitz?" Samuel nodded in appreciation of her genuine expression of condolence. Joan then moved on to a topic she knew she would not share, but she felt that Samuel could be trusted in a moment of confidence. "However, even with your service background, I had to fight for Felicity's application to be accepted because the Ministry of Defence is culling UAS funding, and as I said before, if it wasn't for my father, the boys' club would have prevailed." Samuel reflected on all Joan's words momentarily, then nodded in appreciation. "Well, thank you for calling upon your father's assistance because rejecting her application would have been soul-destroying for Felicity." Samuel then sat forward in his chair to level with Joan. "I don't know if my daughter, Joan, is cut out for the RAF. Sure, she can fly. Indeed, she could probably operate a plane like I can, Joan; however, something has been wrong with her since her last term at Woldingham." Momentarily, Joan wondered whether she had been misguided in fighting for Felicity's acceptance into the UAS. "What do you mean, Samuel? Has she conveyed some contrary position to you?" Samuel shook his head, dismissive of his daughter's verbal ambivalence. "No, Joan. It is nothing, she said. She lost the four-hundred-yard race at Woldingham when she seemed to be the favourite to win. Then something happened at her school prom with a boy whose father I am embroiled in litigation with. And, look, I support her in all her life dreams, but she has her heart set on being the first woman to fly into space. Maybe I am overprotective because she lost her mother when she was an infant. She is an only child, Joan. She was raised around my strict Catholic mother." Joan rolled her eyes, almost as though she had met Catherine. "My sister lives in Australia with her husband and children, so Felicity has not even had her cousins to mentor her. Now, she is on her own here at Cambridge, studying mathematics and science, which I understand includes physics and aeronautical engineering, while also trying to join the WRAF or UAS, or whatever the Ministry of Defence has called the outfit. I worry. She has taken on a lot of studies, which is fine because she is bright, but then she also wants to serve in the WRAF, go into space, and goodness knows what else. That is all, I am worried."

Joan remained silent momentarily, considering every word she heard, and then she raised her open palms to assuage Samuel's concerns. "Do you know my father had a similar discussion with me when I started here, when I was accepted into the UAS? Look, Samuel, Felicity told me about her mother being killed in the Blitz when I spoke to the girls at Woldingham that day, so I can imagine it was a difficult childhood. I was not aware of your mother, but it is not my place to comment, and whatever happened at Woldingham is in the past. In the present and the future, for as long as I remain here – which might be longer than I expected since my fiancé has been accepted as a lecturer on campus – Felicity will have me keeping an eye on her and serving as a mentor. As for her dream, well, goodness knows what the future holds in store for any of us with this goddamned arms race occurring. Nevertheless, she will have me here. Does that ease your concern?" Samuel stared at Joan, then blinked, confirming her words. "Alright, then. The first step I had better take in mentoring your daughter is ensuring she is not tormenting poor Warrant Officer Jones." With those words, Joan stood up and ushered Samuel towards the door. "You first, Samuel. They may be a sexist old bunch of sods at my father's rank in the RAF, but here on campus, it is a new world."

Samuel opened the office door, and sure enough, he could hear his daughter's voice displaying intellectual superiority. He briefly waited outside the office for Joan to walk out, and when she did, it was for a purpose, namely, sorting out why there was such raucous coming from the vestibule. Joan walked briskly into the vestibule, with Samuel only a few steps behind her, and Felicity was standing over Warrant Officer Jones, who almost resembled a trapped little mouse who had been cowered into a corner by an intellectual tiger. "What in heaven's name is going on out here?" Joan's curt words immediately brought Warrant Officer Jones and Felicity to attention, with the latter being the first person to answer. "He is wrong, Joan." Felicity stopped short in her speech to correct herself as she was no longer within the confines of the privacy of Joan's office. "Sorry. Ma'am, he said that jet engines and rockets are the same, but that is not right. They act on Newton's third law, but jet engines need oxygen, whereas rockets don't. It's not rocket science!" Samuel perhaps had no cause for concern; however, Joan had to start teaching Felicity a few facts about campus and UAS life. "Excuse me, Cadet Bennet. Don't ever address a superior member of the UAS and RAF in that manner ever again. It is not 'he' or 'him' or even Drew; you address him as Warrant Officer. Do you understand me?" Felicity realised her folly. "Yes, ma'am. I am sorry, Warrant Officer, but there is an inherent difference between the two types of engines." Joan nodded in approval. "Very well then, Cadet Bennet. The first UAS meeting is scheduled for this coming Friday at 7:00 a.m. sharp. You are otherwise dismissed." Joan turned towards Samuel, revealing the ever-slight hint of a reassuring smile. "Nice to meet you, Mr Bennet." Joan extended her hand to shake Samuel's, which he once again felt awkward accepting. "Likewise, Pilot Officer. Come on, Felicity. I will drive you back to Corpus Christi." Felicity and Samuel then left the cottage, and it suddenly dawned upon Felicity that she was now living in a subservient world of WRAF service.

On the short drive back to Corpus Christi, very few words were exchanged between Felicity and Samuel. When they arrived back at the main entrance on Trumpington Street, they both alighted from the car. Samuel hugged his daughter tightly, almost suffocating her with his love. "Everything will be fine. I am only a telephone call away, and plenty of Quid is in your bank account, so money will not be an issue." Felicity slightly escaped from her father's clutch, and she could see that his eyes had water in them. "I will be fine, Dad. Unless, of course, I strangle that dimwit Warrant Officer." Samuel chuckled; he knew his daughter was right. "Sure. In any event, take care. Stay safe, and I love you, Felicity." She smiled back. "I love you too, Dad." Samuel got back in his car and drove off, looking in the rearview mirror to see his daughter waving goodbye to him. Then he turned onto Pembroke Street, and the image of Felicity was gone.

CHAPTER 14

Asps can be sleek, one of Mother Nature's delights.
However, I warn thee, "Watch out! They bite!"

That first day of university lectures seemed to end as quickly as it began for Felicity. Her first lecture was in physical natural sciences located in the Cavendish Laboratory. The building and rooms revealed their age, and the first-year class was crowded with new undergraduate students, with Felicity being the lone female in a sea of young men's faces. Professor Morris was in charge of the undergraduate physical natural sciences course; however, Felicity's first-year lecturer was Albert Barnsley, and the students had to call him Mr Barnsley. He was a typical man of science; not overly tall, he had developed a belly by his late thirties, and his hair was thinning, so that even with hair oil, it was slightly dishevelled. After introducing himself to his overcrowded class, he commenced writing on the chalkboard without speaking. Felicity immediately began taking notes, whereas some of the male students behind her whispered to one another under their breath for the first five minutes.

Then Barnsley turned around and saw the obstreperous members of the group up the back of the class. He verbally excoriated them before making examples of them by asking them questions to which they did not, and could not, know the answers. One of those young men appeared to come from a family of established hereditary wealth, as his fine clothing displayed the tell-tale signs of tailor-made craftsmanship. He also had fine features, which made him look cute and almost feminine. When Mr Barnsley asked him his name, he responded with the perfected tongue of the landed gentry: "My name is William de Veres, Mr Barnsley." Mr Barnsley detected the landed gentry's arrogance, and it was for de Veres that he displayed his great displeasure with his distracting behaviour. It was immediately apparent to Felicity that Mr Barnsley was a serious man of science and a lecturer who would not tolerate misbehaviour or a lack of academic discipline.

Her natural sciences lecture concluded at 11:00 a.m., giving Felicity enough time before her afternoon mathematics lecture to collect her UAS cadet uniform during the lunch break. The weather was cool and overcast, so she walked from the lecture theatre to Chaucer Road, and even though it took her twenty minutes to do so, Felicity hardly built up a sweat; such was the state of the autumn weather that day. The grey skies were perhaps foreboding of what lay ahead of her in life, but Felicity enjoyed taking in the sights of her new world. Sure enough, when she entered the UAS cottage, Warrant Officer Jones was seated at his desk, and he was immediately on his guard when he saw Felicity walk in. Nevertheless, Felicity saluted him, and her salutation of 'Warrant Officer' had a slight hint of disdain for a person she considered to be a bit of a dill. Warrant Officer Jones returned the salute. "Cadet, I gather you are here to collect your uniform?" She wasn't there for the want of a stimulating intellectual conversation, but Felicity decided condescension was not the best way to start her UAS career. "Yes, Warrant Officer." He then left his seat and walked down the hallway whilst Felicity remained in the vestibule. About a minute later, Warrant Officer Jones returned with a brown paper parcel and a pair of new black leather flat-heeled shoes. "These should fit you, but if they don't, bring them back immediately for urgent adjustments." Felicity eagerly took the parcel and shoes from Warrant Officer Jones, and she somewhat awkwardly saluted him before turning back around and leaving the cottage. Warrant Officer Jones was spared her wit for now.

Felicity could not return to her room fast enough to try on her new uniform. It took her 20 minutes, and while she was walking, a very slight shower passed over, chilling her to the bones. When she arrived at her room, Felicity eagerly tore the parcel apart and changed into her uniform, which, along with the boots, fitted her perfectly. At least Warrant Officer Jones got the measurements right! Felicity looked at herself in the wardrobe mirror. The blue uniform jacket and skirt were fresh-looking, and the Wedgewood blue shirt and navy tie made her outfit look very smart. The cadet cap sat perfectly on her head, and her shoes fitted her perfectly. Felicity imagined she was saluting a superior as she admired the outfit. Her dream felt like it was on the way to coming true; however, there was still a long way to go. Her grumbling stomach signified that she needed to quickly get some lunch into her before her mathematics lecture. Felicity changed into her dress again, and she carefully hung her UAS WRAF uniform up in her wardrobe before making her way for a quick sandwich and lemonade at the cafeteria.

Later that same first day, after the lunch break, Felicity had to attend her first mathematics lecture. This first-year undergraduate mathematics class was taught by Professor Colin Wickham, who had decided to be hands-on with the undergraduates by teaching them in their first year. If Mr Barnsley had presented himself as a man of science, then Professor Wickham presented himself as a mathematician, a late forties man with grey hair perfectly parted on the right side and thick, black Bakelite frames that encased thick reading glasses, suggesting he could not see past the end of his nose. One of the young men exemplified by Mr Barnsley was also in that class: William de Veres. Once again, Felicity was a lone female face in a sea of male faces. William de Veres recognised Felicity from their natural sciences lecture, so he sat beside her, which she found slightly discomforting given his previous behaviour. William did not speak to Felicity at all during that first mathematics lecture. When it concluded, he turned towards her as though he was about to say something, but then he changed his mind and walked out. Felicity was intrigued by this behaviour and was also interested in him because he was cute-looking.

After she had finished her mathematics lecture, Felicity decided she should call her father to report back to him about her first day of university lectures. She had not properly turned her mind to the time, and it was only 4:00 p.m. The fifth ring, the telephone was answered, but it was not her father. "Hello, this is Catherine Bennet speaking." Felicity momentarily froze, and even though she had mended bridges with her grandmother, she knew that Catherine was a volatile soul. "Hello, is anybody there?" Catherine's demanding tone necessitated a response from Felicity. "Oh, hello, Grandma. How are you?" Volatility prevailed that afternoon. "Felicity, why didn't you speak when I initially answered?" Quick thinking was required to try to subdue her grandmother's volatile temperament. "I could not initially hear a response, Grandma, until now, but in any event, how are you and Grandpa?" Now for the interrogation. "We're fine. Have you been to church since you arrived at university?" Felicity wanted to end the call promptly, but she knew there were several more questions to answer. "Grandma, I have only been on campus a few days, but I plan to attend the Fisher House service this coming Sunday. Is Dad there?" There was no easy escape from the Inquisition. "Well, make sure you do, young lady. Have you been praying each day?" Felicity was now becoming slightly impatient with her grandmother's piety. "Of course. Every night before I go to bed. Now, is Dad there, please, Grandma? I want to tell him about my first day of lectures." Still, there was no escape. "No, he is out in the fields with your grandfather. So, tell me. How was your first day of lectures?" Felicity should have kept her response simple. "It was fascinating. I had a natural science lecture this morning and just finished my mathematics lecture. Oh, and I think one of the boys in both lecture classes with me likes me because he sat next to me this afternoon." The sword of Damocles, which had been hanging above her head, now fell. "Interested in you? Did he speak to you?" Her candour drove that sword in deep. "No. No, he didn't." Then, it came from the viper's sharp tongue. "Well, what on Earth makes you think he would be interested in you? You do not have your aunt's looks, so." Felicity immediately cut her grandmother off before she lost her temper with the old woman. "Look, Grandma. I don't know. Anyway, I have to go and study. Please tell Dad I will call him tonight after dinner. Goodbye, Grandma." There was no contrition in reply. "Goodbye, and say your prayers tonight."

After she hung up the telephone, Felicity stood there for a while looking at it, wondering why her grandmother had to be so cruel and, more importantly, wrong about her looks. "Is it because my breasts are small?" She could not answer her question, but she thought she must have some form of attraction for William de Veres to sit next to her. Felicity shook her head and returned to her room at Corpus Christi to study her mathematics and natural science work. Then, she would telephone her father after dinner.

The dining hall at Corpus Christi College was a testament to a time of English grandeur seldom repeated since the Second World War. The polished wood-lined walls stretched fifteen feet upwards on each side, save for several long windows that let in natural light during the day. Where the wood lining finished, the walls extended further upwards for another ten feet of resplendent decorative wallpaper. They then arched inwards for another fifteen feet of polished wood beams and decorative paper, meeting at the ceiling. The far wall from the entry contained the most ornate lead-line crystal arch window, comprised of separate, smaller arched windows that form a giant masterpiece of English craftsmanship. Painted canvas portraits of notable past scholars hung on the walls, a reminder of Cambridge's standing in academia. The formal presentation of the room also required a formal dress code, a college rule. The males had to wear a coat and tie, while the females had to wear a dress and heels. There were three long rows of tables, all covered with fine linen, and each spot had already been set for the evening meal, with silverware and crystal glasses to drink from. The dining hall looked majestic, sparkling like a palace from a fairytale.

As she had done for the previous evenings, Felicity wore a delicate blue cotton dress that extended down to her knees. After the insult she had been subjected to earlier by her grandmother, she had decided to wear full makeup, including rouge and lipstick. When she entered the dining hall, Felicity saw a room of mainly males, except for a few females seated down the far end of the room. Still, they were already surrounded by overly interested males, just like they had been on two previous evenings. So Felicity sat by herself at the end of one of the long tables nearest the entry, trying to hold a dignified poise despite being alone with several unoccupied chairs next to her.

Then, almost as though it was a veritable riposte to Catherine's insult, William de Veres entered the dining hall again dressed in his fine tailor-made suit, cotton shirt and a regal-looking silk tie. He stopped, looked around, and saw Felicity sitting alone at the end of the long table to his right. William looked at Felicity, smiled, and then walked towards her, causing Felicity to become slightly nervous, but not in the same way she had felt for Amelia. William stopped next to Felicity, and she slowly looked up at him. She was too nervous to speak. "Well, since we will be in two lectures, may I have the honour of sitting next to you if nobody else is sitting there?" Felicity stared at him momentarily, unsure how a young woman should conduct herself in these circumstances. William broke the silence. "What is the matter? Has the cat got your tongue? Don't worry, I do not bite." He then took it upon himself to sit down next to Felicity, and when he did, he placed his right elbow on the table to rest his chin and cheek in his right hand as he faced Felicity side-on. "Undoubtedly, you heard Barnsley dress me down in natural science for talking, so you know my name, but what is yours?"

Now, she could not avoid talking to him, so Felicity slightly turned to face William, and his features appeared even more feminine now than they had in the harsh light of the lecture theatres. "My name is Felicity. Felicity Bennet." William grinned, and for a moment, his grin almost resembled Amelia's. He extended his right hand, prompting Felicity to hold out her right hand's fingertips for the customary submissive salutation of English women in the 1950s. "Nice to meet you, Felicity. So, which part of the world do you hail from?" Felicity was polite but short in her response. "Essex. What about you?" William was not shy, nor was he humble. "I am from Hampshire. My family has owned over three hundred acres of estate land there for centuries, as well as land in other southern regions. Overall, we have approximately two thousand acres of land. Eversley Manor is where we reside. My father is an Air Marshal in the RAF, Lord Richard de Veres. What about you?" Felicity was almost embarrassed to respond, as if she had been transported back to Woldingham when she was 12, explaining her circumstances to the far wealthier Amelia. "My family own a grain and cattle farm near Colchester. It was almost a hundred acres, but my father has doubled it in size since World War II to about two hundred acres." Now, it was time for William's Anglican arrogance. "Yeoman! Well done on doubling your handling." Felicity bit at the bait. "We once were not Yeoman. However, the Glorious Revolution, among other matters, saw to the end of that because we are Catholic." William held his hands up defensively. "Sorry. I did not realise it was such a touchy subject. Since we will study two subjects together, how about we be friends? Do not be alarmed; I only have good intentions for Catholics."

Felicity stared at William's face, and his intentions seemed honourable. "Sure. Fine by me. However, I cannot study late on Thursday and Sunday nights because I have UAS service duties early on Monday and Friday." William grinned, almost as though he had won a hand in a poker game. "Well, fancy that? I, too, have UAS service duties. We are going to make a splendid team." Felicity pondered this remark because of her competitive nature. "Team?" She kept her thoughts to herself as she spoke pleasantly to William over dinner before excusing herself to return to her room. When she returned to her room, Felicity thought about William for a while. She did not know what to make of him or whether his intentions for her were pure. However, at least she had companionship in an otherwise large and lonely new world. She said her prayers before bedtime, and just before she went off to sleep, Felicity wondered for a few moments what Amelia was up to. However, this was an ephemeral moment of contemplation because her new world of university was about to become very busy.

CHAPTER 15

To believe that a woman was made from a man's rib,
It is to believe nothing more than men's eternal fib.

As instructed by Joan at the start of the week, Felicity attended the first UAS meeting at 7:00 a.m. sharp. The UAS hangers were located at Teversham Airport, which meant Felicity had to catch a bus at 6:30 a.m. from central Cambridge. As a result, her day began very early, at 4:30 a.m., to allow her to take her morning jog, shower, and change into her cadet uniform before catching the bus. She had missed eating breakfast that morning, but Felicity was too excited to worry about food, and she wondered whether there might even be a flight for her that day. Approximately ten other UAS personnel were on the bus, all of whom were males, but there was one noticeable absence. Namely, William was not on the bus. None of these UAS males spoke to or sat next to Felicity, making it seem as though she was not welcome to sit with them, as they did not even acknowledge her.

Her expectations came crashing down to Earth quickly when Felicity arrived at the UAS hangar at Teversham Airport because there would be no joy flights. Joan met all the cadets outside the hangar. Her first command signalled there would be no flying that morning. "Alright, cadets. You're not in lectures now, so one single line and attention." Felicity knew from the stories Samuel had told from a young age how she had to stand on parade, and she very quickly obeyed the command. In contrast, the other new cadets awkwardly lined up, trying to imitate Felicity's perfect stance. Joan was unimpressed. "Oh, goodness me! Look at this: Cadet Bennet is the only cadet who knows how to line up." Felicity immediately felt like she was one up on her fellow cadets. Joan turned her attention to one of the male cadets whose crumpled uniform underscored his awkward stance. "Goodness me, Cadet Williams. Look at you. Your uniform is a disgrace, and you look like you're waiting for an order at a fish and chip shop. Look at Cadet Bennet. That is how you should present yourself and stand to attention. Now, attention!" Cadet Williams did his best to copy Felicity's stance, and once Joan was satisfied with the line-up, she delivered her next set of orders.

"Alright, this morning I will teach you how to march in perfect formation and…" Joan's words were broken by the sound of a car screeching around the corner of the hangar. Sure enough, there was William behind the wheel of a silver MG. He had the canopy down and a cigarette hanging out of the corner of his mouth. He pulled his car up about thirty yards away from where the other cadets were lined up, and he could immediately see that Joan was unimpressed by his tardiness and his flamboyant entrance. Her command immediately followed the sound of the engine switching off. "Cadet de Veres. Get your miserable body out of that car and over here now, and put out that cigarette."

William knew he was in trouble, just how much he did not realise. He hurriedly made his way over to the parade, and in stubbing out the cigarette under his boot, he only further infuriated Joan. "Cadet de Veres! Pick up that cigarette butt and put it in the ashtray of your car, where it belongs!" William complied with the command, but he then displayed his defiance by placing the extinguished cigarette butt in his pocket rather than the ashtray of his beloved car. Joan was seething with anger, and it was not only about his tardiness and defiance. Her anger extended from a family rivalry that even William was unaware of. "Cadet de Veres! How dare you treat your uniform like a rubbish dump? Place that cigarette butt in your car ashtray immediately!" Joan shouted this command, and her voice seemed to echo around Teversham that morning. William complied with the command, and he reluctantly placed the cigarette butt in the ashtray of his car before dawdling over to the parade of his fellow cadets. William stood next to Felicity, which made her feel slightly uncomfortable because of William's poor attitude. Joan was not finished with him, and she would now punish all the cadets because of William's behaviour. She stood right before William, almost eye to eye, and her loud voice was deliberately directed into his face. "Cadet de Veres, when you are told to be here at 7:00 a.m. sharp, you are to be here by no later than that time. Now, because of you, the whole squad of new cadets will suffer. I was only going to make all of you march for half an hour. However, thanks to the tardy Cadet de Veres, all of you can march for the entire hour!" Sighs emanated from some of the other males, but Felicity remained disciplined and faced forward, in position and quiet. "Now, Cadet Bennet can lead the lot of you. Cadet de Veres, get up the back of the line where you belong!" William moved to the back of the line, and sure enough, Joan marched the cadets around Teversham Airport for the entire hour. She singled out the cadets who marched out of time and praised Felicity for her perfect marching style.

At the end of the first induction of fire for the new UAS cadets, Joan informed them that they had to meet again at Teversham Airport the following Monday at 7:00 a.m. sharp. She dismissed them from her presence but kept a close eye on William, who was siding up with Felicity. William spoke under his breath, but it was not soft enough to escape Joan's keen ears. "God, almighty. What got up her nose this morning? Say, would you like a lift back to college?" Before Felicity could answer, Joan's commanding voice intervened. "Cadet Bennet. I want to have a word with you. Come into the hangar, and you, Cadet de Veres, have been dismissed, so get in the car and remove yourself from this airfield. Now!" With that final harsh command, William went to his car while Felicity followed Joan into the hangar.

The hangar contained one of the RAF's two planes assigned to the Cambridge UAS. An old two-seater Hawker was parked in one bay, and it was a similar model to the aeroplane Felicity had spent her summer in with Charles, earning her thrill-a-moment licence to fly. The engine cover of the Hawker had been removed, suggesting the old silver bird of the sky needed repairs. Felicity followed Joan into the hangar, immediately identifying the Hawker as a similar aeroplane she had recently been flying. Despite being alone around Joan, Felicity maintained her disciplined WRAF stance of respect for coming to attention. Joan immediately reverted to a less formal mode, just like she had many months ago at Woldingham. "You may relax, Felicity. We are not in UAS mode now; it's just me and you, woman to woman." Felicity relaxed and naturally wondered why she had been held back from the rest of the squad. "Why did you want to see me, Joan?" There was a table and chairs near the end of the hangar where the Hawker was parked in its bay. Joan ushered towards it. "Come over here and sit down, Felicity. I need to have a frank discussion with you." Felicity was now even more puzzled about the purpose of their meeting, but as an obedient younger sister would do, she followed the older woman over to the table and sat down.

Joan turned her chair so that she could comfortably speak to Felicity face-to-face. Felicity's curious expression left no doubt that she was unaware of why they were meeting. Joan thought momentarily, her eyes fixed on the old calendar on the wall that had not been updated for a few years; then she returned her attention to Felicity's polite but puzzled face. "How well do you know William de Veres?" It was indeed an unusual question to be asked during her first week of university, and her facial expression underscored her mystified response. "I only just met him this week, Joan. Why do you ask?" Joan had to be careful, as she could not reveal too many facts to a young cadet about the storm clouds that hung over the relationship between her father and William's father in the upper echelon of the RAF. She used his conduct that morning as the excuse for her inquiry. "Why do I ask? You saw how he arrived this morning: late, smoking and displaying an air of insolent defiance. I think he is trouble, and I am just looking out for you, as I promised your father I would." Joan immediately knew she had revealed information spoken in confidence between herself and Samuel. Still, the words were out there, immediately surprising Felicity. "As promised to my father. Is that what the pair of you were discussing the other day?" Felicity's defensive and simmering hostility in her response had to be doused by Joan before the flames of emotion burned too brightly. "Wait just a moment there, Felicity. Do not get too uppity with me. This is a new world for you here at Cambridge, and there are not too many of us women on campus, as you would have seen. So, I promised your father I would be like the big sister you do not have to ensure that none of the men here took advantage of a young woman. That is all." Felicity nodded, but Joan interrupted her before she could speak. "And I promised your father I would not reveal the details of our discussion, so please do not mention this discussion to him." Of course, Joan and Samuel had discussed more confidential information. Still, Joan had succeeded in covering up her error, revealing a moment of confidence between her and Samuel as Felicity nodded in acceptance of the explanation.

Now, Felicity's mind returned to the original topic of William. "I know he is an arrogant and entitled sod, Joan, but he made the opening gesture of friendship to me, even if he did insult me by referring to my family as Yeoman." Joan chuckled under her breath because William was a chip of the old block; he was just as arrogant as his father, Lord de Veres, for whom her father held little respect, as he considered his inferior officer to have been a coward during the war. "Yes, well, that is an insulting remark to make." Felicity was quick to avenge history, even if Joan was an Anglican. "It's arrogant and also untrue, Joan. Had it not been for the history of Catholic subjugation in this country, my father would hold more land and a blessed title." Joan held up her right hand to calm the emotional younger woman in front of her. "There is no need to mention history to me, Felicity. I am well acquainted with it, and as an Anglican, I am upset about it, too." Joan took stock for a while to return to the reason for their discussion; she momentarily stared at the battered surface of the table before returning her attention to Felicity. "In any event, the university is different to secondary school, and there are no nuns here to monitor the conduct between randy young men and women." This was a foreign concept for Felicity: randy young men and women. "He is cute-looking, Joan; however, I can look after myself. As I said before, he extended the olive branch of friendship to me." Joan nodded. "Very well, then. Anyway, I am looking out for you."

Joan was about to get up to leave when Felicity decided to ask her one question that had popped into her mind during their discussion. "Joan, I know you said you would be watching out for me, but aren't you going to leave here at the end of the year when you graduate from medical school?" It was Joan's turn to feel uncomfortable because the question unintentionally delved into her personal life. Still, it was a reasonable question, given their previous discussion at Woldingham. "Well, how best do I describe it? Life's little vicissitudes have dealt me a different hand, Felicity. My fiancé has been offered the esteemed role of Professor of Medicine here, so my plans have changed somewhat." Felicity was undoubtedly surprised on two fronts: Joan was engaged to a staff member, and more importantly, she would not be pursuing her dream of flying for the Royal Flying Doctor Service of Australia. The former revelation entertained Felicity's mind first. "Goodness me, Joan. Your fiancé is a member of the faculty here at Cambridge?" Indeed, it was an unusual arrangement, but Joan's explanation for the former would also explain the latter revelation. "Yes, Felicity. I am engaged to one of my former lecturers, and yes, there was a bit of a kerfuffle here when the news initially broke; we are an item. However, my fiancé, Stuart's father, is Earl de Montesquieu, the same Earl who happens to sit on the General Board and Regent House. So, once the news of the affair broke, we quickly announced our engagement. Naturally, Stuart could not, but had not, assessed my studies anyway. Our wedding date is yet to be formally announced, but it will be in the last month of summer next year, after I have graduated from medical school. I will continue studying general surgery here while remaining a member of the UAS and WRAF. Who knows? Perhaps I, too, might one day become a professor here if the General Board so decrees." This was an unexpected revelation for Felicity, but what troubled her the most was Joan giving up her dream. "Yet, what about your dream, Joan? You told me at Woldingham you, too, had a dream." Joan could not express the facts of 1950s life with anything but the absolute truth. "Felicity, you have a lot of learning to do. Although my father is a knight, I am marrying into nobility, and my future husband will inherit the title when his father passes away. He, too, shall sit on the boards of Regent House and the

General Board while I dutifully fulfil my role as a future countess. My fiancé's career comes first, and I knew that was possible when we started our relationship. Don't worry; my father is delighted about my future union." The hint of sarcasm in Joan's voice was not deciphered by Felicity, whose mind was consumed by the injustice of Joan's dreams being cast aside for those of her fiancés'.

Joan's submissiveness gobsmacked Felicity. "But Joan, what about your dreams?" The more worldly woman smiled. "It's a man's world, Felicity. However, do not be despondent. You follow your dreams. However, I am afraid I made my bed long ago." Joan sighed and stood up; however, Felicity had one last question. "So, Joan, when can I fly an aeroplane here?" Joan threw back her head and laughed. "Oh, Felicity. Welcome to the second world we live in. RAF cadets get to fly first, before WRAF cadets. Now, be on your way; otherwise, you might be late for lectures." The revelation was over, but it lingered on Felicity's mind long after it was over, and she would not give up her dreams for anyone.

University life had commenced for Felicity, and a young adult woman was quickly replacing the schoolgirl. Still, notwithstanding the new world she was now experiencing, there were occasional flickers of thoughts about Amelia. However, Felicity would push those thoughts out of her stream of consciousness, but the feelings for her still existed deep in her heart.

CHAPTER 16

Life, for some, sparkles brighter than a twinkling star,
Whereas for others, life's light fades, as they are too far.

For the next year of university life, Felicity undertook the onerous tasks of studying for a dual degree while also fulfilling her UAS duties. As Joan foreshadowed, the men got to fly the Hawker and the other aeroplane, the Tiger Moth, before Felicity got anywhere near the controls of one. Still, when the opportunity arose, Felicity displayed her exemplary and superior flying skills compared to her fellow cadets. Felicity otherwise kept to herself on campus and had little spare time to socialise. Her mind remained focused on the goal she had dreamt of ever since Sputnik I caused such heightened apoplexy in the Western World: she wanted to one day fly in space.

She remained friendly with William, whose arrogance, defiance and general cavalier conduct could not be subdued by the lecturers or Joan. Felicity did not know William's intentions with her, but she did find herself progressively assisting him in completing assignments. The first occasion was perhaps understandable. It was a late Wednesday afternoon in November 1958, the middle of the Michaelmas Term, when learning was in full swing. Professor Wickham's lecture had run slightly over time, mainly because William was under-prepared for the Mathematical Tripos of Calculus. Indeed, it was apparent that as Professor Wickham pressed William more about the theorem he had written on the board, the young man did not have the slightest clue about the correct approach to answer the question. It was understandable that a student may struggle with the immediate steps to the complexities of Calculus. Still, the particular theorem Professor Wickham was challenging William about was not too complex to attempt its initial components. The exchange between William and Professor Wickham became quite tense. After an agonising ten minutes of argument between them, Professor Wickham realised the lecture had run over time, so he dismissed the lecture group in a fit of frustration, and he shook his head as he sat at his desk, making a note in his file, while the students promptly made their way out of the lecture theatre. Felicity had sat there, witnessing the exchange between the professor and William, feeling embarrassed for William and, more importantly, sympathetic to his being made an example of.

As they left the lecture theatre, William tugged on Felicity's cardigan, causing her to be initially startled. "Don't be afraid, my yeoman friend. I am not going to hurt you." Yeoman friend! It may have been said in jest by William, but for Felicity, it had the same derisive effect as the 'Space Freak' tag she had to endure at Woldingham. "What is it, William?" Her terse reply did not impact her newfound supposed friend's demeanour. "I need help with Calculus. That old bastard is too difficult to understand, and, more importantly, I evidently annoy him." Felicity could detect a degree of ignominy emanating from William's eyes. Still, his arrogance at this moment did not make her inclined to assist him. She stared back at him without speaking, and then he displayed humbleness that he had not shown before. "Please, Felicity! The fact is, I do not have a clue about Calculus, whereas you seem to understand it easily." Her forgiving nature prevailed. Still, she was curious why William could not even grasp the elementary aspects of Professor Wickham's theorem. "Have you ever studied the paper Professor Wickham distributed a few weeks ago, William?" He nodded, but that was a lie. The truth was that William was enjoying the social life on campus more than his studies. "Alright, tomorrow, we do not have any lectures, so I shall meet you at the library at 8:30 a.m., and please, do not be late." With a relieved smile, William turned on his heels and walked away, without a word of thanks, to join a group of young peers and bask in the night away. Felicity shook her head in frustration that he had not even expressed gratitude.

The following morning, Felicity was pleasantly surprised to see William waiting outside the library at 8:30, drawing back on his cigarette and looking slightly under the weather from the hangover of his previous night's social activities. When he saw Felicity, William dropped his cigarette to the ground. He stubbed it out with his shoe and, leaving the butt on the ground where he had just dropped it, he walked over to her with a smile. "I thought you might have stood me up." Felicity quickly retorted. "Unlike whelps like you, we Yeo people have manners." William chuckled, although he did not realise the underlying inference was that she thought he was not a 'Gentleman' in the English tradition of the gentry. They made their way into the library, and Felicity led William to a desk not far from the entrance of the grand building, which had been constructed several decades earlier with the assistance of the Rockefeller Foundation. When they sat down, Felicity opened her notebook to the page where she had taken notes on Professor Wickham's first lecture on Calculus, and then looked up to see William sitting before her; his notebook was closed, which immediately annoyed her. "Open your notebook, please, William, as there is no magic spell to make you suddenly cognisant about Calculus." He took the hint from her terse request and opened his notebook to the first page, revealing that ink had not touched it. Felicity immediately began repeating Professor Wickham's first words, which he had spoken about the topic, and which she had made a note of many weeks ago. "Calculus is all about changes, William. In mathematics, the derivative of a function of a real variable measures how sensitive the function value, which is the output value, is to changes in its argument, the input value. Derivatives are a fundamental tool of calculus." Felicity watched as William made notes, and she continued tutoring him after he finished writing. "For example, William, the derivative of the position of a moving object concerning time is the object's velocity: this measures how quickly the object's position changes when time advances. Are you following me?" He nodded as he wrote down the notes he should have made weeks ago. Felicity continued the tutorial session and wrote on her notepad for William to follow. "So, the derivative of a function of a single variable at a chosen input value, when it exists, is the slope of the tangent line to the function's graph at that point. The tangent line is the best linear approximation of the function near that input value. For this reason, the derivative is often described as the "instantaneous rate of change", the ratio of the instantaneous change in the dependent variable to that of the independent variable. Do you understand what I am saying?"

William's eyes revealed he did not, which intrigued Felicity because this was secondary school mathematics. "William, this is not difficult mathematics to understand. You should have been taught this at school." William shrugged his shoulders, indicating that he probably had been taught this calculus level during his secondary schooling, but he had not bothered to study it. "William, how on earth did you even matriculate into university?" William's condescending grin met Felicity's ignorance about privilege. "Felicity, you are sheltered from the way the world works. My nobility assured me of a place at this university from the day I was born. For centuries, this university has benefited from my family's wealth. I did not have to 'work' to study here, but I must pass my subjects; otherwise, I will be cleaning bins for the RAF."

William's condescending candour had awoken Felicity's mind to many facts, least of all the fact that William needed to understand the basics, so she tried a different approach. She drew a rectangle in her notebook and then added lines at right angles from the edges of either side of the rectangle to create a basic ground image. Then she drew a little stick person on top of the rectangle, making William feel somewhat intellectually inferior and insulted. Still, he remained silent as Felicity provided the tutoring he desperately needed to understand the subject. "Alright, William, this is you standing on top of a twenty-metre-tall building, which, for the sake of this exercise, you are going to jump off so that we can calculate how fast you will be falling after one second. Now, the formula for the distance fallen is d equals five-t squared. So, d equals the distance you have fallen in metres, and t equals the time from the jump in seconds. You jump from the building; therefore, the formula at one second is d equals $5t^2$ equals 5 by 1^2 equals 5 metres. The speed of that fall is calculated in this manner: speed equals distance over time. At one second, speed equals five metres per second. Do you understand the formula?" Eureka! The enlightenment in his eyes was evident, and for the next two hours, Felicity expanded upon the formula to explain to William the difference between averages and exact speed, using the minute value of time and the delta value. It was like drawing teeth; however, William could at least understand Calculus's simple principles during those two hours. He left the library without displaying much gratitude – he may be noble in title, but William would fail if nobility were a subject to study.

Towards the end of the Michaelmas Term, Felicity's faith was challenged by her Natural Sciences study. She was aware from her physics studies at Woldingham of Fred Hoyle's Steady State theory of the universe contrasting with Georges Lemaître's hypothesis of the primeval atom, which Hoyle coined on the BBC in 1949 as the 'Big Bang'; however, in keeping with the school's commitment to the Catholic faith, Woldingham propounded that regardless of Lemaître's 'Big Bang' expanding universe or Hoyle's Steady State theory, God was responsible for the creation of the universe. Now, within the confines of academia, where 'God' was not part of the equation, Mr Barnsley explained the competing theories to the students in greater detail, using the depth of quantum mechanics. "During our previous lecture, I informed all of you that this lecture would focus on the Big Bang and the Steady State theories. These theories may be challenging for those of you whose religious beliefs hold dear to your hearts the biblical notion of a creator; well, all I can say is that you are in the wrong lecture theatre: theology is taught in a different building." Felicity heard William's slight murmur of a laugh as he closed his eyes. "This sounds like it will be fun for you, Felicity. Wake me up when it is over." She turned around to see William sitting behind her, conveniently shielded from Mr Barnsley's view as he indeed went off to sleep. Mr Barnsley's monotone voice continued to deliver the comforting post-lunch tonic for the rest, which William sought. "I shan't be apologising for that. You are here to be people of science. It is a science to which your minds must be dedicated." Mr Barnsley then deliberately cleared his throat, an action which was in vain because there were several William types in the lecture theatre that afternoon. However, Felicity sat forward in her seat with her notebook ready. "Now, one matter common to the two theories is the abundance of hydrogen and helium in the universe and that the universe evolved from a hot, dense state. Still, that is where the two theories depart from one another. Richard Tolman's oscillating universe theory explains that it was an indefinite, self-sustaining cycle of a contracting and expanding universe. I have to concede the position held by some doubters about the oscillating universe theory because of Albert Einstein's general theory of relativity and the singularity; however, Tolman argues that, because of a lack of quantum gravity, the singularity could not be pinpointed as the origin of the universe, and therefore the physical processes that govern the singularity caused the universe to be eternal. Here at Cambridge, we are at the forefront of astrophysics, and the Big Bang is emerging as the more plausible theory for the origins of space and time. It makes sense for the recognised expansion of the galaxies in the universe that it commenced in this dense, hot, almost peach-sized state of expansionism."

Mr Barnsley looked around the lecture theatre in what could only be described as an amateurish performance of enlightenment. "The Big Bang is not a theory of the creation of the universe, and if science has taught us anything, there does not need to be a reason or cause; random events occur without a cause. Yet, Edwin Hubble's evidentiary note that every galaxy is flying away from every other galaxy favours the Big Bang over the oscillating universe. Indeed, when Einstein learned about Hubble's redshifts, he immediately realised that the expansion formula of his general relativity theory must be real. However, he did recant it to return to the cosmological constant. Do you have any questions so far?" There was one lone hand of the solitary female amidst a lecture theatre of uninspired, moribund male minds. "Yes, Ms Bennet. What is your question?" Felicity did not hesitate, and earnest enquiry, although innocent in its framing, illuminated one shortcoming of Catholic education: There must be a creator. "I understand the concepts postulated by Einstein, Hubble and Lemaître, but what created the physical densities in the first place?" Mr Barnsley's furrowed brow foreshadowed the intellectual dismissal to follow. "Created? What a preposterous word to say. We do not talk about the field of creativity; as I said at the outset, theology is taught in a different building, thank goodness." Not to be deterred by intellectual arrogance, Felicity shook her head. "Pardon my faux pas by the word 'create'; I meant to ask this: What existed before the Big Bang?"

Mr Barnsley now understood the premise of the question from the only interested student. "You mean what existed earlier than 10^{-36} seconds?" Felicity's earnest nod conveyed that her mind was trying to calculate something so small that quantum mechanics could not explain without resorting to general relativity. "Ms Bennet, that is where Einstein's singularity is the logical equation to answer that question. A tiny point with a huge mass." Her mind was working overtime. "Yes, but before the singularity, what existed?" Mr Barnsley smiled, not in jest but rather in admiration. "A science cannot answer that question, Ms Bennet, nor can religion because, as I say to our disgruntled theologians whenever they cross my path: 'Who created God?'. There is a limit to physics; however, there is an even greater limitation to the notion of creation. Perhaps Einstein's contracting formula in his theory of general relativity is the mathematical answer to the quantum mechanical question of why particles behave the way they do. Or, perhaps, just like quantum mechanics explains, the subatomic particle of the singularity just popped into existence. Needless to say, before the Big Bang, if the theory is correct and over the coming lectures, I shall explain why we here at Cambridge are leaning in favour of it, but if that theory is correct, a theory in which we do not need a cause, and for which then there was no time in the singularity for a cause to exist, then there was also no time for a creator to exist in. The theists always choke on their soup when I explain the universe's origins to them in that manner."

Felicity's physics class at Woldingham had not explored the singularity in great depth vis-à-vis creation versus perpetuity or the laws of quantum physics. Yet, in the lecture theatre, Mr Barnsley opened a doorway in Felicity's mind that disavowed any notion of 'creation'. General relativity, gravity, quantum mechanics, and singularity made greater sense in Felicity's mind than God because there was no time.

Subsequently, when she attended mass to listen to a sermon propounding the theory of there being a creator who was a ubiquitous presence in the heavens, Felicity found a conflict between many years of devotion to God, as opposed to logical explanations of science, which excluded the existence of the divine. Her grandmother's indoctrination prevailed, so Felicity did not stray from the flock in her heart. Still, Mr Barnsley's cosmological physics appealed to the logical pathways of Felicity's mind.

After the Michaelmas Term, Felicity returned home for the extended break over Christmas before commencing the Full Lent Term in January of 1959. Life back at home was the same as it had been several months before, when she left to attend the beginning of her new life at Cambridge University. Her grandmother would beat her ears about what she had been told about other Catholic girls attending a convent to begin the pathway of their lives as nuns. Her grandfather continued to raid her father's liquor cabinet each night before dinner. Samuel briefly discussed his litigation with Herbert Browne, which in turn caused Felicity to wonder momentarily about Amelia and even start harbouring feelings of her desire to kiss her again. She would then chastise herself and say her prayers, during which she blamed this ephemeral moment of desire on the 'devil's ways'. Paradoxically, she found that she now had a conscience internal conflict about the world of mysticism versus the factual world of science. Still, she obeyed the stoicism of her Catholic upbringing and attended church services with her family.

The first year of university remained extremely busy for Felicity as she balanced studying and her involvement in the UAS. William continued to annoy Joan occasionally, and Felicity often wondered why Joan did not have him dishonourably discharged from the UAS; if only she knew the machinations of the two family relationships and the RAF rivalry behind the scenes. Their friendship continued; the more assistance she provided to William, the friendlier he became with her, but she remained on her guard, as Joan had warned her to do. However, William never attempted to take advantage of Felicity's friendship for anything other than to help him with his studies. Occasionally, he would somewhat reluctantly invite her to join his group of male and female peerage friends for what now appeared to be an obligatory weekend party scene developing within the campus. Still, Felicity would not regularly take up such offers. When she attended one of the parties at a house rented in the village by a postgraduate, she found their Anglican behaviour somewhat footloose and fancy-free, conflicting with the stoic morals of Catholicism that her grandmother had instilled in her since her earliest memories. Whereas she had been excluded from the so-called 'high society' of the Catholic world at

Woldingham, at Cambridge, Felicity found she excluded herself from a different world of people because their morality disagreed with hers.

Felicity studied hard and was inexorably committed to the UAS. She remained dedicated to her physical fitness but was not as stoically devoted to her previous Catholic world of services and nightly prayers. Science began to increasingly resonate in her mind as a logical, factual explanation for how life, indeed, the universe, had started, so the question was posed in her mind: 'Why should I be chained to this antiquated obsequious life of Grandma's?' However, more out of obedience than faith Felicity would continue to attend Sunday services, and what if science was wrong? There was inner turmoil in her mind between the logical calculations of the Theory of General Relativity and the might and awe of the divine, or perhaps it was just her grandmother's condemnation she feared the most.

She did not go home at the End of the Full Lent Term. Instead, she remained on campus, continuing her fierce routine of maintaining her mind, body and soul. She also finally noticed the appearance of some breast development during the Full Easter Term, and there was something else: her menstrual cycle finally began. Felicity saw the campus doctor about the late onset of her menstrual cycle and breast development, only to be told that her strict exercise routine had been the cause and to otherwise 'not worry about it'. They were the exact words her grandmother had spoken to her several years beforehand when the other girls at Woldingham had commenced developing breasts and experiencing their menstrual cycles. "Don't worry about it because it is God's way." There was a contrast as to how it had occurred, but both piety and science formed the same conclusion as to why it happened: don't worry about it.

At the end of the Full Easter Term, which also heralded the conclusion of her first year of university, Felicity watched Joan be walked down the aisle of King's College Chapel by her proud father, Air Chief Marshall Sir Thomas Wilberforce; however, the cadets did not have the privilege of attending the subsequent reception. The injustice of Joan's world still lingered in Felicity's mind as she watched the grandeur of the Anglican gentry marrying into the Anglican nobility. Gone was the regimental Joan on this day, and in its place was this attractive and demure new bride displaying all the signs of servitude Felicity never imagined could exist within Joan's heart and mind. 'Is that what is expected of me?' Felicity asked herself as she watched Joan take her vows.

Her second year of university would eventually herald in the 1960s. Still, life at home seemed to be locked into the moribund mentality of the 1950s. Felicity received high distinctions in her Mathematical Tripos and Natural Sciences examinations, and after the Michaelmas Term, she returned home for the Christmas break. During the break before the Full Lent Term commenced, Felicity continued studying, despite Catherine's chastisement for not saying her prayers and her warning about maintaining chastity. When the weather was fine, she went flying with Samuel, and during those flights, her father allowed her to fly the Cessna. They discussed her life on campus, including her 'friendship' with William de Veres, which Felicity reassured her father was platonic and confirmed to be true. He was cute-looking, but there was no chemistry between them like the chemistry she felt for Amelia. Amelia! Once again, when her mind was not busily occupied with her studies, there were ephemeral thoughts about her; however, Felicity would promptly dispatch them, writing off their night together as a 'silly schoolgirl moment'. Felicity, her father and grandparents welcomed in the new decade that Thursday night at the Old Siege before attending the church that Friday, 1 January 1960, to pray for the 'Sorrowful Mysteries of the Rosary', which Felicity felt was her grandmother's ploy to keep Grandpa away from the liquor cabinet. An exciting new decade may have just been welcomed in, but Grandma was firmly entrenched in her traditional Catholic ways. Otherwise, time quickly passed before Felicity returned to Cambridge on Monday, 18 January 1960, for the Full Lent Term to commence the next day.

Meanwhile, thousands of miles away, across the other side of the English Channel, a contingent of young males aged seventeen and over was commencing their training in Moscow with the Komitet Gosudarstvennoy Bezopasnosti, otherwise unaffectionately known as the KGB in the West, to one day fulfil specialised espionage roles for the Soviet Union in the ever-expanding Cold War. One young male, in particular, Anatoli Sidorov, caught the attention of the KGB hierarchy due to his feminine appearance. Anatoli was an orphan from Kyiv, a ward of the Soviet Union. The KGB had a specific plan for the nineteen-year-old Anatoli, whether he liked it or not.

Life at university appeared to be unchanged by the new decade, although there had been one significant change with the UAS. The WRAF had promoted Joan to the rank of Flying Officer, and with that promotion came a greater degree of stentorian command from Joan if one cadet dared set a foot wrong. William was the first cadet to test the cauldron of her fire when he arrived late for the first UAS drill at the start of that week. Joan immediately exerted her authority, which was now underscored by her entry into the world of the noble classes in her personal life. Her voice boomed across Teversham Airport, even causing Warrant Officer Jones, who was working on the Hawker engine in the hangar, to drop his spanner. "Cadet de Veres! Get your miserable little bag of bones over here." For once, William was promptly compliant, the tone of Joan's commanding voice causing him to become somewhat obsequious as he hurriedly made his way over to where the rest of the cadets were on a parade. He quickly came to attention, but it was a bridge too far as Joan was concerned. "Cadet de Veres, I have had enough of your lackadaisical attitude toward the UAS. Consider yourself now officially on report, and, mark my words, you will be discharged from the UAS for good if I put you on report again." Of course, Joan knew that could not happen because of William's father, but it brought to William's attention the severity of his position if his father had to intervene to save his place in the UAS. "Yes, ma'am!" For once, there was a mark of respect in William's voice, and it was evident to Felicity that the latter had won the 'cold war' between William and Joan.

Felicity returned home to the ever-expanding agricultural world of her father, who had successfully sued Herbert Browne and, consequently, settled his damages award by receiving one hundred acres of additional land. Catherine would still chide Felicity about everything from religion to her virtue. Still, at the end of her second year of university, Felicity detected a noticeable difference in her grandmother's appearance and energy; she was losing weight and vigour. Something was up, but neither Grandpa nor her father would discuss it with her when Felicity asked about her grandmother's appearance. As for Grandpa, well, her father's liquor cabinet was still being depleted like the cattle that drank every drop from the troughs on the farm. During the summer break after her second year of university, Felicity could not wait to return to campus for her third year of life at Cambridge. What a year it would be.

CHAPTER 17

The commencement of the Michaelmas Term at Cambridge was initially uneventful for Felicity, except that she streamlined her studies towards the burgeoning astrophysics postgraduate course she planned to undertake after completing her undergraduate studies, along with another postgraduate degree in aeronautical science. While the RAF had introduced the de Havilland Comet in 1956, a jet used for reconnaissance missions, the Fleet Street press had been reporting for some months before the start of the university year that the United States Air Force and the RAF would be working together more closely, in their Cold War efforts, and that as a corollary of the unified approach it included the RAF moving away from propellers in favour of jets. Felicity's intellect and lifetime goals were stirred by the news of the RAF and the United States cooperating as the United States pursued the space race.

The third year of Felicity's undergraduate course continued in the same vein as the previous two years. UAS drills commenced on the first Friday of the first week of the Michaelmas Term, and try as he might, William still found ways to get under Joan's skin. Felicity could not place her finger on why Joan singled William out for extra-disciplinary attention; it was almost as though an unspoken underlying rivalry between them suggested mere conduct alone was not the source of Joan's ire. William continued to lean on Felicity for help with his studies, and, unwittingly, Felicity came to his rescue like a dutiful wife. This reaction was the antithesis of her life's ethos. By early November 1960, the Americans had elected a young president, whose plans for the space race with the Soviet Union had not been revealed. Still, his presence on the world stage symbolised a bright new future in which the societal shackles of the past could be discarded.

Then, on a cold Wednesday evening in mid-November 1960, Felicity returned to her room to find a note placed under her door, urging her to telephone her father urgently. This was the first time she had ever received a request to call Samuel, including her years at boarding school. Although dinner was being served in the dining hall, Felicity would miss the meal to return her father's telephone call. The dial tone rang twice before the telephone was answered, which suggested Samuel was waiting for his daughter to call. "Hello, Samuel Bennet speaking." It was immediately apparent to Felicity that there was a discernible level of concern in her father's voice. "Hello, Dad. It's me. What is up? Why do I have to call you urgently?" There was a short delay in his response; then Felicity heard the unusual sound of slight distress in her father's voice. "Oh, Felicity! It's you. Thank goodness you called." The trailing of distress in Samuel's voice suggested it was some form of unpleasant news to follow. "Of course, Dad, I would call when you ask me to do so urgently. What is wrong? Did Grandpa injure himself on the tractor?" There was a pregnant pause before Samuel could calm his emotions to speak. "No, Grandpa is okay, sweetie. I'm calling you about your grandmother. She is not well, and her doctor believes she has chronic liver disease, which has transitioned to decompensated liver cirrhosis, causing her liver to fail. The condition is in an advanced stage, Felicity. And her treating doctor believes her condition is incurable." With those words spoken, Felicity heard her father weep for the first time. "Dad! Dad! What do you mean by 'incurable'? Is Grandma going to die?" Felicity's tone was clinical rather than emotional, triggering an unexpected reaction from her father. "What do you think incurable means?"

Her father's tone took Felicity aback, and she did not respond to him, which caused Samuel to experience a further emotional outburst that Felicity had not encountered before. "Why aren't you saying anything, Felicity? Your grandmother is dying, for Pete's sake." Why am I not saying anything? Why am I not upset? These thoughts raced through Felicity's mind. "Dad, I am shocked by this news. Can I call you back tomorrow, please? I need time to digest this news." Samuel's response was crisp. "Sure." He then finished the call.

Felicity was shocked to be told this news about her grandmother, but what troubled her more was that she did not feel immediate grief. After she finished speaking to her father, Felicity immediately took herself to the Catholic chapel on campus, not only to pray for her grandmother but also to seek forgiveness for not feeling upset about the news of her health. Her faith had diminished at the same rate as her acquisition of knowledge about quantum physics; however, attending the chapel was more an exercise in searching her heart and mind than an act of faith. She lit a candle and then took her place in front of the statue of the Virgin Mary, kneeling as she began to pray. "I ask thee, Lord, to spare the life of my grandmother, a person to whom her life has been devoted to thee. I also ask thee, my Lord, to forgive my lack of empathy and…". Felicity then hesitated with her prayer because her lived experience with her grandmother as a child had been an exercise in submission, mental torment and ridicule bordering on, if not being, psychological abuse. She resumed praying. "No, my Lord? To whom am I even trying to speak? I do not seek thy forgiveness for my empty heart. Since I was little, my grandmother has diminished my self-worth. Indeed, she has diminished my value as a woman, and for no good reason; she humiliated me, time and time again. Why is it wrong of me to have no feelings for her health and well-being when she has displayed time and time again to have no feelings for me, to shun my dreams and mock my womanhood? I do not want her to be in pain. Still, I do not need nor do I now seek forgiveness for my indifference to my grandmother's plight. I wish her no harm and for her good health to return, but I do not need to seek forgiveness from a myth for no sorrow in my heart." She did not even mark the holy trinity on herself, and Felicity promptly left the chapel, convinced that her honesty was justified, given the psychological treatment she had to endure, which was meted out to her by Catherine since her earliest memory. When she returned to her room, Felicity knew she needed to speak to her father early the following day to heal his heart and apologise. However, she would not apologise for her feelings. There were many years of scars on her mind and pride from Catherine's psychological abuse.

The following morning, after she had completed her morning run, Felicity rang her father. Samuel promptly answered the call on the first ring, as though he had been awaiting it. "Hello, Samuel Bennet speaking." He sounded tired and low in spirits. "Hello, Dad. It's me. I'm…" Samuel immediately cut Felicity off before she could speak another word. "Oh, Felicity, I'm glad it is you. I feel terrible about how I acted on the phone last night, my little darling, and I am sorry." Felicity was surprised as she felt that she owed an apology to her father, and Samuel's heartfelt apology drew sorrow from Felicity. "Dad, there's no need for you to apologise. I should apologise, Dad, as I didn't mean to sound cold-hearted about this terrible news." Felicity knew she did feel cold-hearted. Still, her sorrow emanated from her feelings for her father's emotional distress. "Felicity, you don't need to apologise. You were shocked. I, too, was shocked. I shouldn't have reacted the way I did last night. The line then went quiet; however, Felicity's sniffle, because of her tears, broke the silence. "It's fine to be upset, Felicity. That is how I felt yesterday, and I still feel that way today. Still, the facts remain unchanged. Your grandmother might live for another six months. She is a tough old woman, as you know." Six months! That was not a lot of time. "Dad, should I come home for the time Grandma has remaining? I will ask the university if I can defer my studies for the Michaelmas Term." That was a genuine feeling from her heart, but it was for her father rather than her grandmother. "No, darling, do not defer your studies. In any event, your grandmother would probably chastise you with even greater vigour." Felicity's father's quip generated relief, and her mind turned to her grandmother's feelings. "How is Grandma coping with the news, Dad?" Her father's slight chuckle telegraphed the answer before he even spoke. "You know your grandmother, Felicity. Everything is God's way. She is stoic in her faith and will be to the bitter end." Hardly surprising news. "What about Grandpa, Dad? How is he coping?" Another slight chuckle, telegraphing the expected news. "He is about a bottle and a half of whiskey upset, Felicity. Your grandfather's feelings are expressed in the consumption of whiskey from my liquor cabinet. I asked him last night how he was feeling, and in his usual manner, he threw up his hand to dismiss the question. He is upset; however, he never confides his feelings in me. The only time I have ever seen my Dad cry was when you lost that race all those years ago, and even then, his reaction would have been more about him than you. He spoke to your aunt for at least fifteen minutes last night. That was fifteen minutes more than he spoke to me. Still, he has always been closer to my sister than me, so it would not surprise me if he opened up his feelings to her."

Now, that was a revelation for Felicity about the relationship between her grandfather and his two remaining children. "How is Aunty Anne, Dad? Did you speak to her? Was she upset?" Samuel scoffed in his response. "Upset! Of course, she is upset, but in the same breath, she told me she won't return until our mother is close to the end of her life. 'I do not want to waste money on plane trips' were her words. She might have good looks, Felicity, but my sister can be cold-hearted. Always has been." Another revelation! Samuel had never expressed his feelings about his sister to Felicity before. "Perhaps she is in shock, too, Dad." The sound of another chuckle. "The only shock for your Aunt Anne would be the cost of an international flight, Felicity, and with the money her husband has, that should not even be an issue. Look, I do not mean to vent my feelings; this call is about your grandmother." Felicity felt she was obliged to ask this next question, even though she did not want to do so. "Should I speak to Grandma now, Dad?" To her immense relief, her father dismissed the idea. "No, Felicity. Even though she says it is God's way, she is noticeably angry, and she is likely to say words to you at the moment that would hurt your feelings. Deep down, she is still coming to terms with the news, and I suspect she might be angry that "God's way' is taking her from this earth sooner than she expected. I will tell her you are upset and, of course, praying for her. However, give her a few more weeks. You can do nothing else here, so you can concentrate on your studies. I love you and am proud of you, my little darling." Samuel could speak those words every second of the day to Felicity, and they would always tug at her heartstrings. She began to sniffle again because she wanted to be with her father, hold him, and reassure him that she was concerned for him. "I love you too, Dad. Promise you will be okay because I am happy to come to help with Grandma." Samuel smiled. "Come on, be brave. That is what your grandmother would want. Now, get to class so you're not wasting my money on your education." He hung up the telephone, and Felicity's mind was overwhelmed that day by her father confiding in her in a manner he had never done before. It made Felicity feel different about herself. It made Felicity feel like an adult, even though she had not turned twenty-one.

Although her father had said she should give her grandmother some space to come to terms with her fate, and even though she concluded in her mind that there was nothing wrong with her thoughts about her grandmother's treatment of her since she was a little child, Felicity nevertheless began feeling guilty that she had not spoken to the old woman. It was evident to Joan the following morning during the UAS drill that her star cadet's mind was distracted. This became apparent when Joan brought the cadets to attention to make an announcement. "I have some important news to announce as our third-year squadron cadets. Indeed, it is an announcement that directly impacts one of you." All the males' eyes, including William's, lit up as the hum-drum of the drill suddenly took on an exciting aspect of important news. Joan could see that Felicity's eyes did not express the same delighted yet quizzical expression as the other cadets. "A significant benefactor of our university will be paying us a visit to the UAS during the Full Easter Term, about a fortnight before the UAS Graduation Ball. Viscount Godwin and his ancestors have donated substantial sums of money over the course of many centuries to Cambridge. Indeed, had it not been for the Godwin family's donations, some of the buildings on the campus might not have been as elegantly designed. Therefore, he is a significant benefactor to the university. This may seem silly; however, it's an indulgence both the university and the RAF are prepared to grant him. Viscount Godwin has requested that he be taken for a 'joy ride' by one of our third-year cadets, and, of course, that means the old Hawker will have to be used, as the Sopwith Camel only seats one person. The university and RAF have decided it would also be an outstanding publicity event to garner ongoing public support for the taxpayers' continued funding of the UAS, so the media will be attending to photograph and film this event."

Heads turned among the males upon the mention of the media attending, whereas Felicity stared straight ahead, lost in her thoughts, a reaction that did not go unnoticed by Joan. Her following announcement would send shockwaves through the squadron. "So, one of you has been selected for additional flight time each week until this momentous occasion, and I do not use the word momentous lightly, which has had a bearing on the cadet the UAS, the RAF and the university have selected to pilot the Hawker for Viscount Godwin's 'joy ride.'" There was a momentary pause; the young males eagerly listened in, although William was already resigned to the fact that he would not be selected. Once again, Joan noticed that Felicity seemed nonplussed about the announcement. "Given this cadet's impeccable record since joining the UAS and grades, we have decided that Cadet Bennet will be the squadron member to pilot the Hawker and take Viscount Godwin on his 'joy flight.' Congratulations, Cadet Bennet." There was a noticeable sigh of disappointment from some of the male cadets. However, Felicity did not appear to demonstrate any joy in her eyes. Joan knew it was time for her to talk privately to her. "Alright, some of you may be disappointed, but this decision has been made on merit. You are all dismissed for the morning, except for you, Cadet Bennet; I would like to discuss your duties with you." The rest of the squadron walked away, displaying their disappointment through various subtle verbal and physical cues, save for William, for whom it was no surprise that he had not been selected for this special occasion. Indeed, his delight was incongruent with the rest of the squadron. "Cheer up, lads; it could have been worse. I could have been selected to fly the silly old sod around." There was some muffled laughter; however, it was evident that the selection of a woman in preference to them was an unedifying moment in their UAS service.

Joan turned on her heels and began walking into the hangar, signifying to Felicity that she must follow her. Inside the hangar, they took their seats at the same old tatty table they had sat at several years beforehand when Joan had expressed her concerns to Felicity about William. Small talk was not the order of the day. "Alright, what is up?" Felicity was surprised by how blunt Joan was. "It's nothing to do with you or the UAS, Joan." Felicity's internal confusion was on display in her eyes. "Is it William? I am not oblivious to the fact that he has been getting a piggyback through his courses from you, Felicity. Has he said or done something?" Felicity shook her head and remained silent. Joan pressed on when perhaps it was not her place to do so, but she promised Samuel to keep a watchful eye on Felicity. "Well, what is it, Felicity? Don't you want the publicity of flying Viscount 'Goodtime' Godwin around?" Joan's sobriquet for the Viscount broke the tension, and Felicity opened up. "My grandmother is dying of chronic liver failure, Joan." Joan immediately felt a sense of regret for pushing Felicity this far. "Oh, Felicity. I am so sorry. I had no idea and..." Felicity held up her hand to quieten her superior officer, a bold move. Still, this was more of a sisterly chat. "No, Joan. There is no need to apologise. I feel indifferent about it all, which I have come to terms with because my grandmother was cruel towards me from a young age." Joan was intrigued. "Cruel?" Felicity nodded. "Yes, Joan. She was cruel. She would ridicule my looks and tell me no man would ever want to marry me. She was adamant that I had to become a nun and considered my dream of flying into space childish. Her idea of a good Catholic woman is that we are either married and pregnant by the time we are twenty or that we are in a convent training to be ordained as nuns." Joan allowed her Anglican upbringing to get the better of her. "Oh, bother me. Silly old Catholic woman mentality."

Joan stopped short, for fear she might have offended Felicity. "No, Joan. It is fine. I tend to agree with you, and the more I study natural science, the more I question the existence of a God above, but I'm still unsure how to express it. I'm religious, but it's only because of her. Anyway, what's troubling my mind is that my dad told me yesterday to give Grandma some space for a while and not speak to her. However, that does not feel right. Yes, she was a cruel woman with her psychological torment of me, but she is still my Grandma; she raised me, and I think I should call her." Joan held up her hands to display that this was territory beyond her domain. "Felicity, I am not going to say your father is wrong. Still, I won't tell you what to do. This is what womanhood is about. Sometimes, we have to decide about personal matters, which is one of those moments for you to decide." Felicity nodded. Joan was right; as a young woman, she had to make a decision. Joan decided to change the topic. "Aren't you excited about being selected to fly Viscount Godwin? This will be a tremendous step for your career path with WRAF." Felicity nodded; however, her mind was otherwise preoccupied. "Yes, Joan. Thank you, and despite you saying it was a group decision, I am not oblivious to the fact that you probably put in a good word for me." Joan remained tight-lipped, but her eyes didn't lie. As for her grandmother, Felicity decided there and then she would call her before Saturday service.

After she had completed her studies that next Saturday, Felicity called the home number at about 3:00 p.m., figuring her father was likely to be in the paddock working. Therefore, her grandmother would answer the telephone. Her assumption was correct, but she was not ready for the state of Catherine's listless voice. "Hello, Catherine Bennet speaking." Gone was the force of the stoic tone of a devout Catholic, and in its place was the spiritless soul. "Hello, Grandma. It's me, Felicity. How are you?" The thought was instantaneous: 'Why did I ask that question? She is dying?' Momentary silence forewarned Felicity that an insult was not too far away. "What a silly question, Felicity. Your father has informed you about my health. Why haven't you called before today?" Indeed, why hadn't she? "Because Dad told me not to do so, Grandma." As Catherine's health declined, logical thought processes had left her, and this response made no sense to her. "Because your father told you not to do so? What a load of nonsense; my son would never be so inconsiderate. I am very disappointed in you, Felicity. I expected you to telephone me the moment your father informed you about my health. So this is all the thanks I get for raising you." Felicity took the bait of the insult. "Wait one moment, Grandma. Are you calling me a liar?" Ask a silly question, and you will receive the corresponding response. "Yes, but it does not surprise me. You were always an ungrateful little witch of a child." Witch? The incendiary nature of that word opened the floodgates of recriminations. "Witch? Witch?!? I have endured countless insults from you, Grandma, since my first memories, but calling me a witch is the pot calling the kettle black. You have disparaged me on too many occasions, and now, when I am being truthful with you, I get called a liar and a witch. Well, I wanted to tell you I love you, Grandma, and I am sorry you are sick, but now, all I can say is that God does not exist, and you have wasted your life on prayer."

Before Catherine could utter another word, Felicity ended the telephone call, and she ran back to her room in tears, where she would remain for the rest of that evening, regretting having called her grandmother. Still, she did not regret telling her grandmother about the state of her faith, and she was glad to have expressed her thoughts in this manner. Back at the homestead, Samuel did his best to comfort his distraught mother after Albert had told him that Felicity had spoken some 'dreadful' words on the telephone. "What did she say to you, Mum?" Catherine could only shake her head from side to side as she slumped into the armchair near the brick fireplace of her cottage. "She said: 'God doesn't exist'. What sort of person says horrible words like that?" He pressed for an explanation. "Why did she say that to you, Mum?" Catherine shook her head, clearly indicating she did not wish to speak about the incident anymore. Instead, her tear-filled eyes fixed on the glow of the warm fire. Samuel knew it was out of character for Felicity to tell his mother that 'God didn't exist', so there must be another side to the story. And why did she call her grandmother when he had expressly warned her not to do so? He would speak to Felicity the next day, once the dust had settled.

Felicity deliberately did not attend the Sunday church service the following day. Indeed, by letting the genie out of the bottle, she decided not to participate in any church services again. The world of physics, and, in particular, the concept of a singularity, made more sense to her than the pious rhetoric of the scriptures. More importantly, the world of physics did not discriminate based on sex, race, or religion. When Felicity looked into the night sky, she saw a universe of hydrogen, helium and other elements; in that universe, it seemed implausible that some divine deity was determining the outcome of life. As for Catholicism, well, all it had brought for Felicity was a lifetime of servitude and unnecessary angst. Over dinner that night in the dining hall, she momentarily felt guilty for telling her dying grandmother that 'God didn't exist'. However, she came to her senses as Catherine had caused her emotions to overwhelm her mind, which was adamant: 'So, do not blame yourself.'

When she returned to her room after dinner, Felicity saw a folded piece of paper slipped under the door. She did not recognise the handwriting, but that did not matter, as the note's content was what mattered: 'Please urgently call your father'. Immediately, the worst thoughts entered her mind: 'Did my words cause Grandma to die? Why is it urgent at this time of night?' Felicity quickly ran to the nearest public telephone in Corpus Christie and called her father's telephone number. The phone rang four times before it was answered. "Hello, Samuel Bennet speaking." Felicity earnestly responded without any delay. "Dad! Dad! What is up? After dinner, I found a note in my room requesting I call you urgently." Samuel was blunt. "Why did you say to your grandmother that God does not exist? Why would you say that in her state of health and mind?"

The fire was met with fire. "Now, just one minute, Dad. How about asking for my side of the story?" There was a momentary delay, and then Samuel's tone changed. "Alright. Tell me your side of the story." Felicity composed herself, and then she spoke. "Firstly, I did not feel comfortable with the idea of not speaking to Grandma after you told me about the state of her health. I am not a little child, Dad, and, to be honest, I felt like a child by not calling her. So, I telephoned her yesterday with good intentions to tell her that I loved her and was thinking of her. Before I could utter a word, Grandma castigated me for not calling her sooner. When I informed her that you told me not to call her, she then called me a liar and a witch: a witch, Dad. I have put up with many insults emanating from Grandma's disappointment in me as a woman; I have even been slapped in the face. However, that was the final straw, Dad, to be called both a liar and a witch. So, I lost my temper and told her that even though I was calling her to tell her, among other thoughts, that I loved her, I had now had enough of her insults, and then I told her what I believed." Samuel's silence was deafening. "Did you hear what I said, Dad?" Then, it was the same tone of voice as in past years when he was the peacemaker. "Okay. I understand why it happened, but why did you say those words to her, Felicity?" Now, it was Felicity's turn to be blunt. "Because it is the truth, Dad." Her adamance surprised him. "You don't really mean that, do you, Felicity?" She did. "Yes, Dad. I do. I am studying science. No, wait; let me express it this way. I am a woman of science, Dad, and science means more to me than religion. I am not going to be some submissive slave to a cultish and antiquated religion. I am not going to be another Grandma. I am a woman, and I am entitled to form my opinions without having to enslave myself to the opinions of other people." There was silence, but this time, Felicity waited for her father to speak. "I see. I will not explain that position to either of your grandparents because World War Three will erupt if I do."

Samuel remained silent for a moment, and then he changed the topic. "So, how is university life going? In particular, how is the UAS?" Felicity realised that in all the drama of the past few days, she had not told her father her news. "University is fine, and yes, I am still helping William. Oh, and by the way, the UAS has selected me to fly one of its noble benefactors around later in the university year. Viscount Godwin." The name did not mean much to Samuel, as he did not spare much thought for the noble classes; however, it was necessary for Felicity to sound mildly excited. "Well then, congratulations are in order.

Anyway, I am tired after working all day and consoling your grandmother for 24 hours. Take care, and I will call you, Felicity. Please don't call the home because your grandmother's mind is slipping faster than her health, and there is no coming back from that discussion. It is going to be an interesting Christmas. Goodnight, and I love you." Felicity smiled. "I love you, too, Dad. Goodnight." They simultaneously terminated the telephone call, but Felicity had one thought on her mind: 'Christmas! Do I want to go home this Christmas?'

As she walked back to her room, Felicity made a decision. She would remain on campus to study at the end of the Michaelmas Term. Going home for Christmas no longer had the same allure as it had in years past, and she knew it would be an unhappy experience. However, nature would intervene in those plans, which meant Felicity had no choice but to return home. The day before the Michaelmas Term was to conclude, Felicity returned to her room after the final UAS drill for the term. When she opened the door to her room and saw a folded piece of paper on the floor before her, she intuitively knew it was not good news. After picking up the paper, she slowly unfolded it as though she knew evil tidings were coming her way. The sentence was simple: 'Please call your father urgently. Your grandmother has passed away.' Felicity immediately felt both the contemporaneous feelings of grief and, more strikingly, relief. Tears rolled down her cheeks as the weight of twenty years of psychological torture lifted from her mind.

CHAPTER 18

Death! Comes for us all, ain't that the truth!
Still, people are cruel, and history is proof.

The sky was overcast, murky and darkening at the farm as the cab drove Felicity up the driveway entrance to her home. She had caught the train from Cambridge to Colchester rather than allowing her grieving father to drive to the university to pick her up. Even the livestock appeared to be in a sullen mood as Felicity looked out of the cab's windows, and the memories of her final words exchanged with her grandmother were on her mind, leaving her in a state of suspense about the reception she would receive at home, particularly from Grandpa. After receiving the news of Catherine's passing from her father, Felicity remained at Cambridge for a further week because Samuel told her, 'there wasn't much she could do, and the funeral would be in ten days to allow my sister to travel from Australia.' Aunt Anne: Felicity barely remembered her as she had emigrated from England at the war's end with her well-heeled Australian husband. Aunt Anne – the woman her grandmother had always pitted her against as the example of a woman who should marry – was the womanhood Catherine had told Felicity she would not emulate, so Felicity was said to become a nun instead. As the cab pulled into the driveway in front of the house, Samuel walked out the front door with his wallet in his hand to pay the taxi driver.

Felicity immediately exited the cab, dropped her small suitcase on the ground, and embraced her father. Her emotions overwhelmed her, and she felt remorse for how her final interaction with her now-deceased grandmother had transpired. "Dad!" Her tear-filled voice seemed to echo in the fields that morning. "Sweetheart!" Samuel's tone was a similar strain of emotion, a sound foreign to Felicity's ears for so many years until lately. He clutched Felicity while the patient cab driver waited for somebody to pay the fare. Samuel let go of Felicity after their heartfelt embrace, and he walked over to the cab driver's door and handed him two one-pound notes, telling him to keep the change – an act of generosity that the driver accepted with glee. As the taxi pulled out of the driveway to take the long cobblestone road to leave the farm, Samuel turned back towards Felicity and motioned with his eyes towards the main homestead. "Come inside and meet your Aunt Anne. The last time you saw her, you were four, but she has not changed too much in looks," and there was a pause; a cold wind began to blow across the fields, and then Samuel rolled his eyes, "nor has she changed much in her attitude, so don't take the bait." Felicity was intrigued. "What do you mean by don't take the bait?" Samuel tilted his head slightly to one side while rolling his eyes. "Your grandfather has been telling her about your final discussion with your grandmother ever since my sister arrived." He held up his hand before Felicity's voice of protest could leave her lips. "Don't worry, Felicity. I told her your side of the story, which I have accepted. However, my sister is; how best do I explain it? Oh, to heck with it! My sister is a bitch. That is the best way to describe her. And a snob, so like I said, don't take the bait."

Felicity nodded but needed to know the next piece of the family puzzle. "Are Uncle Hugh and my two cousins, Angus and Edward, here?" Samuel rolled his eyes, a sure sign that his mother's passing was not important enough for them to attend the funeral, and yet Felicity was the one who had to be mindful of her step. She shook her head in disbelief and sheepishly asked, "How is Grandpa?" Samuel's eyes almost rolled to the back of his head. "Well, obviously, he is upset about losing his wife, but did you hear what I just said? Your grandfather is upset about your final interaction with your grandmother, although deep down, he suspects she probably caused it. Nevertheless, Felicity, do not bite back regarding his behaviour. Normally, by 5:00 p.m., he is so full of my single malt that he goes to bed for the evening. So tread carefully is what I am trying to say."

Felicity anticipated her grandfather would be difficult, and she, too, suspected what her father had just confirmed; her grandfather now did not have his wife's handbrake on his drinking habit. Samuel bent over and picked up Felicity's suitcase, which she had dropped. "My goodness! What did you pack in here? Half of Cambridge?" Felicity smirked. "Come on, then. Let's go in and face the cavalry, and, as I said, don't take the bait.

Samuel led the way into the main house, and, as on previous occasions, the furniture and decor inside the dwelling had not changed; however, a gloominess now seemed to lurk in every crevice with Catherine's passing. Samuel placed Felicity's suitcase next to the stairwell, and then he ushered her to follow him down the hall. "They are in the drawing room, so you had better say hello to them first." The drawing room? Her father never used that room, and apart from occasionally reading some of the books stored there, Felicity had rarely used it during her childhood. Her grandmother used to chase her away from it when she was young, as though the room was too luxurious for a child to play in. When they walked into the room, Felicity could see that the old mahogany furniture had not changed, but she noted one immediate difference. The old mahogany armchair faced the bay windows, and standing in front of those windows, looking out onto the field, was the shapely figure of a well-dressed woman. She turned at the sound of her entry and, sure enough, the beautiful face of her Aunt Anne, with her meticulously styled hair pinned into place and her makeup at least two layers thick, finished off with ruby-red lipstick. Anne was the epitome of post-war conservative womanhood, and her snobbery was easily defined by her eyes narrowing as they focused on Felicity. Then Felicity saw her grandfather's face peer around the corner of the tall back of the armchair before it quickly disappeared again when he saw it was his granddaughter.

Felicity began to walk towards her Aunt Anne, but the woman's words brought her to a dead stop in her stride. "My mother was right about your looks. You should have joined a convent." An insult from the outset; this would not be a pleasant experience, and 'what's wrong with my looks?' Felicity thought to herself. 'Don't take the bait.' She nodded in respect. "Hello, Aunt Anne. It has been such a long time..." Felicity could not finish her sentence as she became emotional. "Too bad you did not display this respect when you last spoke to my mother." Samuel would not tolerate Anne's emotional brutality. "Steady on, Anne. My daughter is just as upset about losing her grandmother as you are about losing our mother, so go easy on her." Anne raised her eyebrows, picked up a fine silver cigarette case, took out a cigarette, and lit it with an equally fine silver lighter placed on the windowsill of the bay window. She blew out smoke as she spoke, looking out the window. "God doesn't exist! I am sure she is upset with herself." Felicity walked over towards the armchair, and although her father had told her not to take the bait, she could not let that comment go unchallenged. "Well, if you spend the same time reading books as you do layering your face with powder, perhaps you would understand what I do. By the way, Aunt Anne, weren't there enough seats on the plane for my uncle and cousins to travel to Grandma's funeral?" Her sarcasm and spunk brought Samuel a wry smile; his daughter may have taken the bait, but she had thrown it back in her aunt's face.

Then Felicity's hand reached out and touched her grandfather's shoulder, but he recoiled away from her. "Don't touch me, young lady. I am not happy about what you said to your grandmother!" Felicity withdrew her hand and dipped her head. "I just wanted to tell you I loved you, Grandpa, but I will leave you alone." Felicity then turned around and walked out of the drawing-room, her father briefly remaining to vent his spleen. "For the love of Christ, Anne. You can be a cold-hearted person, but that wasn't necessary. And you, Dad, I know you're grieving, so am I. And so is Felicity!" Samuel then angrily stormed out of the drawing room and returned to the hallway, where Felicity was about to pick up her suitcase. Samuel took his daughter into his arms. "Just ignore the pair of them, sweetie. I told you your Aunt Anne is a bitch; however, I do admire how you handled her, and it looks as though Grandpa has already started to wipe himself out on the single malt. So, ignore them, and come on, I will take you up to your room."

Her room had so many bad memories, but at least Felicity could avoid her aunt and grandfather by spending some time in her room studying. "I am sorry, Dad." Samuel quickly took his daughter by the shoulders with both hands and looked into her eyes. "Heh, you do not need to apologise to me. I am sorry you had to experience that. Let's go to your room, and you can lie down." Lie down? She had brought course materials with her to study. "Lie down? Life is too short to waste on sleep, Dad. I have brought my study materials with me to read. The world of astrophysics at Cambridge is bristling with discoveries in the cosmos, and nothing has changed in my mind; I want to be the first woman to fly into space." Samuel's eyes displayed the utmost pride in his daughter; nothing would deter her from pursuing her life's goal. "Alright, my little astronaut, do what you like with your time while you are here. However, you're only young once, so do not grow up too quickly." Her father's wisdom was not lost on Felicity, but he did not realise the degree of sexual discrimination that existed in the world she had ventured into. Men like William could idly stroll over hills to achieve their station in life; women had to scale mountains to achieve their dreams. Samuel was living in a world of blissful ignorance.

Felicity lay on her bed reading a physics paper written by an Oxford physics student, who was well on his way to first-class honours. He was considered the leading emerging mind at that time, as Einstein's general theory of relativity was undergoing a renaissance. New mathematical techniques revealed that generic gravitational collapse would, not might, but would lead to infinite singularities, ushering in a new world of physics. Felicity's mind absorbed the genius of the postulated maths and physics theories in that Oxford student's published paper.

She had been discussing the same mathematical equations in her tutorials at Cambridge; however, this young man at Oxford was postulating a new approach to physics that would elevate him to the status of an oracle on various theories. It was a humbling experience for Felicity to read that paper. Still, Felicity had not been too far away from the premise of the reasoning herself, matters she had raised with her lecturers, but to only fall upon deaf ears. Men seemed to be the preferred vessels of new science and maths in England, and it troubled Felicity's mind that afternoon that, as hard as she worked, she would not be given the same academic recognition because she was a woman. A woman. She got out of bed and looked at herself in the mirror, her mind fixated on Anne's hurtful remarks about her appearance. "I'm not ugly", she said to herself. Indeed, she was maturing into a reasonable-looking young woman, but her breasts were tiny, and her hips lacked the curvaceousness that was still the defining hallmark of female attraction at that time.

That evening's dinner was a quiet affair of just Felicity and Samuel. Grandpa had already drunk himself into a stupor, and Anne had put him to bed in his cottage, where she was staying, even though there were plenty of bedrooms in the main home. It only took Samuel a few minutes to reveal why his sister was not joining them for dinner. "So, you're probably wondering why you and I are enjoying this nice brisket this evening?" Felicity was indeed intrigued by the absence of her aunt. She nodded. "Well, while you were studying in your bedroom, my sister decided to chat with me about her share of the farm when our father dies." Even though she had a mouthful of food, Felicity could not help but display her shock as she spoke with a mouthful of food. "You are kidding me, aren't you, Dad?" Samuel shook his head as he ruminated over his plate. "No, I wish I were. I told you my sister is cold-hearted. Our mother is not even buried, and my sister is talking about her share of the farm." Felicity could not believe the callousness of her aunt. "So, what did you say, Dad?" Samuel put down his cutlery and looked straight into Felicity's eyes. "I told her she is a cold-hearted bitch, but she would get what she is entitled to, which will not include other tenements I have acquired." Felicity was still intrigued by the discussion between her father and his sister. "What did she say when you told her that?" Samuel's face displayed his sarcasm, which followed. "Well, why do you think we're eating alone?" Anyway, she was always the favourite child when we were growing up with our late brothers. 'Anne this' and 'Anne that', our parents would say, whereas my brothers and I were treated like no good little toe rags. I have made arrangements for Anne if my dad dies, which is more than she is legally entitled to."

Samuel scoffed at the thought of his sister and returned to eating his meal. However, Anne's comment about her looks could not be removed from Felicity's thoughts. "Dad, am I ugly?" Samuel immediately dropped his cutlery, and with a concerned expression, he reached out with his left hand and took hold of Felicity's right hand. "No, sweetheart. Far from it. You have the sweet face of your mother." Felicity smiled, but she was not convinced. "Come on, truly, am I ugly?" Samuel shook his head. "No, Felicity. You are not ugly; yes, you have the same sweet face as your mum." Felicity smiled; however, she wasn't convinced. "Yes, but look at me. I have hardly any breasts, and I am thin like a boy." Samuel drew his seat closer to Felicity, holding her hand with both of his. "Don't let my sister's comment get into your head. You do not have big breasts and curvy hips. So what? Who cares? Is that going to stop you from flying into space?" Felicity shook her head. "Of course, it won't. Look, your mother was not a glamour queen like my sister, but she had a sweet face and, most importantly, like you, had the most beautiful, kind eyes. Women like Anne may have all the curves, but she lacks one feature your mother and you both have: your kind eyes. And yes, you are not ugly." Felicity's warm smile revealed her appreciation; only her father could make her feel at ease in her skin. They both resumed eating their dinner, and later that night, Felicity looked at herself in the mirror in her bedroom wardrobe. She felt much better about herself. She also had something many women and men did not have: an intellect.

An even gloomier Wednesday sky accompanied Catherine's funeral the following morning, and the unpleasant sky made the whole Catholic funeral ceremony even more depressing. Some distant cousins attended the church ceremony, which was presided over by the now-aging but still vitriolic Father O'Leary. Many people from the local district also participated in the church ceremony. Felicity defiantly did not bow her head for prayers, but her defiance went unnoticed as the others, including Samuel, bowed and closed their eyes in prayer. "What a strange ritual," she thought to herself. Even stranger was the eulogy of her Aunt Anne, during which she spoke about her kind-natured mother. Much to Felicity's internal mirth, one of her grandmother's cousins muttered, "Is this the same Catherine we knew?" Samuel spoke with greater sincerity about his mother, complimenting her for stepping in to assist him with raising Felicity. He admired her stoic nature, which allowed her to remain dignified in the face of losing two of her children during the war. Grandpa wept, particularly so when Father O'Leary accidentally knocked over the goblet of holy wine, and the deep red stain of wine on the altar cloth symbolically underscored the loss of life. Fortunately for Albert, there was plenty of holy wine the altar boys could retrieve to refill the goblet.

Afterwards, at the wake, which was held in the neighbouring church hall, Father O'Leary approached Felicity as she finished pouring herself a cup of tea. It was almost as if the priest had foreshadowed what he was about to say with semaphore flags from afar, as the scowl on his face could only be interpreted in one way. "So, what is this news I've heard that you deny the existence of our Holy Father?" His voice was loud enough for Samuel to hear, and he was standing about ten yards away, talking among a group of local townsfolk. As if the weather had not made the occasion depressing enough, now Felicity had to deal with an impolite priest whilst she was mourning the loss of her grandmother in her heart. "Is this the appropriate time for you to pose that question, Father O'Leary?" Without realising his insensitivity, Father O'Leary persisted. "Whenever it involves a member of the flock straying, it is; it's what your grandmother would have wanted me to talk to you about." Father O'Leary's simple, pious mind had asked for it; Felicity was no longer the submissive little schoolgirl he once knew. "Very well, then, if you want to know, you had better get a pen and pad, as I will teach you some maths and science." Felicity half-turned away, but then she turned back, as she had one more quip. "Oh, and by the way, you'd better take your shoes and socks off because you have to count to more than ten." She then placed her cup of tea back on the servery table from which she had just obtained it, turned on her heels, and walked out of the hall.

Samuel politely excused himself from the group of people he was talking to, checked on his daughter, and then glared at Father O'Leary's way as he walked out of the hall. He found Felicity about forty yards away, leaning against the trunk of an old tree that had shed its leaves, offering another gloomy reminder of the death-like winter environs of East Anglia at that time of year. As he approached his daughter, Felicity turned her head to look his way, and rather than tears, her eyes displayed the fire of anger burning brightly inside her. "Please, don't you say anything to me now about what I said or having to apologise to that old fool." Samuel held up his hands like an innocent man accused of a crime he did not commit. "I'm checking in on you to ensure you're not too upset. I agree with you, Felicity; it was inappropriate for the priest to talk to you like that today." Felicity nodded; she felt vindicated. Samuel could not help but observe his daughter's reaction. "You would have made an outstanding cricketer because that was the best sledging I ever heard." Felicity glanced at her father to ensure she had heard him correctly, and when she saw the smirk on his face, she burst out laughing. "Oh, sorry, I shouldn't be laughing today; however, I wasn't expecting that comment." Samuel placed his arm around his daughter's shoulders, and she snuggled into him. "You will be just fine in life, Felicity Bennet." Felicity hugged her father. "Do we have to go back in there, Dad?" Samuel continued to hug her as he shook his head. "No, let's stay out here for a while. It's nice to be out here with you without having to make small talk with a bunch of people who, deep down, probably do not like my mother." They leaned against the tree trunk and talked, occasionally waving goodbye to one of the parishioners as they left the hall. It was a nice father-and-daughter moment; without realising it, such moments are rare.

Anne left the following day to return to Australia, and in her grand delusions, she did not bother to say goodbye to Felicity. Grandpa remained quiet after Anne left, barely giving his granddaughter a moment's notice. Instead, he remained in his cottage next to the main home, swilling Samuel's whiskey from midday until falling asleep in a drunken stupor in front of the fireplace. Before Felicity left home to return to Cambridge for the Lent Term, she received an unexpected letter from Natasha. Felicity had been so dedicated to her university studies and the UAS that she had not thought much about or had any contact with her old Woldingham school friends. Natasha's letter informed Felicity that she and Heather had recently met up in London. They both wanted to visit Cambridge to catch up with their old school friend, discuss their lives after Woldingham, and find a convenient time for Felicity to see them. That was a difficult question for Felicity to respond to because the Lent Term would be an exceedingly busy time for her, and, indeed, she did not plan on returning home at the end of the Lent Term for the customary break before the Easter Term. Felicity penned a letter in response to Natasha's correspondence, informing her that she would be staying on campus between the Lent and Easter Terms, which made the last week of the break convenient for her. She concluded her letter by informing Natasha that she was excited to meet up with her and Heather. She also mentioned calling the Corpus Christi Bursar's secretary the week beforehand, who would, in turn, pass on a note regarding which day the two women would be visiting. Felicity placed her letter in the postal box near Colchester train station when she left home to return to Cambridge. While she was in the carriage after the train departed from Colchester, Felicity briefly thought about Amelia and wondered what was happening in her life now that her parents were bankrupt. There was also a fleeting moment of remembering their night together after the prom and how soft, gentle, and tender their kisses had been. "Oh, to feel her soft lips and warm embrace." Felicity quickly dismissed these thoughts from her mind as she opened one of her physics textbooks to occupy her mind for the journey back to Cambridge.

In Moscow, Anatoli Sidorov was exposed to the sheer brutality of the Soviet Union's desire to infiltrate the West. Surgeons had performed several operations on him without his consent, and scientists were administering various hormonal therapies to him. The past year had been torture for him, and the hormonal treatment caused him to start developing breasts, which made Anatoli the laughingstock of the other young males held at the KGB training camp. Anatoli had begged the KGB supervisor of the youth training group, Leonid Volkov, to stop treating him like an animal; however, whenever the young man begged for mercy, he would be punished by Volkov by either being denied food, locked in a cell in which there was no light or belted with a strap. Leonid Volkov repeatedly told Anatoli, "You're lucky to be alive and have been granted so many privileges that the other young men do not receive here, so stop complaining." Leonid Volkov had served in the Soviet Union's armed forces during World War II, and like many Soviet soldiers, he had experienced the brutality of the Nazis, a regime he, and for that matter, many Soviet Union people alike, had considered to have emanated from the evils of Western capitalism. The Space Race had begun between the Soviet Union and the United States. Yet, more disturbingly for the West, the Soviet Union was winning another race that was not widely discussed outside the intelligence agencies on either side of the "Iron Curtain": the race for espionage. The KGB was uniquely manufacturing Anatoli to fulfil the role of infiltration into Western society, which Anatoli was unaware of at this time.

CHAPTER 19

Star-crossed lovers – what a terrible fate!
Will love blossom? Or is it too late?

During the first week of the Full Lent Term, a young and inspiring President of the United States of America was sworn into office on 20 January 1961. This Inauguration Day even attracted the interest of the university campus at Cambridge, as it heralded the commencement of an exciting new era for Anglo-American relations in the 1960s. The world appeared to be breaking free from the shackles of the 1950s and all the conservative values that were so prominent during that decade.

Felicity was extremely busy during the Full Lent Term with her studies and UAS duties. Her UAS duties were particularly hectic as Joan heavily scrutinised her flying in the Hawker because of the planned joy flight with Viscount Godwin, which was scheduled towards the end of the Full Easter Term. Joan would accompany Felicity on the flights of her planned route with Viscount Godwin. On one occasion, Felicity asked Joan why she had to fly so often, to which Joan curtly replied: "Because the RAF high command might attend without prior warning during the Full Easter Term to test your skills for this flight of indulgence, so I want to make sure you're capable of handling the weather conditions you are confronted with on that date." Joan was fulfilling her role as a surrogate older sister or guardian for Felicity. Still, the Sword of Damocles also perilously dangled above Joan's head because she had selected Felicity for this flight, despite the protests in the upper chain of command of William's father, who believed his noble bloodline in William should be chosen for this auspicious occasion. Once again, Joan's father pulled rank and rubber-stamped his daughter's decision, but it was on one proviso: "Make sure this girl is capable of flying this silly old fool around."

Felicity was also required to spend more time with Warrant Officer Jones, who was assigned the vital role of servicing the Hawker. No love was lost between Felicity and Drew Jones, as she found his mechanical engineering skills inadequate. Samuel had trained her from a young age, when he serviced his Cessna, so she was well-versed in servicing aeroplane engines. It was not so much that Warrant Officer Jones lacked knowledge; for Felicity, it was more a question of tardiness or forgetfulness in checking every square inch of that aeroplane. She remembered the clipping she received from Joan on her very first day at Cambridge, which included Felicity chastising Drew. However, internally, she was frustrated with him because she thought he was incompetent. When she raised the topic with Joan, she would reply: "Warrant Officer Jones knows what his duties are, so you just watch and learn." Felicity did not know that, deep down, Joan enjoyed a primeval delight in having under her command a timid young man whose skills and intellect would never allow him to progress into the officer ranks of the RAF.

William continued to rely on Felicity for assistance during the Full Lent Term. In return, Felicity did not ask for anything. However, it was satisfying for her to know that a man relied on her intellect to help him obtain the results that ensured he would pass his undergraduate degree. Then, he could be done with university forever. Notwithstanding that she did not request a fee or favour for assisting him, Felicity encountered an unusual request from William on the second-to-last Sunday of the Full Lent Term. As usual, they met at the library at 9:30 a.m. on Sunday, and trigonometry was confounding William on this occasion. Felicity could not contain her frustration. "For goodness' sake, William! Do you listen to the lectures or read the textbooks? You wish to be involved with the RAF in the future, and yet here I am, having to start at the basics with you." William smirked as he raised his nonchalant chin. "Why do I need to listen or read when I have you every Sunday to teach me?" He chuckled as Felicity narrowed her eyes, and her thoughts did not trespass from her lips. "If you weren't so cute-looking, I would punch you right on the end of your nose."

Felicity deliberately cleared her throat out loud to gain William's attention. "The three functions of trigonometry are Sine, Cosine, and Tangent, and they are ratios of one side of a right-angled triangle to another." William's attention was focused on another topic, and he was distracted. "William, are you listening to me?" He nodded, but she wasn't convinced. "Well, what did I just say?" His response belied his previous physical confirmation. "The functions of trigonometry are Sine, Cosine and, let me see." The fateful pause gave the game away. "And, oh, bother, whatever the other silly little name is." Felicity huffed in frustration. "Tangent, William! God damn Tangent!" He smiled and leaned back in his chair. "Have you ever been told that you look cute when you become frustrated?" Felicity was taken aback. "What? Cute. What on Earth are you talking about?" William leant forward. "When you become assertive, you're cute." Felicity remained speechless, and her face openly displayed her surprise. "Haven't you ever been called cute before?" She had, but not by a male. "Tell me something. Who is taking you to the Graduation Ball?" The Graduation Ball? Felicity had not even considered attending it at this time. "I don't know, William. I hadn't thought that far ahead. William sat back in genuine surprise. "That far ahead? It's the next bloody term. When we finish." The thought of finishing was not on Felicity's radar, as she intended to study postgraduate courses at Cambridge. "Oh, that is right. You plan to stay on at this hellhole. I forgot about that. In any case, would you like to be my date for the Graduation Ball?"

The thoughts raced through Felicity's mind at the speed of light, but many seconds had passed without her responding to William's question. "What is the matter? Am I not eligible enough for you?" The question broke Felicity free from her thoughts. "You want to take me to the Graduation Ball?" William's chin rested in his hand as his elbow moved further across the library desk it was perched on. "Well, I would ask the Bursar, but people may talk." His sarcasm broke the ice. A slight hint of a pleasant smile enveloped Felicity's usual serious demeanour. "Why me? Haven't you got all those landed gentry womenfolk on campus for whom you entertain for your amusement rather than studying?" William leaned back in his chair and placed his hands behind his head. "If I ask one of them, they and, for that matter, their families, would interpret it as the first step in me asking to take their hand in marriage. I kid you not. However, I do not have that burden of expectation with a Yeoman's daughter. So what do you say?" Somewhere wrapped inside the insult, there was a compliment. "Why, thank you, William. You're sweeping me off my feet." He leaned forward on the table again, and he now rested his chin between his pointer and index fingers. "What would you like me to do? Get down on my knees and beg? Besides, you deserve the honour, as you have been so kind with your tutelage over the past three years." Felicity considered William's last sentence. 'The honour?' she thought to herself. Then Felicity looked at William's cute face, and she acquiesced. "Sure. Thank you. I accept the honour of your invitation. Now, can we return to the topic at hand?" William smiled and nodded. Felicity's attention returned to teaching William trigonometry, but the surprising request for her to be his 'date' for the Graduation Ball was not far from the forefront of her mind for the rest of their time that Sunday morning. Later, when she returned to her room, Felicity pondered over what had just happened. 'He said I was cute, and then he asked me to be his date for the Graduation Ball. Does William have feelings for me?' Indeed, that was the question.

Time seemed to have slipped by so quickly between the day Felicity placed her letter in response to Natasha's letter in the postal box at Colchester train station and the day she was meeting up with her old Woldingham friends. Although it had only been three years since they last saw each other, for Felicity, it seemed like a lifetime ago, as so much had happened in her life. After exchanging messages through the Bursar's secretary, the three young women arranged to meet at The Anchor Pub restaurant, which offered stunning views of the River Cam and Mill Pond. Its charming, polished wood tables and chairs were complemented by an ornate chandelier hanging down from the ceiling in the restaurant's centre. Its centuries-old charm also offered one further advantage. Namely, it would be quiet on the last Wednesday of the university break before the Full Easter Term commenced. Heather and Natasha were already waiting at the Anchor when Felicity arrived, and she did not need to be told by Natasha what she had been up to. Her distended belly displayed that she was now six months pregnant. Heather had matured into a respectable-looking young woman; however, Natasha's circumstances were the paramount consideration.

"Oh, my goodness, Natasha! Have you already had lunch?" Natasha pursed her lips and tipped her head sideways. "Space freak, you have finally developed a sense of humour." With that exchange, the three women gleefully exchanged hugs, as if they were back at Woldingham together. As they sat at the table, Natasha explained before Felicity could ask the question. "So, this is the product of when Richard and I spent a romantic weekend together at Brighton last September, and, yes, Felicity, I continued to date Richard after we finished school." Felicity could not contain herself. "What did your parents say, Natasha?" Heather sat back and smiled as though she had heard this story many times. "Well, let me see. When Richard and I sat down in the living room at home to explain to my parents what had occurred, it was about 7:30 a.m. on a Saturday, and my dad was still dressed in his pyjamas, gown, and slippers. My mum had been awake for several hours by this stage, preparing my dad's Saturday morning breakfast feast, like she has done for the past twenty-five years, so at least she had changed clothes for the day. My older brother was still asleep because he had been out the night before. When I uttered the word 'pregnant', my dad shouted the word 'scoundrel' on top note and picked up the crystal decanter on the table between the two sofas, immediately moving in Richard's direction. Richard began running immediately, closely followed by my father. They both ran out the front of my house with my father now howling on top note 'dirty rotten scoundrel', which not only caused my hungover older brother to fall out of bed but also caused most of the neighbours in the street to peer out the window as they watched a twenty-year-old man run for his life from a fifty-three-year-old man yielding a sherry decanter as a weapon in his night clothes as he pursued Richard down the street. Eventually, after an ignominious chase and pursuit of about 500 yards, my dad ran out of breath. He probably realised how ridiculous he looked, as his pyjama pants had to be held up with one hand while he was chasing Richard. Anyway, when tempers cooled and serious family discussions took place between my parents and Richard's parents, an urgent wedding was arranged at our Catholic Church for the following week, so that we could 'purify' our circumstances. So, there we go, Felicity; just like on the night of our prom, I was barefoot and pregnant by age twenty. So, what have you been up to?"

Felicity looked at Heather, who was now laughing uncontrollably, much to Natasha's chagrin. "You have to admit, Natasha, the thought of your dad running down the road chasing Richard with a sherry decanter in one hand whilst holding up his pyjama pants in the other is pretty funny." Of course, it was funny, and Natasha laughed out loud as Felicity, too, broke down into fits of laughter. Eventually, they contained themselves, but Felicity's curiosity was not satisfied. "So, where are you and Richard living? What is he doing for work? Can you afford to raise the baby?" Natasha held up her hands to slow down the pace of the inquiry. "Whoa, slow down, my old friend – too many questions at once. As you recall, Richard's father owned a furniture store when we were in school. His dad now owns three stores, including one in Maidstone, where we live. Richard is managing that store under his dad's watchful eye, but we have enough money, and there is a three-bedroom flat above the store, which Richard's dad owns, so we do not have to pay any rent for the first few years until we have saved enough to buy a house in the town. There are worse counties to live in than Kent when you're a 20-year-old couple expecting your first child." Felicity was about to ask Natasha whether she would be happy being married to Richard, but the waiter interrupted them to take their orders.

After ordering their meals, Felicity looked at Heather, who looked like she had a story to tell. "What about you, Heather? What have you been up to since we last saw each other?" Heather blushed and politely cleared her throat, noticing that Natasha smiled like a cat who swallowed the mouse. "Yes, Heather. Please tell Felicity what you have been up to since we left school." Heather sighed. "Well, as you may recall, my parents enrolled me in a deportment school in London after we finished at Woldingham. The course took me one year to complete, and before I finished, the school's owners, who are married, offered me a job as a receptionist." Heather then bit her lip and stopped talking. Natasha would not let her get off lightly, and she awkwardly sat forward. "Come on, Heather. Out with the full story." Felicity was intrigued because there was more to Heather's story than being a mere receptionist. Heather sighed. "So, anyway, after working as the receptionist for six months, John, my employer, asked me to stay back one Friday afternoon for a drink, and one thing led to another, and now I'm dating John." Felicity's eyes opened wide because Heather was the last person she expected to have an affair with a married man. There was still more to the story, which Natasha prompted. "Tell Felicity the entire story, Heather. You're only halfway there." What else could Heather possibly say? "All right, Natasha. Let me tell my story my way. Anyway, Felicity. I am still working as a receptionist at the school. John's wife, Alice, is aware of us, but it seems I am not his first paramour, so she doesn't seem to mind as long as the money is flowing into their coffers, which it is. So, yes, I am dating a 45-year-old married man and working with him and his wife." Felicity needed to know more. "What did your parents say?" Heather looked at Natasha, whose smile had widened as she was about to commence laughing. "They don't know. As far as they are concerned, I am still a prim and proper virgin working as a receptionist and waiting for the right man to marry." Natasha now bellowed with laughter, much to Heather's chagrin.

There was so much news for Felicity to absorb, and she spoke freely without considering what she had to say. "My goodness. I left you pair for several years, and look at what has happened. One of you is pregnant, and the other is dating an adulterer old enough to be her father. The most surprising fact is that I expected that you, Heather, might be married and pregnant, and Natasha, well, anything but married and pregnant." She then realised her words could be construed as judgemental. "I'm sorry that was wicked for me to say." Natasha placed a hand on Felicity's arm. "It is all right, Space Freak. You spoke the truth. Now that we have spilled the beans, what about you? Do you have any interesting news to tell us?" She did, but whether it was interesting for her worldly friends, who had both grown up before their time, was another matter altogether. "Well, I am about to finish my undergraduate degrees in natural sciences and mathematics, and then I will stay here to study aeronautical engineering and astrophysics at a post-graduate level. Oh, and yes, I have been selected out of my UAS corps to take a fuddy-duddy old Viscount out for a joy flight this coming term." Natasha and Heather both had looks on their faces like they had been served two-day-old porridge. Natasha broke the emerging tension in the air. "Come on, we want the juicy stuff. Are you dating any of the men here? Have you lost your virginity?" Now it was Felicity's turn to blush because she had no spicy story to tell. "No. And that is no to both questions. I'm too busy for a relationship, although one of my fellow students has asked me to be his date for the Graduation Ball. He is an arrogant son of a nobleman, and I have been his tutor in both courses for the past three years." Natasha could not resist. "Well, are you going to get with him that night?" Felicity was mortified. "No, Natasha. I won't get with him; I don't do that. Besides, he said he was doing it as a favour for me as the daughter of a yeoman." Now, Heather could not contain herself. "He was that blunt?" Felicity nodded.

Their meals were served before another word could be spoken, and they spoke casually over their lunch. Felicity told her Woldingham friends that her grandmother had died several months beforehand, but it was a relief as she had made her feel miserable for too many years. Natasha was about to ask Felicity why her grandmother made her sad when Heather interrupted them. "Heh, Felicity. Did you hear the news about Amelia?" No, she hadn't. She had tried to bury Amelia in the grave of her past. "No, what news?" Natasha and Heather were stunned, and their faces did not hide their feelings. Natasha nudged Felicity's right arm with her elbow. "Come on, you're joking, aren't you?" Felicity shook her head. "I have not thought of Amelia Speranza since we left Woldingham." It was a lie, but she played a perfect poker face. Heather continued to deliver the news. "It was all over the front page of the newspaper today. She is going to be a movie star in Hollywood." Three years of trying to suppress thoughts and feelings bubbled over inside Felicity. "A movie star? How?" Natasha took over the story. "Haven't you even read a copy of *seventeen*?" Felicity shook her head and thought: 'What in hell's name is *seventeen*?' Natasha held her hands out, as if begging her friend. "It's the defining magazine of our age. You have got to stop burying your head in textbooks and whatever else you read here and try joining the real world. The magazine *seventeen* has been regularly featuring Amelia for the past two years, either on the cover or, in particular, in articles about the trend for our age group in England. She is even featured in an article in this month's magazine edition. According to the newspaper reports, a visiting American producer spotted her in a copy of the magazine several months ago and immediately decided she would suit the role of the English glamour girl for his studio's next teen movie. Her surname is no longer Speranza; it's Tolhurst. Still, it's Amelia, former glamour girl at school, now about to become a starlet. Talking about being born lucky." Felicity was confused because the last time she heard any mention of Amelia's name was when her father was explaining Amelia's father's connection to his litigation. "Didn't her parents end up being bankrupt?" Heather nodded, but Natasha held the floor in the discussion. "Yes, but that has nothing to do with Amelia. She started modelling in London after we left school and was immediately successful. She is scheduled to appear on *The Tonight Show* in America early next week." Felicity was living in a world of blissful academia up until now. "What is *The Tonight Show*?" Natasha rolled her eyes at Heather and then turned back to face Felicity. "Are you joking with me? Steve Allan and *The Tonight Show* are among America's most popular television shows. He interviews movie stars, musicians and, well, anyone who is famous. Amelia is going to be a star."

Significantly suppressed feelings and thoughts started erupting in Felicity's mind. Amelia, the schoolgirl she had a crush on, was someone she could not tell anyone about. Amelia, the schoolgirl who treated her so terribly at Woldingham, yet for one night treated her with such tenderness, their hearts had intertwined since then. Amelia, the girl she had managed to banish to the nether regions of her mind, was suddenly front and centre of her thoughts again. Heather detected that something was wrong with Felicity. "Is there something wrong with your hearing this news, Felicity?" She quickly dismissed it, but the eyes did not lie. "No. Her father vicariously caused my father to incur legal expenses." Heather and Natasha looked dumbfounded by this statement. "What I meant was my dad had to sue her father's business associate because old man Speranza's bad investments meant that person could not pay my dad. It's all over now, and my dad succeeded in court; however, I didn't think about Amelia until now. The news was surprising, given what happened to her father's business."

Heather quickly glanced at Natasha, who did not seem to be witnessing what Heather had seen. "Anyway, enough about Amelia, for heaven's sake, Heather;

we're here to talk about Felicity. So, tell me more about your date for the Graduation Ball." Felicity's mind was preoccupied with Amelia, and her feelings from all those years ago were stirring. "Date?" Natasha's sarcasm could not be restrained, and her facial expression underscored her words. "Yes, your date, Prince Charming, who called you a yeoman's daughter." Felicity's mind was still preoccupied with thoughts of Amelia. "I don't know what more I can tell you. We are studying the same degrees. I helped him gain a pass by tutoring him. We are not seeing one another if that was your question."

Natasha was oblivious to Felicity's demeanour. Still, Heather wasn't. "Oh, Natasha. Look at the time. We had better return to the train station; otherwise, we might miss the last train." With those words spoken, Heather tugged on Natasha's left sleeve, and Natasha was still none the wiser about what was happening. "All right, Heather, but we still have forty-five minutes until the train leaves." Heather was most insistent. "No, Natasha. We need to leave right now." Natasha rolled her eyes in Felicity's way. "Oh well, I guess that means we have to leave, Space Freak. It has been so jolly good to catch up, and please, don't be a stranger." They all stood up, and Natasha hugged Felicity as best she could with her distended, pregnant belly. Heather was a bit more subtle as she hugged Felicity goodbye. "Is everything all right in your world, Felicity?" Felicity nodded. Still, it was apparent to Heather that Felicity's mind was preoccupied. "I am always a telephone call away if you need to speak to me." Felicity gave Heather an extended hug, and then she reached out to grab both women's arms. "I miss both of you and will stay in touch."

With those words, Natasha turned around and commenced to leave the Anchor, and while she followed her, Heather glanced back at Felicity, who seemed to be lost in her little world. Natasha could not resist chiding Heather when they were both outside the Anchor. "Now, why on Earth did we have to leave, Heather?" Heather held Natasha's right arm as she walked down the street to catch a bus to the train station. "Something was wrong with Felicity. Didn't you notice it?" Natasha shook her arm free. "No. I didn't notice it, and, more importantly, there is something wrong with you for dragging us away earlier than we should have." With those words spoken, Natasha continued to march down the street, a few yards ahead of Heather. Still, Heather knew the mention of Amelia's name triggered a reaction with Felicity; however, she was clueless about why Felicity reacted in such a manner.

Meanwhile, Felicity initially looked over the balcony of the Anchor out to the beautiful River Cam. Her mind was whirring with thoughts about Amelia becoming famous, and she had buried that murmur in her heart long ago. After staring at the calm waters of the Cam, Felicity immediately felt the urge to do something she had never done before. She wanted to buy a copy of *seventeen* to see the news for herself and a copy of any Fleet Street paper reporting this news. Felicity walked down Silver Street to Queen's Road, and she hailed the nearest taxi. When she entered the taxi, Felicity told the driver to take her to the nearest news agency and wait for her. Sensing he had engaged a lucrative fare for the afternoon, the driver drove Felicity to Cherry Hinton Road, where she left the taxi to 'wait for her' as she raced into the newsagency. Felicity did not need to look for too long. Near the front entrance of the newsagency, she found the Daily Mirror edition that displayed Amelia's photograph on the front page under the banner headline: 'UK Beauty Becomes American Movie Star'. She picked up a copy of the *Daily Mirror*, and then Felicity searched for a copy of *seventeen*. That search also did not take her too long because on the shelves of the magazine rack was the latest edition of *seventeen*, and whilst the front cover did not state anything about Amelia being a future movie star, sure enough, there was a photograph of her with a caption underneath which said: 'The Look of the New Decade'. Felicity purchased both the *Daily Mirror* and *seventeen*, then returned to her waiting taxi, directing the driver to: 'Take me back to Corpus Christi as quickly as you can'.

That night, Felicity did not leave her room as she read the *Daily Mirror* article repeatedly and looked at the pictures of Amelia within *seventeen*. The newspaper article reported that the Hollywood producer Billy Wilder was visiting London. He had seen photographs of the young English model 'Amelia Tolhurst' in this month's edition of *seventeen* and immediately decided she was the look of the early 1960s he was searching for. Felicity's thoughts were prescient. "She changed her name to ensure there was no link to her father's business failures." However, the more she tried to turn away from looking at photographs of Amelia, the more she found herself transfixed by her image. The images of Amelia in *seventeen* displayed her buxom figure from most angles, wearing various styles of women's fashion. Her face was beautiful, with red cherry lipstick and full-flowing auburn hair hanging down over her shoulders. The images of Amelia opened the door to Felicity's heart, which she thought she had locked away long ago, and no matter how hard she tried to shut that door as the Full Easter Term began at Cambridge, it was too late. Her multifaceted mind concentrated on her studies and her extra duties, flying for the UAS on the scheduled 'joy flight' of Viscount Godwin. However, her multifaceted mind also had images of Amelia at its forefront, and her heart swooned at those images. Whenever a story broke in the newspapers about Amelia's exploits being interviewed on American television, Felicity would ensure she purchased a copy of the Fleet Street rag reporting the news. One late night in early May 1961, Felicity stood outside the grand entranceway of Corpus Christi, looking up at the unusually clear night sky. As she looked out to the stars on the horizon of the Western sky, her heart travelled in that direction, hoping she might one day meet Amelia again.

CHAPTER 20

The heart and mind of a young woman are strong,
With such synchronicity, what could possibly go wrong?

Felicity's emotions were turned upside down and inside out by Amelia's re-emergence in her thoughts. Thoughts and feelings she had suppressed and dismissed as silly childhood feelings consumed her mind. She purchased any magazine that featured photographs of Amelia or articles about her. Soon, her room became a wasteland of magazines and newspapers, either stacked in the corners or spread over her usually tidy study desk. Whilst her studies had not been affected by her infatuation with Amelia, it had become evident to Joan that Felicity's mind was distracted when fulfilling her UAS duties. Her flying in preparation for Viscount Godwin had been impeccable. She had assiduously examined every square inch of the flight path and its surrounding landscape to be acquainted with every detail. Still, her usual discipline during drill routines had been occasionally absent-minded, and there was even an occasion when her uniform shoes had not been polished, which was very unlike the usually meticulous cadet she was.

Joan decided enough was enough by the middle of the Full Easter Term and chose to visit Felicity in her room one Sunday afternoon in May 1961. It was a surprise visit that Joan would not usually make in her capacity as a WRAF officer. The knock on Felicity's door awoke her from an afternoon nap after falling asleep on her bed from reading another edition of *seventeen* featuring photographs and a lengthy interview with Amelia. Without thinking about the state of her room or the edition of *seventeen* open on her bed, revealing the pages depicting photographs of Amelia in her bikini costume for her upcoming Hollywood teen beach movie, Felicity hopped off her unmade bed and walked over to open the door to her unexpected visitor. When she opened her door, Felicity was surprised to see Joan standing there, and the sight of her in her WRAF uniform startled Felicity. "Oh, my goodness, Joan, is something wrong?" Joan's response was earnest and commanding. "May I come in? I must talk to you." Felicity felt obliged to agree to Joan's request. "Of course. Please, come in, but forgive my mess." Joan entered the room, and it was indeed a mess and inconsistent with Felicity's years of immaculate parade presentation. "Interesting state your room is in." She saw the edition of *seventeen* open on Felicity's bed, but she did not take too much notice of the content. "Keeping yourself occupied with interesting reading materials, I see? Take a seat, please, Felicity."

Felicity sat down cautiously on the end of her bed, and Joan brought the chair over from the study desk so she could talk to her. When she sat down, Joan remained quiet, staring into Felicity's eyes. Felicity could not bear the interrogation. "What is up, Joan? Have I done something wrong?" Joan looked briefly out the window of Felicity's room before turning her attention back to her. "You have not been your usual disciplined self this past term, Felicity. Is anything or anyone bothering you? In particular, is that serial pest William bothering you?" Felicity shook her head, but she otherwise remained silent. "Well, what is wrong, Felicity? I have never had to chastise you during UAS drills; however, several times this term, I have noticed your usual standards are not up to scratch. So, please, as a friend and mentor, tell me if something is bothering you." Then Joan remained quiet, staring at Felicity, waiting for her to talk. Eventually, Joan's unwavering gaze caused Felicity to confabulate an unconvincing response. "I had some old Woldingham friends visit me during the break while I remained on campus. One of them is pregnant and married, and the other one, well, let me say she is doing something I never imagined she would do when we were at school together, and, I don't know, I guess how their lives have turned out has been on my mind."

Joan sat back in the chair and searched Felicity's eyes, as her explanation seemed feeble at best. "Why would their lives have such an impact on your life, Felicity? That does not make sense. Look at your room; it's the antithesis of the successful student and cadet I have watched mature before my eyes for the past three years." Felicity wanted to tell Joan the truth; her childhood feelings for a girl had resurfaced, but she could not admit to that. "I can't explain it any more than I have, Joan, but I promise my drill conduct will improve, and to prove it, I will start by tidying up the room right now." Joan was not convinced, but she could not elicit any further information from Felicity, so she took her pen and pocket notepad out of the jacket pocket and began writing. "Very well then. Here is my new address on campus since getting married." She ripped the paper from her pocket notebook and handed it to Felicity. 30, Millington Road. Her final words had an edge to them, suggesting to Joan that a deeper pathology was in play than her prize cadet was otherwise revealing. She stood up to leave the room, but turned around before going for one final word. "May I also suggest you stop reading rubbish like that magazine, *seventeen*? Your mind is far too intelligent to be reading that junk media." Joan then left Felicity's room, much to the younger woman's relief. Her drill performance returned to its usual exemplary standards after meeting Joan; however, Amelia was never far from her mind.

The new American President announced to Congress on May 25, 1961, that his goal was to put an American man on the moon by the end of the 1960s. Felicity's mind comprehended the scale of the endeavour proposed by the Americans. However, she was disappointed to hear the President use the word 'man'. Joan had unwittingly helped sharpen Felicity's focus on her goals again, but to hear a putative 'progressive' leader refer to putting a 'man' on the moon was disappointing. It only entrenched in Felicity's mind that the so-called 'Free World' was still a patriarchal society where women had to toil much harder than men to have even a chance of achieving their dreams.

When the heart and mind are occupied, time seems to race quickly into the future. It was Friday, June 2nd, 1961, and the big day of Viscount Godwin's 'joy flight' had arrived. There had been a surprise visit by the RAF about a fortnight beforehand, and Felicity's flying skills left that male Squadron Leader in no doubt that she possessed exemplary flying skills. Felicity had flown the designated flight path many times and thoroughly studied and memorised its maps. Felicity was ready to fly, and the weather conditions were fine, not a cloud in the sky. Joan had been correct all those months beforehand when she told the UAS cadets the media would be present for this momentous occasion of taxpayer funding being wasted. There were journalists from several Fleet Street newspapers present at the Teversham airfield. Television and radio journalists from the British Broadcasting Corporation were also present. Felicity had arrived early at the UAS hangar that morning to inspect the Hawker Hart with Warrant Officer Jones and to avoid the media reporters, whom she did not have time for. Indeed, Felicity considered the whole 'joy flight' to be a waste of taxpayer funds and, like Joan, she believed the money had more worthy uses within the UAS. Inside the hangar, Felicity's primary focus was ensuring Warrant Officer Jones had properly serviced the Rolls-Royce engine and, of course, to ensure it had a full tank of fuel, for it only had a maximum range of two hours and forty-five minutes flight time. Warrant Officer Jones assured Felicity that he had been meticulous in servicing the aeroplane over the previous days, including checking the fuel pump for her.

Joan arrived at the hangar at 7:30 a.m. and appeared noticeably tense about the occasion. Warrant Officer Jones and Felicity stood to attention. "At ease, Warrant Officer and Cadet Bennet." They both complied with the command, and Joan began where Felicity had left off. "Warrant Officer, has this aircraft been thoroughly checked and serviced?" Warrant Officer Jones stammered in a nervous reply. "Yes, ma'am, it has." Joan looked at him to ensure he was being candid; he was, so she moved on to Felicity. "Cadet Bennet, have you completed your safety checks?" Felicity, too, was unusually nervous in response to Joan's stern voice. "Yes, ma'am." Joan looked at them both. "Very well, then. Viscount Godwin will arrive shortly. When he arrives, you, Cadet Bennet, and I will go outside to greet the media, and I will introduce you to the journalists. I shall do all the talking, but if the journalists ask any questions, it will be about how you feel flying the Viscount today, and you say: 'It's an honour and a privilege'. Do you understand me?" Felicity nodded. "Very well, then. Well, don't look so sombre, the pair of you. Everything will be fine." Joan's tense demeanour had caused them to appear sombre when, in fact, they were nervous. The importance of the occasion had dawned upon Felicity; she would receive national media attention for this flight of fancy. She did not know how much media attention she would receive now.

About 15 minutes after Joan had arrived, the elegant Rolls-Royce Silver Wraith carrying Viscount Godwin arrived at Teversham airfield. The media scrum gathered around the vehicle as the driver alighted from the driver's door to run around to the back left-hand-side door of the elegant car to open the door for His Grace. Inside the hangar, Joan turned towards Felicity, who had now changed into her flying outfit to pilot the Hawker Hart. "Are you ready, Felicity? Do you remember what I told you to say if the press asks you a question?" She nodded. "Okay, Cadet Bennet, let's go face the crowd."

As Felicity and Joan walked out of the hangar, Viscount Godwin finally emerged from the back seat of his Rolls-Royce. He was the epitome of a narcissistic old fool. His distended belly suggested he had spent most of his 75 years enjoying too many fine meals and drinks, and his comb-over grey hair, which was oiled down in place, and his moustache, which was twirled at either end, explained everything Felicity needed to know as to the reason why this 'joy-flight' was occurring. Like William, Viscount Godwin, was a member of a self-indulgent anachronism of English society that still believed the world was like that of the nineteenth century. The viscount had held a senior officer's commission in the British Army since World War I but had never seen active duty. Joan and Felicity walked over to Viscount Godwin, who was now standing on a small podium behind a microphone. Joan saluted him, and Felicity quickly did the same. "Your Grace. I am Flying Officer de Montesquieu, and this young woman is your pilot for today, Cadet Felicity Bennet." A broad smile came over his face as he returned the salute, revealing another abnormal physical attribute: a significant gap between his front teeth. His Grace took both women to the microphone by placing his bloated hands around each of their backs and waists. Felicity did not like being touched this way; however, she did not reveal her inner disapproval.

By now, Warrant Officer Jones pushed the Hawker out of the hangar and onto the tarmac until it came to rest some thirty yards away. The media scrum was already firing questions away before Viscount Godwin spoke. Still, his Grace had been trained since birth to command attention when he was the senior noble present. "People! People! Please be quiet; your questions may be asked when I finish speaking." The numerous members of the media crowd, including the respective television and radio technicians, fell silent obediently. Viscount Godwin cleared his throat, a horrible sound more consistent with expectorating than merely clearing. "It is my great honour today to be afforded the privilege granted to me by the UAS to be flown around in that faithful old symbol of British engineering on display, the UAS' Hawker Hart that has trained many a fine pilot here at Cambridge University." The television cameras and newspaper photographers followed the viscount's extended right arm, which was pointing towards the aeroplane. Some brief filming and photography of the sleek, silver biplane was taken before His Grace resumed speaking. "Today, it is an unusual occasion for this flight to occur because it is the first time a female UAS cadet and, I envisage, a future WRAF officer will have the privilege and honour of flying me around the English countryside. Felicity's mind was boggling with the implied misogyny. "My privilege and honour? What a silly old sod."

His Grace flashed his toothy grin Felicity's way. "May I introduce to you, gentlemen of our press and the BBC, Cadet Felicity Bennet." Felicity stood in her place, but his Grace once again manhandled her by the waist to pull her closer to the microphone. Felicity had to contain her displeasure at being manhandled by the viscount. "She is a little bit shy, gentlemen. However, I am reliably informed by Flying Officer de Montesquieu, who has joined me on the podium today, that Cadet Bennet is not only the best pilot in the UAS but will also be the top of her class in mathematics and natural sciences at Cambridge University when she graduates in several weeks. So, I might receive some much-needed tuition while we are flying." There was a general murmur of laughter among the media. "Seriously though, I think it is quite remarkable that British men are not leading the way either in the UAS or at Cambridge, and I think that is a fact to give us pause to consider, where as a society, we have gone wrong since World War Two." Even Joan's eyes ever so slightly widened at the blatant sexism. Felicity felt like telling Viscount Godwin to sod off there and then; however, she once again contained her anger. "However, the UAS still plays an important role in our armed services, so I implore Westminster to continue funding this fine programme."

His Grace then became silent, and the media present politely smiled back, as if waiting for him to say something further. In contrast, he had finished insulting half of the UK's population. Viscount Godwin could not contain his arrogance or frustration. "Well, come on then. Do I have to come over to tap you on your heads to expel the questions from your mouths?" The first hand shot up from a Fleet Street journalist, for whom His Grace acknowledged by nodding in his direction. "Your Grace, Anthony Smith of the Daily Mirror. Is your Grace suggesting the current government is not funding the UAS enough to keep it operating?" Viscount Godwin lifted his nose in disdain. "Where on Earth did you get that idea from? I said nothing like that. Next question?" The hand of the BBC radio reporter shot up, and His Grace nodded in his direction. "Your Grace, David Jackson of BBC Radio 1. Do you suggest there is a societal problem in this country regarding young males?" His Grace's sarcastic expression was as blatant as his spoken sexism. "Well, of course, my dear fellow. If there weren't, I wouldn't be flown around today by a woman, would I?" Felicity's and Joan's blood temperatures were about to boil over. The hand of the BBC television reporter shot up, and once again, the noble nod of approval was given. "Your Grace, Douglas Ramsay of the BBC television news service. My question is for Cadet Bennet. How do you feel about flying His Grace today?" Felicity wanted to say that she wished there was a bomb bay door to drop Viscount Godwin out of, but she quickly glanced over at Joan, whose slight nod reminded her of her sticking to the script. She was initially nervous, but then Felicity took a deep breath and found her confidence. "It is an honour and a privilege for me to be selected to fly His Grace around the countryside today." Another question was about to be asked by one of the other Fleet Street journalists; however, the arrogant old viscount held up his hands to dismiss any further questions. "That is all the questions for the moment, gentlemen. When we return from our flight, you may have an opportunity to ask some more questions, but I also have a luncheon to attend, so there will not be time for too many questions. Otherwise, Flying Officer Montesquieu has arranged for some refreshments to be served to you in the UAS hangar, so please enjoy that."

And with those words being spoken, Viscount Godwin ushered Joan and Felicity off the podium and commenced his noble march towards the Hawker, where Warrant Officer Jones had also set up step ladders for his Grace and Felicity to take their respective positions in the Hawker. Whereas Felicity quickly scrambled into the cockpit at the front of Hawker, entering the rear cockpit was more of a challenge for the rotund Viscount Godwin. As he struggled to lift his right leg over the cockpit, the Fleet Street newspaper photographers and the BBC television cameraman obtained amusing images of his Grace's awkward attempt to enter the cockpit. Viscount Godwin saw Warrant Officer Jones standing nearby, looking vaguely at His Grace's dilemma. His hesitation drew His Grace's ire. "Well, come on, Warrant Officer! Are your limbs painted on?!? Give me some help, you insight-less young fool!" Even Felicity felt sorry for poor Warrant Officer Jones, and he timidly responded to the demand. Eventually, after enduring Viscount Godwin's ample derrière pressed against his face, he successfully assisted His Grace in entering the cockpit. Then Drew handed him his flying helmet and goggles to put on before quickly returning to the hangar, much to the amusement of the media scrum.

Felicity started the Hawker Hart, and its Rolls-Royce engine let out an almighty roar as the photographers and cameramen stood back to ensure the propeller did not harm them. Joan stood not far from the hangar and crossed her fingers as she said this prayer: "Dear God, please make sure this flight is as smooth as possible." Felicity may have been the star of this 'joy flight', but Joan had made the call to put her into that cockpit, and if it went wrong, it would be Joan's career in the WRAF and perhaps the career of her father in the RAF that would suffer.

Felicity taxied the Hawker into the lane leading to the runway, and she radioed into Teversham tower for clearance. "Teversham tower, this is UAS Alpha Bravo-19 seeking your clearance to enter the runway." There was a momentary silence, enough time for Viscount Godwin to display his aviation ignorance, which he screamed into Felicity's ear. "Come on, young lady! There isn't another aeroplane to be seen." Felicity tapped her headphones to indicate that he should put on his pair, which he did. "Your Grace. Leave the flying to me, please!" Viscount Godwin was not accustomed to being spoken to in that manner by a woman. Then, there was a crackle over the radio. "UAS Alpha-Bravo-19, this is Teversham Tower. You may enter the runway, and you are clear for take-off." His Grace realised his mouth was best kept shut.

Felicity then increased her engine power to move the Hawker into position on the runway. Just as her father had taught her many years before in his Cessna, she went through the same takeoff drill. She lined up the aeroplane with the runway, and she ensured that the directional gyro matched the runway heading. It was a still day, so there wasn't a cross-wind to contend with. Next, she advanced the throttle in about three seconds to full throttle. The aeroplane began to move, and Viscount Godwin called out in excitement. "Now, that is more like it. Give this old girl a good thrashing." Another misogynistic statement. As the aeroplane started moving, Felicity performed a visual check of the instruments to ensure the oil temperature and pressure were in the green zone. She then called out 'power available' as the aeroplane reached the minimum power of two thousand three hundred RPM. The aeroplane's speed continued to accelerate rapidly. Felicity called out 'airspeed alive' as her airspeed indicator reached thirty-five KIAS. She then felt the aeroplane's lift on the runway as its speed increased, and then Felicity pulled back slowly on the yoke as the speed reached fifty-five KIAS. At sixty KIAS, the Hawker's nose lifted off the runway, and Viscount Godwin could not contain himself. "Jolly good show; let's get this old girl up high in the sky!" Felicity was fuming, and her thoughts expressed her feelings. 'Old girl! I wish I could offload this old man!' The Hawker's wheels lifted off the runway, and Felicity lowered the nose slightly to reach a climb speed of seventy-five KIAS. She was flying her initial designated flight path, north-northeast, until she reached an altitude of 5,000 feet. At that time, Felicity's flight path was to turn due East to fly over Bury St Edmunds and fly out to the English Channel after passing over Middleton, when she would then fly South-South-West following the East Anglia coastline before turning due West at Southend-on-Sea to fly an inland loop over Northern London to make her way back to Teversham Airfield. The weather conditions were fine, meaning that at least Felicity could enjoy the clear skies and hopefully hear less from His Grace.

As her father had taught her, Felicity kept her bearings focused on where she was heading, even though she had practised flying this flight path many times. The Hawker had climbed to an altitude of about 2,500 feet when Felicity suddenly felt a strange but momentary murmur through the flight stick, almost like the engine was beginning to stutter. Then, as the Hawker climbed to 3,000 feet, the murmur did become a stutter, suggesting the engine was running out of fuel, which baffled Felicity because she watched Warrant Officer Jones fill the tank. She then checked it to confirm it was full of fuel for the maximum flight time of two and three-quarters hours. The stuttering of the engine alarmed His Grace. "What is going on?" Felicity was also alarmed, but she maintained a calm exterior. "The engine is acting like it is running out of fuel, which cannot be the case because it was filled this morning. I will have to turn the plane around to try to make it back to Teversham Airfield. Otherwise, we will land in a field or on a highway." Viscount Goswin was now overwrought with panic. "Try to make it back. What do you mean? Are we going to crash? I don't want to die?" Felicity needed to call the tower, but she couldn't think with a panicking old man in her earphones. "Please, your Grace. Be calm and quiet." His Grace then became hysterical as the stuttering of the engine transformed into it closing down altogether. "Oh my God! We are going to die!" Felicity had had enough of his hysterics. "Your Grace. Shut up! I mean it! If you want to live, shut the hell up!" Viscount Godwin had never been spoken to like this before, and like a meek schoolchild obeying a teacher's command, he shut up. Felicity tried to restart the engine, but it would not start.

Felicity banked around the Hawker to do what needed to be done: Head back toward Teversham Airfield. As she did so, Felicity operated the radio. "Teversham Tower, mayday, mayday. This is UAS Alpha-Bravo 19. Our engine has stalled at about 3,000 feet. I have banked around to head back to Teversham Airfield; however, I am still calculating the glide and lift-to-drag ratios. Over."

Percy Wilson was the air traffic controller at Teversham Airfield Tower. Warrant Officer Jones had entered the tower shortly after takeoff and heard every word of Felicity's mayday call. Percy had acquired ten years of experience as an air traffic controller, and this was the first occasion in his career that he had encountered an emergency of this nature. He could see that the Hawker Hart on-the-ground approach system was approximately nine miles away from Teversham Airfield. "UAS Alpha-Bravo 19, this is Teversham Tower. Do you hear me? Over." There was an immediate response from Felicity. "Teversham Tower. This is UAS Alpha-Bravo 19. Roger that. The engine has stalled and will not restart. I have banked around to attempt to glide back to Teversham Ground. I'm about nine miles from Teversham Ground. Altitude is two thousand nine hundred. Copy that? Over." The radar was consistent with that. "UAS Alpha-Bravo 19. Teversham Tower; Roger that. Over." Percy turned to look at Warrant Officer Jones; however, he was already dialling the telephone to contact Joan in the hangar.

Joan heard the telephone ring while talking to several journalists in the hangar. She excused herself and answered the call. "Hello, Flying Officer Montesquieu speaking." Her face turned ashen when she heard what Warrant Officer Jones told her, and everyone in the hangar heard her following words. "The plane is going to crash! My God, I will be there in a jiffy!" Joan ran out of the hangar without saying a word to the media present, and she immediately entered the RAF Land Rover and drove off toward Teversham Tower. The media did not need any prompting. Journalists, reporters, cameramen and photographers piled into their respective cars and drove off in hot pursuit of Joan's Land Rover. A dull 'joy flight' was now a potentially tragic air accident, and there was nothing like human tragedy to motivate the media's attention.

Under tremendous pressure, Felicity calculated the Hawker's lift-to-drag ratio of 9,000 feet for every 1,000 feet available. Her altimeter had already recorded that the Hawker had descended to 2,700 feet when she had finished her previous radio communication with Teversham Tower. There were approximately 47,500 feet to Teversham Airfield. She calculated her glide ratio to be only about 24,000 feet. 'Only halfway there,' she thought to herself. Felicity knew there was no alternative; she had to find a straight piece of road that was relatively traffic-free at that time of day to hopefully glide the Hawker to a safe landing. Then she recalled that the southern end of Lode Road, near Long Meadow, had about 800 yards of straight, sealed surface surrounded by quiet, rural fields, eventually leading to Bottisham Village. In the limited time, she had to consider it the best of the available options. Felicity radioed into Teversham Tower. "Teversham Tower. This is UAS Alpha-Bravo 19. Over"

Percy crackled back over the radio, and his voice was distinctly nervous. "UAS Alpha-Bravo 19. This is Teversham Tower. Over." Joan had by now scrambled into the tower, and several BBC and Fleet Street journalists were not far behind her to hear the alarming news to follow. Felicity knew His Grace would panic when she spoke, but she had to be blunt. "Teversham Tower. My glide ratio will not be enough to return to Teversham Ground. I have estimated that my best chance of a safe landing is to glide to the southern end of Lode Road near Long Meadow. Over." Percy quickly glanced at Joan and Warrant Officer Jones, and the look of dread on their faces matched his feelings. "UAS Alpha-Bravo 19. Copy that. I will inform the authorities. Over and out." Percy turned to the telephone to call the police. Joan had already picked up the phone and dialled 111.

Viscount Godwin was alarmed. Indeed, he was consumed with panic. "What do you mean by best chance? We are going to crash, aren't we?" There was too much at stake for Felicity to endure a hyperventilating, panic-stricken seventy-five-year-old man. "Stop panicking, your Grace! I know what I am doing!" Her bellow down the microphone of her headpiece was loud enough to subdue Viscount Godwin's hysteria. As Felicity made the necessary adjustments of the flaps to glide towards Lode Road, His Grace put his face and hands on his cockpit panel, and he started whispering his prayers. Felicity was right about her glide ratio, and the speed and height of the Hawker both began to decline rapidly over the next two and a half minutes as she used all of her flight skills. As the Hawker approached the intersection of Quy and Lode Roads, it was barely thirty feet above the ground, and it narrowly cleared a lorry driving along Quy Road, much to the lorry driver's alarm. About forty yards down the Southern end of Lode Road, the wheels of the Hawker touched down on the surface of the road. However, it was not a smooth surface like Teversham Airfield, and each bump in the road pounded its way up the pneumatic shock absorbers and into the cockpits of the Hawker. It was a hair-raising four-hundred-yard ride, but eventually, the Hawker's speed began to decrease under breaks to a gentle roll and then stop as the siren of a police car coming from Bottisham Village made its way towards the aeroplane.

What should have been a disaster had been turned into a miraculous escape, and His Grace now sat in the cockpit crying tears of joy. Felicity radioed Teversham Tower. "Teversham Tower. This UAS Alpha-Bravo 19. We have successfully landed on Lode Road. Over." Percy's response was brief. "UAS Alpha-Bravo 19, this is Teversham Tower. Well done. Over and out." Felicity then immediately jumped out of the cockpit, and agricultural labourers came running from the nearby fields to arrive at the Hawker, where the police car also arrived on the scene. Joan, Warrant Officer Jones and the media had already left the Teversham Tower when Felicity announced her intention to try to land on Lode Road.

By the time Joan, Warrant Officer Jones, and the media arrived at Lode Road, there was already a crowd of local agricultural labourers, police cars, police officers, an ambulance, and two ambulance officers. The ambulance officers were tending to Viscount Godwin, for whom Felicity had used all of her flying skills to save him from a disastrous plane accident, so that his only injury was shock. He kept looking at her as she stood nearby where he sat with the ambulance officers, and His Grace repeatedly said: "Thank you. Thank you for saving my life." Notwithstanding the crowd that had gathered by now, the television, radio, and newspaper reporters, as well as cameramen and photographers, could force their way through the crowd to where Viscount Godwin, Felicity, and the ambulance officers were. Joan and Warrant Jones were not far behind them. One of the Fleet Street journalists yelled out a question for Viscount Godwin to answer. "Your Grace, do you have anything to say? How do you feel?" Pride cometh before the fall. His Grace awkwardly rose to his feet. "I am not injured, and I have Cadet Bennet to thank for her skill and courage in saving my life. I will make a recommendation to the Queen about this young lady." The BBC radio reporter then asked Felicity to answer a question. "Cadet Bennet. How did you manage to perform this miraculous piece of flying?" Felicity looked briefly at the Viscount, and then she responded. "It was quite simple. I did not panic." Felicity saw Joan, standing not far behind the BBC radio reporter. There was a smile on Joan's face and a look in her eyes, which Felicity could discern as this statement: "Well said, and this news is for us women."

When she returned to her room at Corpus Christi later that afternoon, a message was already left under Felicity's door for her to urgently call her father, as he had heard about her near disaster on the BBC radio news earlier. Samuel was relieved to listen to his daughter's voice, and his words soothed her mind: "I am so proud of you, my little flying ace."

CHAPTER 21

The newspapers, radio programmes and BBC television news broadcast Felicity's miraculous safe landing of the Hawker Hart for the next week, and several American television news reports and newspapers also picked up the story. In Los Angeles, Amelia was sitting in the make-up artist's chair in a studio at Hoener Studios while reading about Felicity's exploits, which had been reported in the *Los Angeles Times*. Amelia had a warm smile, and her heart beat with desire.

Meanwhile, in Moscow, the final surgical operation was life-changing for Anatoli. It was a six-hour surgical procedure that had never been performed in the Soviet Union. Still, at the end of the marathon surgical procedure, the surgeons proudly nodded to the watchful eyes of the KGB bureaucracy. Once he had healed, Anatoli's face was transformed to resemble a female's. However, despite the hormonal procedures that caused him to develop breasts, his genitalia otherwise had not been touched by a surgeon's knife. Several days later, after the medical staff had removed the bandages from Anatoli's head, Leonid Volkov entered Anatoli's hospital room, accompanied by two brutish-looking KGB officers, Nikolai Sokolov and Ilya Aliev. Volkov had trained Sokolov and Aliev, so they retained no empathy or sympathy for people of any age. They were taught to follow orders and, when necessary, kill.

Volkov's words were brief but chilling. "You're coming with us, Anatoli. Tonight you will be held in a tyur'ma." A prison? Anatoli protested. "Why are you doing this to me? After all these medical procedures, why am I now going to a tyur'ma?" There was no response from Volkov. Instead, Volkov clicked his fingers, and Sokolov and Aliev forcibly dragged Anatoli from his hospitable bed. As each of the officers held Anatoli by his arms, pulling him down the hallway of the hospitable ward, the tortured young man struggled and screamed at the top of his lungs: "Why? Why are you doing this to me?" Neither the doctors nor the nurses intervened as they knew Anatoli belonged to Volkov and the KGB.

Anatoli was taken to Butyrka Prison Castle, located on the outskirts of Moscow, by Volkov, Sokolov, and Aliev. Anatoli had not even been changed from the gown he was wearing when he was forcibly removed from the hospital. He had been taken to Butyrka in the back of a UAZ-450 van, where he screamed and yelled in protest, all to no avail. Volkov followed the van in his KGB-issued Lada, not even questioning what he was about to do to Anatoli. Volkov considered Anatoli needed to be hardened and was about to put the poor young man through hell to achieve that objective. When the van stopped outside of Butyrka, Sokolov and Aliev wasted no time, and they promptly removed Anatoli from the back of the van. By now, Volkov had also exited from the Lada, and he walked over towards the entry of Butyrka, where he explained to the guards at the gate who he was and why they were there with a feminine-looking youth. Anatoli screamed at the top of his lungs as Sokolov and Aliev dragged him through the entry gates of Butyrka, and, eventually, he was dragged to a maximum security cell, which held two of the tyur'ma's most heinous inmates and bull queers: Boris Petrov and Pavel Vasilev. Volkov ordered the tyur'ma guard to open the door to Petrov's and Vasilev's cell. When the guard did so, Volkov turned towards Sokolov and Aliev, who were holding a horrified Anatoli, and he gave the order: "Throw him in there." Petrov and Vasilev were lying on their bunks, wondering what was happening. Sokolov and Aliev threw Anatoli into the dirty stone and concrete cell. His body landed heavily on the concrete floor, and Petrov and Vasilev stood up and smiled like they were about to eat their Christmas dessert when they saw Anatoli. Volkov's words were chilling. "Enjoy your room for the night, Anatoli. I will see you tomorrow morning." Volkov then ordered the tyur'ma guard to shut the cell door, and as Volkov, Sokolov, Aliev, and the tyur'ma guard walked away, the only sound to be heard was the high-pitched scream of Anatoli.

The following day, Volkov, Sokolov, and Aliev returned to Butyrka at 7:00 a.m. They were taken to Petrov's and Vasilev's cell by four tyur'ma guards, and when the cell door was opened, the two heinous criminals were lying in their respective bunks. In the corner of the cell lay Anatoli, curled up in a ball, crying. When Anatoli looked towards the light of the open cell door, his bruised and bloodied face told a story of barbarity too hideous for the mind to imagine. Volkov then gave the order to the four tyur'ma guards, pointing at Petrov and Vasilev, as he said, "Take them to the interrogation room." To their surprise, Petrov and Vasilev were forcibly removed from their cells by the guards after they had held them down and handcuffed them both with their hands behind their backs. When the guards had removed Petrov and Vasilev from the cell, Volkov, Sokolov, and Aliev walked in. Anatoli was now half-standing up from the floor with his left hand. His face was severely bruised, and blood came out of his mouth with his saliva as he tried to speak. "Why? Why did you do this to me? I have been violated all night. Why, Volkov?"

Volkov squatted down before Anatoli, and with his gloved right hand, he held up the young man's chin to look him in the eyes. "Do you want to kill them, Anatoli?" He looked confused. "What? What do you mean?" Volkov grabbed Anatoli by each of his ears and dragged the young man's face closer to his. "You heard me! Do you want to kill them?" Volkov's commanding yell was immediately responded to. "Yes! I want to kill both of those pigs." Volkov smiled, and as he stood, he clicked his fingers at Sokolov and Aliev. "Good, Anatoli. Come with us." Sokolov and Aliev picked Anatoli off the cell floor by his arms, but on this occasion, he compliantly walked with them as the three followed Volkov out of the cell. After walking through several corridors and locked security doors inside Butyrka, Volkov stopped outside a door where two of the tyur'ma guards who had taken Petrov and Vasilev from their cell now stood. Volkov didn't waste any time. "Are they restrained?" Both of the tyur'ma guards nodded.

Volkov then turned to Sokolov and Aliev, standing three yards away, holding up a weary and injured Anatoli. "Bring him over here." Anatoli was promptly brought over to Volkov. "You will now have an opportunity to seek your revenge, Anatoli. We are going to enter this interrogation room, and when we do, you are going to kill these two pigs." Anatoli was shocked. "What do you mean?" Tears began welling up in Anatoli's eyes, but Volkov displayed no compassion for him. He grabbed Anatoli by the ears, causing the young man to wince in pain. "I should not have to repeat myself. We are going to enter this room now, and when we do, you will kill these two pigs." Volkov let go of Anatoli's ears and turned to the tyur'ma guards. "Open the door." His command was promptly obeyed, and one of the guards opened the door to the interrogation room. Volkov entered the interrogation room, closely followed by Sokolov and Aliev, who were still holding up Anatoli under his armpits.

When they entered the room, Petrov and Vasilev were hogtied and lying on the cold concrete floor in an area of the room where the interrogation desk would usually be placed. Their mouths had been covered with tape, which had wrapped around their heads several times. The interrogation desk and chairs had been moved up against the unpainted and dirty brick wall of the room. If there had been no light bulb hanging from the ceiling, the room would have been dark, as it had no windows. Volkov walked up to where Petrov and Vasilev were lying on the floor, and their muffled voices suggested they were now overwhelmed with terror. Volkov removed a Makarov pistol from inside his jacket and then motioned with it toward Sokolov and Aliev. "Bring him over." The two KGB agents immediately complied with the directive, and they brought Anatoli over to Volkov and let go of him under his armpits, and then they took a step back. Volkov placed the Makarov in Anatoli's right hand. "Kill them!" His command was met with fear and resistance. "What? You want me to kill them now?" Volkov was in no mood for Anatoli's hesitation, and he grabbed the young man by the arms to turn him around so that he stood behind Anatoli as he screamed in his left ear. "These two pigs mistreated you. They treated you like a pig. Kill them! Shoot them in the head, now!" Still, there was hesitation. "I cannot kill a person, even these two pigs." Volkov's ferocious response met with Anatoli's distress. "Kill these two pigs, Anatoli! Now, or I shall have Sokolov shoot you in the head." Sokolov began reaching inside his jacket with his right hand. Anatoli had tears running down his cheeks. Still, he knew Volkov would order Sokolov to kill him if he didn't shoot Petrov and Vasilev.

Anatoli raised the Makarov so that the muzzle of the pistol was only three inches away from Vasilev's head. Vasilev 's eyes revealed his terror. Anatoli squeezed the trigger. The Makarov fired one round into Vasilev's head, and his head immediately went limp as blood began running out of his nostrils. The sound of a pistol being fired echoed down the corridors of the tyur'ma. Anatoli then moved two paces to his left, where a terrified Petrov was struggling and making muffled sounds of protest. Anatoli lifted the Makarov again so the muzzle was about three inches from Petrov's head, and he squeezed the trigger. The same physical reaction occurred with Petrov as it had just occurred with Vasilev. Both men were dead. Once again, the sound of the pistol being fired echoed down the corridor. The enormity of killing two men began to overcome Anatoli, and then he quickly spun on his heels. He pointed the Makarov at Volkov and squeezed the trigger. No round was discharged. He squeezed the trigger again. Still, no round was discharged. Volkov laughed, and then, with a mighty sweep of his back right hand, he struck Anatoli across his already bruised left cheek, causing him to fall to the floor, where, to his right, Petrov's and Vasilev's blood was pooling. "You silly young fool. Do you think I would be so stupid as to hand you a revolver that had more than two rounds in it?" Volkov turned on his heels and glared at Sokolov and Aliev. "What are you pair waiting on? Pick him up." Sokolov and Aliev promptly obeyed the command and lifted Anatoli to his feet. Volkov began walking towards the door to leave the interrogation room. His words underscored Anatoli's fate. "We will fix you up back at the hospital. Then, you will be trained to be a special agent for the KGB, and eventually, you will be a formidable agent for the Soviet Union." Anatoli had no choice in the matter, and he now realised his life was a matter of kill or be killed.

CHAPTER 22

When the stars align, do dreams come true for thee?
Like nature's laws, is life's narrative ever written flawlessly?

Fame and celebrity status consumed Felicity's life for the next two weeks, so much so that Felicity's mind was not preoccupied with Amelia as much as it had been. She also had the UAS Graduation Ball to attend on the last Friday night before the completion of the Full Easter Term, so she had to find the right evening gown hurriedly, which meant selecting a gown that she would have to wear with padded inserts in a strapless brassiere; otherwise, it would be ridiculous with her flat-chested physique. Felicity had come to terms with the fact of her lack of breast development. Still, it was different when she had to dress for an auspicious occasion, when Cambridge would host the event for all UAS members attending universities throughout the United Kingdom. William had kept to his word that he wished for Felicity to be his partner for the gala event; however, given Felicity's rise to fame because of her miraculous effort in gliding the Hawker to safety, it was a case now of William being her partner.

Felicity still had to appear before an RAF Board of Inquiry into the Hawker incident at the UAS Cambridge headquarters two days before the ball, or at least that is what Joan had told Felicity was the purpose of the meeting. Felicity arrived at 2 Chaucer Street ten minutes early for the 2:00 p.m. inquiry. She was dressed in her complete UAS cadet outfit. Warrant Officer Jones informed Joan that Felicity had arrived, and he told Felicity to wait until Flying Officer de Montesquieu and the other officers were ready to see her. Ten minutes seemed to take an eternity, but eventually, Joan walked out of her office and down the hallway. Felicity stood to attention and saluted. "At ease, Cadet Bennet. Follow me down to my office. Warrant Officer Jones, do not send telephone calls to my office while Cadet Bennet is there." Warrant Officer Jones displayed his usual obsequious nature. "Yes, Ma'am."

Felicity followed Joan down the hallway, and although she had been the heroine on the day, she now felt slightly nervous. When they arrived at the doorway, Joan ushered Felicity into her office. Upon entering her office, Felicity immediately saw a male RAF officer wearing an Air Chief Marshall's uniform standing behind Joan's desk. "Sir." Her contemporaneous salute was duly met. "At ease, Cadet Bennet." His voice was polished but kind in its tone. Joan walked behind her desk, ushering Felicity to sit as she and the Air Chief Marshall sat behind Joan's mahogany desk. "Please sit down, Felicity. You may be wondering who the Air Chief Marshall is; he is my father, Felicity, Sir Thomas Wilberforce." Sir Thomas shook his head in disapproval. "Please, Joan. In the confines of this office, we do not need to delve into titles." Sir Thomas stood up, and then, remarkably for Felicity, he extended his right hand to shake her hand like an equal. "Please call me Thomas, Felicity." Like Joan's hand, Thomas' handshake was comforting and secure. "Before World War Two, I was not only an officer of the RAF, but I also had some involvement in the British Labour Party. Before the war, we members of the Labour Party were not welcome among the gentry, so my title is meaningless in the privacy of a closed office, or at least that is my point of view." Now it made sense to Felicity why Joan's father outranked William's father in the RAF: his political affiliations. "So, while we are in this room together, refer to me as Thomas. Are you comfortable with that?" Of course, and Felicity nodded. "Very well then. Joan, how about you tell Felicity about the cause of the Hawker's stall?"

Thomas' words were news for Felicity because she thought there was some form of inquiry to take place. "Certainly, Daddy." Joan smiled at a slightly puzzled Felicity. "It is nothing for you to worry about, Felicity. The Hawker stalled because the fuel pump broke down due to the aeroplane's age. Simply put, Felicity, the dinosaur of a flying machine, was too old, and neither you nor Warrant Officer Jones could have done anything to avoid its malfunctioning. Accordingly, no blame can be attributed to any member of the UAS. That is my news. Now, Daddy, it is your turn to explain to Felicity why you are here today."

Felicity was contemporaneously relieved by the RAF's findings and intrigued to hear there was a further purpose to this meeting. Thomas looked at his daughter, and then he stood up and walked several paces over to the window to the left of Joan's desk, and he momentarily gazed out of it before he spoke. "As you might know, Felicity, we, that is, the United Kingdom, are joined with the Americans in a state of Cold War with the Soviet Union." Thomas turned on his heels and stared directly at Felicity. "You are obviously aware of that." Her head slightly nodded because you would have to be living on Mars not to know otherwise. "Of course you do. As a result of our alignment with the United

States during the Cold War, members of our armed services work alongside American armed services; for the sake of convenience, let's call it an ongoing exercise in training and development of military personnel for both sides of the Atlantic. Are you following me?" Felicity nodded but did not know where Thomas was going with his story. "Ordinarily, the personnel swap regarding the RAF," Thomas held his hand up to pre-empt any objection from his daughter. "And the WRAF is limited to serving officers. However, you have created quite a media storm, Felicity, because of your courage and skill in safely landing that dinosaur, as my daughter so inelegantly described the Hawker."

Thomas turned towards Joan and smirked; she rolled her eyes in response; the father-daughter exchange was enlightening for Felicity. Thomas then walked over to Felicity's side of the desk and casually sat on the corner. "Yes, you are a media star of the UAS, the WRAF and the RAF. Indeed, a star of the UK Armed Services, not to mention Viscount Godwin, has also discussed you with Her Majesty the Queen. In turn, Her Majesty has spoken to the Prime Minister. So, the Minister of Defence made a significant decision based on his discussions with the Prime Minister and high-ranking RAF officers, including me. Indeed, this is a first for the RAF." Thomas awkwardly turned in his seated position to look at Joan, causing her to respond petulantly. "Oh, for goodness' sake, Daddy! Don't keep the poor young woman in suspense in mid-air like that. Out with it." Thomas grinned at his daughter's feisty nature, then looked at a confused Felicity. "Out with it, she says, just like her mother. You're being promoted to Flying Officer. How does that strike you?" Felicity was stunned, and her chin dropped to reveal her surprise. She was about to speak when Joan intervened again. "Tell her the rest of the news, Daddy." Felicity was now speechless, and there was more news. "Of course. Given your celebrity status and in keeping with Her Majesty's desire to see greater involvement of women in our armed forces, you have been selected to participate in the armed forces exchange programme with the United States Air Force. You will be deployed to McGuire Air Force Base in the State of New Jersey, where my daughter will take over the story about why it is that particular base."

Before Joan could speak, Felicity instinctively expressed her concerns. "What about my studies? I intend to commence my post-graduate studies here when the Michaelmas Term commences later this year." Joan smiled. "Felicity, do not be alarmed about your studies, as that is part of the WRAF deployment." Felicity's confusion interrupted Joan's explanation. "How do I study here and be deployed to an Air Force base in New Jersey, Joan?" Joan nodded. "That is a fair question, and the answer is you will not be studying here." Joan held up her left hand as it was apparent Felicity was about to interrupt her again. "Now, wait a moment before questioning me and let me speak. It is well-known throughout the campus that you are disappointed enough that you have not been given credit for your work in physics and mathematics, Felicity. It also annoys me that Cambridge is going to roll out the red carpet to a male student from Oxford in the post-graduate courses, in preference to your work. It annoys me deeply, but I have no control over that, nor does the WRAF or RAF. However, as part of your deployment to McGuire Air Force Base, you will be offered the opportunity to undertake post-graduate study at Princeton University, paid for by the UK Government." Felicity was impetuous. "Why Princeton University? Cambridge is leading the field in astrophysics, Joan." Joan held up both hands as a display of dominance. "Let me finish, please, Felicity. Princeton University offers excellent postgraduate courses in astrophysics, mathematics, and aeronautical engineering. However, this information is important, and it impacts your career goals. At Princeton University, NASA is conducting specific testing regarding the psychological effects of astronauts travelling into space. You will be involved in that research programme as part of your post-graduate studies, which means you will get to place a foot in the door of NASA."

Felicity sat there speechless. America, Princeton, NASA – her dreams were coming true. Still, moving to another country would limit her opportunities to see her father and friends. It also meant she would not be undertaking postgraduate studies in astrophysics at Cambridge, which included leading scientific academics in exploring the heavens and searching for proof to support the 'Big Bang' theory. Still, at Princeton, she would work alongside scientists and NASA experts. At McGuire Air Force Base, she might be able to fly a jet-propulsion aeroplane rather than the UAS 'dinosaur', and the WRAF had accelerated her elevation in the officer ranks so that she would skip the rank of Pilot Officer and become a Flying Officer. Joan mistook Felicity's mental calculation of the pros and cons of the proposal as a sign of ambivalence. She stood up and walked around to Felicity's side of the desk. "If you need time to think about the proposal, Felicity, we can revisit it in several weeks when the university year has concluded." Her mind had only taken several minutes to calculate the pros and cons of the proposal. In her inimitable style, she boldly made a decision, and Felicity shook the idea of delay off. "No, Joan. I will do it.

As you said, it allows me to get a foot in the door with the National Aeronautics and Space Administration. Here, I will be playing second fiddle to an Oxford University star. In the United States, my dreams will come true. Here, they won't, so I will do it."

Felicity's eyes began to well with tears as the gravity of the moment overcame her, and she looked towards Thomas initially. "Thank you, Thomas. I know this would not be happening if it were not for you." Thomas was a modest man who originated from modest circumstances and looked over towards his daughter. "Thank you, Felicity. However, it is my daughter who deserves the thanks. Every single day since you originally submitted your application to join the UAS until now, Joan has fought tooth and nail for you. She put you in that pilot's seat to fly Viscount Godwin. Joan argued that you should be accepted into Princeton University because it would place you a step closer to fulfilling your dreams. I am just an old rubber stamper; my daughter has made this happen for you."

Joan had by now made her way around to Felicity, and to her surprise, the younger woman turned around and flung her arms around Joan. Her tears flowed freely; her voice emanated from her heart. "Thank you, Joan. Thank you. You have been like a big sister to me since the day we met..." Her emotions overcame her, and Felicity cried tears of joy as Joan clutched her close, holding back her own tears. "Heh, come on, this is a time to be happy. And, yes, I have done some things to help you along, but this has all happened because of you, Felicity. Do not ever forget that." Felicity clutched Joan firmly. "Besides, I do not have a little sister, so who else can I argue a case for?" She held Felicity back and smiled into her eyes. "Come on, now. Stiffen the upper lip, my girl. You're soon to become the same rank as me in the WRAF, so we cannot allow the world to see a future Flying Officer with tears rolling down her cheeks and snot falling out of her nose." Felicity laughed, and Thomas handed over his military-issue handkerchief at the same time. "There we go, clean yourself up with this hanky. Don't worry, it is clean. There are plenty more where that came from."

Felicity took the handkerchief from Thomas and wiped her eyes and cheeks, then blew her nose. "Can I just ask one small favour?" Both Thomas and Joan answered the question simultaneously. "What is that?" Felicity meekly smiled. "May I break the news to my dad first because he was surprised enough when I told him I wanted to attend Cambridge rather than Oxford years ago, so that this news will blow his socks off?" Joan smiled. "Of course. We intend to announce the news at the UAS Ball tomorrow night, so you had better tell him now, because the media will also be attending that gala event. Use my telephone." Joan began to walk several paces towards the door, but then she turned to her father, who was standing in the same spot. "Well, come on, Daddy. Give the woman some privacy. We'll be in the boardroom, so come and see us. You need to sign some initial paperwork for the Defence Ministry." Thomas retrieved his hat from the hatstand and followed Joan out of her office. Thomas may have been the superior officer, but Joan outranked him in the father-and-daughter relationship. Thomas muttered loud enough for Felicity to hear. "She is as bossy as her mother. Heaven help her husband."

Felicity picked up the receiver of the black Bakelite telephone on Joan's desk. As she went to dial her father, she paused and asked, "What am I going to tell him?" Physics had taught Felicity that travelling back in time was impossible. Still, here she was, just as she had been at Woldingham, about to break the news to her father about a change in her academic plans; however, this news was far more consequential. She dialled the number, and on the ninth ring, her father answered. He had run from the shed. "Hello, Samuel Bennet speaking." Felicity mistook his breathlessness for a problem at home. "Hello, Dad. It's me. Is everything fine at home?" Samuel took a couple of deep breaths. "Yes, Felicity. I was working in the shed, so I had to run to answer the telephone. Since your grandmother passed, I have installed a bell outside that rings when there is a telephone call; however, a forty-yard dash at my age is like a four-hundred-yard dash at your age. Anyway, how are you?" There was a momentary pause. "I am fine, Dad. However, I have some news for you." Samuel immediately thought it was bad news because of Felicity's hesitation. "What is it, my sweetheart? Are they blaming you for the Hawker incident?" Felicity giggled. "No, silly. What on Earth would make you think that? This is good news, but it may come as a surprise. I am promoted to Flying Officer in the WRAF and moving to America."

The silence was deafening. It was apparent that Samuel was in shock, as evidenced by his silence. "Are you there, Dad?" The news had not sunk in. "Say that again, please, Felicity. Are you being promoted in America? Is that what you said?" She laughed again. "No, Dad. The WRAF will promote me to Flying Officer because I avoided a catastrophic crash. As part of the military exchange programme between the United States and us, I will serve at McGuire Air Base in New Jersey." Samuel interrupted her. "What about your post-graduate studies at Cambridge? Are you still going to undertake that study?" Now for the important news. "Well, no, Dad; however, that is the good news, you see, as I will undertake my post-graduate studies at Princeton University, and this is the exciting news: I will be assisting NASA at Princeton. I have put my foot in the door of the space programme."

The opposite end of the receiver was silent as Samuel digested this surprising news. Then he spoke. "Are you going to be an astronaut?" Felicity smiled, but she would not mislead her father about this issue. "No, Dad. However, working with NASA scientists opens the door for me to be perhaps accepted into their astronaut training programme. I know there are no guarantees in life, but my instincts tell me I have made the right decision." There was silence from her father. "Do you have any problems or concerns about what is happening, Dad?" His following words would leave an indelible imprint on her heart and mind. "Of course not, sweetie. I am so proud of your achievements. However, I would be proud of you no matter what you do in life. When you said all those years ago you wanted to be the first woman to go into space, I believed you would accomplish it because when you set your mind to a task, you give it one hundred per cent of your effort and commitment. I am just saddened that in doing so, there will now be an ocean between us. Nevertheless, if you believe you are making the right decision, I unequivocally support you." No other person could touch Felicity's heart like her father. Her voice began to quiver as she responded. "I love you, Dad. Thank you for being so understanding. And don't worry, I will call you as often as I do now. I had better conclude this call, as I have documentation that the Defence Ministry need me to read and sign. You are my rock, Dad." Samuel smiled. "Goodbye, my little darling. Never stop reaching for the stars."

Felicity hung up the receiver and had to use Thomas' handkerchief again before she left Joan's office to join her and Thomas in the boardroom. Tomorrow evening, she would attend the UAS Graduation Ball, where it would be announced that she would be elevated to the office of a Flying Officer. She would attend Princeton University, work with NASA, and make one giant leap forward for women. Still, there was one issue for her as a woman that concerned her, and that was that her body had not developed like other women's bodies: her chest was still relatively flat compared to that of other women, and her menstrual cycle was irregular.

CHAPTER 23

Because of the announcements that would be made about her at the UAS Graduation Ball, Felicity went out of her way to present herself as nicely as she could because, after all, this was going to be a special occasion for her regarding her newfound fame and the announcements that would be made. It also reminded her of the Woldingham prom, but on this occasion, she was the partner of the eligible William. However, as she looked at herself in the mirror, with her hair professionally styled by a hairdresser, her evening gown complemented by slender, long white satin gloves, and her makeup carefully applied, thoughts of Amelia flooded her mind. Felicity wished Amelia were present tonight to see the woman she had matured into. Then her thoughts started remembering their night of passionate but soft kissing after the prom, and Felicity's mind started questioning that desire. "Stop that. You were just barely a woman. You cannot have feelings for another woman." As much as she tried to tell herself to forget about that night with Amelia, the more she wanted to return to it. "Why tonight, of all nights?" She shook her head to remove the thoughts from her head, but they were embedded in her memory.

The UAS Graduation Ball was held in The Hall of St John's College. It was only a seven-minute walk from Corpus Christi. However, William had insisted he would drive Felicity to the venue because his father had purchased him a new vehicle as a gift for successfully graduating from Cambridge and for being accepted into officer training at RAF Cranwell in Lincolnshire. William had arranged to collect Felicity at 6:00 p.m., even though the ball did not officially commence until 6:30 p.m. William, being William, wanted to show off his new car to Felicity (and, for that matter, anybody walking the streets of Cambridge) by taking her for a drive. William was already parked (illegally) on Trumpington Street when Felicity walked out of the arched entranceway of New Court, the building's centuries-old carved sandstone columns forming two turrets and the arched glass windows encased in their own carved sandstone arches that appeared at different levels above the central arch, adding to the elegance of Felicity's presentation. Even William was surprised. "My goodness, where have you been hiding all these years?" Felicity smiled. "So, what does a woman have to do? Dress up to be interesting for you." William shook his head. "No, it's just that for once, you don't look like..." William stopped short of finishing his sentence. He didn't need to bother because Felicity finished it for him. "A boy, William? I can read you like a book, so you might as well finish your sentences."

For once, William was gallant around Felicity, and he opened the car door to his sparkling E-type Jaguar. "Nice car. Is your father buying me one as a reward for helping you graduate over the past three years?" William scoffed with a mocking laugh as Felicity sat in the passenger's seat. He raced around to the driver's seat to move the car as the driver of an approaching small lorry started honking its horn to warn William he was blocking the carriageway. William retrieved a cigarette from his jacket pocket and drove off at a great rate of knots. He turned to Felicity. "Hold the wheel for a second; I just need to light this up." Felicity had no choice; she had to grab the steering wheel while William quickly lit his cigarette with his sterling silver lighter. Then he took back over the steering wheel. "William, you know how to show a girl a good time, don't you? Blowing that stinking smoke in every direction!" He looked at Felicity out of the corner of his eye as he simultaneously inhaled his cigarette between his lips and spoke. "What is the matter with you? You have never complained in the past about my smoking." Felicity hoped William might display some manners for once, but she gave up on that. "Don't worry about it. So, how long do we have to drive around in your toy?" Pride comes before the fall. "As long as I wish to drive around. You're the star cadet now, so take it all in, as people will notice you in my car." If she hadn't found William cute looking, Felicity would have asked him to let her out now; however, she found William physically attractive, and tonight he satisfied her self-esteem.

Eventually, after approximately twenty minutes of sheer vanity, William pulled into a parking bay on St John's Street across the other side of the street from St John's College and The Hall. It appeared to Felicity that it was only a temporary parking bay for passengers to drop off or pick up. "Are you sure you can park here, William?" His egotism and arrogance were on full display after that unnecessary car ride. "Of course, I can park here. What are they going to do? Do you believe they will tow away an E-Type Jaguar in this precinct of Cambridge? Don't concern yourself about these matters." Felicity rolled her eyes.

However, then William displayed some unexpected gallantry by approaching the passenger door and opening it for Felicity, offering his right hand to take hers to assist her in alighting from the sleek, low-set sports car. "Thank you, William. That is the most admirable act you have ever performed for me." He smiled, admiring her slender body as she gracefully exited the car. "Well, I could not let the world see such an attractive woman getting out of my chariot alone, could I?" His rhetorical response was flattering, and whatever thoughts about Amelia may have been lingering in the back of Felicity's mind were swept away by a smooth side of William's nature Felicity had never experienced before.

William fastened the top button on his dinner jacket, then placed his left arm on his side, which was out of etiquette for Felicity to hold onto. He walked her across St John's Street and through the magnificent centuries-old carved sandstone 'Great Gate' arched entranceway to St John's College, a testament to a time when stone masonry represented all that was grand of English society. From across the other side of the well-maintained lawn courtyard, Felicity caught the eye of Joan, waiting out front of the entrance to The Hall with her husband, Stuart de Montesquieu. Felicity had not formally met Stuart before, as Joan typically maintained a distance between her personal life and campus life at the university. Joan's eyes narrowed when she saw William, but they quickly changed to delight as Felicity became her sole focus as she and William walked closer to the entranceway. "Felicity! Don't you look stunning tonight?" Another compliment. For once, Felicity felt like a lady. "Thank you, Flying Officer." Joan turned to Stuart. "Stuart, this is Felicity Bennet, our hero of the Cambridge UAS. Felicity, this is my husband, Professor Stuart de Montesquieu." Stuart extended his right hand to take Felicity's right hand by the tips of her fingers, and to her surprise, he bowed and kissed her gloved hand before restoring himself to his upright stance that only many generations of nobility could hold with such elegant poise. "Joan is far too formal. Please, call me Stuart."

Stuart then looked at Joan and quickly glanced to signal her to focus on William. "Oh, yes. This is William de Veres, one of our graduating UAS cadets. William, this is my husband, Prof..." Joan checked her introduction. "Since formalities are not required, this is my husband, Stuart de Montesquieu." To Joan's and Felicity's surprise, Stuart extended his right hand to shake William's, accompanied by an air of familiarity. "You're Richard's eldest lad, aren't you? How is that old fox?" Fox? This was news to Joan. "Is there a connection here I don't know about, Stuart?" He turned to smile at his wife. "My father and Baron de Veres are old Trinity College students and members of the victorious First-Eight of The Boat Race of 1921. He was called Foxy by the other team members because he always seemed to win the hearts of the lady admirers, and he didn't marry until he was in his late thirties. I have had the pleasure of meeting Lord Richard several times over the years. You never told me Foxy's boy was a member of the UAS, Joan."

Stuart was oblivious to the family dynamics regarding the Attlee Government, which promoted Thomas over Lord Richard within the RAF hierarchy. "Well, you are not involved in the day-to-day operations of the UAS, darling, and I never knew there was some previous Cambridge connection between your father and William's father." The tension in the air could have been cut with a knife, so Stuart decided it was best to move on from the subject. "Anyway, you pair make your way inside. They're seated at table number one, aren't they, Joan?" Joan nodded. "Very well then, head on inside, as several UAS graduates are already inside with their partners for the evening." Stuart's elegant sweep of his right hand ushered Felicity and William in through the entrance of The Hall. When they entered, he turned to his wife. "What was that tension about? I felt like you were staring darts at Foxy's son." Joan shook the question off with a brief response. "Let me just say my father does not see eye to eye with old Foxy; however, that is a discussion for another time." Stuart now understood why Joan had previously controlled the compilation of the guest list for their wedding.

When they entered The Hall, Felicity was enraptured with the splendour of the reception room. It was built in the sixteenth century and featured fine old linen-fold panelling and a ceiling consisting of beautifully carved wood archways. At the far end of the room, where almost the entire wall consisted of fine linen-fold panelling, there was, in the middle of the wall, an oil portrait of Lady Margaret Beaufort. The portrait appealed to Felicity's sense of emerging womanhood. In front of that back wall, a makeshift podium with a lectern and microphone was set up. The grandeur of the room took Felicity's breath away. William detected Felicity's awestruck demeanour, and he leaned close to her right ear to whisper. "This is nothing. You should see my family manor." Felicity revealed her origins. "I am sorry. It's just that I have never seen such a magnificent room like this one before." William's slight smile was more condescending than understanding. "As I said, this is nothing."

The room had been arranged in two rows of ten rectangular tables, with ten people able to sit at each table comfortably. Each table was covered in a fine linen tablecloth, and each seating arrangement was set out with exquisitely crafted silver cutlery for a three-course meal, along with delicate crystal glasses for water and wine. Very soon, the room was filled with UAS graduates from the numerous universities at which the UAS was established, several RAF dignitaries, including Thomas, and finally, some Fleet Street journalists to whom the RAF had extended an invitation, as a special announcement would be made during the formal ceremony of the night. Behind the very last row of tables, there was enough space left for the graduates to dance after the formal ceremony, and the RAF had provided a quartet of serving musicians to play dinner music and then dance music.

The meals of the UAS Graduation Ball were served within fifteen minutes of the last guests taking a seat, and approximately an hour and a half later, as the dessert was being served, Joan took to the podium as the senior officer on campus to introduce none other than her father to make the formal speech. Thomas made his way up to the podium, wine glass and all, to a round of applause from the graduates and guests. Thomas retrieved a set of prepared notes from his pocket as he stood at the lectern. He then observed the guests in the room, took in deep breath, and began his speech. "It is not often at events such as these that I am introduced to the room by my daughter, for whom I have the utmost pride in her service to the WRAF, the UAS and Cambridge University. Indeed, one day, I shall be bowing and scraping to her. On behalf of the RAF, I welcome everyone here tonight for this special occasion, for which we celebrate the cadets' graduation from their UAS service at many of our esteemed universities. First, would you all be upstanding as we pay homage to Her Majesty, the Queen?"

Everyone in the room stood up. Thomas held up his wine glass. "God save the Queen!" The cacophony that followed as the entire room said the exact words was amplified by the high ceilings, which seemed to instil a richer tone to acknowledge the monarchy. "Please be seated, ladies and gentlemen. You will have to endure my words for a few further moments." A murmur of laughter went around the room. "I wish to acknowledge all the officers of the RAF and WRAF attending here tonight who dedicate their time to the critical functions of the UAS, which ensures each cadet is skilfully trained, should they wish to continue their service to their country when they have graduated. In that regard, I congratulate the many fine cadets tonight who have successfully applied to be trained as RAF and WRAF officers at Cranwell. Would those successful applicants be upstanding?" Approximately twenty UAS cadets stood up, including William. "Please give them a haughty round of applause."

Once again, the cacophony of the clapping caused by The Hall's tall ceilings seemed to amplify the noise. "Well done to each of you. Your country is thankful for your ongoing service. Please take a seat." Obediently, all of the successful cadets sat down immediately. "Now, there is one special announcement I wish to make regarding one of your many fine cadet colleagues attending here tonight. As you know, we had a little incident here at Cambridge several weeks ago that attracted a fair amount of media attention after it occurred." At that instant, it felt to Felicity like every eye in the room was focused on her now. "Indeed, it was more than just a little incident; it was one of the most brilliant displays of aeronautical skill that turned an inevitable disaster into a celebrated miracle of survival. Still, the word 'miracle' is unkind because this cadet displayed exemplary skill as a pilot, courage that many others would not. Finally, this cadet displayed a calm temperament and composure during a perilous moment, which elevated her to a level of skill surpassing that of many trained officers. Cadet Bennet, please be upstanding."

As Felicity stood up, she knew Thomas' following words would send the room into a spin. "Cadet Bennet, your skills in safely bringing the Hawker to a landing not only saved your life but also the life of Viscount Godwin. In consultation with senior members of the RAF and WRAF, the Minister for Defence and the Prime Minister, Her Majesty the Queen, has agreed that commencing tomorrow, you shall receive a commission as an officer of the WRAF in the rank of a Flying Officer." A gasp of astonishment and a murmur of softly spoken words made their way around the room. "Please, honoured guests, there is more to be said. In addition to her elevation to the rank of Flying Officer, Cadet Bennet will also be deployed to McGuire Air Base in the United States of America in the coming weeks, where she will perform her officer service as part of the armed services exchange programme the United Kingdom has entered into with our allies and, yes, there is more, while performing her service at McGuire Air Base, Cadet Bennet will commence her post-graduate studies at Princeton University, and while studying at that institution she will be working with personnel from NASA, assisting them with the United States space programme. So, given her exemplary service to the UAS, her courage and skill, and her immediate appointment to be an officer serving in our vital exchange programme, I would kindly ask all of you to be upstanding as we celebrate this marvellous cadet's achievements." The room rose to their feet, and Thomas led them in three rounds of boisterous cheer.

When the celebration concluded, Thomas ended the formal ceremony in the room. "Well, once again, thank you, cadets, and please, everyone, enjoy your dessert; the RAF band's music shall now play, and you are all welcome to get up on the floor and dance. Thank you." The room applauded Thomas, and the band began playing waltzing music as the waiters served dessert. When Felicity sat down, she immediately noticed William was smiling, and it was the same smile Amelia had displayed that night in Felicity's boarding room many years beforehand. The similarity was uncanny and also slightly unnerving for Felicity. "What are you smiling about?" William leaned over towards her to speak in her ear and be heard. "Well, not only do you look ravishing tonight, you're also quite the superstar." Ravishing? 'Is William telling me he likes me?' she thought, as she politely smiled back, but before she could speak, the invited Fleet Street journalists assembled around Felicity, firing questions her way like the Spitfires fired bullets in the sky during World War II. William once again leaned over to whisper in her ear. "I am afraid I will have to leave you on your own with the press while I go and have a cigarette, but when I come back, I would be honoured if you would join me in a dance." Felicity's mind was buzzing with the thought that William liked her. However, she had to answer the journalists' questions.

William did come back and dance with Felicity. Indeed, he danced with her until the ball was over. Joan had already left with Stuart, and many UAS graduates had already departed or were in the process of doing so. William then took Felicity's hand in his. "Come with me. Let's go for a walk. It is a clear night sky, and then the moon is out, so I want to take you for a walk." William had been so charming since they arrived at the ball that she could not resist the offer to walk in the moonlight. "Of course. You lead the way." William did lead the way. Indeed, he walked Felicity out of St John's College as they talked and led her across Kitchen's Bridge, which led them to the opposite side of the River Cam. William continued walking Felicity along the River Cam's sparkling water until they came to a cosy bench seat under some trees in a secluded spot for that time of night. William assisted Felicity in sitting. He then sat beside her and looked into her eyes. "I wanted to come to this spot to talk because I wish to tell you something I did not want the others to hear." Felicity was intrigued. "What is it that you wanted to say?" William smiled, gently stroking Felicity's fringe with his left hand. "You are quite stunning tonight, and out here in the moonlight, your radiance is lighting up the world."

Felicity's heart started skipping; William was being sweet. "William, I don't know what to say." His left hand gently moved from Felicity's fringe to behind her right ear. "Don't say anything." William's left hand then moved behind Felicity's head, and he gently brought her head closer to his, and then his lips softly kissed hers. His lips felt just like Amelia's did so many years ago. This was the first time a male had kissed her. She pulled her head back several centimetres to make sure it wasn't a dream and that she was kissing Amelia. "Did I scare you?" She shook her head. "No." He then leaned in again to kiss her lips. Amelia's lips were gentler, but his lips were soft and inviting. Amelia's face seemed to appear in the form of William's face as Felicity softly kissed William's lips like she had kissed Amelia's. Her heart beat, and she felt like she had found a male version of Amelia.

Their closed-mouth kissing was mutually receptive for several minutes, and her eyes closed as she felt his lips meet the corner of hers. It was sweet and tender, and her heart now beat like it had at Woldingham many nights ago. However, his kiss then became more forceful, and his lips pressed harder against hers. She continued to kiss him, but Felicity no longer associated William's actions with those of Amelia's; she remained gentle all night long; he had been gentle for an ephemeral moment. Now, his lips parted, and his tongue forced its way into Felicity's mouth. Then his right hand slid down Felicity's left leg on the outside of her evening gown before his fingers found the hemline of her dress and began to forcibly lift her evening gown upwards to expose her stockings, which covered her legs whilst she now tried to pull her head away from his, but couldn't because his left hand was firmly cusped behind her head. She tried to speak through a tongue that was deeply embedded in her mouth. "No, William." His tongue and saliva muffled her words, and William's mouth firmly pressed against hers. His right hand had managed to lift her dress so that her thighs were now exposed. She began to struggle as his right slid up the inside of her right thigh. Then it happened – a violation like she had never experienced before. William's right fingers began tugging at her underwear to try to pull them down. Felicity continued to struggle, but William became more aggressive, and he tugged on her underwear and was now forcing his body onto hers. The final straw; she felt his fingertips brush near her groin, not far from her vulva. She pushed William backwards with all her might and broke free of his grip. Then instinctively, she punched him with her left hand in his upper right cheek, not far from his right eye.

William winced in immediate pain and grabbed his cheek. "You bitch! Why did you do that?" Why did she do that? Felicity was incensed. "Why did I do that? Why did you do what you just did?" He was still holding his upper right cheek and eye in pain. "Because I thought you wanted to try some noble blood in your Yeoman's mixture." He tried to force her to have sex, and now he was degrading her, an insult in addition to an injury. Felicity's anger overwhelmed her, and along with her distress, she then punched William with her right hand in the corner of his left nostril, causing him to fall sideways. Felicity stormed off in tears, pulling her overstretched underpants up as she hurriedly walked away. William's final words were most unedifying for her and were the final nails in her broken heart. "Where are you going, you dirty little slut. How dare you treat me like this!" The 'S' word. She knew where she was heading – Joan's house on campus. Twenty minutes beforehand, she had been this fine, shining figurine in the pale moonlight. Now Felicity was distraught and felt like a cheap, chipped porcelain doll being fobbed off at a thrift store.

CHAPTER 24

There was some distance for Felicity to travel between St John's Meadow and Millington Road; however, in her distressed state, Felicity had taken off her heeled shoes on the meadow and walked briskly, which then became a run, holding her dress up as the tears rolled down her cheeks. She felt betrayed and violated by William because she had dedicated substantial time to helping him graduate from university, despite his otherwise cavalier approach to his studies. He betrayed her because he believed he could use her for his gratification, whether she wished to participate willingly or not. Violated because he had come very close to touching her where no other person had touched her before; not even Amelia had tried to feel that region of Felicity's body that night at Woldingham.

It took her approximately fifteen minutes to run to Joan's house. Her stockings had been destroyed so that they had rolled up over her ankles. Joan's matrimonial home was a substantial two-story detached home on a quarter of an acre of established gardens. In the master bedroom, Joan and Stuart were enjoying a moment of intimacy after what had been a delightful social occasion for them. With their busy respective lives, it was a rare moment of intimacy. Still, it was certainly one that did not require them to rise at an early hour the following day. With Joan's academic career nearing its end in her post-graduate medical studies, she and her husband were now wishing to start a family. They were in the full throes of passion when suddenly the doorbell rang. Stuart initially froze. "What on Earth is that?" Joan did not care as she was too lost in the moment. "Who cares? Don't stop." Stuart started making love to her again, but after about two minutes, the doorbell rang, pressing twice this time. "Oh, blast it." Stuart rolled off Joan, whose body was covered in their combined sweat. As he put on his robe and slippers, Stuart expressed his disapproval. "There had better be a damn good reason why we are being disturbed at this time of night." He flicked on the lights as Joan sat upright in bed, naked and disturbed to be interrupted in such an intimate moment.

Felicity did not know that married couples might have been enjoying each other's company this time of the evening. Joan had previously provided her address to her on the understanding of 'Whenever you need to talk.' The front porch light turned on, followed by Stuart opening the door to see a distraught young woman in bare feet. His frustration was interwoven with surprise. "Felicity! What brings you here at this time of night? What happened to you? What is wrong?" His Gatling Gun delivery of questions elicited a meek and tearful response. "I am sorry to disturb you. Is Joan here, Stuart? It is urgent." Stuart could tell by the young woman's presentation that it was indeed a matter of utmost importance and urgency that had disturbed the moment of intimacy. "Of course, Felicity, come into the study, and I will go and get Joan. Come on, come in out of the cool night's air." Stuart showed Felicity to the study, a splendid room that contained fitted oak bookshelves and an assorted collection of bound books. "Take a seat on the chaise lounge here, and I shall go and get Joan." Felicity sat as Stuart quickly left the study to fetch his wife.

Joan had already commenced putting on her night gown, robe and slippers as Stuart entered their former den of intimacy. "Who is it?" Alarming words for Joan followed his concerned face. "It's Felicity. She appears quite distressed; her clothes are dishevelled, and her stockings are tattered. She wants to speak to you urgently. I have taken her into the study." Joan was indeed alarmed, as she was with William the last time she had seen Felicity. "Oh, cripes." She hurriedly put on her slippers and quickly left the bedroom to head downstairs. "Do you want me to come with you?" She turned her head back towards Stuart. "No, darling. Wait here for a moment. However, I might need you, so I will call out if I do."

Joan quickly made her way downstairs and entered the study, where, sure enough, Felicity was sitting on the chaise lounge, sobbing and presenting just as Stuart described her. "Felicity, what has happened?" Felicity bound off the chaise lounge into Joan's arms, crying as she spoke. "I am sorry to disturb you, Joan. It was horrible, it was ra..." She could not finish her words; however, Joan knew it was more than mere angst. "Come over here to the desk and take a seat. Do you want a glass of water? You look like you ran here." Through tear-filled eyes, Felicity nodded. Joan briefly disappeared from the study, and when she returned, she gave Felicity a glass of water in a cut crystal glass. Joan then sat in the fine timber and leather swivel office chair on the opposite side of her desk, and from a lower drawer, she retrieved her WRAF issue official notebook. "Tell me in your own words what happened. Here, take a tissue." Joan handed over a brass box, which contained tissues. Felicity took a moment to compose herself to speak, wiping her nose and mouth as she spoke. Joan held a fountain pen in her right hand, ready to make a formal notation of complaint. "After the ball, I went for a walk with William. He had been so charming for most of the evening, and he was being so sweet." She began to cry. Joan reached across the desk, and like a big sister, she comforted Felicity by holding her right forearm in her left hand while still holding the fountain pen in her right hand, which was finalising the initial notation. "It is all right, Felicity. You can tell me. What happened?" Felicity took another tissue from the brass box, wiped her eyes and nose, and continued. Joan's pen was synchronised to move with the first syllable. "He was being so charming, so I agreed to go for a walk. We walked across the bridge to St John's Meadow, which was so beautiful in the moonlight. We found a bench seat in a quiet area, and then William told me how nice I looked. He was being so sweet. He kissed me on the lips and..."

Once again, Felicity broke down into tears. Joan continued to comfort Felicity by holding her forearm with her left hand as she wrote down the version of events. "Come on, be brave. Tell me what happened next. I need to know everything, Felicity, including your thoughts and feelings." Be brave. Tell her everything. Alright then, everything. Felicity opened up her heart, mind and mouth without any barriers. She looked up to the ceiling to speak as though she was opening her soul to the heavens above. She felt Joan's hand release its grip on her forearm, signalling her to speak candidly. "So, he kissed me on the lips, and it was so soft and sweet, just like Amelia had kissed me at school. Indeed, Amelia has been on my mind ever since my old Woldingham friends visited me, before the Full Easter Term commenced, and that is why my room was strewn with magazines and newspapers, because Amelia is now famous. I love her with all my heart. Williams's kisses reminded me so much of my night with Amelia. I had never kissed a boy before, but I kissed him because he felt like Amelia. However, he wasn't like Amelia at all. He began to force his tongue into my mouth and held my head to his while he did so. Then he reached down with his right hand and pulled the bottom of my ball gown to reveal my stockings up to my underwear. It was all happening so quickly, and I tried to say no whilst he kissed me, but he was overwhelming me physically. Then he started to pull my underwear down, and his hand touched my groin, not far from my private area. Amelia never did that to me. She was so gentle and loving. William was being rough, and it was obvious he was trying to force me to make love to him out in the open on a bench seat. When his hand came so close to my private part, I struggled free, and I punched him near his right eye. He insulted me again, so I punched him with my hand near his nose. I might have hit his nose. I began to walk away to come here, and William levelled another insult at me by calling me a slut. I was distraught and had nowhere else to go but here."

With those words being spoken, Felicity's eyes descended from the ceiling to look at Joan, and to her surprise, Joan was sitting in her seat with her arms crossed. It appeared she had stopped making notes quite early during Felicity's recital of the facts, as the open notepad contained fewer words than Felicity had spoken. "What is it, Joan? Don't you believe me?" Joan shook her head. "No, Felicity. I believe you. Still, I cannot comprehend what you have just told me." Felicity detected a disapproving tone in Joan's voice. "What do you mean by comprehend? William was trying to force me to have sex with him. That is unlawful, Joan. Why are you looking at me like that?" Indeed, Joan's facial expression conveyed disapproval of Felicity, or so it seemed. Joan looked towards the bookcase to her left, then refocused on Felicity, and her eyes narrowed. "Homosexuals and lesbians are not allowed to serve in Her Majesty's forces. Indeed, it is an offence against military law, and the consequences are dishonourable discharges. Are you a lesbian, Felicity?" She could not believe what Joan was telling her, nor could she understand her inquiry. Felicity had just described an attempted rape, but it appeared she was being accused of committing a military offence. "What do you mean, Joan? William tried to rape me. That is the offence, isn't it?" Joan's gaze remained fixed on Felicity. "Maybe he was trying to. However, from the details you just told me, it appears that you have admitted to an offence under armed services law. So, I am going to ask you again, Felicity, and in doing so, I bear in mind that many people, including my father and me, could be caught in an unnecessary scandal, and your skyrocketing career could come to an abrupt end. Now, look me square in the eyes, and answer my question. Are you a lesbian, Felicity?"

Felicity was mortified. She did not want to make love to every woman. Her thoughts were scrambled, confused and drowning in the fear of an inquisition. 'The only woman I have feelings for is Amelia, but that doesn't mean I'm a lesbian, does it?' Joan's left pointer finger began to tap on her right forearm. "Please answer my question, Felicity." At that moment, Felicity realised her life could head in only two directions. Say yes, and her career was over, but she might still be able to cross those stars in her heart to be with Amelia again. Say no; her future was safe, but her love was unrequited. She shrewdly, and with the voices of protest in her head ringing out loud, chose the latter. She shook her head. "No. Joan. I am not a lesbian. I must have been lost in stupid tabloid magazine insanity." Joan stared at Felicity for an eternity, then sat forward and spoke to her. "Fine, then. I will not make an official report about this and pretend that this conversation never happened. However, listen to me carefully. Suppose you want to be accepted into NASA. In that case, you are going to have to marry a nice 'All-American' man, and any hint of sexual impropriety on your behalf will be the end of your career as far as the Americans are concerned. So, I will write all this 'Amelia business' off to a bit of champagne and a young prat to whom some vicarious consequences are coming his way via my father. You have my support, Felicity, but I cannot dishonour my oath as an officer, and neither can you. So, your answer denying a lesbian inclination is enough for me. Now, wait here, and I will put on some clothes to drive you back to Corpus Christi."

Joan walked back upstairs to her bedroom, where Stuart was reading on the bed. Given her facial expression, he realised any chance to return to a moment of intimacy might be unrealistic. "Is the young woman alright, dear?" Joan shook her head. "No. However, the situation is resolved. I am going to drop her off at Corpus Christi." Joan detected the disappointment on her husband's face. "Do not worry, Romeo. We both have a free day tomorrow. So, we can revisit making the next generation of de Montesquieu's in the morning." Joan quickly changed from her night clothes into a casual summer dress and flat-heeled shoes. She then left the bedroom, but not before kissing a slightly disappointed Stuart on the lips with the promise: 'Tomorrow morning'.

Hardly a word was spoken on the drive back to Corpus Christi. Still, Felicity was disturbed that she was almost raped, but she seemed to be the villain. However, Joan's words were prescient about life as she knew it. It was far worse to declare her feelings from her heart, and to fulfil her dreams, she would have to marry an American man, even if she did not love him. When they arrived at the entranceway to Corpus Christi on Trumpington Road, Joan finally decided to speak about an issue that had been on her mind after Felicity's revelation. "When your father spoke to me alone on your first day of university, he told me that you had told him that you had your heart broken or, words to that effect, by a boy. However, I now realise that you had your heart broken not by some boy but by Amelia." Felicity's ashen face clearly expressed her embarrassment and fear. "Do not worry, Felicity. What you just told me remains between you and me. Now, it is none of my business to tell you to stop if I have transgressed into an area of your life that you do not wish to discuss with me; however, may I suggest that you never reveal to your father what you revealed to me. He idolises you, Felicity. I understand the hormonal influences of your teenage years, as I am a woman, but your father's generation of men probably does not. It also seems his litigation involved resentment about a young man's behaviour, which your story reveals never occurred. So, don't ever tell him. Do you understand me?" Felicity nodded. "Yes, Joan. And thank you for not reporting me." Joan shook her head. "You don't have to thank me, Felicity, and I was also serious back at my house. William will surreptitiously get his comeuppance at Cranwell." Joan's smile was undercoated with wickedness that suggested she would surreptitiously make William's days at Cranwell a living hell.

Two days later, Felicity affirmed her oath of allegiance to Her Majesty the Queen, thereby becoming the youngest female Flying Officer in the history of the WRAF. William's attempted rape was playing on her mind as she took the oath, when this day should have otherwise been one for Felicity to savour.

CHAPTER 25

Shortly thereafter, the Full Easter Term concluded and life as Felicity knew it at Cambridge University came to its regrettable ending. She had learnt so much at Cambridge, but in particular, she had learnt immense lessons about life and womanhood. Regarding the latter, she had to climb the mountain because she was a female. The preferential treatment given to a male scholar from Oxford by Cambridge's mathematics and science courses had enlivened her mind to the discrimination; having to cover up an attempted rape sheeted home the reality of her existence in a patriarchal world. William did not show his bruised face around Cambridge in those few remaining days; the bruising was an ephemeral injury, but the damage to his pride was an indelible imprint on his mind, an imprint that would stew into a lifetime of animosity.

Felicity returned to her home for two weeks with her father before she departed for America. Grandpa's mind was declining quickly since Catherine had passed, and Samuel now engaged the full-time services of a carer for his father as his flourishing agricultural business around the county often saw him spending nights in the dwellings of other farms he had purchased. Still, these were two weeks he had devoted to spending as much time as possible with Felicity because soon she would be flying to America at the behest of the Defence Ministry. They would talk about general matters: how it was unfair for Cambridge to select the Oxford male student over her so that she assumed the position of being an underling in the post-graduate course; the following stages of Samuel's agricultural plans, which included a business model he had studied at Oxford many years beforehand regarding vertically integrating an agricultural undertaking that Samuel envisaged him now expanding into the secondary production of abattoirs; Felicity's studies at Princeton University, which she understood would include a new experiment into the world of sensory deprivation. Felicity quickly dismissed the Graduation Ball as a dull stepping stone to the next stage of her life.

The day before Samuel would have to drive Felicity to Heathrow Airport for her departure to America, he asked her to sit down with him under an old oak tree in the field on their centuries-old farm, which he now devoted to fattening either cattle or sheep before they were transported to an abattoir. It was a warm summer's day, and the tree's shade provided a tranquil and private environment for him to talk frankly. "It sure is warm today, isn't it?" Felicity nodded. Samuel briefly gazed upon the infant who had quickly grown into a woman, and he decided to reveal to Felicity a personal endeavour he had been following since she was a baby. "Ever since you were little, I have spoken to your mother up above in the heavens each night that I have something on my mind about you. I never told you that before, did I?" Felicity shook her head. "I have been speaking to her about you quite often lately." Samuel gazed into the distant horizon of undulating agricultural fields of varying colours. "She does not come down from the sky and appear before me as an apparition of her once physical being. However, I feel her whenever I question myself as a father." Felicity interrupted him. "You have always been a wonderful father, Dad." Samuel smiled. Still, his eyes slightly glazed over as he responded. "No, Felicity. I have not been. I should have been stronger around my mother from the moment she started chastising you, from the moment she commenced belittling you, from the moment she tried to destroy your dreams. I apologise for failing to protect you from my Mum's vicious streak." Felicity cuddled into her father's left arm. "You're not to blame, Dad. You were a single parent trying to run a farm. Grandma and Grandpa were all you had in life to assist you."

Samuel cuddled his daughter tightly with his left arm. "You're not emotionally affected by my mother's treatment?" Felicity lied by shaking her head, but she did not want her father to be blamed. Her grandmother had a profound impact on her mind in many ways, including her self-esteem and self-image. Samuel closed his eyes and was relieved by Felicity's response. "Your late mum was a tougher soul than me; my mother tried to start chastising her not long after we were married, and in her stoic Irish manner, she very quickly let your grandmother know it would be unwise for her ever to try that again. I see a lot of your mother's spirit in you, Felicity, particularly as you have matured into a young woman." They both smiled at one another, but there was a further matter he wished to air at this time of soul searching. "When you told me the news about the RAF or WRAF – honestly, I cannot understand why they still differentiate between the sexes." Felicity was pleasantly surprised to hear her father's growing discontent with the discrimination. "In any event, when you told me the news about your sudden elevation to an officer's rank to be deployed to America, I panicked."

Samuel noticed his daughter's confused expression, prompting him to clarify or refine his feelings. "Panicked is not the correct word. I was both elated and concerned. Does that make sense to you, Felicity?" She shook her head. "Well, obviously, I was elated about the opportunities that have come your way. However, I was concerned because what you are embarking upon is a world of deceit, power play and trepidation. It's a world where Americans and Soviets live in a polarised cone of hypervigilant anxiety about the progress of their perceived antagonist. Goodness knows the newspaper reports consistently describe a world of spying and mistrust, I thought we had put behind us the moment Berlin fell in 1945. I worry about you. My daughter is getting caught up in that world with this armed services exchange alliance we have entered into with the Americans; so, several nights ago, I could not sleep, and I went for a nighttime walk down to the front gate, looking up to the clouded heavens and asking your mother for guidance like I always have when I questioned myself as a father. My heart, or as I like to think, the spirit of your mum, told me to let you live your life and go, even if it breaks my heart for there to be an ocean between us."

Felicity threw her arms around her father's chest and held him tightly. "I will miss you, too, Dad. However, there might be an ocean between us, but the sky above us truncates that degree of separation." They held each other tightly in a display of love that a father and daughter would soon infrequently share.

Felicity then looked away into the fields for a moment, and it was obvious to Samuel she had something on her mind. "What is up, my little darling? You have that look in your eye as though the Luftwaffe are approaching." Felicity continued staring at the horizon for about two minutes. She wanted to tell her father everything: the attempted sexual assault by William, her concern about her lack of breast development; it was Amelia who had broken her heart at Woldingham. She wanted to open her heart and mind to her father, but Felicity could not, mainly because she had to suppress her desire and feelings for another woman. A door opened in Felicity's heart in those two minutes, only for her to shut it again. "You have nothing to worry about, Dad. I am not oblivious to the world we live in, nor am I oblivious to the peril of this baffling 'Cold War' we have entered into. I can assure you that I am fit enough to look after myself in a dangerous situation. Indeed, heaven help any person who would try to hurt me."

At that moment, she wondered what colour the bruising was on William's face; probably yellow, in keeping with his nature.

A slight breeze blew across the fields as the world continued its perpetual rotation into its bulging oceans. Felicity half turned her head towards Samuel, and there was a discernible steely glint in her eye that he had not seen before. "I want you to know that I realise this is a man's world, and I will change that when I chase my dreams. Men may think they're stronger; however, we women are tougher." The invincible spirit of Felicity's words seemed to be collected by that breeze, to perhaps be carried across the waters to what was once described as the 'New World'.

"New Worlds Discovered"

CHAPTER 26

The tale told on paper seldom reveals the truth about thy future,
Dreams being carved up, indeed diced, like meat before a butcher!

Felicity had thought the UAS was a disciplined and committed undertaking. However, life at McGuire was an enlightening revelation of not only the actual British Armed Service discipline but also the remarkable commitment displayed by American Armed Service personnel, including what should have been the liberating experience of service in the sky. Yes, the British were committed to their protocols, obsequious observance of rank and attention to detail; however, the Americans displayed not only the extreme of military protocols but also a style of boisterous command communications that could drown out a foghorn.

It had been a long, hot summer on the East Coast of the United States in July and August of 1961. When Felicity arrived on the East Coast in late August 1961, that heatwave had not abated, and the weather conditions seemed to match the disposition of the people she encountered on the base.

Her direct RAF commanding officer was Squadron Leader Reginald Stonehouse, whose actual wartime experience had caused him some mental duress. Still, he was a person who displayed extreme intelligence and training. When she arrived at McGuire Air Base, Felicity's first service detail was reporting to Stonehouse. His office and, for that matter, as she was soon to discover, her office were located in the same building at the base as the American Air Force personnel. However, there was a clear demarcation between the two countries' occupation of that building. The RAF was located in the left corridor, leading to the staffed reception of the building, while the Americans were in the right corridor, in more spacious offices. Felicity informed the young American Airman operating the reception desk who she was and that she was reporting to Squadron Leader Stonehouse. The young Airman saluted her, a gesture which had been absent when she first entered the reception, undoubtedly missing in action because she was a woman. The Airman dialled three numbers on the reception telephone and informed the person answering the call that Flying

Officer Bennet had arrived to report to Squadron Officer Stonehouse. He received his response instructions and promptly ended the call. "Sir." Felicity immediately interrupted him, "Where I come from, we are addressed as Ma'am." The young Airman was embarrassed. "Yes, Ma'am. Proceed down the corridor to my left, and open the door when you reach the end. That is where the RAF officer contingent serves on this base." Felicity nodded, and then she proceeded down the hallway.

Felicity followed the instructions the Airman had given her. As she walked down the long, dimly lit corridor, Felicity began to feel exhilarated by the thought that her dream of flying into space was within her reach. Or so she thought. She opened the door at the end of the corridor, and it was like she had walked through the other side of the wardrobe to re-enter the United Kingdom. Whereas she observed a high level of anxiety among the American Air Force service members from the moment she set foot on McGuire Air Base, the same orderly, calm, and dignified atmosphere of her home country pervaded the RAF offices at the base in the UK. There was also a marked difference between the RAF and UAS offices at Cambridge. It was still fresh in her memory. The UAS office was situated within a cottage, which created a homely atmosphere. In contrast, the RAF office at McGuire was formal and serious, lacking familiarity with the UAS headquarters' home environment in Cambridge. Still, the British approach to life within the RAF offices at McGuire was a welcome atmosphere.

Felicity approached the communications desk staffed by a male Warrant Officer, who appeared older than Felicity. There were several female faces among the open-plan office, and those women were busily typing correspondence, memoranda, or other official documents at modern desks. The fine, classical wooden furniture in the UAS office was also a readily observable difference in the office's environment. These women were not wearing uniforms, which Felicity inferred meant they were likely local American women performing administrative duties as civilians. Each of these women contemporaneously looked at the unique sight of a woman dressed in an officer's uniform entering the RAF office. The sight of a uniformed female RAF officer was foreign to them. A small wooden plaque on the desk identified it as belonging to Warrant Officer Smith, who was on duty. The Warrant Officer shot to his feet and saluted Felicity immediately upon recognising the insignia on the coat of her uniform. "Ma'am." Felicity returned the salute. "As you were, Warrant Officer Smith. I am Flying Officer Bennet, reporting in for duty to Squadron Leader Stonehouse."

By now, the Warrant Officer had retaken his seat. He dialled a three-digit number. "Sir, Flying Officer Bennet has arrived to report for duties." There was a momentary delay, and then the Warrant Officer responded. "Yes, sir." He placed the receiver back down again. "Squadron Leader Stonehouse is just finalising some official paperwork for the Americans, Ma'am. Please sit in the waiting area, and he will see you in approximately five minutes." Warrant Officer Smith's outstretched right hand pointed towards a rudimentary waiting area to his left, in which six cheaply made modern chairs surrounded a similar cheaply made coffee table, upon which a small terracotta pot containing a cactus sat as an afterthought of decoration. A portrait of Her Majesty was hung on the far wall of this area. Otherwise, like the rest of the open-plan area of the RAF administrative centre, it was a very clinical presentation, much like the foyer of the headquarters at McGuire. 'Thank goodness for the English disposition,' Felicity thought to herself as she absorbed the bland presentation of the RAF offices.

Approximately five minutes after she had taken a seat, a door to a closed office opened, and a handsome man in his forties walked out. It was immediately apparent from his insignia that this was Squadron Leader Stonehouse. Notwithstanding his looks, it was immediately evident to Felicity that he was a pleasant but serious man, undoubtedly a product of years of RAF service, perhaps even combat service. She rose from the chair and saluted. "Sir. Flying Officer Felicity Bennet, reporting in for service." The Squadron Leader returned the salute. "At ease, Flying Officer. Welcome to McGuire Air Base." His pleasant nature engendered a similar response from Felicity: "Thank you, Sir." The Squadron Leader then turned on his heels and ushered with his right hand towards his office. "Please, Flying Officer. Come into my office to discuss some matters before I show you around the office." His hand remained outstretched, indicating that he expected a woman to enter his office first – a gentlemanly gesture.

Felicity entered the Squadron Leader's office, and he promptly followed her into the room, closing the door behind him as he entered. "Please. Felicity, isn't it?" She nodded. "Please, Felicity, take a seat." His informality surprised her as his presentation outside of the office was different. "Thank you, Sir." As she sat, he shook his head and walked around to his side of the desk. "When we are out of sight and earshot around here, please call me Reg. Like you, I am away from home, and you will soon find out the only way to endure the pugnacious Americans is to be serious in public, but then for us RAF officers to be relaxed behind closed doors." Reg did not discriminate by referring to her as WRAF, which was another pleasant surprise. "Thank you, Reg." There was an uncomfortable silence as Reg and Felicity looked at each other, waiting for the other to speak. Reg broke the ice. "Well, I see from the communications sent to me from RAF Headquarters back home and, of course, from the newspaper reports that you are quite the hero. Tell me, did you panic at any stage when it was apparent the Hawker's engine could not be restarted?"

Felicity had not troubled her mind too much about her initial reactions since that famous day. The press and other people's inquiries focused on how she managed to land the aeroplane safely and efficiently. She shrugged her shoulders. "Oh, perhaps for a fraction of a second, when I realised the old dinosaur was extinct. However, I had been trained by my father and his RAF instructor, and having flown that aeroplane and route so many times, my mind immediately switched to emergency landing mode." Reg nodded. "Outstanding. You mentioned that your father was trained for the RAF. Did he serve during the Second World War?" Felicity nodded. "Yes, he did, initially. He was a Pilot Officer flying Hurricanes at the start of the War, but then he received a compassionate discharge after my mother was killed during the early stages of the Blitz." Reg held up his hands to acknowledge his regret for opening the traumatic pages of her history. "I am sorry to hear that news. My apologies, Felicity, if I opened any old wounds." She immediately dismissed the thought of his transgressing into areas of her life he perhaps shouldn't have. "Don't be silly, Reg. It was a long time ago. I was a baby. It was the War." Felicity then quickly changed the subject. "Did you see active service during the War?" Reg nodded. "Yes, but not until close to the end of the War, when it wasn't a fair fight for the Jerries in the air. I was a young pilot officer with Bomber Command, and much to my regret, our incendiary missions were nothing short of bloody-minded intent to seek revenge for the Blitz." She had heard her father mention this fact when she was younger, but she did not say anything, as it was evident Reg's incendiary missions towards the end of World War II still played on his mind.

Reg then focused on the business at hand. "Right, well, we had better discuss what your duties will entail while you are deployed here, shall we?" Felicity nodded. "As you are aware, Felicity, our purpose here at McGuire is to acquire skills and knowledge from the United States Air Force and share our skills and experience with them. It's a minor matter, but when drafting documentation, refer to the American Air Force as the USAF for clarity." Minor detail noted. "Because of the escalation of the Cold War, the Americans have developed a supersonic jet interceptor named the Delta Dagger. Have you heard about that jet fighter?" Of course, she had. Felicity nodded. "Very well then, I don't need to descend into minutiae about that fighter. We, the RAF, are considering various options that the American Government is making available to us to purchase the jet fighters they produce. Here at McGuire, we are examining the utility of the Delta Dagger. We also have several Avro-Vulcan pilots gearing up to participate in a joint national air defence exercise with the USAF in October; however, we, RAF personnel here at McGuire, are not. There is also a dual purpose to our attachment here at McGuire concerning RAF Fighter Command's assignment to the North Atlantic Treaty Organisation. You are aware of NATO, aren't you?" Of course. Felicity impatiently nodded, wanting to know precisely what she would be doing at McGuire. "So much of our work here is observation, instructional and reporting. Do you understand that?" Felicity did, but she needed to clarify one issue. "Sir." Reg held up his right hand and slightly shook his head to remind Felicity that, in the confines of the privacy of his office, she did not need to address him in that manner formally. "Sorry. Reg, does the observation mean I will be trained to fly the Delta Dagger?"

It was a genuine question, but Reg almost choked on his glass of water. "You? Fly? Felicity, notwithstanding your exploits in England, it was difficult enough for us to convince the Americans we were serious about including a woman as part of our outfit here. Only highly experienced RAF pilots get an opportunity to fly the Delta Dagger, and I am talking about RAF pilots with at least five years of pilot experience. There will be opportunities for you to train in the American O-1 Bird Dogs over the next twelve months, but I emphasise the word 'some.'" Her petulance got the better of her. "The O-1 Bird Dog is a slow, propeller-driven aeroplane made by Cessna. I learnt how to fly in a Cessna years ago, as my father owns one. I thought Her Majesty wanted to see women advancing in opportunities open to them by the RAF." Reg leaned forward on his desk and raised his right pointer finger. "I know why you are here, Felicity. However, the USAF call the shots about who is eligible to fly in their state-of-the-art jet fighters, and a woman famous for avoiding a catastrophe in a Hawker is not at the top of their eligibility list." Felicity took a deep breath to calm her emotions, and once she had cooled her passions, she nodded. Reg concluded the briefing about her duties by changing the subject to the positive attributes of her deployment. "In any event, your time here will be regularly interrupted by the requirements of your post-graduate studies at Princeton University, and, as I understand my briefing note, you are going to work with NASA as well at that university, so you are right in the thick of some historical events taking place here in the United States." Felicity nodded to acknowledge that opportunity, but was still disappointed to receive the news about her lack of opportunity to fly a jet aircraft.

Reg then stood up as he spoke. "Good. Now that we have covered your duties at McGuire, let me show you your office." He ushered Felicity out of his office and walked across to the other administrative side, where there was an office with a plaque named 'F/O Bennet'. Reg flicked the light switch on the wall outside Felicity's office, then opened the door. Felicity did not need to enter the office to see that she had been allocated an office none of the male officers wanted – it was an artificial light dystopia with no windows. "Come on in, Flying Officer." The artificial tones of excitement strained Reg's voice as Felicity entered her office. There was a gunmetal grey desk, the 'Metal Tanker Desk,' featuring an artificial wood light brown desktop and a slightly worn Beefy Steelcase Banker desk chair for her to sit on. On the opposite side of the desk were two nondescript wooden office chairs. In one corner of the office stood a tall, four-drawer gunmetal grey filing cabinet with a combination lock on the top drawer for security. In the opposite corner stood a wooden office bookcase, made before World War II, that was almost overflowing with RAF and USAF manuals on various topics. The clutter of the bookcase suggested the office had been used as a storage room before word had filtered through that Felicity was being deployed to McGuire. On the front wall of her office, an electrically operated clock was placed in the middle to remind the occupant of time ticking away on their life.

To complete the dystopian office presentation, a black Bakelite telephone was placed in the top right corner of the desk. Reg conveyed a final bit of news, hoping it might change Felicity's apparent lack of interest in her office. "You can use the telephone to make one personal call back to the UK weekly. There should be a piece of paper in one of the drawers of your desk that records how you can make an international call via the telephone exchange." Felicity nodded her head and then turned back to Reg, saluting him. "Thank you, Sir. I had better use that telephone call to inform my father that I have arrived safely at McGuire." Reg nodded. "Of course, Flying Officer Bennet. When you have finished your call, ask Warrant Officer Smith to show you to your barracks – oh, and one last detail. The Americans are a bit more robust than we are in terms of their conduct, including the use of loudspeaker systems located throughout the base. Therefore, you must be patient with their operating methods, Flying Officer. As you were and at ease."

Reg then closed Felicity's office door, and she muttered the words she had wanted to say. As soon as she had been shown to the office, no other male officer had wanted or been assigned to occupy. "Oh, crap. I may as well have joined the administrative pool because at least they get windows to look out of." Felicity then took a seat in her Beefy office chair. Even through the tough fabric of her WRAF uniform, she could feel the plastic seat cover crack open, which immediately annoyed her. "Delightful." Felicity then placed her shoulder bag on her desk and opened it to retrieve her indexed notepad of telephone numbers and addresses from her former world across the Atlantic Ocean. She opened the top left-hand drawer of her desk, filled with pens, pencils and other small stationery items that seemed to have been tossed in there for several years. The top right-hand drawer was at least clear, and the instructions for making international telephone calls were typed on a piece of paper, which had been fastened down to the drawer by sticky tape. It was 2:00 p.m. at McGuire, which meant it was about 7:00 p.m. back home in Essex.

After successfully negotiating the telephone passageway out of the United States, Felicity heard the familiar ringtone. On the seventh ringtone, Samuel answered the phone. "Hello, Samuel Bennet speaking." Four of the sweetest words in the world right now for Felicity to hear. "Hello, Dad. It's me. I have arrived safely here at McGuire Air Base in the good old USA." Her sarcasm in her pronunciation of the final three words was easily discernible to Samuel. "Oh, Felicity. I am so glad to hear that you have arrived safely at your base in America. However, I couldn't help but notice the delightful strains of sarcasm in your voice. Is everything alright?"

Just as Felicity was about to answer her father's question, the loudspeaker system Reg had warned her about seemed to boom out in every square inch of the British section of the airbase headquarters. "All airmen are to note that, being a Friday, there will be a screening of the movie *From Here to Eternity* at 1900 hours, so dinner in the mess hall will not be served after that time. That is all." Felicity's eardrums seemed to be still pulsating as she responded to her father. "Well, as you might have heard, the American airmen are watching *From Here to Eternity* tonight."

She already knew her father's response after he heard that loudspeaker booming away before he spoke. "Good lord! They are a loud bunch. I had little to do with them during the war. Anyway, coming back to my question – are you alright?" She had already let the cat out of the bag, so it was better to be candid. "No, Dad. It isn't. Putting to one side Sergeant Barge Arse we both just had to endure, I have reported to my Squadron Leader, whom I might add is a nice fellow in a male version of Joan, but I have reported to him to find out for the first time that most of my duties will be generating paperwork, and that I might in the first twelve months get several opportunities to fly the American Air Force version of your aeroplane, so jets seem to be a distant future opportunity, if the Americans trust a woman to fly one, and, to make matters worse, I have been allocated an office without windows which make an MI5 interrogation room appear more hospitable. Goodness knows what the barracks are like, but they couldn't be any worse than my office." The excitement about the opportunity he had heard in his daughter's voice many weeks beforehand had been replaced by dejection. "I hear you, sweetie. All I can say is, welcome to the RAF. Still, it could be worse – you could be an American Airman." His attempt at humour was met with further sarcasm. "Oh, very funny. But seriously, Dad, the deployment to McGuire was never explained to me by Joan and her father to be like this. For Pete's sake, a O-1 Bird Dog, a pigeon, could fly faster than that aircraft. Anyway, I will be in the seat of Delta Dagger before any of them expect it to occur."

Samuel smiled. His daughter's motivation to succeed in life could never be subdued. "Well, I don't doubt that fact, sweetie. However, you have to learn how to crawl before you can walk, and now, you don't have Joan there, so obey your orders, and the RAF will look after you. Remember, you have Princeton University commencing soon, and you will be working with NASA there as well, so be patient, and everything will work out for you." Samuel always seemed capable of illuminating her world when the world seemed bleak. "You're right, Dad. I won't let the lumbering wheels of the machine get to my mind. Anyway, I have to be shown to my quarters in the officers' barracks, and where I go to eat. When it comes to the Americans, I need to be mindful of where I can and cannot sneeze. I had better get off this call, which, by the way, the RAF very generously allows me one international call a week to make when I am at McGuire. So, why don't we make it 7:00 p.m. your time every Tuesday, whether I am here at McGuire or on Campus at Princeton?" The arrangement was set in stone. "Sounds fine to me. Take care, sweetie. Remember, be patient with the machinery of the armed services, and, as always, I am proud of you and love you." As always, her heart felt warm. "I love you, too, Dad. Goodbye."

Subsequently, Warrant Officer Smith escorted Felicity around the base, showing her where the officer barracks were located, particularly her quarters, which, like all other officers' quarters, had a bathroom. She was also taken to the officers' mess. She was informed by Warrant Officer Smith which table the RAF officers sat at, rather than the tables for the USAF officers. Segregation in the officers' mess was an interesting proposition for Felicity. Still, America was a country in which segregation because of race was still in place in some states, particularly in the South. Even though Reg went out of his way to introduce her to every officer in the officers' mess that night, she found herself isolated when she sat down for dinner at the RAF table. The male officers talked among themselves, showing little interest in the heroine from back home in the UK.

As she sat there eating alone, little did Felicity realise that she had caught the eye of one of the young USAF officers that evening. First Lieutenant Dwight Hoover came from a military background, as his father was Four-Star General Ted Hoover, first in command of the USAF. The Hoovers were supposedly 'good southern white Baptists' from Virginia, and twenty-five-year-old Dwight was a star on the rise in the USAF, although other Airmen whispered, out of earshot, that he had a foot up from his daddy. Dwight's star had risen to him becoming a test pilot and, if fortune favoured him, a future intake in the astronaut program of NASA. Dwight had heard about the daredevil young English UAS female cadet, now WRAF, a woman who had miraculously brought her doomed aeroplane to a safe landing, and he liked the look of Felicity. Dwight did not possess movie-star good looks, and his strict Baptist upbringing meant he was timid with women. He wished to go over and introduce himself to Felicity; however, segregation existed everywhere in America, including, strangely, between the USAF and RAF.

Later that night, Felicity penned letters to Natasha, Heather and Joan. Her correspondence to Joan commenced in a manner that would leave little doubt about what the tenor of the rest of the letter would be like:

Dear Joan,

I have arrived at McGuire Air Base and am concerned about the US Air Force.

CHAPTER 27

If thee believed that there was an alluring life in the New World, that's too bad,
The reality is that it's harsh and inhospitable, and as for progress, that's absurd!

In September 1961, three lives, out of a multitude of lives worldwide, embarked on separate paths, the end of which was yet unknown in time and place.

Within the strictly guarded confines of the KGB headquarters of the *Lubyanka Building,* located in Lubyanka Square in downtown Moscow, Anatoli had recovered from the physical injuries he had endured several months beforehand; however, Volkov was manipulating the young person's psychological injuries for him to evolve into a KGB agent the likes of which were unknown to the world of espionage at that time. As promised by Volkov, he was treated like a prince in the fourth-floor room allocated to him within the *Lubyanka Building*; however, on the second floor of that building, he would regularly be required to participate in either auditory or visual or, occasionally, both, psychological manipulation the effect of which was to generate hatred and a pathological desire to kill anybody from the other side of the Iron Curtain.

In California, Amelia's first 'teen movie', *Summer Beach Party*, had premièred and was a box office success as young men, in particular, flocked to see on the silver screen this 'English beauty' whose costume throughout the film mainly consisted of her wearing a daring two-piece bikini, heralding the liberation of the younger classes from the restrictive lifestyle of the 1950s. With the movie's success and Amelia's meteoric rise to fame came the hedonism of life in Los Angeles, or, as it was known, 'Tinsel Town'. Since arriving in Tinsel Town, it was expected that she would sleep with the males who dominated the cinema industry there, and Amelia was very quickly introduced into another social stratum of Tinsel Town's hedonistic society: the pursuit of lascivious activities at private parties with either gender so desiring the temptation of her pretty body and beautiful face. It was difficult for Felicity to avoid images of Amelia, whether on American television programmes, billboards advertising *Summer Beach Party*, or, in particular, Airmen hanging her posters in public spaces at McGuire Air Base, which the USAF officers considered appropriate. As much as her heart tried to sing out for Amelia, Felicity remembered Joan's frank discussion, and Felicity's mind was adamant: "You don't love her. You're not a lesbian. You must find the right man; William was anything but the right man."

Felicity had settled into life at McGuire Air Base, although she was dissatisfied with the flying opportunities. As she had done at Cambridge, Felicity maintained her early morning exercise routine, running around the grounds of McGuire each morning; she was as fit, if not fitter, than any other man on the base. 'They might limit my time in the air; however, the sods are not going to beat me on the ground,' were regular thoughts as she ran.

Now that it was September, the time had come for Felicity to resume her academic life. At Princeton University, Felicity embarked on her postgraduate studies in aeronautical engineering and astrophysics, and, of course, assisted the Department of Psychology in their research on the psychological aspects of sensory deprivation. There was one aspect of Princeton that Felicity found to be not only too similar to Cambridge but indeed worse: the ingrained discrimination from its history as a 'male-only' institution. Princeton had only allowed its first civilian woman to study there that year, and that was at a post-graduate level. Indeed, on Campus, Princeton had no accommodation available for single women. Hence, the Defence Ministry had to pay for her to stay at The Peacock Inn whenever she was required to be on campus for consecutive days. If Felicity were only required to attend the campus for part of a day, she would have to drive the twenty-six miles to campus beforehand and then return to the base that same day. This meant she had to quickly come to terms with the novelty of driving on the right-hand side of the road, and, more importantly, in a left-hand drive car. All she was told by the Airman providing the USAF Jeep to her was: "Be careful out there. Most foreigners have a car accident within the first ten minutes of driving." That was the extent of her 'driving instructions'.

Felicity had to be on campus for three consecutive days at Princeton University in the first week of September, as the Graduate School held orientation for its students on the first two days. Then, early on the third morning, she had to report to the Department of Psychology for the research programme. During the limited time Felicity had been deployed to the United States, she had discovered that many Americans could be two-faced – outwardly pleasant but internally unpleasant. The woman on the front desk of The Peacock Inn reinforced that perception when she checked Felicity into her room. Felicity had travelled from McGuire in her uniform, so there was no doubt about her occupation. The check-in receptionist was a plump woman in her mid-fifties, but her presentation was professional. The name plaque on her desk informed guests that her name was Prudence. She stated the obvious as soon as Felicity approached the counter. Felicity's ears were not soothed by Prudence's heavy American accent, suggesting she was from one of the Southern States. "Good afternoon. I see you're from England." Felicity barely managed to display a slight, polite grin. "Yes. There should be a three-night booking in the name of Flying Officer Felicity Bennet." Prudence took some time searching through a bundle of paperwork on her desk. Finally, she found the document she was looking for. "Oh, yeah, here it is, right where it shouldn't have been. Flying Officer Felicity Bennet. Oh my golly, a woman can be an officer in England." Felicity was surprised by Prudence's inquisitive statement. "Yes. I am a member of the Women's Royal Air Force." Prudence continued to talk rather than promptly checking Felicity in. "Wow! Here in America, women cannot become officers in our Air Force. Indeed, where I come from, coloured people are not allowed to attend our universities."

Felicity was already aware of Princeton's history, but not the separate issue Prudence had raised about 'coloured'. "I am aware of Princeton's history, but unaware of what you said about your home state. What state are you from, and what do you mean by coloured?" Prudence was surprised and spoke in a sotto voce tone to answer Felicity's question. "I am from Alabama, and we don't allow the nig…" Felicity held up her hand to stop Prudence in mid-sentence. "I understand." However, Prudence had not finished venting her mind, once again in a sotto voce tone so that she could not be heard by anyone other than Felicity. "And now we have that damn Catholic in the White House. He wants to take away our Jim Crow in the South, but I will tell you, he will be dead before we allow that to happen." Felicity could not bear the woman's ignorance and wanted to escape her as quickly as possible.

Prudence continued to indulge in idle chit-chat about Felicity's rank in the WRAF. "Wow! I'm impressed that you're an officer in the English Air Force. We have always thought of your country as being a bit. What is the right word? It's old-fashioned." Felicity tried to politely move the discussion on to checking in. "Oh well. I'm sure there are many things Americans do for women that make us English look old-fashioned to Americans. My stay is for three nights." Prudence didn't catch the subtle hint to move on. "Oh, no, we are very behind your country regarding being a woman. For example, this university has only recently permitted women to study there. They do not have accommodation for single women." This was news to Felicity, but she did not express her thoughts. 'Most Americans think they are progressive compared to us? They're a bloody colonial outpost!' Finally, Prudence attended to check her into her room. "Alright, you are in room 5 on the second floor. You have your own bathroom facilities in your room. A complimentary breakfast is served in the dining room on the ground floor from 6:00 a.m. to 8:00 a.m. If you wish to dine here, please book a seat in advance. Dinner is served from 6:00 p.m. to 9:00 p.m. Would you like me to book a table for your dinner for the next three nights?" Felicity didn't know a soul, so she nodded. The check-in was finally completed, and now Felicity could escape from the annoying southern drawl of Prudence, as well as the woman's bigotry.

Whilst Princeton University was not steeped in Cambridge's history dating back to the thirteenth century, it was nevertheless an Ivy League institution that had celebrated its bicentennial during the previous decade, so the architecture of the buildings had a slightly similar carved stone presentation to that of Cambridge. The celestial observations of Felicity's post-graduate studies in Astrophysics at Princeton were to be undertaken by her at the Halstead Observatory and offices constructed during the 1880s. The telescope was now an antiquated piece of machinery compared to other observatories, but it sufficiently served her purposes for postgraduate studies. The Department of Aeronautical Engineering was established at Princeton as a stand-alone course in the 1940s. By the early 1960s, it had been affiliated with all the American armed services for over a decade in postgraduate courses for young officers in jet and rocket propulsion. The Department of Aeronautical Engineering also benefited from the construction of new state-of-the-art facilities, which helped it undertake important academic and practical research work. This course attracted Felicity's mind to the proposal made by Joan and Thomas. She was the only female post-graduate student in either course, making her somewhat of a novelty to the staff and students at Princeton University.

Notwithstanding the RAF representations about her research work with Princeton's Department of Psychology being undertaken in conjunction with NASA staff, that fact did not materialise upon her first attendance in September 1961. Felicity had been at Princeton for three days when she was finally required to undertake the research work in the antiquated surroundings of Eno Hall.

As the North-East experienced the effects of the long, hot summer, it was a hot at 9:00 a.m. on Thursday, September 7, 1961, when Felicity reported in for the sensory deprivation research at Eno Hall. She wore her WRAF uniform to impress what she thought were NASA personnel conducting the research. Dr John Hernan, the head of the research programme, greeted her in the reception. He was a slimly built man in his late thirties and of average height. He liked to be called Jack, even though his badge referred to him as 'Dr John Hernan'. "Good morning, Flying Officer Bennet. I'm Jack Hernan, head of this research programme." Felicity remained formal, in keeping with her RAF training. "Good morning, Dr Hernan. It's a pleasure to meet you." Jack Hernan immediately dispelled the necessity for any formality with him. "Call me Jack, please, Flying Officer Bennet. We're a pretty relaxed crew undertaking this research." Felicity was relieved to hear that detail. "Thank you, Jack. Please call me Felicity. I only wore my uniform today because NASA staff will be present." Jack raised his right eyebrow. "NASA staff? Who told you that NASA staff are involved in this research?" Felicity was both alarmed and adamant in her convictions. "I was informed by senior RAF officers that NASA personnel are involved in this research programme to determine the potential impact of sensory deprivation on astronauts."

A smile crossed Jack's face, which did not bode well for the news to come her way. "Felicity, I apologise if someone from this Department of Psychology has communicated the incorrect information to the RAF. However, we do not have NASA personnel working with us here on this research programme. Some of our research will be provided to NASA. Still, the only people working on this research programme are the various Doctors of Psychology from psychiatric hospitals, and Evelyn Grant from the National Science Foundation, whose husband, Roger, is an aeronautical engineer employed by NASA. Still, he occasionally lectures undergraduate students in aeronautical engineering here. Perhaps that is where the confusion has arisen in exchanging information dispatched from our department to the military. And, of course, there is also me. Our research into the effects of sensory deprivation will be provided to the Air Force, Army and Navy because it is a changing world, and the humane treatment of prisoners of war is a concept we fear our enemies will oppose. Please note that our research, which incorporates your observations and reports, will be submitted to NASA. However, NASA primarily operates a research facility at the Aerospace Medical Laboratory, located at Wright-

Patterson Air Force Base in Ohio." Felicity was confused. "Ohio?" Jack nodded. "Yes, the State of Ohio. However, as I said, we do share information with NASA about our research, and Evelyn, in particular, does that via the National Science Foundation."

Jack could see by the expression on Felicity's face that she was perplexed. "There is obviously relevant work for you military personnel to observe, and as I understand it, you are also studying other courses here on a post-graduate level, aren't you?" Felicity nodded. "Yes, I am. I'm studying Astrophysics and Aeronautical Engineering." Jack's smile widened. "Oh, well, our Post-Graduate Aeronautical Engineering course is the leading one in the country. Anyway, Evelyn and two doctors from separate psychiatric hospitals are working today, so I will take you to our research centre to introduce you to them. Come on, follow me."

With those words spoken, Jack led the way through a series of hallways, up a set of stairs to the second floor of Eno Hall and down more hallways until they came to a recently reconstructed area of Eno Hall. The building's interior was old and tired-looking. Without any intention to do so, its presentation added to Felicity's concern and disappointment that Thomas' and Joan's recommendation for Felicity to pursue their proposal was poorly executed or, even worse, misinformed by details from the Ministry of Defence in the UK. Still, at least there was this person, Evelyn, who had a vicarious connection to NASA. Eventually, in the back left corner of the first floor of Eno Hall, they arrived at the purpose-built area; the fresh state of its construction stood in stark contrast to the tired presentation of Eno Hall.

Jack opened the door for Felicity to enter. When she entered the room, she saw a collection of tables, some machinery and piles of paperwork and textbooks. As Jack had told her, three people were already in the room. One of the two men immediately stood up. The other man and woman remained in their seats as though Felicity's entry was an ephemeral interruption to their work. "Everyone, this is Flying Officer Felicity Bennet from McGuire Air Force Base. She is the UK officer I mentioned would be assisting us from time to time with our research project. However, we can call her Felicity." Jack introduced her around the room to the other people present, commencing with a balding elderly man closest to her left. "This Dr Walter Wood, but we call him Walt." They shook hands. "Next over here at this desk is Dr Peter Benson, but, once again, we call him Pete." Pete finally stood up and walked over to shake her hand. Like Walt,

Pete was at least in his fifties; however, he had a full head of hair. Felicity was pleasant. "Pleasure to meet you, Pete." His response was cordial. "The pleasure is all mine, Felicity." Then Jack turned to the woman, who did not get out of her seat but was eyeing Felicity up and down, which Felicity found unsettling. "And finally, this is Evelyn Grant. She is the person we were discussing whose husband occasionally lectures undergraduate students here when he is not working for NASA. Evelyn, this is Felicity, and she has some interest in NASA, so you two should get along fine."

Evelyn remained seated, but it was evident from her presentation that she was not as progressive as most American women. She wore a blouse and skirt; however, the blouse had the top two buttons done up. She was an overly curvaceous woman with huge breasts and large lips covered in a conservative hue of coral pink lipstick. Unlike other American women Felicity had encountered, Evelyn's hair was not styled. Instead, her auburn hair was in a tight beehive bun. Her glasses were the only odd feature of her presentation. They were quite goggle-shaped with an inner pale blue rim that seemed to flow out in every direction, made of thick tortoiseshell plastic that hugged her skin above and below her eyes. It was the only razzle-dazzle in what was otherwise a 1950s presentation of women's office fashion. There was a hint of a cold smile; however, there was something else about her, an indefinable trait that seemed to emanate from her eyes as she looked Felicity up and down. "Hello." Felicity knew she would have to work on developing a relationship with her if she wished to meet her husband. She walked over to her. "Hello, Evelyn. Nice to meet you." Evelyn didn't smile back. It was apparent Felicity would have to prove her worth to Evelyn on this project to have any chance of establishing a relationship. Evelyn turned back around and resumed scribbling notes in her notepad.

Jack then ushered Felicity over to a door on the far back wall. "And over here, Felicity, through this door, is the sensory deprivation room or, actually, rooms." He walked over and opened the door, revealing the rooms. "This first room is where the male subjects participating in our experiment will use a chemical toilet. It's still a sensory deprivation room, but it is not soundproofed like the next room, which you can see through the open door at the end. In this sound-proofed room, well, that is where our male subjects sleep, eat and spend all of their time. Come on into the main room here, and as you can see in the partial light, there is a mattress on the floor where the subject males will spend their time. On the wall, he can push a distress button if it becomes too overwhelming for him, and next to that switch is a tiny light the male subject can play with if they are bored." Felicity could see from the light filtering through that the confines of the soundproof room were very cramped, designed to simulate a person enduring a dark and confined space. Still, she was intrigued by one element of Jack's presentation to her. "Jack, you specifically said male subjects. Have no women volunteered to participate in this project?" Evelyn let out a scoff, evidently mocking in its tone. Jack narrowed his eyes at Evelyn, whose back was turned on him, and then he responded to the question. "Felicity, we do not have any females in our undergraduate course, so no."

Felicity found this fact remarkable but saw an opening to prove her mettle. "Well, since I am going to be involved in the research for the RAF, I am happy to be one of the guinea pigs." Evelyn and the other two men put down their pens and looked at her. By the looks on their faces, Felicity knew she had immediately proved her mettle. Evelyn smiled at Felicity for the first time, but did not smile invitingly to suggest a thawing of the ice between them. No, this smile was akin to: 'Good luck with that.' And there was still that obtuse character attribute projected from her eyes again. "She looks like one tough, sour bitch", Felicity thought to herself as she turned away to follow Jack over to a desk where he was now waiting for her. "Now, here are the questionnaire forms we are working on for our research; when each male has finished their time in the room, whether prematurely because they need to escape the environment or for those who can endure the entire time, we then interview them. It's a work in progress, and naturally, as you are attached to the Air Force, please feel free to include questions that you believe may be relevant to the armed services."

Jack had not provided information about when Felicity had to draft her questions. Indeed, Jack had not offered a date for when the first male would be entering the sensory deprivation rooms. "Jack, when do you need me to provide the questions?" He shrugged his shoulders. Another sign that the research programme was not the fantastic opportunity that Thomas and Joan had portrayed was evident. "I don't know. I guess when we have volunteers sign up to participate in our research, I don't know, but maybe a month."

After spending several hours with Jack and the rest of the sensory team going through various aspects of the research project, it was time for Felicity to leave. She was looking forward to returning to McGuire Air Base, as it was her home. She was not overly impressed by what she witnessed at Princeton University over the past three days. In particular, she was disappointed to find out today that she would not be working side by side with NASA personnel. She would write another letter to Joan that evening when she returned to her quarters at McGuire, and once again, this item of correspondence unequivocally expressed her concerns.

CHAPTER 28

In life, men can bore tunnels through mountains to get to the other side,
Whereas women have to scale the peaks, only to meet a rising tide.

When Joan received Felicity's second letter, she was annoyed because her father had told Felicity she would be working with NASA personnel, which was not the case. Joan sat at her desk in her home study, considering both of Felicity's letters. She inferred from the tone of Felicity's letters that she felt Joan and her father had betrayed her, and Joan could not allow those feelings to manifest themselves in Felicity's mind. She decided to speak to her father immediately. Joan retrieved her telephone directory from the top drawer of her desk, which included Thomas' new telephone number at RAF Andover, which was now Command Headquarters.

When she was put through to her father by his assistant, Joan wasted no time in raising her concerns about Felicity's letters. "Hello, Joan. What a delight to receive a telephone call out of the blue from you today. How is Stuart?" Her tone was sharp. "Daddy, he is fine. Why did you mislead Felicity about her deployment?" Thomas was taken aback by his daughter's tone of voice and her allegation. "Now, just wait a minute. What do you mean by misled? I did nothing of the sort." Joan's response was sharp, quick, and to the point. "You told her she would assist NASA personnel at Princeton, Dad. I received a letter from her today informing me that this was not the case. Indeed, NASA has limited dealings with Princeton's research project, which you raised with Felicity several months ago. And I should also mention that I received another letter from her about a week and a half ago. She will not be flying much at McGuire, and if she does, it will be in a 01-Bird Dog, a propeller plane we are not even using. It is apparent from her letters that she feels misled, and I cannot have that young woman thinking I misled her. So, please tell me why you made the representations to her about how beneficial it would be for her to accept moving to America when that does not appear to be the case?" Thomas would not be accused of misleading anyone when that was not true. "Now listen here, Joan. I do not know what you are talking about, and, more importantly, I do not like being accused of doing something that I did not do. Now, contain yourself, young woman."

Joan took a couple of deep breaths. Could it be that the Ministry of Defence misinformed her father? Perhaps that might be the case. "I am sorry. But look, she is hardly going to receive much of a progression in her military career flying a single-engine aircraft made by Cessna, and as far as working with NASA personnel is concerned, one of the research personnel at Princeton is married to a man who works for NASA, when he isn't lecturing undergraduate students at Princeton University. It's also apparent from Felicity's second letter that she feels Princeton's post-graduate courses are not a patch on Cambridge University's courses. So, I can understand her disappointment, Dad."

There was nothing but silence from Thomas for what seemed like an interminable time. "Dad. Are you still there?" He was. Still, he was just as surprised and disappointed as Felicity. "Yes, Joan. I will have to think this whole mess through because it is all news to me." There was more silence, and then, before Joan could utter a word again, there was a response from Thomas. "Alright. Here is what needs to be done. I will make some enquiries with the Minister's office about these matters. In the meantime, you relay a message to Felicity to let her know we have spoken. Explain to her that it is just as surprising for us to receive this information because I was not informed of it, and I am looking into it. Will that suffice?" Joan knew Felicity too well. "I can only hope so, Daddy. And I am sorry for speaking to you like I did moments ago." Thomas knew what was genuinely motivating his daughter. "Thank you for your apology, Joany. But I know this young woman is like the sister you never had, so I can understand your being upset for her. Now, let me sort this mess out, and I will get back to you soon. Goodbye."

Joan did not have the luxury of free international telephone calls, and goodness knows, the UAS didn't have the funding to pay for them. She had to see her doctor that day about the blood test results, which would reveal whether she was pregnant, so she sent a telegram to Felicity from the Post Office.

When she arrived at the Post Office, Joan wrote down a message that she hoped would settle Felicity's mind:

Dear Felicity,

I have received both of your letters. I am surprised by this news. I have spoken to my father, who is also astonished by it.

My father will talk to the Ministry of Defence. I will send you another telegram once my father responds. Please be patient and do not panic, as I am confident my father will resolve these issues.

Take care,

Joan

She hoped the telegram would allay Felicity's concerns and any feelings she may have held that Joan and Thomas had misled her. The news was positive when Joan saw her doctor; she and Stuart would indeed be parents. Her concerns about Felicity were replaced by her elation at being informed she was expecting. After she told Stuart the good news, Joan also had to telephone her father. Thomas was excited to hear the news that he would be a grandfather. Suddenly, the urgency of Felicity's circumstances seemed to dissipate in Thomas's mind. Joan, too, was swept away in the joy of the news. There was now an ocean between Felicity and the concerns Joan had earlier expressed to her father.

The following day, the telegram was delivered to Felicity at McGuire Air Base. The document that Joan had sent to her was marked on the outside. Her pulse increased in the excitement that Joan's telegram would say the RAF had resolved all the issues Felicity had raised in her two letters about the base and the university, and that the dream she had been promised several months ago would come true. She quickly but carefully opened the telegram, and as she read it, her excitement declined rapidly, almost as though a lead weight had been tied around her heart. She sat motionless in her office chair for several minutes; eventually, tears began to well up in her eyes as she looked at the picture of Her Majesty hanging on the wall near the doorway. Her door was closed to let out her emotions, followed by her words being expressed directly towards the Monarch's photograph. "Speak to the Ministry of Defence! By the time they finish speaking, I will probably have finished studying at Princeton without having had one single opportunity to come my way in the skies above or, for that matter, the space beyond that sky. Best of British, bloody luck to me." She then retrieved a handkerchief from her skirt pocket and wiped her eyes.

Days turned into weeks and then into months. Although her aeronautical engineering postgraduate studies provided intellectual stimulation, Felicity was otherwise confronted at McGuire Air Base with the meaningless tasks of drafting memoranda and observation reports about fighter jets she was not permitted to fly. Felicity would call Samuel every week, and every week, Samuel would tell his daughter to be patient and let Joan's father resolve the problems. So, Felicity remained patient, hoping each day that some news would come her way about an opportunity to fly jets or work alongside NASA personnel. However, with each new day came its disappointing conclusion of no news.

Patience may be a virtue; however, the temptation of curiosity surrounded Felicity everywhere when it came to Amelia's new movie, *Summer Beach Party*, including at Princeton University. The film was screened at the Princeton Garden Theatre. On a cold autumn night in early November 1961, Felicity had an overnight stay at the Peacock Inn due to study commitments the following day. She decided to watch the film to find out what all the fuss was about regarding Amelia. Whether it was around McGuire Air Base or on campus at Princeton, Felicity would repeatedly overhear men talking about the 'English goddess.' Felicity was late for the 6:00 p.m. cinema session when she arrived at the ticket booth, located at the entrance to the Princeton Garden Theatre. The booth operator told her there were spare seats in the last two rows, but she had better hurry to the door, as the usher would soon be closing it. Felicity hurriedly made her way to the cinema door, where the young male usher was indeed about to close the door. She entered the cinema theatre with the usher, and the one-thousand-seat room was in complete darkness as the curtains began to rise for the movie to start. With his tiny torchlight, the usher took Felicity to her seat in the theatre's far left second-to-last row. The last two rows of the far left side of the cinema were empty, and in the darkness of the theatre, with her eyes still adjusting to the change of lighting conditions, Felicity could not see who was sitting in the final two rows of the central aisle of seats.

When the credits had finished, and the movie began, it was not long until Felicity discovered why so many young men were talking about Amelia. In the opening scene on the beach, Amelia was dancing with other young adults in her two-piece bikini, and she looked like a goddess on the silver screen. Joan's voice rang in Felicity's mind about her burying her desire for Amelia, but as the movie played out on the screen, Felicity's fantasies played out. Impulsively, she began to feel her arms, imagining she was feeling Amelia's arms. Then her right hand moved to her chest, and she started feeling her tiny breasts, touching her nipples through her clothing and brassiere, as the scenes began to depict Amelia close-up, discreetly but pointedly permitting the viewer to focus on her voluptuous body. Her pulse was racing, and her right hand then began to move down her abdomen, before Joan's voice rang in her thoughts: 'Lesbians are not allowed to serve in the WRAF'. Felicity's response in her thoughts was as quick as her right hand moving away from the lower half of her abdomen, where it had stopped: 'I am not a lesbian.' She decided it was best to leave the theatre immediately and hurriedly stood up to descend the stairs. Had the lights come on, Felicity would have seen that Evelyn was seated several seats from the end in the last row of the central aisle. She was writing her PhD about the psychology of young men's fascination with the modern era of cinema, depicting screen goddesses like Amelia in the manner that this film was doing so, and out of the corner of her eye, she had caught sight of Felicity's actions. Evelyn watched Felicity quickly depart down the theatre's stairs, tapping her chin with her left index finger as she pondered and watched Felicity disappear into the darkness. Later that night, as Felicity sat in her room at the Peacock Inn, she repeated the same short sentence over and over again in her mind: 'I am not a lesbian.'

The sensory deprivation programme had not even started by December of 1961 when the United States entered another war in Asia. Felicity attended two meetings with Jack and Evelyn, each involving different academic research psychologists. Evelyn was still as cold as ice, and still, from her eyes, emanated that same indefinable attribute Felicity could not decipher. However, after the night of her briefly watching Amelia's movie, Felicity also observed a strange hint of a smile on Evelyn's face whenever their eyes met. It was unnerving for Felicity. Still, she did not want to upset Evelyn because of Roger's connection with NASA, so she did not ask her why she smiled at her in that manner. During the second meeting, Jack announced that the first group of six male students had finally been found to carry out their work. However, to permit these students to settle back in after the Spring Term commenced, the first subject would not be tested until the third week of March 1962. After their tedious bureaucratic meeting of two hours had concluded, Felicity decided to try to take matters into her own hands by speaking to Evelyn. As everyone stood up to leave for the afternoon, Felicity talked to Evelyn. "Excuse me, Evelyn. May I have a word with you for one moment, please?" Evelyn's eyes seemed to expand outside the perimeter of her large glass frames. Even Jack was surprised by the direct nature of Felicity's approach. "Is there something I can help you with, Felicity?" She shook her head as she partially turned her head his way. "No, Jack. I only need to speak to Evelyn." Jack shrugged his shoulders in his typical manner and then left, deeply engrossed in discussions with his fellow visiting researchers.

Once they had left the room, Felicity turned back to face Evelyn, standing with her arms folded, displaying an obvious sign of impatience about being requested to stay back and talk when her work was done. "How might I help you, Felicity?" Her intellectual arrogance underscored her tone. "It won't take too long, Evelyn. Please, come over to my desk and sit, and we can talk." She reluctantly sighed and complied with Felicity's request, and once they were both seated, Evelyn sat there with her arms folded, waiting for Felicity to speak. Eventually, Felicity broke the ever-increasing tension that had built up in the void of silence. "So, I understand from speaking to Jack that your husband works for NASA when he is not lecturing undergraduate students here." Evelyn slowly nodded, a curious expression enveloping her face as she did so. "Yes. And why is it so important that you wanted me to stay back here to talk this afternoon?" Her tone was condescending, causing Felicity to think to herself: 'What is her problem? Did I offend her?' Felicity nervously hesitated as she looked down at the desk before deciding she might as well get to the point. "Well, I raised him because I, too, would like to one day work for NASA." This news surprised Evelyn, and she leaned forward in her seat to ask for further information. "And what do you wish to work on at NASA? Engineering? Is that why you wish to speak to Roger?" Now was not the time to dilly-dally around the truth – get straight to the point. "No, I want to go into space. I want to be an astronaut."

Momentarily, Evelyn sat motionless and emotionless, not saying a word. Then, a faint smile followed her, becoming consumed with laughter as she tried to speak. "You have to be joking? An astronaut, have you been smoking pot?" Felicity was mortified by being mocked in such a manner. "No. I am absolutely serious. I want to be an astronaut." Evelyn continued to laugh as she spoke. "Oh, honey. You have a lot to learn about the United States of America. I don't know what it is like back in England, but women are expected to be in the kitchen, not on a rocket here." Felicity was not going to be subdued by patriarchal stereotyping. "Well, it is what I want to do and will do. And how can you, as a woman, accept such an ignominious set of affairs? Indeed, as a woman of science, you must be disgruntled with such chauvinism." Evelyn gathered herself together since it was apparent that she was dealing with a sincere yet misguided young woman. "There is no woman more offended by sexism than I. I had to marry twenty-five years ago to a man ten years my senior when I was nineteen, and I also had to have two children. Eventually, ten years ago, Roger agreed I could attend the University of Richmond, where he was lecturing, to study psychology. And I was born into wealth! So, nobody knows more about a woman's lot in life than I do. However, I can tell you that NASA is a men's club of test pilots. That is why I am laughing. I am not laughing at you; instead, I am laughing out of frustration."

Felicity looked quite forlorn as she absorbed this eye-opening information from Evelyn. The older woman could observe the noticeable signs of disappointment and dejection in the younger woman's demeanour. Felicity's genuine nature appeared to appeal to Evelyn, breaking down the ice wall she had deliberately put up for her peace of mind. Then, Evelyn did something quite out of the ordinary; she placed her right hand on Felicity's left knee and squeezed it. "Look, I am a member of a Women's Group. Well, it is better to call us the bitter housewives' club. When it is convenient, and one of our husbands is away, we meet for the night and discuss women's issues, including making societal changes." She then rubbed Felicity's knee, which Felicity was not shocked by but found an invasion of her personal space. "We also have some drinks and a bit of fun. Why don't you join us the next time we meet?" Felicity politely moved her knee to disconnect physically, but the invitation to discuss women's issues interested her. "Sure. I would be happy to discuss the sexism in the RAF. I am sick of men telling us what we can and can't do in our lives. When is your next meeting?" Evelyn's eyes lit up, and she eagerly responded. "Roger goes away fishing in the Rocky Mountains with a group of his old college buddies for a week just after Christmas, so we are meeting on New Year's Day at my house at 6:00 p.m. to start 1962 with some food, some drinks and a bang of women's power. What do you say? Would you like to join us?" She had nothing else to do on New Year's Day, and arranging leave with Reg would not be problematic. "Okay. I am in. Let's start 1962 with a good old bang of women's power. I like the idea of that." Evelyn smiled and nodded. Then, she took her pen from her coat pocket, wrote down the details for Felicity, including her address, and handed them to her. Felicity read the address details: 696 Princeton Kingston Road, Princeton. She had been attending Princeton long enough by now to know it was a well-heeled suburb of Princeton City, and Felicity wondered how two public servants could afford to live in that suburb. She had not absorbed Evelyn's comment about her family's wealth.

Evelyn stood up, turned to walk away, but then stopped and turned back around. "By the way. You do not need to book a room for the night. My boys are grown up and do not live at home so that you can stay in one of our spare bedrooms." Felicity nodded. She felt content, innocently believing she might be one step closer to NASA by befriending Evelyn and her group of like-minded feminists. If only Joan's father could do something about that blasted lack of flying at McGuire Air Base.

There was a telegram shoved under the door to her quarters to entrench the hopelessness in her mind about the state of the RAF and USAF when Felicity returned to McGuire Air Base that cold December evening. She opened her door and picked it up. It was from Joan, but for some reason, the fact of a telegram from her did not augur good news at all. Felicity entered her room, closed her door behind her, and then sat on her bed to read the telegram. The words chilled her spine:

Dear Felicity,

I apologise for the delay in writing to you. I have some lovely news and some not-so-nice news to share with you, and I've decided that the not-so-nice news should come from me rather than my father.

It appears there was a terrible miscommunication between our Ministry of Defence and the American Secretary of Defence. The USAF allows women to sign up to serve, but they do not permit any women to fly their aircraft, let alone their jet aircraft. Neither my father nor I knew this when we spoke to you at Cambridge. We are both upset for you and annoyed with the bureaucrats. Please do not give up on your dreams; when you return to England, you will be promptly trained to fly jet aircraft.

As for Princeton, the wires about who you would be working with were again crossed. One of the research team members is married to a NASA engineer who also lectures at Princeton. Once again, my father and I are tremendously upset and annoyed. However, the research work is beneficial for the RAF's purposes, so do not despair, that will count towards your long-term prospects with the RAF and, who knows, perhaps even NASA.

I am sure my news is relatively insignificant given how upset you must be reading these preceding matters, but I am now through my first trimester of pregnancy. I must resign from the WRAF, as my time will be devoted to being a mother.

Please try to enjoy your Christmas, and do not give up on your dreams.
Sincere, warm wishes,
Joan

Felicity sat on her bed. Various emotions and feelings were spinning around inside her. Anger won out in the end. "Damn those bastard men in the RAF and USAF. January 1, 1962, will be women's power, as they have never known it before."

CHAPTER 29

A rare life lesson; however, an innocent one, beware!
If thee dance around a cauldron of sin, hell might be waiting there.

Christmas was heralded at 6:00 a.m. by the loudspeaker system ringing out all over McGuire: "Good morning, all USAF and RAF personnel. Merry Christmas. A reminder for Airmen that your Christmas lunch will be served at midday, so do not be late, as there is only a limited supply of turkey for you." Felicity had just returned to her room from her daily 5:00 a.m. jog around the air base grounds. The booming voice of the American Airman penetrated through the walls of her quarters from the speaker system in the hallway. She could not get used to that overbearing American tone of voice, and Felicity ground her teeth until the announcement was completed. Christmas goodwill was exchanged in the officers' mess between all the USAF and RAF officers at breakfast, and of course, their Christmas lunch would be a feast compared to the slim pickings provided for the Airmen. However, Felicity was missing her father, so she quickly went to her office after breakfast to telephone him for Christmas. They spoke for half an hour, and, of course, she discussed again her frustrations about the contents of Joan's last telegram. Samuel reminded Felicity to be patient and enjoy the Festive Season, even though it was complicated by her being on the opposite side of the Atlantic Ocean.

Within the blink of an eye, it was New Year's Day 1962, and with it, the opportunity for Felicity to attend Evelyn's 'women's meeting', where she could start venting her fury about being a woman in the armed services. In several months, she would be turning twenty-two years old, but in her brilliant mind, she felt like a disgruntled fifty-year-old woman, robbed of her opportunities to achieve her life's dreams. Reg had agreed to issue a leave pass for her that night, as she told him a little white lie that she and Evelyn were working on a specific component of the sensory deprivation programme that would be relevant to prisoners of war, and this was the only window of opportunity they had to meet before the first male participated in being locked in the room, as Evelyn and her husband were going away on some much-needed leave. Reg issued the leave pass and granted her the authority to use a USAF vehicle without further questions. More concerning issues were occurring in the world for Reg to consider, such as America's commitment to the war in Vietnam. At the same time, the United Kingdom had decided it was an irrelevant conflict for the British Isles to concern itself with.

As previously arranged, Felicity arrived at Evelyn's house at 6:00 p.m. sharp. It was almost the middle of winter, and even though Felicity was dressed in her warmest civilian clothing, the open-air design of the USAF Jeep allowed the wind to penetrate the four layers she was wearing easily. To her surprise, when Felicity arrived at Evelyn's house, she saw that it was an impressive three-level wooden heritage structure and, most importantly, there were two chimney stacks at either end of the sprawling home pumping white smoke out into the night's air, suggesting that a warm, inviting and luxurious interior awaited her.

Felicity picked up her small carry bag from where she had left it on the Jeep's front passenger seat. She had brought a change of undergarments, a change of blouse and, of course, her toiletries. The short driveway from the street led to a large, half-oval-shaped courtyard. It was apparent in the darkness that sprawling grounds surrounded the impressive house. As she walked closer to the home, it was evident to Felicity that other women had already arrived, as she heard the raucous laughter of American females. 'Why are they always so loud?' she thought to herself as she approached the front stairs of the house. The short flight of about six steps led to a covered porch with two carved columns supporting the front of the enclosure. Felicity knocked on the solid grey timber door, and she heard Evelyn's voice ring out from inside the house: "Hold on one moment, I'm coming." Several moments later, the large wooden front door opened inward, revealing Evelyn in a presentation style that contrasted with the cold, bureaucratic look she maintained on campus. Her hair was let down, free-flowing, and held back from her forehead with a pretty blue-pink headband. Her blouse was also the same colour as the headband; however, the top three buttons were down, revealing the parting crease line of her enormous breasts. She was not wearing a coat, which also revealed that her hips were wide from multiple childbirths. Her light grey skirt finished just above her knee line, a difference from her campus skirts that covered her knees. Evelyn's face was entirely made up, and her lipstick matched the colour of her blouse and headband. She eerily looked like an older version of Amelia, a similarity Felicity had not previously noticed.

Upon seeing Felicity standing before her at the front door, Evelyn was unusually elated and inviting, throwing her arms open wide to greet her. "Happy New Year, my young British friend." Her arms immediately embraced Felicity, pulling her tight into her body, much to the younger woman's surprise. Felicity slowly embraced Evelyn, and she was more reserved with her salutations. "Happy New Year to you as well, Evelyn." Evelyn immediately let go of Felicity, and with her left hand, she took Felicity by her free right hand to bring her inside the house as she spoke. "Come in out of the cold. You will freeze outside; it is nice and toasty warm in here." The hallway from the front door revealed the impressive and historic nature of this house. The walls were made of plasterboard that had been painted white, and the polished wooden floorboards were at least six inches wide. They complemented the hallway presentation, which was otherwise lined with old paintings and mirrors on the walls, along with some antique furniture. Guests could sit here before being invited into one of the many rooms that led from the hallway. About halfway down the hallway, there were a flight of stairs with elegantly carved bannisters supporting the handrail, leading to the home's second level. Above that stairwell, a sizeable, delicate glass chandelier hung from the high plaster ceiling, with its lead cord surrounded by an elegantly moulded ceiling rose.

Indeed, this house screamed out old East Coast North American money. Still, before Felicity could ask any questions, Evelyn dragged her by her hand to the first entranceway on the righthand side of the hallway, which led to a large sitting room where an open fire blazed away in a carved marble fireplace, where four other women including, unusually for American society at the time, a pretty African American woman, sat on the two comfortable sofas. This room was lined with bookcases on one side of the wall, and next to the wall, a long, wood-and-leather-covered coffee table sat between the two sofas. It was covered with various plates of food and long-stemmed glasses of champagne. Evelyn wasted no time in introducing Felicity to the room. She pointed to a middle-aged, red-haired woman who sat at the near end of the left sofa. "Felicity, meet Dolores Adams. Dolores' husband, John, is a lawyer who works in Mercer, but they live here in Princeton." Dolores warmly smiled towards Felicity; however, she remained seated. "Hello, Felicity. Evelyn has been talking about you." Had she? That was news to Felicity. "Hello, Dolores."

Evelyn then extended her right hand towards a blonde-haired woman sitting at the opposite end of the couch, where Dolores was sitting. She had an attractive face, lit up by a warm smile, and looked to be in her mid-thirties. "This lovely young woman is Jennifer Warren, and her husband, Ted, is a high school principal in Mercer. They used to live here until recently, when Ted was appointed the school principal." Jennifer's greeting was joyful in the stereotypical style of a 1960s television sitcom. "Hello, Felicity. I am so glad you can join our group tonight." A bit of a ditz, but pleasant enough. "Hello, Jennifer." Then Evelyn turned her hand towards the woman at the far end of the opposite couch, who appeared more conservative with her tied-back black hair and a long-sleeved dress paired with an equally long skirt. "Now, this delightful woman is Annette Mason, and she is married to Bob, the Chaplain of our Lutheran Church, where we all or almost all initially met." Annette may have appeared conservative, but her manner was anything but. She held up the glass of champagne she had been slurping on to greet Felicity. "Nice to make your acquaintance, Felicity. I sure am glad we have someone like you involved with our group." The champagne glass promptly returned to her lips. Felicity was intrigued: 'Someone like me? English? RAF? What on Earth does she mean?'

Finally, Evelyn's hand was directed toward the pretty African American woman sitting near them, at the opposite end of the same sofa where Annette was seated. Her clothes were not as expensive as the other women's, but what she lacked in sartorial elegance was made up for by her very pretty face and ringlet-curled hair. "And finally, this gorgeous young woman is Annabelle. Her husband, Sidney, was appointed last year as the first black manager of the Post Office, and we were very fortunate to meet Annabelle at our parish of the Lutheran Church." Annabelle was initially shy, but she stood up almost subserviently, and her smile soon revealed a warm and keen welcome for Felicity. "Hello, Felicity. I am thrilled to meet you." That was nice yet strange. "Hello, Annabelle." Before Felicity could speak, she was again dragged by the same hand Evelyn had held since they met at the front door. "Now, come with me, Felicity, and I will show you to the loft room where you will be staying tonight."

As she walked up the stairs with Evelyn holding her hand and leading the way, Felicity could not resist commenting on the exquisite home. "You live in a very nice house, Evelyn. How long have you lived here?" Evelyn spoke as she walked up to the top of the first flight of stairs. "All of my life. I told you at Princeton that I was born into wealth. Weren't you listening? Oh, it doesn't matter. This house has been in my family for five generations. When Roger and I married, he moved into the house, and my mom moved into the loft. Although it is my family's house, Roger was the man of the house." Evelyn did not let go of Felicity's hand, almost like she was leading a child to their room. "What about your father?" She immediately felt Evelyn's grip slightly ease, although she did not release it entirely as they approached the next stairs. "My father died from the Spanish Flu not long after I was born." Her voice had a tinge of sadness, and Felicity immediately felt like she had strayed into Evelyn's personal life, which was out of bounds. "I'm sorry. I should not have pried." Evelyn turned back towards her as they approached the top of the stairwell leading to the loft. "Don't be sorry. It was a fact of life at the time. He left behind enough money for me and my mom to survive." They had now arrived in the loft, which, save for one room, was an open-plan area of two separate rooms separated by a wide archway and a wall. The room they first entered was a small lounge room with windows at either end. Evelyn continued to drag Felicity by the hand through the archway. "So, this is where you can sleep tonight, and that doorway at the far end is your bathroom." Evelyn then sat on the made-up bed, which was larger than the single bed Felicity had in her quarters at McGuire. "The bed is a king single, cosy and fun to sleep in." She had that strange look in her eyes again. 'Fun to sleep in?' Felicity thought as she placed her small carry bag on the bed.

Evelyn immediately hopped off the bed, and then, without any invitation from Felicity, she removed her large woollen overcoat. "You will cook in this house tonight wearing that garment, and, oh my goodness, you don't need that sweater on either." Evelyn commenced undoing the buttons on Felicity's sweater, but then Felicity stepped back to take it off by herself. "Thank you, Evelyn. I have got it from here, and, yes, you're right, it is toasty warm in this house tonight." Evelyn smiled, but then she invaded Felicity's space again. "And, oh my goodness. Here, undo those top buttons on your blouse. We're not going to church tonight." She reached up to undo the first button, and after she had done so, Felicity undid the next. "Thank you again, and yes, this is more comfortable."

Evelyn reached out with her left hand and took Felicity's right hand, immediately walking out of the room. However, as they walked, Felicity could not resist her curiosity. "Evelyn, I appreciate your hospitality and inviting me to join your group. But I am curious about your change of heart towards me, as I thought you did not like me when we first met." An unexpected inquiry in which honesty was the only answer. She turned and faced Felicity and took her left hand with her right, peering through those oversized glasses, inside Felicity's eyes. "You're English, my dear young girl. We might have been allies in two wars, but we have not forgotten 1776. It felt as though the RAF had demanded that you participate in our programme without giving us any options to decide. However, when I saw the disappointment in your eyes when I told you that NASA was a boys' club, I saw the same look of disappointment that women in this country endure, and also there..." Evelyn stopped short in her sentence and let go of Felicity's left hand, but started walking again, dragging her by the right hand.

Felicity once again complied like an obedient schoolchild being dragged to the classroom by her teacher, though she was curious about what Evelyn intended to say beforehand. "Also, there was what, Evelyn?" She did not turn around. Instead, she walked Felicity down the flight of stairs from the loft to the second level, quickly responding over her shoulder. "Don't worry. You will find out in due course. Anyway, let's hurry back downstairs because I'm thirsty for champagne, and there is much to discuss and do tonight with the other women." Another curious statement for Felicity to think about: 'Do what? Oh, cripes, hope we will not sew and weave blankets.'

They entered the drawing room, where Annette was fiddling with the radio dial, tuning the device into some jazz music. "Oh, Annette, can you turn that down for a moment? There will be plenty of time for us to have fun with the music later on." Annette obeyed Evelyn's request and returned to where she had been seated when Felicity arrived. Evelyn then turned towards Annabelle. "Excuse me, Annabelle, honey, would you please move down the other end of the sofa so we can sit here?" Annabelle politely smiled and shuffled with her champagne glass to sit next to Annette, who threw her left arm around her shoulders to cuddle her. "Come here, my darlin'. Aunt Annette will look after you tonight." Evelyn picked up an unused glass from the coffee table and selected an open bottle from a large silver champagne bucket containing six bottles, leaving just enough for one glass. She poured the champagne and virtually shoved the glass into Felicity's hand. "There you go, Felicity. That glass will refresh you, and don't worry, there is plenty more where that came from." Felicity was not a drinker of alcohol, but she thought it would be rude to refuse Evelyn's gregarious gesture. She took a sip and discovered it was a fine, smooth, and easy-to-drink beverage. "Thank you and, well, yum, Evelyn. This champagne is delicious!" Evelyn smiled. "It should be. It's Dom Pérignon. It's just one of the benefits of us meeting here tonight." Annette, who still had her arm around Annabelle's shoulder, lifted her glass. "Let's drink to that, girls. Bottoms up, pardon the joke." Save for Felicity, all the other women giggled like it was some trite joke they had heard before.

Evelyn then sat down right next to Felicity. For Felicity, it almost felt as though Evelyn was mothering her. However, she was in her own house, and, of course, Roger was a key figure in Felicity's acceptance into NASA in some capacity. It was time to get down to business. "Right, ladies, if I can use that term, as Felicity is new to our group, so could you please tell her about your lot in life and what you wanted to be if it wasn't for this patriarchal world we were trapped in." Evelyn gestured towards Dolores, who was seated directly opposite her. Felicity noticed for the first time since returning to the room that Jennifer had moved down the sofa to be seated closer to Dolores. "Dolores, you're first, and then we will go around the room until Felicity can be lucky last."

And so the stories began. Dolores explained that she had wanted to be a stage actress, but at eighteen, she had to marry her father's business partner, John, who was twenty years her senior. Dolores told the group that it was almost twenty-five years ago, and after having given birth to four children, she had lost any opportunity to pursue a stage career because she was not young. So, now she has to wash dirty clothes, clean a house, cook meals and, because of her husband's age, endure a non-existent sex life with him. She finished by telling the group, "There is a whole new era of women who are about to suffer the same lost dreams as me, and that is why we must remain militant to try to change this world of male domination." As Dolores finished her spiel, Evelyn grabbed another bottle of Dom Pérignon, quickly opening it and recharging Felicity's glass without asking her.

Jennifer spoke next, and her story was similar to Dolores' regarding her dreams being taken away from her because of the expectations of society. Jennifer told them how she had started teaching at the New Jersey State Teachers College just after World War II, where she met Ted, who was about fifteen years older than her and worked as a lecturer. She was innocent and immature, but he was so dominant that she agreed to marry him. She had two children, a boy and a girl, who are still in high school. She wanted to return to teaching, but Ted wouldn't let her. Indeed, they had argued about it, and Ted had slapped her several times, so she no longer raised it. And, yes, she explained that she hates Ted for taking away her dreams, for hitting her, and that they rarely have sexual intercourse because he seldom can sustain an erection, telling Jennifer it's her fault because she is not as attractive as when they first met. Her final comment was far more ferocious than Dolores': "Fuck those sons of bitches, ladies. They deny us our dreams, use us as playthings until they're too old to please us and otherwise expect us to be maids for them. We're better off without them." Felicity was surprised by Jennifer's vitriol but also angered to hear about her physical abuse. By now, Evelyn had recharged Felicity's glass of champagne for the third time, and apart from hors d'oeuvres on the coffee table, she had not eaten a meal since lunch, so she was becoming slightly tipsy.

Annette's story was not too dissimilar to Felicity's life with her late grandmother. Annette told the group that her father was a Lutheran preacher, and her mother told her from an early age that she had no choice but to marry another preacher. She wanted to attend an artists' college to become a painter because she was fascinated by the female form. She explained that in high school, she used to sketch the other girls in her class in various stages of undress in her schoolbooks. This was until her teacher discovered it, and her mother was called in to see the principal. She was expelled from school at the age of fifteen. That night, her mother whipped her with the handle of the feather duster and told her she was evil. By the age of sixteen, she was married to Bob. Over the years, they had five children and travelled all around the East Coast for twenty years until Bob finally secured the role of parish minister in Princeton, where they have lived for the past ten years. She told the group, "I haven't painted or drawn since I was expelled from school, but I bet I could do some masterpieces for you fine ladies. We should not give up our dreams to be baby factories, girls." Felicity's champagne glass was recharged again by Evelyn.

Annabelle's story was tragic. She had been born into poverty in Harlem. By the age of thirteen, her alcoholic father was either sexually abusing her or beating her when she said no, so she ran away from home just before her fourteenth birthday. She found work in a laundry in Trenton and started attending the Lutheran Church, where she met Sidney, a postal worker twenty years her senior. They had one child together, a boy who was six; however, she disliked the way Sidney expected her to have sex when he wanted it, and without being too impolite, it felt like he was going to the toilet. When she was a little girl, she wanted to be a ballerina, but her mom told her that black children were not allowed to do ballet. If it had not been for this new president, they would probably still be struggling to survive on the poverty line. Still, since Sidney was appointed the first black manager of a Post Office here in Princeton, they can afford new, albeit cheaper, clothing and eat three square meals every day. Annabelle was adamant, "Our bodies belong to us, not to them, and we women should be able to decide when we want to have sex." That was quite blunt for Felicity and close to the bone, given her experience with William. Annette placed her left arm tightly around Annabelle's shoulder and cuddled her close into her chest again, an occurrence with which Annabelle seemed comfortable. Another recharge of Dom Pérignon, and the alcohol was fuelling Felicity's rage.

Then Evelyn informed the group that she had already shared her story with Felicity. Still, like the rest of them, she was sick of the patriarchy in America. Evelyn turned to Felicity, and she knew from her intoxicated eyes that the young woman had a story to tell. "Well, it is your turn now, Felicity, to tell the group your story." Felicity was intoxicated on both liquor and vile bile on her liver about many issues, for which, in a state of sobriety, she might not otherwise discuss. She looked around the room, and when she stared back, she saw not just faces but also the sisters of a bonded sisterhood. She stood up, initially unsteady on her feet, as the alcohol-fuelled blood rushed to her head. Still, she steadied and then opened her heart. "My mother was killed in the *Blitz* shortly after I was born." Gasps followed by multiple voices saying, 'That is dreadful' and 'How sad' emanated from the sisterhood audience. She continued. "My late grandmother psychologically tormented me about my physical presentation, repeatedly telling me to join a convent because nobody would marry me. However, at Cambridge, a cute young man in my class seemed to be interested in me, but now I realise he was using me to help him pass and, even more disturbingly, he tried to rape me."

Gasps seemed to come from every corner of the room. Evelyn asked the obvious question. "Did you report it to the authorities?" Felicity's eyes began to glaze over. "Yes, I did, and, to make matters worse, I was told it could not be reported." Felicity should not have answered Evelyn's next question. "Why on Earth were you told it could not be reported?" She tried to resist answering the question, but she felt so embittered about her treatment by the UAS, the WRAF and the RAF that, combined with the alcohol, the words passed through her lips. "During my interview, I revealed that when I was a schoolgirl, I had a crush on another girl, and that crush confused me regarding the intentions of the young man for whom I had some feelings. My superior officer told me that I would be dishonourably discharged from the WRAF if I were a lesbian, which I am not, and that it was best, given the circumstances of my version of events, that I didn't report it because then my superior officer would be compelled to document my state of mind. Before that incident, I had been elevated to the rank of Flying Officer because I had saved the life of a Viscount by avoiding a catastrophic plane crash. I was redeployed to McGuire and to study here at Princeton based on working with NASA scientists, which, no offence, Evelyn, has been the biggest bureaucratic catastrophe in the history of bureaucracy." The women sat in silence, still contemplating the gravity of what they had been told. Then, Evelyn broke the silent contemplation, taking Felicity by the hand to sit her back down again. "Well, we are not concerned by your thoughts, Felicity. Indeed, we welcome them."

Evelyn then stood up and walked over to the radio Annette had been fiddling with earlier. She turned to the dial, and the tunes of swing music from the 1940s echoed out from the speaker across the room. "Come on, ladies; it's time to have fun." With those words being spoken, Annette immediately rose from her seat and started to dance freely, waving her arms around in the air as she talked in tune with the group. "Yes, come on, girls. Let's dance like it is World War II all over again, when the men were away." With those words being spoken, Dolores, Annabelle and Jennifer all stood up and joined in the drunken yet overly joyful dancing with one another. At the same time, Felicity sat back, unsure of what to do in this strange new world she had entered. They jived and then jitterbugged. Then, the music show played a calmer waltz, a song with which Felicity was unfamiliar but for which Evelyn displayed the greatest delight. "Oh, it's The Tennessee Waltz. Felicity, come on over and join us. You can be my dance partner." Dance partner? Now, that was different. Still, Evelyn's outstretched hand and warm, inviting smile suggested she was in safe hands. Felicity rose unsteadily to her feet, and whether it was the music or the champagne, she was easily lured over to join Evelyn as her partner for the waltz. "I don't know how to waltz", she told Evelyn. The older woman smiled and pulled her closer into her body, so that Evelyn's ample breasts were pressed hard up against Felicity's chest. "Don't panic, and don't try to do anything; just let the music flow over you, and I will lead you in this gentle dance." She then gently swayed with Felicity, who watched as the other couples waltzed, slowly turning around to the music.

The words to the song were romantic, and as she began to glide slowly but surely with Evelyn, the evening started to take on a stranger dynamic. She thought she saw Jennifer and Dolores kiss as they twirled in their slow anti-clockwise spin. Then, as she was drawn closer to Evelyn's chest by that other woman, who drew her in with a two-step twirl, it happened again: Dolores and Jennifer began kissing each other. Another half twirl, and sure enough, Annette was now passionately kissing Annabelle's inviting and full lips while running her hand up the woman's back to the zipper on the back of her dress, which she began to pull down slowly. Felicity was so confused by what was unfolding before her eyes that she did not notice that Evelyn had slowly two-stepped into a corner of the room so that Felicity's back was slowly pushed up against the wall by Evelyn's breasts. Then there were images of Jennifer pulling down Dolores' skirt as she said aloud: "Let me see that burning bush of yours again." Annette's long, almost early pilgrim-style dress quickly fell from her shoulders to reveal fancy undergarments in contrast to her conservative top garments.

Then Felicity was gently forced back into the wall altogether by Evelyn, whose face was painted with an amorous glow. Felicity tried to pry herself away from Evelyn, but the older woman's enormous breasts seemed to press her more securely against the wall. "Don't panic, Felicity. I told you these evenings are also fun." As she said the word fun, Evelyn thrust her pelvis into Felicity's and began to rub herself slowly, pelvic joint to pelvic joint, against the young woman as her lips moved closer towards Felicity's. "What are we doing, Evelyn? I thought this evening was about discussing…" She could not finish her sentence as Evelyn's left index finger rose like a serpent over Felicity's chin to close her lips gently. "I was there that evening." Which evening? What was she on about? "What do you mean?" Felicity responded. Evelyn's face drew closer so that her nose tip was millimetres away from Felicity's nose tip, and disturbingly, she seemed to form the appearance of an older Amelia as she spoke. "I was in the cinema that evening, watching that same movie you were watching, and I saw you commence touching yourself as you watched that actress on the screen." Her final word was almost a mere whisper of air as her fulsome lips touched Felicity's. Felicity's frozen bewilderment met that action. Still, as Evelyn's soft lips began to take the same smooth and gentle form as Amelia's lips once did, Felicity started to respond momentarily before the alarm of Joan's voice rang out in her mind: 'Are you a lesbian, Felicity?'

Her negative response was once again her answer. She pushed her left hand against Evelyn's sizable right breast in an attempt to move away. "No, Evelyn. I do not want to do this." However, Evelyn's lustful desire was fuelled by alcohol and the misguided belief that, as old East Coast American money, her will was her way. "Do not resist it, Felicity. I know it's confusing, yet it is also the most tender moment when two women make love." Once again, her lips began their magnetic pull into Felicity's lips. Evelyn's left hand quickly made its way up under Felicity's skirt, and just as quickly, her fingers then entered Felicity's underwear. They made their way to her vagina, which quickly became an exercise of stimulating her vaginal area. Felicity felt for the first time in her life the sexual stimulation of having this region of her body touched, even though it was against her consent that Evelyn was touching her there. As Evelyn's lips pressed harder against Felicity's mouth, her tongue began to part Felicity's lips while her index finger began to part Felicity's vulva. Confused feelings of lust began to enter Felicity's mind; however, just as part of her mind was about to give in to that lust, in another part of her mind, Joan's voice was present: 'No, Felicity. Get out of there!' The mind was more substantial than the power of the older woman's dominating, curvaceous body and stimulating touch. Felicity used both her hands to push Evelyn backwards forcibly. "I said no, Evelyn! I am not a lesbian."

Felicity's words interrupted the four other women, who were now in various stages of undress, fully intertwined with their accompanying paramour for this moment of the evening. Felicity had freed herself from Evelyn, and as she walked out of the room, she adamantly stated her position. "I am not a lesbian. I did not come here tonight for some form of ritualistic orgy." The other women remained motionless as they awaited Evelyn's response. After a moment of silence, Evelyn smiled and shrugged her shoulders. "Oh well, ladies. I was mistaken. I thought she would become a member of our club." With those words being spoken, Evelyn had walked over towards Annette and Annabelle, and, seemingly without a care, she had removed her blouse and brassiere by the time she reached the two naked women on the sofa. She smiled in delight as she joined the other women on the couch. "Just what I need; black and white." With that, the five women all resumed their passionate ritual.

Meanwhile, Felicity returned to the loft. She was initially quite drunk as she sat on the bed, wondering why this had happened and, regrettably, feeling guilty as though she had done something wrong. Americans can be loud in social settings, but the noise was almost deafening as the sounds of women making love seemed to snake their way up the stairs to the loft. The mouths of usually respectable women descended into a language of pure vulgarity, followed by sounds of pleasure that seemed as forced as the laughter of the television sitcoms. Felicity's empty stomach began to reject the abundant supply of champagne. She quickly made her way to the bathroom and vomited into the toilet bowl once, twice and a third time. As she reached into the bowl, the overly loud orgasmic sounds seemed to echo through the entire home. "Why are they so loud?" she said to herself.

After an hour, Felicity began to feel better. Her repeated emptying of her stomach had removed some of the excess alcohol. Nevertheless, she did not want to remain in this house because it felt eerie and only made her long to return to the base she now had to call home. She opened her bag and took out her toiletry pack. She brushed her teeth three times, swirling water around her mouth and gradually drinking water from the tap as her stomach settled and her senses returned.

As Felicity finished packing her carry bag, she felt another presence in the room. She turned from the bed where she had just closed her bag to see Evelyn standing in the open arched entryway, separating the loft's sleeping area from the sitting room. Evelyn was naked, a symbol of the frenzy Felicity had heard for the past hour, with her makeup smeared all over her face. Still, she had her glasses on, tied back her hair and leaned against one of the outcrops of the archway, assuming an air of superiority as she crossed her arms like a disappointed employer. "Well, I see you're about to do what I was coming to say. You should leave Felicity, and I want you to know that everyone here tonight is very disappointed with you." Disappointed with her? A dystopian orgy of *Macbeth's* witches had just played out to a cult, yet disappointment was to be her burden. Felicity was just about to protest when Evelyn chilled her to the bone. "Now, don't go blabbering to anyone about my women's group and what we do because it will only work out in tears for you." It was a threat, but it carried a venom that scared Felicity. "What do you mean by tears for me? How could it end up in tears for me?" That same cold, imperious demeanour Evelyn had initially displayed when she first met Felicity had returned to their relationship. "There are four other respectable women in this house who will all swear to the fact that they witnessed an arrogant and, by her admission, a sexually confused young British officer try to abuse a young black woman sexually." Felicity was stunned. "You wouldn't dare say that. It is a despicable lie."

Evelyn stood there, staring at Felicity with an aloof smile. Felicity repeated herself. "That is a terrible lie. You would not dare say that." Evelyn closed her eyes, smiled a devious smile, and then abruptly opened them as she spoke. "Wouldn't I? You will be out of Princeton, out of McGuire, and out of America quicker than muck going through a duck, Felicity. You're not in England anymore." Evelyn turned away, swaying her full buttocks with each step before she turned around for one last verbal arrow to be shot at Felicity's way. "Oh, and don't think remaining silent means an introduction via Roger NASA." Evelyn then grabbed her bare pelvic region with her right hand. "You have to go via here to get there. Now, leave my house as a redhead is waiting in my bed." Evelyn then walked down the stairs from the loft, calling out on the top note. "Oh, Dolores. I'm coming, ready or not."

Felicity quickly left Evelyn's home with her belongings. Although she was still under the influence of the champagne, she drove back to McGuire Air Base as swiftly and as safely as she could, the cold night air helping her during the half-hour drive to sober enough so that the American Airmen raised no eyebrows on guard at the front gates of McGuire. She made her way quickly to her quarters, and as soon as the door was closed, she flung herself onto her bed and cried. "Why does my life seem to go from bad to worse here?" However, through the feelings of trauma and despondency, Felicity's mind began to wander into an existential question about her proclivities. "Am I a lesbian? No, I can't be. It's wrong, isn't it?" she asked herself on several occasions through her tears before eventually falling asleep on her bed shortly after the clock turned over January 2, 1962. Happy New Year, indeed!

CHAPTER 30

1962 seemed a long, drawn-out nightmare for the world and Felicity. She was stuck at an airbase in a foreign country that treated women worse than her home country. She had only been allowed to fly the wretched 01-Bird Dog on a few occasions and spent most of her time on base observing jet aircraft as they were serviced or took off and landed. While excelling in post-graduate studies at Princeton University, she would nevertheless read university papers about the significant advances the Cambridge University Astrophysics Department was making in its quest to discover the universe's formation. Instead, Princeton's Astrophysics Department and Post-Graduate course took toddler steps in examining the Sun. At least there was some utility in her post-graduate studies in aeronautical engineering, as they helped her gain a more comprehensive understanding of the USAF's jet engines. However, the sensory deprivation studies of the Psychology Department were hampered by young male volunteers who could not remain in the darkroom for longer than two hours. As the university year ended in the middle of the year, there were fewer volunteers for the next round of examinations when the new university year was set to resume in September 1962. And, of course, there was Evelyn. Felicity did not say a word about that night at Evelyn's house, nor did she take the forbidden fruit that would expedite her access to NASA. The male psychologists did not detect the frozen arrows being cast out from each woman's eyes, but men rarely possess the intuition to read the unspoken language exchanged between women. Venus and Mars orbited around the clinical environment of a psychological torture chamber.

Amelia's world of Hollywood fame began blossoming as she became a regular screen goddess, with her second teen beach movie released just in time for the summer break. By now, Amelia's life was well and truly caught up in the web of the trappings of fame, a never-ending sea of casting couches upon which she had to give up her body to men for whom nature had not been kind in their physical appearance. Still, for their money and power, she would not have even entertained the idea of fornicating with them. Then there were the parties, which seemed to be a natural consequence of garnering fame in Hollywood. With the parties came the vice, not only the plentiful supply of liquor but also narcotics. However, her life was now managed by a man almost twice her age, and he was gay. Walter Melville moved to Los Angeles from Detroit towards the end of 1945. Walter had fortuitously not been inducted into the United States military during World War II because he had contracted polio as a child, which led to muscle wasting in his left leg, which in turn meant he had a limp caused by muscle drag. Walter was 23 when he arrived in Los Angeles, and although he carried the physical disability of his slight limp, he hoped that the 'Silver Screen' would immortalise his troubled life. Regrettably, it didn't, and even though he gave his body to the not-discussed side of Tinsel Town, movie roles did not come his way, no matter how powerful the man he slept with was in his attempt to achieve his dream. Now, he found himself being an unhappy parasite surviving off the good fortune of others who had beaten the odds to become a star. By the time Amelia's agent had secured her second role for her, Walter had emerged within the hallowed gates of Horner Studios as the most appropriate candidate to manage the shooting star from England. It did not take Amelia long to discover Walter's secret regarding his sexual proclivities, and his closeted lifestyle meant Amelia could hide a secret about her life in the fast lane of stardom – her bisexuality.

Felicity could not help but wonder what life was like for Amelia as her fame grew in Hollywood. Felicity couldn't escape Amelia's ubiquitous presence as the Airmen swooned for the young English goddess, and it seemed as though a day did not go by that she at least once heard a mention of her name. Still, Felicity paid credence to Joan's words, and she would distract her mind from thinking about Amelia by devoting her thoughts to her studies at Princeton and her monotonous duties at McGuire. The monotonous duties and her disappointment about Princeton University were never far from her lips when she spoke to her father. However, Samuel reminded his daughter that she had impetuously signed up for this life in America, so she had best fulfil her duty if she ever wished to achieve her dreams.

Not too long after the new university year began at Princeton in the fall of 1962, Felicity made up her mind about her ongoing participation in the Psychology Department's darkroom experiment. She took Jack aside on a

Wednesday afternoon in early October after Evelyn and the other researchers had left for the day. They sat at his desk, and her earnest expression immediately told Jack something was up with her. "Okay, Felicity. I am all ears. What is it that you wanted to discuss with me?" Felicity's eyes briefly glanced at the door leading to the darkroom; then she looked back at Jack. "Jack, no offence to you, but it seems to me that young American men are either unsuitable guinea pigs for this experiment or, more importantly, perhaps this experiment is already a self-fulfilling prophecy that its environment is too harsh for the men's minds to cope with." Jack was slightly offended by Felicity's opinion. Still, he was intrigued by the direction this discussion was heading in. "So, what are you saying, Felicity? Are you suggesting we finalise our studies and report on the cases we have examined?" She shook her head to dismiss that proposition. "No, Jack. I am not suggesting there is no further utility to your experiment." Then there was silence. Felicity was hesitant to reveal what was on her mind. Eventually, Jack cracked their cone of silence. "Well, for heaven's sake. What are you suggesting?" Felicity stared deep into Jack's eyes. "I have previously made this request; however, I guess I will have to make it again. Please put me in the darkroom. Put me in the darkroom because I cannot see what possible use for the RAF or USAF I can be if I do not experience what life is like inside the darkroom."

They stared into each other's eyes. She looked for signs of sexism. He looked for signs of psychological weakness. If there was one mental attribute about Felicity that could not be defeated, it was that she could stare down a man. Jack acquiesced to her request. "Okay, you will be our first guinea pig, as you so described it, for the university year. Be here at 7:00 a.m. on Monday, October 15. We will conduct our standard debrief, as we did with our previous participants, and then place you in the darkroom. Will the Air Force hierarchy permit you to be off the base on that day?" Of course, they would. "If it involves me being exposed to some form of prisoner-of-war torture technique, Her Majesty's Air Force would be more than glad for a woman to be subjected to it." Felicity's ironic sarcasm and subtle disdain for the RAF were obvious to Jack, who smiled in acknowledgment. "Alright then, I understand. Well, Flying Officer Bennet, you will be our first subject for the university year. I shall let the other research team members know you have volunteered to be our first participant for the university year. Who knows? Perhaps some brave, strapping young All-American male students might volunteer once they hear a woman is going into the room." Now it was Felicity's turn to smile because she detected the undertones of disappointment in Jack's voice when he referred to 'All-American male?'

Later, when Jack informed Evelyn that Felicity had volunteered to participate, she scoffed and then laughed. Jack could not determine why Evelyn seemed to hold such contempt for Felicity; however, he was not brave enough to confront a brutal 'Ice Queen' like Evelyn.

Just as Felicity foreshadowed to Jack, Reg was more than accommodating of her having time away from the base to be subjected to the world inside the darkroom. As Felicity drove out of McGuire Air Base on the afternoon of Sunday, 14 October, little did she realise what was occurring within the hierarchy of the United States military after one of their spy planes had flown over Cuba.

It was about 5:30 p.m. when Felicity arrived at The Peacock Inn. In what was an ominous sign of what was stirring in the wind of the Cold War, a very cool blast of air blew at Princeton late that afternoon, and the leaves of trees fell around Felicity's jeep as she parked it in the residents' bay of The Peacock Inn. Unfortunately, Prudence was working at the reception desk that afternoon, and as she had done on the prior occasions, Felicity had the misfortune of being greeted by her; Prudence told her how terrible it was that 'That Catholic President of ours is allowing coloured people to have rights like us white folk'. Felicity politely smiled, then rolled her eyes, disgusted at the ignorant woman's racism. Felicity was tired as she had been strangely nervous the prior evening at McGuire when she thought about being locked in the darkroom; she had previously seen numerous male subjects hit the distress button and then subsequently explain the terror they experienced in that room. Felicity asked Prudence for her evening meal to be immediately brought to her room, and, in the off-chance someone from the base tried to call her, not to put any calls through to her because she needed a good night's rest. However, Felicity tossed and turned in her hotel room bed that night. She did not want to make a fool of herself, especially in front of Evelyn. Reg had also tried to call Felicity to forewarn that something was stirring in the winds of the Cold War, but Prudence peremptorily told him she could not put any calls through. An American receptionist told an English officer she would not put his call through to a room; what on Earth was happening in this world?

Felicity arrived at Eno Hall at the designated time of 7:00 a.m. She was exhausted after two sleepless nights and still quite apprehensive about how she would react once locked in the darkroom. However, as soon as she saw the smirk on Evelyn's face, whatever feelings of fatigue and apprehension inside her body and mind fortified themselves into an iron will – no way on Earth would she give that lesbian the satisfaction of watching her succumb to the demons of the darkness. Indeed, there was an emeritus professor formerly of the Harvard Psychology Department there that day, Professor Robert Brady, for whom Jack held high regard and for whom the task of examining a woman's reaction to the darkroom had lured him out of retirement. The initial orientation session took place, and while Jack explained everything she already knew about the room to Felicity, she could not help but notice Evelyn standing in the background, her smirk now an almost indelible feature on her face. And then Felicity entered the darkroom's meal and toilet exchange room, and the main door was shut behind her. She then felt her way into the darkroom, and after closing the door, she moved over to the mattress and lay down. Her thoughts were racing in that darkness; however, there was one thought she kept repeating: "Don't give in to that damn woman outside. Don't fail!" Felicity quickly drifted into a profound sleep, undisturbed by any sensory stimulants in that environment.

Like a bolt of lightning, Felicity sat up in the darkness. She did not know how long she had been asleep, but five hours had drifted by in the outside world. She was thirsty, and in the darkness, she found the steel jug and steel cup, which had been placed in the corner of the room, safe from her accidentally knocking them over while she slept. She gulped down a cup of water, followed by another one. Then she felt the urge to empty her bladder, so once again, she crawled on hands and knees to another corner of the room where the bizarre little chemical box was kept. When she opened the lid, the smell of formaldehyde offended her nose, an unexpected reaction. 'Imagine what it will smell like after a day,' she thought to herself as she urinated in the darkness, squatting on top of a box of toxic chemicals. And then she crawled back over to the mattress and sat alone in the dark, with only her thoughts to keep her company.

After fifteen minutes of idly thinking about her childhood, during which she briefly contended with the voice of her late grandmother chastising her again about her chosen career path, Felicity decided to use the little light box on the front wall. It was the only sensory stimulation available to her in the darkroom. She crawled over to the front wall, stood up and felt her way with her hands around it until she found the lightbox. The light box was six inches long and four inches high. It should have contained a card with some squiggly lines and a dial she could turn, which would activate a light on a board outside the darkroom, signalling to the observers that she was using the device. The round dial was there; rather than a card of squiggly lines, there was a black-and-white picture of Amelia's face. Felicity did not need too long to work out who was responsible for that picture being there – 'Evelyn, you bitch' she thought to herself as she quickly closed the box. However, the deliberate act of psychological torture that Evelyn had surreptitiously placed in the lightbox began weaving its spell in Felicity's mind. The more she tried not to think about Amelia, the more the images of her on the silver screen in her bikini played out in Felicity's mind. The images of Amelia in Felicity's mind began to transform from her wearing a bikini to being naked. Then Felicity did something she had never done before in her life. She placed her hand down into her underpants. She began to feel her vagina as her mind imagined Amelia's naked body pressed against her now, and she parted the pubic hairs to allow her fingers to feel all the physically stimulating components of her vaginal region. Then, like another sensory stimulant, Joan's voice echoed throughout what was just previously a universe of carnal desire: "Felicity, are you a lesbian?" She quickly withdrew her hand from her underpants and shook her head. "Damn that bitch Evelyn. I am not a lesbian," she said to herself in the darkness.

Felicity was initially angry with Evelyn for playing her little psychological game. Then, after about five minutes of stewing on her anger, Felicity decided to turn the tables on her torturer. She crawled in the dark once again, and eventually, she found the lightbox. Felicity opened it again, and Amelia's face stared back at her. She glanced at the picture briefly, and then Felicity spoke to the faint image of Amelia. "I am sorry. I love you, but I'm unable to make love to you. I am not like that." And then her return serve of torturing Evelyn began. Felicity began to turn the round dial, and sure enough, a light lit up on the board in the examination room, immediately bringing a smirk of enjoyment to Evelyn's face. However, Felicity did not stop turning that dial. Indeed, as she looked at the image of Amelia, she turned that dial without stopping for what seemed like a short time in that room, whereas outside, it had been flashing for 90 minutes. By now, Evelyn was seething as she realised Felicity was playing with her mind. Eventually, after two hours, Felicity stopped turning that dial as there was a bell buzzing in the darkroom to inform Felicity that food was waiting for her in the exchange room and for her to bring the little chemical toilet to that room so that it could be subsequently emptied and a fresh stew of chemicals returned to her.

Felicity's mind had prevailed, and by 6:00 p.m., she had lasted longer in the darkroom than any of the previous male subjects. Jack, Evelyn, and Dr Brady all went home for the evening. A male final-year psychology undergraduate student had to sit guard in the examination room until the following day to deliver more food and a fresh chemical toilet to Felicity, and to assist her if she had to press the distress button. However, Felicity did not become distressed in the darkroom. Instead, she sat there thinking about her supposed predicament regarding being deployed to America by the RAF. Her disappointment about not working with NASA personnel in the darkroom experiment transformed into a determination to stay in America, be accepted into NASA, and become the first woman to travel into space. At some point that evening, she fell asleep, and there were no thoughts or dreams about either Amelia or Evelyn. There was just the bliss of her mind imaging the sensation of being in space and looking back out of the space capsule's window to look down upon the world.

She must have slept for almost eight hours, but Felicity was abruptly awoken to the sound of banging outside the darkroom door, a most unexpected event. The banging did not stop, and then she heard a muffled voice screaming through the door, which she soon recognised as Jack's. "Felicity, can you hear me?" Felicity crawled over to the darkroom door and shouted back through it. "Jack? Is that you, Jack? Why are you banging on the darkroom door?" She heard Jack's voice through the darkroom door, and his words were foreboding of doom. "Felicity, nuclear war is about to break out with the Soviets. We have to shut down the experiment and go home now." Felicity was just as surprised by the news as she was by the broken protocol of the banging on the darkroom door. 'Nuclear war about to break out? What can I do to avoid the apocalypse? Go back to an airbase which will be one of the immediate targets?' she thought. "No, Jack. I am not leaving the room. Go away, and leave me be."

On the other side of the door, Jack could not believe his ears. "Felicity, are you insane? I said nuclear war is about to break out, so you must leave this room!" His shouted command was met with steely determination in response. "No, Jack! I am pretty content in here. Now, go away, and when I am ready, I will leave the darkroom." Jack did not know what to say. Not only had Felicity lasted longer in the darkroom than any other person, but she also resisted leaving that room in the face of a nuclear apocalypse. However, it was an experiment, and if the war did not materialise, as Jack was hoping it wouldn't, he would have an excellent test case on which to base his subsequent research. He acquiesced to the contentment of the RAF officer. "Alright, Felicity. Have it your way. I will leave you some snacks, water and a fresh chemical toilet in the exchange room. I will return here later today or tonight if war does not break out. If it does, then heaven help all of us." Jack left the exchange room and returned with the food, water and the fresh chemical toilet. After closing the exchange room door, he pushed the buzzer to inform Felicity he had left the supplies for her and then quickly made his way home to duck and cover under a kitchen table.

In the darkness, Felicity thought about nuclear war breaking out, and she initially panicked for fear of her father's safety. Still, her mind fought through the panic again and found clarity in this thought: 'What on Earth could I do here in America for Dad in England? If they blow us to kingdom come, so be it. Dad knows that I love him.' So, she sat there in the darkness, thinking about her father and waiting for the sound of a nuclear blast pushing its way through the walls. However, that nuclear blast did not materialise, and Felicity's mind resumed thinking about being in outer space. Inside the darkroom, Felicity's mind was able to venture into an imaginary world where she felt weightless and, unlike the world outside, in space, her mind felt at one with her body; feelings of physical inadequacy because of her small breasts and thin hips did not occupy her mind. Whereas people like William and Evelyn tried to take advantage of her in the outside world, Felicity felt invincible in the darkroom as she began to gain insight into the telltale signs of those who wish to feed off you instead of those who nurture you. But whereas she was blind, could she now see?

She slept again, and when she awoke, she ate the food and drank the water Jack had left for her and, of course, disposed of her stinking chemical box for the new stinking chemical box. Eventually, just before midnight, the buzzer went off to inform Felicity that more food and water had been left for her in the exchange room, along with another stinking box. As the world sat on tenterhooks for four days until being relieved to hear the crisis was over, Felicity maintained her vigil in the darkroom, stunning every single member of the research team, the RAF and the USAF, and even the NASA researchers who were undertaking far fewer challenging experiments with the astronauts. Reg was particularly surprised during the four days of the crisis that despite his repeated requests for her to return to base, Felicity disobeyed those orders and remained in the darkroom. Felicity's mind contemplated life and death, religion and science, love and hate. She accepted that religion was a manifestation of human beings' innate fear of death and, most importantly, there was no 'afterlife' as the world of any religion tried to instil in her psyche. In her imaginary world of being in space, she accepted that after she had taken her last breath in life, she would give back her molecular structures to the universe from which she had borrowed them. Eventually, on Tuesday, October 23, 1962, Felicity pressed the button to inform the research team she had had enough of being in the darkroom.

During those eight days, Felicity explored every square inch of her psyche and felt more at ease with herself than at any previous moment. Once again, she was famous, but only among military personnel, academics, and some NASA personnel. For the rest of the world, it was not even an event worth mentioning in the media. A woman had proven she was made of more resilient matter than a man, but it did not attract any media attention. However, she had defeated Evelyn with mind games, and Jack agreed that her contribution to the study should be enshrined in an academic paper on how the mind can defeat the torture of the darkroom.

As for meeting Evelyn's husband, Felicity did not wish to anchor herself to that woman's strange cult of misconceived feminism, which only pursued carnal desire and, indeed, involved another act of sexual assault Felicity had to endure but could not report. In Evelyn's world, how could Felicity make her way into the world of NASA without having to give up her body to the cult of closet lesbians? She informed Jack that once she had completed her paper, she would continue to participate in his research program; however, her participation would now be infrequent, as she had acquired enough information to assist the RAF and USAF in understanding how the use of the darkroom could compromise the fragile minds of servicemen. She believed that it was the best decision she could make about her future to try to extricate herself from Evelyn's cauldron of sexual servitude. This broth seemed to be the only remedy Felicity could take if she wished to gain access to NASA. Nevertheless, fewer interactions with that woman had to occur because Felicity was adamant in her mind that, unlike Evelyn, she wasn't a lesbian.

When she returned to McGuire Air Base, Felicity had to report to Reg immediately. During her vigil, which included the time she spent at The Peacock Inn, Felicity had not reported to Reg, even though, during the world crisis, almost entering a nuclear holocaust meant that all RAF personnel had to return to base. That Tuesday afternoon, the air was cold, and when she knocked on Reg's office door, his commanding voice to enter sounded stern. Felicity opened Reg's office door, and his eyes immediately narrowed as she stepped in and saluted him. "Sir", she said with utmost respect but also courage. Reg stared at her; his narrowed eyes slowly began to reopen before he responded. "Shut the door, Flying Officer Bennet." She obeyed his command but noticed he had not invited her to sit. After shutting the door, Felicity turned around and resumed her stance of coming to attention before a superior officer. "I don't believe I need to express in too many words my dismay and anger that you disobeyed a direct order to return to base. I was almost at the point of issuing a Court-Martial for your recalcitrant conduct on the second day of the crisis. However, the head of the research programme informed me that you had outlasted all the male participants' tolerance of that isolation. He requested that I forgive you, as there were benefits for the armed services in allowing you to remain in that room for as long as you wished. Therefore, you will not be the subject of a Court-Martial I might have issued. Still, take this acknowledgment of your deeds as a warning: when I issue a direct order for you to do anything, you must obey it. Are you clear about that?"

Felicity had never seen Reg display such hostility, and it occurred to her that he perhaps felt humiliated by her mental endurance displayed in the darkroom. Nevertheless, she had to respect the rules if she wished to get into NASA. "Yes, sir. I am sorry, sir, and it won't happen again." Reg nodded. "Very well, then. You had better write that research paper immediately, as the American intelligence agency, the RAF, and the USAF all wish to review it. Indeed, every bloody military and intelligence office wants to know why and how a woman could outlast a man. So, write that paper, post haste." Once again, she displayed her genuine respect for her superior officer. "Yes, sir." Reg then resumed entering his manual and dismissed Felicity from his presence. "Very well then, at ease, and you may leave."

Felicity was about halfway out of Reg's office when he called out to her. "Oh, before you go, Flying Officer. I have a telegram here for you from Joan de Montesquieu. It arrived this morning." Felicity took the telegram from Reg's outstretched hand and immediately returned to her barracks.

Felicity sat down on her bed to read Joan's telegram. She had not received any correspondence from Joan for almost a year, which she inferred as a sign that she was stuck at McGuire. She felt nervous about reading the contents of this correspondence, as she anticipated that the news would not be good after such a lengthy break in hearing from Joan. Felicity felt it was best for her to read it rather than delay the obvious:

Dear Felicity,

I hope America is treating you well, and I do hope you were not too unnerved by the recent missile crisis between the Americans and the Soviets.

I apologise for not writing to you sooner. My excuse for the delay is personal because Stuart and I became the proud parents of a baby boy two months ago. He was eight pounds and six ounces in weight and eight and a half inches long, a big bouncing boy. We have named him Charles Stuart de Montesquieu. My recovery from having Charles is progressing well, and Stuart and I have decided to try for another child in a few years, but for now, we are content with our little fellow.

Regrettably, this correspondence also brings you some terrible news. Notwithstanding all my father's efforts, it appears the Americans will not permit a woman to fly their jets. My father feels awful about the bureaucratic mistake and wants me to tell you that you could be redeployed back home to England. Still, that means removing you from the opportunity to pursue your dreams with the American space programme. Daddy and I are sorry for this mess, Felicity. Please forgive us.

Take care, and please know I am proud of you.

Love,

Joan

Felicity pondered this news about her career options for a moment. Although she was disappointed by the 'bureaucratic mistake', there was some merit in Joan's subtle words of wisdom. Returning to England would remove her from the country where her desired career path might become a reality. In the darkroom, she resolved to remain in America despite the disappointment. That decision was now evident in her mind; she could only leave this planet and go into space by remaining in a foreign country. And so it was, she wrote back politely to Joan to inform her that she would stay in America, continue studying at Princeton, and try with all her might to pursue her dream. Felicity congratulated Joan on becoming a mother and said she looked forward to meeting him one day.

So, she would remain in America to pursue her dream, and Felicity hoped 1963 would be a better year than 1962 had been. She also completed that paper post haste for Jack as she had been ordered to do by Reg, and, in her usual style, Felicity concluded by forthrightly stating the female mind is far more resilient than the male mind. However, lingering in the background was Evelyn and Felicity's encounter with her, which had been demoralising, confusing and now challenging for her regarding her pursuit of her dream.

CHAPTER 31

If thou had any faults, then this solitary fact was certain,
Entering relationships without love is an unnecessary burden.

A New Year means new beginnings. Felicity's new beginning materialised when a new lecturer was appointed to her post-graduate aeronautical engineering class at the start of the Spring Term in January 1963. Professor Ronald Golding was a former Princeton student, having completed his PhD in aeronautical engineering there after his studies were interrupted by his service in the USAF during World War II. He had returned to Princeton after lecturing at Yale for several years, and, most importantly, he also worked for NASA. Misfortune had become good fortune for Felicity; whereas 1962 seemed to be shrouded in darkness for her, at least the Sun had come out for Felicity at Princeton University regarding her aeronautical engineering course.

The drudgery of her astrophysics course, which examined the Sun, had not changed. She even politely asked the course's professor if they could turn the telescope around to study the lunar surface or, perhaps, Mars. Anything other than repeatedly studying solar flares. The response was always a firm no.

From the very first aeronautical engineering lecture, Felicity and Professor Golding formed a healthy student/ teacher bond. The first topic was a historical discussion, following his introduction to the class and an explanation of his impressive credentials. "So, how about we discuss the difficulties the USAF has experienced with Delta Dagger or the Air Force referring to it as the Deuce? Who can tell me what Convair got wrong about the first supersonic aircraft?" This question was right up Felicity's alley, as she had spent the past fifteen months of almost daily repetitive drudgery reviewing the pros and cons of the Delta Dagger as part of her duties for the RAF. She earnestly shot up her hand, and when he looked at his student roll, it was not hard to find the only female student in what was otherwise an all-male class. "Our British friend, Flying Officer Bennet, seems quicker than the Deuce lads."

A murmur of laughter went around the lecture theatre. "Seriously, though, what is your answer, Flying Officer?" There was nothing Felicity enjoyed more than one-upmanship. "Right from the outset, there were problems, Professor. There were problems with the original airframe and fuselage design because it overlooked basic aerodynamic principles. Then, there were several ongoing problems with propulsion, radar, and fire-control systems. The aircraft encountered issues with drag when approaching the transonic speed zone, so the engineers had to redesign the wings. Subsequently, it was discovered that the fuselage was not optimised appropriately for the transonic flight profile, resulting in excessive drag that prevented breaking the sound barrier. The redesign of the plane introduced maintenance complications, and the design phase devolved into a prolonged struggle with the fundamental physics of flight. The final design surpassed Mach 1; however, it could only do so under optimal circumstances because actual operational use rarely makes this possible due to concerns about structural integrity, fuel consumption, and reliability."

There was silence in the lecture theatre as Felicity concisely summarised the historical problems the USAF had experienced, and to a lesser extent, still experienced, with the Delta Dagger. A broad smile broke out on Professor Golding's face, and he genuinely acknowledged her comprehensive knowledge. "There we go, boys. Our British friend has succinctly summed up the problems with the Deuce. Soon, she will be teaching me about the problems with the Saturn-1 rocket." More murmurs of laughter broke out in the lecture theatre. Still, Professor Golding admired Felicity's comprehensive knowledge, and it was immediately evident that she was the 'teacher's pet' student. He turned back towards the blackboard and began both writing and lecturing his class simultaneously. "The basic aerodynamic principle with the Deuce that Flying Officer Bennet referred to is the area rule; it's designed to minimise wave drag, which starts to appear as aircraft near Mach 1. We engineers discovered that as an aeroplane approaches Mach 1, the air flowing around the fuselage and wings begins to exceed Mach 1. This is known as the transonic speed range, which the Flying Officer so elegantly referred to before. As the supersonic flow develops around your aircraft, shock waves form, creating boundaries of pressure where the airflow transitions from supersonic to subsonic flow. These shock waves generate immense drag and require significant thrust to overcome. The solution was to taper the fuselage where the wings spread out, balancing the total cross-sectional area and minimising wave drag. So, that is the area rule, and during this term, we will examine the design of many military aircraft to see if we can identify design flaws and develop solutions." Professor Golding then discussed various other topics of aeronautical design, mentally noting Felicity's eager note-taking compared to the more lackadaisical approach of her fellow male students.

After the lecture, Felicity was the last student to pack their bag. She was unexpectedly interrupted. "Excuse me, Flying Officer. Do you have a moment?" Professor Golding had walked over to where she had been seated without noticing. She was slightly startled. "Oh, my goodness, please excuse me, Professor, for I was frightened as I was not expecting you." Professor Golding held up his open palms to apologise physically. "You don't ever have to worry about me, and please, when the others are not around, call me Ron, as long as I can call you Felicity." Felicity smiled. "Of course, Ron. Felicity is fine by me." Ron nodded in appreciation. "I don't know if you noticed, but I was watching you throughout that entire lecture, Felicity." She hadn't noticed and shook her head with a puzzled expression. Ron continued to speak. "Well, I was, and that is because people like me are always on the lookout for a student whom the gods of engineering have blessed with a superior understanding of aeronautical engineering. You strike me as that type of student, Felicity. So, tell me, what are your career goals? Do you want to continue studying, or should I please pardon me for intruding into your personal affairs? Will you enter the commercial aircraft field after serving in the RAF?"

It was almost as if she had been taken back in time to Woldingham, many years ago, when Joan had asked her a similar question. Candour had served her well back then, and now it was time to be candid with a man from NASA. "Well, to be frank, Ron, and please don't laugh at me, but I want to work for NASA or, oh, to hell with it – Ron, I want to be the first female astronaut to go into space." Felicity waited for the older man to laugh; however, he pondered over her words before speaking. "That is a tall order, Felicity. Don't get me wrong, I am on your side. However, we Americans are not permitting women to fly our fighter jets, let alone become astronauts. But do you know something? I believe in you, Felicity. I believe in you because you are a thorough and attentive student who knows her facts about jet fighters, such as the Delta Dagger. I bet you are probably writing a report for the RAF advising them not to spend a penny on purchasing those jets from Convair." She wrote the report but could not reveal those details to Ron. "Don't worry; I do not expect you to answer that question. Anyway, I wanted to talk with you to see if you were interested in doing extra credit work with me studying the design problems of the Saturn-1 rocket?" Felicity's eyes lit up like a slot machine that had just turned all its slots to the jackpot. "Are you saying I will get to work with you at NASA?"

There was a momentary delay, and then Ron held up his hands like a grandfather trying to calm down an excited grandchild at a candy shop. "Whoa, slow down there. You must learn to crawl before you can walk, let alone run. No, I'm not saying work with me at NASA. Still, the extra-credit studies might – I stress the word, might – get you in the door for employment there. So what do you say?" There was only going to be one answer. "Of course, Ron. I would be delighted to do this extra credit work with you." He smiled. "Good. I was pretty sure you would say yes. I will speak with you after class about our first small project from our lecture. Now, you had better get out of here as you probably have to return to McGuire Air Base before dinner time." Felicity nodded and smiled before leaving the lecture theatre. And sure enough, when they finished the following lecture, Ron spoke to Felicity about their first research project with the Saturn-1 rocket.

Time seemed to slip by quickly for Felicity, and in May of 1963, Princeton University had its usual end-of-the-university-year recess. Reg had assigned her the task of examining some new Delta Dagger jet aircraft that the USAF were proposing the RAF purchase from them, and he was aware that Felicity had been performing extra credit work in her post-graduate studies with Ron, so if anybody were going to detect aeronautical problems with the Deuce, it would be Felicity. Felicity inspected the Delta Daggers in the USAF hangar on a warm Wednesday afternoon. She had access to the engineering designs for the previous iterations of the Deuce. Notwithstanding the USAF's assurances to the RAF that this new design had addressed all the engineering issues, Felicity was not convinced that the design had resolved the previous problems with the area rule.

As she was writing down her notations at a desk at the back of the hangar, Felicity heard the overpowering boom of a USAF officer's voice. "I don't care who your daddy is, Captain Hoover, nor do I care that you are now on the shortlist for the next round of potential trainees for NASA's astronaut program. If I tell you during a training dogfight not to depart from my wing as my wingman, and you break that order again like you did today, you will be out of the USAF quicker than shit through a goose! Do you understand me?!?" The mention of NASA caught Felicity's attention, so it was evident to Dwight Hoover that she was watching him out of the corner of his eye. "Yes, sir, Major sir!" The Major was about six inches shorter than Dwight; however, his superior rank demanded that Dwight be obsequious to him, and the Major was not done with his verbal excoriation of him. "And, don't think the boys at NASA will not hear about today either. I am recording your disobedience on your personnel record, so you will have some explaining to do come July. Do you understand me, Captain?" Dwight had to take the short man's medicine. "Yes, sir, Major Sir!" By this stage, Felicity had risen to her feet, and as the Major turned on his heels, he caught a glimpse of her, including her RAF officer's uniform. "Who do you think you are looking at, you Limey? This is none of your business." Limey? Felicity had not been called that old World War II-era slur before.

In his brisk, short man's stride, the Major stormed away on a mission to record his disobedience in Dwight's personnel file. Dwight took off his flying helmet, and his head dipped down as he looked over towards Felicity, who was still standing behind the desk in shock. "I suppose you heard every single word of that, ma'am?" His Virginian drawl was polite and endearing with its undertones of embarrassment. Even though it was a rhetorical question, Felicity nodded. A hint of a smile came over Dwight's face, and he lifted his head so that he didn't look so emasculated now that his superior officer was out of sight. He began walking over towards Felicity as he spoke. "Oh shoot, don't worry about little Major Hopgood; as my Daddy says, short men have no place in the Air Force. Still, he shouldn't have called you a Limey, ma'am. That was impolite." By now, only the desk separated Dwight and Felicity. "I'm Dwight; Dwight Hoover. You don't need to introduce yourself to me, Flying Officer Bennet. I know who you are and what you did back home. All of us on base know about your miraculous flying in England." Felicity was surprised by Dwight's comment because even though she had seen him occasionally around the base, he had not previously introduced himself. All the USAF officers knew about her, yet they had not fraternised with her. She did not know what to say, so Dwight had to draw the words from her mouth. "What's the matter? Has the cat got your tongue?"

Embarrassed by her silence, Felicity caught her nerves to respond to the tall, well-built USAF officer. "No, not at all. I was processing what you told me. I'm sorry, I didn't mean to sticky-beak into your business with the Major, Captain Hoover." The smile broadened on Dwight's face. "Heh, you can call me Dwight. And don't worry about the knee-high major. My Daddy will find out what he called you, so if anyone's personnel record is going to have a red mark, it will be his." Felicity now felt more at ease, and even though his facial features were plain, Dwight had an alluring aura because of one word she heard – NASA.

"How impolite of me. It's nice to meet you. Please call me Felicity." She held out her right hand to be shaken; however, Dwight, in his Virginian manner, just extended his fingertips to grip Felicity's fingertips. He had soft skin, which felt nice to Felicity.

They looked at each other momentarily, neither knowing what to say. Eventually, Dwight built up the nerve to ask her a question he had been wanting to ask for a while. "Say, I have a leave pass for the evening until midnight. I don't know what the rules are like with you Brits, and if you don't feel comfortable, let me know, but would you like to join me for dinner tonight at Papa Joe's Pies in Trenton?" Felicity's eyes widened in surprise, which caused Dwight to awkwardly assure her that he did not mean to be forward. "Hey, don't be worried. My invitation is friendly. It's not like I'm asking you..." He had to bite his tongue, as he knew what he had asked her was what he was trying to deny. Felicity smiled as she watched his eyes get confused. "On a date?" Dwight smiled. "Yeah. It's not a date. It's just a chance to chat and eat some of the best pizza in New Jersey. So, what do you say?" Felicity's guard was up after her experiences with William and Evelyn. However, Dwight seemed to be honourable enough, and besides that, she was intrigued to learn more about him being shortlisted for NASA. "I think I can easily arrange a leave pass with my superior, so what time and how do we get there?" Dwight smiled. "I have a car. So why don't you wait outside the Terminal building at 6:00 p.m.? It will take about thirty minutes to get there." Felicity nodded. "Sure, Captain Hoover. See you at 6:00 p.m." They walked away from each other in opposite directions. He thought about how fortunate he was not to make a fool of himself in getting her to come out for dinner; she thought about NASA and how he might be the key to the door.

Reg's attitude about a dinner pass for Felicity to catch up with one of the Yankee USAF officers was typical. "I couldn't care less. Eat some pizza with a Yank. I care more about Delta Daggers. Are they a worthwhile investment for the RAF?" Felicity was brutally frank. "Reg, they were a piece of junk a year ago and are still a piece of junk. I would not pay a shilling for them." Reg did not need to ask any further questions, because if Felicity opined that they were not worth spending a penny on, that was enough for him.

At 6:00 p.m. sharp, Felicity stood outside HQ in her civilian dress, and right on time, Dwight drove up in his sky blue 1960 Chrysler 'New Yorker,' an elegant looking 'Yank Tank' with splayed wings running from above the front door handle on either side back to the car's end, and, of course, white-walled tyres. The car seemed to be a contrast to Dwight's personality; it was elegant and sleek, whereas he was awkward and lacked style. After their initial greeting, Felicity and Dwight didn't speak for the first ten minutes of the half-hour drive to Trenton. The gentle light of that spring afternoon glistened against the freshly sprouted leaves of the Tulip trees, which seemed to overhang the scruffy Pitch Pines. Finally, Felicity broke the nervous silence, and her tone pressed him for information. "So, Dwight. Would you please tell me more about NASA?" Dwight glanced sideways, more out of nerves than reacting to Felicity's importunate query. "What do you want to know?" Felicity would have to extract the information from him. "Well, for example, what did you have to do to be short-listed for the astronaut program?" He shrugged, both hands keeping a firm grip on the steering wheel. "Well, I had to log hundreds of hours in high-performance aircraft. You could say I've been flying at Mach 1 for most of my aviation career in the USAF. Why do you ask?"

The moment of truth. Would he turn the car around and return to McGuire, believing she was insane? "Because I want to be an astronaut." Felicity waited for Dwight to react; however, he didn't even take his eyes off the road. Ten seconds seemed like an hour, but Dwight did not respond. "Did you hear me, Dwight?" He nodded. "So, what are your thoughts?" Now, a response. "I can't see why not. You would have to be qualified. What are you checking out on?" That expression was foreign to Felicity. "Checked out on? What do you mean by that phrase?" Dwight realised the Brits probably didn't speak like that in the RAF. He momentarily took his eyes off the road and looked at Felicity. "What aircraft has the RAF let you fly?" Now came the shame. "A O-1 Bird Dog." Dwight chuckled in his inbred sexism. "You ain't going to fly a rocket after only flying a Cessna. The USAF ain't going to allow a woman to fly an F-110, let alone the Deuce." Felicity looked away, forlornly pondering the woods. Dwight knew she was upset, and he desperately searched for ideas to rescue himself from his faux pas. "You're studying, am I right?" Felicity nodded as she looked out the side window of the car. "What are you studying?" Felicity turned back to look Dwight's way, and as she spoke, she waited for the slightest hint of male chauvinism. "I'm studying postgraduate degrees in astrophysics and aeronautical engineering."

It was salvation through education for Dwight. "Well, there we go, then. NASA needs a large number of people who have studied those subjects. Who knows? Perhaps your university studies will be far more critical to the program in future intakes than guys like me who fly by the seat of their pants." Felicity interrogated him to determine whether he was indulging her dreams. "Do you believe that, Dwight? Do you truly believe NASA will care more about brains than just brawn?" He didn't. Still, he liked this British girl, so he lied. "Of course. My Pa tells me that NASA employs women to do all types of work for them." Felicity couldn't resist responding to the 'all types of work' comment. "Sure. However, NASA isn't employing women to enter the Gemini rockets, are they?" There was no spinning his way out of the web he had woven himself into. Instead, Dwight shook his head and focused on the road ahead.

About ten minutes later, Dwight parked in the street before Papa Joe's Pies. Dwight quickly exited his car to go around and open Felicity's door for her. Still, she beat him to that by opening the door for herself and getting out. Felicity detected that Dwight was disappointed she had done this, so she assured him it was fine. "That's very gallant of you, Dwight. However, I'm not the type of woman who expects men to open doors for her." As bad luck would have it, at that moment, Evelyn walked out of Papa Joe's Pies with Roger, where they had spent the afternoon eating and drinking. Initially, Felicity froze as she saw Evelyn's cold stare directed at her. Even Dwight could feel the crisp breeze from the older woman's cold eyes. Felicity quickly put her arm inside Dwight's, much to his surprise and delight. "Come on, Dwight. Let's go inside. It's too frosty out here for humans." Cutting words, even for the uninitiated, and said loud enough for Evelyn to hear. As they walked into the pizza restaurant arm-in-arm, Dwight could not help but ask what the Cold War was all about. Felicity dismissed the topic out of hand; however, Evelyn's threatening eyes and foul stench lingered in the back of her mind.

Over dinner, Dwight told her how his Daddy and Granddaddy had served in the Army Air Forces during World War I and World War II, as well as how his older brother, Hank, had been shot down and killed during the Korean War. He explained to Felicity that his great-grandfather had been a Major General in the American Army. So, it was expected of him and his late older brother to serve in the armed forces. His older sister, Shirley, had married a United States Army Colonel, Bob Sanders. He didn't initially get the joke when Felicity laughed out loud about Shirley marrying Colonel Sanders. Still, as she continued to convulse in fits of laughter, it dawned on Dwight for the first time that his sister had married a man whose name was synonymous with a fast food outlet – Felicity could not believe that his entire family had not made that connection. She told him about her life in England, including her mother being killed in the Blitz. He explained how his family members were Baptists, and they were from Norfolk in the south of Virginia – Felicity's mind sighed in relief: "Thank goodness they are not Lutherans." She told him her family was Catholic, which didn't seem to trouble him. He told her his family were staunch Republicans; she told him her family were Liberal Democrats. And, of course, they talked about NASA. They enjoyed the night at Papa Joe's Pies.

Later that night, when Dwight dropped her back at the RAF barracks, he couldn't help but ask for another night out again. "So, how about we go back there at the same time next week? It's a great place to eat, isn't it?" Felicity smiled back at him. "Yes, and yes." Like a child being told they were getting a new bicycle for their birthday, Dwight closed his eyes and grinned, then leaned over as if to kiss her cheek; however, Felicity put out her right hand, allowing him to kiss it instead. And so it began. They began to see each other every Wednesday night for pizza at Papa Joe's Pies. It was a long, hot summer, but in late September 1963, Felicity finally permitted Dwight to kiss her on the lips after one of their Wednesday nights at Papa Joe's Pies. Dwight felt like he had won the lottery. Felicity felt like she was one step closer to her dream. The kiss was gentle and sweet, yet it lacked the spark of her first kiss so many years ago. They were chalk and cheese, the odd couple of the combined Cold War service, but at least for Felicity, she felt the intermittent questions about her sexuality had been answered, or so she thought.

CHAPTER 32

Felicity entered the final year of her post-graduate studies in September 1963, during which three positive events occurred. Yet, the autumn winds were blowing in a foreboding warning.

Her academic career with Ron in aeronautical engineering had steered her on the pathway to an Advanced Degree, and he, indeed, implored Felicity to continue her studies to obtain a doctorate. Ron had already mentioned Felicity's name among the powers-that-be of NASA's aeronautical engineering division as a talented candidate for the future expansion of the space programme's engineering workforce. Still, there were always two issues those faceless people would raise as an obstacle regarding Felicity's employment: she wasn't an American, nor was she married, let alone married to an American; the RAF deployed her for the joint Cold War military cooperation commitment between the RAF and USAF, which meant she could be ordered back to the United Kingdom upon completing the tenure of her service at McGuire Air Base. Ron candidly discussed the feedback he received from his superiors at NASA with Felicity, including her marital status. It frustrated Felicity as a woman that she was expected to be married. While her mind told her it was demeaning to her status as a woman, it only affirmed that she needed to do whatever was required to remain in America to fulfil her dreams. By early October 1963, Ron also informed Felicity that he would be assuming the position of head of the Aerospace and Aeronautical Engineering Department at Stanford University when the new academic year commenced in August 1964.

Ron wanted Felicity to follow him to Stanford to obtain her doctorate; however, this step would present another obstacle for Felicity regarding her evolving relationship with Dwight. Their relationship had formed a close personal bond between two loners at McGuire Air Base. He was the son of the highest-ranking officer in the USAF, and that familial tie made other USAF officers jealous. They were steadfast in their belief that Dwight was an average aviator whose good fortune in rising through the ranks and being short-listed for NASA's astronaut programme occurred because of his father. There was some merit in those officers' steadfastly held beliefs. Among the RAF, Felicity was seen as a sideshow attraction due to her daredevil deeds while a member of the UAS. The other male officers took a superficial interest in her presence, and even now, her leading supporter, Reg, seemed to find her presence a distraction rather than serving any utility for the joint Cold War commitment.

Felicity felt that her tie to NASA, vis-à-vis Dwight, could be severed if he were not selected for astronaut training. The evolution of their relationship had been born out of a shared goal: The desire to be an astronaut. She had remained celibate with Dwight, yet felt an attraction to him. The attraction was the ever-increasing likelihood he would be accepted into NASA's astronaut programme, and that attraction had manifested into a committed relationship. Felicity kept him focused on his goal. Dwight's raging hormones wanted the relationship to go to the next level; however, after having suffered previous sexual assaults, Felicity had one barrier in her mind: No sex with Dwight. However, as their relationship blossomed, so did the nauseating pet names. He called her Honey Bunny; she called him Teddy Bear. Dwight was now an additional reason why Felicity believed she needed to stay in America, but her reasoning was flawed by the seed it had germinated.

If one autumn wind by the end of October 1963 had brought warmth to Felicity's world, it was the news that the Psychology Department had decided the darkroom studies had acquired enough information for Jack's doctoral paper, and the combined Cold War military intelligence of the Americans and British, which meant Evelyn was no longer required on campus. The day Evelyn left the Psychology Department with her box of documents and materials coincided with Felicity's delivery of her final observer notes to Jack. As Evelyn marched out the doors of Eno Hall, Felicity remained within Evelyn's observable field of vision, and the smirk on the younger English woman's face only ingrained animosity, indeed hatred, into Evelyn's heart. Evelyn's husband had already decided to take up employment in the private sector, which meant that for Felicity, the forbidden path to NASA via Evelyn was no longer an issue.

During the second week of November 1963, one of the reasons for the foreboding winds manifested itself in an urgent telegram Samuel had sent to Felicity. She had returned from working with Ron on an engineering task, applying her expertise to the next generation of rockets he was developing for NASA. It was a cold, late fall afternoon on Thursday, November 14, 1963, when Felicity arrived back at McGuire Air Base. As she entered her barrack, there was the haunting presence of an international telegram on the floor, which some careless Airman had shoved under the door. An urgent international telegram did not need to be opened to reveal its gloomy news. Felicity could feel the blood draining from her extremities and the chill running up her spine as she picked up the lonely piece of paper from the floor. She saw on the back of the telegram that her father had sent it, and she expected the worst. Sure enough, when Felicity opened the telegram, the news was grim:

Dear Felicity,

At 6:00 a.m., I went to the cottage to see why Grandpa had not come into the kitchen for breakfast. To my sorrow, I found my father dead on the floor of his bedroom. The doctor said he probably died on his feet before he managed to go to bed, and I will not describe the rest of the details for you because they are too ghastly for me to reduce into writing. The funeral is scheduled for next Friday, 22 November 1963. I have allowed this time for you and, regrettably, my charming sister to make your respective ways back home.

Love always,

Dad

Although her grandfather held nothing but cold eyes for her when she last saw him more than two years beforehand, grief began to overcome her, and she immediately ran to her RAF office to call her father, even though it was not a designated day for Felicity to make such a call. Once the international connection was made to the telephone at her father's home, it rang only twice before Samuel answered; the emotion in his voice was enough of a trigger for Felicity. "Hello, Samuel Bennet speaking." Felicity's tears immediately met his tearful voice. "Dad, it's me. I just read your telegram about Grandpa and…" She could not finish her sentence, and at the opposite end, Samuel, who was traumatised by finding his father in the manner that he had, also broke down into tears before being able to gather himself together to respond. "I know, my little sweetheart, it is dreadful news, and I am sorry you had to find out this way."

Felicity reached out with her left hand to extract a handful of tissues from the drawer in her desk, which she used to wipe her eyes and nose before responding to Samuel, who had broken down again. "Dad, it's okay. There was no other way you could tell me. I am just sorry for you because you discovered Grandpa in that state and…" She once again could not finish her sentence, her grief manifesting itself in not only the passing of her grandfather but also being an ocean away from her father. Samuel once again gathered himself to speak. "It's fine, my darling, let the tears out." He waited several moments to hear Felicity calm down on the other end of the line. "I know he was horrible to you when you last saw him. However, deep down, he loved you, Felicity. I gather you were able to read the entire telegram?" Through a snuffled response, she confirmed she had. "Yes, Dad. The funeral is being held next Friday." She felt a wave of grief again, prompting Samuel to ask about the information she had intended to volunteer beforehand. "Will you be able to obtain leave to attend the funeral?" Her response was immediate, even though she had not asked Reg. "Of course, Dad. I will be there." Samuel's final words were telling for Felicity. "Good. I will need you there. I feel like an orphan. Indeed, I am one, and, to make matters worse, my sister will be attending with her husband, who has a form of paralysis, but you will discover in due course why I called him that. Anyway, my little darling, I don't feel like talking much about anything. I want to have a couple of stiff brandies and then try to get some sleep. I love you." Felicity began to break down again. "Goodbye. Daddy. I love you, too."

The call ended, and Felicity was not only suffering the grief of loss but also the grief of hearing her father's traumatised voice. She immediately went in search of Dwight, for whom there was one lonely place he liked to sit on Thursday night – at the USAF Officers' Club bar. Felicity was not ordinarily entitled to enter this club; however, she did not care on this occasion. Much to the surprise of Dwight and the several USAF officers at the club that night, Felicity walked straight into the club and up to Dwight, throwing her arms around him and breaking down into tears once more. "Hey, Honey Bunny, what's the matter?" His alarmed southern Virginian drawl seemed to drown out the sound of Doris Day playing on the jukebox. "Just hold me, Teddy Bear, please." She would later pour out her heart to Dwight about how a chapter of her life had unexpectedly closed and, in particular, how her Grandpa used to make her train every day since she was a little girl to be a runner, which is why she still kept to her daily routine of jogging around McGuire Air Force Base. However, she could not open up to Dwight about the trauma she suffered because of her grandmother's disparaging remarks about her physical attributes.

The RAF granted Felicity urgent bereavement leave to travel back home to England for her grandfather's funeral. Fortuitously for Felicity, the RAF had an Argosy *AW660* departing from McGuire Air Base at 6:00 a.m. on Tuesday, 19 November 1963, which meant that, with all the various stops to top up fuel, including Nuuk in Greenland, the journey would take several days. Then, upon her arrival at RAF HQ at Andover, eventually, after a series of changing train lines, she arrived on the train at Colchester Station at 5:00 p.m. on Thursday, 21 November 1963. Samuel was waiting for Felicity outside the train station in his recently acquired maroon Jaguar Mark X saloon. After initially hugging her father tightly, Felicity remarked on the impressive motor vehicle. "My goodness! Dad! You must have broken the bank to purchase this car." Samuel smiled and opened the front passenger door for his daughter. "I purchased it about a month ago, and it's second-hand. The agricultural business has been kind to me, whilst the years have not, and, in any event, I always wanted a nice town car. Come in before the cold night's air gives you a chill."

It was not a long drive home, but it was long enough for Samuel to share some further regrettable family news with Felicity. "So, my sister and her husband arrived yesterday." His tone of voice immediately signalled there was terrible news in the wind. "Oh, yes." Felicity's tone signalled that she anticipated some lousy news coming her way; however, she did not expect what followed. "It was about mid-morning, and they had arrived without calling me from Colchester Station to tell me that they were on their way in a cab. Hugh had his usual nonchalant air of Australian arrogance as he walked into my house without an invitation, closely followed by your Aunt Anne, who was holding an envelope. I had just finished cleaning up the breakfast room from having my morning tea when I walked out to the hallway to see them walking through the front door. Ironically, your snot-nosed cousins had not been brought with them."

Felicity sounded even more concerned about the direction this news was heading in. "Oh dear, please don't tell me something awful occurred, did it, Dad?" Samuel nodded as he drove along the road that would lead to the entrance of the farm. "Yes, after a very brief and cold greeting from them, Anne handed me the envelope she was carrying. I knew immediately it would be about my father's estate; my sister always had a sinister glint about money when we were children. Anyway, inside the envelope was a letter from a solicitor in London whom they had engaged through Hugh's solicitor in Adelaide and, without fail, the letter set out her expectations that any money I had acquired through the business operations of the farm that is, my other farms and the abattoir, should be divided equally by a payout or they would litigate for a sale of everything." Felicity's jaw almost dropped. "You are joking, aren't you, Dad?" He shook his head. "I wish I were. Our father is not even buried in the ground, and they want their share of his estate. Apparently, old Hugh's vineyards have suffered from some dry conditions in Australia, and they need a few quid, or at least that is what they told me, which doesn't make sense because they have already dropped a few pounds on solicitors' fees." Felicity was still shocked, but she sensed there was more to the story. "So what did you say, Dad?" Samuel flashed a hint of a grin and then momentarily looked at his daughter. "I told them to leave my house and return to Colchester. I rang the same cab operator who dropped them off, and about thirty minutes later, he took them back to Colchester to stay there. So, tomorrow will be another barrel of laughs, just like when we buried your grandmother."

Felicity still needed to know the other side of the impending Probate Court melee. "Well, what are you going to do, Dad?" By this stage, Samuel had turned the Jaguar into the entranceway to the farm Felicity still called home. "Don't worry. I had planned for this to happen for many years. I have enough Quid tucked away to pay Anne her share of Dad's estate, but she will never get her hands on the businesses I have acquired, as corporate trustees own them, and I, too, have good solicitors and accountants. So they can accept my offer and go back to buggery in Australia." Felicity raised her eyebrows, and her thoughts were only those of admiration for her father's business acumen. 'Oh, my. Who would have thought you had such a killer instinct in you?' When they arrived at the farmhouse, Felicity had an early supper and went to bed early, exhausted from almost three days of travel. Tomorrow would be a day to say goodbye to her Grandpa and, hopefully, Aunt Anne.

The next day would be one Felicity would never forget. She arrived with her father at the Colchester Catholic Church at 10:00 a.m., and Father O'Leary was already glaring her way as Felicity walked in. The undertakers had already brought Grandpa's coffin to the church, even though the service was not scheduled to commence until 11:00 a.m. Samuel had some brief words to say to Father O'Leary, and then after that, Samuel sat in the front pew with Felicity, waiting for friends and family to arrive. They chatted briefly. "There was something I didn't tell you yesterday, Dad. I didn't tell you because I was shocked by your news about Aunt Anne's conduct." Samuel's eyes had been focused on his father's coffin, but now he turned to face his daughter. "What is so important that you wanted to tell me now?" Felicity shrugged. "Knowing our family, this service or the gathering afterwards could become farcical, so I had better tell you now. I have met someone in America, Dad." She waited for his reaction, and after a momentary silence, he raised his open palms to encourage Felicity to speak. "He is a USAF Officer short-listed for the next astronaut intake training programme at NASA." Momentary silence. Then, Samuel raised his eyebrows. "Does this American fellow have a name? Or should I just refer to him as Captain America?" Felicity dropped her eyes in disapproval of her father's mocking tone. "His name is Dwight; Dwight Hoover, and his father is first-in-command of the USAF." Samuel rolled his bottom lip over and nodded his head before he responded. "Well, just don't mention to your Aunt Anne that Dwight's father holds such an important office; you never know, Old Man Hoover might also be served with a letter of demand from her solicitor." It was not meant to be an occasion for merriment, but Felicity could not help giggling under her hand at her father's backhanded swipe at his greedy sister.

Soon enough, Anne and Hugh arrived, along with some distant cousins, the few remaining friends of Albert and Catherine who were still alive and the various town and county acquaintances who came to pay their respects. Anne and Hugh sat on the opposite side of the aisle in the church, which did not worry Samuel or Felicity; indeed, Felicity was relieved that she might get through the day without having to talk to her despicable aunt. Father O'Leary launched into his customary piety, pointedly looking Felicity's way when he discussed Albert's and Catherine's unwavering commitment to their faith. Felicity rolled her eyes at the ceiling in response, momentarily unsettling the old priest. Then there was the gathering afterwards, where people politely ate cake and sandwiches while drinking their tea, before the family gathered at the cemetery for Albert's coffin to be buried next to Catherine's. Once again, no words were exchanged between Samuel, Anne, Felicity, or Hugh. They stood at opposite sides of the grave, and, true to form, Anne turned on the tears to attract the sympathy of the people who gathered for the sombre occasion.

Then, in keeping with Albert's wishes, there was a small wake at the tavern they always spent their New Year's Eve dinner at in Colchester. Finally, shortly before 7:00 p.m., Felicity and Samuel returned to the farmhouse. Felicity walked upstairs to her old bedroom, intending to take off her funeral clothing and put on her pyjamas for the evening. However, she heard Samuel calling for her to come downstairs urgently. She quickly ran back down the stairs, fearing that her aunt and uncle had the temerity to show their faces at the farm. Instead, Felicity heard her father calling out from the family room, where the brand-new television was located. Felicity raced into the family room to see the television turned on, and Samuel held his hand up to his mouth. "What is it, Dad?" a terrified Felicity screamed out. Samuel pointed at the television screen. "The President of the United States has been shot." They remained glued to the BBC television news that evening as the following reports were announced about the President being dead and the Vice-President being urgently sworn in as the new President. The handsome young president who proposed to put an American on the Moon was dead, and the world had changed.

The following morning, after the sad and dreadful events of the previous day, Felicity finally had some quiet time at her father's home during breakfast to talk about her life in America. As she sipped her cup of tea, Felicity could see that her father's mind was working over some issues. Eventually, she had to enquire about what was entertaining his mind. "What's up with you this morning, Dad?" Samuel's gaze was diverted from his teacup. "I am worried about you being in America, Felicity. That country has a violent history, and the events of yesterday have only confirmed my fears about them as a country. And who is this Dwight? Is he a decent man?" Felicity smiled, placed her cup of tea on the saucer, and reached out with her right hand to grip her father's left hand, which was rolled up in a ball of tension. "It's okay, Dad. I am a woman now, and Americans might be strange compared to the English, but Dwight is harmless, and, most importantly, he acts like a gentleman towards me." Samuel unravelled his left hand to hold onto Felicity's hand. "He might be a gentleman, but how do you feel about him? Are you sure you're not distracted by his background and future career to see who he is?" Samuel had touched a raw nerve within Felicity because it was for those exact reasons she was interested in Dwight. She withdrew her hand and resumed sipping her cup of tea. "Give me some credit in life, Dad. I am old enough now to know who is right for me." However, did she?

Subsequently, when Felicity returned to McGuire Air Base, the shockwaves of the assassination of the former president were still reverberating around the base. Dwight was not a Democrat supporter. Still, even he was shocked that a president could be so easily killed by one lone gunman who was also now dead, thanks to a mobster's supposed act of revenge motivated by the sight of a grieving widow. America mourned their loss, and the hope and goodwill of a new decade was buried with an assassinated president. Felicity's life would now be subject to the new world she had returned to.

CHAPTER 33

From the rancid bowels of Hell, where there's only eternal suffering, Lucifer emerged,
The embodiment of sin was among the madding crowd, and henceforth evil surged.

By February 1964, when Anatoli celebrated his twenty-fourth birthday, Volkov decided it was time for the young man to undertake his first assignment. Medical science had transformed almost all of Anatoli's body into that of a woman's. He had well-formed breasts, and if he were in a women's hosiery store in the West, he would comfortably fit a C-cup brassiere. The years of hormonal therapy caused Anatoli's Adam's apple to recede into his throat, so he presented a feminine neckline without a trace of masculinity. Anatoli's buttocks and legs were also feminine, and if it were not for his retaining his penis, he would pass for a pretty young woman.

Nevertheless, Volkov had also subjected Anatoli to years of torture of all kinds: physical, sexual and psychological. Anatoli had endured numerous occasions of being sodomised since he was cruelly left in that gaol cell for a night. Some of the other KGB agents had been permitted to have their way with Anatoli to the point where he had become accustomed to being violated. Eventually, he learnt that the less he resisted, the more likely it would be that he would not suffer anal bleeding. His physical torture was far more targeted towards his capacity to endure pain and not crumble, thereby ensuring no secrets could pass his lips. Anatoli's psychological torture varied from intoxicating him with psychotropic medication to propaganda films that contained rapid image changes depicting violence, which was also accompanied by music manipulation.

Volkov had also trained Anatoli to master hand-to-hand combat so that, if necessary, he could kill any person with his bare hands or, his preferred option, a knife. Anatoli had undergone speech training to pass as a French woman and had learned French, along with English, which opened the door to the world for him to quickly assimilate into Western European culture.

Anatoli had become a well-trained agent for whom pain knew no threshold and whose desire to kill a fellow human being had evolved from revenge to just being a cold and direct function of his orders. His first assignment required him to travel to France, where KGB intelligence had suggested that on Thursday, 27 February 1964, top American Central Intelligence Agency officers would meet with the Israeli Foreign Minister, Yosef Saar, the details of which were top secret but the Soviets' most reliable information sources obtained from their covert agents in Tel Aviv suggested it would be related to America's race for space. The Israeli Foreign Minister was a closeted bisexual man whose sexual proclivities included a fetish for transsexuality. The likes of Anatoli would be a dream come true for Saar – a mixture of a woman and a man. Yosef Saar might have publicly presented himself as a deeply religious family man. Still, in the underground club nightlife of a big city like Paris, he could quickly disappear into the crowds as an unknown participant in acts of sexual gratification – pure by day – impure by night.

Sokolov and Aliev accompanied Anatoli on this assignment. Their roles were to follow Saar from his hotel to the underground bar, where the Israeli was known to visit whenever he travelled to Paris. Because of his closeted sexual proclivities, Saar would refuse to be accompanied by any security personnel when he travelled abroad. He would only be accompanied by his secretary, a fifty-five-year-old Polish Jewish woman, Frajda Michnik, who had survived the Nazi holocaust and would keep to herself in her hotel room once her work for the day had been finished. Frajda never questioned Yosef about his after-hours activities; however, even she suspected some form of infidelity would be on the agenda.

Anatoli would accompany the other two KGB agents in a car, following Saar to his nighttime den of iniquity, the Chez Ma Cousine cabaret restaurant and bar, which was located behind the Moulin Rouge. Once Saar had entered Chez Ma Cousine, Anatoli would make his grand entrance, with his face heavily made up and glamorously dressed in a body-hugging one-piece dress, high heels, and a long black wig. If the events played out as planned, Saar and Anatoli would return to Saar's hotel room. Sokolov and Aliev would wait until Anatoli emerged with any classified documents he could obtain from Saar after Anatoli had 'discreetly' killed him, and then be whisked away from Paris before the French police, Mossad and the CIA could find Anatoli. There was one express detail Volkov ordered Anatoli to obey: Saar could sodomise Anatoli; however, Anatoli must not sodomise Saar.

The information sourced by the KGB agents in Israel informed Sokolov, Aliev, and Anatoli that Saar was staying at the elegant Les Bristol, a 1920s icon of French elegance. Sokolov, Aliev and Anatoli waited one hundred yards down from Les Bristol on the Rue Du Faubourg Saint-Honoré in the black Citroën 2CV, which Sokolov had stolen hours beforehand from the Rue De La Gare, where some poor unsuspecting Parisian rail worker had parked his car for the afternoon, oblivious to the fact that it would not be there when he finished his shift at midnight. Anatoli sat in the backseat of the 2CV, looking glamorous; even the ordinarily emotionless Aliev had commented upon how attractive Anatoli looked. At 6:00 p.m., Saar walked out of the front doors of the Les Bristol onto the pavement of the Rue Du Faubourg Saint-Honoré. He was of medium height and build, and Saar's curly, short black hair had enough grey running through it to make him look distinguished. He was wearing a tan suit, a white shirt and no tie. Yosef Saar presented himself precisely as Volkov had described him to Anatoli – a respectable-looking Jewish family man. Not long after he had exited from the hotel, a Renault 4CV taxi pulled up. After Saar entered, the taxi slowly began its journey to Chez Ma Cousine, with the stolen 2CV following not too far behind. The taxi took about fifteen minutes to travel to Chez Ma Cousine. After Saar exited the taxi and walked into the Chez Ma Cousine, the 2CV waited on the Rue Norvins for fifteen minutes before Anatoli emerged from the backseat of the car, turning the heads of passing-by Parisian men who were walking down that street.

Upon entering the Chez Ma Cousine, Anatoli could see why Saar had chosen this restaurant and bar as his nighttime entertainment venue in Paris. It was not an overly large room, and the small cabaret stage was tucked away to the left of the restaurant's front doors. The restaurant was overcrowded with rows of booth seats and two-seater tables, all decorated with red tablecloths. Running down the entire length of the low-set ceilings were several dark brown stained timber joists supporting the floor for the next level above the cabaret restaurant, which not only made the room feel much smaller but also set the tone for the transsexual cabaret performer sitting on a stool on the small stage, singing a dirty ditty which entertained the male crowd of gay men, and the transsexuals who met up there to engage in paid for sexual activity in the privacy of the destinations of Paris they were taken back to by their male companions. Heads turned as the attractive Anatoli entered the Chez Ma Cousine, especially Saar's head. Anatoli sat at an empty table near the cabaret stage, where Yosef Saar sat. As Anatoli slowly crossed his left leg over to his right, the split in the middle of his dress revealed he was not wearing any panties, and Saar was able to catch a glimpse of Anatoli's genitalia. Anatoli had hooked his catch of the day.

Yosef Saar's blood pressure elevated quickly with desire, and after he spoke to the old waiter serving him, Saar then made his way over to Anatoli's table. Saar presumed the Parisian transsexual appearance of Anatoli meant the young transsexual spoke in French, so in his best heavy Israeli accent, he said in French to Anatoli, "May I sit here with you?" Anatoli's French accent was impeccable. "Of course, darling. Take a seat." The word darling was said with enough passion to stir Saar's pulse to greater levels. Saar then introduced himself. "Thank you. My name is Yosef." Anatoli held his right hand for Saar to kiss, like a French female socialite. "My name is Sophie." Saar kissed Anatoli's right hand and sat at the table. "Thank you. May I buy you a cocktail?" Anatoli revealed a hint of a smile as he replied. "Of course, darling. You can buy whatever pleases you to do so."

Whatever pleases you, those words were a signal to Saar that Anatoli would engage in sex for money. He signalled to the old waiter, who promptly made his way over to the table. "Two Daiquiris for me and my friend, please." The waiter nodded and walked to the kitchen, where the drinks would be promptly made. Yosef Saar stared longingly into Anatoli's eyes, not knowing what to say next. So, Anatoli decided to cut to the chase. "I suppose you want to know how much it would cost for whatever pleases you?" Saar nodded, his gaze transfixed on Anatoli's deep blue eyes; however, no words were forthcoming, so Anatoli had to ask the question. "Well, what would please you?" Saar looked over his shoulder to make sure nobody was listening, and then he leaned in closer over the table to lower his voice just enough to be heard. "I want to have sex with you, and then I want you to have sex with me." Anatoli had never had sex with any person before where he was allowed to insert his penis into another person's orifice. Indeed, Volkov's orders for this mission expressly ruled out Anatoli sodomising Saar. However, he realised it provided an avenue for him to carry out his orders and, for the first time in his young life, sexual power. Anatoli leaned closer to the table so Yosef could only hear his words. "Because you want twice the pleasure, twenty new francs will be the cost." That was forty American dollars, a significant sum, an expensive service Saar was willing to pay for because Anatoli was driving Saar wild with desire. Saar nodded to agree to these terms.

Saar was about to speak when the old waiter returned carrying a tray of Daiquiris in two long-stemmed glasses. The old waiter spilled the tray down Saar's back in his nervous state of trying to serve the drinks. "Idiot!' he roared in French. Anatoli feared the incident would attract too much attention if he did not extricate himself and Saar from the farcical turn of events. He looked at the timid waiter, who must have been in his late 50s. "What is your name, old man?" Anatoli's voice was calm. The old waiter now fully viewed Anatoli's unforgettable blue eyes. "Lucien. My name is Lucien. I am sorry; I will replace your drinks." Anatoli held up his left hand and, simultaneously, wiped down Saar's back with his right hand, using a serviette as the cabaret show played on. "Do not bother with that. We are leaving, and if anybody asks what happened, tell them I accidentally bumped you." Anatoli reached into his stylish evening bag and extracted two new francs. "Here. This is for the two drinks." Lucien nodded in appreciation, as one of those new francs would be his tip. Anatoli turned and looked at Yosef, whose face seemed bewildered by Anatoli's actions. "Well, don't look surprised, darling. I do not want to be the centre of attention, and, in any event, we must get you home to get you out of these wet clothes." Saar smiled because getting out of their clothes was precisely what he wanted to do. They left the Chez Ma Cousine, and Saar hailed a Renault 4CV taxi on the Rue Norvins. They entered the taxi, and then it set off to Les Bristol. Anatoli glanced over his shoulder and saw Sokolov and Aliev following in the 2CV.

Anatoli relaxed his entire body as he lay on the bed on his haunches, his buttocks pointed upwards and out so that Saar could easily sodomise him. In his evening bag, which he kept near him on Saar's hotel bed, Anatoli carried a small tube of lubricant, which he applied to his anus for comfort. As Saar's penis was inserted into his backside, Anatoli made soft groaning noises. As Saar began to thrust his penis quicker and harder into Anatoli's anus, the louder the young man moaned. Within five minutes, it was all over as Saar reached a climactic orgasm, and he ejaculated inside Anatoli's anus. Afterwards, he breathlessly held his position behind Anatoli, holding onto Anatoli's breasts as the sweat from his chest dripped onto Anatoli's back. Saar then removed his penis from Anatoli's backside, and then he turned around to face the bedhead, sprawling out on his haunches and presenting his anus to Anatoli. "My turn." Saar's voice was full of glee as he requested Anatoli to sodomise him. Anatoli dragged his evening bag closer to him as he turned around to the sight of Saar's anus presenting itself to him. "Alright, my darling. Just let me prepare myself and you, and then I will give you a sensation you have never experienced." The thought of sodomising a man repulsed Anatoli; however, he had been trained to overcome any feelings for the sake of completing an assignment, so performing sodomy on Yosef was just a step to take in this assignment. As Anatoli lubricated his penis with his left hand, causing his penis to become erect, he also lubricated Saar's anus with the lubricant he had applied to his right fingers. The sensation of Anatoli's fingers being inserted into his anus stimulated Saar, and he was also impatient. "Hurry up! I want to feel your penis inside of me." Anatoli's penis was now erect enough to insert it into Saar's anus, and he did so with an almost bloodthirsty delight. Finally, Anatoli was the giver rather than the receiver. As he thrust his penis harder and quicker into Saar's anus, the Israeli begged for more. "Please. Harder and quicker." Anatoli thrust his penis harder and faster into Saar's anus, as demanded, and as he did so, he surreptitiously slid his right hand into his evening bag. Anatoli retrieved a silver-handled switchblade from his evening bag as he continued to thrust his penis harder and quicker into Saar's anus. Then the feeling of orgasm came over Anatoli, and he felt his penis enlarge into an almost solid iron bar, which also caused Saar to roar with pleasure. Anatoli then gripped Saar's hair locks and pulled his chin upwards as he ejaculated into his anus, and while Saar enjoyed the ecstasy of enjoying Anatoli's warm fluids enter his anus, Anatoli pushed the button on the handle to release the blade, reached around and slit Saar's throat from left to right, pulling his head even further backwards as the man shrieked and then Saar's blood spurted out from his neck and onto the bedhead, then onto the wall. Anatoli removed his penis from Saar's anus and let go of his hair as he watched the bleeding man grip his throat to try to stop the blood. However, it was all to no avail as the incision was too deep; Anatoli, in one precise sweep of the blade, had severed the left and right common carotid arteries, and Saar quickly bled to death on his hotel bed.

Now, he had to move quickly, as Anatoli did not know whether anybody had heard Saar's blood-curdling shriek. He promptly entered the ensuite and wiped his penis clean, and then washed the blood off his right hand and the switchblade. Anatoli promptly got dressed and packed the switchblade and tube of lubricant into his evening bag before fixating his eyes on what he had been assigned to get from Saar's room – his leather briefcase, which was neatly positioned on a writing table in the corner of the hotel room. Anatoli grabbed the briefcase by the handle, and then he quickly made his way over to the door to the room. Anatoli slowly opened the door so that he could peek into the hallway to see if anybody was standing there. It was clear. He then poked his head around the corner of the door to look down the opposite direction of the hotel hallway, and once again, it was all clear. Anatoli quickly approached the stairwell instead of waiting for the elevator. He promptly walked down the three flights of stairs to the hotel's foyer and just as quickly exited from it out onto the Rue Du Faubourg Saint-Honoré, where Sokolov and Aliev were waiting for him in the 2CV.

Anatoli, Sokolov, and Aliev quickly made their way to the wharves of the Seine River, where they boarded a boat large enough to travel down that river, out to the English Channel, and then to the Atlantic Ocean. A Soviet naval submarine would collect them just before dawn so they could eventually return to Moscow. While travelling on the Seine River, Aliev opened the leather-covered briefcase. Inside, there was a letter on the official letterhead of the President of the United States of America, signed by the newly sworn-in President. The President's letter was addressed to the Israeli prime minister, and its words were an enigma for those who read them:

Dear Prime Minister,

Thank you for agreeing to participate in Project Zeus.

The attached envelope contains further details about Project Zeus and the mutual benefits your participation would bring to our nations.

There wasn't an envelope inside the briefcase. Saar may have led a double life; however, he was risk-averse when he ventured out into the night for his sexual gratification. The envelope had been left in safekeeping in Frajda Michnik's room.

By 9:00 a.m. the following day, Frajda was highly distressed that Yosef Saar had not come to collect her for their flight back to Tel Aviv. She asked the hotel manager to open the door to Saar's room because she had been knocking on it, and he did not answer the door. When the hotel manager opened the door and Frajda entered the room, she saw the horrific sight of Saar dead on his blood-soaked bed and the blood that was all over the bed and walls. She let out a high-pitched scream that could have shattered a pewter mug, and then she fainted. Subsequent investigations by the French police and the Mossad investigation team, led by Aharon Kohen, traced back to Chez Ma Cousine, where poor little Lucien could identify Saar from his photograph. Still, otherwise, all he could say about his companion was that the woman had dark hair and the most beautiful blue eyes he had ever seen. A subsequent autopsy performed on Saar's body discovered traces of seminal fluid inside his anus. Kohen and his fellow Mossad investigators were intrigued by this discovery; however, the only evidence they could obtain from their investigations was that Saar had been murdered by a man and a woman or, more disturbingly for Saar's family, by one of many transsexual men of Paris. For Aharon Kohen, who had survived the Holocaust to only live with the haunting memories of the rest of his family being murdered by the Nazis, this abhorrent and unedifying killing of Saar became his mission in life to discover the culprit, and as the Old Testament so proclaimed, exact revenge by an eye for an eye. The hunt was now on to find Saar's killer.

When the news filtered back to Volkov that Anatoli had sodomised Saar and left behind traces of his seminal fluid, he had Anatoli locked away in solitary confinement for six months to punish him for his indiscretion in leaving a potential clue as to his identity. It would be several years before Volkov could order Anatoli to participate in another KGB assignment in France. However, Volkov successfully argued on behalf of Anatoli to the Politburo that his operative's life should be spared, as there were plenty of other countries around the planet to which he could send his unique undercover agent. Sokolov and Aliev would also need to be separated as long-standing team members, with Aliev being redeployed to replace an undercover agent in America, whose identity had been compromised. At the same time, the former would continue his subterfuge in France. Volkov believed he had diffused a potential problem. Still, Mossad would never give up on finding the person responsible for the murder of Saar.

CHAPTER 34

Oh! How much do thou wish to be immortalised on that silver screen?
Immortality comes at a price, terms for which thee couldn't have foreseen.

By early March of 1964, Amelia's shooting star appeared to be in jeopardy of burning out entirely. The previous year, a pencil-thin English woman referred to as 'The Shrimp' was turning teen culture upside down, and the curvaceous look of the screen goddesses of the 1950s seemed destined for obscurity. To add to Amelia's misfortune, the third movie of her contract with Horner Studios had already been filmed, yet it was not released, as the new waif-thin look was taking hold of America. The movie would be released at some stage, but not during Easter peak season; it was slated to be released as a filler the following month. Her agent was out and about searching the studios of Tinseltown for another contract. Still, there were plenty of gorgeous young women in Los Angeles on the books of numerous agents, and television was affecting the volume of feature film production. Sitting around in a living room watching a wooden box became more popular in the USA than sitting in a crowded movie theatre, listening to other people slurping soft drinks or chewing popcorn.

Amelia sought Walter's advice about her predicament. He was brutally honest as her manager. Through his effeminate voice, Walter observed some home truths about the industry he fed off. "This town chews people up and spits them out quicker than the seasons come and go, my little English beauty queen. Sure, you were the flavour of the month; however, since The Shrimp became the year's model last year, the type of woman the studios are looking for is demure and waif-like. In contrast, fulsome-figured women like you, and don't get me wrong, sweetie, because if I were a heterosexual guy, I would adore you, but fulsome figures are not the 'look' for the teen movie market. If I were you, I would start taking profound acting lessons because the teen market is over for you." Amelia was not comforted by this news, and she glared at Walter with disapproval. "Take some profound acting lessons? Are you suggesting I am a bad actress?" Walter shook his head. "No, not at all. However, you are a one-trick pony. Your range is typecast, and, to be honest, once you are typecast, it is tough to change the minds of the studio bosses and casting agents. You might have to consider performing some roles that are not glamorous characters, and you might also have to delve into some brazen sexual acts to obtain those roles."

Amelia turned away from gazing at Walter to look out the window of her plush Beverly Hills home. The air was thick with pollution that day; however, Amelia's mind was even more polluted with the hedonistic world she had experienced since moving to Los Angeles. Walter stood up and walked over to Amelia, and when he stood next to her, he grabbed both of her shoulders and looked her in the eyes. "When I said brazen, what I meant to say was also depraved." Amelia freed herself from Walter's grip and turned away to stare out the window again, looking towards the Hollywood Hills, where she longed to live in a more private setting than that of the peering eyes around Beverly Hills.

Amelia pondered Walter's final sentence. 'What could be more brazen and depraved than the sex I have been exposed to already?' she asked herself. Amelia turned back towards Walter, who had returned to sitting in the same armchair of Amelia's living room, where he had been sitting when Amelia initially sought his counsel. "What brazen and depraved sexual acts could be any different to what I have had to endure here? I have had to sleep with more old, saggy men than I have had dinners. What could be more brazen and depraved than the promiscuity I am expected to perform to stay in the good books of studio bosses, directors and casting agents?" Walter stood up again and walked over to Amelia, and when he stood next to her, he grabbed both of her shoulders again and looked her in the eyes. "There is promiscuity, and then there is depravity. I can introduce you to the avant-garde world of cinematic production, Amelia. However, the question that entertains my mind is, Are you ready for that world?"

Amelia was puzzled by Walter's question. In the past few years, she had endured treatment, which consolidated in her character an additional layer of despair to that of her unfortunate experiences as a child. "What do you have in mind?" Walter turned away from Amelia and momentarily stared out the living room window, searching his mind for the answer. Then, like an epiphany, he saw the window of opportunity. "Through one of my ex-lovers, I know Old Nick Martin at Independent Artists' Studios." Amelia immediately recoiled in horror. "Independent Artists' Studios? They make B-grade artsy-fartsy crap, Walter. Do you expect me to do their work?" Walter shrugged his shoulders. "Who else will you get work from? Your agent is knocking on locked doors. If you do not sign a contract soon, the banks will change the locks on these doors. And then both of us will be out of a job."

Amelia was desperate because her shooting star appeared to be fading; a year earlier, she might have dismissed Walter as her manager. But now she needed him; she walked over to him by the window and placed her hand on his shoulder. "What do you say is so depraved about Old Nick Martin, Walter? Please, tell me." Walter closed his eyes, and then he turned and faced Amelia. "It's not just Old Nick Martin alone; it's also his wife, Lilith. It's all about his wife. Old Nick may make you another victim of his couch; however, Lilith runs the creative content of the studio. She is the creative genius of the operations and also a closet dyke. But not any everyday type of dyke, God knows we have plenty of those in this dirty old city. No, Lilith will make you her whore for the term of your contract."

Amelia looked into Walter's eyes to determine if he was telling the truth. He appeared to be, and with her life at Horner Studios appearing to be spat out on the pavement like a piece of chewing gum, Amelia knew she had little choice but to go with the option of seeking a contract through Independent Artists' Studio. The prospect of the ignominy of returning to England as a has-been she could not entertain. 'So what if I have to be a dyke's whore. How bad could it be?' Her rhetorical final thought perhaps should have been verbalised because Walter could have expanded upon the nature of Lilith's proclivities. "What the heck. Let's do it. Make the arrangements, Walter. However, they should ensure that they contact me through my agent. I have a reputation to uphold." Amelia walked away to her bedroom without saying another word. Walter shook his head and mumbled in a high camp mocking tone, "Oh, thank you, Walter. What would I do without you, Walter?" He then went to Amelia's home office and dialled the direct line to Old Nick Martin.

Penny Long had received a firm no for several weeks as she desperately tried to find Amelia a film role. She was trying to make her way as a casting agent in Hollywood, and when she secured Amelia as a client two years ago, she thought that would be her breakthrough to the top of the agent's tree in Los Angeles. Now, her meal ticket looked like it was vanishing when Amelia's career seemed to be over. As her casting agent, Penny had a lot to lose if she did not find a new role for Amelia. When she received the telephone call from Old Nick Martin informing her that Independent Artists' Studio was interested in offering Amelia three movies, she was filled with great excitement. Penny had heard through industry gossip that Old Nick and his wife were difficult for young actresses to work with; however, this was a three-movie contract, and with it would hopefully come the ancillary deals of advertising roles and television appearances. Penny's hopes of reaching the top of the tree meant more than the welfare of her clients. After Penny had spoken to Old Nick Martin, she excitedly telephoned Amelia to tell her that she had secured an opportunity to audition for a three-movie contract with Independent Artists' Studio. Although she knew the audition offer was forthcoming, Amelia acted with the appropriate degree of surprise and elation upon receiving this news. Penny informed Amelia that Independent Artists' Studio wanted her to audition at 11:00 a.m. the next day at their studios in Burbank. When asked what she would wear, Penny told Amelia to dress in her finest outfit because the role was aristocratic.

Amelia arrived for her 'audition' at Independent Artists' Studios the following day. She did dress in her finest day dress, which not only revealed the beautiful lines of her cleavage but also showed the rest of her fine, young and curvaceous figure. She looked exactly like a movie star. Walter had driven her there in her Lincoln Continental Convertible, a luxury which she would also lose if she did not secure the contract on offer. She took the scarf off her head, which she had worn to ensure the wind did not dishevel her perfectly styled hair. As Amelia exited the sleek car, Walter's words were prescient: "Get ready for it because Old Nick and Lilith are bad eggs." Amelia disregarded the words of warning because she was on a mission to maintain the presence of her shooting star in the murky skies of Los Angeles. The studios were not as large or elaborate as Horner Studios. Although there was a flurry of activity with grips, leading hands, and cameramen walking in and out of the three sound stages, the buildings were old, run-down, and in need of some tender loving care. The studio office was small compared to Horner Studios, and the receptionist was a beatnik rather than the doll-like personnel employed at the more prestigious studios.

After a half-hour wait, Amelia was shown into Old Nick Martin's office, and now she had realised part of Walter's words of warning. Old Nick was an overweight, middle-aged slob of a man, and his business shirt was hanging out from the right side of his roll of fat over his trousers. He had a half-eaten chocolate doughnut sitting on top of a pile of film scripts, which were scattered over the tabletop of his polished oak executive desk, which looked out of place in the otherwise cheap-looking, gaudy red-velvet furniture, including the infamous casting lounge Walter had warned her about. He did not get out of his chair. Instead, he slumped backwards in his tatty leather office chair and momentarily eyed Amelia's luscious figure up and down, like she was a cattle carcass on display in an abattoir. Old Nick picked up the receiver of his office telephone, pushed an intercom button, and within seconds, he spoke. "Yeah, she is here. Are you ready for her?" He heard the response, nodded and then placed the receiver back on his telephone.

Old Nick then looked Amelia up and down again, still standing in the same spot in his office after she had entered it several minutes before. Then Old Nick undid the belt on his trousers, pulled down his fly and finally spoke. "Get down and crawl over here." Amelia was startled by this grotesque display of chauvinism. "What? You want me to do what?" Old Nick did not even blink. "You fucking heard me. Get down on all fours, crawl over here, or otherwise scram." Begrudgingly, Amelia obeyed the disgusting man's command, and she placed her designer Gucci handbag down on the shag pile carpet before commencing the ignominious task of crawling towards Old Nick.

As she was halfway across the floor of the office, Amelia saw Old Nick pull his uncircumcised penis out from his underwear, which the roll of his rotund belly almost entirely hid from view. Amelia knew what Old Nick was expecting, and the thought of performing fellatio on this grotesque man sickened her. Then, just as she was within a few feet of him, Amelia heard his office door open. She turned her head to see who it was, and an attractive woman in her early forties stood in the doorway, dressed in black lingerie, and, disturbingly, tied between her legs was some form of smooth metal device that resembled a penis. It didn't require an introduction for Amelia to realise the woman must be Lilith Martin. "What are you waiting for? Continue to crawl over here and then suck it!" Old Nick Martin's voice had that edge of depravity to it that only a perverted and wicked man could speak. Amelia crawled over to him, and as she extracted his penis from under his belly, she felt the hem of her dress being forcibly lifted over her buttocks, followed by her panties being ripped down.

Half an hour later, Amelia emerged from the office block of Independent Artists' Studio, and she was wiping tears away from the corner of her eyes with the cotton handkerchief she kept in her handbag. Her stylish sunglasses did not hide the mascara that trickled down with those tears. She walked briskly to the Continental, where Walter sat in the driver's seat, half asleep in the early fall sun. She startled him as she robustly opened the rear door and then slammed it shut in a matter of seconds as she took up her place in the middle of the back seats. Walter turned around and immediately knew the Martins' perverted behaviour had upset the young actress. "Are you okay, Amelia?" It was a silly question. "Well, obviously, I am bloody well not, but before you ask your next silly question, yes, I have secured the contract. Now get me the hell out of here!" The sting to her words was underscored by the tragic sounds of a person being simultaneously violated and demoralised.

Later that afternoon, Amelia received an excited telephone call from Penny, informing her that Independent Artists' Studios had selected her for a three-part eighteenth-century movie series to be filmed in France and Los Angeles over the next six years. Amelia was still despondent after her ignominious casting session, and she barely paid attention as Penny rattled off how the news of this contract would open the doors to television roles when she was not required to be on set for Independent Artists' Studios. Amelia had experienced a lot of unpleasantness in her relatively young life; however, the events in Old Nick's office that day had been too disturbing for her to take too much notice of Penny Long's greed-driven drivel. She politely thanked her for the call and then went to her bedroom for the night without even acknowledging Walter, who was slaving away in the kitchen, cooking her a crab soufflé to celebrate her success. Walter heard the telltale sound of the bedroom door slamming shut. He shook his head and mumbled. "Well, it looks like it's just me, the bubbles, and you, Mr Souffle, tonight. I warned little Miss Priss." Tinsel Town might have glittered to the outside world, but in reality, it was a murky pit of sleaze that made the hazy skies of Los Angeles look deceptively bright.

CHAPTER 35

Dreams can be easily broken by men, as though they're disposing of trash,
But when it comes to matters of the heart, young maiden, don't be rash!

The week leading up to Good Friday in 1964 was one Felicity would never forget. If the universe could ever contract back to a central, incendiary and profound moment, it could be compared to this fateful week of Felicity's life.

Felicity's life on Monday, March 23, 1964, commenced in its usual daily manner of her punishing her body as she ran repeated laps around the perimeter of McGuire Airbase. Dwight had previously queried why she started her day by running almost a marathon. Her response had been, 'It has been my daily routine since I was a little girl.' Her morning duties were mundane, and she enviously looked out the window of the RAF administrative offices, watching her male RAF officer colleagues taking off in the new state-of-the-art F-111 jet aircraft. The USAF was still vehemently opposed to women flying their jet fighters, a position in which Felicity had expressed her frustration to Dwight on several occasions. Then, after lunch, she received an unexpected visit to her office from Dwight, who would not usually venture into RAF territory. Dwight smiled from ear to ear, and he was as excited as a small child on Christmas morning as he held a piece of paper in his hand.

Felicity had just been finalising one of the many meaningless reports she had to complete that week when Dwight came bounding into her office, and his unexpected visit startled her. "Oh, for the love of God, Dwight. You scared the life out of me!" Dwight was excited and could not utter his words in an intelligible sentence. "I've done it!" Felicity was perplexed, and she stood up to settle him down. "Just calm down, Dwight. You are not making any sense. What have you done?" Dwight unfolded the piece of paper. "Look at this letter. NASA has confirmed it in writing. I am officially accepted into the NASA astronaut programme." Felicity quickly shut the door to her office and inspected the letter Dwight held in his hand. Sure enough, the letter confirmed that effective Tuesday, March 31, 1964, Dwight would be a member of NASA's astronaut training programme in Flagstaff City. Felicity looked up from the letter to Dwight's face, and his eyes revealed his soul was burning brightly with excitement. "Well, congratulations are in order." Dwight's eyes widened. "Congratulations?" Then, without warning, he picked Felicity up off the ground and kissed her on the lips for only about five seconds. Still, the smell of garlic, which he had consumed only half an hour beforehand at lunch, was more overpowering for Felicity than his impulsive behaviour.

"Whoa there, cowboy, put me down before you make me giddy." Dwight's smile was now underscored with slight surprise. "Aren't you excited for me, Honey Bunny?" He looked like a small child seeking approval from a cool-tempered parent. Felicity smiled and hugged him, her feet planted on the ground. "Of course I am, Teddy Bear." The smell of garlic from Dwight's breath was still overpowering; however, an important question now needed to be asked. "So, Flagstaff City is in Arizona, isn't it?" Dwight immediately realised the implications of Felicity's question and slightly released his grip to look at her face. "Yes, I know. It means I will be on the country's opposite side." They looked at each other; both were bewildered by the apparent tyranny of distance. Then, like a light bulb had switched on in his mind, Dwight's eyes lit up. "Say, why don't you see if your Brit boys will redeploy you to a base on the West Coast?" Felicity was puzzled by Dwight's impulsive reasoning, and she slightly tilted her head to the right while displaying her surprise. "Dwight, I have to finish my studies at Princeton first." Dwight nodded, realising the folly of his impetuosity. "Sorry, I forgot about that. Still, don't panic. I will work something out." He then let go of Felicity and walked towards her office door. "Where are you going?" Her words did not bring him to a halt; instead, he looked back over his shoulder as he opened the door. "I am going to call my mom and dad. They will be over the moon when they hear this news. Don't panic, I will work something out." With those words being spoken, he walked out the door believing Felicity was overjoyed for him; however, Felicity only felt more isolated now as a woman trying to achieve her goals in a man's world.

The following day, Felicity went to Princeton to complete her additional credit work with Ron. While working together on the rocket engine components, Felicity could tell Ron had something on his mind. Eventually, after about forty-five minutes, Felicity had had enough; she needed to know why her mentor was so distracted. "Ron?" He looked up from the bench where he was working. "Yes, Felicity. What's up?" She displayed her feelings of disbelief. "What is up with you? Since I arrived here this afternoon, you have been acting like your mind is distracted by something." He got off his stool as he spoke. "It's that obvious?" Felicity nodded. "Okay then, I had better deal with the issue now than when we're finished. My superiors at NASA want you to continue working with me at Stanford University. Now, I have informed them that you are serving with the RAF so that they will make the decisions regarding your deployment. Still, it is a genuine suggestion by the boys at NASA that we continue working together, and you can obtain a Doctorate in Aeronautical Engineering at Stanford. So, if there is some way the RAF could redeploy you, it would be a hell of an opportunity for you."

Felicity's breath was taken away; NASA wanted her to continue working with Ron. However, her acceptance of the RAF proposal, which Thomas and Joan had previously discussed, was limited to being deployed at McGuire Air Force Base. She had no ties to the USAF, and if the RAF's discretion militated against Felicity being redeployed to another base after she had acquired her advanced degrees, her options to study at Stanford involved her seeking a discharge as an RAF officer and live in a country which she would have to seek a visa to continue living in without employment, or to remain at McGuire hoping that one day a door to NASA might open. She realised the latter was an unlikely event. Despite all of her efforts to date, including her unwavering patience with the inefficiency of the bureaucracy in the Ministry of Defence, Felicity knew she would have to plead her case with the RAF to be deployed to a yet-to-be-determined base, which was also an unlikely event. Ron could detect that something was now troubling Felicity's mind. "I thought you would be excited to hear this news, Felicity. What's up?" She smiled back at him, but it was not filled with glee. "Ron, I am honoured to be offered the opportunity to continue studying under you at Stanford. However, I will have to seek an indulgence from the RAF to be redeployed to the West Coast, and as far as I am aware, the RAF has not deployed any personnel to air bases there. So, I must beg to be redeployed because I do not want to be discharged from the RAF."

Ron nodded and realised Felicity's obstacles in studying at Stanford University under him. "Well, the opportunity is there. I can write a letter for the RAF if need be. It's a tremendous opportunity, Felicity. While I cannot guarantee NASA would even employ you, let alone accept a UK woman into its astronaut programme, it does open the door to possibilities. Nevertheless, I understand your sense of loyalty and duty, so while I would not be upset if the RAF refused to indulge you, as you put it, I would be disappointed for you.

Anyway, you speak to your superiors." When Felicity returned to McGuire Air Base that evening, it was too late for her to speak to Reg. She would have to raise Ron's proposal with him immediately the following day.

Wednesday is often the most demanding working day of the week for civilians, whereas, ordinarily, it is just another day in the armed services. As Felicity undertook her usual run that morning, she knew it would be a critical day in her quest to conquer her Everest – to become the first woman to fly into outer space. Without fail, she saw Reg as soon as she entered the RAF office. She figured that at 9:00 a.m., he would be far more receptive to her than towards the end of the day, when he too became tired of addressing the endless stream of bureaucratic paperwork that crossed his desk. The door to his office was closed, so Felicity knocked on it. "Come in," were the commanding words of invitation.

Felicity entered Reg's office, and when he looked up from the pile of paperwork, his face foreshadowed terrible tidings. "Oh, Felicity, I was going to come and see you shortly, so it is an opportune time for us to meet. Take a seat, please." She sat at his desk, expecting the news would not be favourable. "Felicity, you have been essential to the RAF's Cold War collaboration with the Americans. Indeed, if it were not for your well-educated eye, we might have purchased the most unreliable jet fighter ever to be manufactured by the Americans. Your service will be properly recognised in that regard." Reg stopped short of speaking his following sentence as he fumbled for his following words; however, Felicity spared him the anguish of exploring English. "My time is ending here, isn't it?" Reg nodded. "Yes, I'm afraid it is. After finishing your university year at Princeton, you will be redeployed to the UK. I know you had your heart set on your ultimate career goal, but I am afraid Her Majesty requires your services back on home soil." Felicity sighed; from the moment she arrived in America, she had been repeatedly disappointed, but she would not give up. "NASA wants me to continue assisting Ron when he moves to Stanford University at the start of the new university year in August. I want to seek a further term of deployment in America by the RAF, as it is an opportunity that is too good to refuse. If need be, I will write to Air Chief Marshal Wilberforce"

Reg shook his head, which was another indication of bad news coming Felicity's way. "It's too late, I'm afraid. The communication I received was from Air Chief Marshal Wilberforce himself." Reg held out the official letter he had received from RAF HQ in the UK. Felicity took the letter from Reg and commenced reading it:

Dear Felicity,

I refer to your current duties for the Royal Air Force stationed at McGuire Air Base in America.

The tenure of your deployment to America as a member of the RAF's joint Cold War service programme with the USAF will conclude on July 1 this year, after you have completed your Advanced Degrees at Princeton University. The RAF is scaling back its involvement in the joint training exercise, so this decision will not only affect you but also others.

I sincerely thank you for your fine work over the past three years, particularly your meticulous examination of the United States Air Force's jet fighters. Indeed, had it not been for your superb aeronautical engineering skills, Her Majesty's air force would have purchased fighters from the Americans, which would not have been fit for the purpose.

You were disappointed that the Americans did not permit you to train in their jet fighters. That matter was totally beyond the Ministry of Defence's control. However, suppose you decide to continue serving in the RAF upon your return to the United Kingdom. In that case, I am confident that we will be training excellent female officers, such as yourself, to fly our fighter jets at some point in the next decade.

Yours faithfully,

Air Chief Marshal Sir Thomas Wilberforce DSO DFC

Felicity looked quite forlorn as she folded the letter and placed it in her jacket pocket. It was evident to Reg that this news was devastating for her, so he remained quiet for a moment to allow Felicity to process the news. After about one minute, she took a deep breath to ensure that when she spoke, her tone would be respectful yet also display her disappointment regarding how the RAF permitted one of its female officers to be treated by the USAF. "I have to be frank, Reg. I am disappointed with this news. Sir Thomas says in his letter that the RAF is scaling back its involvement in the joint programme with the USAF. Still, it does seem evident that my gender is also a significant issue that is at play in the decision-making process." Reg tried to interrupt Felicity to dispel notions that gender played a role in her redeployment back to the United Kingdom. However, Felicity defiantly held up her hand to convey she was not finished speaking. "Please, Reg. I need to get these words off my chest, and you are one of only two people on this base who have taken the time to speak to me. I will continue to carry out my duties diligently until July 1; however, this decision significantly impacts several matters related to my ongoing service with the RAF. I have an opportunity that the stroke of a pen has now taken away. To say that I am bitter is an understatement. Still, I will observe protocols and fulfil my duty until July 1. When I return home, I will decide on my long-term plans regarding whether or not I will continue serving with the RAF. In any event, it's nothing personal with you, Reg, as you have been an excellent leader for me to serve under, and yes, I am grateful that my country has paid for my ongoing university study for the past three years." Reg remained silent for several seconds before boldly speaking in reply to Felicity's venting of her spleen. "Felicity, I will not enter into a debate with you about gender-based decision-making. All I wish to say is that if you decide to continue serving the RAF when you return home, I am confident that one day, you will be flying our jet aircraft and, undoubtedly, elevated to Squadron Leader. So, please, do not make any rash decisions."

Although he did not mean to do it, Felicity felt like a powerful male was manipulating her. Thomas' letter also made her feel the same way. Felicity nodded, stood up and saluted Reg, who returned the salute. Reg did not formally dismiss Felicity from his presence, in keeping with his relaxed command style, as it was now taken for granted that once they had exchanged words in this private setting, she could leave his office. Felicity walked proudly to her office with her head held up high, and after she closed the door behind her, her emotions got the better of her. She began to cry, then sob, and as she did so, her solitary thought was impotent frustration: "What does a woman have to do to achieve her dreams in a man's world?" She should have telephoned her father immediately, as her emotions and dejected thoughts left her vulnerable to making rash decisions.

Subsequently, Felicity met with Dwight for their usual Wednesday night dinner date at Papa Joe's. She had committed herself to a relationship with Dwight, and even though she remained celibate with him, she had developed feelings for him, which would now be another shipwreck on this dark day. During the drive from the base, it was evident to Dwight that something was on Felicity's mind. However, he had been dating her long enough to know that she would first broach the subject when she was ready. Dwight discussed his plans with NASA and how he would use every spare leave day to travel back to McGuire to see Felicity, because she meant a great deal to him. She quietly took in his words as she tried to process how the world seemed to be tumbling down around her.

They had been seated at their usual table at Papa Joe's for about fifteen minutes when Dwight could no longer hold his tongue; he had to find out why Felicity was so quiet. "Okay, Honey Bunny, what is up?" Felicity was confused about her life and could not tell Dwight that she either had to leave the RAF, which, despite everything that occurred in America, she did not want to do but had to if she wanted to have any chance of joining NASA, or she remained in the RAF, which meant tearing them apart and waving goodbye to the opportunity Ron had offered her. "I cannot tell you at the moment, Teddy Bear. I need to think through a problem." Dwight was genuinely concerned, and he leaned forward and took her right hand in both of his. "What problem?" Felicity pulled her hand away. "I just cannot talk about it now. I need time to think. Dwight was frustrated by Felicity's obstinacy. He ripped the pull-tab off his can of Coca-Cola with such force that it caused some soft drink to hit his uniform. "Oh damn it. Now look at what you've made me do. Look, Honey Bunny, my Pa, whom you will get to meet one of these days, told me when I was a child, 'Son, there is no problem in this world that cannot be solved.' And do you know what? He was right. So, please, Honey Bunny, talk to me."

Felicity momentarily turned away because she wanted to choose her words wisely. Several seconds went by as she thought, and then she sighed. "Alright, I will tell you since you wanted to know now. Ron has told me that NASA wants me to continue studying under him at Stanford." Dwight threw his hands up in delight. "Well, that is excellent news, Honey Bunny. Some of my training will be at Stead Air Force Base. You can get your British superiors to transfer you there, which will solve the time away from each other." Felicity furiously shook her head. "No, Teddy bear. That will not happen because the RAF want me to return to England on July 1. Therefore, there will be no transfer to Stead. I want to pursue my PhD under Ron at Stanford, but I do not want to relinquish my officer's appointment with the RAF. I earned that rank through sheer hard work. And before you say it, yes, I also do not want to be torn away from you. Can you understand the conundrum I am in, Dwight?" He did. He ruminated over the pull-tab he still held in his right hand. Then, like a bolt of lightning, Dwight had a moment of inspiration, and a smile came over him as he reached out with his right hand and took hold of Felicity's left hand. He lowered his voice below the cacophony of the restaurant. "Honey Bunny, you might think I am insane, but I want you to know this is coming from the bottom of my heart. Flying Officer Felicity Bennet, will you marry me?" Felicity was stunned and unsure she had heard Dwight correctly because he had lowered his voice. "What did you say? Did you ask me to marry you? I have yet to meet your parents." Dwight nodded. "Yes. Don't worry about Ma and Pa; they will adore you. Anyway, if we get married, you can transfer your rank to the USAF and, of course, be deployed to Stead Air Force Base. My Pa can make that happen, and, in any event, you would make me a happy man if you were to be my wife. Imagine the headlines: an aspiring astronaut marries an English flying ace. So, what do you say?"

Felicity was surprised and simultaneously confused; she liked Dwight a lot, but did she love him? However, the thoughts of opportunity and ambition overwhelmed this essential existential question. Felicity had felt since she was a young girl that her gender was an obstacle to her ultimate career and life goal. Her decision was rash, but she wanted to hear Dwight ask again. "Please ask me again, Teddy Bear." He held out the pull-tab in his left hand. "Felicity 'Honey Bunny' Bennet, will you marry me, please?" By now, several neighbouring tables were watching, a circumstance both Felicity and Dwight were oblivious to. She smiled. "Yes, Dwight 'Teddy Bear' Hoover, I will marry you." The pull-tab was placed on Felicity's ring finger. The eavesdroppers at the surrounding tables applauded, causing Dwight to acknowledge them in a celebratory response, whereas Felicity blushed. Indeed, Dwight was in a very celebratory mood. "Heh, Papa Joe, my gal just accepted my marriage proposal. Two glasses of your finest champagne." Felicity was concerned about Dwight's impetuosity. "Teddy Bear. We are in uniform in public. We cannot drink alcohol dressed in uniform." Dwight scoffed. "Maybe you Brits can't, but I'm an astronaut. Who will see us here?" Two glasses of Korbel were brought out, and with the pull-tab still on her finger, Felicity clinked her glass with Dwight's to acknowledge their rash engagement. Over dinner, Dwight told her it was best that they get married before the end of June so that her transfer to the USAF could be finalised before her RAF transfer. Later that night, as she went to bed, Felicity assured herself she was making the right decision for her future.

The following morning, Felicity rang her father before breaking the news to Reg. She was slightly apprehensive about breaking the news to him about becoming engaged, an emotion that should have been a warning beacon for her; however, she was an ambitious young woman whose desire to fly into space outweighed some of her inner emotions. Fortuitously, it was raining in Essex, so Samuel spent his late morning catching up on some overdue bookkeeping work. He answered the telephone on the second ring, almost as though he was expecting a telephone call. "Hello, Samuel Bennet speaking." Felicity was circumspect about how to break the news to her father about her engagement to Dwight. "Hi, Dad. It must be a typical Essex day for you to sit by your telephone." As always, Samuel was delighted to hear his daughter's voice. Still, they usually spoke to one another at the start of the week, which they had not done because of Dwight's news on Monday. "Felicity, it is so nice to hear your voice. It must have been a hectic week because you didn't call me on Monday." Samuel was right about Felicity's week, and she decided the best way to break the news to him was to do so chronologically. "It certainly has been a remarkable week, Dad, so let me tell you about it. On Monday, Dwight told me that he had been accepted into the next round of NASA's intake for the astronaut programme, which meant he would be leaving McGuire next Tuesday. On Tuesday, Ron informed me at Princeton that his superiors at NASA had requested that I continue studying and working under him at Stanford University in California to pursue a PhD. When I spoke to Reg on Wednesday about seeking a transfer to California to continue studying and working with Ron, he handed me a letter from Joan's father stating that the RAF would transfer me back to England from the beginning of July this year..." Samuel was delighted by the news that his daughter would return to England, or so he thought. "Oh, Felicity. How wonderful it will be to have my little darling return to England in several months. I miss you every day." Felicity quickly interrupted her father's premature elation. "Dad, I haven't finished yet." Samuel could tell by his daughter's voice that perhaps he had misjudged what the future held for him. "Sorry, keep on talking."

Felicity took a deep breath because now she had to tell him the pointy end of the news. "So, by last night, when I went out with Dwight for our usual Wednesday night dinner date, I was coming to terms with the news that the RAF would be denying me the door of opportunity that had opened on Tuesday and that news was devastating. I told Dwight about my predicament regarding the RAF's decision. He proposed to marry me, which, of course, I accepted. Marrying Dwight will allow me to transfer from the RAF to the USAF, enabling me to remain in America to study under Ron at Stanford, while still keeping the door open for opportunities at NASA. So, that is my news." If Felicity expected an instantaneous response from her father, she was surely mistaken. Samuel remained quiet for at least half a minute as his mind processed this surprising and, in some respects, disappointing news. Eventually, Felicity broke the silence. "Dad, are you still there?" Samuel was awoken from his mind's whirlwind of thoughts. "Yes, sweetie, I am. So, let me get this right in my head. You are now engaged, which means you won't be coming back home; you will be attending Stanford to study and, if I heard you correctly, somehow transferring to the USAF, all to keep an opportunity open with NASA. Is that right?" Felicity could tell by the tone of her father's voice that he was troubled by this news. "Yes, Dad. That is right. But do not worry; everything finally worked out for me in America. Aren't you happy for me?" Samuel had to be blunt. "I'm happy that you believe you are happy with these surprising events, Felicity. But tell me this: where was the word love?" Felicity was perplexed by Samuel's query. "What do you mean, Dad?" Samuel's thoughts were confirmed. "What I mean is quite simple, namely, where is the word love regarding your engagement to Dwight?" Felicity was petulant when she should have been perceptive. "Well, Dad, I would not have said yes to marriage without love!" Her harsh yet adamant tone abruptly brought Samuel's inquiry to a halt. "Alright, well, I guess it is good news. Congratulations. Have you set a date?" Now came the news that fortified Samuel's mind that his daughter was making a rash decision. "Saturday, June 13. This year."

Again, there was no response from Samuel. "Dad, did you hear me?" Samuel was reluctant to rechallenge his daughter. "Yes, Felicity. I was checking my diary to ensure the date doesn't conflict with anything related to the farming business here, which it doesn't. So, I will come to America several days before June 13 to meet Dwight and his family. Have you met his family yet?" Felicity knew her father was looking for problems. "No, but I will. And Dwight tells me they're lovely, so that everything will be fine, Dad." Despite his reservations, Samuel had to take his daughter at her word, as he wrote in his diary. "Very well then. I have entered the dates in my diary to arrive in America on June 10 to meet Dwight and his family. Anyway, I'm glad life has worked out for you, sweetie. Please have a nice Easter. I love you." The three magic words that had yet to come from Dwight's mouth had the usual effect on Felicity. "I love you, too, Dad. Bye." In those few minutes after the call, Samuel felt he should ring his daughter back, tell her to wait, and not rush into marriage too quickly. His finger hovered above the telephone as his mind deliberated whether he should interfere. However, he reckoned that it was her life to live, not his, and against his better judgment, he did not call Felicity back.

Later that morning, Felicity broke the news to Reg about her engagement, marriage, and transfer to the USAF. He was surprised by this turn of events, as he did not realise Felicity's and Dwight's relationship had been ongoing for that long, which was just further confirmation for Felicity about her decision being the right one. She also sent urgent telegrams that same day to Joan, Natasha and Heather, asking them if they could do so to be her bridal party and, notwithstanding all the problems the Ministry of Defence had caused, she, in particular, asked Joan to be her Maid of Honour because she was, after all, like a big sister to her. Her urgent telegrams were responded to the following Tuesday after Easter, each confirming they could attend, congratulating her and, in Joan's case, thanking her for the honour of being her Maid of Honour. Felicity also said goodbye to Dwight temporarily that Tuesday afternoon, with the understanding that they would meet at his family home in the City of Norfolk on Friday, April 17, so his parents could meet the future bride over the weekend.

So, Felicity would soon have a new life in the new world. The only lingering question to be answered was whether she had made the right decision to accept Dwight's marriage proposal.

PART 5

"Love"

CHAPTER 36

To be a bride requires the ultimate submission of a young lass,
Be sure of thyself, and watch out for those who display some sass!

The hands on the clock of time seemed to tick more slowly as Friday, April 17, 1964, drew closer. Whereas Felicity's mind had been occupied with study and her RAF duties for the first fourteen days of April, suddenly, as it dawned upon her, she would soon be meeting Dwight's parents, and those thoughts began to consume her mind regarding what they would think of her. The derisive and derogatory comments about her looks, which she endured from her grandmother, left an indelible self-doubt in Felicity's mind. The attempted sexual abuse of her by William and Evelyn had left her confused about relationships and wary of people. The only people she had ever genuinely felt comfortable with were her father and perhaps Dwight. She kept deluding herself about the importance of marrying him now for numerous reasons, primarily because he was an essential link to her career dream of becoming an astronaut.

Acknowledging the importance of the big moment in meeting her future parents-in-law for the first time, Felicity had dressed nicely in a knee-length light blue dress, the sleeves of which came halfway down her arms to the crook. She wore a light pink cardigan that remained unbuttoned but covered her noticeable lack of cleavage. She had taken the time at McGuire Air Base that morning to style her hair and apply appropriate makeup to her face before departing for Trenton-Mercer Airport in a taxi. She wore two-tone pink and blue semi-heeled shoes with tan stockings, presenting a demure appearance rather than her usual WRAF uniform. For once, she presented herself as a stereotypical 1960s housewife rather than a dedicated RAF officer.

Dwight was waiting for Felicity at Norfolk Municipal Airport after she disembarked from flying down from New Jersey in a Piedmont Airlines jet aircraft. Reg had granted her leave for that weekend. It was an unusually cool Spring day as Felicity walked across the tarmac, and the chill of the wind hitting her back exacerbated her apprehension about meeting Dwight's parents. The good people of Norfolk were proud of the relatively new airport terminal. This plain, two-level red brick construction housed the tower on a narrow third level of the terminal building; however, when it was opened in 1951, it epitomised America's post-war confidence as it entered the 1950s. Dwight had flown into Norfolk about two hours beforehand, and he surreptitiously caught a taxi to take him to Baker's Fine Jewellery & Gifts in Norfolk, where he collected a surprise before his fiancée arrived. When she walked through the terminal doors from the tarmac, Dwight was waiting by the arrival gate, smiling like the cat who had just swallowed the mouse. Felicity returned the smile, wondering why he was smiling in that manner as she walked towards him. "Teddy Bear! It's so nice to see you again. Why are you smiling at me..." She did not get to finish her sentence as Dwight lifted her off the floor and twirled her around in his arms before kissing her. "Oh, Honey Bunny, I missed you!"

Felicity was overwhelmed by being picked up with such ease and embarrassed as the other passengers on her flight stared at the dynamic display of public affection. "Okay, Teddy Bear, I missed you, too, but please put me down as people are watching." Dwight realised his impulsiveness was perhaps too passionate. However, he was excited to see his fiancée after almost three weeks of separation and couldn't wait to give her the box he had collected, which he had in his pocket, shortly before she arrived. He put Felicity down, then grabbed her left hand with his right to start walking her towards the terminal cafeteria. Felicity was both surprised and puzzled by Dwight's impulsive behaviour. "Teddy Bear, where are we going? What about my bag?" Dwight looked back over his right shoulder, smiling with a sense of reassurance and purpose. "It will be alright. I want five minutes of your time over here before we go to my Pa's and Ma's house." Felicity was clueless about what was happening; however, she complied with her excitable fiancée's request. Dwight walked Felicity to the terminal diner, where a table had been set to one side of the room. On the table was a cheap glass vase containing a single red rose. Dwight pulled out one of the cheap wooden seats, ushering as a sign of gallantry for his fiancée to sit down. Felicity was flattered by Dwight's gallantry, although a side of her believed she was perfectly capable of seating herself at the table. As Dwight took his seat, enough was enough for Felicity; she had to know what was occurring. "Teddy Bear, this is very nice. Still, what on Earth is going on? Aren't we meant to be heading to your parents' house?" Dwight held up his hand and shook it from side to side, almost as though he was dismissing the idea. "All in good time,

Honey Bunny. Something must be done now before we go to meet my parents." He smiled but stopped speaking for a moment. Felicity was perplexed by what was occurring. "Well, don't stop speaking, Teddy Bear. What is so important that we had to come in here?"

Dwight reached into his right pant pocket, and when he pulled it out, he was holding a small polished wooden box in his hand. "Honey Bunny, I couldn't let your engagement ring be a pull-tab off a Coke can, so I went to the local jeweller and purchased this for you." As he finished his sentence, he opened the box, revealing a sparkling round-cut diamond one-carat engagement ring encased in 18-carat gold. Felicity's eyes lit up with joy and tears of happiness. Their engagement had been so transactional that she did not have a moment's thought about an engagement ring. "Oh, Teddy Bear. You shouldn't have spent so much money, you silly boy." Dwight handed Felicity a paper napkin with his left hand as he picked the ring up from the box with his right hand. "I couldn't take my fiancée home to meet Ma and Pa without a ring on her finger. Now, come on, give me that ring finger so that I can give this little gem a home." Felicity held her left hand across the table, and Dwight placed the engagement ring on her finger. She looked at the sparkling beauty on her finger; never had she ever dreamt of wearing a ring, let alone an engagement ring. The diner waitress, who had been busily eavesdropping at a nearby table, clapped her hands, the only sound of celebration in an otherwise empty diner. "Congratulations," she said in her distinctive Virginian voice.

Felicity threw her arms around Dwight's neck and kissed him on the lips. "Thank you, Teddy Bear. I don't know what to say." Dwight stood up and retrieved his wallet from his pocket. "You don't have to say anything; however, we'd better get going as Ma and Pa expect us." Dwight handed two one-dollar bills to the waitress as a tip for allowing him to use the diner's table without purchasing anything. They collected their respective bags and caught a taxi outside the terminal. Dwight gave the directions to the taxi driver – 1212 N Fairwater Drive, Larchmont-Edgewater. The address was meaningless to Felicity. Still, the taxi driver's response was a partial revelation: "The fancy end of town." For almost the entire fifteen-minute drive, Felicity could only stare at the pretty, sparkling, expensive engagement ring she had just received as Dwight pointed out local landmarks that hardly drew her attention. How could the majesty of one item of jewellery possess the mind of an otherwise independent and strong-minded young woman? Perhaps Felicity was like any other young woman of the 1960s – struggling for independence but still subordinate to societal norms and expectations.

Her attention was on her engagement ring, and she was distracted by Dwight pointing out that they were crossing the beautiful, blue, sparkling waters of the Lafayette River, which meant they were minutes from his family's home. The taxi turned right onto Hampton Boulevard immediately after crossing the bridge onto Fairwater Drive. About two hundred yards down the street, it pulled up in front of 1212 N Fairwater Drive. Dwight had not told Felicity how majestic his parents' home was. As she exited the taxi, she saw before her an impressive three-story red brick loft home on the southern shore of the Lafayette River. Built by Dwight's parents towards the end of the Great Depression, just before the war commenced in Europe, the grandeur of the house represented the generations of family wealth acquired through serving in the highest ranks of the United States Army and Air Force. The majesty of the home was complemented by the sprawling front lawn, which was divided into two halves by a stone pathway extending from the entrance to the front door.

The taxi driver carried their bags from the taxi down to the pathway to the front door, where Dwight then paid him the fare and a tip. Felicity was now strangely nervous and felt as though she was entering Evelyn's home again, which was otherwise eerily similar in style to the Hoover family's home, save for the bricks. Indeed, the wooden grey door was too familiar, but she hid her fears from her fiancée and smiled at him as he approached. Within seconds, Dwight knocked on the brass door knocker, and "Ma and Pa", as Dwight called them, opened the front door. Lucille Hoover was in her late 50s, and her most striking feature, beyond her heavily made-up face, was her 1950s hairstyle, which time should have forgotten. Her tinted grey hair was shoulder-length; however, she had pinned it back on either side, and the top had been rolled inwards to meet a part down the middle, which accentuated the grey hair rather than the tints. Being her 'baby boy', Dwight was her natural favourite, mainly because he looked like her. She threw her arms around Dwight and cuddled him tightly. "My darling little astronaut is home. Oh, I have been waiting for you to return, my darling boy." In what was an ominous start to her relationship with her future mother-in-law, Felicity noticed she received half of a glance out of the corner of Lucille's left eye as she cuddled her son.

Four-Star General Ted Hoover followed his wife through the front door, but rather than going straight over to Dwight, he approached Felicity. She instinctively saluted him, as if they had met on McGuire Air Base rather than at her family home. He immediately waved his left hand, signalling she did not need to display the formality of saluting him. Felicity withdrew her salute, feeling embarrassed by her instinctive reaction to the officer-in-charge of the USAF. Ted extended his hand in the typical Southern gentlemanly manner, his son had done when he first introduced himself to Felicity. "You must be the famous Felicity Bennet, the miracle flight pilot of the UAS. Our home doesn't require formalities; you can call me Ted. Welcome to the family, Felicity." Indeed, Ted had been studying every RAF service record about Felicity since Dwight first informed his parents the previous Christmas that he was 'going steady' with a famous English RAF officer. Ted Hoover was tall, like his son; however, his forehead was heavily lined for a sixty-four-year-old man, and, in keeping with the sleepless hours, he kept dealing with people as high up in the government as the President, other United States military top brass or the directors of the CIA and NASA, his hair was white without even a hint of colour. Felicity felt comfortable with Ted from the moment she met him. "Hello, Ted. It's nice to meet you."

With those words being spoken, Lucille broke away from Dwight, and she eyed Felicity up and down, immediately fixating her eyes on the young woman's underdeveloped breasts as though she was inspecting a dairy cow whose teats suggested they were unsuitable for producing the milk of life. "Well, aren't we a skinny young girl?" Felicity was immediately on edge and wary of Lucille. "Girl?" she thought to herself before putting the tips of her right fingers out to greet Lucille. "It's a pleasure to meet you, Lucille." Dwight's mother slowly reached out to take the tips of Felicity's fingers, displaying her apparent wary disposition about whether this young woman was worthy to be her son's wife. "Pleasure to meet you." Her accent was too similar to Prudence's from The Peacock Inn, suggesting that Lucille had 'married up' when she wed Ted.

Ted held his arms to his son to embrace him, but not with the same vigour as Lucille. "Boy, welcome home. And congratulations on NASA, although we knew that would be a likely event, didn't we?" The remark had a disparaging tone, suggesting to Felicity that there was a yet-to-be-discovered history of this father-and-son relationship. Dwight dipped his chin, and it was evident to Felicity that Dwight was never his father's favoured child, which immediately made her feel sympathetic for Dwight. Nevertheless, it was Ted who displayed genuine warmth towards Felicity. "Come on into our house, Felicity. We have some food and drinks out back to celebrate your joining the family, and the waterfront is splendid at this time of year. Dwight, you take the bags up to the rooms. Felicity, you can sleep in our daughter's former bedroom, which has a lovely dressing table where you can put all your items. Dwight, your mother has made up your bedroom for you, and make sure you treat it like your barracks room, boy." There was a history to the father-son relationship, evident from Ted's command and Dwight's obsequiousness. "Okay, Pa. Honey Bunny, you go out the back with Ma and Pa. I will show you to your room later."

Dwight entered the house first, carrying items of luggage, followed by his mother, and then Ted ushered Felicity in through the front door. "Come on in and make yourself at home." When she entered the home, Felicity was immediately struck by its grandeur. The walls were light blue plasterboard from floor to ceiling, offset by American white cornices and doors. Halfway down the hallway was the impressive white battened stairwell, which wrapped its way up to the second floor and then continued to the third-level loft. What made the stairwell even more remarkable was the Royal Blue Persian-style rug carpet, the edges of which were fastened in place by a brass moulding. The furnishings were contemporary for the 1930s. Ted walked down the hallway with Felicity as he explained the history of the home. "We built this home here in 1937 when I was stationed at Langley Air Force Base. My daddy had unexpectedly passed away that year after a heart attack, and I was the only surviving child of three boys. My eldest brother had died in battle on the Western Front in World War I, and my other older brother died from the Spanish Flu in the early 1920s. My mammy very kindly passed on a lot of my daddy's money to Lucille and me so that we could build a house for our three children. Dwight was only a baby then, and my late son, Hank, was six. My daughter was two, so we built the loft to contain two extra bedrooms. One was for our servant, Ethel, who helped Lucille raise our children while I was away at war, and the other was for my mammy, in case she ever wanted to move in with us. However, she didn't and remained living in Chesapeake, where I was born and bred, until she passed only several years ago at the ripe old age of eighty-eight."

By now, Lucille was opening the glass doors of the rear sunroom, which led out to a paved courtyard. When Felicity followed, not far behind her, the courtyard revealed that it led onto lawns and gardens extending another fifty yards down to the stonewall separating the property from the shores of the Lafayette River. Lucille and Ted had set up an outdoor wooden table, covered in a fine linen tablecloth, with a platter of cheese and biscuits, and a silver champagne bucket containing a bottle of Moët on ice. Ted pulled out one of the wooden chairs for his wife to sit in, then pulled out another for Felicity. All the chairs had tied cushions, making the experience of sitting out there on that cool spring afternoon a comfortable one.

As Felicity took her seat, Dwight briskly walked out the back door, immediately engaging his father's derision. "Well, what took you so long, boy?" Dwight was short of breath after lugging two bags up several flights of stairs. "Sorry, Pa. I quickly unpacked my bag in the loft room after I placed Felicity's bag in Shirley's old bedroom." Dwight pulled the remaining chair out to sit on as Ted leaned over to speak to Felicity. "That loft bedroom was my late son Hank's old room. You would have liked Hank; he was a fine, stylish man." Lucille leaned over and placed her right hand on Dwight's left arm. "But it is Dwight's room now, and we're so proud of him being accepted into NASA's astronaut programme. Aren't you proud of him, Felicity?" She nodded as she reached out and held Dwight's hand in a sign of solidarity. "Of course, Lucille. I am very proud of Teddy Bear." Lucille permitted a slight smile. "Teddy Bear. What a delightful pet name for my baby boy." Lucille's words were underscored with a hint of sarcastic commentary. As he spoke, Ted leaned over and took the champagne bottle out of the bucket. "Let's celebrate our son's engagement to this fine young English Flying Officer." With those words, the cork popped, and a small spout of champagne flowed out of the bottle, landing just near Lucille. "Oh, careful, Ted. I'm wearing silk." Felicity could tell Lucille had married up in life, as English women did not need to describe their clothes to display their class. Ted poured four glasses of champagne and then toasted the newly engaged couple.

After placing their champagne flutes on the table, Lucille turned to Felicity. To commence her earnest inquisition about her future intentions. "So, Felicity. You're a Flying Officer, which Ted tells me is a Second Lieutenant in our Air Force. But, of course, I imagine you will start having a family after you and Dwight get married, which means the end of your service career." Felicity was stirred by Lucille's assumption about her future intentions. "Far from it, Lucille. I intend to continue serving in the USAF and studying at Stanford, child or no child." Lucille raised her eyebrows. "But how do you expect to serve as a mother while Dwight is training for NASA?" Felicity leaned forward, and as she did, Dwight held onto her knee under the tablecloth to restrain his fiancée;

however, Felicity had been down this path in life many years before with her late grandmother, and she was not about to back down. "Lucille, I believe a woman is entitled to maintain her career and be a mother at the same time. At Stanford, I will be pursuing a PhD in Aeronautical Engineering under the guidance of Professor Ron Goldman, including conducting work for NASA that may help ensure the safety of astronauts like Dwight when they are flying in space. That is just as important as cooking a roast chicken and vegetables." Ted intervened, evidently taking the side of Felicity. "I agree with Felicity. The RAF considers her an outstanding officer, so it would be a shame if our Air Force were denied the opportunity to use her skills."

Ted's words immediately silenced Lucille on the career line of questioning; however, much to both Ted's and Dwight's dismay, Lucille continued her inquisition. "What religion are you and your family, Felicity?" The religious question: What could she say when she had long ago rejected the existence of God? "I was raised in a Catholic family." Dwight had not mentioned Catholicism to his parents, who were both devoted Baptists. He decided to try to hose out the flames of this line of questioning because he did not even know Felicity's religious beliefs. "Felicity knows we're committed Baptists, Ma. Our wedding will be held in our parish church here in Norfolk, isn't it, Honey Bunny?" Dwight's nomination of a church wedding had not been previously discussed with Felicity. While her eyes lit up with disbelief that Dwight had assumed she would marry in any church, she could tell by the pleading expression of his eyes that she should reluctantly confirm this detail. She decided to quickly save a deteriorating start to her relationship with her future mother-in-law by affirming Dwight's comments. "Yes, well, Dwight and I were going to break that news to both of you this weekend, so we may as well confirm it now." Felicity could see an internal sigh of relief emanate from Dwight's eyes. Lucille's demeanour changed immediately, and she leaned over and hugged Felicity, much to the younger woman's surprise. "Oh, well, that is wonderful news. It's joyous news. Wait until you meet Pastor Ford on Sunday, Felicity. He will be delighted to hear you are joining our flock." Felicity contained her surprise, but her thoughts shouted into every cavity of her head. 'Church on Sunday? Joining their flock?!?' However, she constrained herself, as it was necessary to marry Dwight for many reasons.

Subsequently, over dinner, Lucille was far more convivial towards Felicity, who, in return, remained respectful to maintain peace between her and Dwight. Then, after dinner, Ted suggested they all sit down to watch Steve Allen's *Tonight*

Show. This was a novelty for Felicity, as she did not watch television at night while stationed at McGuire because she would be studying instead. They sat in the cozy living room in front of the colour television. The show began with Steve Allen's usual introductory comedy routine, which Dwight and his parents found funny, but Felicity thought it was droll. Then Steve Allen announced his first guest for the evening, and much to Felicity's disbelief, it was Amelia. She looked stunning as she walked out onto the stage in front of the studio audience, wearing a miniskirt and knee-high boots. Her hair was slightly shorter and she was less curvaceous than Felicity had seen her on the big screen at Princeton. However, she looked beautiful, and Felicity's heart immediately began beating with desire, just as it had at Princeton. Lucille and Ted commented on Amelia's beauty, and Lucille couldn't help but comment on Amelia's ample breasts. Like the studio audience, the Hoover family marvelled over a movie star returning from potential obscurity with an Independent Artists' Studio movie contract. Additionally, ABC developed a television show. Felicity sat there yearning for those soft, fulsome lips to kiss hers again. Then, she was mortified by the feelings she was experiencing, hoping that none of the family, especially Dwight, had noticed. Felicity got up quickly and excused herself, telling Dwight and his parents she was tired after a long day.

Felicity raced up to the bedroom she was to sleep in for the night. She placed her face into the pillow and muttered to herself, "Why? Why am I having these silly thoughts? Grow up, Felicity! You were a child back then. And damn you, Amelia, as all you did was break my heart!" It took Felicity about ten minutes to put the Amelia genie back into its bottle; however, the lid could never be fastened shut. She then looked at her engagement ring, and the memories of Lucille's afternoon discussions flooded her mind. "But am I just expected to be Dwight's baby factory? What about my goals? What about my dreams?" She started questioning the notion of marriage, but what would she do if she were redeployed to the UK by the RAF? She loved the English countryside; however, they did not have a space programme. "And what about the opportunity at NASA, the door Ron opened, inviting me to study under him at Stanford? There will not be a door opening for me like that back in an English university?" She became annoyed about the predicaments women experienced. "I am a Cambridge University graduate. I am soon to be a Princeton University graduate. I can fly an aeroplane better than any man, yet all I have been able to do here in America is fly the God damn O-1 Bird Dog! And all that is on offer for me back in the UK is that I might one day get to fly a jet fighter! Dwight's just a pilot, yet he gets selected for the Astronaut programme because of who his father is." While she pondered these thoughts of inequality, it suddenly dawned upon Felicity that the only way a woman could get ahead in life was to be anchored to a man. In Dwight's case, he was not a nefarious viper. Dwight was now training to be a NASA astronaut. Ron was offering her the opportunity to enter NASA through Stanford University. As much as it pained her as a woman, she accepted that she would have to take this path if she wished to pursue her dream, just as Joan had told her several years beforehand.

Subsequently, Dwight knocked on her door to make sure she was okay. By this time, Felicity had reconciled in her mind; it was just a momentary lapse of immaturity again about Amelia and that she was not a lesbian. Her only options in life were to marry Dwight and to study at Stanford or, alternatively, not marry Dwight and not study at Stanford. She told Dwight she was almost asleep and would see him in the morning.

On Sunday, she attended the Hoover family's local Baptist church, which was an eye-opening experience for her as she observed the unusual religious rituals. She bowed and closed her eyes when people were asked to pray, but she did not speak to any imaginary sky fairies. Afterwards, she met Pastor Ford, who did not press her on her belief because she was in the company of a prestigious family who regularly attended his church. Pastor Ford told Lucille that Felicity would make an excellent wife and mother. The pastor's blessing suppressed Lucille's concerns about Dwight marrying an English catholic woman.

After attending the church service, Ted, Lucille, Dwight, and Felicity returned to Fairwater Drive, where lunch would be served before Felicity and Dwight had to separate at Norfolk Airport. Shortly before lunch, Ted sat down with Felicity and Dwight to discuss Felicity's future with the USAF. They sat down in the same living room from which Felicity had walked out two nights before while they were watching Amelia on *The Tonight Show*. That room harboured bad memories for Felicity, and the tone of Ted's voice when he asked her and Dwight to join her did not sound promising. Ted poured himself a Jack Daniel's as he commenced talking. "Now, Felicity, my impetuous son has told you before speaking to me that I can perform miracles regarding USAF appointments." Ted stopped mid-speech and glared at Dwight, who dipped his head. "By the way, would you like some Jack Daniel's?" Felicity shook her head, finding it strange that Ted would drink bourbon before midday. "Anyway, why did I want to talk with you? Dwight might have told you I could arrange a transfer from the RAF to the USAF." Felicity nodded and glanced sideways at Dwight, whose head was still dipped. "The answer is I can; however, it isn't to the regular USAF. Under the exchange programme, I can arrange a transfer to our Women's Air Force, but it would not be as a pilot. You will hold the rank of Second Lieutenant, which is comparable to your current RAF rank. Still, you won't be allowed to fly a jet fighter. That is not my decision; that is a matter of military law in this country. Is that a problem for you?" Felicity glanced at Dwight, who finally lifted his chin. His eyes displayed genuine remorse. Felicity was angry that Dwight had oversold what his father might be able to arrange; however, studying under Ron at Stanford mattered the most to her. "No, Ted. It isn't a problem if my rank is comparable to my current office with the RAF. As for not flying jets, I would be lying if I said I am not disappointed. Nevertheless, that is the same barrier I have encountered with the RAF. Mind you, I am not happy about it. Still, I did think Teddy Bear was perhaps a bit overexuberant when he regaled me with the might and power you held in the USAF. So, in answer to your question, it's not a problem for me per se, but it sure is a problem for women in general."

Ted drank the rest of his bourbon and then left the room. Dwight began to apologise. "I am sorry, Honey Bunny, for..." Felicity held up her hand to silence her fiancée. "There is no need to apologise. You only tried to look after my best interests, Teddy Bear." Dwight hugged her in appreciation of his reprieve, and then he left the room. Felicity could only fume about a woman's life. Still, there were Ron and Stanford. Where there is a door, there is hope.

Later that day, Dwight and Felicity went their separate ways at Norfolk Airport. Dwight was the first to leave on his American Airlines flight, which he had to change over at Houston to fly to Los Angeles, where he would again have to change to fly to Flagstaff. His shirt had the stitched logo of "NASA" on the left side of his shirt pocket, which left no doubt to whom he belonged in that world. On the Norfolk to Houston route, he was the only person seated in first class that afternoon, which meant the attractive, shapely, young redhead hostess could pay him more significant attention. After takeoff, and when the captain of the Boeing 707 had announced that passengers could move freely around, the redhead airline hostess came over to Dwight's seat to offer him a refreshment. "Hello, sir. My name is Jolene, and since the flight isn't full this afternoon, you have me all to yourself. Can I offer you something today?" Her Texan accent carried a hint of seduction, which caused Dwight to break out into an embarrassed smile as he shook his head sideways to decline the drink. Jolene couldn't help but notice the NASA logo stitched onto Dwight's shirt. "I hope you don't mind me asking, sir, but are you a scientist?" Jolene's Texan accent made the seductive undertones of her voice sound all the more enticing to Dwight. "No, ma'am, I don't mind you asking. By the way, my name is Dwight, so you don't have to call me sir. To answer your question, I'm training to be an astronaut." Jolene's eyes lit up like the light on a Bally 'Money Honey' slot machine. "An astronaut! Wow, aren't you the pride of the nation, Dwight?" Dwight broke into another embarrassed smile and felt inclined to talk to Jolene. "No, I don't know about that. I have to go into space before I can make that claim." There was momentary silence, and then he spoke again. "So, Jolene. Do you often fly this route?" Jolene smiled the seductress's smile. "Not often. I usually fly the L.A. to Houston route and back. I live in Houston, where you can find NASA boys working. Am I right about that?" Dwight nodded. "Some of the time. I'm in training at Stead Air Force Base, but I also have to travel to Houston for my training." Jolene's final words and smile left no doubts about her intentions. "Well, I might see more of you in the future." She slowly swivelled her hips to turn around, giving Dwight a long look at her shapely legs and backside as Jolene made her way slowly and deliberately to the cockpit to refresh the pilots.

On her flight back to Trenton-Mercer Airport, Felicity kept repeating, 'I am doing the right thing. Dwight is a good match for me. Life will be fine.' But after Steve Allen's show, could she genuinely say life would be acceptable? And what were Dwight's intentions about Felicity maintaining her career goals? Ted had just told her she would not be better off in the USAF than the RAF. And would Ron continue to argue her case at NASA? Flying into space seemed simple when Sputnik 1 encircled the Earth in 1957. In the real world of 1964, it appeared that climbing Mount Everest would be a relatively more straightforward task for a woman. There were more questions than answers, but they would have to wait as Felicity had a wedding to plan and a career to pursue.

CHAPTER 37

History should have taught thee that a woman's place is at the head of the queue,
Yet, for reasons that defy nature, the feminine species submits to saying 'I do.'

Time passed quickly between April 19, when Felicity returned to McGuire, and June 9, her last day at McGuire Air Force Base. During those seven weeks, she appeared to be arranging her wedding more than performing any work for the RAF. Ted processed the officer exchange programme papers so that Felicity could start with the WAF immediately after the short honeymoon Dwight arranged for them in Anaheim, which allowed him to take her to Disneyland. It was not precisely Felicity's choice of honeymoon vacation destination, but their time was limited.

Not long before she departed from the RAF, Felicity was finally acknowledged by the RAF for her almost three years of service. Reg arranged a ceremony to be held at McGuire, which was attended by a small contingent of RAF officers remaining at the base, many of whom had befriended Felicity over the past several months. It was not lost on Felicity that perhaps their belated attempts at friendship germinated from a relief that 'the boys' club' was no longer being infiltrated by the opposite sex. However, it was recognition for her service. In return, Felicity's wedding guest list expanded to include her fellow officers, many of whom, like her, were alone in a new world. The final words of her parting speech underscored Felicity's disappointment with the armed services in the so-called democratic world of the RAF: "Women must be permitted to progress also to touch the sky, and not merely be the all-seeing eye of the machinations of its bureaucracy."

Samuel had already wired the money to Felicity so that he could cover the cost of the wedding reception. Lucille had insisted that the wedding reception be held at the Monticello Hotel, the oldest and most prestigious hotel in Norfolk. This choice would not only benefit from the use of its ballroom for the wedding reception but also accommodate the number of rooms guests had booked for two nights to attend the wedding itself. Numerous VIP guests would be attending this wedding, including top American military personnel,

NASA directors, the Deputy Director of the CIA, an old USAF friend of Ted's and members of Congress. Not to be outmatched, Felicity had Sir Thomas Wilberforce attending, Reg, her fellow officers from McGuire Air Base and most importantly, her Maid of Honour, whose husband, Stuart, was now officially the Earl de Montesquieu, after his father had passed away earlier that year, making Joan the Countess de Montesquieu. Even Viscount Godwin was attending the wedding after receiving Felicity's invitation because, as he described it in his reply, "I owe my life to you, so it is not inconvenient for me at all to travel across to the land of the Yankees for such an important moment in your life." Ron had also been invited to be one of Felicity's guests, a list which contained far fewer people than Dwight's family's list of guests. Notably missing from Felicity's guest list was her aunt and uncle in Australia, both of whom she had disowned after they pursued her father for money. Lucille had also ensured there would be plenty of press coverage about her son's marriage, including a reporter from the Washington Post. Samuel almost fell out of his chair in his home office when Felicity told him that the wedding cost would be two thousand pounds sterling.

Felicity had a local dressmaker in Trenton create her white satin wedding gown, which featured sewn-in cups to accentuate the full breasts she did not naturally possess. She also had the same dressmaker make the bridesmaids' dresses, which required urgent telegrams to be sent back and forth across the Atlantic Ocean. Joan, Natasha, and Heather were each separately measured by dressmakers in England, all of whom required a fee for their services. The wedding gown and bridesmaid's dresses were shipped in advance to 1212 N Fairwater Drive, to arrive there on June 9, when Felicity would fly down from Trenton-Mercer Airport to Norfolk, so that she could be in Norfolk on June 10 when Samuel would arrive to spend two nights at the Hoover household to become acquainted with not only his future son-in-law, but also his family.

Dwight, his sister, Shirley, and her husband, Colonel Bob Sanders, had already settled in at Fairwater Drive when Felicity arrived at Norfolk Airport, where Dwight was waiting for her. After the overly gushing greeting in the terminal, Dwight and Felicity returned to Fairwater Drive, where she knew her future sister-in-law and brother-in-law were waiting to meet her. Lucille had already spoken to her daughter about the 'English woman being very strident in her views about maintaining her career, as opposed to being a dutiful housewife.' The poisoned chalice had been drunk before Felicity could fill Shirley's cup with womanly wisdom. When Dwight and Felicity arrived at

Fairwater Drive, his family were waiting for them on the back patio, enjoying an afternoon glass of champagne. After their initial pleasantries of meeting, which included Felicity, doing her best trying not to laugh when Ted introduced Bob as 'Colonel Sanders', it didn't take long for Lucille's words to emanate through the lips of Shirley as they all sat down, sipping champagne as the beautiful blue waters of the Lafayette River meandered by. "So, Felicity, my Mom tells me you will start studying at Stanford University this August." Felicity politely smiled, unsure of where the conversation would lead. "Yes, that is right. I am pursuing a doctorate in aeronautical engineering under the guidance of Professor Ron Goldman. As part of my studies, I will be working with him on projects for NASA." Shirley smiled politely; however, her next question was not so polite. "But of course, that might all have to be delayed when you have children with Dwight, won't it?"

Felicity couldn't help but notice Lucille, sitting to Shirley's left but supposedly listening to three men talk, slightly turning her head towards Shirley and Felicity. It was evident to Felicity that Lucille had been discussing her future intentions with Shirley. "Well, no, Shirley, and I do not understand why I cannot be a mother, student and worker." Shirley was now treading too close to her future sister-in-law's personal life. "But who will raise the child? Dwight will be busy with NASA. How can you raise a child, study and work?" Felicity was now stirred. "Look, Shirley. We have just met, so I assume your query's genesis is genuine. However, I am not like 'other' women. I believe a woman can be a wife, a mother, and, most importantly, maintain a career. Did it occur to you, as a woman, that perhaps I might one day be flying into space?" Shirley naively laughed. "You English with your unique sense of humour."

Felicity leaned closer so that she could be heard; given the look of disdain emanating from her eyes, she would likely shout if she did not stare down Shirley's feeble submissiveness. "Who on Earth would think that was a joke?" There was enough bite to Felicity's voice to cause the three men to stop talking and turn her way. That did not deter Felicity from making her point. "As for Dwight being busy with NASA, well, who knows? Perhaps he might have to share the load if I become too busy with my career!" Dwight immediately stood up to intervene, for fear that Shirley would respond with a question that would enrage his soon-to-be wife. "Heh, Honey Bunny, how about you come inside? I have something in my bag that I wanted to give you at the airport, but I forgot to take it with me." He had something in his bag that he wanted to give to Felicity the day before their wedding: some earrings that he wanted her to wear with her dress. However, he now had to use that gift as a circuit breaker.

Felicity followed Dwight into the house, but Shirley's voice was loud enough to follow them through the doorway. "Well, isn't she a first-class bitch! I hope my brother knows what he's doing!" Ted and Bob were too busy discussing military matters to be disturbed by the women's quarrels. Lucille nodded at her daughter but lowered her voice. "I told you, Shirley, she's a strong-minded young woman. Nevertheless, your brother likes her, and she does seem to know several people holding English titles, which will benefit your brother's reputation." Shirley lifted her glass of champagne as she spoke. "As long as she provides him with children for the next generation of the Hoover name to live on, she can otherwise take her career and shove it..." Lucille put her hand on her daughter's arm to interrupt her, fearing that her daughter's final words would not be pleasant.

Dwight led Felicity upstairs to his bedroom, almost dragging her by the hand. When they entered his bedroom, he quickly closed the door and tried to hug her, but she resisted his hold. "Please, Dwight. Not now. I cannot believe your sister had the nerve to speak to me like that." Her voice was irritated and loud, causing Dwight to lift his finger to his mouth to shush her. "Calm down, Honey Bunny. She did not mean anything personal by the way she spoke to you. My sister believes a woman must be a wife and a mother. She is old-fashioned that way." Felicity looked long and hard at Dwight, trying to determine whether he held similar views. Eventually, she spoke. "Do you believe that is what I should be, Teddy Bear?" He did, to some extent, but he also believed that his future wife should be able to pursue her dreams. "I won't lie to you, Honey Bunny. Of course, I want to have children, but that doesn't mean I want you to put your career on hold. No way on God's Earth I would not expect you to stop working with Ron." Her career aspirations sought to scale greater heights than working with Ron; however, Felicity accepted his candour, and then she hugged him. "I am sorry I lost my temper with your sister, Teddy Bear." He then broke free of their hug and retrieved a gift he had purchased for her from his bag. Upon opening it, he handed over a small box and revealed a pair of sapphire earrings. "Here you go, Honey Bunny. Something blue for you to wear on our wedding day." Felicity hugged him tightly. "Thank you, Teddy Bear. But you shouldn't have spent so much money." Later that night, the family dinner was a very contrived civil affair. However, an underlying tension existed between Felicity and Shirley, which permeated the atmosphere of superficial harmony.

Dwight and Felicity welcomed Samuel the following day upon his arrival at Norfolk Airport. As he walked through the arrival doors of the terminal, Felicity leapt into his arms, a reception which Dwight noticed he never received. "Dad. Oh, how glad I am to see you." His embrace was just as comforting as it always had been. "It's so good to see you, my little sweetheart." After embracing her for about fifteen seconds, Samuel realised the tall man standing near her should be acknowledged. He let go of his daughter and shot out his hand to greet Dwight. "And you must be the famous Dwight I keep hearing about?" Dwight took Samuel's right hand, and his grip was soft, which slightly worried Samuel. "Mr Bennet, it is so nice to meet you, sir." Samuel gripped Dwight's hand with greater force. "Please, it's Samuel. Nice to finally meet my future son-in-law. I had heard my daughter talk so much about you, but I wondered whether you were like Godot." Felicity giggled at her father's Beckett reference. Still, the humour was lost on Dwight, which was another niggling matter of concern for Samuel: the cultural divide between Americans and the English. Was this man the right person to marry his daughter? Felicity was adamant that he was a good man, so Samuel would keep his thoughts concealed for the moment. "Come on, we'll get your bags, and then you can come back and meet my folks, my sister, and her husband."

Samuel took in the splendour of the Lafayette River as Dwight drove the three of them in his father's Cadillac back to the Hoover household. When they arrived, the greetings were pleasant between the two families; however, Samuel detected a cold streak running through the veins of Dwight's parents, sister and her husband. He found Lucille to be reeking of poor girl made good, Ted to be a hardened career military man, just like Bob, and Shirley, well, he found her to be a bitch. The dinner was civil, but Samuel flinched when he heard Ted mention, 'How glad we are that damn Catholic was no longer in the White House.' Still, he did not utter a word that night to Felicity when they bid each other goodnight before retiring to their separate rooms. Samuel remained polite and quiet the following day as he mingled with the Hoovers' extended family members who came to greet the new additions to their family. He noticed Dwight seemed very passionate when he cuddled Felicity, whereas his daughter did not appear to display the same affection. 'Is it just her way?' he thought to himself.

Everything about the Hoover world rang alarm bells for Samuel. He sat quietly in the front seat of the Cadillac as Dwight drove Felicity and her father to stay at the Monticello Hotel for the night before the wedding. It was his daughter's life, but he felt like he owed a duty to his wife to extricate the one remaining light from heaven of her still on Earth – the daughter she brought into this world who had given him so much joy. 'However, what can I say?' he asked himself as they checked into the Monticello Hotel the day before the wedding. 'It is too late because all the guests from England have arrived, but there doesn't seem to be any warmth displayed by my daughter. 'What do I do?' Samuel thought as the bellhop carried his bags to his hotel room. It was not only too late to prevent the wedding from going ahead, but it was also too late, as the soiree at the Hoover household meant that it was 10:00 p.m. by the time he and Felicity had checked in for the evening.

Natasha, her husband, and their two spoiled British children had already checked into the hotel. Heather, along with her philandering boss, had also checked in. However, Felicity briefly caught a glimpse of her in the hallway as she entered her suite for the night, while Heather was rushing to get some ice. Heather waved at her friend and gestured from afar that she would see Felicity the next day.

Countess Joan, the Earl, and their entourage of nannies, who would assist their two children, had checked in. Joan's father was in an adjoining room with the grandchildren, allowing his daughter and Earl to enjoy some private time. Even the pompous old Viscount Godwin had arrived and checked into a deluxe suite with his long-suffering wife, Countess Margaret.

Everything about this wedding screamed a mistake to Samuel, but he felt helpless now, as the wedding was scheduled for the next day. Little did Samuel realise that as he tossed and turned that night before the wedding, Felicity was doing the same in her hotel room. Dwight was kind, and she had feelings for him. "But is this love?" she asked herself repeatedly. His kisses were gentlemanly, but there was no spark like when she kissed Amelia's lips. "Amelia!" Her words were spoken in anger as her mind had wandered back to that night. Finally, there was her run-in with Shirley about being a career woman and a mother. That angered her and made Felicity determined to prove Shirley wrong, when it should have served as a warning. Eventually, she fell asleep a little after midnight, telling herself these were routine questions brides asked themselves the night before their wedding. She didn't realise the most significant mental challenge awaited her from the person she least suspected of challenging her the following day.

CHAPTER 38

It was not so much a taming of a shrew, which matrimonial life expected,
No, it was an age-old problem: the risk of love being neglected.

Later that morning, at 7:00, Felicity was awakened by a knock on her room door. She thought she might have heard someone else's door being knocked on, but within a minute, there was knocking again. She quickly got up, put on her complimentary robe, and hurriedly approached the door. "Who is it?" There was a prompt response. "It's me, Heather, Felicity. May I come in?"

Felicity opened her bedroom door to her friend and bridesmaid, who was also dressed in a hotel robe. Heather looked as though she had had a big night, as she was dishevelled, as one might be after being in the throes of passion for a considerable time. Felicity flung her arms around her old school friend. "Heather, it is so nice to see you!" Heather was slightly more reserved. "Nice to see you too, Felicity. I know it's early, but may I come and speak with you for a moment? Felicity detected the earnest tone of her old friend's voice and was worried that something might have occurred between her and the love interest in their room that night. "Of course. Please, come and sit on the sofa." Felicity's father had paid for a suite because the bridesmaids would be getting ready in that room later that morning, so ample space was available to sit comfortably in the plush lounge area. They both sat down, and Heather remained quiet as she tried to distil how she would tell Felicity what was worrying her. Felicity could tell something was on Heather's mind, and she immediately thought it might be related to her partner in life. "Has John done something to you, Heather?" Heather shook off the notion that her relationship was troubling her; however, she did not know how to express her concerns about Felicity. Felicity probed for answers. "Well, what makes you look so concerned this morning on my wedding day?"

The magic words had opened the door to the cave of insight dwelling in Heather's mind. She turned and looked deep into Felicity's eyes. "You deliberately lost that race because you loved Amelia, right?" Right then, Felicity felt her friend could see a world in a grain of sand because she had unlocked a vault of guilt that Felicity had stored away years ago. Her face turned ashen, a clear giveaway of the truth. However, to cover up the truth, Felicity displayed imperious disdain. "What on earth are you talking about, Heather?" Heather was not going to accept intellectual bullying because this was a matter of trying to save her friend from what she felt was a grave mistake. "Don't use that intellectual superiority on me, Space Freak. We have known each other for far too long. I know it's your wedding day, and I'm not trying to cause any trouble, but as your longtime friend, I knew from the day we had lunch at Cambridge that you loved Amelia. I could see it in your eyes the moment her name was mentioned. And now I have seen written all over your face this morning. I put two and two together after lunch at the Anchor that day because I still, up until that moment, couldn't work out how you could have lost that race at school. Then it dawned on me that day at lunch, when I saw the look on your face, that you love Amelia, which is fine with me. However, I don't want you to marry just for the sake of it if your heart belongs to someone else. I can't, as a friend, let that happen to you."

Felicity felt like a mouse cornered by a cat. And of all the people to possess such insight as her friend Heather, who was not as academically accomplished as she was. Felicity stood up and walked over to the nearest window to the right of the sofa. Her mind was whirring with the thoughts of what she had just been confronted with. But it was too late to reveal the truth. And what if her confession leaked out via Heather confiding in Natasha, whose mouth knew no boundaries? She closed her eyes, took a deep breath, and told herself to be brave as she faced her interrogator. Then she turned around, displaying an imperious smirk, as though her friend was a fool. "My goodness! What an imagination you have there, Heather. Is this a result of living a double life with John that you would think these things? I mean, honestly, a simple poor start to a race, and you have so many years later concocted in your mind some love conspiracy. Are you being serious? Or are you joking with me? One thing is sure: I am as nervous as any bride could be on her wedding day, so please don't come interrogating me about some silly idea you've hatched in your mind." Her words were cutting, but they had worked. Suddenly, Heather felt like she was a fool and an impolite intruder. "I'm sorry, Felicity. I didn't mean to upset you on your special day. I was wrong to ask these questions. I was wrong to think these thoughts. Please forgive me."

A hint of tears filled poor Heather's eyes, which made Felicity feel worse for browbeating her. She walked over and sat down beside her friend, placing her arms around her shoulders and consoling her. "Heh, don't cry, Heather. I am not angry at you. I was surprised, but you are just being a good friend. I do not love Amelia, and I never have. She tried to bully me at school, and whenever her name is mentioned, it makes me uncomfortable because of the bullying. That is why I might have looked funny at the Anchor when you mentioned her that day. Now, come on. Grab some breakfast, and then make sure you're here by 10:00 a.m., as the hairstylist is arriving at 10:30 a.m. Heather hugged her old school friend. "I'm sorry, Felicity. Please don't tell Natasha about this." As if she would tell Natasha. "Come on. Go and get some breakfast. I am sure John needs some sustenance after the night you pair have had." Felicity's remarks brought an embarrassed smile to Heather's face, and then she got up and walked over to the door, turning to smile at Felicity to seek assurance, which she was granted in response. Heather then left the room. Felicity fell back onto the sofa. "Cripes, that was all I needed. Get out of my mind, Amelia. This is my day, not yours." The day's frenetic pace would soon partially remove thoughts from her mind about Amelia, but her friend Heather was right: she did, indeed, still have feelings for Amelia. She just had to try to bury them, as Joan had commanded her to many years ago.

Joan was the first member of her bridal party to arrive at the room at 10:00 a.m. Room service had only just taken Felicity's breakfast away. Joan's words were comforting and forthright. "Well, Flying Officer Bennet. How proud I am of you today." Felicity hugged Joan, just as a younger sister would. "Joan! How good it is to see your face right now." Their embrace was a fleeting moment of comfort as Felicity pulled away from Joan and walked over to the bed, where her wedding dress now lay. Joan detected Felicity's confused state of mind. She walked over to her and placed her left hand on her right shoulder. "What is up, Felicity? You look like your mind is grinding away on all the world's worries. Is there anything wrong?" Joan's hand gently squeezed Felicity's shoulder, encouraging the bride-to-be to turn around. Felicity dropped her eyes because what she would say next would only be half of the truth. "Am I doing the right thing getting married so fast, Joan?" Joan then used her left hand to lift Felicity's chin. "Do you want to pull out of the wedding, Felicity? If you do, you had better let people know now, although I imagine an outcry will be heard back to England. Don't you want to marry Dwight?" How could she tell Joan that Heather had stirred a hornet's nest in her mind about her feelings for Amelia and that her real motivation to marry Dwight was to stay in America as NASA awaited her at Stanford? How could she say that she was an atheist who was about to pretend to take a vow? She closed her eyes again to hide the truth in her heart. "No, Joan, and yes, I do want to marry Dwight. I am just nervous. If you had asked me a year ago if I thought I would be married by now, the answer would have been no. It's just wedding day nerves." Joan placed her hands on Felicity's shoulders and gently shook her to open her eyes. "Felicity, look at me, please. Do you want to marry Dwight?" She did and she didn't; however, if she learned anything about herself in the darkroom, it was that she could quell her emotions. Felicity smiled and contemporaneously nodded. "Yes, Joan. It's just wedding day nerves." Joan nodded as a sign of accepting Felicity's word. If only she had pressed her for more information or, more importantly, been present when Heather interrogated Felicity earlier that day, things might have turned out differently. She might have elicited the truth from Felicity's heart rather than the lie fabricated in her mind. Felicity then turned around and picked up her wedding dress, a full-length garment that covered her entire body. "Can you please help me put this on over my petticoat, Joan? I cannot reach the zipper at the back, and it is tight around my neck, so I have to put it on before the hairstylist arrives."

Joan assisted Felicity in putting on her dress. As she finished helping her, Natasha came bursting through the door, cigarette in one hand and a bottle of champagne in the other, heralding the acceleration of the day's festivities. "Bloody hell! Aren't I glad to have a few hours' break from those brats of mine." She then realised Joan was in the room. "Oh, cripes! I didn't see you there. I remember you from Woldingham. Joan, isn't it?" Joan nodded politely, although she was used to being acknowledged as Countess. Natasha's bluster continued as she hurriedly poured four glasses of champagne as Heather arrived, followed immediately by the hair and make-up stylists. Two hours seemed to fly by in the blink of an eye, and then Samuel arrived on time at 1:00 p.m. to walk them all down to the Monticello Hotel entrance, where two black Cadillac Sixty Special cars waited for them. Samuel accompanied his daughter in the back seat of the first car, and the three bridesmaids sat in the back seat of the second car as they journeyed to the Freemason Street Baptist Church. During that journey to the church, Samuel did not speak to Felicity about his concerns regarding the family she was marrying into. Like Joan, had he forcibly pressed his daughter's heart and mind at that time, he might have elicited the truth; however, Samuel was used to Felicity's steel-trap mind, and when she had made her mind up to do something, nobody could persuade her to do otherwise. If only he had realised how vulnerable she felt at this time. When they arrived at the church, Samuel turned towards Felicity and finally spoke. "Well, this is a day a father has to acknowledge his little girl has grown up. I am proud of you, sweetie." His words soothed her mind as Felicity looked up at the daunting tall church steeple, but he had one more thought for the day. "By the way, Felicity. I know you are an atheist, but obviously, the Hoovers and Dwight don't know that fact, so a word of advice – close your eyes during the prayers." She smiled because at least that piece of advice settled her mind.

From thenceforth, the day sped through the bizarre rituals of Baptists, which the Catholics and Anglicans from England alike found mildly amusing. As Felicity took her marriage vows, she spoke the mumbo jumbo to keep up the façade of marrying into a well-connected southern white family. Then, there was the reception at the Monticello, where Lucille displayed her gushing common American traits around the stable of English nobility guests. Cameras flashed as the press took their photographs of the gala wedding event. Within an instant, the crowd was saying goodbye to the man and wife as they left the Starlight Room of the Monticello to go upstairs to the deluxe room Dwight had booked for them to spend their first night together in. Dwight opened the door, then picked up his slightly tipsy new bride to carry her over the threshold. The hotel staff had already moved Felicity's clothes and belongings to this room. As she walked over to her suitcase to pull out her pyjamas, she did not notice that Dwight had quickly stripped out of all his clothing, leaving him naked. Felicity turned around to ask for help with getting out of her wedding dress; she was startled to see Dwight standing beside the bed, naked. "Oh, my goodness! Teddy Bear, why are you naked?" Dwight was just as surprised by Felicity's candid query. "Honey Bunny, we have to consummate the wedding."

Now it dawned upon Felicity what her impetuous wedding required of her, which she had not turned her mind to. Sexual intercourse. She was a virgin bride in more ways than one, and the whole notion of actually allowing a man's penis to enter inside of her troubled her; indeed, it scared her. 'But what can I do?' she thought to herself. She had to consummate the marriage, and it was expected of her to have sex with her husband. "Sorry, Teddy Bear, it must be the champagne. Can you help me get out of my wedding dress? Dwight gleefully assisted his new wife in taking off her wedding dress. He then started to take off her petticoat, but Felicity stopped him. "Teddy Bear, I will do the rest. Go over and turn the light off, and I will meet you under the covers." Felicity was embarrassed by her small breasts, so she felt more comfortable being naked if the lights were off. "Okay", said Dwight as he quickly turned off the lights so that only the faint moonlight streaming in through the partially open curtains slightly illuminated the room. Felicity removed the rest of her clothing, then nervously ambled to the bed and slid under the covers. Before she could say a word, Dwight was on top of her, kissing her mouth heavily before prising her legs apart with his right hand so that he could insert his penis into her vagina. There was no tenderness, just the blunt force of Dwight pushing his erect penis immediately into Felicity's vagina. There was no natural lubrication because she was not enjoying the full and awkward feeling of his penis thrusting in and out; there was too much girth, as Felicity did not feel right; she did not feel stimulated. And then, as quickly as it was all reaching the point of her wanting to stop, Dwight ejaculated inside of her. It felt warm, kind of like someone was urinating inside of her. Dwight's body shuddered and then rolled off her as though his work for the evening was done. Felicity lay there, feeling strange about the encounter, which felt foreign to her. Through his panting breath, Dwight spoke. "Thank you, Honey Bunny. That felt great. How was it for you?" Felicity could only lie about the experience. "It felt great, Teddy Bear." He leaned over, kissed her, and then returned to his pillow to sleep.

Meanwhile, as Dwight snored away, Felicity remained awake for at least an hour, realising that she did not enjoy sexual intercourse with a man. However, her mind worked overtime considering these grave questions: "Is it now the case, by being married, that I have no choice as far as society is concerned? Am I to have sex with my husband even though I don't enjoy it? Yet where is the tenderness? Where was that spark I felt when Amelia's lips had touched mine? Oh, where art thou, Amelia?" As the clock that counted the time approached midnight on Saturday, June 13, 1964, there were more questions than answers in Felicity's mind, but at least there was one certainty – Stanford University was where she had to be in life if she wished to fulfil her dreams. Joan's words of life and career advice seemed more insightful than ever before as she went off to sleep: 'Marry an American and you will enter NASA'.

The following Monday, as Felicity and Dwight boarded their Pan Am flight to embark upon Dwight's chosen destination for their honeymoon of Disneyland, Amelia was waiting with Lilith at the departure gate at Los Angeles

International Airport for the direct TWA flight to Paris. After many months of Lilith's significant sexual abuse, which Amelia had to endure whether she liked it or not, the time had come for the filming of her first epic period drama set in France. To avoid speaking to Lilith, Amelia had purchased a copy of the *Los Angeles Times* to read. Politics and business news did not initially interest her, so she immediately skipped to the 'Society' pages. To her immense surprise and stirring passions, there was a photograph of Felicity and Dwight leaving the church as newlyweds under the caption of 'Top Trans-Atlantic Marriage'. She looked at the picture of Felicity in particular, and her heart skipped a beat as she wished for her to re-enter her life. How many times had she wished she had kept in contact with her, even for a fleeting moment, so that she could feel the tenderness of her lips again? Innumerable moments she could not count, but they were always after her sexual liaisons with men and now Lilith. Oh, how the mere presence of that woman repulsed Amelia; however, she was caught in a trap which, if she managed to extricate herself from now, her film career was over. Subsequently, little did Amelia realise that as her TWA flight was departing Los Angeles International Airport, Felicity's Pan Am flight was taxiing into the arrivals section of Los Angeles Domestic Airport. They were so close, yet also so far away.

Two days later, Aliev brought a copy of *The Washington Post* into Volkov's office and placed it on the desk in front of him, with the 'Society' page specifically opened. Volkov looked up at Aliev. "Why have you brought this piece of American trash to me?" Aliev pointed at the picture depicting Dwight and Felicity. "He is about to become an astronaut. But look at her. Doesn't her face remind you of somebody we know?" Volkov studied the picture for several moments and read the article, which mentioned that Felicity would be commencing her doctorate at Stanford University and assisting NASA. Then, like an epiphany, his eyes lit up. "Anatoli! Her nose is finer; however, comrade, you are right! She looks like Anatoli. But how can we use that regarding her work at the university?" Aliev shrugged his shoulders. Volkov leaned back in his chair and closed his eyes to think momentarily. Then, there was another epiphany-like moment, and he sat bolt upright and crashed his closed right fist down on top of the photograph. "Tell some of our undercover agents in Europe and America to watch this Felicity Hoover closely. In the meantime, I will speak to our surgeons to see if they can refine Anatoli's nose." Aliev nodded at his superior and left his office. Volkov's gut instinct was telling him that maybe, just maybe, there was, in the future, perhaps a link between the mysterious Operation Zeus and Felicity. Oh, how marrying for the wrong reasons can sometimes deliver more poison to the chalice.

CHAPTER 39

Almost three years of the antithesis of marital bliss in their home in San Jose rolled by in the blink of an eye for Felicity. San Jose was close to Stanford University, and Dwight had chosen for Felicity to live there, even though he spent much of his time in Houston for NASA. 1468 Hopkins Drive, San Jose, was a plain-looking single-story three-bedroom home. However, it was an affordable home for them, located close to Stanford and Travis Air Force Base, where Felicity had been stationed, performing the mundane duties of a female United States Air Force officer.

Initially, Felicity and Dwight were genuinely trying to have a child, without success; however, Dwight's sexual contact with her lacked tenderness, and Felicity's mind wandered back to that traumatic night at Evelyn's house, and in particular Annabelle's description of her sexual relationship with her husband being akin to him making her feel like he was going to the toilet. That was how Dwight made Felicity feel when they had sex – like he was going to the bathroom. Not only did she not enjoy their sexual contact, but Felicity also started experiencing a slight change in Dwight's attitude. Gone were the nauseating pet names for one another, and they referred to each other on a first-name basis. It was just another warning signal about their declining marital relationship. Still, she had promised Dwight a child, as he wanted a successor in life. Felicity's clinical, scientific mind told her that something might be wrong in her body, so she increased the duration of her punishing daily running routine.

To add to the pressures of her marriage, Dwight's mother and sister were becoming increasingly invasive about the reasons why Felicity had not fallen pregnant. After a family reunion during Easter of 1965, Lucille and Shirley spoke to Felicity following an excruciating Baptist service on Easter Sunday, asking why she and Dwight had not announced any news about having children. Felicity responded sharply: "Well, it's not as though we are not trying. Goodness knows, down below, I feel like I have been stabbed more than Julius Caesar. You will be the first to know as soon as the next era of the Hoover baby factory commences operating." Felicity's remark only served to maintain the simmering tension between herself, her mother-in-law, and her sister-in-law. Dwight was unhappy with Felicity when Shirley told him how his wife had responded to her and her mother. They argued about it, but Felicity refused to apologise to either woman. When Felicity subsequently spoke to her father about Lucille's and Shirley's intrusion into her personal life, Samuel told his daughter she was entitled to defend herself, and the two women had no right to intrude into her marriage. Samuel stopped short of telling his daughter what was on his mind – he did not like the family and was unsure about Dwight being a suitable husband. However, Samuel did not wish to intrude on his daughter's marriage to that extent. Time would tell whether his judgment call was correct.

Adding to Felicity's misery was watching Amelia's shooting star take off again after the release of her first film for the Independent Artists' Studio towards the end of 1965. The period epic set in France, *Une Vie Pas Si Belle*, or as translated for American cinemas, *A Not So Beautiful Life,* garnered critical acclaim for its portrayal of Amelia as a miserable and tortured wife of a French aristocrat. It was undoubtedly a case of art imitating life because Amelia continued to be sexually mistreated by the Martins, in particular, Lilith. During the filming in France, which lasted for a year, Amelia was humiliated by Lilith as she was exposed to Lilith's predilections for kinky sex. When they were not filming, Lilith insisted that Amelia escort her to the underground lesbian club life in Paris of Le Monocle, where Lilith would often find a young Parisian woman to force Amelia to have sex with, whilst Lilith sat back and watched for her pleasure before joining them in bed. Amelia's character in the film had to suffer the ignominy of France's aristocratic class, knowing her husband was sleeping with another woman, so the misery Amelia was being subjected to in real life by Lilith oozed out of her skin in front of the camera. Her pain felt so real to the film critics as they watched her performance unfold on the big screen. Still, there was one positive outcome in Amelia's life from the humiliation she had endured: her agent had secured her a television role as the doting All-American housewife and mother of a family life set in San Francisco. A major American network had agreed to broadcast the television series for at least one year, with filming to begin in the fall of 1966. However, Amelia still had to fulfil her contract to finish filming the other two films for Independent Artists' Studio.

Regrettably, the role of the television series did not give Amelia any power to resist the Martins' depravity. Lilith threatened to reveal Amelia's liaisons in Paris to the media if she did not obey the Martins' whims. Walter, of course, had always replied, "I told you so", whenever Amelia reported back to him about the abuse and threats she endured.

The more marital relations Felicity and Dwight had, the blander their sex life became. On one occasion, when he was having sexual intercourse with her, Dwight said, "Perhaps we could fall pregnant if you moaned?" Felicity's retort underscored the lack of sexual chemistry between them. "What? Like a moose, Dwight?" He was not as intelligent as Felicity to comprehend the mocking put-down, which was just another problem in what was otherwise portrayed in the media as the 'fairytale wedding of an English flying ace and a future American astronaut'. And the most significant stress was that, still, Felicity was not falling pregnant as the summer of 1966 drew closer to its conclusion.

Dwight was also spending more time in Houston, as his training required him to be around Mission Control. He had found an apartment in Hermann Park, near Rice University, and he would often refer to it as home when speaking to Felicity. Dwight's faux pas about where he considered his nest to be did not go unnoticed by Felicity, but they had more stressors to argue over than the issue of separate nests. Notwithstanding their strained marital relations, Felicity would not reveal to anyone, including her father, how unhappy she was in her marriage. She had made her bed and now had to sleep in it.

At least Felicity's study for her doctorate under Ron at Stanford gave her some comfort from her mental anguish, and after three years, she had been exposed to many of the powers-that-be at NASA. However, the Machiavellian nature of her impetuous decision to marry Dwight now haunted her with all the pressures and expectations of being a 1960s wife.

The calendar had well and truly turned over to the two-year point of their marriage when Dwight decided that his wife should see a doctor about her inability to fall pregnant. The weather was 95 degrees Fahrenheit on Wednesday, September 28, 1966, when Dwight broached the subject with his wife. When Dwight knocked on the open door, Felicity sat at her desk in one of the spare bedrooms she converted into a home study room. Felicity turned around in her chair, and she could tell from the expression on Dwight's face that his mind was occupied. "Dwight, you don't have to knock on an open door in our house." Dwight did not say anything; instead, he stood in the doorway, fumbling for the right words. Felicity was intrigued by the silence after being first disturbed. "Now, what is troubling you, Dwight?" Eventually, after a further uncomfortable fifteen seconds of silence, he spoke. "Felicity, I know you have been trying hard to have a child for us, and I am grateful for that." Grateful was perhaps not the right word, but Felicity did not take offence. "Well, thank you for your gratitude, Dwight. However, something else is obviously on your mind, so speak." Her wish was his command. "I want us to see a doctor."

Felicity was now the one to remain silent as she processed her husband's request. Dwight could tell his wife was perplexed by his statement. The heat of the day made him sweat profusely with nerves. "I meant to say that I want you to see a doctor. An obstetrician." Felicity was surprised. "Just me, Dwight? Who says the problem with us falling pregnant rests with me?" Dwight turned his eyes to the ceiling, trying to conceal the truth behind them. Felicity was not deterred by his reticence to talk; he had opened Pandora's Box. "Dwight, don't turn your eyes away from me. Now, tell me, why do you say that I have to see a doctor? How do we know that it is not a problem with you?" Dwight dropped his chin, and finally, he was candid. "That is because I have already had my boys down here in my loins tested at NASA several months ago, and the doctor there tells me there is nothing wrong with them. So, that leaves you and your eggs." Felicity was initially irritated by the thought of Dwight having a fertility test without informing her. Still, she suspected in the back of her mind that something might be wrong with her. She took a deep breath, and then she spoke. "Alright, well, you could have told me sooner. I suppose you already have somebody in mind, don't you?" The truth would set him free. "Yes, I do. He is also a member of the faculty at Stanford's medical school. A NASA doctor told me he was one of the best doctors on the West Coast for addressing pregnancy problems. His name is Dr Arnold Loewenstein." Felicity pondered the notion of having a member of the Stanford Medical School examine her; however, at least it meant she did not have to travel far to get the unpleasantness out of the way. She nodded. "Alright, Dwight, I will see Dr Loewenstein."

Subsequently, Felicity made the arrangements to see Dr Lowenstein. He was a highly experienced specialist doctor, but at sixty-nine, he presented more like a mad scientist than a medical professional. His wiry white hair shot somewhat from either side of his head, whereas on top, he was balding. And, due to his Jewish ancestry, his prominent nose had a significant bump in the middle, which meant his round spectacles were neatly rested just before the bump. Still, he was highly regarded, and he immediately set out to find the answer to why Felicity had not fallen pregnant. She underwent a series of tests, and a comprehensive medical history was taken. She also had to undergo the ignominy of a gynaecological examination. A further appointment was scheduled for her to see Dr Loewenstein in three weeks, when Dwight would return to San Jose after a training exercise in the Mojave Desert.

Felicity occupied herself with her studies at Stanford University and her rudimentary duties at Travis Air Force Base. Still, that dreaded clock ticked with an ominous precision of foreshadowing doom each day. Then, the fateful day of infamy arrived, Thursday, October 27, 1966. Dwight was scheduled to fly back to Houston at 3:00 p.m., so the appointment with Dr Loewenstein had been moved forward to accommodate Dwight's plans. Felicity and Dwight met with Dr Loewenstein in his office at Stanford University at midday. Upon entering the doctor's office, Felicity did not need Dr Loewenstein to tell her the results because she could tell by the look in his eyes. The doctor stood up and introduced himself to Dwight. "So, you must be the famous astronaut Felicity told me about. Arnold Loewenstein." Felicity was surprised by the simplicity of the introduction, as she had only been given a formal introduction. "Dwight Hoover, doctor. And no, I am not an astronaut yet, as I have not flown in space." They both then sat down as the doctor resumed his seat. After an initial ten-second uncomfortable silence, Dr Loewenstein delivered the news to them. "Sadly, there is no way for me to say this other than honestly. Felicity, after all of the tests, my medical examination of you and the history I have taken, I am afraid you cannot have children."

It was like her heart of glass shattered into a thousand tiny pieces in that instant. Felicity had always found an answer to a problem, but now she was being told a definitive no regarding her ability to fall pregnant. Tears began to well up in her eyes; however, she turned her head, shook off the emotion, and then confronted Dr Loewenstein. "What do you mean by 'I cannot have children', doctor? Surely, there must be a medical explanation." Dr Loewenstein nodded. "Yes, Felicity. There is an explanation. You are what we used to call a barren woman." Felicity was mortified by the suggestion of her being barren. "How could I be barren, doctor? I have maintained a healthy lifestyle all my life. I hardly drink and exercise daily." Dr Loewenstein seized the moment. "Precisely. You have overexerted yourself with exercise since you were little, Felicity. When I took your personal history, alarm bells rang in my mind, suggesting that your grandfather's influence introduced you to a daily regimen of punishing running from a young age. I am afraid that your daily routine has affected your ovaries to such an extent that you are barren. I am sorry to say this, Felicity, but there is nothing medical science can do for you. I am sorry for you, Dwight, as well. However, my diagnosis is certain; you will never have children." If there was a moment for Dwight's hand to hold his wife's hand, it was now. Instead, Dwight became very introverted, almost as though he was disappointed with his wife.

They did not talk to each other on the drive back home to San Jose. Felicity felt defeated by events out of her control for the first time. Eventually, after they entered their home, Felicity spoke. "I am sorry if I have disappointed you, Dwight. However, it would have been nice if you could have comforted me rather than being silent, as if I had done something wrong." Dwight barely turned to speak to his wife as he walked away. "I don't blame you, I am just disappointed I cannot be a father." His lack of compassion at this time bewildered and angered Felicity. "Where in the name of Christ are you going?" Dwight immediately stopped and turned around. "Don't blaspheme like that in this house, Felicity. I know you're not religious, but I am. And I will call my mom because she is waiting for this news." Felicity was now infuriated with her husband, and she let her emotions speak for once. "Fine. Go and speak to your 'Mom' and tell her how it is all my fault!" With those words released at the top of her lungs, Felicity walked to their bedroom and slammed the door behind her. She immediately broke down into tears, and she lay on the bed crying into her pillow as she heard Dwight's muffled voice piercing through the doorway as he explained to his mother that his wife was 'barren' and that 'no, the family name will not carry on through me', words which only confirmed for Felicity that her husband did blame her.

About an hour later, Dwight went to the bedroom to retrieve his bag, which he had packed previously that morning. Felicity was still lying on the bed, looking out the window and comprehending the world she was now trapped in. Dwight's parting words were brief. "I have to head to the airport now to catch my flight. I don't blame you, Felicity. We can work our way through this problem." Felicity half turned her head on the pillow. "Thank you for your concern. Now, you had better go because I would hate to be the one to cause you to miss your flight." Dwight was about to respond to her, but instead, he thought it best to leave Felicity alone at this time. He closed the bedroom door, then dialled a taxi to take him to the San Francisco Airport, where he would catch a direct flight to Houston.

Three hours later, Felicity called her father, even though it was 1:00 a.m. in England. She had to find sympathy from someone in this world. Eventually, on the eighth dial tone, the gruff voice of her father answered the telephone. "Hello, Samuel Bennet speaking." Felicity immediately opened the floodgates of tears. "Hi, Dad. I am sorry to call you at this hour, but I have some terrible news." Samuel was immediately alarmed. "What is wrong, sweetie? Has Dwight been hurt?" The mention of Dwight irritated her tearful voice. "No! The news is about me, Dad. I cannot have children because Grandpa made me run every day since I was a little girl. It has nothing to do with my self-centred husband!" Samuel had to address three life issues with his daughter. "Oh, my little sweetheart, I am so sorry to hear this news. I know how hard you have been trying to have a child, and I cannot imagine how you feel inside, darling. Still, I want you to know this: I will always love you, regardless of whether or not you can have children." They were the comforting words Felicity expected to hear from her husband; however, he had left a world of self-absorbed emotional pain, disregarding how his wife felt. Felicity tried to stop crying, but the tears flowed with the words. "Do you mean that, Dad?" Samuel smiled on the other end of the line. "Sweetheart, you could have married the most hideous person on Earth, and I would still love you unconditionally." Samuel had opened the door through which Felicity could have let him into the secret she had buried for many years; however, Joan's words that night at Cambridge about her not disappointing her father echoed in her mind as she then, regrettably, decided to keep her psyche and her genuine heart locked in that vault. They talked for the next two hours, and eventually, Felicity could go to bed comforted by the words of the only man who had ever reached into her heart.

While Felicity was speaking to her father, Dwight looked out the window of his American Airlines aeroplane, lost in disappointment about not being a father. He had initially been booked on a Pan Am flight, but it had been cancelled at the last moment. Fortunately for Dwight, American Airlines had a spare seat on its 6:00 p.m. direct flight to Houston. His flight had only taken off ten minutes beforehand. Still, he was too morose to notice the people around him. Suddenly, a familiar, sweet, alluring tone interrupted his thoughts. "Well, howdy, Mr Astronaut. Why are you looking so glum on such a beautiful evening?" It was the beautiful stewardess, Jolene, whose path he had not crossed since their meeting over two years ago. She looked like a woman who was ripe for having children with her shapely body and ample cleavage. Dwight sheepishly smiled at her. "I remember you, ma'am. You're Jolene, aren't you?" She nodded. "You look upset. What could be bothering such a fine specimen of an astronaut like you, honey?" The word honey was so sweet in his ears. He shook his head, more to clear it than to dismiss her. "Oh, just personal stuff. Nothing to worry you about." Jolene then leaned in closer, to lower her voice whilst also bringing her ample breasts within Dwight's personal space. "I'm a good listener, and this is my last flight for the night. So, how about a nice boy like you buy me a drink, and I will solve your problems for you, honey." Forbidden fruit had been offered in the Garden of Eden, and Dwight's smile broadened.

CHAPTER 40

There is perhaps no other vicissitude of life that the female psyche can be challenged by more than the news that a part of her body, over which she believes she has total control, has been taken away from her because of her submission. In allowing Grandpa to live vicariously through her, Felicity had unwittingly robbed herself of the ability to reproduce. Had it not been for her study at Stanford University under Ron and his work on improving rocket design technology for NASA, which brought her into contact with the agency at ever-increasing exposure rates, Felicity might have fallen into an immense depression.

For the next year, her marriage to Dwight descended into the realm of almost being tenants sharing the occasional time under the same roof. Although she did not yearn for it, they had only engaged in sexual intercourse on one occasion, when Dwight forced himself upon her during the middle of the night whilst she was initially asleep. Although she reluctantly consented to having sex with him, Felicity did not enjoy the experience. She was a form of trophy wife for Dwight – the pseudo-celebrity status of their wedding required her to publicly present herself as the doting and proud wife of an astronaut candidate whose family history was steeped in American Military service. Her military service as an officer in the USAF also brought her no joy, as she was still not allowed to fly a jet fighter, even though her duties required her to study the aeronautical engineering of the aircraft.

To add to her mental anguish, she could not escape the images of Amelia's revived fame on her television series, which had engaged the American public's imagination about what stable family life should be in a landscape where the country was now challenged by becoming involved in an unnecessary war that had sparked outrage among the younger generations. Amelia was even engaged to one of Hollywood's most eligible leading men, Bud Walker, but little did the public know that the purported relationship was a sham, to cover up their proclivities for same sex partners. Amelia might have been portraying the 'happy housewife' on television; however, Lilith Martin's lesbianism had converted Amelia or, perhaps, liberated her.

Meanwhile, in Moscow, Volkov continued to seek further information about Project Zeus. Indeed, the Kremlin was overwhelmed by the mention of the mysterious project for which the only piece of information they had received was the letter Anatoli had taken from Saar's room that fateful night he had murdered him. The murder of Saar had hindered the KGB's espionage activities because Mossad was working closely with the CIA to find the culprit for Saar's murder, and that meant the KGB's double agents in Israel and the United States were constrained in their dealings with Mossad and the CIA. Any mention of Project Zeus by the double agents was sure to give away their true identities, and with it, other valuable field information about America's ever-increasing arsenal of nuclear weapon technology. Anatoli's rhinoplasty surgery had successfully refined the shape of his nose so that his facial features were eerily similar to those of Felicity's, so that even though the powers-that-be in the Kremlin were displeased with Anatoli's interruption of information lines because of Saar's murder, Volkov could nevertheless protect him from being executed as he was able to convince his superiors there was a potential utility to having an agent who presented remarkably similar facial features to those of the wife of a potential NASA astronaut who herself had some connections with that agency. Still, Project Zeus was a mystery, and the Soviets did not like being left out in the cold as to what the Americans and Israelis were up to.

In late November 1967, Felicity returned home to San Jose after a two-week stint at Stead Air Force Base. She was on her own as Dwight was in Houston, where he spent more time as the year drew closer to its end. It was a crisp Wednesday night at the end of the Fall. Felicity felt cold and alone in that empty house as she was studying to prepare her thesis, which she hoped would bring Stanford's imprimatur, so that she could hold an esteemed Doctorate in Aeronautical Engineering. She had fallen asleep at her desk when the telephone rang, and it awoke her. Through her tired eyes, she looked at the clock on the wall of her home office, and to her surprise, it was 10:00 p.m. Felicity walked out to the empty living room, which was dark. Felicity answered the call, still half-asleep, wondering who could be calling her. "Hello, Felicity Hoover speaking." It did not take her long to know who the caller was and what their state of mind was. "Felicity. It's me, Dwight. Did I wake you up?" He sounded like he had been drinking alcohol; there was the sound of music playing somewhere in the background, and his speech was slurred. "Dwight. Why are you calling at this time of night? Are you drunk?" Dwight was indeed drunk. "I sure am. I'm hammered like I have never been before, honey bear." He even got the nauseating pet name wrong, indicating to Felicity her husband was indeed 'hammered', as he so described it. "Dwight, why are you drunk, and why are you calling me now?" His response was self-righteous. "I'm calling because I can whenever I want to, and I thought you should hear the news now, before it's announced tomorrow. Do you want to hear the news?" Only an inebriated person could ask an asinine question about what had been discussed so far. "Well, of course I want to hear the damn news. You have called me this late in a drunken state." There was a pause, and Felicity heard the sound of Dwight drinking. Then he spoke. "I'm going into space, Teddy Bunny. What do you think of that?"

Felicity absorbed the news; her husband was going to fly into space. The momentary silence irritated Dwight. "Why are ya so damn quiet? Aren't you happy for me?" She realised he was drunk, so Felicity did not bite back in response to his impertinence. "Well, congratulations are in order. I am very proud of you, Dwight. When did you find out?" Felicity heard the distinct sound of him slurping liquid before he spoke. "They told me, Chip Gatley and Bobby Mozley, at 4:00 p.m. that we would orbit the moon early next year. Launching on May 15 from Cape Canaveral. You're going to be the wife of an astronaut. What do ya think of it?" He was hammered; Felicity left his poor grammar be for the moment. "I told you, I am very proud of you. However, Dwight, you're extremely drunk. I think you had better go to bed." His rambunctious reply unsettled her. "I'll go to damn bed when I'm ready, and I ain't ready yet!" Felicity decided it was best to let him savour the moment. "Alright, Dwight. You enjoy the moment. We will speak tomorrow, when you have sobered up. Have a good night."

As she went to hang up the receiver, she heard Dwight's voice, and it sounded like a woman's voice was also calling out his name, but she couldn't be sure because of the sound's fleeting nature. Felicity was not too concerned because Dwight was at a bar. She rubbed her eyes and then decided to go outside for a moment, to look up at the night sky. It was a clear night in San Jose, and the stars twinkled brightly, almost as though they were sending her an invitation. Felicity thought about what the future now held for her. There would be attention from the press as she was an astronaut's wife, which also meant she might be one step closer to achieving her dream. However, she also had a dreaded feeling that Dwight's success might hinder her future; his success might make her a background figure, expected to be the dutiful and proud wife in a marriage, proving to be a source of unhappiness for her. Then there was Dwight's disapproving mother and sister, whom she would have to contend with, as undoubtedly they would snipe about Dwight not having a child he could proudly hold in his arms for a press photograph. These feelings of dread occupied her mind until she went to bed and fell asleep sometime after midnight.

As certain as the day follows the night, the press harasses an astronaut's wife after NASA announced that Dwight had been selected as part of the three-man team for the mission to orbit the Moon. Television and newspaper reporters showed up on the front lawn of Felicity's home. A NASA representative had already contacted her to explain what to say: proud, happy, and excited. She had to wear a 'feminine housewife' style dress – bright yellow with polka dots. Cameras flashed in her eyes, and microphones were held up to her face, yet through all of the attention, a reporter did not ask Felicity about her career. It was half an hour of her life that she managed to maintain a happy smile, despite being miserable inside. Felicity knew it would be the first of many media engagements she would have to endure. At least there were Ron and Stanford to look forward to over the following months, she thought as Felicity sought shelter inside her house from the press frenzy outside. Later that afternoon, Felicity spoke to Dwight, and on this occasion, he thanked her for handling the press so well. It was the first compliment he had paid her since that harrowing day of her finding out she could never have children.

That evening, in Los Angeles. Amelia enthusiastically watched each news broadcast on television, featuring a segment of Felicity's interview. Walter, who was about to finish for the evening, fulfilling his dual role of manager and butler for Amelia, could not contain his curiosity when he saw Amelia change the channel on her television to find another news report featuring the 'doting wife' Felicity Hoover. "Why are you watching the same news story repeatedly, Amelia? Do you know that woman?" Amelia nodded, without looking away from the television screen. "Yes. We went to school together. We had a..." Amelia momentarily paused because she had never been asked to describe her feelings for Felicity. Walter was now curious, like a gossip columnist, and wanted to extract the truth from Amelia because every piece of information he heard or saw about Amelia's private life ensured he remained employed by her. "You had a what together?" Amelia realised she had opened Pandora's box, and Walter would harass her until she revealed the truth. "We had a thing for one another." Walter was now hooked and sat on the leather sofa opposite the marble coffee table to interrogate Amelia. "Oh, do tell me. I do like to hear these stories about your past."

Amelia pulled a cigarette from her sterling silver case, placed it in the long stem holder, and then lit it. Her eyes returned to meet Walter's as she puffed smoke between them. "Why are you so interested in my past?" He promptly responded, but it was a lie. "Because then I know what landmines I might need to circumnavigate in the future." Amelia stared at Walter; each vein in her body told her not to proffer too much personal information, but she couldn't contain her feelings. "Well, since you must know, she is the only person who has ever touched my heart. My school group saw me as the pinnacle of the school hierarchy, while Felicity was just some intellectual nerd to tease, yet for whom I felt an attraction like no other, then and now. She was always trying to beat me in athletics, and indeed towards the end of school she had done so in one race, but then deliberately lost the next for me." Walter threw his hands in the air in disappointment. "Is that it? Why on Earth would she lose a race for you?" His disparaging tone had an incendiary effect on Amelia's passions. She stubbed the cigarette out in anger in the fine crystal ashtray on the coffee table and stood up. "Because I knew she liked me, and I took advantage of it! We subsequently had a night together, and no, it wasn't sexual, so to speak. It was tender; we kissed, and it felt like electricity passed through every inch of my body whenever our lips touched that night. Then I turned around and broke her heart the next morning, and I have regretted it ever since. Are you happy now? Does that satisfy your little faggot curiosity, Walter?" Amelia then stormed out of the room. Meanwhile, Walter sat back in the lounge and smiled to himself. Nothing like information to keep oneself in gainful employment in the vicious zoo of Hollywood.

CHAPTER 41

Thou was such a pure-hearted innocent child, and thy dreams were just as pure;
However, selling thy soul might be a mistake, an error for which there isn't a cure.

The hands of the clock spun quickly as Felicity ferociously devoted her time and mind to acquiring her Doctorate in Aeronautical Engineering. On April 2nd, 1968, she proudly accepted her doctorate in the Frost Amphitheatre of Stanford University. Samuel had travelled from England to watch proudly in the audience as his daughter was awarded her doctorate. Dwight, too, was present but seemed preoccupied with some matter, which Felicity attributed to his imminent departure into space the following month. Indeed, Dwight departed immediately after the ceremony, but not before the press photographers took a staged photograph of the supposed happy astronaut kissing his doctorate-holding wife on the cheek. There may have been a perception that they were a happy couple, but Samuel could see right through it. However, he would ask questions later, as he had now joined Ron and Felicity for a celebratory dinner in Encina Hall.

Over dinner, Ron chose to break the news to Felicity that he had kept secret for about a fortnight. The three of them were finishing off their main meal when Ron spoke. "So, Felicity. I have some news for you and me that I have kept secret until now." Simultaneously, Felicity and Samuel placed their cutlery on the fine China Dinner Plates. "Secret? What on Earth are you talking about, Ron?" Even Samuel was intrigued by the 'secret', but he wondered whether it was appropriate for him to hear it. "Should I be taking a stroll outside for some fresh air? Is this news something I should hear?" Ron nodded. "Of course you can stay, Sam. This ain't going to be a secret by tomorrow. Indeed, there was another reason why the press photographers were here today beyond you being awarded a doctorate." Ron stopped for a moment, causing Samuel to speak impetuously. "Well, come on, old boy. You cannot leave us hanging in mid-air like this. What is the God damn news?" Felicity placed her right hand on her father's forearm to constrain his enthusiasm.

Ron took a deep breath and then spoke. "Well, it is news for both of us.

I have been promoted at NASA to head the Aeronautical Division. My former superior is being transferred to Mission Control in Houston, and they asked me who I thought would be the most suitable person to take over my role in rocket propulsion development. So, of course, I told the boys at NASA it was you, Felicity, and they have agreed that you are now officially an actual NASA engineer, not just an assistant to me in a university laboratory. Congratulations, Felicity, you are a step closer to your dream." Ron stopped speaking, and for a moment, he was puzzled by the blank faces of the father and daughter to whom he had just broken the news. Then, they both broke into smiles simultaneously, followed by a jubilant hug. Felicity spoke through tears of joy as she hugged her father. "Dad. I told you that one day I would fly in space." Samuel gripped his daughter tightly. "Well done, my little sweetheart. I knew that you could do it. I have never doubted you, and your mother would be looking down on you now with tears of joy."

Felicity held her father for another half a minute, then immediately let go and hugged Ron, much to his surprise. "Oh, Ron, thank you. I could not have achieved this without you." Ron was not accustomed to being hugged, as his world of science had always been a disciplined journey of the mind, rather than the body. "Thank you, Felicity, but this appointment concerns your fine work. My recommendation was only made because we have worked around each other for so long, and nobody else could come close to your ability." Ron then managed to prise himself free of the delighted young woman, and Felicity managed to constrain herself. "Sorry, Ron. I must have startled you to grab hold of you like that. We English do not normally express our emotions like this, but after everything I have gone through, this is the best news I have heard in years." Samuel immediately twigged to his daughter letting the cat out of the bag; however, now was not the time to broach the subject with her.

Ron continued with his news. "Well, there is still more of the story to be told. We will both be working in Canoga Park, in the San Fernando Valley." Felicity was immediately taken by surprise. "Canoga Park? San Fernando Valley? Why are we going to have to work from there, Ron? Why can't we work from here? Dwight and I own a house here, even though he is hardly ever home, it's still our home." The old scientist held up his hands to reveal an aspect of NASA that Felicity was unaware of. "I know. It sounds off, but this is the United States, and even NASA contracts work out to companies. Rocketdyne is the company benefiting from our work together, and indeed, our work is being used as we speak to build the Hercules rocket that will send your husband into space next month. There is more work for us to do beyond what we have accomplished here, which I have not yet been made aware of. The boys at NASA have told me that you and I need to be working out of Rocketdyne's facility at Canoga Park for the next two years." Felicity raised her eyebrows as Samuel watched on in interest. "Two years? Why so long?" Ron held up his hands to show he knew as much as she did. There was another new region of the United States for Felicity to live in, and she did not even know why.

When they arrived back at Felicity's home in San Jose, Samuel felt it was time to ask his daughter the questions on his mind. They were seated in the living room, and Felicity had just served up an early evening drink of single malt scotch for her father, while she drank a cup of tea. Samuel was looking at her, and it unnerved Felicity to the extent that she had to speak up. "Alright, Dad. What is on your mind? You were quiet in the car on the way back here, and now I feel like you are looking right through me. What is on your mind?" Samuel took a good swig of his whiskey, then placed the cut crystal glass on the lamp side table next to his chair. "What is going on in your marriage, Felicity?" Felicity sat back on the couch, spilling tea on her dress without noticing. "What do you mean?" Her voice was indignant, but Samuel was not going to be deterred. "Look, I hardly get to see you and Dwight together. However, I have lived long enough to see a loveless marriage when there is one, particularly when it happens to be my only child's marriage. The way you and Dwight have interacted since I arrived has been an eye-opening experience for me. You don't hug each other, other than that staged farce I watched at Stanford today for the sake of the press photographers. So, I did not come down in the last shower, Felicity. Are you and Dwight happy?" Of course, they were not, but Felicity was too proud to reveal to her father that she had made a mistake marrying Dwight, and, more importantly, she did not like having sex with men. "I don't believe this is any of your business, Dad. If I were unhappy with Dwight, I would not be living under the same roof as him."

Samuel reached for his glass, had another swig of the drink, and then spoke. "The thing is, sweetie, you don't live under the same roof as him. Dwight has been stationed in Houston. You virtually live on the opposite side of the country from him, and your lives together seem to be an ephemeral moment of interactions to keep up appearances for the press. More importantly, keeping up appearances for the American way of life." Her father was right; however, Felicity could not tell him that she felt exactly as he described – a woman keeping up appearances for a foreign country, her one goal in life. She stood up and defiantly dismissed his line of questioning as she walked to the kitchen to clean the tea off her dress. "I am a grown woman, and I can look after myself. We are fine, but we are also busy people. And look at what you have made me do. It is a new dress." Samuel was not persuaded, but his daughter had always been headstrong.

The following day, at 6:00 a.m., Felicity attempted to call Dwight to share her news about NASA. The telephone in Dwight's apartment at Hermann Park rang out, which Felicity found odd because Dwight was not expected at NASA's headquarters that day, having taken his last leave before his mission to watch Felicity receive her doctorate. Half an hour later, she tried calling him again, but the telephone was unanswered. Samuel had arisen from his slumber by now, for he had to catch a flight from San Francisco Airport to New York to catch a connecting flight to London that evening. He watched his daughter try to call Dwight again within ten minutes of her previous attempt, and he could not resist asking her why she seemed so worried. Felicity curtly told him to mind his business, so Samuel did as he was told and returned to his room to pack for his trip home.

After breakfast, Felicity drove her father to the San Francisco Airport. For the first twenty miles of the thirty-mile drive, it was quiet, sombre, and Samuel could sense that his daughter was concerned about something. The only sound was the hum of Felicity's two-door Ford Falcon engine. Samuel had to enquire about his daughter's state of mind before he left to go home. He carefully chose his words. "Look, Felicity, I apologise for interfering in your life yesterday. My impertinence was motivated solely by one fact: my love for you, as your father. Still, I apologise that I meddled in any way in your personal life."

While keeping one eye on the road, Felicity half-turned towards her father. "That is alright, Dad. I am not angry at you today. It's just odd that Dwight did not answer the telephone call early this morning, as today was the leave day he had before his mission, so he should have been home." Samuel carefully corrected his daughter. "You mean in his apartment." Felicity displayed a hint of a smile. "Yes, Dad. I meant the apartment. Home is in San Jose. We have not spent much time together there over the past four months, but our house in San Jose is home." Samuel could not leave the subject alone. "Well, now that you are required to work in Southern California, what will you do with the house in San Jose?" Felicity had not even considered that question until now. She momentarily thought about her answer, then spoke candidly to her father. "I had not thought about the issue until you raised it, but I am inclined to tell Dwight we should sell it. My goal is still to be accepted into the astronaut programme, as much as the prospect of that occurring in this patriarchal world might seem to be beyond my reach." Samuel placed his hand on Felicity's right shoulder and gently rubbed it, just like he used to do when she was upset as a young girl. "You will be accepted into that programme, sweetie. You keep reaching for the stars like you have always done since childhood, and your dream will come true." Felicity smiled, and she felt comforted by her father's hand.

When they arrived at San Francisco Airport, Felicity exited the car at the curbside collection and baggage drop-off bay, even though she was meant to remain in her car. In the cold world of her personal life, she found comfort in seeing her father, yet she felt sadder than before about his return to England. Tears welled up in her eyes, and then she started to cry as she hugged him goodbye. "I am going to miss you, Dad. I wish we didn't have an ocean between us." Samuel held his daughter tightly in his arms. "I am going to miss you as well, my little darling. However, you are going to be fine, and besides, you have been accepted into NASA, and your husband is going to fly into space soon." Felicity pulled away from Samuel and wiped her eyes with her hands. "Look at me. Crying like I'm a child. Still, you are right. I have a lot to look forward to in life." Samuel could see the baggage handler was approaching them, and the look on the young man's face suggested Felicity had better get back in her car. "Now, you had better get back in your car and leave before you get into trouble." Samuel held his hand up to the baggage handler to indicate his daughter was leaving.

After Samuel retrieved his luggage from the boot of the Falcon, Felicity drove off. Still, she began to cry again as she watched her father in her rearview mirror hand over his luggage to a curbside luggage collector and then walk into the terminal. Yes, she had much to look forward to, but her heart felt empty again.

Later that evening, she spoke to Dwight and asked him where he had been earlier that morning because she had tried to call him at the apartment. Dwight took a moment to answer her question, and then he told Felicity he had gone for a walk because the mission was on his mind. He did not sound convincing, but Felicity did not want to start an argument by accusing him of lying, so she refrained from questioning him again about that issue. She then broke the news to him about her acceptance into NASA, and although Dwight congratulated her, he did not sound particularly jubilant. Felicity explained to Dwight that she would be working at Canoga Park for several years, developing NASA's rocket technology, so the house in San Jose would no longer be needed. They discussed selling the San Jose house because she would now have to look for a home near Canoga Park, a proposition which Dwight did not object to. During the telephone discussion, Dwight seemed to be preoccupied with other thoughts. She went to bed that night wondering why her husband seemed uninterested in her news.

Felicity had to fly to Houston a fortnight later to be inducted into NASA's service. It was a hectic schedule, spending the day at NASA's Manned Space Centre in Clear Lake, south of Houston, where Ron would be waiting for her, before departing with him the following day to fly back to Los Angeles and make the long trek out to the San Fernando Valley to Canoga Park. California. During that fortnight, Felicity had to make arrangements for the San Jose house to be placed on the market by the realtor and pack up her office at Stead Air Force Base. She also had to urgently make arrangements with a realtor in Winnetka to rent a two-bedroom house while she waited for the San Jose house to sell. Felicity told Dwight she must stay with him that night in Houston. Once again, Dwight seemed preoccupied with other thoughts when Felicity spoke. Indeed, he was so preoccupied that Felicity had to ask Dwight if he wanted her to stay the night in his apartment. He told her he did, and when she questioned him about why he didn't sound thrilled to have her staying the night, he explained that some issues with the mission were on his mind. She accepted his explanation. Still, once again, Felicity was not convinced by Dwight's explanation. If she had time to dwell on the topic, perhaps Felicity might have broached the subject more with Dwight and asked him whether he still wanted to be married to her. But she had barely a second to arrange her affairs, let alone worry about matters of the heart. All the personal items she needed to take to Winnetka were collected by a courier van the day before she departed for Houston. So, all Felicity had to take with her on the flight was enough clothing and personal items for two days.

Then the moment of her life arrived as the taxi arrived at NASA's Manned Space Centre in Clear Lake, twenty-five miles south of Houston. It was midday, and Felicity had been in transit from San Jose Airport since early that morning. Even though her time there would be for only one day, Felicity was awed by the momentous occasion, and while the main building was a two-storey, unimpressive design, the mere fact that she was now a NASA employee brought home to her the hope that one day she would be boarding a rocket in Florida to fly into space. She proudly walked through the building doors and informed the young woman at the main reception desk that she was reporting in and that Ron Goldman was waiting for her. The receptionist dialled a number, and when it was answered, she told the person on the other end that Felicity Hoover was reporting in for service. The receptionist told Felicity to sit and that one of the directors would greet her soon. 'A director of NASA!' she thought as Felicity sat in reception. 'My appointment must be a special one.'

After about five minutes, a man in his mid-forties, who had lost most of his hair on top of his head and otherwise had the paunch of the good life, with his stomach protruding outwards through his short-sleeved shirt, walked into the reception. He walked up towards Felicity, who immediately stood up to greet him. He held out his hand to shake Felicity's hand, a gesture she was not used to in the world outside, where women had to hold out their fingertips like it was still the nineteenth century. She took the man's hand as he spoke. "Hello, Dr Hoover. My name is Theodore Purvis, and I am the director-in-charge of this centre." His tone was very official and earnest, but Felicity remained poised and confident, even if her nerves were boiling. "Hello, Director Purvis. Nice to meet you." Theodore seemed to be worried, and he was quite curt in his tone. "Come with me, please; there is an important meeting we need to have before I introduce you to some of the rocket development team. Ron Goldman is also waiting here, but won't join us for this meeting." Felicity was intrigued and unnerved by the terminology of 'important meeting'.

Felicity followed Theodore down a long hallway from the reception doorway, where she could see various offices with mainly men working at their desks. Although the hallway was only forty yards long, it felt like a mile to Felicity as she followed Theodore, wondering what the crucial meeting was about. Theodore stopped in front of the doorway at the end of the hallway and opened it, ushering Felicity into a large boardroom. To her surprise, Dwight and his father, Ted, were seated at the opposite end of a long, light coloured veneer boardroom table, surrounded by twelve boardroom chairs. Felicity could not contain her words. "Dwight? And Ted? What are you doing here?" Theodore ushered Felicity down to the end where Dwight was sitting, but on the opposite side of the table. "Take a seat here, please, Mrs Hoover. We have something confidential to discuss between the four of us." Felicity did what she was told and sat in the boardroom chair Theodore had pulled out. She looked at Dwight, but he turned away as though he was ashamed of her. Ted then stood up, his full military attire signifying that this was official business they had to discuss. He considered his words, glared at his son, and then turned back towards Felicity and leaned over the boardroom table, placing his hands in front of him on the table to support himself. Ted looked at Felicity momentarily, then spoke to her like a commanding officer rather than a father-in-law. "Felicity, you are undoubtedly surprised to see me here. And I have to say that I am not happy that I have to be here in these circumstances, but you see, my idiot son has caused a major problem to arise, which could have compromised his mission, the reputation of NASA and my family name." Ted stopped talking for a moment. Still, Felicity had absorbed enough information to realise Dwight had done something terrible. Ted shook his head and turned away to look out the window as he talked. "Yep, my entire family history could have been soiled. I have never had to deal with this immorality, and I cannot believe it." The word immorality was enough information for Felicity to join the dots. "Alright, Dwight. What have you done behind my back? I have suspected something was up with you. Don't make Ted have to tell me. Look me in the eyes, Dwight! I want to hear it from you!"

Felicity's voice had enough venom to cause Dwight to look at her. Ted turned back around and looked at his son. "Tell your wife, Dwight." Dwight's face displayed pure shame, and he looked at Theodore, who gestured with his eyes for him to tell Felicity. Dwight took a deep breath and let the truth free him, or so he thought. "I have been seeing another woman here in Houston, Felicity. I'm sorry, but I could not help it because you and I have not been getting along for a while now and..." Felicity immediately cut Dwight off. "Don't you blame me, Dwight. If you have been unfaithful to me, that is all of your own making!" Dwight nodded. "You are right. I am responsible for my actions. I am sorry, Felicity. But you see, this woman understands the pressure I have been under ever since I found out you could not have a child." Another blame game, and Felicity would not stand for it. "Dwight! Don't blame me! Yes, I cannot bear you a child. However, that is no excuse for you being unfaithful." Dwight nodded, then dropped his eyes, signifying his more profound shame was yet to surface. Ted beat Felicity to the mark in speaking next. "Tell your wife the entire story, son. She deserves to know the whole truth." The whole truth caused Dwight to close his eyes. "She is pregnant, Felicity. Four months pregnant. We have decided to keep the child." Felicity was stunned. "Pregnant! We, Dwight? You mean the mystery woman and you." Ted nodded, and then he answered Felicity's next question. "When Dwight says we, he refers to me, his mother and his sister. Now, before you become too angry, Felicity, don't worry, we disagree with Dwight's infidelity. However, we cannot allow our family name to be tainted by the thought of terminating a pregnancy, and as the grandparents, we will pay for the child's upbringing. When Dwight told me the news two months ago, I had to take all the necessary steps to contain the damage that such an unfortunate occurrence could cause everyone, including you, Felicity. I have already spoken to the young woman, and based on us paying for her and the child to live comfortably, she will hold her tongue and live in Norfolk, far enough away from here, so that the rumour mill and press will never know. All I ask, Felicity, is that you keep up appearances of the happy wife of an astronaut who is about to make history in a few weeks by being part of a mission to fly around the Moon and back. In return, the USAF, NASA, and even the Secretary of Defence have arranged for you to work here on a top-secret project, on the condition that there is no divorce and this messy business stays secret." Felicity was furious. She was being bribed to remain quiet, and it now appeared that her dream of coming true was just a means to an end, covering up a scandal. She did not take her wrathful glare away from Dwight as she spoke to Ted. "So what is the top secret project, and how does it benefit my career, Ted? What is so special about it that I should have to eat Dwight's shit pie, pardoning my French, Ted?"

It was time for Theodore to intervene. "Dwight, I think it is an appropriate time for you to step outside for a moment. I will let you know when you can return to the room." Dwight could not leave the room quickly enough, and he felt each poison arrow from Felicity's eyes hit his body as he stepped outside, closing the door behind himself. Theodore looked at Ted, who nodded to him to proceed. "Look, Felicity, I know we have only just met, but I am unhappy about hearing this news. However, you pair are our golden-haired couple as far as the press and the public are concerned. So, here is the deal, and I should say that even Ron Goldman is not aware of this, and he never will be. We are working on a project with the American Defence Force to give the United States an advantage over the Soviets, in the event of an actual nuclear war, God forbid. The name of that work is Project Zeus, and the work you are being assigned to do at Canoga Park is to develop the technology for it, and when it is ready, you will be one of the crew members to take Zeus up into the heavens, into space. This is not a bribe, Felicity. It is a career progression that no other woman on Earth has available to them. The project is top-secret, and the Israelis have been assisting by running a decoy for us on the Soviets. Regrettably, one of the top members of Israel's government paid the ultimate price with his life for this decoy. Still, it has the Soviets looking everywhere except for Canoga Park. So, now that you know what is on the table, will you play ball and keep it all smiles and happy families for NASA and America?" Felicity's mind was spinning out of control; the genesis of her dream coming true was because of her stupid husband's infidelity. Still, how could she say no to becoming the first woman to go into space? If only she had not been so rash, she could have appreciated that the malodorous odour of immorality fuelled her impetuosity to fulfil her dreams. Felicity looked at Ted and then at Theodore. There was still one question she wanted Dwight to answer. "Well, Director, and Ted, of course, it is yes. It's no secret that I want to join the astronaut programme. I didn't expect it would because my husband impregnated another woman." I want Dwight to answer some final questions for me. Ted held out his hands and nodded. He walked to the boardroom door, opened it, and spoke to Dwight, who was waiting outside like a naughty student who had to see the principal. "Come back in, Dwight. Your wife wants to speak to you." Dwight walked back into the boardroom, and Ted closed the door behind him. Ted gave a command to his son that only a General could provide. "Go back down to your seat and face your wife like a man. She has a question you must answer." Dwight walked the ignominious walk of shame back to his seat directly opposite where Felicity sat, and he sat down and faced her. "What is it, Felicity?" Her eyes narrowed at him "Who is she, and how did you meet?" Dwight looked at his father, who nodded to confirm he had to answer. He looked at Felicity. "The lady's name is Jolene, and I met her on a flight some years ago as she is an airline hostess." Felicity threw her head back and laughed out loud in a mocking tone. "An airline hostess. You were unfaithful to me with an airline hostess named Jolene. Oh, Dwight, you are an idiot!" Dwight dropped his chin in shame.

Theodore had one more request for Felicity, although he was uncertain how she would respond after witnessing her reaction to her husband's revelation that he had been unfaithful by sleeping with an airline hostess. Better to broach the subject now than in several weeks. "Felicity, there is one more matter I need to discuss with you from a public relations viewpoint. When Dwight's mission is launched, we want you to fly to New York that same day to appear on the *Ed Sullivan Show* later that evening. This television appearance would have occurred regardless of the unfortunate news that your husband has just broken to you. The fact is clear to us: despite the civil unrest occurring around this country these days, the media still views you and Dwight as a beacon of everything good about America. Your appearance on a nationally broadcast show will help convince Congress to increase our funding. The studio wishes to announce, in advance of the launch, that you will be a special guest – the wife of one of the astronauts who will be the first men to fly around the Moon. You're working with NASA now, which makes you publicity gold for us. Goodness knows, there are several congressmen for whom spending money on us does not sit right with their perspective on the efficient use of public revenue. Will you also do that for us?" She was being asked to eat a lot of humble pie, but the bait of her flying in space suppressed her urge to tell them that she wanted the world to know how much her husband had wronged her.

She mulled over the news and the 'bribe' that would keep her quiet. She closed her eyes as she thought through the consequences of selling out her principles, but the attraction of space won out in those two minutes of contemplation. Felicity turned towards Theodore. "Alright, Director Purvis. You have my word. I shall maintain the 'front' of a happy wife, and I will not mention this to anyone. Now that I have been shamed, might we please go and meet the other rocket development team members, including poor old Ron, who must be wondering where I am right about now." Theodore nodded, and they both stood up. After they turned around to walk away, Felicity turned back towards Dwight. "By the way, Dwight. I will not be staying at your apartment tonight. So, if your little Jolene is in town, go and get rid of your extra cargo in her for the night. Ted, thank you for being candid with me, and don't worry about the family name, I will not tell a soul about this surprising news, not even Ron."

Felicity then strode out of the boardroom, quickly followed by Theodore. Theodore had allowed Felicity half an hour to come to terms with Dwight's betrayal of trust, and in that time, she had managed to constrain her emotions. Subsequently, that afternoon, Theodore introduced Felicity to the Rocket Development team, which included Ron as her direct supervisor, although he, too, was unaware of Project Zeus. She was the only female member of that NASA division, although Theodore explained to her that other women held important scientific roles within NASA. Felicity remained true to her word in not revealing to Ron the inner turmoil she felt. Before he left Felicity in Ron's reassuring hands for the afternoon, Theodore quietly told Felicity he needed to see her at 7:00 a.m. tomorrow, in the same boardroom they had just left, to discuss their 'top secret assignment'.

Humiliated. If Feliciy had felt infuriated by Dwight's unfaithfulness when she first heard the news, she felt humiliated that night in her lonely room at the Holiday Lodge Hotel. It was evident to her that Dwight's family liked Jolene. Otherwise, they would not be moving her to Norfolk. Felicity felt she had compromised her principles by promising Theodore and Ted to remain silent in exchange for her elevation to the astronaut corps, which involved working on the mysterious Project Zeus. Felicity needed to speak to her father. She sat on her hotel room bed for approximately two minutes, holding the telephone receiver in her hand, and questioned whether she should call her father and let her heart break over the phone to him. Samuel was right when he had seen Felicity and Dwight together several weeks beforehand. Still, if she spoke to her father, Felicity knew he would try to talk her into coming home, and the lure of space was too attractive a proposition for her to say no. Felicity decided to leave her father out of her life, the wisdom of which only time would tell whether she had made the right decision.

CHAPTER 42

Living a lie! It comes at a price when thou sets out to deceive.
For thee has thrown thy principles out for the world of make-believe.

The following day, at 7:00 a.m., Felicity met with Theodore in the NASA foyer. He walked her down to the boardroom, and, to her surprise, when she entered that room, Ted was already in there, almost as though he had not left from that regrettable meeting the previous afternoon. Also present were the head of the CIA, Frank Derham, and the Secretary of Defence, Peter Waller. Felicity recognised Director Derham from watching him on the television news several weeks beforehand, being interviewed about the nation's security risks posed to America by the presence of double agents within the CIA, an allegation which he dismissed as mere gossip among the press corps. Felicity was familiar with Secretary Waller's face from her service in the USAF. Now, both of these high-ranking officials were in the same boardroom as her and Theodore, which she inferred meant that the meeting Theodore had requested her to attend earlier had more serious overtones. Both men were unaware of Felicity's and Ted's personal life crises.

Along with Theodore, Ted, Director Derham, and Secretary Waller spent an hour impressing upon Felicity the top-secret nature of Project Zeus and how her involvement in it might jeopardise her safety. Despite the supposed absence of double agents within the United States, there were actually many, and therefore, she should be cautious and trust no strangers. When Felicity asked the four men what it was about Project Zeus that attracted such secrecy on one side, and such fervent curiosity on the other, she was curtly told by Theodore that 'in due course, she would find out'. A second alarm had rung out in the twenty-four hours, perhaps foreshadowing evil tidings that might lie ahead for Felicity. Still, the intrigue of Project Zeus lured her in, and it also assisted her that morning in restoring her broken ego caused by Dwight's unfaithfulness. Just like the previous day, Felicity vowed to maintain the confidentiality of Project Zeus. Ted, Director Derham and Secretary Waller were satisfied with the adamant undertaking, and the three men quickly made their way out of NASA before business as usual resumed around the facility – space, spies, and secrets – three words that now consumed Felicity's life.

While Felicity and Ron were in transit later that night, flying back to Los Angeles to commence work the next day on the development of the Hercules Rocket, which would eventually take astronauts to the Moon, the *Ed Sullivan Show* announced a special show in two weeks. Amelia was in her countdown mode that night, as her last film engagement in France with Lilith would see her departing from JFK Airport the day after Dwight departed for his trip around the Moon. Amelia was looking forward to France again, where she could revisit her character for the final film of her contract and explore the hedonism of Paris' lesbian clubs, which she could flee to when she was not expected to be Lilith's paramour for an evening. Amelia had decided, out of boredom, to watch the show that Walter never missed. None of the guests or acts appealed to Amelia. Still, then, during the final moments of the show, her interest was steadfastly engaged by the words old Ed spoke: "Ladies and gentlemen in the audience, indeed to all you good folks watching at home, we're excited to announce that two weeks from tonight we have an extra special show in store for you because we are going to interview here in the studio the wife of Astronaut Dwight Hoover, Mrs Felicity Hoover. So buckle up for a space adventure in two weeks, viewers. It will be one hell of a great show."

Walter had noticed out of the corner of his eye that Amelia suddenly sat forward in the chair when Ed Sullivan mentioned Felicity's name, and he sensed a command would follow immediately after the commercials commenced playing on the television screen. He turned towards Amelia, and her delight was immediately evident in her eyes. "Let me guess, you want me to arrange that somehow, you also want to be a guest on the show that night, right?" Amelia nodded enthusiastically, and her voice was filled with excitement. "Walter, I will increase your pay if you can arrange for me to be a guest that night. I must be on the same night as Felicity, not the night after or before. That very same night. I must fly to France from JFK Airport the next day, for my last tango in Paris with Lilith, and I must see Felicity Hoover. Do you understand?" Walter sighed as he exited the armchair he had found comfort in for the past hour. "Alright, just keep your hat on. I will now call one of my former lovers who works in the production team, and ask him for the return of the favour he has owed me for about five years now." Amelia was both excited and curious. "What favour did you do for him that could get me on that show that night,

Walter?" He smiled a devilish smile. "I have never told his wife, nor anyone for that matter, until now, of course, that we were lovers for several years before he married. As you know, Amelia, in the world of film and television, it isn't who you know that matters; it's who you're sleeping with that makes a difference. Let this old queen say that I am owed several return favours if I may. And before you ask, consider it done. I shall ensure you stay in the same hotel as Mrs Hoover that night." Walter then hobbled out of the room to call The Ed Sullivan Theatre in Manhattan. The world of espionage and NASA may have been a world of secrets. Still, there were also secrets in the entertainment industry and, more importantly, opportunities, if you knew the right people. Walter called his former lover, David Otlowski, who nervously agreed to let Amelia Tolhurst make a last-minute surprise guest appearance. Walter was able to make all the arrangements, including the room at the hotel in Manhattan, which would place Amelia as close as possible to Felicity.

After receiving Walter's telephone call, Otlowski tapped his fingers on his desk. The actress Amelia Tolhurst had to be on the *Ed Sullivan Show* the same night as Felicity Hoover and stay in the same hotel. Otlowski knew this would be valuable information for his undercover contact. He picked up the telephone and dialled a telephone number in Boston. After the fourth dial tone, it was answered. "Hello, Emil speaking." The unrefined mixture of a Russian accent impersonating a German one agitated Otlowski's fragile nerves. "Aliev, that German accent needs more work because it sounds like metal grating on metal at the moment." Aliev grunted. "What do you want, comrade?" Otlowksi proceeded to inform the Soviet agent about Walter's telephone call. "I have some interesting news about Felicity Hoover, and you'll have to come to New York immediately." Then he divulged to Aliev all the details he knew from speaking to Walter, and upon Aliev's request, assured him that he could arrange a job at the Hilton Hotel. The dies was cast before anybody knew it because there were never any secrets in show business.

For the next two weeks, Felicity and Ron worked around the clock at Canoga Park to examine the current Hercules rocket plans and determine what modifications would be necessary to fulfil its future destiny of landing astronauts on the Moon. NASA wanted some indicative data and plans prepared before Dwight's mission took off for its lunar flyby. Felicity still felt the pain of betrayal in her heart, and, of course, there was the lingering secondary thought about what on God's Earth the secretive Project Zeus was about. Ron had noticed that

Felicity's mind seemed to be preoccupied on occasion when they were speaking; however, whenever he asked her whether something was wrong, Felicity would attribute it to her concern about Dwight's mission, as NASA did not have an unblemished record when it came to the safety of their astronauts.

Subsequently, it was expected of Felicity, as the doting wife of an astronaut, that when she arrived in Orlando the day before his mission launch, she would call Dwight to wish him well, just as the other astronauts' wives did. Theodore had told Felicity during a telephone discussion that it would be noticed by other NASA staff if she did not make the obligatory 'doting wife' telephone call – more vile bile for Felicity's heart and mind to accept.

Dwight's secure room at Cape Canaveral had a telephone that Felicity could call in on to wish him well, knowing full well that the call was undoubtedly being monitored by the CIA, NASA, and the Defence Department to ensure Felicity was still keeping her word to play the devoted wife of a brave astronaut. They had not talked since Dwight told her about him being unfaithful, and Felicity had a strange feeling in her belly as Dwight answered her call. "Hello." Whereas his voice on the telephone once brought her comfort, it now delivered the feelings of wrath that she had to suppress. "Hello, Dwight." There was a momentary silence, then he spoke to break the chill enveloping the connection. "Felicity? Is that you?" Oh, brother. He could be stupid at times. "Of course, it's me, Dwight. Who else would be calling you the night before your important day?" He detected a slight sarcastic edge in her voice, so Dwight changed the subject to discuss her work. "How is it going there at Canoga Park? I have been so busy, I have not had a chance to call you." Now for the surprise he was not expecting. "Canoga Park is working out fine. Still, I am not calling you from Canoga Park because I am in Orlando." Dwight's next question underscored his lack of understanding of simple life matters. "Orlando? Why are you in Orlando?" It was hard not to mock him, so Felicity decided to do so through a giggle. "Oh, you silly man. I am in Orlando to watch your launch tomorrow at Cape Canaveral. Where else would I be on such a special day?" She might have spoken through a giggle, but Dwight detected condescension when he heard it; he decided it was best to end the call quickly, for fear that she might say something unpleasant if he tried to make small talk. "Well, I am glad to hear your voice, Felicity, because naturally I am a bit nervous. Anyway, I'm glad you will watch the launch tomorrow; my parents and sister will too. However, I have a very early start tomorrow, so I had better finish this call, as I need to go to bed. Goodnight and thanks for calling." It was evident to Felicity on the other end of the line that Dwight was surprised she had called and that she would be watching him the next day. She was surprised that Theodore had not forewarned her that Dwight was not expecting her call. Unwittingly, to all those ears listening in, Felicity passed the test of loyalty which would permit her more freedom than she might have otherwise received. She was otherwise not thrilled by the prospect of seeing Dwight's mother and sister. It would be a restless night for both of them.

There is no greater envy in life than watching another person live your dream. As Felicity sat in the VIP stand, watching that rocket launch with Dwight and his fellow astronauts about to make history by orbiting the Moon, all she could feel was envy that a man with fewer talents than hers, who had been unfaithful to her as well, would from here on bask in the glory of making history. To add to her envy, Felicity also had to endure the ignominy of sitting with Dwight's family, watching him live her dream. At the same time, she knew they must be aware of his infidelity and his bastard child, which another woman was carrying in her belly. Then, the countdown commenced, and the Hercules' giant rockets ignited on the launch pad, forcing large plumes of white smoke sideways as the rocket lifted off. As the Hercules rocket cleared the tower, Felicity caught a glimpse of Ted out of the corner of her eye. His attention was focused on her, making her feel uncomfortable and simultaneously aware that some members of NASA and the Defence Department would be monitoring her every move at Cape Canaveral. She still had to fly to Manhattan to appear on the *Ed Sullivan Show* that night, where her every word would be monitored again. When the rocket was over a minute into its flight, it reached a velocity of 2,195 feet per second, and as it disappeared further into the sky, so too did Felicity disappear from the stand to be whisked away to Orlando Airport, where she would commence her journey of a lifetime.

CHAPTER 43

Felicity had not been to Manhattan before. Her life in America had seen her visit several parts of that nation, but she had never been to the Borough of Manhattan before this night. She now understood the public's fuss about the splendour of Manhattan as the chauffeur driven Cadillac crossed the Brooklyn Bridge because the glow of the city's lights lit up the island like it was some fairytale world, where Felicity could escape from the austerity of her married life, escape from the life of living a lie for the sake of NASA, and escape from the nightmare of a life playing second fiddle to her imbecile husband who was now flying in space, inside the cramped conditions of the command capsule that was heading towards the Moon. Indeed, when the Cadillac was halfway across the Brooklyn Bridge, the image of the Full Moon began to lift above the top of the Manhattan skyscrapers, bringing Felicity back down to Earth, as she realised that she now had to wear a fake smile on her face for several hours at the Ed Sullivan Theatre, before she could eventually escape to the confines of her room for the night at the Hilton Hotel. This fall back to Earth for Felicity was about to deliver her a surprise she was not expecting.

The Cadillac pulled up at 1697 Broadway at 53rd Street, and Felicity was met at the doors of the building by David Otlowski. He presented as a very conservative television show executive, and little did Felicity know that his belly was twirling because Walter was also inside the Ed Sullivan Theatre that night, accompanying Amelia, who Felicity was still oblivious to the fact that they were about to be reacquainted with each other for the first time in almost a decade. David recognised Felicity immediately and walked over to her as she walked towards the doors. "Hello, Mrs Hoover. My name is David Otlowski, and I am one of the show's producers tonight, and also in charge of making sure you go to the right makeup room, so our makeup artists can style you before you go out on stage for your interview." Felicity smiled politely and otherwise followed Otlowski as he led her into the building. As they approached the studio's dressing room assigned to Felicity, Otlowski informed her about the arrangements and guests on the show. "Okay, Mrs Hoover." Felicity interrupted him. "I do not mean to sound precious, but I am a doctor in aeronautical science, so perhaps if you could pass those details on to Mr Sullivan, I would be grateful. However, sorry that I interrupted you; what were you saying?" Otlowski nodded to acknowledge her correction. "My apologies, as NASA didn't pass on that information about your title being Dr Hoover. Anyway, as I was about to say. This is your dressing room, where the hair and make-up stylist is waiting for you. When it is your turn to go on the show, I will come and get you. It's a bit of an English theme tonight. We have a new English pop band appearing first, followed by an English actress, and then you. Your travel bag and purse can stay in the dressing until the show is over." Otlowski turned to walk away; however, Felicity was curious after hearing him speak. "Mr Otlowski, before you leave, I have two questions arising from your spiel. You mentioned an English actress is on the show tonight before me. Who is that person?" There was a detectable quiver to her voice, which intrigued Otlowski. "It's Amelia Tolhurst." Otlowski noticed Felicity's cheeks blush. "Is that a problem for you, Dr Hoover?" Felicity's pulse was heightened by the excitement of her finally making contact with Amelia after almost ten years. She was embarrassed by her blushing, which she had to conceal. "Oh, no, there isn't a problem. I have known Ms Tolhurst from my school days back in England. It must be almost a decade since we last saw each other." Otlowski smiled. "You mentioned a second question, Dr Hoover?" Felicity needed to escape the obvious discomfort she was displaying as she tried to shield her emotions. "Oh, I can't remember now. It was probably trivial." Otlowski nodded. "Excellent. I will let Ed know about the school history. Now, hurry up and go and get styled for the show. We're starting in half an hour."

Felicity had mixed emotions as she sat in her dressing room, waiting for Otlowski to knock on the door. The stylist's fifteen minutes of work on Felicity's make-up and hair distracted her; now, she was alone, and one question was: 'Will it be obvious on television that I am naturally attracted to her?' Time would tell now, as there was a knock on the door. Felicity sat in her dressing room, frozen by the contemporaneous thrill of being near Amelia again, yet terrified her beating heart would win its battle against her steel-trap mind. Joan's words at Cambridge all those years ago repeated themselves over and over in her mind. "Are you a lesbian, Felicity?" Her pulse intensified as she thought about that glorious night at Woldingham and how nobody had been as tender with her as Amelia since then. She looked at herself in the mirror; her light blue dress was complemented by the bra padding she wore. Her make-up stylist made her look pretty, a housewife pretty. However, nobody could make her mind stop torturing herself. She begged to lie. "No, Joan. I am not a lesbian." Then came the second knock on the door, which was forceful, indicative of the knocker's impatience. Then Otlowski's voice broke the debate, pounding away in Felicity's mind. "Dr Hoover. Hurry up, please. You're on when the next commercial break is over."

His voice was a crack of thunder in Felicity's mind. She got up quickly from her chair, stammering a few words. "Okay, I heard you the first time!" The command in her voice assured her she could survive the five to ten minutes of being on live television, sitting a seat away from her heart's desire. She opened the door to an anxious Otlowski standing directly before her. "Come on, Dr Hoover. We have ninety seconds until the commercial break is over. "Alright, Mr Otlowski. Just keep your hat on. A woman is entitled to check her appearance before she goes on live television." Otlowski raised his eyebrows, and then, without warning, he took Felicity's right hand and almost dragged her to the wings of the studio some thirty yards down the hall, where the stage director, an old would-be actress, waited nervously, smoking a cigarette as Felicity raced into the wings. When they approached, the stage director coughed out a plume of cigarette smoke. "Thank goodness. You're on in thirty seconds. You walk between these blackout curtains as soon as I tap your back. It's about ten paces, and then you will be on set. Smile and wave at the crowd as you walk towards Ed." There was a crackle of sound in the stage director's earphones. "Okay. Here we go. Five, four, three, two, one." Felicity felt the firm push to her back, signalling her to walk. Each step was one small step for a person. Still, for Felicity, each step was like one giant leap forward, and as she came within a step of entering the studio stage, she heard Ed's unforgettable tone ring out to the audience. "Put your hands together, ladies and gentlemen, for Dr Felicity Hoover!" With her name being mentioned, Felicity's timing was immaculate as she walked out onto the studio stage, slightly blinded by the lights; she waved and smiled at the audience. Out of the corner of her eye, she saw Amelia, and she felt her pulse intensify as she walked up to Ed Sullivan to shake his hand in a lady's manner.

The next few moments seemed like an eternity for Felicity as Ed introduced her to the live studio audience and viewers at home. Then he escorted Felicity to the lounge, where she was reacquainted with the woman who broke her heart when they were school colleagues. Felicity's pulse began to increase as she looked into Amelia's beautiful yet broken eyes; little did she realise that Amelia's pulse was accelerating, even though she kept her calm exterior. Felicity also maintained an emotionless exterior; however, the look in their respective eyes told the other no lies about an unrequited passion that burned brightly inside both of them.

It didn't take long for Ed to break the secret of their former school ties. "Folks at home, these two lovely British gals share a past life back in their home country by attending the same school, but they haven't seen one another for, am I right, almost a decade?" Amelia broke the tension in her typical show business style by leaping to her feet, hugging Felicity in a friendly manner, and speaking to Ed. "That is right. Ten years, Ed. Space Freak has changed a lot since we last saw each other." Felicity was mortified to be called Space Freak again, and just as she felt the flames of anger ignite in her mind, Amelia reached out and held her hand, with the etiquette and elegance for which only English women have an innate and effortless ability to do. The touch of her gentle hands soothed Felicity's passion. As they resumed their seats for the next ten minutes to be interviewed by Ed, Felicity was lost in a world of nervous tension, playing the role of a doting wife to a famous astronaut. Her mind barked out a command to reveal to the world that her so-called heroic husband was a swine, a scoundrel, and an imposter in a role for which she, as a woman, had more skill and intelligence. Yet, there were also the barking words of Project Zeus and the promises she had made to the American military and NASA to keep her silent. There was a battle in her mind between the assertive eighteen-year-old and the pragmatic twenty-eight-year-old, and the latter won out over the former.

Time seemed to be bent around the gravitational pull of Amelia's presence, but before Felicity knew it, her time was up, and she was ushered off the stage first, as Amelia remained on stage to sing with the new emerging English pop band, The Butterflies. Their reunion was over, and just as it had been at Woldingham ten years beforehand, Felicity was disappointed that this was the extent of her surprise reunion with the only person who held the keys to her heart. However, she knew that must be the extent of their reunion because she had spent almost a decade of her life persuading herself she was not a lesbian. If she were to allow her true feelings for Amelia to be revealed, as Joan had previously warned, that would end her life in the military and, most importantly, at NASA. As she walked out of the wings of the sound stage, Felicity could not see Otlowski.

Little did she realise that Walter and Otlowski were reacquainting themselves with one another in the privacy of Otlowski's locked office, two floors below. David Otlowski might now be a respectable family man, but he, too, was living a double life, and Walter was more than happy to be the brief receiver of David's pent-up sexual frustration. There would be one more surprise for Walter, which Otlowski had in store for him that night; however, that was later, for a promised rendezvous at the Hilton.

Subsequently, when she was settling into her room at the Hilton, having changed into her nightie, Felicity was still dealing with her disappointment of having spent only about ten minutes with Amelia. Felicity's head kept reminding her it was the right outcome for her career. Still, her heart was yearning for Amelia, like it had yearned for no other. She was just about to turn off the light in her room to go to sleep for the night when she heard a knocking sound on the door. Felicity opened her room door, only to discover nobody was there in the hallway. She closed her hotel room door, and then there was a knocking sound again, which she now ascertained was emanating from her adjoining room door. She cautiously walked over to the door and spoke to the stranger who was knocking on the opposite side. "Hello. Who are you and what do you want?" It didn't take long for the mystery person to identify themselves. "Open the door, Space Freak. It's me." Only Amelia could use the sobriquet 'Space Freak' with such a luxurious, rich and inviting voice. Felicity's pulse increased rapidly as she opened her side of the adjoining room door, revealing the stunning beauty of Amelia dressed in her white silk nightie, the fabric of which was so thin that Felicity couldn't help but see Amelia's large but perfectly shaped breasts. She then stared into her eyes, nervously trying to work out what to say. She didn't need to bother because Amelia made the first move by gripping her hands behind Felicity's head and pressing her lips against hers. It felt so natural, so sweet, and so tender that Felicity dropped her guard, and she started passionately kissing Amelia back. 'To hell with Joan,' she thought as the electricity passed between their lips.

Their kissing was intense, as if they were instinctively catching up on a decade of separation. Yet it was so sweet, tender and loving that Felicity hardly noticed they had ended up on her bed. Then Felicity felt Amelia's body gently press against hers to push her head back towards her pillow. As her head fell gently onto the pillow, it was followed by Amelia's voluptuous body resting against hers and their 'pashing' became even more furious in its delight. She then felt

Amelia's hand touch her left breast. Amelia further stimulated Felicity's desire for her, and then her hand quickly but gently found Amelia's large right breast. It felt natural for Felicity to feel the other woman's breast. Then she felt Amelia's other hand make its way up underneath her nightgown, and initially, Felicity felt nervous as she partially withdrew her tongue from Amelia's mouth. "What are you…" Felicity's words were simultaneously interrupted by Amelia's hand, which was now making its way under her nightdress as she partially spoke through their kissing. "Shush, it's okay; I will look after you." Her words were too alluring, and Felicity resumed her uninhibited kissing with Amelia as the other woman's hand now gently felt Felicity's breast. The feeling of Amelia's skin touching her excited Felicity. Almost as if she were experienced in affection, her left hand made its way under Amelia's nightdress, and she gently felt onto her large right breast. Their hands undid buttons on their respective nightgowns, and very soon, they were both topless and kissing each other deeply as their hands simultaneously caressed each other's breasts. After several minutes, Felicity then felt Amelia's hand make its way under her panties, and she felt her soft fingers stroke her vagina. Felicity was frightened and tried to pull away, but Amelia used her body to overwhelm her, and her voice once again liberated Felicity from her inhibitions. "It's okay; I know what I am doing and, if you want, do the same to me." She gave in to her as Amelia pulled down her panties. Felicity felt erotic, and she very quickly responded in kind by doing the same with Amelia's panties. Then they threw away all their inhibitions, and the two women became naked and kissed each other's bodies before finally bringing each other to the sensation of ultimate pleasure. They continued their passion for another two hours, and finally, in their exhaustion, they fell asleep in each other's arms. It had only taken seconds for Amelia to break down the wall Felicity had built up in her mind over a decade. Still, for either woman, it was the most tender lovemaking they had experienced; it was pure, it was feminine, and it was natural. It was star-crossed love.

While Amelia and Felicity had been passionately making love in Felicity's room, Walter was eagerly waiting for David Otlowski to arrive, as he promised he would. As Felicity and Amelia were falling asleep in each other's arms, Walter heard a knock on his hotel room door, and he enthusiastically hobbled over to his door to open it, expecting to see David there for what he promised would be a lengthier encounter than their brief interlude in the office. Walter swung open the door and said excitedly, "Hello, darl…". The cat immediately took his tongue, as Otlowski was standing there with another man who had the harsh look of a man of Balkan heritage, dressed in the uniform of a Hilton Hotel bellhop. Otlowski could tell Walter was surprised and confused by the presence of another man, so an explanation was required. "Walter, I was not totally honest with you when I promised you earlier in my office that we would have more time together tonight, which, eventually, we will. However, before then, we need to talk. Meet Emil, or, actually, it's Aliev. And Aliev, this is Walter, the guy who is the manager of the movie star, Amelia Tolhurst." Walter was perplexed as he extended his hand to shake Aliev's, whilst he looked into Otlowski's eyes for answers. Aliev's handshake was firm and brutal; immediately, Walter knew there would not be a third person joining him in the bed that evening. David was determined that the three of them would enter the confidential confines of Walter's room. "May we come in, please? Aliev and I wish to discuss a matter of grave importance with you." Walter nodded and moved sideways for the men to enter his room. Aliev let out a command in his rough imitation of a German accent, which still grated on Otlowski's nerves. "Shut the door!" Walter shut the door to his hotel room, and then for the next hour, he listened to both men speak. By midnight, a promise was made by Walter in return for a financial reward, and then Aliev left the room to return to his supposed 'work' as Otlowski made true on his promise for him and Walter to have more than a one-sided, fleeting sexual rendezvous.

The following morning at six o'clock, Felicity awoke before Amelia. They were both still in each other's arms, naked, where they had fallen asleep about six hours beforehand. Felicity initially panicked, thinking that they were somewhere other than the hotel room where hearts had entwined sub rosa to an otherwise unsuspecting world. When Felicity realised she was still in the safety of her locked hotel room, her focus returned to the splendour of Amelia's beautiful soft skin, perfectly shaped eyelashes and those ruby red full lips which she had revelled in hours before.

She studied her face for about ten minutes, and then, just as alluring as her face had been in its slumber, Amelia's eyes gently opened to reveal the icing on the cake, her stunning blue eyes. They momentarily looked at each other, and then Amelia smiled. Her head gently leaned over Felicity's, and the sweet touch of her lips immediately sent tantalising pulses of power to every inch of Felicity's body. "Good morning, Space Freak." Amelia's loving smile revealed no malice to her words, and Felicity kissed her again for about ten seconds before responding. "Good morning to you, too. And I mean it, it is a good morning." They both stared into each other's eyes, and then Amelia gently reached up with her right hand and, with her index finger, moved some of Felicity's hair, which was hanging down too close to her left eyebrow. "How long have you been awake?" Felicity didn't want to say the words, but she could not resist being open and honest with Amelia. "I don't know, but it's a while. Perhaps ten or so minutes. I just wanted to look at your beautiful face while you slept, to make sure this was real, and not a dream." Amelia used her right leg to entangle herself closer to Felicity's body. "Why did you think it was a dream?" Felicity could not help but be candid as she too twisted her body closer into Amelia's. "Because for the past decade I have been telling myself that what we did at Woldingham was wrong, then I would say it was right, but it could not happen while all the time deep down I wished to feel your lips against mine again." She paused momentarily, waiting for Amelia to respond, but none was forthcoming. "Did that sound strange to you, too?" Amelia softly wiggled her nose tip against Felicity's. "Of course not. It sounded so sweet. And, deep down, I have wanted this moment to occur again ever since our night together at Woldingham. You don't know how excited I felt when I read about your miraculous flight, and then, like a miracle, you were in the news again, this time marrying... oh, whatever his name is. It doesn't matter; I knew I had to be on that show last night if ever I would meet up with you again." Felicity's eyes slightly widened in pleasant surprise. "You arranged to be on the show especially for me?" Amelia gently nodded, rubbed her nose tip on Felicity's and then gently kissed her lips for about fifteen seconds before removing them to be millimetres away from Felicity's willing lips. "Of course. I had my manager urgently arrange all of this; the television appearance and the adjoining room, as this was a tiny window opportunity." Felicity slightly raised her head off the pillow to look more deeply into Amelia's eyes. "Why did you say a tiny window of opportunity?"

Amelia smiled without her eyes departing from Felicity's earnest gaze. With her left hand cupping behind Felicity's neck, she touched their lips again for another ten seconds of electrifying and tender kissing before answering the question. "I have to fly to Paris later this afternoon to film the third, and thank God, the final instalment of that classical epic. I will be away for about nine months of torture with..." She stopped short of mentioning Lilith's name and the sexual torture she had endured since that ignominious day at the studio. "It doesn't matter. So, I knew that if I did not meet up with you again last night, we might not have the opportunity to do so again." Felicity could not conceal her disappointment at hearing that, after allowing a decade of denial to be broken down, Amelia would soon be departing for France, and with her departure, the imminent return of her misery to a loveless marriage. Amelia gently stroked the back of Felicity's neck with her right hand as she brought the tips of their noses back together again. "Heh, it's only nine months and then I will be back, and I promise you this time, we will be together again. Now, we have a few hours before checkout, so let's make love again." Felicity needed no further encouragement, and once again their lips met, which soon became the electrical spark of love as they passionately made love to each other for the next hour and a half, before they both breathlessly climaxed whilst still maintaining their passionate bond with their eyes.

Subsequently, after they showered and changed their clothes, Amelia asked Felicity for her telephone number. When Felicity wrote her number down on the hotel notepad, Amelia did the same, promising she would call her from France as soon as she knew she would return to Los Angeles. They gently kissed each other again, ensuring neither of their made-over faces was disturbed by this gentle kiss. Then Amelia left first, to meet up with Walter, who would, on this occasion, accompany her to Paris to ensure Lilith did not go too far with her sexually depraved ways of dominating the beautiful young actress. Once ten minutes had passed and the coast was clear, Felicity emerged from her hotel room to resume living the lie, which was the life she had to endure to chase her dreams. However, at least now, there was hope – that was the hope that, by fulfilling her career goal, she might now be free to nourish her heart. Regrettably, in those two minutes as she marched out of the doors of the Hilton to catch her taxi back to JFK Airport, Felicity, on this occasion, buried in the back of her mind the voice of reason of Joan. Her thoughts were adamant: 'There is nothing wrong with me; I have loved her all my life. In any event, if Dwight can cheat on me, why can't I cheat on him? Surely the heart can only lead me down the right path?'

Later that day, through a series of covert Soviet operatives stretching from the United States through to Syria, and then directly to Moscow, a coded telegram was sent by Aliev to Volkov, which, upon being decoded, read as follows: 'Amelia Tolhurst's manager is secured as an informant, thanks to our comrade Otlowski. Her manager mentioned that Tolhurst and Dr Felicity Hoover are old-school lovers. Although I'm not certain if the relationship has resumed, her manager told me that Tolhurst attempted to rekindle it last night. Tolhurst has left for Paris today, to make her last film in France. Her manager also told me the producer, who is a lesbian, has been using Tolhurst for her sexual fantasies. At the same time, they also frequent underground lesbian bars in Paris, including multiple participant orgies. I suggest Sokolov monitor Tolhurst in France, and when the opportunity arises, Anatoli should be sent to Paris to liaise with Tolhurst, once her manager confirms a relationship has resumed with Hoover.' When Volkov finished reading the telegram, he reclined back in his chair and smiled at the ceiling in his office. His instincts had proven him right in all aspects of the decisions he had made for years; he had been right by arguing that Anatoli's life should be spared after the debacle of the sodomy murder of Saar; he had also been proven right that Aliev should be deployed to America as a covert operative, because now there were several channels of information about Dr Felicity Hoover. The only missing piece in the puzzle was to uncover the true intentions behind the Americans' and Israelis' involvement in Project Zeus. He picked up the receiver of his telephone to be connected to the Politburo, so that he could speak to the Minister of Defence and inform him about the probable light at the end of the tunnel that led to the mysterious 'Project Zeus'.

Two nights after their reunion on the *Ed Sullivan Show*, Heather was watching the BBC television evening news, which broadcast a segment of the show under the pretence of 'old school friends reunited'. It might have only been about ten seconds of footage of Felicity and Amelia. Still, Heather immediately detected the glint in Felicity's eyes that she had detected over a decade ago whenever she was near Amelia. Although Felicity denied holding any feelings for Amelia on the morning of her wedding day, Heather's suspicions were reignited by the television footage. The eyes truly are the mirror to a person's soul.

PART 6

"Space"

CHAPTER 44

Dwight had returned from space as a national hero, and Felicity was ordered to be the doting wife to greet him in Houston, once he had been released from the Mobile Quarantine Facility. After the press, television, and radio reporters had finished their public relations interviews and returned to their respective organisations to shape the news as their editorial teams saw fit, Felicity hastily departed from NASA's headquarters to return to Canoga Park. Dwight might have been a hero as far as the public was concerned. Still, to Felicity, he was a no-good philandering husband who had impregnated another woman, with whom his time was devoted. She knew he didn't want her to remain in Houston, and in any event, she now felt vindicated by having an affair with the only person who had touched her romantic heart.

Time, space, gravity, thrust and light seemed inconsequential for Felicity for several months after her heart, mind, and body reunited with Amelia. Although a continent and an ocean separated them, telephone technology kept them in contact, work schedules permitting. Felicity's work environment at Rocketdyne's Canoga Park facilities was bland and uninspiring. Still, when she returned home to Winnetka, the intercontinental telephone romance with Amelia brought new life to Felicity's damaged heart and mind. When they telephoned one another, they would discuss how much they missed the other's touch, whether it be as simple as cuddling into their arms or the more salacious details of the night of making love and how they both wished to feel and explore every inch of the other's body. There was only one subject they did not discuss: work. Felicity could not discuss it because of national security reasons; Amelia did not discuss her work because of the ignominy of being Lilith's organic sex toy.

In those few months following her night with Amelia, Ron noticed that Felicity seemed much happier after her trip to Cape Canaveral and New York, as did Samuel when he spoke to his daughter on the telephone. When asked about the delighted disposition she presented, whether in person or over the phone,

Felicity would respond that every day she worked with NASA brought her one day closer to achieving her life goal. Her lie satisfied the enquiries; however, she did not realise how that lie might come true. Her work on Project Zeus at Canoga Park seemed as mystical as Godot, because she and Ron seemed to be working only on improving the functional capabilities of the Hercules Rocket. Felicity felt that Space and Zeus were separated from her by the powers-that-be of the patriarchal system of American institutions and agencies.

In late August of 1968, Theodore rang Felicity at Rocketdyne for several reasons. He had the unenviable task of delivering the news to her that Dwight was now the unofficial father to a nine-pound, one-ounce baby boy, who had been born several days beforehand. That news was met with silence from Felicity. Regarding the additional reason for his call, Theodore was also to the point: Felicity had to take the first Pan America flight from Los Angeles to Houston the next morning, as she was required for a 'special meeting' about Project Zeus. Felicity was given one extra direction, which made no sense to her, given Theodore's knowledge of the state of her marriage. Theodore told her that she would need to stay at Dwight's apartment for the night. Felicity was gobsmacked. "What? You want me to what, Theodore?" He might have presented himself as a science nerd, but Theodore could be quite commanding when the moment required him. "I said you must stay at your husband's apartment for the night. You and he are both needed for a press conference tomorrow, followed by a meeting with me and the Secretary of Defence the next day. And I do not care about what he has done to you or who he is in love with. As far as the American public is concerned, you and Dwight are NASA's golden couple, which helps us maintain our mainstream funding for the space programme. So, sleep on the sofa as far as I am concerned, because I do not want some snooping journalist to report that you are staying at a hotel when your husband has an apartment. Do you understand me, Felicity?" She felt like telling Theodore where he could stick his golden-haired couple propaganda; however, she sensed that the press conference was an important milestone in her goal to become the first woman in space, so she acquiesced, no matter how foreign it felt to her resolute sense of what it meant to be a woman.

The following day, when Felicity arrived at NASA's headquarters, she felt as though a cloud of humiliation surrounded her. After being made to wait in the reception of the administrative centre for about twenty minutes, Theodore emerged from the entrance to hallway that eventually led to the boardroom, and his keen eyes displayed appreciation when he saw Felicity's packed travel bag, which had an identifying tag recording in capital letters Dwight's address on it, a subtle hint that she would comply with Theodore's direction made the previous day. Felicity rose from her seat as Theodore motioned with his hand for her to follow him, and his words were spoken with their usual clinical and emotionless tone. "Felicity, come with me, quickly, please. We only have a quarter of an hour until the media arrives."

She gathered her travel bag and followed Theodore through the doorway leading down to the ignominy at the end of the hallway, awaiting her. When they arrived at the closed entrance to the boardroom where she had been told several months ago about her husband's infidelity, Theodore turned around to glare at Felicity, and his tone was even colder and emotionless. "Right, your husband is on the other side of that door. I know how you feel about him, but for the next fifteen minutes, you are going to become reacquainted with him, so don't play up because you then have to regale the media with the news I am about to discuss with both of you, which will be the announcement made at the impending press conference. Do you understand me?" Felicity nodded, but internally, she was seething with rage about the humiliation awaiting her as she became 'reacquainted' with Dwight. Theodore opened the doorway to the boardroom, revealing to Felicity Dwight sitting at the far end of the table. His eyes displayed discomfort as he knew his wife was there. Theodore's next direction surprised Felicity, but it had to be obeyed because she sensed the importance of the announcement in achieving her career goals. "Go in, please. And sit next to Dwight." Felicity's eyes showed hesitation; however, Theodore's return glare spared no sympathy for her feelings. She nodded and commenced the walk of anger down towards Dwight, who could not look her in the eye because of his shame. What a debacle a fairytale wedding had turned out to be.

Felicity pulled out her chair and sat down next to Dwight. Theodore pulled out a chair on the opposite side of the boardroom table from them and sat down. Theodore's next direction surprised both Felicity and Dwight. "I want you to hold each other's hands as I explain what we will announce to the media soon." Felicity's and Dwight's voices both rang out in unison. "What?" Theodore shook his head in defiance. "You heard me. Dwight, you reach out with your right hand, and Felicity, you reach out with your left, and I want the pair of you to hold hands." There was still an uncomfortable hesitation. "Do it!" Theodore's bark immediately caused Dwight's right hand to extend towards Felicity, whereas she reluctantly extended her left hand until they both somewhat uncomfortably held hands together. Theodore then delivered his news to the odd couple sitting across from him at the table. "You look like a pair of first graders going on a school trip, but in any event, keep on holding hands. I am about to inform both of you that we will announce the news to the media in approximately ten minutes, so please prepare accordingly. Felicity, you have partial insight into Project Zeus, but Dwight is being told about it for the first time. Dwight, this is news to you, but your father is aware of it because it involves our defence forces. NASA is working on a space mission we have named 'Project Zeus'. Felicity has been working on upgrading the thrust of the rockets at Rocketdyne for our mission to the Moon, but even this announcement is news to her. What neither of you knows is that NASA and various federal institutions, including the Department of Defence, are working on developing a new design of spacecraft. I cannot reveal the full details to you now, other than it will include a scientific laboratory to be maintained in space. The news aspect for today's purpose is that both of you will be the team to fly Zeus into space, where it shall remain in Earth's orbit as long as Congress decides it is feasible to fund the programme. Essentially, Zeus is a space station, which, with your academic background, Felicity, you will help design at Rocketdyne's Reno facilities, but still being primarily located at Canoga Park, where you will continue working with Ron Goldman on the Hercules Rockets, which will be the technology we use to launch Zeus into space. Dwight, your job will be the commander of this seven-day mission in space, and, if you do not impregnate any other women, you might even be included as a mission member for one of our future Moon landing missions. The pair of you will be the first husband-and-wife team to fly into space together, emphasising the importance of the family unit to the current White House Administration and Congress. That is the extent of the announcement to the media today, and it is also why I wanted you to portray at least some form of a happy family unit. Do either of you have any questions?"

Felicity was consumed with ambivalence; her dream of becoming the first woman to fly into space had now become definite. However, that dream was clouded by the thought of having to endure seven days in space with Dwight as the flight commander. While holding Felicity's hand, Dwight shot up his left hand, like a first-grade school student. "Does this mean Felicity and I will have to live together?" Theodore raised his eyes to the ceiling, but Felicity was just as interested in hearing his reply. "From time to time, yes, you will have to stay at each other's residences to maintain the illusion of one big happy family, whether the pair of you like it or not. That also means, Dwight, that any liaisons between you, Jolene and your baby boy will have to be done surreptitiously, at night and not out in public, for the next few years. And, yes, Dwight, Felicity knows that you are now a father. Do you understand me?" They both nodded, but they were both afflicted with ambivalence, for differing reasons. Theodore then gave them the next set of directions. "Alright, the show must go on, so let's walk across to the hangar where the media will now be waiting, and you pair are to continue holding one another's hands until you take a seat at the desk we have set up in that hangar, which will include Congressman Tebbe, who is part of the oversight committee monitoring the funding of Project Zeus, so for goodness sake, smile as well as holding hands." Felicity did not know she could hold Dwight's hand with the customary familiarity of a couple in love. Instead, as best she could, she pretended she was holding Amelia's hand, which at least permitted her hand and arm muscles to relax enough to look convincing.

Subsequently, Felicity had to endure the press conference from hell when it was announced that she and Dwight would be the first married couple to enter space as part of a bold new scientific programme for NASA named Zeus, scheduled to launch in the early 1970s. No mention of the importance of Felicity being the first woman to fly into space. The announcement was premised on her subservience as the astronaut's wife, despite her intellectual superiority to the hapless Dwight and her aspirations to become an astronaut. Congressman Tebbe told the madding crowd of journalists that family values mattered just as much to America in space as they did on the terra firma of the United States. In the cacophony of questions, cameras clicking, lights blaring, and the whirring sound of film cameras recording, the irony of 'family values' was not lost on Theodore or Felicity. In contrast, Dwight nodded in ignorant bliss to the antithesis he had created with Jolene.

After the press conference, Felicity wanted to run to the telephone to call her father, breaking the news before he eventually heard it on the BBC's late news service. Still, Theodore, in the presence of Congressman Tebbe, explained there was a reason why she had to remain in Houston for the night, and that was because the entire Congressional Oversight Committee would be meeting 'the first couple in space' the next day. Felicity was eager to get to a telephone. However, after dismissing Dwight from their presence, Theodore directed Felicity to follow him back to the boardroom, where he told her they were to meet with Secretary Waller, a meeting for which she had no idea of the purpose.

By now, Felicity's mind was whirring with thoughts of maintaining an illusory marriage, whilst also comprehending that her future mission to fly into space was underscored on the premise of preserving family values as an astronaut's wife rather than acknowledging her feat as the first woman to achieve this milestone, all while she was in the early stages of a relationship with another woman whom she loved for many years. So when she entered the boardroom, Felicity was hardly cognisant of Secretary Waller's presence. Theodore brought her to her senses with his commanding voice. "Felicity, I know it's been a surreal day for you; however, perhaps you might pay Secretary Waller the courtesy of saying hello to him?" Felicity shook her head in a signal of opening her mind to her surroundings, and she shook the outstretched hand of Secretary Waller, who was standing next to his seat at the boardroom table. "My apologies, Secretary Waller. Theodore is correct; it has been a surreal day. How are you?" The Secretary of Defence clutched her hand firmly to ensure she was receptive to him and the discussion they were about to have. "I am fine, Dr Hoover. Please, take a seat next to the Director. We have some important matters to discuss."

Although her mind had been consumed with many thoughts, the mention of the word 'important' engaged Felicity's attention, and she promptly sat next to Theodore's right side, who sat at the head of the boardroom table. When they were settled, Secretary Waller opened a manila folder and handed Felicity a bound forty-page document. Before she could commence reading it, the Secretary of Defence spoke. "Don't worry too much about this document; it is an overview of what we shall discuss now. Project Zeus is what we have portrayed it to be to Congress, the American public, and the rest of the world, consistent with everything announced to the press beforehand. However, there is a secondary purpose that only I, the Director, along with several heads of our Defence, including your father-in-law and the President, am aware of. And now, of course, you. Not even your direct superior, Ron Goldman, knows about this information, and he can never know. Do you understand me?" Felicity nodded. Secretary Waller blinked to acknowledge her undertaking of secrecy, and then he delivered the news he hoped would not dismay this ambitious British woman. "In two months, it will be a year since we signed off on the Outer Space Treaty, a treaty which we will break because we do not trust the Soviet Union, and we believe they are probably in the final stages of weaponry development to be deployed from space, a programme which our covert operatives inform us has been on the Soviet's drawing table since the first Sputnik was launched over a decade ago. However, we plan to outdo them at their own game, and that is where Project Zeus comes into play. Indeed, the Hercules Rocket work you are undertaking at Canoga Park will be an integral feature of Project Zeus. Have you heard of the term 'Fractional Orbital Bombardment System', or FOBS for short?" Felicity shook her head. "I didn't think so. Its concept has only been known at the top end of the Defence establishment, and, of course, the White House. A FOBS is a nuclear warhead delivery system that uses a low Earth orbit to reach its target. Still, before reaching its target, it deorbits using a retrograde engine burn." Felicity nodded and spoke with some reservations. "I understand, but that is a ballistic missile launched from Earth, right?" Secretary Waller nodded and continued his spiel by patronising Felicity. "That is right. You are a clever girl."

Girl. 'I'm a woman.' If only her thoughts could have been heard. Secretary Waller continued. "Rather than launching the missile from Earth, it is launched from low Earth orbit. The FOBS is launched from Zeus, a hypersonic glide space craft or, as we refer to it, an HSG space aircraft that also uses retrograde rockets to re-enter Earth's atmosphere. Zeus is a test spacecraft, and given the United States' commitment to the Outer Space Treaty, we will test the HSG technology in high Earth orbit, effectively out of sight. We can at least surreptitiously conduct our tests to refine the technology without the Soviets knowing, and that is where the Israelis enter the picture." Felicity impetuously interrupted him. "But won't the Soviets detect the HSG's entry, and perhaps conclude that Zeus is performing more than scientific experiments in space?" Secretary Waller smiled at Theodore. "She is a bright girl. Yes, Dr Hoover, and that is where Israel enters the picture. You might have heard about the brutal murder of one of their government ministers several years ago?" Felicity vaguely remembered the news. "Yes, well, as the HSG descends from high Earth orbit, Israel will fire a FOBS, which, in coordination with the timing of the HSG entry, should keep the Soviets guessing. The HSG will return to high Earth orbit, whereas the FOBS will harmlessly land in the middle of the Atlantic Ocean. The Soviets' radars will be blind to your movements. We need you to work on these systems at Aerodyne's Reno facilities while continuing to work under Ron Goldman at Canoga Park. However, the programme must remain top secret, so we will not reveal the truth about Zeus to your husband until just before the mission."

Secretary Waller's words sent a chill down Felicity's spine. She was knowingly involved in breaking an international treaty. However, the lure of space, even if it was only in high Earth orbit, had a stronger gravitational pull on her mind than the morality screaming out from her heart. However, the doubt about the morality of Project Zeus still lingered.

Then, Felicity was also immediately consumed with fear about her relationship with Amelia. "What about visiting friends? For example, I recently reestablished ties with an old classmate from Woldingham days who is now a movie star. Amelia Tolhurst, you would have seen us on television several months ago. Am I able to maintain friendships with people outside of our clandestine little world?" Secretary Waller shook his head. "Don't be silly, Dr Hoover. Live your everyday life as you normally would. Visit your friend in Hollywood or wherever she lives. Visit the Queen of England, as far as I am concerned, I couldn't care less. Just don't mention your work. There is no need to be paranoid about your everyday life." That was a relief for Felicity because she and Amelia had already agreed their relationship could only occur behind the closed doors of Amelia's Hollywood Hills mansion.

Notwithstanding that her relationship with Amelia would not be closely scrutinised as they were only 'old school friends', Felicity had reservations about designing Zeus and testing it in space to be a spacecraft capable of launching FOBS. Theodore detected Felicity's discomfort, and he then turned his chair to face Felicity directly so that he could look her in the eyes. "Do you have a problem with what we're asking you to do, Felicity?" Of course, she did and had to express her thoughts verbally. "So, after years of service, whether it be when I transferred over to the United States Air Force or, working here at NASA, you're telling me that my pathway to fulfilling my career goal of flying into space requires me to design a spacecraft that can be deployed for military purposes to by stealth launch a nuclear warhead at the Soviet Union, and consequentially kill tens of thousands of people. Am I right about that fact?" Theodore didn't blink an eyelid as he returned her stare. "Yes."

Felicity stood up and walked over to the windows of the boardroom. The sky outside was beginning to look inhospitable as dark storm clouds started rolling in and the wind picked up. Nature appeared to be howling the word 'no'. Still, it was a guaranteed ticket to fly into space. Yet the consequences of this action were that the military and NASA were able to develop a spacecraft capable of being deployed for war, despite its purported noble purpose of advancing science. "She turned towards Theodore and Secretary Waller. "Give me a moment, please, to think this through." Secretary Waller stood up. "Take a few minutes to think about your role, but remember, as far as the world is concerned, you will be flying into space in several years, so I don't know how NASA will feel if you pull out of this history-making flight." Theodore and the Defence Secretary then stepped out of the boardroom.

If Felicity felt ambivalent before the press conference, she now felt trapped in a world of subterfuge, from which she would go down in history as the first woman to fly in space, albeit on the pretence of being the supposed wife of an astronaut, embedding the American myth of 'family values' into a society oblivious of its leaders' nefarious ways. Her heart told her to resign, divorce Dwight, and live happily with Amelia in any part of the world where they could in the bliss of anonymity. Still, her mind asked her how either of them could be anonymous? They were recognised faces worldwide. She had dreamt of flying in space since Sputnik first tormented the West with its presence. And as for Dwight and Amelia, well, Dwight was an oaf; she would have to continue to endure. Amelia had already discussed the need to keep their relationship within the confines of presenting to the public that they were 'old school friends reunited'. Once again, Felicity was allowing her impetuous nature to dictate her decisions rather than giving herself more time to think things through. 'Damn it, I will do it.' Then there was a knock on the door, followed by Theodore and Secretary Waller entering the boardroom. They didn't get a chance to ask the question, as Felicity already had the answer. "I am in." Secretary Waller smiled. "Excellent. We will meet again at Rocketdyne's Reno facilities in a fortnight, where you will be introduced to a handpicked team who will construct Zeus under your direction." Felicity nodded. "A fortnight; that is fine. Now, may I please go and telephone my father back in England, as I envisage the BBC News has probably already broken the news?" Both men smiled at each other and then nodded to permit Felicity to leave the boardroom.

That was one ordeal out of the way. Still, Felicity had to maintain a cheerful tone for her father and not reveal the sinister side of her mission. Then there was dealing with Dwight for a night, and many more in the years ahead. At least there was one pure light in her life: Amelia. However, even that light was dimmed by the circumstances of their working lives. If only Felicity had taken a few more minutes to think matters through.

CHAPTER 45

Thy arrow was dipped into the cauldron's poison to contaminate another's heart,
Yet, by venturing into that dark universe, thou sowed bad seeds from the start.

In the maze of the internal office spaces of NASA's administration building, Felicity found an unused office and a telephone to contact Samuel. It was 3:00 p.m. in Houston, which meant it was 9:00 p.m. back in Essex. The telephone dial tone barely rang once, and Samuel promptly answered it on the other end. "Felicity? Is that you calling?" The poor fellow had been waiting by the telephone for over an hour since the BBC had broken the news about his daughter being selected to fly into space. "Yes, Dad. It's me." His voice was jubilant. "Oh, I have been waiting for you to call. The BBC announced that you have been selected to fly into space with Dwight in a few years. Is that right about the time?" Felicity knew her father was intelligent, and his mind would have already questioned why there was such a long delay. "Yes, Dad. That is right." Samuel's jubilation could not be contained. "Oh, my darling baby. I am so proud of the woman you have become, and now you are achieving that dream you revealed to me years ago, when Sputnik was encircling the Earth. I almost cried tears of delight when I first heard the news, and I know you have discarded faith, but I can tell you now your mother would proudly smile down upon you."

Would she? Nevertheless, preserving the façade of American values required Felicity to maintain the confidentiality of her mission's true purpose. "Thank you, Dad. You always know how to make my heart glow. And, yes, Dwight and I will become the first husband-and-wife team to fly into space. And, yes, the Americans are delighted by the prospect, as am I." Her delighted tone even surprised herself in its authenticity. "My goodness, what a fantastic achievement. I know it was hard for you to come to terms with being unable to have a child; however, maybe that was a sign that your childhood dream would come true. I am so proud to be your father, Felicity." His words brought tears of joy to Felicity's eyes, yet pangs of guilt in her heart. "Oh, Dad, you don't know how much those words mean to me, even now." Samuel's curiosity could not be contained. "Tell me, please, sweetie, why will it take several years for your mission to become a reality?" Indeed, her father was intelligent. Time for the big lie to be told. "Well, Dad, isn't it obvious. The Americans are currently focused on landing the first man on the Moon, so there is a priority queue. Still, in two or so years, my mission will occur, and you can sit in the grandstand of Cape Canaveral and watch my rocket launch into space." Samuel would never have known that his daughter was also designing the spacecraft, nor would he have known Zeus's true purpose. "I understand, sweetie. The American ego must be satisfied first by landing a man on the Moon. Still, I will be excited for several years, waiting for the big day to arrive. In any event, I imagine you have many people to call, and it is still work time in America, so I had better end this call." Felicity longed to tell Samuel the truth about every detail of her life, but she couldn't. She had sold her principles for a ticket to fly in space. She had followed her heart to love another woman. She was trapped in a foreign land, living by her instincts, and she had sown the seeds of her destiny. All she could say was that at least one element of the truth remained in her life. "I love you, Dad, and I miss you." Now it was time to face Dwight.

It was 5:00 p.m. when the taxi arrived outside Dwight's apartment block. Felicity was not looking forward to spending the night in the premises with her estranged husband. She understood that from hereon, whenever she was required to attend NASA's headquarters, she would have to stay under the same roof as Dwight. Similarly, when he was required to travel to Los Angeles to participate in an event in Canoga Park, he faced the same dilemma. Felicity pressed the intercom for apartment number 666, and after a brief delay, Dwight answered. "It's Dwight. Who's there?" Who did he think was there? Felicity bit her tongue and attempted to be pleasant. "It's me, Dwight." Without any further words being spoken, the buzzer on the door alerted Felicity to it being remotely opened. With dread, she entered the building and caught the elevator to level six.

Felicity took a deep breath as she walked out of the elevator. The apartment block was relatively new, so it still had a lingering smell of fresh materials. The wallpaper in the hallway was the latest fashion of the 1960s, with large, brightly coloured flowers set against a background of white and thin lavender stripes. The wallpaper was very feminine and totally out of character for Dwight. Apartment 666 was right at the end of the long hallway, which was accompanied by the wallpaper, almost making the walk along it like a stroll in Alice in Wonderland, except there would be no tea party for Felicity to look forward to. When she arrived at the end of the hallway, Felicity saw that the two doors were closer together than the apartment doors she had passed by earlier in the hallway, and apartment 666 was on the right. Soon she would discover why. Still, she now had to build up her strength of diplomacy to make it through this evening.

After taking another few deep breaths, Felicity knocked on the woodgrain door. Moments later, Dwight opened the front door. He had a smile on his face like when they first started dating, which only made the moment even more difficult for Felicity to maintain a pleasant exterior. "Hi. Come on in." Dwight did not even bother to offer to assist Felicity with her travel bag. She stepped over the threshold of the apartment, a threshold that felt like it belonged to another woman. Then the décor immediately inside the apartment revealed that another woman's touch had been applied, as feminine-framed prints of flowers hung on the wall of the short entrance hallway. The apartment was small, featuring only one bedroom, one bathroom, an open-plan living area, and a combined dining and kitchen space. Opening the door to the bedroom revealed an unmade bed, a typical sight for Dwight. In the open plan area, two large windows looked out onto parkland and houses down the street. There was also a lounge, which Dwight had stopped in front of. "This sofa makes a pretty comfortable bed." Felicity looked at the sofa, and it looked new and clean. Dwight broke the silence. "I didn't think you would want to sleep in the bedroom, because that is where I..." He didn't finish his sentence. Still, he didn't need to because Felicity could finish it for him. "Because that is where you and Jolene slept together, Dwight. What did you think? That we would sleep together again?" Dwight did not sense sarcasm or understand that it was a rhetorical question. "Well, we are still married." Felicity raised her eyes to the ceiling, and then she turned around and placed her travel bag on the round dining table to retrieve the material Secretary Waller had handed to her during their meeting.

Dwight stood in the same spot where he had just been given the deserved cold shoulder by Felicity. There was no food in the apartment for dinner, and he wanted to speak to Jolene, so he found an excuse to leave. "I don't have any food in the fridge for dinner, and there is a nice pizza restaurant, which is about a five-minute drive from here. Do you want me to get you some pizza for your dinner?" As Felicity extracted the bound documents from her travel bag, she half turned back towards Dwight. "Yes, please. Pepperoni will be fine, thank you. "Felicity turned back around, and as Dwight picked up his car keys from the coffee table in front of the sofa, Felicity had one final blunt parting message. "Oh, Dwight,

I forgot to say, take as long as you want to call Jolene from wherever it is you are going to. I imagine you might have a bit of explaining to do with her about our, what is the word I'm looking for? Arrangement. Yes, explain to her it's an arrangement rather than a reconciliation." With those crisp words spoken, Dwight left the apartment, slamming the door in a feeble display of dominance.

Felicity found the electric kettle, a clean cup and, typical of Dwight, a box of teabags in one of the kitchen cupboards. After her tea, Felicity sat down and studied the material Secretary Waller had provided her that afternoon. The concepts that NASA and the Department of Defence had considered regarding the FOBS were feasible; however, the HSG spacecraft's engineering design and functionality were a mess. Designing a new HSG spacecraft meant Felicity had a lot of work to do if Zeus was to be launched in about two years. She realised she would be the only trained astrophysicist and engineer in the crew being assembled at Reno, meaning she would have to handle all the design work. This would likely involve living out of a travel bag in Reno for as long as she worked at Canoga Park. "Oh well, at least there will be fewer occasions for me and Dwight to be together", Felicity said in mocking relief as she started making notes in the document.

Dwight returned with the pizza at about 7:00 p.m. When he entered the apartment, Felicity could not contain her tongue. "That took a long time. Did you have much explaining to do with wife number two, Dwight?" He put the pizza box in front of her, which had begun to sag because of the heat. "Yes, I did have a lot explaining to do. However, eventually, Jolene was fine, and I also got to speak to Dwight Junior." The mystery baby's name had finally been revealed. "Well, that must make your mother and sister happy that he is named after you." Dwight huffed at Felicity's apparent barb at his family. He sat on the sofa, eating pizza from his box while watching the news on TV, while Felicity retrieved a plate from the kitchen cupboard and a knife and fork from the drawer to eat her pizza. Dwight otherwise displayed little interest in the material Felicity had been studying at the dining table.

After several minutes, Dwight leapt to his feet, and with a piece of pizza in his right hand, he pointed at the television in great excitement and hollered out loud. "Heh. There we are. We're on the news." Felicity was slightly startled by Dwight's unusual display of jubilation about them being on the news, but soon she realised he was jubilant about himself. She could not put up with the arrangement without asking Dwight some necessary questions. "Dwight, while you're in a good mood, I wanted to ask some questions, please." He sat heavily on the sofa, disappointed that he was being interrupted while watching himself on television. "What is it, Felicity? Can't we make this work, without asking questions that I know will be about me, Jolene and the baby?" Felicity crossed her arms as she shook her head. "No, Dwight. I deserve to know the answers. At least give me that tonight, and I will never ask you again." He reluctantly nodded. "Okay. Fire away."

Fire away. He asked for it, so he shall receive. "What attracted you to Jolene so much that you did not even have the decency to tell me our marriage was over before you had sex with her?" A blunt question received a blunt reply. "She fulfilled my needs that you couldn't do." Needs? The ambit of Dwight's needs could be anything from opening a packet of crisps for him, through to having to endure his mechanical sexual interaction. "Enlighten me about the 'needs', please, Dwight." He dropped his eyes to the floor, a sure sign he would lie. "Don't look at the floor, Dwight. Look me in the eye and tell me about these needs. If we are in space for at least a week, at the very least, tell me the truth about why I could not fulfil your needs. Was it that I could not have a baby?" He looked her in the eye. "Yes. Okay, that was part of it. And Jolene makes me feel sexual in bed. I felt like I was on top of a starfish with you." Felicity had an inkling it was a sexual attraction, and as for a baby, there were no surprises there, either. "I thought so. Is she pretty, Dwight? Do your mother and sister approve of her?" He nodded. "It's yes to both of your questions." Felicity had one more question to ask him, which she needed to ask to heal her wounded pride. "Did you ever intend to honour your wedding vow? I mean, not enough, it seems. No. I meant to ask why you asked me to marry you. Why, Dwight?" His answer surprised her. "Because you were good for my career. I would not have made it through my training as an astronaut if I didn't have that brain of yours to call upon. And, you wanted to stay in the country to have a shot at NASA, so I guess it was a mutual favour. I was not a ladies' man, Felicity. I was a goofball son of a father who had lost his firstborn pride and joy in a war. You were nice to me. When we found out about you being unable to have a child, I immediately realised I had made a mistake. I met Jolene, and for the first time in my life, I had someone who genuinely appreciated me. Let's be honest with you: I was a ticket to NASA. We even acknowledged that when I proposed to you. Did you ever love me, Felicity?" Her response was prompt, a lie intended to wound his heart and make him submissive to what she claimed was the truth. "Yes, I did. But you cheated.

So, now I don't feel that way." Dwight was made to feel an inch high. Felicity had her answer, which strangely made her feel better about herself and reinforced the importance of her relationship with Amelia. After momentarily processing Dwight's words, she broke the nervous tension and guilt he was suffering from. "Well, thank you for your honesty. Now, I want to go to sleep soon, so I will have to use that sofa as soon as you have finished eating."

The following day, Felicity and Dwight pretended to be the excited husband-and-wife team wishing to preserve America's family values in space when they appeared before the NASA oversight committee. As far as the committee was concerned, Project Zeus would be funded by Congress.

Eventually, when she returned to Winnetka, Felicity called Amelia for her much-needed satisfaction. They talked for several hours without discussing their respective work lives. Amelia tantalised Felicity's eroticism by telling her how she would gently make love to her when they met up again. Felicity responded in kind. Each of their words had a loving intention, which only made the recipient hunger for the other's heart more. If only Amelia could have revealed her circumstances in France and how Lilith was treating her, Felicity would have moved heaven and earth for her to escape that woman's iniquitous ways. Perhaps Amelia would not have continued to be jettisoned down the flightpath as a broken bird.

CHAPTER 46

Lucifer unleashed an armoury of evil as the horsemen ascended from hell,
And his whore would pay the price, as his deathly hand tolled the bell.

A yearning heart can only be interrupted by a fervent mind consumed with creating a monster to satisfy its goal in life. Felicity's first meeting at Reno with the crew of men who would construct Zeus was as clinical as it was certain. Theodore attended that meeting, and each man was left in no doubt that Felicity was in charge of them. Finally, after years of submissiveness, Felicity would be in charge. However, behind closed doors, Theodore told her that authority was limited to the men on the floor. Otherwise, she was answerable to him, Secretary Waller, Ted, and, of course, the President.

When working with Ron, Felicity contemporaneously examined the functionality of the Hercules rocket, the retrorocket used to slow the command module for lunar orbit, and the descent rocket used for landing the lunar module on the Moon's surface. Ron was impressed with Felicity's dedication, but he was not his usual self. He seemed not as sharp-witted as he had once been, physically weaker, and his mind was distracted. Felicity would inquire about his disposition; however, he would dismiss it, attributing it to his constant work for NASA and several universities over the past decade. The notes Felicity made about the Hercules Rocket and its other components destined for the Moon would be utilised by her when she worked at night in the privacy of her home in Winnetka or, when she was required in Reno, at Rocketdyne's facilities in that city. Her work ratio had been so imbalanced that she hardly noticed that almost six months had passed since the infamous announcement of the Zeus mission. When Ron pressed her for information about Zeus, Felicity would play dumb by telling him it was above her pay grade.

The moments arose when she had to either stay in Dwight's apartment in Houston or have Dwight remain at her home in Winnetka. They were civil to each other in private, but otherwise, they were very much estranged. Outside of their respective homes, they kept up the public image of the happy married couple preparing to embark on their journey into space at some future time.

By early April 1969, the final contractual film for Independent Artists' Studios that Amelia was working on had almost been completed. Sokolov had been deployed to Paris by Volkov several months beforehand. Through Otlowski, Walter contacted Sokolov shortly after the KGB agent had arrived in Paris. He informed Sokolov that Lilith usually kept a tight rein on Amelia, and her work schedule on this film had been gruelling, so he did not anticipate there would be much spare time for the young actress until towards the end of her filming schedule. However, Walter did reveal to Sokolov that on the infrequent occasions when Amelia was free to explore the lesbian culture of Paris, she would attend New Moon, a lesbian cabaret and bar located in Place Pigalle; however, because she was committed to Felicity Hoover, Amelia had not had any liaisons with the lesbians attending the club. Sokolov was content to bide his time, and unbeknownst to Walter, he surreptitiously followed Amelia when she was not filming to understand her activities outside the confines of film production. It did not take Sokolov too long to ascertain that Amelia had expensive tastes and was likely to be lured by the source of all evil: money.

Amelia had agreed with Walter to send him back to Los Angeles two weeks before the end of filming, both of them believing she no longer needed him to chaperone her. How misguided of them to have thought so would be measured by the events to follow in those final weeks of filming. Although the production of the final contracted film was coming to its conclusion, Lilith was not finished yet with having her way with Amelia, and she was already setting the wheels in motion to undermine Amelia's ability to work for any other studio. Lilith was obsessed with Amelia, considering her to be her property; such was the deranged and depraved claim she believed she had over the actress. When she heard the new French director, Raphael Leroy, whom she had hired for the final instalment of the trilogy of period setting epics, was in concert with Penny Long trying to secure Amelia a contract with the French film production company Les Films Corona, Lilith seethed in a tempest of paranoia, obsession and revenge to destroy Penny Long's agency back in Los Angeles, and undermine Amelia's reputation in Tinsel Town, so that her options for work would be restricted to Independent Artists' Studio. The undermining of Amelia's career in America had suddenly materialised in Amelia's television series, inexplicably replacing her in the lead role. Penny Long informed Amelia about the role replacement. Penny could not explain why this had occurred, and she, too, felt Lilith's cruel and invisible influence in

Hollywood, as her agency was losing actors and actresses to other agents. The Martins might have been seen as an avant-garde studio, but they held a position of power in Hollywood that made or broke people.

Lilith had not finished endeavouring to punish Amelia for her conduct, which she considered the height of disloyalty. She changed the script for the final scene, much to Raphael's protestations. Lilith's script change would transform the movie's conclusion from depicting Amelia as a heroine who escapes the Medieval church's reign of terror to portraying her as a victim burned at the stake. To add to the drastic change in the script, Lilith wanted Amelia's hair to be totally shaven all over her body as she perished in the flames. Raphael found the notion of changing the plot and altering the appearance of the movie's heroine an unnecessary and illogical conclusion to the trilogy. Yet it was Lilith's film, and she had her way, although she required Raphael to swear to silence about the change or else the final instalment of his salary would not be paid. The director cursed at her in French when Lilith threatened him; however, he was young and needed the money, so against his better judgment, he agreed to hold his tongue.

Amelia was oblivious to the changes to the script and the requirements for her appearance, which meant her trademark hair would be removed and her head shaved. Her hair had defined her screen career in any role, and Lilith knew it would torture Amelia to remove her hair. Lilith's sadomasochistic proclivities inflicted on Amelia had already gone beyond the ambit of previous conduct with the young actress. Still, she drew pleasure from the idea of not just removing the hair on her head, but also removing all her bodily hair, before then exposing Amelia to the most depraved sexual activity yet. Amelia had been summoned to attend Lilith's villa by 3:00 p.m. on the last Friday before the last week of filming. Only Lilith was present when she arrived at the villa. She handed Amelia a cocktail that had been laced with diazepam. By 4:00 p.m., Amelia had passed out in a drug-induced sleep.

Amelia started waking up from her drugged state at about 9:00 p.m. Through her blurred vision, she could see that she was on a four-post bed. She recognised enough features of the bed to presume it was Lilith's. However, Amelia could not move her arms and legs, which had all been chained to the four posts of Lilith's bed, leaving her spreadeagled and immobile. Her blurred vision revealed the figure of a woman standing at the end of the bed. Although she could not see her head, Amelia could feel that it had been shaved, as had her vaginal hair and eyebrows. Her vision soon detected the outline of Lilith's facial features. Amelia immediately felt alarmed. "What are you doing to me, Lilith? Why have you chained me to your bed? Why have you shaved my hair off? You bitch!" Lilith slowly began to walk closer towards Amelia. When she was close enough, Amelia saw that the costume she was wearing was a Nazi officer's uniform, and the ominous sign of a man-like bulge under her trousers. Lilith's tone was cold and calculated. "Did you think you could sneak away from me, you little whore? If it weren't for my husband and me, you would be doing advertisements in Arkansas by now. So now you will finish the film as a filthy whore being burned at the stake; there will not be any triumphant finish for you. I will make you pay for being so disloyal to me." For the remainder of that evening, Lilith sexually abused Amelia and, descending to even more depraved levels, she tortured her physically and mentally. At about midnight, the abuse broke Amelia; her mind would never be the same again.

It was 1:00 a.m. on Saturday when Amelia eventually returned to her rented apartment on the banks of the Seine. She was distraught, and when she looked in the mirror to see her bald head and missing eyebrows, she was simultaneously consumed by grief and hatred; grief that Lilith had taken away her lifelong beautiful hair, and hatred for Lilith that manifested in a desire for revenge for her years of abuse. She was oblivious to being watched and followed from a distance by Sokolov the previous afternoon and that morning, but he had noted her missing hair when he saw her leave Lilith's villa.

Sokolov had arranged for Anatoli to enter France via Monaco about a fortnight before the filming was scheduled to conclude. After the debacle with Saar, Anatoli was kept waiting in a Haussmannian apartment just south of Montmartre in Paris, awaiting deployment to make his presence known to Amelia when the opportunity arose. Over the past few months, Sokolov had observed Amelia occasionally attend New Moon, but she never left the establishment in the company of another woman. On this particular Saturday morning, when he observed Amelia's state when she left Lilith's villa, his instincts informed him that Amelia was unlikely to return to Lilith's that night. Having observed Amelia's emotional state, Sokolov's instincts told him that she was likely to go out Saturday night to New Moon, and regarding her state of mind, she might be vulnerable enough to be seduced by Anatoli. He slept in the car near her apartment. He followed her when she subsequently emerged from the building in the late morning of that Saturday, with her head covered by a scarf tied around it. He observed her enter a wig shop, and about an hour later, she emerged wearing a long red wig and carrying a bag that appeared to contain another wig. Then Sokolov followed Amelia to a beautician's shop, and about half an hour later, he saw her leave that shop with what appeared to be perfectly applied fake eyebrows. He surmised the young actress was more than likely to attend New Moon that night, which meant it was time for Anatoli to be deployed to the fashionable club.

As sure as night followed day, Sokolov's instincts were correct. At about 8:00 p.m., he observed Amelia leave her apartment. Shortly after stepping outside, a taxi arrived, and she entered it. He followed the taxi and, eventually, as he had previously surmised, the taxi arrived outside New Moon. Amelia exited the taxi and quickly made her way into New Moon. Sokolov parked his car around the next corner on Rue Victor Masse. Sokolov briskly walked to the nearest public telephone and called Anatoli. His message was simple: It was now or never, so get to New Moon at 66 Rue Pigalle as quickly as possible.

It was 10:00 p.m. when Anatoli arrived in a taxi, looking his glamorous best, and speaking with his finest, feminine French accent. Sokolov showed Anatoli a photograph of Amelia again, so her image was fresh in her mind. Still, he was also told that she was wearing a distinctive red wig. Anatoli then entered New Moon, and it did not take him too long to discover Amelia leaning against the bar, being harassed by a woman in her fifties who wished to take advantage of the intoxicated actress. As Anatoli walked towards Amelia, her eyes lit up with delight, because as far as she could tell, Felicity was walking towards her. But as Anatoli drew closer, Amelia began to realise this person, who looked remarkably like Felicity, was not her at all, as her breasts were noticeably larger than her girlfriend's back in California. She was committed to her relationship with Felicity. However, she had spent so much time on the telephone talking to Felicity about their next liaison, and Lilith had broken her mind, that now, notwithstanding her feelings for Felicity, she desired anybody who closely resembled that tender woman. Anatoli opened the exchange with the starlet. His accent sent electric waves through her intoxicated senses. "May I buy a special cocktail for the most beautiful woman in the room?" He had hooked his fish. "Sure. Buy me anything you want, but please, what is your name?" Anatoli effortlessly provided his false name. "I am Josephine; Josephine Durand. And you?" Amelia smiled sheepishly at this person who looked remarkably similar to Felicity. "Surely you must know who I am?" Anatoli shook his head while holding up twenty francs. "No, I don't. Still, I want to get to know you very well tonight, and save you from these old hags trying to misuse your beautiful face and body."

The old barman was a face from Anatoli's past: Lucien. Anatoli's face might have been surgically altered, but Lucien could never forget those eyes. Anatoli did not recognise Lucien, as the man had aged, and their previous encounter with each other had been an ephemeral moment in Anatoli's life of murder sprees. Lucien nervously asked Anatoli for the order. Two French 75s were ordered. Anatoli turned back to Amelia, whose eyes displayed an obvious amorous intent as she spoke. "I have a girlfriend back in California who looks just like you. I shouldn't be talking to you since I am committed to her, but what the heck. I am in another country, I am a little bit drunk, you look just like her, and I am feeling filthy tonight. Would you like to get filthy with me?" Circumstances were unfolding more quickly than Anatoli had anticipated. Still, his mission was to become involved in Amelia's life, because unbeknownst to her, Walter had made contact with Sokolov, and in doing so, he informed him that Amelia was definitely in a relationship with Dr Felicity Hoover, so if Anatoli looked anything like Felicity, Amelia would be like putty in his hands. Lucien served the 75s, and Amelia threw caution to the wind and consumed her glass in one gulp. Her back was turned to the bar, so Lucien never got a proper look at her face; however, the distinctive red wig was noticeable. After Amelia gulped down the cocktail, she then passionately kissed Anatoli's lips. "Come on, Josephine. Let's not waste any more time around these old dykes. Take me home to your house and make love to me all night. I want to be filthy with you." Anatoli placed his cocktail glass on the bar and walked out of the club with Amelia, dragging him. She hailed a taxi outside New Moon, and when they entered, Anatoli provided the address of his apartment. Meanwhile, Lucien thought that he should visit the police the next day to report his sighting of the person whom the authorities believed had murdered Saar several years ago.

When they entered the apartment, Amelia wasted no time wanting to make love to her newfound friend, Josephine. She stripped down the top of Anatoli's silk dress to reveal her perfectly shaped breasts. The surgery had been so delicate that there was no visible hint of a scar. Amelia grabbed Anatoli's breasts with glee while inserting her tongue into his mouth. Anatoli had never made love to a woman before, and he was slightly unsure about what he should do. However, that all changed when Amelia reached down under Anatoli's skirt, and in placing her hand under her panties, she was surprised to find a penis where a vagina should be. Anatoli thought this discovery would scare Amelia. Instead, her eyes lit up with delight. "Oh, you are a dream come true. I have never made love to a transvestite before. Tonight is my lucky night, but Josephine, please, can I call out my girlfriend's name, to add to the splendour of being with you?" Anatoli felt aroused by Amelia's delicate fondling of his penis; unlike the men who had brutally used his body before he disposed of them, this was tender. "Sure. You can call me whatever name you like." They wrapped their arms around each other, and as promised, Amelia was filthy with him, yet also tender. Her tenderness had struck a chord in Anatoli's otherwise cold heart.

CHAPTER 47

*Thou shalt not kill, thundered the Omnipotent from the top of the Mount;
However, money is like honey, and it's acquired too many souls to count.*

Anatoli opened his eyes the following morning. The sunlight was bright, signifying that he had overslept. He felt a body next to him, and when he turned in the bed, the exposed naked body of Amelia was still sleeping next to him. His heart had never felt the strange sensation that ran through it now; he felt attracted to this woman – indeed, he had felt the mesmerising touch of love that had been missing from his life. Amelia Tolhurst was only meant to be a target; however, Cupid's arrow had unwittingly struck Anatoli, and he had never felt more confused in his tortured life.

Anatoli reached for the packet of cigarettes he kept next to his bed, and after lighting one, he felt a soft hand on his back. He turned around as he blew a puff of smoke out. Amelia's eyes were partially opened, and her head was slightly sore from consuming too much alcohol the previous night. She smiled as her eyes focused on Anatoli's face. "Goodness me, you look so much like Felicity, it is uncanny. Can I have a puff on that, please?" Anatoli handed her the packet of cigarettes and a box of matches. "Take one for yourself. How is your head?" After Amelia had lit the cigarette, she coughed as she spoke. "It's been better." She drew on the cigarette again and then sat on the bed. "Your name is not Josephine. I mean, that is obvious. But who are you? And why do you look so much like my girlfriend?"

Anatoli stood up. His naked body was so feminine, so perfectly shaped, that his penis otherwise looked out of place. Considering the lengthy and frenetic sexual activity he had participated in with Amelia, he felt the moment was right to reveal his identity and what he could offer her in return for her assistance. But he was meant to be menacing her, whereas all he could do now was obsequiously implore her. His smooth accent transitioned from French to Russian, like a person could effortlessly change their shirt. "My name is Anatoli. I am a KGB agent. I have been moulded to look like a woman since the KGB first took me in as a young man because they wanted to have a trans man out in the field, ready to liaise with men who sought the pleasure of a transvestite. My face has often been operated on many times to make me look more feminine. Still, the last operation was several years ago, after my commanding comrade saw a newspaper picture of your girlfriend, Dr Felicity Hoover. Thanks to your manager, we know she is your girlfriend." Amelia stubbed out her cigarette in anger, surprising Anatoli with her vicious tone. "That horrible little faggot. Who else has he talked to about my relationship with Felicity? I could stab that little faggot right in the heart if he were standing here now! Who else has he told?" Her eyes revealed the truth; she could kill Walter right now. The irony of the circumstances; the trained killer was alarmed by the killer look in Amelia's eyes. Anatoli placed his right hand gently on Amelia's arm, a physical reaction that even surprised him that he was capable of such tenderness. "Don't worry; only the KGB knows about your relationship with her." Amelia's mind might have been broken, but this news about the breach of privacy committed by her manager angered her. "Damn, Walter! Goddamn him!"

Amelia got out of bed and paced back and forth naked and in anger, which only seemed to arouse Anatoli more, as his eyes savoured every inch of Amelia's immaculate skin. She was furious about her manager's deceit. Still, while her mind was occupied with anger, a graver question than her manager's failings began to emerge. She stopped pacing and turned towards Anatoli. "So, why were you sent to New Moon to meet me?" Anatoli's response was clear. "I need you to inform us about what Dr Hoover is working on with NASA, and in return, we will pay you more money than your sick studio bosses are paying you. We will pay you more money than anyone in Hollywood would pay you." Reveal her girlfriend's work to an enemy? Amelia was about to speak, but Anatoli persisted with the offer. "And, if you agree to help us, we will help you, and we will protect you, including, if need be, killing anyone who tries to harm you." Anatoli's eyes fixed on Amelia to determine how she would react, because if she said no, he had been ordered to kill her; however, he was conflicted now, as he couldn't do that, as, on this occasion, he was the spider caught in her web. He was taking a considerable risk, but if she said no, he could not kill her. However, he sensed from her eyes when he mentioned killing a person that her mindset had changed from surprise to interest.

She shook her head to clear it and opened her eyes to reveal the information overload running through her mind. Eventually, she spoke. "Well, you certainly don't mess about being candid with people. So, what you're asking me to do is help you spy on America by using my girlfriend and me. Is that correct?" Anatoli nodded. Amelia took a deep breath. She turned to face the window, and as far as Anatoli was concerned, the faint light coming through the window shone like a halo around her head. She loved Felicity. 'How could I betray our love?' Then, as a cloud blocked the light beams, the reality of her career being in ruins clouded her mind. She had been poor once before when her parents were bankrupt, and now she was at risk of being poor again.

It seemed like an eternity, but eventually, after half a minute, Amelia turned around again to face Anatoli, and her eyes were as menacing as any that Anatoli had seen. Her voice was as cold as ice. "How much?" Her cold disposition surprised Anatoli; little did he realise that Amelia had already sensed that he was enamoured with her. "We will pay you $60,000.00 monthly into your chosen bank account. However, might I suggest you select one in Switzerland because that will make the transaction easier to accomplish and more difficult for your CIA to detect. Your manager can help you, as he has already opened an account for himself." The news of Walter's misdeeds was overwhelmed by the sum of money on offer. $60,000.00 a month! That was more than Amelia could make in a year from her movie and television contracts. She picked up Anatoli's cigarette packet and lit another cigarette. She blew out the smoke, and in doing so, she stared down Anatoli. "Are you serious? Will the Soviet Union pay me $60,000.00 a month to acquire information from Felicity about her work?" Anatoli nodded again. Her quizzical expression revealed to Anatoli the question even before it was asked. "Well, what if she won't tell me anything? She has told me numerous times that she cannot discuss her work for national security reasons. What happens then?" Anatoli walked over to her side of the bed to meet her eye-to-eye. "If she won't tell you anything, introduce me to her, and I will obtain the information. We need to know what the Americans are up to with Project Zeus before it launches into space. So, you have about eighteen months to work away on her." Amelia put out her cigarette in the ashtray next to the bed. To obtain the roles she had to date, Amelia had to effectively sell her body to Hollywood executives, and every actress has a limited shelf life. Yet, Lilith's evil ways had prematurely truncated her shelf life, and, in addition, she had been treated in such an unedifying and ignominious way by that bitch. "Well, I want proof that you will act on my wishes by killing someone for me, now. If you do so, of course, it's a yes."

Her eyes revealed a pain that unwittingly played to Anatoli's sense of indignation about his treatment. Still, Anatoli was not expecting to have to kill another person right now. "Who do you want me to kill?" Amelia forcibly removed the red wig from her head, which the shop had glued in place the previous day. "The bitch who did this to me. My film producer. Lilith Martin. And she is living here on her own as her grotesque husband is back in L.A. I hate her, and I want her dead. If you are being honest with me, then will you kill her for me?" She fluttered her eyelashes like a damsel in distress, snaring Anatoli's heartstrings in the process. Anatoli could tell by the look in Amelia's eyes that she was deadly serious. He nodded. "Okay. I will kill her tonight. However, it will be obvious to the police that people working around her are suspects, and your missing hair will likely attract their attention. You need an alibi for the next twenty-four hours. Is there anybody you can stay with?" Indeed, there was. There was a person who wanted her to work with him on more French films. "Yes. Yes, there is. The director of my film. Raphael. He is married, but I have met his wife, and she knows I am no threat to her. I could ask him to come and stay with him until we resume filming. He won't suspect anything and, in any event, he also hates Lilith." Anatoli nodded about the arrangement, but then he checked to ensure she was serious about assisting the KGB. "Alright, consider it done. But once I have killed this woman, there is no turning back for you. You are one of us. Do you understand me?" His sinister voice underscored the deadly outcome of reneging on the deal. Amelia's mind was broken, so she did not even think about the consequences if she reneged on the agreement. "I understand you." As Anatoli was about to leave, Amelia revealed the grave nature of Lilith's sexual abuse, and her distress was genuine, which only instilled malice in Anatoli's heart. "She sodomised me on Friday evening, Anatoli. It wasn't the first time she had subjected me to that. However, on this occasion, she had humiliated me by shaving my hair off, and, to make it worse, she was dressed in a Nazi uniform as she sodomised me with that metal thing she ties around herself. You kill that Nazi bitch, Anatoli. You kill like you have never killed anybody in that manner before." Another chord inside Anatoli was struck as his mind wandered back to the night in the gaol cell. The thought of the Nazi uniform only embedded his vicious intent. He was now motivated by hatred to subject Lilith to degrading treatment before slitting her throat. He nodded at Amelia to confirm the deal was done.

Amelia then got dressed and caught a taxi back to her apartment. She was lost in the world of greed and revenge. When she called Raphael to ask if she could stay at his home for the next few nights, she explained that Lilith had told her on Friday to remove all her hair. Now, having done so, she felt vulnerable and needed some company. Raphael agreed that she should stay with him without asking her further questions. She packed her bag with two nights' worth of clothing and her makeup and applied the glue to her head to put on the black wig. Before leaving, Amelia called Walter back in L.A. and told him in no uncertain terms how unhappy she was that he breached her trust. Walter was very matter-of-fact in response – "Sack me and I go straight to the authorities and turn you in, so get over it." Amelia was displeased with him, but she needed to protect herself by establishing an alibi. Whether she liked it or not, Walter was now entangled in her iniquity. She then caught a taxi to La Courneuve to stay with Raphael and his wife, where she would explain to them that Lilith had told her about the change to the film's ending on Friday. Her best acting to date was portraying her reluctant agreement to the script change, and Lilith cutting off her hair on Friday evening, much to the dismay of Raphael and his trusting wife, Eloise. Eliose, a committed feminist, congratulated Amelia on her bravery in pursuing her art. They were none the wiser to the fact that, as they sat down to dinner, Anatoli was brutally murdering Lilith after having sodomised her in an ill-thought-out act of revenge for that woman's treatment of Amelia. Like Saar, he had unwittingly left traces of seminal fluid for investigators to find.

Lucien had attended the nearest police station to his home that Saturday afternoon to report his sighting of Anatoli, only to be told to come back on Monday when the detectives could be contacted. It was lazy police work, providing an unexpected opening for Anatoli to slip out of France after killing Lilith.

Lilith's body was not discovered until Sunday morning, when the la femme de chambre returned to the villa after her night off. The French police officers contacted Raphael, who was shocked to hear the news, and they told him it appeared from the doctor's examination as though Lilith had been murdered sometime the previous evening. When asked whether he suspected any of the film crew or actors, he could not identify anyone. The central star had been staying with him and his wife since approximately 1:00 p.m. on Saturday. The alibi was unimpeachable in its veracity. Some specific details about Lilith's murder remained a matter of police secrecy, and her death was not revealed to the French media until late on Sunday.

Eventually, during the middle of the morning the following day, one of the detectives who had worked on Saar's murder case spoke to Lucien. When Lucien informed the detective that he was positive Saar's murderer had been at New Moon the previous Friday evening, a call was immediately placed to Mossad in Tel Aviv. The call was promptly sent to Aharon Kohen, who informed the police he would catch the next flight to Paris and asked them to hold Lucien until he arrived later that night. Subsequently, during their interview, Lucien told Kohen that the woman whom he saw with Saar that night was murdered, had left New Moon with a red-headed woman, whose face he had not had a proper opportunity to view on Friday evening. The French police told Kohen that an American film producer had been murdered during the evening of Saturday just passed, and the doctor performing the autopsy had detected semen in her anus. Still, there were no suspects, and everyone working on the film had alibis. However, notwithstanding the bumbled handling of Lucien, Kohen suspected there was a link between Saar's murder, Lilith Martin's murder, and the members of the cast and crew of the film. Kohen noted that the last member of the cast or crew to see Lilith alive was Amelia, and that was about twenty-four hours before her murder. She might have an alibi, but Kohen would now closely monitor Amelia Tolhurst's activities. He did not wish to share his suspicions with the CIA, as Kohen considered them to be just as clumsy as the French authorities. No, he and his team at Mossad would now closely monitor Amelia, without informing the Americans. The French police had to be involved, but Kohen would control them.

As for the film, filming continued that week, including the rewritten final scene. In the meantime, Amelia signed a contract to star in two movies for Les Films Corona, to be made over the next two years, with Raphael as their director. The contract was not as lucrative as the American contracts, but it was still film work. She would remain in the lion's den of Paris for another month to assist the costume and production department of Les Films Corona for the commencement of filming the first movie in four months. Kohen was watching and, with the help of the French police, listening.

CHAPTER 48

Thou had made thyself complicit in amassing Hell's Armageddon,
And for thy sins, thou might incur the consequences of that burden.

When the news broke in the United States about the murder of Lilith, Felicity was in lockdown at Rocketdyne's Palomino Valley facilities, which were not only secured so that nobody could enter the facilities, but also there was an information blackout to the outside world. Rocketdyne and NASA staff lived onsite, and the production facilities were state-of-the-art, compared to the aging facilities at Canoga Park. White walls and ceilings were the uniform colour throughout the Reno facilities, whether in the workspaces or the accommodation. In consultation with Rocketdyne's staff regarding what could feasibly be manufactured for Project Zeus within the remaining eighteen-month timeframe, Felicity could draft a complete set of plans for Zeus, which included the HSG and FOBS, by the end of April 1969.

Felicity returned to Winnetka in early May 1969, having been in lockdown at Reno for six weeks. She called Amelia's home number in Los Angeles, only to be informed by Walter that Amelia was still in France. He told Felicity that Amelia had secured a two-movie contract with Les Films Corona in France, which meant she would need to spend more time there over the next two years; therefore, she had rented a small villa on the French Riviera. Still, he anticipated she would return to Los Angeles in about two months, for a three-month stay before jetting off to France again to produce the first movie. Then, Walter broke the news to Felicity about Lilith's murder, which came as a shock to her because she had been under an information lockdown. Felicity was alarmed to hear this news, and she asked him whether he had Amelia's new telephone number. Of course, he did, and Walter provided Felicity with the contact number for Amelia in France. 'She must be earning a fortune,' Felicity thought to herself as she wrote down the telephone number.

At 9:00 a.m. on Saturday, May 10, 1969, Felicity called the new telephone number in Paris for Amelia, which Walter had provided to Felicity the previous evening. Although it was 6:00 p.m. in Paris, Kohen and the French police were monitoring and recording the call – a telephone call that would go down in infamy. After four dial tones, Amelia answered the telephone. Her voice had the distinct sound of being under the influence of liquor. "Hello, it's Amelia, darlings." It was a unique way to answer a telephone call, and Felicity was unequivocally sure Amelia was drunk. "Hello Amelia, it's me, sweetheart. Are you alright?" There was the distinct sound of crystalware clinking against the telephone receiver, followed by a slurping sound. Undeniably drunk. "Felicity, my sweetheart. Where have you been the past month? I have been trying to call you, so that I could hear the sweet sound of your voice as we talk about making love to each other again." Two French police officers and Kohen looked at each other; Amelia Tolhurst and another English woman, Felicity, were making love.

Felicity was brief in her response. "Amelia, I have been busy with work." Amelia's intoxication subtly militated against her. "What have you been working on, darling, that you cannot tell the best lover you've had?" Felicity changed the topic of her discussion. "You know we can't discuss my work. Anyway, Walter told me about the murder of Lilith Martin. I had not heard that news until this morning. Are you coping?" Amelia giggled before responding. "I will be better when I get to kiss those lips of yours again, my sweet little Dr Hoover." Simultaneously, Kohen and one of the French police officers made a note: 'Amelia Tolhurst and English woman Dr Felicity Hoover talking about kissing each other.' The name Dr Felicity Hoover sounded familiar to Kohen, but he could not identify why.

Felicity tried to keep Amelia focused on the question she had asked her. "Amelia, sweetie, please answer my question. Are you okay after Lilith Martin was murdered?" Amelia was petulant in her intoxicated state. "Of course I am okay. That bitch had it coming to her. I hope the guy who did it was brutal with her." Kohen made a note that confirmed the thoughts of the two French police officers. 'Tolhurst says a 'guy, as in male, killed Lilith Martin. French police did not release the details about the sex of the killer. How does Tolhurst know the killer's sex?' Felicity was momentarily lost for words before she spoke again. "Amelia, darling. Don't talk like that. That is not the sweet and tender woman I know." Another slurping sound followed by the distinct clinking sound of crystalware on the receiver again. "I am sorry, my darling lover. I will not speak like that again. Anyway, I'm back in about two or three months, so I hope you will be around because I want to kiss every square inch of your body." Felicity blushed at the thought of making love to Amelia. "Unless something comes up with my work, I will be home in Winnetka for three weeks." Kohen made a further note. 'Dr Hoover works in Winnetka. What is near Winnetka?' Amelia then nonchalantly responded. "I will call you when I am back. Make sure you're wearing your prettiest undergarments, as I want to take them off with my teeth, my sweet Felicity. Now, I am going to take a hot bubble bath and think about you. Goodbye, my sweet." Although she knew Amelia was drunk, Felicity felt aroused by the thought of Amelia's beautiful body being immersed in a bubble bath. "Goodbye to you as well, you lascivious queen of my heart."

The call was concluded; however, Kohen was only getting started. He told the French police not to act on Tolhurst's apparent knowledge of a male killing Lilith Martin. He wanted to discover who Dr Hoover was, why she could not discuss her work, and, most importantly, ensure that the French police continued monitoring Amelia Tolhurst's calls while she was in France. Then he, too, would be travelling to Los Angeles. When he called Mossad's headquarters in Tel Aviv, Kohen could have been knocked over with a feather when he was informed who Dr Felicity Hoover was – the wife of Astronaut Dwight Hoover and a flight team member of Project Zeus. Kohen's thoughts went into overdrive. 'Saar's killer stole a letter that briefly referred to Project Zeus. Amelia Tolhurst seemed to know the sex of Lilith Martin's killer, who, coincidentally, was murdered similarly to Saar. Amelia Tolhurst and Dr Felicity Hoover are lovers.' Kohen pieced together a puzzle that had been in the making for more than four years. 'Saar's killer might be a KGB operative. The Soviets are interested in Project Zeus.' NASA might be compromised, which meant that at some stage, Kohen would have to inform his contact at the CIA. However, he needed more evidence before he involved the clumsy CIA. Still, Kohen was like a bloodhound picking up the scent of a man on the run.

The following week, Felicity flew to Houston to meet with Theodore and Secretary Waller about her final plans for building Project Zeus. They were very detailed and consistent with Felicity's meticulous nature; she had reviewed them several times since returning from Reno to spot any flaws that might be present. Zeus would be a formidable machine, both in its design and purpose. It was a masterpiece of Felicity's scientific and engineering brilliance. However, the idealistic dreams of the 1950s child had given way to the pragmatism of the Machiavellian woman of the late 1960s. She did not believe in the soul, but somewhere in the cosmos of spacetime, a child cried out to its adult self: 'Means do not justify the ends,' and that Zeus was a misnomer, as the Greek god 'Eris' embodied the moral duplicity of her creation. Nevertheless, in space, nobody can hear you, so that idealistic child remained mute as Felicity zealously pursued her dream at any cost.

CHAPTER 49

Sweet, pure and eternal love re-entered thy complicated world,
Whereas thy true and trusted friend would soon leave your fold.

Sometimes the mechanical ring of a telephone can bridge the gap from the monotony of machinery to the ethereal and lonely universe of unrequited love in some human hearts.

Felicity and Dwight had come to terms with the reality that they were living a lie for the American public, indeed, the entire free world. During the summer of 1969, when mankind's feet first touched the surface of the moon, when they were occasionally required to appear together in Houston to promote the purported virtues of Project Zeus to Congressmen or the media, Felicity would endure Dwight's presence at night by sleeping on the couch in his apartment. Dwight's knowledge about Project Zeus was still limited to his being the commander of a future space mission of the supposed 'scientific' laboratory. It was ironic that Ted knew more about Zeus than his son. Still, if it were not for Ted, Dwight would not be a NASA astronaut, let alone the proposed flight commander for this future mission. What particularly repulsed Felicity about Dwight when they had to spend time together was his occasional comments about still prioritising her best interests in life. Her simple reply was to chide him about trying to ride two horses with the one backside, and that his best interests were his mistress and his child, who were living in Norfolk.

During the two months that Amelia was in France, Felicity would speak to her on the telephone; however, Amelia only gently pressed her secret lover for information about Project Zeus, as she felt that was a topic best left for the next rendezvous. Their next rendezvous, oh, how each woman would titillate the passion of the other as they spoke passionately over the telephone about how they would next make love. Kohen was listening to every word they said, noting how Amelia would occasionally gently press Felicity to reveal more about her work. He sensed there was a rat in the henhouse, and he was the cat who lay in waiting to catch that rat. He would also hear Amelia talking to Walter, and his suspicions were confirmed when Walter told her that he would inform their mutual friends that she still had not elicited any details from Felicity about Project Zeus.

Now, after two months, as the Sun's radiance had moved to that last week of the first month in the fall, when the evening's breeze was warm like a lover's embrace, Felicity's home telephone rang. Although she hoped it would be Amelia, Felicity had to maintain a professional telephone manner just in case it was a member of NASA personnel calling her. Despite her best efforts, her inner fear and excitement expressed themselves in her slightly trembling voice. "Hello, Felicity Hoover speaking." There was a pause, a silence and for a moment, her heart had perhaps got its wires crossed in reaching out to that mechanical ring of the telephone's bell. Then the silence was broken. "You always sound so sexy, yet so serious, but still edible when I hear your professional telephone manner." Felicity's heart started beating faster, like it had many times before, as it was her star-crossed lover. She exhaled a nervous breath before she spoke. "Amelia, I so hoped it was you because I cannot stop thinking of you. Are you back from France?" Amelia smiled on the other end of the line, as she knew time and distance could not break her grip on her paramour's heart. "Well, Mae West would say at this moment: 'Are you happy to see me?' but, honey, you don't have a gun." Felicity laughed, almost like an infatuated teenager. "You silly little thing. Where are you?" Her eagerness for her heart's desire was apparent, but Amelia wished to play more with her. "I'm back in L.A., honey, where I am waiting for you in my cutest little black negligée that you can remove as you kiss my shoulders."

Felicity giggled with delight. "Only you could say such a wicked thing yet make me grin. How was Paris?" The sound of Amelia's lips making a fake flatulence release was all Felicity needed to know. "That place? Well, it pays the bills. And Walter's salary, mind you, I don't know why I even bother paying for that old queen's bag of bones to be my manager, particularly as..." Amelia held her tongue as she almost contemporaneously let the cats out of the bag about Lilith's murder and the KGB. Felicity detected that Amelia had deliberately cut her sentence short. "What is it, Amelia? What were you going to say?" Amelia dismissed the topic. "I don't walk to talk about it, but I do want to show you something that will add more spice to our time together." Amelia's reply caused Felicity to giggle again. "Stop being so silly. So, when am I going to see you again?" The response seemed to return to her ear before her words had finished echoing down the telephone line. "Tomorrow night. I want you to spend the entire weekend with me at my home, as I have some special treats planned for you." Felicity had not visited the glitz and glamour of Hollywood, let alone spent time at Amelia's house. "Will we be safe there?" Amelia laughed with delight. "Oh, you are adorable. We're not going to be on show to the world, darling. I said my home; we're not going to be parading down Sunset Boulevard together. We both have public reputations we need to maintain, and secrets to share in the privacy of my home." Secrets? Felicity thought Amelia was referring to their burgeoning relationship.

She hung up the telephone, and then the guilt of what she was about to do came to the forefront of her mind. She had castigated Dwight several times for cheating on her, indeed, leading a double life, with Jolene and his bastard son. And here she was, surreptitiously having an affair with a woman, indeed, falling madly in love with her. Then she thought about what her father might think of her if he were ever to find out about her affair with Amelia; she had not even told him about the parlous state of her marriage. However, her heart swiftly overcame her mind, and she went to sleep that night, dreaming about her body being intertwined with Amelia's again. It was a delightful dream that night; however, it did not usurp her lust for space flight.

The following day, time seemed to slow down at Rocketdyne as Felicity waited for her rendezvous with Amelia to become a reality. Towards the middle of the afternoon, Ron approached Felicity while she was working furiously away, redesigning the F-1 rockets used on the first stage of the Hercules Rockets. She did not even notice Ron approaching her, so he had to clear his throat to gain her attention. She looked up, slightly startled by his presence, and what he might have seen her working on. "Oh, Ron. You took my breath away in fright just now." Felicity could see his eyes were glassy. "What is wrong, Ron?" He pulled out a chair from the opposite side of her desk and sat down. His glassy eyes were accompanied by a look of disbelief that had enveloped his face. He searched for his words, and then he looked into Felicity's eyes, revealing the fear that hid behind his glassy eyes. "I'm dying, Felicity." She was stunned to hear this news. "What? What do you mean by dying, Ron?" He momentarily closed his eyes and then opened them again to reveal his inner horror. "I have been ignoring problems with my breathing for some time, putting it down to my age. However, it appears I have a rare medical condition caused by cellular dysfunction – it's called Multiple Organ Dysfunction Syndrome. Had I addressed the symptoms earlier, I might have survived, but now the condition has advanced too far and my physician tells me I only have a matter of months or, worse, weeks, to live."

The news rocked Felicity to her core. "Oh, Ron. This is dreadful news. Are you sure that nothing can be done? Surely there must be a cure?" He closed his eyes as he shook his head. "No, I let myself go for far too long. There is nothing that can be done to save me, Felicity. It's my stupid fault for disregarding the warning signals. So, this is my goodbye. I have informed the relevant authorities at NASA that, due to my health, I must resign immediately. Anyway, we have put a man on the Moon, and Hercules is now in your reliable hands. And, most importantly for me, you are now on the pathway to fulfilling your dreams by being a crew member of Project Zeus and exploring the wonders of science in space." Felicity kept a poker face, so she did not blink an eyelid in response to Ron's words about Zeus, even though a cosmic voice in her head suggested she should discuss it with him. Ron did not know, and he could not know, what Zeus's true purpose was as a spacecraft.

Felicity rarely revealed her emotions; however, this news about his health was devastating to her. Thoughts about her personal life escaped her as she spoke to Ron for the next hour. In a pseudo-fatherly manner, he pulled himself together to urge her to concentrate on forging ahead with her career at NASA. Still, it ephemerally dampened the fire that was burning inside of her to see Amelia. Ron's sudden departure would elevate Felicity's general standing within the Aeronautical Engineering Department of NASA; however, it also meant that a critical supporter had left the patriarchal world in which she worked, the consequences of which could only be assessed in the future.

CHAPTER 50

After coming to terms with Ron's news, Felicity then embarked upon her journey into her desire and her heart. On the drive to Amelia's house, Felicity tried to rationalise Ron's sudden departure from her world at NASA. He had been an influence on her becoming a NASA scientist and engineer, and in what was a world of intrigue, at least he had been her rock. Now he would be gone, and she would have to forge ahead, not only as the sole responsible party for the engineering of the Hercules Rocket Mission but also for the surreptitious and morally compromised Project Zeus. Nevertheless, the closer she drove towards Amelia's house, the more her thoughts became occupied by the realisation she was about to liaise with the woman she had held up on a pedestal for most of her life, and what their second journey into their carnal desires for each other would be like.

9029 Hollywood Hills Road was tucked away on a secluded lot and hidden from street view. The house gradually revealed itself through a private approach, and as she drove closer to the entrance, the elegance of the home's 1950s architecture revealed itself to her. Amelia was right, her house was secluded, and they could not be seen. A tremulous quiver enveloped Felicity, as it had been many months since she had seen Amelia, and she had longed to feel their naked bodies together again, gently making love all night long. Now that the moment had arrived, she was strangely nervous. For two minutes, she sat in her car, asking herself whether she should go in. Her mind told her that what she was doing was dangerous. Her heart was telling her that her soul mate awaited her. Emotion was more potent than reason, an unusual outcome for a person of science.

The breeze was unusually cool in Los Angeles that late September evening; however, Felicity's passions within her warmed every inch of her body, and her heart skipped a beat as she exited her car with her bag of personal belongings and walked towards Amelia's front door. After she pressed Amelia's doorbell, Walter opened the door. He was wearing a leopard-skin pattern suit, a bright fluorescent green shirt and alligator-skin shoes. Walter's eyes lit up when he saw Felicity because he knew his employer was about to turn her house into a playground of lascivious games. Whilst Walter had no interest in the female form, he nevertheless loved it when depravity was on display, and, more importantly, that Felicity might reveal the information he and Amelia had sold their souls to obtain. "Felicity?" They talked on the telephone, but had never met each other before. To her surprise, he then flung open his arms like a long-lost Beverly Hills hairdresser, having his dream client come back to him. Felicity initially accepted his over-the-top embrace, then politely prised herself free, as she was more interested in where Amelia might be. "Hello, Walter, and thank you for that lovely welcome. Where is Amelia?" Walter drew in closer to Felicity to ensure his words could be spoken in a sotto voce manner. "She is in the formal lounge, and my sweet girl, she has been waiting for you." He then winked, as only an American could wink. There was something about Walter that unsettled Felicity; he had that sleazy male demeanour about him, which so turned Felicity off the man.

As she walked through Amelia's home, Felicity could not help noticing it was looking a bit tired, a little bit unloved and perhaps reflecting the mood Amelia may be in. All of that changed when Walter opened both doors to the formal lounge, and as Felicity walked in her heart went from beating to almost stopping because there lay Amelia on the chaise lounge, wearing a figure-hugging black negligee that came down to a few inches above the knees, and what appeared as her beautifully hairdryer blown dark hair seemed to match the undergarment she was wearing. Amelia held her long cigarette holder. Felicity froze after having walked a few paces into the room. As Walter closed the doors to the room to leave them in privacy, Amelia slowly and seductively got up from the chaise after placing her extended cigarette holder in the crystal ashtray, and then came the walk that sold over a million movie tickets as her gorgeous hips swung. At the same time, her ample breasts stood up proud. Felicity did not even get a chance to say a word, as Amelia's lips met hers, followed by deeper and even more passionate kissing. They did not even go to the master bedroom; they had both disrobed relatively quickly, and Amelia took off her wig, quickly explaining to Felicity that she had to shave her head for the final scene of her previous film. They proceeded to make the most ardent love to each other for the next hour, on the floor of the lounge room, then on the lounge, and even on the chaise.

It was a highly charged interaction of making love, which formed an even stronger bond between two hearts that had not been together for a very long time. After her third orgasm, Felicity needed a break; she may be a fit person in training to be a crew member of Project Zeus, but Amelia seemed to have greater stamina than she did. Even when they stopped making love, nothing was said; instead, they just softly kissed each other's lips and looked into each other's eyes as their hearts did all the talking.

Eventually, they put on their panties and walked around to the master bedroom, leaving their clothes where they lay on the floor of the lounge room. Before closing the bedroom door, Amelia called out to Walter for her order: "Champagne, cheese, fruit and, oh, whatever, just make it nice, Walter and if we are fucking leave it outside of the door." When she walked into the bedroom, Amelia saw that Felicity was slightly ashen-faced. "What is wrong, my sweet?" She knew what was wrong; Felicity was not used to her vulgarity. "You just spoke to him like a wharf manager would speak to his worker, Amelia. Is that what happened in France?" Amelia no longer cared for politeness or convention. She walked up and grappled Felicity's tiny breasts, almost like she was sculpting them. "I will show what I learned in France, namely not to be so fucking demure and to let yourself enjoy sex with another woman or man." Felicity was perplexed and jealous of Amelia's candour. "What do you mean by 'Enjoy sex with another woman or man?' I thought we were exclusive?" Amelia laughed in a mocking tone. "Oh, you're still as sweet and innocent as you were at Woldingham. I do not work in your world. Studio and television executives, male and female, use younger women for their pleasure, honey. But, yes, we're exclusive, so don't fret, my pet." Amelia's revelation about her working life enlightened Felicity, who nodded to acknowledge her understanding. Still, jealousy's curse lingered in the background of her mind.

Amelia then reached out with her right hand and grabbed Felicity's left forearm, thereby dragging her close into her body. "Now, let me show what I learned in France, which with you is even better because I love you." As Amelia said the 'L' word, her right hand slid down behind Felicity's back to slink its way into her panties and then grabbed her left buttock cheek firmly, pulling her closer to her so that she could passionately kiss her. Then, without warning, she brought both hands up to Felicity's chest height, and in the blink of an eye, she lunged forward to shove Felicity backwards onto the queen-sized bed.

Felicity was initially startled by her uncontrollable fall backwards. Still, when she realised she was safe on that luxurious bed, she began to feel stimulated by her desire for Amelia. "So what are you going to do to me now? Devour me, like you used to say to me on the telephone?" Amelia smiled the same grin she would smile as a teenager when she was about to lead a person astray. "I am going to do to you what Lilith did to me in France. Lay down." Her gentle command was obeyed, and Felicity lay there while Amelia retrieved some scarves from her bedside drawer. Upon seeing them, Felicity could not help but be glib. "Oh, what have you got in mind? Play dress up." Amelia brought her finger up to her lips to quieten her lover, and then she made her second command. "Put your hands up behind your head, and don't panic; this is all about trust." Felicity was compliant with the command, and to her surprise, she felt one of the scarves being tied around her wrist. Before she could speak, Amelia had tied the other end of the scarf to the bed end. "What are you doing...".Amelia's hand covered Felicity's mouth, and then she withdrew it, kissing her as she spoke. "Trust me, this will be great." Felicity threw open her trust, and without fail, both of her hands were soon tied to the bedhead behind her. Then Amelia started kissing her way down Felicity, nibbling certain spots to cause her to squeal in delight, before she removed the woman's panties and tied a scarf to her left foot. "What are.." Amelia sat up, her voluptuous breasts almost swinging in tandem with her words. "Please have some trust, as trust is essential for the adventure I am about to take you on." Felicity could only giggle because it sounded erotically fun.

Within moments, both of Felicity's feet were tied to the other end of the bed. When Amelia spoke, it was as though an evil spirit was residing in her soul, as her eyes narrowed and her voice became deliberately low to speak into Felicity's ear. "I am going to show you how much I love you." With those words being spoken, Amelia began to kiss Felicity's neck softly, and Felicity felt the delight of being restrained. "Oh, Amelia, that feels so..." Amelia put her hand over her lover's mouth. "Be quiet, and just go with the moment." She then untied Felicity, and they resumed making what was far more pleasurable and stimulating love. Every time Felicity looked into Amelia's eyes, she saw the same love she had for her staring right back at her. Later, in bed, they would eat some of the food, drink some champagne, and eventually fall asleep in each other's arms with the bedroom lights still on bright. Neither of them awoke to the sound of Walter surreptitiously setting up the microphone under the bed, the cord for which he and Aliev had previously installed in the wall that then fed its way the wardrobe in Walter's neighbouring bedroom and makeshift office, where one of the EMI

TR52/2 two track reel to reel systems was now operating, waiting to record the two women's words when they awoke the next morning.

The next morning, they continued to lie in bed together. Both of them had missed each other's gentle embrace, and Felicity was not restricted in this house; she could be who she was: an intelligent woman, a member of the Project Zeus team, and a woman who just happened to be in love with another woman, as she had always been. However, she had some things to say about their childhood, or, to be blunt, some gripes she wanted to get off her chest. She stared at Amelia for half a minute, which caused Amelia concern. "What is up with you? Why are you staring at me like that?" Felicity had to speak. "That morning after we kissed each other at school, you broke my heart by being so cold in telling me we could not be partners. Why did you do that to me?" Amelia was not expecting this question, so she thought it was best to be truthful. "I was a very mixed-up young woman back then, Felicity. Please don't judge who I am now on that previous iteration of me." Felicity nodded her head, but she wanted answers. "I know, and so was I, but why did you not even speak to me for two minutes after our night together? And why did you treat me in such a mean way before then for so many years?"

Amelia rolled over so that she could look into her lover's eyes and be candid. Amelia's eyes began to fill with genuine, heartfelt and sorrowful tears. "I was being sexually abused by my parents' butler from the age of thirteen. I was confused, angry and emotionally unstable, my darling. My parents were hardly home when I returned from Woldingham on school holidays, and if they were, they were regularly hosting their 'high society' parties and displayed little time or attention for me. So, more often than not, I was left alone with a horrible creep of a man, who abused my body with his fingers, and then threatened me if I ever opened my mouth. I had to portray this image of being the supremely confident product of two charlatans when deep down I just wanted to scream out in pain. At school, I quickly picked up on your childhood infatuation with me, and in my troubled state of mind, I made you a target for my inner despair. Deep down, I liked you as well, Felicity, but I had to be the 'shining star' of a 1950s girls' catholic school, so I had to suppress my feelings and draw on my anger. I am so sorry. However, after our night together after the prom, how could we have been girlfriends back then? Even now, as the so-called 'swinging sixties are coming to their conclusion, we cannot publicly be seen in a lesbian relationship. But, I am truly sorry for being a cold-hearted bitch to you."

Tears began rolling down Amelia's eyelids towards the pillow, and Felicity embraced her tightly. The injustice of what happened to Amelia brought back faint memories of Felicity's feelings of injustice after William's treatment of her. However, she could not let that Jeanie out of the bottle; instead, she consoled her paramour. "Oh, you poor darling. If only I had known you were being abused, I would have told my father, as he would have spoken to your parents. My Dad is so tenacious and honest that he would not allow anyone to be subjected to that type of abuse." Amelia began to sob as she snuggled her head under Felicity's chin during this moment of vulnerability. "My life has been a rollercoaster of abuse ever since then."

Felicity held Amelia's head close to her chest for several minutes, stroking her hair, before Amelia lifted her head to stare deeply into her lover's eyes, as it was now her turn to ask some questions that had to be asked. The switch from vulnerable to deceitful was as quick as a supernova. "Why did you marry Dwight? I mean, honestly, you could have done better than him." Amelia's condescending tone about Dwight prised open the vault in Felicity's mind. "Dwight was, and still has to be, a means to an end. I started dating him immediately after one of the female staff members at Princeton sexually assaulted me." Amelia's eyes shot open wide in surprise. "What?" Felicity nodded. "Yes. But she didn't do anything other than touch my private area, before I resisted her. Then, she, too, threatened me. I quickly latched onto Dwight as a means to prove to myself I was not a lesbian, even though you were always in the back of my mind. Then, I needed to stay in America, as the RAF wanted to redeploy me back to England, and he proposed to me. I should have said no, as I didn't love him, although I pretended to my heart that I did. However, sex with him was so revolting, and then when we found out I could not have children, the stupid idiot went off and had an affair with an airline hostess, and he knocked her up. They have a young boy. So, yes, I have been living a lie, first for my heart and now for NASA. Fortunately, I hardly have to see him too much because when I am not working at Canoga Park, I am in Reno..." Felicity had not told Amelia about Reno; however, Amelia's mind was distracted by the former revelation, not the latter one.

Felicity's first solemn promise of silence had been broken; she had revealed too much information, even to an intimate partner whom she loved with all her heart. This discussion had to be closed down quickly. However, Amelia was stunned that her sweet and supposedly innocent girlfriend could be so duplicitous, and she sat bolt upright in bed, gazing down at her lover. "You evil little thing! Are you serious that you married that dork to stay in the United States?" That cat was out of the bag, so Felicity nodded. "Yes. I should not have told you that, Amelia, as I…" Felicity almost let the word promise out. Amelia shook her head with delight. "I didn't realise you could be so devious. What else are you hiding from the world? What is happening at NASA? Tell me more about Project Zeus. Are you going to have to spend a week in space with your dork husband? What are you going to do for a week?" Amelia had crossed a line, which slightly annoyed Felicity. She quickly sat up in bed. "Come, come. I have told you that I cannot discuss my work. Zeus is exactly what NASA has told the world – it's a science laboratory in space." Amelia could tell by the look in her lover's eyes that she was not being candid.

Felicity hopped out of bed and hurriedly put her panties on from the night before. Amelia was disappointed that Felicity had not told her the truth about Project Zeus, particularly as she had opened so much of her heart and soul to Felicity. Amelia crawled to the bottom end of the bed, like a feline taunting its Tomcat. "Where are you going? We haven't had morning sex as yet?" Felicity had no clothing to put on, as Walter had not brought her bag into the bedroom. "I am hungry. We barely ate any food last night." Amelia reached out with her left hand and grabbed onto Felicity's panties, stretching them back towards her. "Walter will bring breakfast in when I tell him. But come back to bed. I promise I won't ask any more questions. Don't you want more of these for your lips to touch?" She gently puckered her lips, knowing full well they were a physical feature Felicity had taken delight in. Her enticing grin was too much to resist, and Felicity gave in to her desire. "Alright then, you know I cannot resist those lips." She jumped back into bed, and the two women made love for another hour, until Amelia summoned Walter to deliver them breakfast in bed. After he had offered them breakfast, Walter went to his wardrobe. He changed the reels on the tape machine, hoping that Amelia might prise the information from Felicity, that the KGB so desperately wanted to find out.

And so that is how their personal life proceeded for several months. When Felicity was not required at Reno, Canoga Park or Houston, she would spend weekends secretly making love to Amelia inside the woman's supposed fortress of secrecy. Amelia would subtly try to pry information from Felicity's lips about Project Zeus. Still, she would fail, whereas Felicity was more than happy to discuss details about her 'dork' husband, his mistress and their bastard son. When they were apart, they spoke on the telephone. Kohen had not yet spoken to the

CIA, so Mossad's agents in Los Angeles were not monitoring these calls. Still, they had followed Felicity's car on enough occasions to the Hollywood Hills to establish that she was only travelling to one destination. Kohen would wait until Amelia returned to France, where the French authorities had given him total autonomy to monitor Amelia's telephone calls from her villa. Meanwhile, Walter would explain to Aliev back in the United States that Felicity was a hard nut to crack, but he was certain Amelia would soon prise the truth from her. The clock continued to tick down toward the eventual launch of Project Zeus, and the Soviets were growing increasingly impatient. Felicity should have listened to that cosmic voice of her childhood self, imploring her for several seconds outside of Amelia's home that first night to turn around and go home. Felicity had a two-minute window of opportunity to escape that treacherous world. Still, now she was unwittingly in too deep, and, in particular, she was now too deeply in love with Amelia. What a mutual web of desire, intrigue and uncertainty these two star-crossed lovers had woven

CHAPTER 51

Too late, as thy heart had consumed the forbidden fruits of desire and envy;
However, could it be that thy yearning heart was also thy insidious enemy?

Love and deception cannot coexist in harmony. Whereas the former emanates from one's heart, the latter is a toxic product of the dark recesses of the inner space of the human mind.

Meeting up with Amelia was complicated by Felicity's work on Project Zeus, as well as Amelia's commitments to the film studio in France. Nevertheless, at least once every three weeks, they would have a moment in heaven together where they could display their love for one another. However, now, in the season of goodwill, it was their final rendezvous of love, a weekend of unbridled loving desire, before Amelia would depart for France, where her film schedule had been extended out to May 1970. Notwithstanding Amelia using all of her subtle charm to elicit from Felicity more details about Project Zeus, no secrets could be prised from her lips. Aliev was vicariously informing Amelia via Walter about the Soviet Union's patience beginning to wear thin, and the threat of turning off the gravy train now loomed large in Amelia's life. Walter implored Amelia to use all of her charms to obtain the information from Felicity now, as her feared Aliev's threats of turning off the money supply might evolve into more deadly intentions.

They had spent their entire last Sunday morning gently making love to one another. It was 2:00 p.m. when, out of exhaustion, the two women finally spoke without their lips meeting, their lips barely touching as they whispered sweet words to each other. Christmas Day was only four days away, and both women would be spending it alone, with an ocean and a continent separating them. Amelia stared lovingly into Felicity's eyes; her heart and mind conflicted as she did love her, but her fear of losing her Soviet gravy train was never far from the forefront of her mind. Amelia then turned to her right and opened the drawer to her bedside table. With just as much smooth movement with her left hand, she took a small, gift-wrapped Tiffany's box out and turned back to Felicity, whose puzzled expression revealed her ignorance of the time. "Merry Christmas, my sweet." Felicity had forgotten to purchase Amelia a gift. "I am so sorry, my sweetheart, for I have totally forgotten about Christmas." Amelia gently placed her right index finger on Felicity's lips. "Hush, my darling. You don't need to give me a gift; spending time together this weekend is a gift in itself. Now, open it." Felicity carefully opened the gift wrapping, and when she opened the box, a delicate twenty-four carat gold bracelet containing rose coloured quartz hearts glimmered in the soft rays of the winter sun, which now filtered through the windows of Amelia's bedroom.

Felicity's eyes began to fill with tears, and then Amelia softly kissed her lips, and then she stared deeply and lovingly into her eyes. "Do not cry, as this is my moment of delight. I have to tell you, because I can no longer resist doing so. You are the love of my life, Felicity." Felicity was overwhelmed by emotion to hear Amelia's heartfelt and magical words. Felicity did not know how to respond, and after all that she had been through with Dwight and others, she could not hold back her tears. She wanted to scream the exact words back to Amelia. Instead, Felicity initially looked into Amelia's eyes and then gently kissed her lips. Then she permitted her heart to open wide. "I love you, too, my beautiful sweetheart. I always have. Even on my wedding day, all I wanted in my life was you." Her words were meek and vulnerable, revealing her lifelong feelings. Still, they were also recorded on the two-track reel in Walter's wardrobe.

Amelia looked into Felicity's eyes, and her eyes transformed from projectors of love to vessels of earnest inquiry. Amelia proceeded to ask Felicity the question she had been trying to answer for many months. "What is Project Zeus all about, Felicity? And don't insult my intelligence by suggesting that it is a science laboratory in space because your eyes always reveal that you are holding back a secret from me." Felicity was shocked that Amelia would question her about her work, not only because she had told her on several occasions that she could not discuss Project Zeus, but also because she had only moments ago lost herself in a world of open expression. Felicity hurriedly sat up in bed, her face changing from love to irritation. "Why do you keep on asking me that question, Amelia? I have told you, on several occasions, that Project Zeus is a scientific undertaking by NASA to explore the ability of life to be sustained in space. It is a scientific laboratory that will hopefully one day lead to deep space travel. How come you keep on asking me the same question, even though I provided that same answer to you beforehand?" She had not revealed this level of depth before about the duration of life in space, another clue being recorded several rooms away in Walter's wardrobe.

Amelia sat upright in bed, her frustration evident. "I have previously told you about a secret from the bottom of my heart, and yet you deliver to me the answer to a simple question that, as I see it, is a piece of NASA propaganda. You are working around the clock, and I admit that is your current working life. However, for the rest of my life, I do not want to spend it with anybody other than you, Felicity. So, when you continue to tell me Project Zeus is nothing more than a scientific experiment in space, and we have shared our hearts and bodies so much, it is not hard for me to see through the propaganda and to perceive that there is a greater purpose to Project Zeus than you are willing to reveal to me."

Felicity hurriedly got out of bed, and she was now exasperated that Amelia continued to press her about a matter which she had previously told her on so many occasions she could not discuss. "What is it with you, Amelia? Why do you continue to press me for answers when I am telling you the truth?" She wasn't, and her eyes revealed as much. Still, her frustration could not be tamed, and her tone increased in volume. "I have told you precisely what my work is about. You tell me that you love me, and yet you do not believe me? Why is that so?" Amelia similarly raised her voice to the days when she would be tormenting Felicity at Woldingham. "I really cannot understand why you continue to treat me like a child about your work. Felicity, I just want to know what is going on in your world. I share with you everything about my world, including my childhood experiences. If you cannot be open with me in this relationship, please let me know now, because I cannot see a future with someone I love who doesn't trust or love me. Do you trust me and do you love me, Felicity?"

It was Woldingham revisited, and she shouted her retort at Amelia. "I can tell you, Amelia, that I, too, cannot see a future with a person who does not believe what I have to say! I put up with a lot of torment from you when we were younger. You broke my heart after our prom. Yet, notwithstanding that treatment, I have only ever felt love for you. I have even accepted that in your work world, you probably have to be unfaithful. In contrast, I only dedicate my body to you. I am not hiding any secrets from you about Project Zeus, so, if you cannot accept my word, then let's call it quits here, and I will get on with my life, and you can get on with your life, rather than us fighting about something which you do not believe me about." Amelia was enraged that Felicity would speak to her in this manner, especially when she blatantly continued to lie to her. "Get out of my house, Felicity! You and I have shared many wonderful nights and days in this house, under circumstances where we both agreed that we couldn't tell the world about our relationship. Surely, after all of our time together, you would show more trust in me. However, you do not trust me, and it seems that you also hold a lot of resentment towards me, after I've explained to you the abuse I suffered as a child. So get out of my house, Felicity!" The rage in Amelia's voice startled Felicity; however, she, too, was filled with rage. She screamed at the top of her lungs. "Fine! I will. And keep your stupid little present." Amelia always had to say the final word. "Fine. I will keep the present, and I might even give it to somebody else in the future who trusts me. Now, get out of my bloody house, and don't come back again."

By now, Felicity had put on a skirt and was doing up her blouse. She was enraged by how Amelia had spoken to her, and she was not going to accept that imperious tone like she had received when they were schoolgirls at Woldingham. "Alright, Amelia, I will get out of your house, and I will never disturb you again. If you cannot accept my word, then I may not be the right person for you. Everything about Project Zeus has already been announced in the media. You do not believe me, and I must say, I do not understand why you continue to question me about it. But this is it! I have had enough of being hurt by you."

Walter had been standing outside the door of the bedroom for several minutes, listening to the argument that had ensued between the two women. Walter was dismayed to hear that they might be breaking up, as he could foresee problems for both him and Amelia if they did not deliver what the KGB was seeking: the truth about Project Zeus. Within thirty seconds of the last words being shouted between the two women, Felicity stormed out of the bedroom to see Walter standing not too far away from the door. She quickly glared at him and spoke condescendingly. "Did you enjoy listening to that, Walter? Do you get your cheap thrills out of listening to people's arguments? In any event, tell Amelia when she calms down that I might speak to her again, but in the meantime, do not contact me."

Felicity cried for most of the drive home, and her heart was breaking. She could not understand why Amelia had changed from being so tender to suddenly interrogating her about Project Zeus. Life in America had seemed perfect for the past few months. Yet, now, it seemed her life was as cold as the weather outside.

Walter knew he had to speak to Aliev urgently because if the news filtered back to him that the two women had broken off their relationship, there would be blood on the floor. He was hoping the information he passed on to Aliev about Project Zeus, which tested the duration of life in space, would be received with approval. In contrast, he was told it was not good enough. When he broke the news to the Soviet agent about the fight between the two women, which seemed to push them further away from the objective the Soviets were seeking, Aliev left Walter with little doubt that back in Moscow, they would not be pleased to hear this news. Walter knew this meant more than the tap of funds being turned off. He told Aliev to assure his superiors in the KGB that he would get the two women back together again because their relationship was deeper than mere sex; he just needed time for their passions to cool.

It was cool and partially overcast Christmas morning in Winnetka. Still, in Felicity's heart, there was a blizzard blowing through her veins, as she regretted her argument with Amelia. She telephoned her father at 9:00 a.m. to wish him well for Christmas. It was 5:00 p.m. in England, so Samuel was about to sit down to Christmas dinner on his own. Felicity maintained a brave front even though she wanted to tell him every single miserable fact about the world she was now living in.

In Paris, the temperature was freezing that Christmas night as Amelia spent the night by herself, regretting that she had spoken to Felicity as she had. Amelia wanted to pick up the telephone and call Felicity. Still, her manipulative side told her to wait, as she knew Felicity's anger would soon turn to desire again.

Through the espionage grapevine, Aliev conveyed all of Walter's information back to Volkov in Moscow. After much deliberation, Volkov unilaterally decided to maintain the status quo rather than turn off the money tap and dispose of Walter and Amelia. More importantly, he decided that it was time for Aliev to leave the East Coast, as it appeared that Dr Hoover was working on something far more sinister than a mere space science laboratory. The Soviets were aware that Rocketdyne's facilities in Reno were top secret, and Volkov wanted every move that Felicity made to be monitored by Aliev. The agent was redeployed to Los Angeles, where he could find available casual 'work' at the Hilton Woodland Hills when necessary, ensuring he maintained a regular work schedule for his visa.

CHAPTER 52

Living a lie means sooner or later that the truth might be nigh.
Still, thy whole world is a lie; it might likely all blow sky-high.

Felicity's heart was no longer filled with delight, and she did not realise that by early January 1970, she was being followed by Aliev, remaining out of her direct sight. Aliev had purchased a Plymouth Valiant in Los Angeles so that he could surreptitiously follow Felicity as she drove to Canoga Park. There, Aliev would park down the road from the facility, making notes about her work patterns. Then, in early February 1970, Felicity left her home later than usual and drove a completely different route, which Aliev followed to Los Angeles Airport. Her mind was too preoccupied with thoughts about Project Zeus and Amelia for her to notice that the Plymouth was tailing her. Aliev followed Felicity into a long-term parking bay at Los Angeles International Airport, and he parked in the bay adjacent to hers. He closely followed her to the curbside check-in for American Airlines, where he heard her tell the baggage handler she was flying to Reno on the midday flight. Aliev purchased a ticket for the same flight to Reno that she flew. After they arrived, he followed her in a taxi from Reno Airport to Rocketdyne's facilities in the Palomino Valley, where, sure enough, Felicity was permitted entry to the secure facility. Aliev then had the taxi driver return him to the Bank of America branch in Reno, where he handed the driver a twenty-dollar bill for what was only a twelve-dollar fare. Upon being served by the teller, Aliev handed over his passbook and withdrew one hundred dollars to hire a car and stake out Rocketdyne for several days.

It only took Aliev twenty-four hours to gather all the information he needed about Rocketdyne in Palomino Valley. As late as the following evening, he saw a truck pull into the security gate, bearing the familiar seal on its secure crate of the United States Atomic Energy Commission. He had all the information he needed at that time. Aliev returned to Los Angeles the following morning, and the information he passed on to Moscow through the information channels was simple: 'Dr Hoover is working with nuclear material at Reno.' When Volkov read the message, he knew his unilateral decision to deploy Aliev to Los Angeles had paid dividends in information.

Project Zeus was a massive spacecraft; indeed, it was too large to convince anyone that its sole purpose was scientific research. However, that is where Felicity's brilliant mind satisfied all the relevant United States agencies that she was the right person for this mammoth and nefarious undertaking. Towards the end of February, Felicity met with Ted, Theodore, and Secretary Waller at the Palomino Valley facility, where she walked them through the nuclear fission mechanisms of the space nuclear propulsion system, or SNP, as it was known at NASA, which she had designed and overseen the construction of at Palomino Valley.

All three men expressed their gratitude for Felicity's work. Still, Secretary Waller then spoke the words that were on every other man's mind. "Felicity, Zeus is an enormous spacecraft. I think I can say for my colleagues here by expressing concern about its size. Aren't we flagging to the Soviet Union that the United States is launching something into space that has another purpose other than being a scientific laboratory?" Felicity smiled. "Yes. Yes, we are. However, Ted, Theodore, and Secretary Waller, my explanation for the size of Zeus is simple: it is both a scientific research lab and a secondary HSG designed to re-enter the Earth's atmosphere and descend back to Earth using retrograde rockets powered by nuclear electric propulsion, which uses heat from the fission reactor to generate electricity, similar to nuclear power plants. That electricity is then used to ionise a gaseous propellant and electromagnetically accelerate it, generating thrust that propels a spacecraft or, for this mission, the retrograde rockets, thereby preserving the central rocket machinery for future use. Regarding the so-called scientific laboratory of Zeus, which would be separated from the component of the spacecraft returning to Earth, the SNP would power it. As far as the press and the Soviets are concerned, the HSG's size can be explained because it has a separate reactor and a compartment for taking future payloads into space to the laboratory." Ted interrupted Felicity. "Where are the FOBS launched from?" Felicity pointed to the shell of the HSG that was under construction in the enormous manufacturing hangar of the facility. "The payload section of the HSG; however, the fission generator has to be turned off and blast shields lowered around it when it is in low Earth orbit at the time of the FOBS' launch because there is too much risk that the heat will cause an explosion."

Secretary Waller questioned Felicity about one component of the HSG. "What is that area of the payload container that looks like a separate compartment? What is that area designated for?" Felicity raised her eyebrows in mocking contempt for his ignorance, which was then reflected in her imperious English tone. "We cannot descend in retrograde without a safety chamber for the astronauts in the circumstances of a fission malfunction. That section is a pod that can separate from the HSG and descend back to Earth much like the Hercules re-entry module. It is also a lifeboat in space, if some unforeseen disaster should occur, which won't be the case; however, astronaut safety must be a priority, and this little pod is my baby, gentlemen."

Theodore was the next person to ask a question to attract Felicity's intellectual ire. "Well, what about the HSG? Do we just let it re-enter anywhere when it's malfunctioning? That could lead to a catastrophic outcome if it were to return to Earth and explode." Felicity's wrinkled brow displayed her disdain for the Director of NASA's ignorance. "No, Theodore. We have a dual manual and automatic remote-controlled self-destruct button built in the central control room of the laboratory, the cockpit of the HSG and the pod. It permits the astronauts a maximum of two minutes to get to the pod from any part of the spacecraft when it is one complete object or after its separation into two parts, and yes, I have timed it so that it can be detonated in fewer seconds if necessary."

Ted understood the genius behind Felicity's design. "This spacecraft is excellent, gentlemen. The HSG can launch its nuclear missile from low Earth orbit and then return to dock with the space laboratory, and the Soviets will never know where the FOBS was launched from. The HSG can subsequently return to Earth days after it has launched the FOBS and be reloaded." Felicity interrupted her father-in-law. "Alternatively, it can be loaded with scientific equipment, such as satellites. The HSG can be used to launch commercial satellites." Ted nodded at her. "Of course, it can also be used for that purpose." Secretary Waller, who had to explain the cost to Congress, importunately questioned Felicity. "Okay. I get the HSG part of the spacecraft, but why do we need a space laboratory as large as this one?" His outstretched hand was riddled with tension, yet Felicity remained calm. "Well, it's obvious. If you are going to fool the world about the purpose of Project Zeus, you're not going to do so by sending a laboratory into space that is the size of a telephone box. We want the Soviet Union to believe we are conducting scientific research in space. To achieve this, you need to send something into space that resembles a laboratory, which will sustain various forms of life, and, of course, a team of scientists for weeks or months. Once it is in space, the SNP can propel the entire spacecraft around the moon and back."

Secretary Waller then delivered the unexpected news, which even Ted had not been informed about at this juncture. "Well, the President wants Zeus launched by the beginning of this coming August." Felicity was surprised by the news. "But I thought we were proposing a launch date in April 1971? Now you want us to launch eight months before then, is that correct?" Secretary Waller nodded. "Congress wants the Hercules missions to end early next year. The following year is an election year, and the President does not want a fight in Congress over funding Zeus after the Hercules mission is terminated. He wants it launched this year, so that he can campaign on the footing that under his administration, America rules the heavens. So, you'll have to double your efforts secretly and get this ship built in time. Additionally, the construction of this ship on its current set of plans is too expensive, so we've had another aeronautical engineer amend your plans to reduce the costs." Felicity was astonished. "You have done what? Are you telling me that I am being ghosted behind the scenes about the design of Zeus?" Secretary Waller was blunt. "Yes. Yes, I have. The new plans will be delivered here in several days. In the meantime, I will explain the cost factors to the Congressional Oversight Committee."

Secretary Waller turned on his heels to leave the hangar, closely followed by Ted, whereas Theodore remained behind to speak to Felicity. He waited until the two men exited the hangar, then turned to face Felicity, who was still contemplating the news about the new design plans and, more importantly, how she would safely construct Zeus for an expedited launch. "Felicity, that was news to me, as well. Secretary Waller's news surprised me just as much as it must have surprised you. Still, that isn't why I stayed back to talk to you." Felicity raised her eyebrows. Theodore's demeanour became somewhat maudlin as he took a deep breath. "Ron passed away in the early hours of this morning at Cedars-Sinai Medical Centre." Felicity's emotions froze at another, more disturbing piece of news. Theodore placed his right hand on Felicity's left shoulder to awaken her benumbed senses. "Did you hear me, Felicity? Ron is dead." Her emotions began to overwhelm her now. "I didn't know he was in the hospital. I didn't get a chance to say goodbye." Theodore gently squeezed her shoulder to comfort a now visibly distressed Felicity. "Neither did I. His sister broke the news to my secretary this morning, while I was flying here from Houston." Ron was her friend, and she could not hide her grief. "When is the funeral?" Theodore withdrew his hand from her shoulder. "There isn't going to be a public funeral ceremony. Those were Ron's wishes; it will just be a closed, family ceremony. But listen to me, if he were here now, he would tell you to keep on going. And that is even more so now, as we have to build this behemoth within six months. Ron would have told you to get the job done, so do it for him; build this monster of a ship, and God save all of our souls." Theodore then turned away, and he, too, left the hangar to enter the Rocketdyne limousine, where Ted and Secretary Waller patiently waited to return to Reno Airport.

Felicity now felt more alone in America than ever before. She and Amelia were not talking to one another. Dwight was living out his double life between Houston and Norfolk. Her father might as well be living on the other side of the galaxy, such was the tyranny of distance that separated them. And now, her mentor, and her rock since she had been living in the United States, was dead. The dark void of space was minute compared to the void in Felicity's heart. Still, on she must go because her moment was about to arrive; sooner, rather than later, she was about to become the first woman to fly in space. However, a darkness lingered over Project Zeus, a darkness more profound than that of space itself.

CHAPTER 53

Thou hast entangled thy web with too many other arachnids, my dear,
And there are too many demons and serpents now drawing near.

Time. Neither Felicity nor Amelia had enough of it. One woman was desperately trying to build her enormous spacecraft. The other woman was trying to finalise the monstrosity of her deception. When it came to the latter, she had the menacing impatience of the Soviet Union hanging over her head, the proverbial sword of Damocles. For the former, she had the hands of time working against her, and the new plans, along with the tightening of her budget to construct Zeus, led Secretary Waller, Ted, and even Theodore to discard safety measures they considered unnecessary given the risk ratio. Felicity protested about discarding these safety measures, as she believed that where there was even a slight chance of risk, safety must prevail. Yet, her protestations were to no avail. Even some of the handpicked construction team in Reno were asking Felicity about why such obvious potential design flaws were being implemented – all she could say was that they were expediting the launch date. The only remaining feature of her designs that had not been altered was the powering of the pod's emergency beacon in space, which bureaucrats, focusing on costs, deemed a relatively inexpensive device adapted by Felicity from classical innovation.

Amelia was surprised and disappointed that since she returned to France, Felicity still had not called her after their fight. By late February, Amelia had repeatedly tried calling Felicity's house, but the telephone would ring out on each occasion without an answer. Before leaving Los Angeles, Amelia ordered her long-suffering manager to continue trying to call Felicity. Aliev had been regularly contacting Walter to ascertain what was going on. And now, in France, Sokolov had paid Amelia a surprise visit while she was on set, simultaneously introducing himself whilst also warning her that the KGB's patience was wearing thin. Amelia didn't hesitate to call Walter as soon as she returned to her villa that evening. The telephone conversation between Amelia and Walter was being listened to by Kohen. After the pleasantries, if they could be described that way between the pair of them, she bluntly got to the point. "Well, has she answered any of your calls?" Walter sighed. "No. And I have even been driving by her house in Winnetka, but it seems like she has not been home for months."

Months! Amelia's instincts told her something was afoot with Project Zeus. "A member of the KGB paid me an unexpected visit on the set today, Walter." Kohen's ears perked up like a hare's in a field. "He told me the KGB is becoming impatient with us and, in particular, me, because Felicity has not revealed to me the true purpose of Project Zeus. He claimed we have not provided them with one single valuable piece of information. I was scared by that man today, Walter." Walter was dismayed by Amelia's news. "What? You were threatened on set. Oh, my God. Are you sure it was a threat?" A silly question received a comparable answer. "No, Walter. I was off my head on opium. Of course, it was a bloody threat. When he said, 'We will get Anatoli to pay you and your faggot manager a visit,' then, in those bloody circumstances, Walter, it's a threat!" Walter's ears were still ringing from Amelia shouting down the line at him, but he persisted with his inquiry. "Who is Anatoli?" A momentary pause, and then Kohen heard the words to connect the dots. "Anatoli is the KGB's transsexual agent, for whom I owe my thanks for Lilith's throat being cut from ear to ear, Walter. Anatoli looks like Felicity, and I picked him up at New Moon thinking he was her, only to have the best of three worlds. He was the agent who informed me that you had already reached a deal with the Soviet Union. He was the agent who brought me in to deceive my girlfriend, with whom I am no longer in contact. When I told him how Lilith had treated me, he visited her and treated her in like manner, except he cut her throat."

Walter was panicking. If the KGB were impatient with Amelia, then they were also impatient with him. "Well, what do you want me to do, Amelia?" Her tongue was like a viper's. "What do I want you to do? What do you think, Walter? Speak to Aliev and tell him that Felicity's house appears to be like she hasn't been home for months, which means something is going on with NASA and Project Zeus. Felicity is fastidiously tidy, to the point of being regimental. If her house is looking unkempt, then that means something is going on with Project Zeus. Secondly, speak to NASA and ask them to pass on a message that her 'best friend' from the television show is desperately sick in Paris. That, hopefully, will cause her to pick up the telephone and call me. Do you understand me, Walter?" Every single syllable. "Yes, Amelia. I will call Aliev, or drive to the Hilton at Woodlands, as the KGB have moved him to L.A., which concerns me even more now that I have been told that you were threatened today. Don't worry,

I will take care of everything." Kohen had enough information now to speak to the CIA. In the meantime, Walter completed both tasks as his tempestuous employer instructed him.

When Volkov was informed about the two women being at loggerheads with each other, and there seemingly being no further information beyond what had been announced in the press about Project Zeus, he informed Sokolov that it was time to bring Anatoli into the equation; that when the two women met up again in America, Anatoli was to be present as well, and if Dr Hoover did not tell him the truth about Project Zeus, then in those circumstances, he was to kill both of them. Because the French police had not released critical information about how Lilith Martin died, Sokolov had not connected the dots to Anatoli, which meant Volkov was also in the dark about those essential details. Volkov sent a message through the KGB's grapevine to Aliev, outlining his plans in light of the information about Dr Hoover's home. According to this, Anatoli and Sokolov were to be brought into the United States via South Africa. Aliev was also ordered to warn the crippled manager that if Dr Hoover did not see Amelia, or she did not tell her the truth about Zeus, they would all die. They would both be killed by Anatoli, and the same fate awaited him if he was to be so stupid as to forewarn anyone about the KGB's plans.

About six weeks before the new launch date, NASA announced to the press that Project Zeus would be launched on August 8, 1970, eight months ahead of schedule. The media world went into meltdown over the surprising news. Even astronauts, including Dwight, were surprised by the news. Still, Theodore ordered Dwight to immediately dive into training regarding the operations of Zeus' command module, which were not too dissimilar to those of Hercules' command module. For the sake of keeping the peace in training, it was decided to keep Dwight and Felicity apart until the final fortnight before launch. In any event, she was still finalising the audacious spacecraft's construction, and thus, learning to flick switches was not a priority. Samuel and Joan both sent separate messages to NASA stating that they would be attending the launch.

Upon hearing this surprising news about the new launch date, Aliev visited Walter one evening in the Hollywood Hills, after Volkov's message had been passed on to him. Aliev's words were brief, but they were as cold as Ten Kelvins travelling down Walter's spine. When Walter informed Amelia about Aliev's message, she responded in desperate fear: 'Send a message to Felicity and tell her my health is ailing!' Walter sent a further telegram to NASA, which assuaged the Soviets by making arrangements for Amelia to return from France and meet with Anatoli in Las Vegas. The only missing piece from the deadly puzzle was to lure Felicity to Las Vegas. There were too many moving parts for Walter to cope with, and Kohen detected his distress by listening in on his calls to Amelia. The proposed meeting point was in Las Vegas, which was a much easier destination for Anatoli and Sokolov to reach. It was time for Kohen to call his old contact at the CIA, Bill Granger.

CHAPTER 54

Thy instincts told thee not to trust that crippled piece of ham,
For he is crippled in both body and mind, and is hardly a 'man'.

Love is the 'nuclear pasta' of the human heart. Indeed, the crust of a neutron star undoubtedly pales into insignificance compared to the substance of love. It has brought humans together, even when some sweet thing might have come along. It was love that Amelia now waged all her hopes on.

The snail-pace speed of Walter's message being delivered to Felicity by NASA could be measured in light-years. There was a month to go until Project Zeus launched into space. Felicity had been working her team around the clock to build Zeus, and she had also been punishing her body to train for her mission into space. It was 7:00 p.m. on Wednesday, 8 July 1970, and there were only four-and-a-half weeks left until Zeus's launch date, when Felicity read Walter's second telegram; she immediately made a telephone call to Amelia, disregarding any rules or regulations. No matter how much Felicity's heart had been hurt in the past by Amelia, Cupid's arrow always struck its target. The line seemed to ring forever on the other end of the line before Amelia answered the call in an alcohol-fuelled haze of being awoken from her sleep. "If that is you, Walter, I am going to kick your backside up and down Sunset Boulevard when I return, because it's 1:00 a.m." Felicity momentarily froze as the slurred, vicious tone of Amelia's voice disturbed her. Amelia was impatient. "Walter, what's the matter with you? Has the cat swallowed your tongue?" Felicity took in a deep breath to regain her composure, then she spoke politely. "It's not Walter, Amelia. It's me, Felicity." Amelia's mind immediately changed from anger to manipulation. Her intoxicated state underscored Amelia's sigh of relief. "Oh! Oh! Finally. Where have you been? I have been trying to call you for months."

Felicity's impetuosity got the better of her. "I have been working at Palomino Valley for many months. What is going on, Amelia? The telegram I received from Walter said your health is ailing. What is wrong? What is happening to your health? You sound like you have been drinking?" Too many questions for an intoxicated mind to process. "One question at a time, please, Felicity. My health is not good. I have to return from France for treatment in Las Vegas in two weeks. I have felt terrible since our argument. I need you to be with me, Felicity, in Las Vegas. I don't know if I can go through with the operation." Operation! This was serious news, or so Felicity thought. "Amelia! An operation! Oh, my darling, what is wrong with you?" Indeed, what was wrong with her? She ad-libbed the response like a seasoned stage performer, drawing upon the script of her latest film for the medical condition. "It's complicated, my sweet Felicity. It's a rare uterine condition. I think the doctors have said that if I do not have my uterus removed, I will die within a year. I believe the name of the condition is 'sarcoma', or a term of similar effect. I need someone who understands me to be with me, but if you are too busy, then I will understand." The tremors of fear and imminent distress were the synthesised music that accompanied her manipulative words. Felicity was mortified to hear Amelia imply that she would abandon her in her hour of need. Feelings of regret for not being with Ron in his hour of need consumed her, along with feelings of guilt. "Oh, Amelia. Don't be silly. What kind of person would I be if I weren't there for you? Of course, I will be there, but why Las Vegas?" Another valid question, which called for another impromptu reply. "Felicity, you do not think like a screen star. If I were to be admitted to a hospital in Los Angeles, the press would be in the room before the doctor even arrived to operate. That is why I need the one closest to my heart to be by my side. Vegas is the loneliest place in the world when you are on your own. Will you be there for me?"

It was another impromptu performance worthy of an Oscar, and the gravity of the moment elicited the response from Felicity that Amelia, despite her intoxication, was hoping to achieve. "Of course, my sweet. I will move Heaven and Earth to be there with you. When do I need to be there?" Amelia then played the next card from her thespian bag of tricks, and she began to cry. Friday, 24 July. However, I am checking into The Dunes Hotel the day beforehand. Will you stay the night with me then, please?" Amelia's tearful words flowed like a waterfall over into the depths of Felicity's kind heart. "Consider it done. Do not worry. I will be there for you, my sweet." Amelia's final words drove Cupid's arrow deeper into Felicity's heart. "Thank you, my darling. I'm sorry for what I said to you before last Christmas. I love you." Felicity had missed those words for over seven months. "I love you, too. Now, I have to get back to work. Be brave, and I will see you at The Dunes on the twenty-third. Goodbye." Felicity put the receiver back on the handset; she would have to convince Theodore somehow to permit her a leave of absence for forty-eight hours, only two weeks before the launch date.

Back in France, Amelia immediately called Walter to inform him that she had succeeded in reestablishing her relationship with Felicity. She also made Walter attend to all the necessary arrangements, including booking her into a medical facility in Las Vegas for her staged operation and informing the KGB. When Amelia concluded her respective calls, Kohen put down his listening device and turned to Bill Granger, smiling like the cat who caught a mouse. Granger was a hardened former Korean War army officer, and he was not convinced that Dr Felicity Hoover posed any national security threat. "Why are you smiling? Okay, granted, the wife of an astronaut might be leading a double life by having some kind of relationship with an old friend from the UK. But, so what? I didn't hear anything to suggest that they are a couple, Aharon. They're English, and they speak differently to everybody else." Kohen was astonished that Granger could be so dismissive about the consequences of a NASA scientist and future astronaut being potentially linked to the KGB. "Are you fucking insane, Bill? Didn't you hear that slut of an actress mention she is arranging for the KGB to be in Las Vegas in two weeks? What more evidence could you need?"

Granger threw his hands in the air in frustration as he stood up in the office that the French police had devoted to Kohen's monitoring work. He looked out the open window of the Prefecture de Police to the tree-lined streetscape of Rue de Lutèce. The glorious nineteenth-century architecture of the neighbouring buildings did not bring any joy to Granger's mind that a pair of British lesbians might compromise his country's national security. He turned back and faced Kohen, who remained standing in the same spot, and he was still displaying an astonished demeanour. "Alright, Aharon. I admit it. That telephone call between those two women sounded a bit suspicious. But, a NASA scientist consorting with the KGB? I don't buy that. Dr Hoover has been fully screened by our military, the CIA, the FBI, and NASA. If she were working with the KGB, we would have found out long ago." Kohen was about to speak his mind to dispel any notions that the Americans' intelligence and law enforcement agencies were competent; however, Granger held up his hand to silence his Israeli counterpart. "I had not finished yet. I will speak to my superiors about you and some of your Mossad colleagues being granted a right to operate on American soil to potentially, and I stress, potentially, track down the killer of Saar. I doubt that request will be resisted, given Israel's assistance with Project Zeus. However,

I am not going to shoot from the hip and allege Dr Hoover is consorting with the KGB or that she is a dyke. What we, and yes, the CIA, or, more specifically, I, will be doing is working with you and your team, and I suggest that the first step we take when we're back in the US is that we pay a little visit to that faggot manager of Tolhurst's. If we catch Saar's killer, then Mossad can do what they please with the person. Is that proposal kosher with you?" Kohen nodded. He had to agree within the purview of his authority to do so; otherwise, Mossad would be alienating the CIA. He was one step closer to tracking down Saar's killer – an eye for an eye.

Granger had to handle the discussions with his superiors within the CIA very delicately. A potential link between the Hollywood movie industry and the KGB was one matter; however, to raise the slightest hint of there being any connection between Dr Hoover and the KGB, and, for that matter, alleging she might be a lesbian, when the country was brimful of excitement about the first husband and wife team flying into space was totally out of the question when he had only a scintilla of evidence. Granger's superiors within the CIA agreed to allow Kohen and two other Mossad operatives to operate on US soil. Still, it was on the condition that Granger called the shots on the steps taken.

Subsequently, Walter awoke early on the morning of Wednesday, July 22, 1970. He would be meeting up with Amelia the following day at Los Angeles International Airport, where they would both take a domestic flight to Las Vegas. It was his last day of bliss before he had to endure Amelia's volatility. Also, the looming peril of the KGB operatives, Aliev and two of his colleagues, whom Walter had not met before and did not relish the thought of meeting now, was concerning. At about 10:00 a.m., he took a drive down Sunset Boulevard to Ben Frank's Coffee Shop, where he enjoyed some coffee and apple pie before returning to his car to drive back to Amelia's house. At no stage did Walter realise he was being followed by a 1965 light brown Oldsmobile Vista Cruiser driven by Granger, with Kohen and two of Kohen's handpicked Mossad agents to work with him in the United States: Benny Goldberg and Abner Levi. Walter turned into the driveway of Amelia's home, still oblivious to the Oldsmobile that had been following since he left the café; an Oldsmobile Vista Cruiser was a dime a dozen around Los Angeles. The Oldsmobile pulled up outside of Amelia's house, and the four men all quickly alighted from the car. Before Walter could close the door to his car, he was apprehended by Granger, who put a hand over Walter's mouth while pulling his left arm sharply behind his back. And

Goldberg simultaneously yanked Walter's right arm behind his back, causing him to scream in pain and fright, while muzzled by Granger's big left hand. The two men proceeded to frog-march Walter to the front door of Amelia's house, closely followed by Kohen and Levi. Granger's tone was menacing. "Alright, my old queen friend. Which pocket are the house keys in?" Walter's scared, muzzled voice was accompanied by his eyes looking down at his left trouser pocket. Granger looked at Kohen and directed his eyes to Walter's left pocket, and the Mossad agent quickly retrieved the house key chain from Walter's left trouser pocket. Kohen hurriedly opened the front door of Amelia's house, and Walter was bundled into the house by Granger and Goldberg, closely followed by Kohen. At the same time, Levi closed the front door behind them after he also entered the house, and he remained there like a sentry.

Granger and Goldberg threw Walter onto the living room sofa, the older man screaming in fear and pain as he twisted his crippled foot. "Don't hurt me, whoever you people are. There is plenty of money and jewellery in this house. Take that, but please, don't hurt me." Kohen walked over towards Walter, his deliberate, slow footsteps matching his menacing stare. He stopped before Walter, and then Kohen bent down to peer directly into his eyes. Kohen waited momentarily, sizing up the man – or lack thereof – before him, and then he spoke. "Shut up, you little faggot. If we wanted to kill you, it would have occurred hours ago when you were watching the younger men at the café. Yes, we know everything about your sordid life." Walter stated the obvious. "You're not American. Who are you?" Granger stepped beside Kohen, and he cuffed Walter across the top of his head with his war-hardened right hand. "He told you to shut up, faggot. And I am American. I'm Agent Granger from the CIA. My friend here is Katsas Kohen from Mossad, and the other two are his colleagues, Katsas Goldberg and Katsas Levis. And you, you miserable excuse for a patriot, you're a traitor as far as the CIA are concerned, so shut up and listen to Katsis Kohen."

Walter nodded obsequiously away, tears beginning to well up in his eyes as he realised he was in a lot of trouble. Kohen looked around at Goldberg, who opened his jacket to reveal the Beretta in the holster under his left arm. Kohen turned back to stare down Walter. "As I was saying, if we wanted to kill you, we would have done so hours ago. I have been listening to you and that little slut you work for talk to each other over the telephone for some time, whilst she has been in France. I am aware of everything regarding your dealings with the KGB.

The CIA knows everything about your dealings with the KGB. I have listened to your discussions with the one who calls himself 'Aliev'. The only reason you're not in a jail cell is that we need your help." Walter raised his eyebrows in surprise. "Help?" Kohen brought his closed fist down hard on Walter's knee, causing him to scream in pain. "Yes, help! We know that you and Tolhurst have arranged a staged medical emergency in Las Vegas, to lure Dr Felicity Hoover so that your KGB friends, or should we say, your benefactors, can try to extract from her information about America's top secret Project Zeus. One of those KGB operatives killed our Foreign Minister several years ago." Walter remembered the story, and he nodded to acknowledge he understood. "Yes, I thought you would remember the horrendous murder of Foreign Minister Saar. We have reason to believe one of the KGB operatives attending your little staged escapade is Saar's killer, a transvestite named Anatoli. I have heard Tolhurst mention to you that she arranged with the KGB to kill Lilith Martin in Paris. What we don't know is where you have arranged for the KGB to meet up with Tolhurst and Dr Hoover. We also don't know who the KGB operative is that you have been liaising with in this country, or, for that matter, any other people in your line of work who are sympathetic towards the Soviet Union. If you assist us and the CIA, then my colleague, Goldberg, will keep his pistol in his holster. However, if you don't tell us everything, well, Agent Granger will be distributing parts of your body to the fish out in the ocean. Do you understand me, faggot?" Walter nodded, and then, for the next hour, he divulged every piece of information about the arrangements for Las Vegas, informing Granger about the identities of any of his entertainment industry friends who were communist sympathisers. Walter had bought his freedom and life, and in return, Mossad and the CIA had all the information they required. Viva Las Vegas!

CHAPTER 55

To worship thy libertine sister is tantamount to unwittingly trading thy soul;
For her heart is but an empty chamber, the darkest universe of them all.

Felicity had convinced Theodore to grant her thirty-six hours of emergency leave for her to support her 'friend' in her hour of need. In truth, Felicity had been wishing all along, since their fight, that she and Amelia would mend their rift and return to the unconditional love affair that had finally been granted limited sunlight to blossom. Deep within her conscience, Felicity knew that she had traded her morals to remain in America, to join NASA, and to fulfil her dream of flying into space. Nevertheless, deep down in her heart, she also knew that Amelia was her soulmate. While that woman may not have been the perfect partner, whenever their lips met, the electricity generated by their passion was the pure, clean energy of their hearts. Zeus was not how she had envisaged fulfilling her goal of being the first woman to fly into space when she was eighteen. Contrastingly, Amelia was the only person she ever desired to be her life's passion since that age.

On Thursday, July 23, 1970, as Felicity's aeroplane taxied out towards the runway of Houston Airport as the first direct flight for the day to Las Vegas, Kohen's Mossad team and Granger's expanded team of two additional CIA agents were installing the listening devices in room 1015 of the Main Tower of The Dunes Hotel, which were then carefully fed through the ceilings down to room 1017, where Granger and his team, two young agents in Ed Reynolds and Burt Hackman, waited with him and Kohen, while Katsas' Goldberg and Levi remained downstairs in the hotel carpark under the pretence of being asphalt repairmen, waiting for Walter to appear at the service doorway to usher in the KGB operatives. The CIA had moved heaven and earth to make these arrangements over the past twenty-four hours, which, if all went well, would result in Aliev being finally intercepted, along with his other comrades, including the elusive Anatoli, whose scalp belonged to Kohen. Walter had been compliant with his undertaking to cooperate, making all the arrangements with Aliev the previous afternoon, after Kohen and Granger had threatened him. Walter even spoke to Felicity that last evening to inform her about the room number that he had booked for her to be with Amelia.

As Felicity's flight was taking off at Houston Airport, Sokolov was instilling in Anatoli's ears Volkov's strict orders to Anatoli in unequivocal terms in their room at the Sands Motel, where they had checked in the previous afternoon under the pseudonyms of Mr and Mrs Cronje, a newly wed South African couple en route to Las Vegas after having commenced their honeymoon in Mexico. "We are taking a significant risk in entering the United States, Anatoli. Volkov does not want there to be a bloodbath of women with their necks cut and evidence left behind that they have been interfered with by another man." Anatoli interrupted his superior. "I do not sodomise women; I only do unto men as they have done unto me." Sokolov sarcastically smiled at Anatoli. "Spare me the moral bullshit, Anatoli. Your sociopathic tendencies need to be reined in on this occasion. You are to elicit from Dr Hoover all the information that you can about Project Zeus, and that is all you are required to do. If she does or doesn't speak, you put a bullet through her head and that of Amelia Tolhurst's, with the silencer attached to your pistol. Do you understand me?" Anatoli hesitatingly nodded. Sokolov detected some form of weakness in Anatoli's eyes. "Don't tell me you have a soft side for Tolhurst, Anatoli. She is a manipulative little English slut." Anatoli had reconciled that attribute of Amelia's from their previous liaison, and he would not let it happen again. "I promise, if Dr Hoover does not talk, I will kill both of them, and there will be no bloodbaths with my knife."

Anatoli retrieved his knife from his handbag and placed it in front of his comrade. Sokolov stared at Anatoli to ensure he had understood Volkov's strict orders. "Very good, then. We shall meet with Aliev at the Golden Gate Hotel in Las Vegas at 1:00 p.m. Tolhurst is checking into The Dunes at 1:30 p.m., and Dr Hoover should arrive at about 2:30 p.m., so you need to be in the room before then. And might I remind you one more time, if Dr Hoover does not speak, you kill both her and Tolhurst." Anatoli had one further question. "And what about that little cripple who Tolhurst employs as her manager? Do I shoot him as well?" Sokolov shook his head. "No. He is staying in a separate room in The Gold Tower. Volkov needs him as a contact in America, regardless of the outcome today. He will not be in the room while you are there." Anatoli nodded, and then he finished styling his long fawn-coloured hair and applied his make-up, so that he looked like an over-made-up version of Felicity Hoover. They then departed, en route to the Golden Gate Hotel and then The Dunes.

When Walter broke the news to Amelia that Anatoli would be visiting them at The Dunes, Amelia felt a chill go up her spine, without Walter needing to explain why the KGB had taken the extreme step of sneaking Anatoli into the country. Amelia's mind was too consumed with her own concerns about Anatoli to notice that Walter's mind was preoccupied. Amelia was sure that she would lose Felicity forever when she discovered her lover's deception. Amelia was also confident Anatoli would kill Felicity if she did not reveal any further details about Project Zeus. For once in her life, Amelia had no answers to solve a problem; there was nobody she could seduce; there was nobody she could offer up her body to; there were no knights in shining armour to save her from particular peril; there was not a chance in Hades that Felicity would give up her dream this time to save Amelia.

Sokolov drove the silver Buick GS350 into the car park of The Dunes. The KGB had not been too discreet at all regarding the car Sokolov hired after he and Anatoli had crossed the border. Goldberg put down his shovel and walked around to the back of the white Dodge A100 van. From inside the van, he messaged Kohen. The instructions from Kohen were explicit: wait for Walter to meet the people at the service entry, then they would be certain it was Saar's killer and his comrades. Within five minutes, Walter exited from the service entry to The Dunes, leaving the door ajar, and the Buick drove over to a parking bay that was closer to that entry point of the hotel. Goldberg returned to the back of the van and confirmed to Kohen the identities of three KGB agents. Two of the males remained waiting by the service entry, while a female, who closely resembled Lucien's description in Paris, had entered through the service entry.

Anatoli entered Amelia's room, and she immediately detected a menacing air about him. Walter had already scurried back to the safety of the Gold Tower after he had led Anatoli to the tenth floor. Amelia fluttered her eyelids and flicked back her hair in a staged display of seduction. It helped her performance that Anatoli was almost the spitting image of Felicity. "Why, Anatoli, what on earth had happened that you hold such a grim greeting on your face for me?" Anatoli turned sharply around to face Amelia. "Do not play your silly little movie games of seduction with me, Amelia. Save your performance for your movie cameras. You have let down the Soviet Union, and you're not going to seduce my heart like you did in Paris." Anatoli then walked over to the armchair of the petite lounge, which was included in the suite Amelia had hired for this dangerous liaison. He sat down and held his handbag close to his right side. Amelia did not need to be expressly told that inside Anatoli's bag there would be a weapon. Now, they waited for the imminent arrival of Felicity.

It had been over seven months since Felicity had last seen Amelia. During her flight from Houston, Felicity had been consumed with mixed feelings about seeing Amelia again and her imminent mission on Project Zeus. Felicity missed Amelia and wondered whether her estranged lover's illness was nature's message that they should openly display their love for one another; she was already stuck in a sham marriage, the purpose of which was to maintain appearances for a family she was not particularly enamoured with. However, her mind then reengaged with her lifelong goal, bringing it almost to fruition. How could she jeopardise that opportunity? That word, opportunity, began to gnaw at her mind when she was in the taxi taking her from Las Vegas Airport to The Dunes. A young girl's voice in the back of her mind was telling her she had sold out morality for an opportunity. Too many forbidden fruits had been consumed by Felicity by now, and her pragmatic iron will told her Project Zeus was a priority in her life.

Felicity took in a deep breath of air as she walked up to the door of room 1015. She did not know what to expect when she saw Amelia again, nor did she know the state of the beautiful woman's health, nor whether the symptoms of her internal illness were now affecting her appearance. She knocked on the door, and within seconds, she heard the familiar words of Amelia call out, "I'm coming." Amelia opened the door to her room, and her physical appearance displayed no noticeable signs of deterioration from her supposed inner illness. As soon as Amelia saw Felicity standing at the door, carrying her familiar cabin bag, she immediately reached out and dragged her into the room by her left arm. Then, as quickly as she dragged Felicity into the room, she closed the door, pressed her up against the wall and commenced passionately kissing her mouth. Felicity could not help melting into those beautiful lips once more, although she had hoped their greeting might resemble something like the passion now on display. What Felicity was not expecting on this occasion was that Anatoli would accompany Amelia. During their passionate kiss, she heard a person make a noise to announce their presence.

Felicity pulled away from Amelia and looked around the corner of the entrance to the suite, and there, sitting in the armchair, was what she thought was another woman who looked almost like her twin, except for the breasts. She was surprised, and Felicity immediately turned back towards Amelia, whose face had changed from one of amorous intent to embarrassment, and, peculiarly, slight fear. "Amelia, who is this person who looks remarkably like me?" Anatoli's voice clearly conveyed to Felicity that she was not looking at a carbon copy of herself, as his deeper tone of voice was still male. Anatoli stood up and began to stroll with Felicity, his remarkable resemblance now bearing a distinct difference: the menacing look of a trained killer. "Don't say another word! Sit down on the bed. Now!" Anatoli's voice was so commanding that Felicity felt compelled to sit on the bed. Amelia turned around and looked at Felicity. "Sweetheart, I'm sorry, but this could not be avoided. This is Anatoli, and I imagine you have numerous thoughts running through your mind, including why he looks like you." Felicity raised her eyebrows. "You might say that, and perhaps an explanation could be provided." Anatoli glared at Felicity. "Don't speak. This meeting is for a specific purpose. I am KGB, and your lover here should've told you long ago that she was mixed up with me." Felicity looked at Amelia, searching for answers in what was still a bewildering set of circumstances for her. "What does he mean by mixed up, Amelia?" Anatoli once again commanded obedience. "Shut up! You, Dr Hoover, are only permitted to answer questions. Don't ask them! And don't move."

In room 1017, Reynolds instinctively leapt to his feet, for fear of serious harm being perpetrated on Felicity. Kohen promptly grabbed him by his left arm. "Sit down. Be patient. The KGB agent is presently trying to instil fear in the women."

Felicity was initially shocked by how threatening Anatoli's words were, yet now she found the fortitude to resist them. "How dare you speak to me like that. You have no right to..." Anatoli took a step forward and took out a PSM pistol from his handbag. "I said shut up. If you continue to speak when I tell you not to, you will not survive this meeting." Tears began to well up in Amelia's eyes, and she sat next to Felicity. "I am sorry, my darling, but this is the reason why I've been asking you for so long what Project Zeus is about. I had no choice." No choice! Felicity's condescending facial expression underscored her disbelief. Amelia's tears began to roll down her cheek, signifying her embarrassment and shame.

Meanwhile, Granger and Kohen continued to listen to the unfolding drama while also recording the conversation. Granger feared the level of hostility was indicative of a sociopath about to commit acts of murder, so he, too, now leapt to his feet. "We have to end this. This agent sounds too volatile for my liking!" Kohen grabbed him by the back of his shirt. "Don't go anywhere. We need all of this conversation to be recorded before any action is taken." Granger did what he was told; however, he remained alert for the slightest hint of escalating violence.

Anatoli's PSM remained fixed on Felicity's head. Amelia continued sobbing while also seeking Felicity's understanding. "Sweetheart, with my career looking like it was going to be a fading star, I sold my soul to the KGB. I am so sorry; I love you, Felicity, and please don't hold it against me. What I did was done out of desperation, but also in the hope that perhaps I could have enough money for you and me to run away from this life and find somewhere in this world where we could be together without anybody judging us for loving one another."

Anatoli had heard enough of Amelia's teary performance. "Shut up, Amelia! Your tears are not enough to save your life. So, enough, I tell you. You have been paid a lot of money for too long now, and we must find out the truth." Anatoli stared at Felicity, and then he approached Amelia to hold his PSM about one foot away from her head. "You, Dr Hoover, you need to tell me now what Project Zeus is about, and if you don't, I will kill her right in front of your eyes before I then kill you." Felicity now felt the chill of fear go up her spine, because she could see in the eyes of this KGB agent that he meant precisely what he was saying, namely that he would kill Amelia if she did not speak. "What do you mean? Sorry, that isn't meant to be disingenuous. Project Zeus is a scientific laboratory in space. It's nothing but that." Anatoli shook his head. "That is a lie. If you do not believe me, I will prove it to you right now." Anatoli placed the muzzle of the PSM against Amelia's forehead. Felicity sprang up from the bed and cried out to prevent Amelia from being murdered. "Don't. Please, don't kill her. I will tell you whatever you need to know, but please do not kill this woman." Anatoli looked Felicity in the eye. "Tell me now, Dr Hoover, otherwise I will shoot her between the eyes before doing the same to you."

Felicity held up her hands in a sign that she would finally reveal the truth about Project Zeus. "Alright, I will do whatever you say, as long as you promise me that you will not kill Amelia or me." Felicity's display of genuine selflessness and love ignited the embers of what remained of Anatoli's humanity. Sokolov had ordered Anatoli that he could not allow either of them to live, even if Dr Hoover had spoken. However, Anatoli harboured a deep sense of sympathy for these two women, stemming from a gentler side of his psyche. This was a place where his lost innocence still prevailed. He often ruminated about how the world perceived him and now wished to be like Dr Hoover. He nodded. "You have my word. If you tell me the truth, I will not kill Amelia. Now, for the final time, tell me the truth about Project Zeus." Felicity knew that she should not reveal the truth about Zeus, but her love for Amelia was too powerful. "This is the truth. We know that in the Soviet Union, you are planning on building space weaponry to be used against the United States and its allies. Although we have a covenant between the two countries, we did not trust you, and accordingly, Project Zeus is our first line of defence against you. Project Zeus is both a scientific space station and a spacecraft capable of re-entering low orbit to launch intercepting warheads, which will destroy your missiles at a safe height above the Earth. There, that is the truth. Does that satisfy you?" Anatoli stared long and hard into Felicity's eyes, and he could see nothing but the truth emanating from within her. The Oscar for best actress belonged to Felicity at that moment, for she had been able to use half the truth convincingly. Anatoli slightly nodded, and then he withdrew the muzzle of the PSM from Amelia's forehead. "Your eyes do not lie. I will not kill you or her, but if either of you reveals we were here, my comrade in Los Angeles will track both of you down, and he will kill both of you." Felicity nodded to confirm that she would maintain her silence.

With those words being spoken, Anatoli walked towards the door of the hotel room, but before he opened the door, he turned back towards both of them, and then walked back over to Felicity and Amelia and faced them one more time. "Do you understand my words? I mean that you tell no one, including your NASA, that I was here and that you have spoken to me about your mission. And as for you, Amelia, your life has been spared out of my sympathy for you, but you, too, must maintain your silence; otherwise, I will be back with my knife and I will cut you up like I did to your former boss." Amelia nodded, causing her tear droplets to fall freely to the floor. Meanwhile, Kohen smiled as he had his man.

Anatoli opened the hotel room door and walked out, closing it behind him, and he quickly started making his way towards the fire escape steps so that he could stealthily remove himself from the building without being seen. The stairs led down to the service entry, where Sokolov and Aliev were waiting outside the door. Anatoli exited the building. Goldberg radioed in to Kohen to seek permission to move, but Kohen told him to wait until the KGB agents were about to leave in their car. Sokolov promptly sought a briefing from Anatoli. "Did Dr Hoover speak?" Anatoli nodded. "Did you kill both of them?" Anatoli shook his head. "No. They promised to maintain their silence." Sokolov was simultaneously shocked and angered by Anatoli's recalcitrance and gullibility. "You have orders. Go back up to that room and kill those women, Anatoli, otherwise you will end up in the ocean. You're an idiot. Maintain their silence! How old are you? Two? Get back up there and finish the job. Now!" Sokolov's scathing vitriol snapped Anatoli out of his humane mindset. He felt like an idiot for permitting them mercy. "Yes, I understand. I shall finish the job." He turned around and re-entered the service entry.

When Anatoli was previously interrogating the two women, Levi had carefully driven the van over towards the service entry to commence their next stage of supposed work. From this vantage point, they could quickly apprehend and bundle Aliev and Sokolov into the back of the van. Meanwhile, Granger, Kohen, Hackman and Reynolds had surreptitiously followed Anatoli down the stairwell to apprehend him from behind. When Anatoli swung open the door to the service entry, he was surprised to see the four men standing there. They all froze momentarily, and then Anatoli reached into his handbag to retrieve his PSM. However, Hackman and Reynolds were quicker off the mark, and they had grabbed him and tackled Anatoli into the asphalt, cracking his head on that surface and also grazing his back. Granger and Kohen leapt into action to apprehend Sokolov and Aliev, but as they turned to try to flee, they were immediately set upon by Goldberg and Levi. It was a perfectly coordinated manoeuvre by the Mossad and CIA agents. Within several minutes, all three KGB agents were hogtied in the back of the van, which then sped off quickly, leaving Granger behind to collect the tape recording equipment from room 1017, and when it was appropriate, apprehending Amelia Tolhurst, whom he wished to interrogate.

While all the drama was occurring downstairs, in room 1015, Amelia was sobbing and seeking forgiveness from Felicity. Felicity sat on the bed in silence for five minutes as Amelia babbled and wept before her; Amelia was imploring Felicity to forgive her, but Felicity was not hearing a word she was saying. Instead, she tried to come to terms with what had just occurred; a gun had been pointed at her face, and she had broken her oath of silence. Amelia then sat next to Felicity on the bed, who remained in a state of shock for several moments, but then she snapped to and spoke. "Why? Why did you do what you did? You have not only compromised your life but also mine. Why didn't you tell me about this dilemma a long time ago, when you were asking me the questions that I refused to answer?" Amelia tried to explain through her tears what she had done. "I had no choice. Lilith had destroyed my career. I would lose my home and my career. Lilith drugged me, shaved my body and then sodomised me with her tied-on penis, like she had done before. I was humiliated, destroyed and desperate. Then along came Anatoli in Paris, who looked virtually the same as you. I was drunk, and I took her, or him, home. The next morning, he revealed who he was, what the KGB wanted me to do about finding the truth from you regarding Project Zeus and in return, they paid me a fortune, and also killed Lilith for me. In doing so, I made myself vulnerable not only to him but also to anyone else who found out what I had done. They offered me a fortune, Felicity, and I am so ashamed of what I have done, but please, please, help me. I beg you, do not hold it against me."

Felicity stood up and walked away from the bed. She then turned around and looked at Amelia. "Why didn't you tell me this at that time? Had you told me back then, I would have done something about it. I, too, have been living a lie with that stupid oaf of a man that I am supposedly married to, when all I wanted to do was fly into space and otherwise love you. God Almighty, I only married that big troglodyte to stay in America. I never loved him, and even on our Wedding Day, all I dreamt of was you. That is how much I love you, Amelia. If you had told me that your life was in danger, I would have done something about it to protect you and shield you because you are the love of my life. And look how we ended up; you lured me to this city under the pretence of a supposed illness. Yes, don't try to convince me that you are genuinely sick. I know. I know." Amelia looked up from her hands, which she had been crying into. "And you are the love of mine. Please. Please forgive me, Felicity. I only wish to spend the rest of my life with you. Forget the stardom. Forget the glitz. It is just you." She then fell to the floor at Felicity's feet and clutched them while simultaneously begging forgiveness under her breath.

Felicity stared at Amelia for several moments as the pitiable woman begged at her feet; how the worm had turned since that infamous morning at Woldingham. Her heart wanted to sweep Amelia up and take her away to some quiet little town in the world where they could secretly live out their lives together. But then, where could they go? NASA, the RAF, the USAF, and numerous other agencies would eventually find them. And there was her mission. Her dreams of spaceflight were beyond that door, yet at her feet was the woman she always loved, but a star-crossed relationship was doomed to fail. Reason prevailed over emotion. She managed to free her feet from Amelia's hands, and Felicity then picked up her carry-on bag, which she had dropped when she first saw Anatoli. "Amelia, I will never stop loving you, but I cannot be with you." Amelia reached out to implore forgiveness once more, but Felicity held out her open palm to silence her begging. "No, please don't, Amelia. It's beneath you and, indeed, me, for you to act like this. I have always succumbed to your seduction, given in to your will, and held you up on this pedestal because I have loved you unconditionally, both from afar and when we were together. However, you're an anchor, Amelia, and my ship must sail. I cannot live a life with you, but I will always love you. Now, goodbye." Felicity then turned and walked out the door to the sound of Amelia screaming out in desperation for her to come back, only to be muffled by Felicity pulling the hotel door shut firmly behind her. Felicity returned to the lobby of The Dunes and requested that they order a taxi to take her to the airport. Within several minutes, the taxi arrived and took Felicity to Las Vegas Airport, where she caught the next available flight back to Los Angeles. Halfway through that short flight, Felicity momentarily broke down into tears. She had closed the door on Amelia, but the door to her heart remained open for her. However, she now had looming in the back of her mind, what should she do? If she told Theodore, Ted or Secretary Waller that she had told a half-truth about Project Zeus to a KGB agent, her ticket to space would likely be taken from her. Like she had many times before, Felicity made a rash decision; she rashly chose that silence was the best option when, in reality, the truth might set her free.

Eventually, Amelia pulled herself together to start packing her bag to leave Sin City. She was about to call reception to connect her to Walter's room when there was a knock on the door. She presumed that must be her manager, coming to check on her. Amelia raced to the door and opened it. Standing before her was Granger, and his grim face revealed her fate. "Ms Tolhurst. I'm Agent Granger. I'm with the CIA, and you, young lady, have some explaining to do." Granger slammed the door behind him, a door that would never open to the same world again for Amelia.

Subsequently, Aliev and Sokolov were detained in one of the CIA's secret detention centres in Iowa. If they thought they had travelled many miles in their lives until now, they did not anticipate how long the road ahead of them would be to be held for interrogation by the CIA. Meanwhile, in the middle Atlantic Ocean, on an Israeli frigate, Kohen extracted his country's revenge on Anatoli for the murder of Saar. After many days of torture, during which Anatoli was physically pulverised with beatings, yet he did not talk, Kohen carried out the final act of revenge. He placed a plastic bag over Anatoli's head and then tied it around his neck, so that slowly, over about the next ten minutes, he eventually died by asphyxiation. Kohen ensured the execution was filmed to satisfy the Israeli government. Goldberg and Levi then severed Anatoli's body into several parts and threw them progressively into the Atlantic Ocean, where the sharks would dine on the tragedy of a wasted life.

CHAPTER 56

When the end of that prolonged road draws near,
The only people left are those that thou holds dear.

When Felicity returned to Houston, she felt as though she was walking on thin ice. Yet, within the first twenty-four hours, it appeared that nobody knew about what had occurred in Las Vegas, and slowly but surely she began to relax into a false sense of safety. Her mind warned her to be on her guard. Still, after those first twenty-four hours, she thought that, despite the secrecy surrounding Project Zeus, nobody, including NASA, suspected anything other than Felicity had urgently compassionate leave to assist an ill friend. Even when she bumped into an unsuspecting Theodore at Houston, he innocently asked her about her sick friend's operation, to which Felicity replied: "It was successful." After that, little did she realise that as she was preparing for the imminent launch of Zeus, Granger was carefully preparing a brief for the newly appointed Director of the CIA, Ben Seymour.

Felicity had minimal time to train Dwight in Houston on the finer details of Zeus' operations. She had not yet been given clearance to discuss the purpose of the HSG, except to explain that it could be reused to bring supplies to the space laboratory. Additionally, she informed Dwight that it relied on nuclear propulsion for the retrograde operation of its rockets. Dwight was cavalier about each instructional session. It was unsettling enough that he had to spend a week in space with a woman he referred to as his wife. Yet, he had been living with his secretive de facto wife for a very long time. The thought of enduring seven days in space with Felicity lecturing him about the simple job of pushing buttons and manoeuvring gimbals did not excite him. For Felicity, it was like trying to train an old pig to sit. Fortunately, their physical training was separate, so there were fewer hours in the day when they were together than when they were apart. Three days before the launch, they were flown to Cape Canaveral, where they would isolate themselves to prevent contracting any viruses or bacterial infections. Telephone contact with close family members was permitted.

Ted and Theodore had both been summoned to The Pentagon, in Arlington, Virginia, by Secretary Waller to meet with him at 7:00 a.m. on Friday, August 7, 1970. Neither man knew why they had to attend the meeting, nor did they know they would both be present. When they were taken separately, but simultaneously, to the door of Secretary Waller's office by security, each man expressed surprise to the other that they were present. One of the security officers knocked on the door, and the muffled voice of Secretary Waller could be heard through the door, commanding people to enter. Both Theodore and Ted were further surprised to see two other men in the office, one of whom was well-known to them as the CIA Director, Ben Seymour. The other face neither man knew – it was Bill Granger. The three of them were seated around Secretary Waller's round meeting table, a stylish post-war, polished oak desk, which had a dual-reel tape deck placed in its centre. Secretary Waller stood up. "Ted and Theodore, come in and sit down." Secretary Waller nodded at the security personnel, who then closed the double doors and guarded the hallway entrances to prevent anyone from entering until the meeting concluded. "Ted and Theodore, if you haven't met Ben before, I am sure that you recognise his face. And seated next to him is Bill Granger, one of the CIA's more senior agents." Bill and Ben, the CIA men. Ted was acquainted with Ben and nodded in recognition. Ted and Theodore didn't need to be rocket scientists to understand that something dire was on the meeting agenda.

They all shook hands and then took their seats around the table. Secretary Waller's anxious demeanour set the tone for the meeting. "Ted and Theodore, after Ben contacted me yesterday, I considered it would be more appropriate for us all to meet here, so that you can hear from both Bill and, most particularly, Ben, some top secret information that is... how can I best describe it? Alarming. There is no other description. I have been briefed and have listened to the critical evidence. Without sounding too melodramatic, it's too damaging to be released into the public domain, let alone to the President. So, Ben, it is over to you." Ben Seymour was a former army officer of Ted's vintage, and they had known each other during their early careers, so he was more inclined to display sympathy for Ted. "Ted. I have known you since we were junior officers, so I am going to try to be as delicate as I can, as the information involves a member of your family." Ted immediately thought it was his halfwit son, Dwight, who had done something stupid. "Tell it as it is, Ben. If my son has been up to no good, I can handle the news." Ben shook his head. "No. It's not about your son, Ted. It's your daughter-in-law, Dr Felicity Hoover. And the salacious details of her behaviour might shock you, but they have to be told."

This revelation was a shock for both Ted and Theodore, as they had considered her to be a model example of military discipline, honour, and, in particular, trustworthiness. Ben took a deep breath and then proceeded to tell them the broad details. "Many years ago, the Israeli Foreign Minister was murdered in Paris, an event you both probably remember. He had been killed just after agreeing to assist the United States with Project Zeus, by using their upgraded Jericho missiles as a decoy for the Soviets. At the same time, we would simultaneously test Zeus' HSG capabilities after the launch tomorrow. Mossad had been investigating Saar's murder from the first day his body was discovered. Even though we knew a letter written by our former President had fallen into the hands of the KGB, we did not know the lengths they had gone to in order to find out Project Zeus' true purpose. The letter was deliberately vague to maintain secrecy. Fortunately, Saar was smart enough to separate the President's letter from the remainder of the information we had exchanged with him during our meeting in Paris. Anyway, a Parisian waiter eventually identified Saar's killer, and his information led to Mossad making a connection between the KGB and the English actress, Amelia Tolhurst, or more importantly, your daughter-in-law's supposed close friend. That was when we were contacted by Mossad, and from here-on-in I will hand over the floor to Agent Granger, who will try to be as delicate as possible, won't you, Bill?" Granger nodded as he leaned into the round table. "Mossad's information suggested Dr Hoover and Tolhurst were a pair of dykes." Granger was as delicate as a crown of thorns. Theodore's and Ted's chins dropped in unison. "Don't take my word for it, listen to this edited version of tapes that were handed over to us by Tolhurst's manager, a despicable old, crippled homosexual who has consorted with commies and worked in the entertainment industry for years. We've given him immunity in return for his assistance; however, these tapes were originally made by him to be eventually handed over to the KGB. I will let the tapes do the talking for the next few minutes." Granger turned on the tape deck, and for the next two minutes, Ted and Theodore grimaced as they listened to recordings of Felicity and Amelia making love, and Felicity's condescending, insulting and disparaging remarks about Dwight, including her broken promise by revealing Dwight's double life to Amelia.

Granger turned off the tape deck. "So, Tolhurst was being paid a fortune by the Soviets to try to elicit information from Dr Hoover about Zeus for the Soviets. They had a lovers' tiff, so Tolhurst then arranged a meeting in Las Vegas, which, to be fair to Dr Hoover, was on the pretence that she, Tolhurst, was gravely ill. Dr Hoover attended the designated meeting point at The Dunes, and waiting for her in the room was Tolhurst and Saar's killer, a transvestite named Anatoli. Under duress, Dr Hoover revealed that Project Zeus' design included nuclear propulsion for the HSG, but it would not take the Soviets too long to work out the true purpose of Zeus if that information was delivered back to them. Fortunately, we apprehended Anatoli and his two comrades, who accompanied him to The Dunes, so the Soviets are unaware of the information Dr Hoover leaked. However, the security breach occurred, and that's where I will hand back matters to Ben." Ben then stood up and stared at the ceiling before turning to face the naturally shocked and disappointed faces of both Ted and Theodore. "So, we have a problem, gentlemen. Dr Hoover is a dyke, and she breached a promise to both of you about your son. And, when under pressure, she revealed top secret information to the commies. Thankfully, the Soviets are none the wiser about Zeus, but it's only a matter of time until the truth emerges about her sexuality. The mission has to go ahead, but what are we going to do about this powder keg that is likely to explode?"

Theodore was too disturbed by the information to suggest anything. However, Ted, being the head of the military, knew what had to be done. Notwithstanding the respect he had for Felicity as an officer, she had crossed a line, and he knew that if she were to be arrested, she would be likely to reveal every fact, including the family shame of his son's infidelity and bastard child. He tapped the desk with his right index finger to garner every man's attention, and, when he had done so, he spoke. "Zeus is meant to be in space for a week?" Except for Granger and Seymour, the other men nodded. "Well, why don't we change the plans and fly Zeus around the Moon? We will explain to Felicity and Dwight that the Israelis are not willing to launch a rocket, so the only other option is testing the HSG on the far side of the Moon. Its nuclear propulsion system can direct its flight path towards the Moon. When it's on the far side of the Moon, under instruction from me, my son can cause there to be a little 'accident', which nobody will receive any transmission about, and my supposed daughter-in-law will be sadly lost to the cosmos. My distraught son will return to Earth, mourning the loss of his wife. Ben, I imagine the CIA has already taken care of Tolhurst?" Ben nodded. "Yes, Ted. We have her doped to the eyeballs in a mental institution in Paris, where she will be held for the rest of her life for the murder of her former producer, Lilith Martin. Yes, there is another salacious story there I don't wish to share with you and Theodore." Everyone turned to look at Theodore, who was struggling to comprehend the very notion of NASA losing an astronaut in space. "Why are you all looking at me? Of course, there is no other solution than the plan that Ted has suggested. But who is going to speak to Dwight?" Ted didn't need any prompting. "I will do that at Canaveral tomorrow, just before they suit up. Bill, I will need a copy of that tape." Granger nodded. Ted finalised the details of which team member would break the news to Dwight and Felicity about the change in their flight plan. "Before I speak to my son, Theodore, you can explain to both of them the change in the plans, that way Felicity won't suspect that there is an ulterior purpose." Theodore nodded his head, but the gravity of purposely losing an astronaut in space did not delight him. Secretary Waller called the meeting to an end. "I have had some interesting briefings in my time, gentlemen. However, this one is a doozy. We all know what needs to be done, and may God have mercy on our souls."

It all seemed so simple as taking out the trash, but Felicity's mind lit up like a fireworks display on Guy Fawkes Night when Theodore arrived at Cape Canaveral later that day to explain the change to the mission's plans. Dwight didn't think twice about it, as he was disappointed about spending a week with Felicity in space when he would rather be in Norfolk with Jolene and his son. He had yet to be told about Zeus carrying missiles, let alone the powder keg of information Ted would share with him the following day. Eventually, Felicity accepted the change of plans, and, in any event, seeing the entire surface of the Moon was an additional experience for her. However, she was concerned that Zeus' launch date was being rushed, and her early flight experiences after the near miss at Cambridge instilled in her the need to be cautious, careful, and meticulous when inspecting any craft. She also had Amelia niggling away in the back of her mind; no matter how hard she tried to forget her, Felicity still worried about Amelia, and she still loved her. And, of course, the dangerous liaison in Las Vegas was not far from her mind. Yet, she naively did not suspect that anyone knew about the events in Las Vegas.

That evening, Felicity was sitting in her quarantined room, reading over the new flight plans, when the telephone rang. She had only provided her telephone number to one person. She quickly raced over to her bedside table to answer the phone. She did not know her calls were being monitored. "Hello." It was her father. "Hello, my little astronaut. How are you tonight?" She was concerned about Zeus, but she had to cover up her feelings. "Oh, Dad. My goodness, didn't I need to hear your voice tonight?" Alarm bell one for Samuel. "What is up, sweetie? You sound like the weight of the world is on your shoulders when you should be jubilant. Is there something bothering you?" Alarm bell number two was incoming. "No, Dad. I am reviewing my flight plans. It's nothing, just last-minute NASA stuff. We Brits are far more organised than the Americans." Her upbeat voice was easily heard over the telephone line by her father. "Felicity, is everything alright about the flight? Is NASA asking you to do something you don't want to do?" How in the hell did he deduce that, she wondered. Of course, they were, but she maintained secrecy. "No, Dad. Why do you always assume the worst? No, it's just me doing what you taught me to do since I was little, namely, always to be aware of every little fine detail when it comes to flight. Only now, there is the extra fine detail of space to contend with." His daughter's voice did not entirely convince Samuel, but he accepted her word. "Well, look, you are only doing what any RAF officer would do. You will be fine, and I know that because you are doing your preparation work tonight. And, while it's fresh in my mind, I am so proud of you, my little darling. Who would have thought all those years ago, when Sputnik was beeping away in space, and you declared at the dinner table that you wanted to be the first woman to fly into space, that that dream would come true? Well, I did, because I know you, and whatever you put your mind to, you can achieve, so I am the happiest dad on the planet tonight."

As always, only her father could touch her heart in that way. Felicity's voice began to tremble as the events in recent weeks finally started taking their toll on her. "Oh, Dad. Only you can make me go watery-eyed and snotty-nosed like that. I wish I could hug you right now. And yes, I am alright, just a little bit of last-minute nerves." Nerves. Alarm bell number three for Samuel, as Felicity was always such a forthright and confident girl and woman. Nevertheless, rather than pressing the topic, which might have opened her heart and mind at that moment, Samuel remained positive. "Nerves are natural. I would always get nervous before I took to the air to fight the Nazis." Felicity laughed, much to Samuel's relief. "Dad, I am not fighting the Nazis, but I take your point. Anyway, I had better finish my study, Dad, because I'll have an early start tomorrow. So, until I touch down in over a week, I love you, Dad." Samuel smiled on the other end of the line. "I love you too, my little astronaut. Oh, and make sure to tell

Dwight I'm proud of him as well." Dwight! She had forgotten that she had to endure his presence in space for a week. "I will, Dad. Goodnight."

Granger stopped listening to the call when Felicity's receiver was hung up. He did not know her like Samuel, so there were no security breaches as far as he was concerned.

CHAPTER 57

In the abyss, there is nothing but silence, for that is space,
That has always been the consequence for thee to face.

Dwight walked out of the briefing room after meeting with his father. Ted had informed him about the KGB, Amelia and Felicity, and he had played the same tape-recorded discussions he had heard the day before. Dwight could not get out of his head that his wife had been unfaithful to him with another woman. Nor could he remove from his mind the various belittling comments Felicity had made about him. As far as Dwight was concerned, he had been duped from the start by a manipulative, dirty little lesbian. He understood his orders, which were to jettison Felicity when they were on the far side of the Moon. However, he felt so betrayed by Felicity that he wished to make the whole experience for her a terrifying one. His hypocrisy was palpable, and his misconceived desire for revenge was just one of his lifetime of deadly sins.

Secretary Waller confidentially informed his Israeli counterpart about the change in plans regarding Project Zeus, as the Israeli official was already anticipating this might be the case after receiving a briefing note from Kohen.

Felicity entered the vacuum-sealed room to put on her spacesuit. She had hardly slept after studying the new flight plans until the early morning. Then her mind replayed all the minute details of the flight plan until, around 4:00 a.m., she fell asleep for three hours from sheer exhaustion. It was only now, when she was putting her spacesuit on, that Felicity finally started getting lost in the glory of the moment to be the first woman to fly into space. She was too overwhelmed, distracted with excitement, to detect the deranged look in Dwight's eyes. Once the launch crew had fitted her helmet and oxygen pack, Felicity was encased in her little universe for the next few hours, until eventually she could remove her helmet once Zeus had safely made its way out of the atmosphere and into space.

About half an hour before liftoff, Samuel took his VIP seat in the stand with Joan, not too far away and in the same row as Dwight's parents. Samuel nodded at Dwight's mother, who also returned the courtesy of an acknowledgment.

However, Ted would not look over Samuel's way to acknowledge him, even though his wife so blatantly tugged on Ted's arm and whispered into his ear. Samuel didn't think much of it at the time, as he did not like the family.

Inside the cockpit, Felicity and Dwight were too busy talking to Mission Control in Houston to be bothered with talking to each other. Then came the two-minute countdown point, where there was no going back. Felicity's pulse began to race with excitement. Mission Control then pre-empted the excitement to go for Felicity. "Mission Control to Project Zeus, we are good to go for launch." And then the launch rockets began to engage as the ten-second countdown arrived. "Ten, nine, eight, seven, six, five, four, three, two, one, and lift off!" The sensation of the massive Hercules rockets thrusting Zeus upwards was a pure adrenaline rush for Felicity. She had dreamed about this moment since she was a schoolgirl, and now it was her reality. Mission Control then announced the successful liftoff. "Project Zeus, you have cleared the tower. Rockets are full thrust."

In the grandstand, Samuel stood up and started feverishly applauding his daughter. "Bon voyage, Dr Felicity Hoover. Your mother in heaven is proud of you!" Tears rolled down Samuel's cheeks as one of the dignitaries attending the launch turned around. "Congratulations. You must be a proud father. I can't even get my daughter to go to the convenience store for me." They were trifling words for a father overcome with immense pride as he watched his baby, whom he had held in his hands many years ago, make history as the first woman to fly into space. Samuel politely smiled for a moment, and then he watched the giant Hercules rockets drive the enormous spaceship higher and higher into the sky. Joan, in a rare moment of emotion for her now as a Countess, hugged Samuel and whispered her congratulations to him, and also informed him how proud she was of Felicity.

Back inside the command module's cockpit, both Felicity and Dwight then felt the next burst of thrust, as the Zeus three giant rockets injected larger volumes of fuel into their combustion chambers, causing an increase in the G-force as Zeus now climbed to its maximum upright height before it rolled to take it downrange, defeating the Brachistochrone Problem and taking advantage of the Earth's curvature to help propel it higher into the atmosphere to reach orbit. When Zeus reached the Karman Line, its speed had reached eighteen thousand miles an hour, and Mission Control officially announced it on the speakers of Zeus' cockpit, and it was also announced on the speakers in the grandstands at Cape Canaveral. "This is Mission Control to Zeus. Your thruster rockets are now disengaging as you have crossed over the Karman Line. Congratulations, Dr Felicity Hoover, on becoming the first woman to enter space. Congratulations, Mr and Mrs Dwight Hoover, as you are the first married couple to enter space as well. God's speed to both of you." The speakers were then silenced for the madding crowd at Cape Canaveral. Mission Control then reverted to radio contact with only Zeus' cockpit. "Alright, Zeus. This is Houston. In ninety minutes, you will complete one full orbit of the Earth. At that moment, you will need to fire up the nuclear thrusters of the HSG so that you can slingshot your craft towards its new trajectory. Until then, this is Houston. Over and out." With those words being spoken, Dwight flipped open the latches on his helmet, and he looked at his flight manual without acknowledging his estranged wife. Felicity followed suit and flipped open the latches on her helmet. Now began the great silence. However, Felicity had the joys of weightlessness to enjoy. And there was that feeling of satisfaction that she had conquered a mountain which no other woman had done before her. Notwithstanding how she got there, Felicity felt the satisfaction that she would go down in history as the first woman in space.

About ninety minutes went by, and then Houston contacted Zeus. Felicity, by this stage, was inspecting the pod's safety hatch, which she found difficult to close quickly due to its design. The first defect issue was identified due to the expedited construction time. "Zeus, this is Houston. Over." Dwight answered the radio. "Houston, this is Zeus. We hear you. Over." Now for the next set of flying orders. "Zeus, you are about to complete one full orbit in one hour and twenty-nine minutes. Fire up the HSG's nuclear engines and direct your pitch as prescribed in the manual for a thirty-second burst of thrust that will take you straight towards your lunar target. Over." Dwight flicked the switch to fire up Zeus' nuclear engine. He then angled the gimbal before pressing the button to fire the thrust from the powerful HSG engine. In the weightlessness of space, Felicity felt the thrust of the HSG's nuclear engines for thirty seconds before they fired down. Now, there was a three-day journey to the Moon ahead of them; three days of the great silence inside and outside of Zeus. However, Felicity had plenty of tasks to do to keep her busy, and then there were also plenty of moments for her to look out of the spacecraft's viewports to observe the wonders of space. Felicity felt at ease in space, marvelling at the clarity of distant stars and galaxies compared to the vision from telescopes on Earth.

She felt calm in space. Felicity felt at peace in space. She finally felt good about herself while she was in space.

Meanwhile, down on the beautiful blue planet, Volkov was arrested and charged by the KGB for having compromised three of the agency's agents because of his unilateral decision to send Anatoli to the United States. The Soviets remained suspicious about Zeus' true purpose, but Volkov's actions had triggered a chain reaction of their own, as covert agents were arrested in America for espionage.

Three days went by, and Felicity couldn't avoid being around Dwight. The silent treatment by Dwight, which Felicity had endured for the past three days, had become infantile in its extreme, to the point where they had to converse before Zeus reached lunar orbit because there were some manoeuvres the spacecraft had to perform when it reached Lunar Orbit, so that the HSG could separate from the laboratory. The gravitational forces were not the same in lunar orbit, and even though they were not as extreme as Earth's gravity, Felicity wanted to ensure Dwight considered these variations when operating the HSG. Zeus was now about to enter radio blackout as its first lunar orbit was approximately thirty minutes away from the far side of the Moon.

Felicity had to break the silence out of need because she had to drain the build-up of hydrogen and oxygen from the separate reactor room to generate nuclear energy, which powered the laboratory. The engine room had been operating for the past three days to create sufficient power for the botany room of the scientific laboratory. The reactor for the HSG shared the same exhaust vacuum as the laboratory, which was a result of Congress's cost-cutting measures to rein in Zeus's costs during the frenzied construction stage. It was not an ideal design, because the HSG could not power up its engines until the hydrogen had been drained from the laboratory's reactor room, a task that should have been completed before reaching orbit. However, the last-minute compilation of the new flight plan overlooked this detail.

Felicity initiated contact from the laboratory after opening the ventilation that led to the vacuum. "Dwight, can you hear me?" Ten seconds ticked by, and there was no response. "Dwight, can you hear me?" Ten seconds went by, and there was still silence. Felicity had had enough of Dwight's immaturity. "Dwight Hoover. Would you stop acting like the village idiot? I might not be a ditsy airline hostess for you to play with, but you can at least act like a grown-up and speak to a crew member rather than acting like an immature three-year-old." Felicity's imperious and condescending tone struck the bullseye of Dwight's rage, which had been simmering beneath the surface ever since his father played the CIA's tapes to him before the launch. "Don't you speak to me like that, you filthy little slut." The word 'slut' was one of the words that ignited Felicity's anger ever since that infamous evening in the confessional box. "Dwight! How dare you use that word to speak to me like that? I don't deserve to be called that name." His retort answered a question that had been on Felicity's mind since the infamous Las Vegas incident. "I heard the tapes of you having sex with that 'friend' of yours. You're a dirty, low and sneaky lesbian slut, Felicity!" What tapes? Felicity was unaware of any recordings. "What on earth are you talking about, Dwight? What do you mean by tapes?" Dwight's reply revealed the extent of surreptitious conduct that Felicity was oblivious to. "The CIA have tapes of you screwing that Amelia Tolhurst, who was involved with commies, as were you. You're a dirty lesbian commie, slut!"

The extent of spy agency subterfuge surprised Felicity; however, she was more surprised and annoyed by Dwight's hypocrisy. "Dwight! You pitiful hypocrite! You were 'screwing' a stupid airline hostess behind my back. You have no right to call me a hypocrite when my relationship with Amelia commenced long after you were unfaithful to me!" The full extent of the taping then materialised. "Don't lie to me, Felicity. You had a relationship with her while you were at school. I have even heard you tell her that you were thinking of her on our wedding day, and that you would think of her when we were having sexual intercourse. And, you were using me! You were using me right from the very first day we met. You even lied about loving me!"

The CIA indeed had an extensive collection of tape recordings of her discussions with Amelia. Still, Felicity was not going to be browbeaten by a halfwit American. "Well, you, too, would have to dream of somebody else making love to you if you were stuck under a plank of wood like I was whenever you had sex with me. And at least I am not a halfwit who has only progressed up through the rank and file because his daddy was head of the military! You're an idiot, Dwight. An idiot who would not be on this mission if it weren't for your father. You're also an idiot who knocked up a lowly airline hostess!"

Felicity's verbal excoriation of Dwight sent his enraged mind into an irrational, homicidal rage. He had not studied the vacuum design of Zeus. He had not studied the consequences of firing up the HSG's nuclear reactor when it was still connected to the sector of the spacecraft where Felicity had only just commenced the drawn-out process of draining the atomic reactor room of the laboratory's NSP. He screamed in anger as he imprudently pushed the button to fire up the HSG's nuclear reactor. "You're a dirty, lying, sneaky commie lesbian slut, Felicity, and you are going to pay for your sins now!" Felicity heard Dwight's fateful act of starting the HSG reactor. She knew that she only had seconds to race to the safety pod. Unlike Dwight, Felicity knew the HSG's payload compartment stored two nuclear warheads, so a reactor explosion in the HSG was more likely than not to compromise those two FOBS. She yelled out a command as she ran out of the reactor room. "Dwight! You moron! You were not meant to start the HSG reactor. You are going to blow up the entire spaceship. Quick, get out of the cockpit and race to the safety pod. Now!" Dwight had become delirious in his ignorant and homicidal state. "No, you're the only person who is going to die, Felicity. I'm taking the HSG out of here." Another design flaw was that the two sectors of the craft could not separate when the air-lock doors between the scientific laboratory and the HSG were open. Dwight's pushing of the lever to immediately separate the HSG malfunctioned and became static in error mode. He now screamed in panic. "What is going on? Why can't I separate from you?" Felicity was five yards away from the safety pod, and her breathless voice underscored Dwight's perilous actions. "You can't separate the two sectors unless both hatches are closed. I was in the laboratory reactor room. The doors are open, Dwight. Run because we have two FOBS on board, which are armed!" It was too late for Dwight to make his way to the safety pod; he had wasted time trying to separate the HSG from the laboratory. As Felicity scrambled into the safety pod, she heard the fateful warning signal of the laboratory reactor about to explode because of the hydrogen and oxygen that had not been drained. As she struggled to eventually close the safety pod hatch, the laboratory reactor room exploded, which then set off a chain reaction back up the exhaust to the HSG reactor, and the hydrogen had not drained from its reactor room, which had been opened to the environs of other sectors of the spacecraft during the journey to the Moon. The last sound Felicity heard through her headphones was Dwight's brief scream as the two FOBS then exploded. Zeus's interior explosion violently jettisoned the pod away from the rest of the craft, and in doing so, Felicity, who had not had time to put on her safety harness, was thrown headfirst against the ceiling of the pod, instantly knocking her unconscious from the severe concussion.

The President's desire to expedite the launch of Project Zeus was the genesis of the spacecraft's obliteration. Had Felicity been permitted the time she wanted to iron out all the possible defects, the exhaust systems to drain hydrogen and oxygen would have been separated. However, what she could never have foreseen was that, for once in her life, she would permit her heart to prevail over her mind, the consequence of which was that her estranged husband would break down into a delirium of rage and sociopathic emotions while they were in space because of the subterfuge of the Americans and Soviets. However, while she lay on the floor of the escape pod, which had been subjected to enough force to generate an escape velocity to break free of the Moon's gravity, and was now hurtling towards the general direction where Mars' gravitational force might capture the pod years from now, there was one further manufacturing defect that was the product of penny pinching and impetuosity: the explosion had pierced the outer shell of the pod. It cracked the oxygen tank, and oxygen had been rapidly leaking for the two hours that Felicity had been knocked out.

At Houston, Mission Control was expecting Zeus to have come back into radio range approximately forty-five minutes beforehand. There was nothing but radio silence every time an attempt was made by Mission Control to contact Zeus. There were only five people who knew the true purpose of the change in Zeus' mission plan. Unbeknownst to anyone back on Earth, Dwight was dead, and the pod only had an emergency beacon because it was not expected to be deployed beyond medium Earth orbit. A frenzy of NASA officials was now trying to understand what had gone wrong. Theodore suspected something had gone awry on the far side of the Moon, but he was not going to confess to conspiracy to murder an astronaut.

Eventually, Felicity came to on the floor of the escape pod. Her head ached from striking the ceiling, and she was confused about her surroundings as the effects of the concussion still militated against her proper cognitive functioning. Nevertheless, there is nothing quite like the sound of an emergency alarm to help the mind focus. The oxygen level alarm was beeping with an ear-piercing sound that only aggravated her headache. Felicity flicked the off switch to turn off the alarm, and then, to her dread, her eyes focused on the oxygen level gauge, which recorded that she only had two minutes of oxygen left in the pod's tank. She crawled to the nearest viewport to see where the escape pod was located relative to the Earth. There were only the lights of distant galaxies and stars that she could see out of that viewport. Felicity then dragged herself over to the other viewport on the opposite side of the pod. When she looked out of that viewport, she saw, to her horror, that the escape pod was about forty thousand miles away from the Moon, moving away from the Earth. Newton's three laws, Einstein's theory of relativity and every other physics principle informed her that she was now on a trajectory to perhaps one day come within the gravitational field of Mars as the escape pod travelled away from the Earth, Moon and the Sun.

Felicity floated within the dark and cramped confines of the escape pod. She knew she was doomed as the oxygen level dropped below the two-minute supply. She wasn't afraid; being a scientist, she believed there was no heaven, and she did not fear death, although she would have liked more time. Her time in the Dark Room at Princeton had conditioned her mind to cope in the dark and confined space of the pod, which she now found herself in. She began to ruminate over her life. She wished she had not been so harsh with her grandmother, despite Catherine's cruelty to her. She wished she had not deliberately participated in losing that race at Woldingham, as it saddened her to see her grandfather so distraught. She wished she had told her father about her love for a woman, not a man, because he would have intervened to prevent her marriage to Dwight. Perhaps, life would have been different for her and Amelia, whom she still loved deeply. Finally, as the oxygen tank became completely depleted, she wished that she could cuddle into her father's arms one more time, just one more time to feel the loving bond of the only man she had loved and trusted. As she began to lose consciousness, Felicity whispered one last sentence of her life, "I love you, Daddy, and I will miss you." Felicity then passed out, and not long after, in her unconscious state, she died.

In the years that followed, after NASA had announced that an inexplicable disaster must have occurred on Zeus when it was on the far side of the Moon, a High School was named in honour of astronaut Dwight Hoover, and quietly his son, Dwight junior, was recognised within the Hoover family as his son, and Jolene was recognised as the wife Dwight should have married. The President tried to close down the space programme, but he lost the 1972 Presidential Election, and his successor announced that a new space exploration named 'Columbus' would be undertaken by NASA; Columbus would comprise two unmanned probes that would explore the solar system, the first of which was launched towards the end of 1974. Meanwhile, Amelia remained intoxicated on psychedelic medications in a French asylum, where she would spend the rest of her life in a drug-induced vegetative state. And as for Walter, he lived out his life under a pseudonym in the Caribbean, free from the worry of the life he had led.

Samuel did not accept NASA's explanation that it was an inexplicable error or that Zeus had suffered a mysterious catastrophe. He recalled the three warning signals from his final telephone conversation with Felicity, and he spent much of his fortune over the following three years trying to uncover the truth about what had happened to his daughter. Eventually, all he had left was the farm that his father had passed on to him, and he lost both the financial capacity and the will to continue investigating the alleged 'accident'.

The CIA, the Department of Defence and NASA locked all the evidence away from the whole sorry tale of the KGB, Amelia Tolhurst, Felicity, Anatoli, Aliev, Sokolov, Walter and any other communist sympathiser they had apprehended. The CIA liaised with MI5 in the United Kingdom, and all evidence related to the saga was mutually agreed to be permanently sealed as 'Never To Be Released Classified Documents'.

As for Felicity, neither the United States nor the United Kingdom paid homage to her exploits of becoming the first woman to fly in space. There was no state funeral, no high schools named after her, and no statues erected in her honour. The bravest pioneering young woman of the space age was virtually deleted from the history books. It was a man's world. Indeed, in the United Kingdom, Baron William de Veres now presided over the classified records division of the RAF. He had carried the lifetime mental scars of torment of his punishment meted out at Joan's behest for his treatment of Felicity, and now, as he read Felicity's classified file before marking it never to be opened, he remarked with vain callousness: "Typical! She was a bloody dyke! That explains everything." He then threw her records into a metaphorical bottomless box of materials, never to see the light of day again.

PART 7

"The Light"

CHAPTER 58

The announcer at NASA's auditorium made the same comment again about the beeping noise, about two minutes after he had first commented, "What on Earth is that beeping noise?"

After about three years of travel, Columbus 1 had reached the orbit of Mars and its two moons, Phobos and Deimos. NASA had invited approximately 100 guests to its auditorium in Houston to witness the first images that Columbus 1 was sending back to Earth as it approached Mars' gravitational field. It had been an exciting event for the VIP guests and NASA staff. Still, this unexpected development had interrupted the celebration of those images, and a confused crowd looked around at each other, unsure of the cause of the sound. Some of the guests began espousing wild theories that there might be life on Mars, and the sound was taken as evidence of such life.

The noise was not coming from Mars and its moons, nor was it coming from any other celestial objects. Indeed, sound cannot be heard from space. One person among the one hundred or so people knew precisely what the cause of the noise was. Theodore knew that the escape pod of Zeus had one marvel of genius explicitly made for it by Felicity; she had designed an oscillating battery on similar principles to the Clarendon Dry Pile, which meant the beacon battery had a very long life, and the electronic pulse of the beacon drained very little energy from the battery. Columbus 1's plasma wave instrument was detecting the electron waves of the beacon travelling through the ionised gas of the Martian ionosphere. That data was being beamed back to Earth and converted into the deafening sounds booming from the speakers in NASA's auditorium. The escape pod was caught in a High Martian Orbit, out of sight of the cameras, but still fulfilling its lifeless purpose of being a pod, and in its interior were Felicity's remains. She had travelled further in space than any other person, trapped in her permanent celestial tomb.

Theodore quickly made his way to the announcer's room, where he flicked off the switch of the speakers. And then Theodore had a brief word with the announcer, which he in turn informed the guests about the cause of the noise. "Sorry for that noise, folks. It appears that we've encountered some technical difficulties with the plasma instrument on Columbus 1, which our scientists are now addressing. Still, it means that we have to shut down the entire broadcast for today as our scientists work on the problem. But, heh, didn't we see some great sights of the solar system and the universe up until then?" Although disappointed by the broadcast coming to an unexpected, abrupt end, the audience started applauding and then cheering. The announcer fed their jubilation. "That's right, folks, let's show our thanks in the usual manner to our brilliant scientists at NASA, and God bless the USA." Patriotism! The last refuge of the scoundrel!

At that moment, back in Essex, Samuel stood in the middle of the long laneway that led from the farmhouse to the main road. He looked up at the clear December night's sky, and he remembered back to the 1950s when he stood in almost the same spot with Felicity, as she marvelled about the wonders of Sputnik circling the Earth, and declaring that one day she would be the first woman to travel into space. Samuel's heart had broken twice in his lifetime: the first occasion was when his wife was killed during the Blitz; the second occasion was when he came to terms with the fact that the baby he had nurtured and loved all of her life had perished in space as an astronaut, fulfilling her life's dream. While he felt there was a terrible injustice on so many levels about Felicity's death, his lifelong commitment to his Catholic faith gave him some comfort. He looked at the Moon, and then spoke some words in tribute to his brave little explorer. "Enjoy the life you are now experiencing with your mummy, Felicity, and one day we will be together again."

More powerful than all men, the wisdom of one woman is an infinite, invincible, and ubiquitous power throughout the universe that emerges from pain, which forever rises from the ashes of men's inhumanity.

9 781923 441255